Clive Barker's Books of Blood
Volumes 1–3

Here are the stories written on the Book of Blood. They
are a map of that dark highway that leads out of life towards unknown destinations. Few will have to take it.
Most will go peacefully along lamplit streets, ushered out
of living with prayers and caresses. But for a few, a chosen
few, the horrors will come, skipping, to fetch them off to
the highway of the damned . . .

Available at last in an omnibus edition

D1347270

Also by Clive Barker in Sphere Books:

CLIVE BARKER'S BOOKS OF BLOOD VOL 1
CLIVE BARKER'S BOOKS OF BLOOD VOL 2
CLIVE BARKER'S BOOKS OF BLOOD VOL 3
CLIVE BARKER'S BOOKS OF BLOOD VOL 4
CLIVE BARKER'S BOOKS OF BLOOD VOL 5
CLIVE BARKER'S BOOKS OF BLOOD VOL 6
BOOKS OF BLOOD VOLUMES 4–6
THE DAMNATION GAME

VOLUMES 1–3

CLIVE BARKER

Every body is a book of blood;
Wherever we're opened, we're red

SPHERE BOOKS

A *Sphere* Book

Books of Blood Volume 1, Volume 2 and Volume 3
first published separately by Sphere Books Ltd 1984
First published in this omnibus edition 1988
Reprinted 1989, 1990 (twice), 1991, 1992 (twice), 1993

Printed in England by Clays Ltd, St Ives plc

ISBN 0 7474 0164 0

Sphere Books
A Division of
Macdonald & Co (Publishers)
165 Great Dover Street, London SE1 4YA

BOOKS OF BLOOD
VOLUME 1

To my mother and father

ACKNOWLEDGEMENTS

My thanks must go to a variety of people. To my English tutor in Liverpool, Norman Russell, for his early encouragement; to Pete Atkins, Julie Blake, Doug Bradley and Oliver Parker for theirs rather later on; to James Burr and Kathy Yorke for their good advice; to Bill Henry, for his professional eye; to Ramsey Campbell for his generosity and enthusiasm; to Mary Roscoe, for painstaking translation from my hieroglyphics, and to Marie-Noëlle Dada for the same; to Vernon Conway and Bryn Newton for Faith, Hope and Charity; and to Nann du Sautoy and Barbara Boote at Sphere Books.

CONTENTS

Introduction

by Ramsey Campbell

'The creature had taken hold of his lip and pulled his muscle off his bone, as though removing a Balaclava.'

Still with me?

Here's another taste of what you can expect from Clive Barker: 'Each man, woman and child in that seething tower was sightless. They saw only through the eyes of the city. They were thoughtless, but to think the city's thoughts. And they believed themselves deathless, in their lumbering, relentless strength. Vast and mad and deathless.'

You see that Barker is as powerfully visionary as he is gruesome. One more quote, from yet another story:

'What would a Resurrection be without a few laughs?'

I quote that deliberately, as a warning to the faint-hearted. If you like your horror fiction reassuring, both unreal enough not to be taken too seriously and familiar enough not to risk spraining your imagination or waking up your nightmares when you thought they were safely put to sleep, these books are not for you. If, on the other hand, you're tired of tales that tuck you up and make sure the night light is on before leaving you, not to mention the parade of Good Stories Well Told which have nothing more to offer than borrowings from better horror writers whom the best-seller audience have never heard of, you may rejoice as I did to discover that Clive Barker is the most original writer of horror fiction to have appeared for years, and in the best sense, the most deeply shocking writer now working in the field.

The horror story is often assumed to be reactionary. Certainly some of its finest practitioners have been, but the tendency has also produced a good deal of irresponsible nonsense, and there is no reason why the whole field should look backward. When it comes to the imagination, the only rules should be one's own instincts, and Clive Barker's never falter. To say (as some horror writers argue, it seems to me defensively) that horror fiction is fundamentally concerned with reminding us what is normal, if only by showing the supernatural and alien to be abnormal, is not too far from saying (as quite a few publishers' editors apparently think) that horror fiction *must* be about ordinary everyday people confronted by the alien. Thank heaven nobody convinced Poe of that, and thank heaven for writers as radical as Clive Barker.

Not that he's necessarily averse to traditional themes, but they come out transformed when he's finished with them. 'Sex, Death and Starshine' is the ultimate haunted theatre story, 'Human Remains' a is brilliantly original variation on the doppleganger theme, but both these take familiar themes further than ever before, to conclusions that are both blackly comic and weirdly optimistic. The same might be said of 'New Murders in the Rue Morgue', a dauntingly optimistic comedy of the macabre, but now we're in the more challenging territory of Barker's radical sexual openness. What, precisely, this and others of his tales are saying about possibilities, I leave for you to judge. I did warn you that these books are not for the faint of heart and imagination, and it's as well to keep that in mind while braving such tales as 'Midnight Meat-Train', a Technicolor horror story rooted in the graphic horror movie but wittier and more vivid than any of those. 'Scape-Goats', his island tale of terror, actually uses that staple of the dubbed horror film and videocassette, the underwater zombie, and 'Son of Celluloid' goes straight for a biological taboo with a directness worthy of the films of David Cronenberg, but it's worth pointing out that the real strength of that story is its flow of invention. So it is with tales such as 'In the Hills, the Cities' (which gives the lie to the notion, agreed to by too many horror writers, that there are no original horror stories) and 'The Skins of the Fathers'. Their fertility of invention recalls the great fantastic painters, and indeed I can't think of a contemporary writer in the field whose work demands more loudly to be illustrated. And there's more: the terrifying 'Pig-Blood Blues'; 'Dread', which walks the shaky tightrope between clarity and voyeurism that any treatment of sadism risks; more, but I think it's almost time I got out of your way.

Here you have nearly a quarter of a million words of him (at least, I hope you've bought all three volumes; he'd planned them as a single book), his choice of the best of eighteen months' worth of short stories, written in the evenings while during the days he wrote plays (which, by the way, have played to full houses). It seems to me to be an astonishing performance, and the most exciting début in horror fiction for many years.

Merseyside, 5 May 1983

The Book of Blood

The dead have highways.

They run, unerring lines of ghost-trains, of dream-carriages, across the wasteland behind our lives, bearing an endless traffic of departed souls. Their thrum and throb can be heard in the broken places of the world, through cracks made by acts of cruelty, violence and depravity. Their freight, the wandering dead, can be glimpsed when the heart is close to bursting, and sights that should be hidden come plainly into view.

They have sign-posts, these highways, and bridges and lay-bys. They have turnpikes and intersections.

It is at these intersections, where the crowds of dead mingle and cross, that this forbidden highway is most likely to spill through into our world. The traffic is heavy at the cross-roads, and the voices of the dead are at their most shrill. Here the barriers that separate one reality from the next are worn thin with the passage of innumerable feet.

Such an intersection on the highway of the dead was located at Number 65, Tollington Place. Just a brick-fronted, mock-Georgian detached house, Number 65 was unremarkable in every other way. An old, forgettable house, stripped of the cheap grandeur it had once laid claim to, it had stood empty for a decade or more.

It was not rising damp that drove tenants from Number 65. It was not the rot in the cellars, or the subsidence that had opened a crack in the front of the house that ran from doorstep to eaves, it was the noise of passage. In the upper storey the din of that traffic never ceased. It cracked the plaster on the walls and it warped the beams. It rattled the windows. It rattled the mind too. Number 65, Tollington Place was a haunted house, and no-one could possess it for long without insanity setting in.

At some time in its history a horror had been committed in that house. No-one knew when, or what. But even to the untrained observer the oppressive atmosphere of the house, particularly the top storey, was unmistakable. There was a memory and a promise of blood in the air of Number 65, a scent that lingered in the sinuses, and turned the strongest stomach. The building and its environs were shunned by vermin, by birds, even by flies. No woodlice crawled in its kitchen, no starling had nested in its attic.

Whatever violence had been done there, it had opened the house up, as surely as a knife slits a fish's belly; and through that cut, that wound in the world, the dead peered out, and had their say.

That was the rumour anyway . . .

It was the third week of the investigation at 65, Tollington Place. Three weeks of unprecedented success in the realm of the paranormal. Using a newcomer to the business, a twenty-year-old called Simon McNeal, as a medium, the Essex University Parapsychology Unit had recorded all but incontrovertible evidence of life after death.

In the top room of the house, a claustrophobic corridor of a room, the McNeal boy had apparently summoned the dead, and at his request they had left copious evidence of their visits, writing in a hundred different hands on the pale ochre walls. They wrote, it seemed, whatever came into their heads. Their names, of course, and their birth and death dates. Fragments of memories, and well-wishes to their living descendants, strange elliptical phrases that hinted at their present torments and mourned their lost joys. Some of the hands were square and ugly, some delicate and feminine. There were obscene drawings and half-finished jokes alongside lines of romantic poetry. A badly drawn rose. A game of noughts and crosses. A shopping list.

The famous had come to this wailing wall – Mussolini was there, Lennon and Janis Joplin – and nobodies too, forgotten people, had signed themselves beside the greats. It was a roll-call of the dead, and it was growing day by day, as though word of mouth was spreading amongst the lost tribes, and seducing them out of silence to sign this barren room with their sacred presence.

After a lifetime's work in the field of psychic research, Doctor Florescu was well accustomed to the hard facts of failure. It had been almost comfortable, settling back into a certainty that the evidence would never manifest itself. Now, faced with a sudden and spectacular success, she felt both elated and confused.

She sat, as she had sat for three incredible weeks, in the main room on the middle floor, one flight of stairs down from the writing room, and listened to the clamour of noises from upstairs with a sort of awe, scarcely daring to believe that she was allowed to be present at this miracle. There had been nibbles before, tantalizing hints of voices from another world, but this was the first time that province had insisted on being heard.

Upstairs, the noises stopped.

Mary looked at her watch: it was six-seventeen p.m.

2

For some reason best known to the visitors, the contact never lasted much after six. She'd wait 'til half-past then go up. What would it have been today? Who would have come to that sordid little room, and left their mark?

'Shall I set up the cameras?' Reg Fuller, her assistant, asked.

'Please,' she murmured, distracted by expectation.

'Wonder what we'll get today?'

'We'll leave him ten minutes.'

'Sure.'

Upstairs, McNeal slumped in the corner of the room, and watched the October sun through the tiny window. He felt a little shut in, all alone in that damn place, but he still smiled to himself, that wan, beatific smile that melted even the most academic heart. Especially Doctor Florescu's: oh yes, the woman was infatuated with his smile, his eyes, the lost look he put on for her . . .

It was a fine game.

Indeed, at first that was all it had been – a game. Now Simon knew they were playing for bigger stakes; what had begun as a sort of lie-detection test had turned into a very serious contest: McNeal versus the Truth. The truth was simple: he was a cheat. He penned all his 'ghost-writings' on the wall with tiny shards of lead he secreted under his tongue: he banged and thrashed and shouted without any provocation other than the sheer mischief of it: and the unknown names he wrote, ha, he laughed to think of it, the names he found in telephone directories.

Yes, it was indeed a fine game.

She promised him so much, she tempted him with fame, encouraging every lie that he invented. Promises of wealth, of applauded appearances on the television, of an adulation he'd never known before. As long as he produced the ghosts.

He smiled the smile again. She called him her Go-Between: an innocent carrier of messages. She'd be up the stairs soon – her eyes on his body, his voice close to tears with her pathetic excitement at another series of scrawled names and nonsense.

He liked it when she looked at his nakedness, or all but nakedness. All his sessions were carried out with him only dressed in a pair of briefs, to preclude any hidden aids. A ridiculous precaution. All he needed were the leads under his tongue, and enough energy to fling himself around for half an hour, bellowing his head off.

He was sweating. The groove of his breast-bone was slick with it, his hair plastered to his pale forehead. Today had been hard work: he was looking forward to getting out of the room, sluicing himself down, and basking in admiration awhile. The Go-Between

3

put his hand down his briefs and played with himself, idly. Somewhere in the room a fly, or flies maybe, were trapped. It was late in the season for flies, but he could hear them somewhere close. They buzzed and fretted against the window, or around the light bulb. He heard their tiny fly voices, but didn't question them, too engrossed in his thoughts of the game, and in the simple delight of stroking himself.

How they buzzed, these harmless insect voices, buzzed and sang and complained. How they complained.

Mary Florescu drummed the table with her fingers. Her wedding ring was loose today, she felt it moving with the rhythm of her tapping. Sometimes it was tight and sometimes loose: one of those small mysteries that she'd never analysed properly but simply accepted. In fact today it was very loose: almost ready to fall off. She thought of Alan's face. Alan's dear face. She thought of it through a hole made of her wedding ring, as if down a tunnel. Was that what his death had been like: being carried away and yet further away down a tunnel to the dark? She thrust the ring deeper on to her hand. Through the tips of her index-finger and thumb she seemed almost to taste the sour metal as she touched it. It was a curious sensation, an illusion of some kind.

To wash the bitterness away she thought of the boy. His face came easily, so very easily, splashing into her consciousness with his smile and his unremarkable physique, still unmanly. Like a girl really – the roundness of him, the sweet clarity of his skin – the innocence.

Her fingers were still on the ring, and the sourness she had tasted grew. She looked up. Fuller was organizing the equipment. Around his balding head a nimbus of pale green light shimmered and wove –

She suddenly felt giddy.

Fuller saw nothing and heard nothing. His head was bowed to his business, engrossed. Mary stared at him still, seeing the halo on him, feeling new sensations waking in her, coursing through her. The air seemed suddenly alive: the very molecules of oxygen, hydrogen, nitrogen jostled against her in an intimate embrace. The nimbus around Fuller's head was spreading, finding fellow radiance in every object in the room. The unnatural sense in her fingertips was spreading too. She could see the colour of her breath as she exhaled it: a pinky orange glamour in the bubbling air. She could hear, quite clearly, the voice of the desk she sat at: the low whine of its solid presence.

The world was opening up: throwing her senses into an ecstasy, coaxing them into a wild confusion of functions. She was capable,

4

suddenly, of knowing the world as a system, not of politics or religions, but as a system of senses, a system that spread out from the living flesh to the inert wood of her desk, to the stale gold of her wedding ring.

And further. Beyond wood, beyond gold. The crack opened that led to the highway. In her head she heard voices that came from no living mouth.

She looked up, or rather some force thrust her head back violently and she found herself staring up at the ceiling. It was covered with worms. No. that was absurd! It *seemed* to be alive, though, maggoty with life – pulsing, dancing.

She could see the boy through the ceiling. He was sitting on the floor, with his jutting member in his hand. His head was thrown back, like hers. He was as lost in his ecstasy as she was. Her new sight saw the throbbing light in and around his body – traced the passion that was seated in his gut, and his head molten with pleasure.

It saw another sight, the lie in him, the absence of power where she'd thought there had been something wonderful. He had no talent to commune with ghosts, nor had ever had, she saw this plainly. He was a little liar, a boy-liar, a sweet, white boy-liar without the compassion or the wisdom to understand what he had dared to do.

Now it was done. The lies were told, the tricks were played, and the people on the highway, sick beyond death of being misrepresented and mocked, were buzzing at the crack in the wall, and demanding satisfaction.

That crack *she* had opened: *she* had unknowingly fingered and fumbled at, unlocking it by slow degrees. Her desire for the boy had done that: her endless thoughts of him, her frustration, her heat and her disgust at her heat had pulled the crack wider. Of all the powers that made the system manifest, love, and its companion, passion, and their companion, loss, were the most potent. Here she was, an embodiment of all three. Loving, and wanting, and sensing acutely the impossibility of the former two. Wrapped up in an agony of feeling which she had denied herself, believing she loved the boy simply as her Go-Between.

It wasn't true! It wasn't true! She wanted him, wanted him *now*, deep inside her. Except that now it was too late. The traffic could be denied no longer: it demanded, yes, it *demanded* access to the little trickster.

She was helpless to prevent it. All she could do was utter a tiny gasp of horror as she saw the highway open out before her, and understood that this was no common intersection they stood at.

Fuller heard the sound.

'Doctor?' He looked up from his tinkering and his face – washed with a blue light she could see from the corner of her eye – bore an expression of enquiry.

'Did you say something?' he asked.

She thought, with a fillup of her stomach, of how this was bound to end.

The ether-faces of the dead were quite clear in front of her. She could see the profundity of their suffering and she could sympathize with their ache to be heard.

She saw plainly that the highways that crossed at Tollington Place were not common thoroughfares. She was not staring at the happy, idling traffic of the ordinary dead. No, that house opened onto a route walked only by the victims and the perpetrators of violence. The men, the women, the children who had died enduring all the pains nerves had wit to muster, with their minds branded by the circumstances of their deaths. Eloquent beyond words, their eyes spoke their agonies, their ghost bodies still bearing the wounds that had killed them. She could also see, mingling freely with the innocents, their slaughterers and tormentors. These monsters, frenzied, mush-minded blood-letters, peeked through into the world: nonesuch creatures, unspoken, forbidden miracles of our species, chattering and howling their Jabberwocky.

Now the boy above her sensed them. She saw him turn a little in the silent room, knowing that the voices he heard were not fly-voices, the complaints were not insect-complaints. He was aware, suddenly, that he had lived in a tiny corner of the world, and that the rest of it, the Third, Fourth and Fifth Worlds, were pressing at his lying back, hungry and irrevocable. The sight of his panic was also a smell and a taste to her. Yes, she tasted him as she had always longed to, but it was not a kiss that married their senses, it was his growing panic. It filled her up: her empathy was total. The fearful glance was hers as much as his – their dry throats rasped the same small word:

'Please – '

That the child learns.

'Please – '

That wins care and gifts.

'Please – '

That even the dead, surely, even the dead must know and obey.

'Please – '

Today there would be no such mercy given, she knew for certain. These ghosts had despaired on the highway a grieving age, bearing the wounds they had died with, and the insanities they had slaughtered with. They had endured his levity and insolence, his idiocies, the fabrications that had made a game of their ordeals. They wanted to speak the truth.

Fuller was peering at her more closely, his face now swimming in a sea of pulsing orange light. She felt his hands on her skin. They tasted of vinegar.

'Are you all right?' he said, his breath like iron.

She shook her head.

No, she was not all right, nothing was right.

The crack was gaping wider every second: through it she could see another sky, the slate heavens that loured over the highway. It overwhelmed the mere reality of the house.

'Please,' she said, her eyes rolling up to the fading substance of the ceiling.

Wider. Wider –

The brittle world she inhabited was stretched to breaking point.

Suddenly, it broke, like a dam, and the black waters poured through, inundating the room.

Fuller knew something was amiss (it was in the colour of his aura, the sudden fear), but he didn't understand what was happening. She felt his spine ripple: she could see his brain whirl.

'What's going on?' he said. The pathos of the enquiry made her want to laugh.

Upstairs, the water-jug in the writing room shattered.

Fuller let her go and ran towards the door. It began to rattle and shake even as he approached it, as though all the inhabitants of hell were beating on the other side. The handle turned and turned and turned. The paint blistered. The key glowed red-hot.

Fuller looked back at the Doctor, who was still fixed in that grotesque position, head back, eyes wide.

He reached for the handle, but the door opened before he could touch it. The hallway beyond had disappeared altogether. Where the familiar interior had stood the vista of the highway stretched to the horizon. The sight killed Fuller in a moment. His mind had no strength to take the panorama in – it could not control the overload that ran through his every nerve. His heart stopped; a revolution overturned the order of his system; his bladder failed, his bowels failed, his limbs shook and collapsed. As he sank to the floor his face began to blister like the door, and his corpse rattle like the handle. He was inert stuff already: as fit for this indignity as wood or steel.

Somewhere to the East his soul joined the wounded highway, on its route to the intersection where a moment previously he had died.

Mary Florescu knew she was alone. Above her the marvellous

boy, her beautiful, cheating child, was writhing and screeching as the dead set their vengeful hands on his fresh skin. She knew their intention: she could see it in their eyes – there was nothing new about it. Every history had this particular torment in its tradition. He was to be used to record their testaments. He was to be their page, their book, the vessel for their autobiographies. A book of blood. A book made of blood. A book written in blood. She thought of the grimoires that had been made of dead human skin: she'd seen them, touched them. She thought of the tattooes she'd seen: freak show exhibits some of them, others just shirtless labourers in the street with a message to their mothers pricked across their backs. It was not unknown, to write a book of blood.

But on such skin, on such gleaming skin – oh God, that was the crime. He screamed as the torturing needles of broken jug-glass skipped against his flesh, ploughing it up. She felt his agonies as if they had been hers, and they were not so terrible . . .

Yet he screamed. And fought, and poured obscenities out at his attackers. They took no notice. They swarmed around him, deaf to any plea or prayer, and worked on him with all the enthusiasm of creatures forced into silence for too long. Mary listened as his voice wearied with its complaints, and she fought against the weight of fear in her limbs. Somehow, she felt, she must get up to the room. It didn't matter what was beyond the door or on the stairs – he needed her, and that was enough.

She stood up and felt her hair swirl up from her head, flailing like the snake hair of the Gorgon Medusa. Reality swam – there was scarcely a floor to be seen beneath her. The boards of the house were ghost-wood, and beyond them a seething dark raged and yawned at her. She looked to the door, feeling all the time a lethargy that was so hard to fight off.

Clearly they didn't want her up there. Maybe, she thought, they even fear me a little. The idea gave her resolution; why else were they bothering to intimidate her unless her very presence, having once opened this hole in the world, was now a threat to them?

The blistered door was open. Beyond it the reality of the house had succumbed completely to the howling chaos of the highway. She stepped through, concentrating on the way her feet still touched solid floor even though her eyes could no longer see it. The sky above her was prussian-blue, the highway was wide and windy, the dead pressed on every side. She fought through them as through a crowd of living people, while their gawping, idiot faces looked at her and hated her invasion.

The 'Please' was gone. Now she said nothing; just gritted her teeth and narrowed her eyes against the highway, kicking her feet forward to find the reality of the stairs that she knew were there. She tripped as she touched them, and a howl went up from the crowd. She couldn't tell if they were laughing at her clumsiness, or sounding a warning at how far she had got.

First step. Second step. Third step.

Though she was torn at from every side, she was winning against the crowd. Ahead she could see through the door of the room to where her little liar was sprawled, surrounded by his attackers. His briefs were around his ankles: the scene looked like a kind of rape. He screamed no longer, but his eyes were wild with terror and pain. At least he was still alive. The natural resilience of his young mind had half accepted the spectacle that had opened in front of him.

Suddenly his head jerked around and he looked straight through the door at her. In this extremity he had dredged up a true talent, a skill that was a fraction of Mary's, but enough to make contact with her. Their eyes met. In a sea of blue darkness, surrounded on every side with a civilization they neither knew nor understood, their living hearts met and married.

'I'm sorry,' he said silently. It was infinitely pitiful. 'I'm sorry. I'm sorry.' He looked away, his gaze wrenched from hers.

She was certain she must be almost at the top of the stairs, her feet still treading air as far as her eyes could tell, the faces of the travellers above, below and on every side of her. But she could see, very faintly, the outline of the door, and the boards and beams of the room where Simon lay. He was one mass of blood now, from head to foot. She could see the marks, the hieroglyphics of agony on every inch of his torso, his face, his limbs. One moment he seemed to flash into a kind of focus, and she could see him in the empty room, with the sun through the window, and the shattered jug at his side. Then her concentration would falter and instead she'd see the invisible world made visible, and he'd be hanging in the air while they wrote on him from every side, plucking out the hair on his head and body to clear the page, writing in his armpits, writing on his eyelids, writing on his genitals, in the crease of his buttocks, on the soles of his feet.

Only the wounds were in common between the two sights. Whether she saw him beset with authors, or alone in the room, he was bleeding and bleeding.

She had reached the door now. Her trembling hand stretched to touch the solid reality of the handle, but even with all the concentration she could muster it would not come clear. There was barely a ghost-image for her to focus on, though it was sufficient. She grasped the handle, turned it, and flung the door of the writing room open.

9

He was there, in front of her. No more than two or three yards of possessed air separated them. Their eyes met again, and an eloquent look, common to the living and the dead worlds, passed between them. There was compassion in that look, and love. The fictions fell away, the lies were dust. In place of the boy's manipulative smiles was a true sweetness – answered in her face.

And the dead, fearful of this look, turned their heads away. Their faces tightened, as though the skin was being stretched over the bone, their flesh darkening to a bruise, their voices becoming wistful with the anticipation of defeat. She reached to touch him, no longer having to fight against the hordes of the dead; they were falling away from their quarry on every side, like dying flies dropping from a window.

She touched him, lightly, on the face. The touch was a benediction. Tears filled his eyes, and ran down his scarified cheek, mingling with the blood.

The dead had no voices now, nor even mouths. They were lost along the highway, their malice dammed.

Plane by plane the room began to re-establish itself. The floorboards became visible under his sobbing body, every nail, every stained plank. The windows came clearly into view – and outside the twilight street was echoing with the clamour of children. The highway had disappeared from living human sight entirely. Its travellers had turned their faces to the dark and gone away into oblivion, leaving only their signs and their talismans in the concrete world.

On the middle landing of Number 65 the smoking, blistered body of Reg Fuller was casually trodden by the travellers' feet as they passed over the intersection. At length Fuller's own soul came by in the throng and glanced down at the flesh he had once occupied, before the crowd pressed him on towards his judgement.

Upstairs, in the darkening room, Mary Florescu knelt beside the McNeal boy and stroked his blood-plastered head. She didn't want to leave the house for assistance until she was certain his tormentors would not come back. There was no sound now but the whine of a jet finding its way through the stratosphere to morning. Even the boy's breathing was hushed and regular. No nimbus of light surrounded him. Every sense was in place. Sight. Sound. Touch.

Touch.

She touched him now as she had never previously dared, brushing her fingertips, oh so lightly, over his body, running her fingers across the raised skin like a blind woman reading braille. There were minute words on every millimetre of his body, written in a multitude of hands. Even through the blood she could discern the meticulous way that the words had harrowed into him. She could even read, by the dimming light, an occasional phrase. It was proof beyond any doubt, and she wished, oh God how she wished, that she had not come by it. And yet, after a lifetime of waiting, here it was: the revelation of life beyond flesh, written in flesh itself.

The boy would survive, that was clear. Already the blood was drying, and the myriad wounds healing. He was healthy and strong, after all: there would be no fundamental physical damage. His beauty was gone forever, of course. From now on he would be an object of curiosity at best, and at worst of repugnance and horror. But she would protect him, and he would learn, in time, how to know and trust her. Their hearts were inextricably tied together.

And after a time, when the words on his body were scabs and scars, she would read him. She would trace, with infinite love and patience, the stories the dead had told on him.

The tale on his abdomen, written in a fine, cursive style. The testimony in exquisite, elegant print that covered his face and scalp. The story on his back, and on his shin, on his hands.

She would read them all, report them all, every last syllable that glistened and seeped beneath her adoring fingers, so that the world would know the stories that the dead tell.

He was a Book of Blood, and she his sole translator.

As darkness fell, she left off her vigil and led him, naked, into the balmy night.

Here then are the stories written on the Book of Blood. Read, if it pleases you, and learn.

They are a map of that dark highway that leads out of life towards unknown destinations. Few will have to take it. Most will go peacefully along lamplit streets, ushered out of living with prayers and caresses. But for a few, a chosen few, the horrors will come, skipping to fetch them off to the highway of the damned.

So read. Read and learn.

It's best to be prepared for the worst, after all, and wise to learn to walk before breath runs out.

The Midnight Meat Train

Leon Kaufman was no longer new to the city. The Palace of Delights, he'd always called it, in the days of his innocence. But that was when he'd lived in Atlanta, and New York was still a kind of promised land, where anything and everything was possible.

Now Kaufman had lived three and a half months in his dream-city, and the Palace of Delights seemed less than delightful.

Was it really only a season since he stepped out of Port Authority Bus Station and looked up 42nd Street towards the Broadway intersection? So short a time to lose so many treasured illusions.

He was embarrassed now even to think of his naivety. It made him wince to remember how he had stood and announced aloud: 'New York, I love you.'

Love? Never.

It had been at best an infatuation.

And now, after only three months living with his object of adoration, spending his days and nights in her presence, she had lost her aura of perfection.

New York was just a city.

He had seen her wake in the morning like a slut, and pick murdered men from between her teeth, and suicides from the tangles of her hair. He had seen her late at night, her dirty back streets shamelessly courting depravity. He had watched her in the hot afternoon, sluggish and ugly, indifferent to the atrocities that were being committed every hour in her throttled passages.

It was no Palace of Delights.

It bred death, not pleasure.

Everyone he met had brushed with violence; it was a fact of life. It was almost chic to have known someone who had died a violent death. It was proof of living in that city.

But Kaufman had loved New York from afar for almost twenty years. He'd planned his love affair for most of his adult life. It was not easy, therefore, to shake the passion off, as though he had never felt it. There were still times, very early, before the cop-sirens began, or at twilight, when Manhattan was still a miracle.

For those moments, and for the sake of his dreams, he still

12

gave her the benefit of the doubt, even when her behaviour was less than ladylike.

She didn't make such forgiveness easy. In the few months that Kaufman had lived in New York her streets had been awash with spilt blood.

In fact, it was not so much the streets themselves, but the tunnels beneath those streets.

'Subway Slaughter' was the catch-phrase of the month. Only the previous week another three killings had been reported. The bodies had been discovered in one of the subway cars on the AVENUE OF THE AMERICAS, hacked open and partially disembowelled, as though an efficient abattoir operative had been interrupted in his work. The killings were so thoroughly professional that the police were interviewing every man on their records who had some past connection with the butchery trade. The meat-packaging plants on the water-front were being watched, the slaughter-houses scoured for clues. A swift arrest was promised, though none was made.

This recent trio of corpses was not the first to be discovered in such a state; the very day that Kaufman had arrived a story had broken in *The Times* that was still the talk of every morbid secretary in the office.

The story went that a German visitor, lost in the subway system late at night, had come across a body in a train. The victim was a well-built, attractive thirty-year-old woman from Brooklyn. She had been completely stripped. Every shred of clothing, every article of jewellery. Even the studs in her ears.

More bizarre than the stripping was the neat and systematic way in which the clothes had been folded and placed in individual plastic bags on the seat beside the corpse.

This was no irrational slasher at work. This was a highly-organized mind: a lunatic with a strong sense of tidiness.

Further, and yet more bizarre than the careful stripping of the corpse, was the outrage that had then been perpetrated upon it. The reports claimed, though the Police Department failed to confirm this, that the body had been meticulously shaved. Every hair had been removed: from the head, from the groin, from beneath the arms; all cut and scorched back to the flesh. Even the eyebrows and eyelashes had been plucked out.

Finally, this all too naked slab had been hung by the feet from one of the holding handles set in the roof of the car, and a black plastic bucket, lined with a black plastic bag, had been placed beneath the corpse to catch the steady fall of blood from its wounds.

13

In that state, stripped, shaved, suspended and practically bled white, the body of Loretta Dyer had been found.

It was disgusting, it was meticulous, and it was deeply confusing.

There had been no rape, nor any sign of torture. The woman had been swiftly and efficiently dispatched as though she was a piece of meat. And the butcher was still loose.

The City Fathers, in their wisdom, declared a complete close-down on press reports of the slaughter. It was said that the man who had found the body was in protective custody in New Jersey, out of sight of enquiring journalists. But the cover-up had failed. Some greedy cop had leaked the salient details to a reporter from *The Times*. Everyone in New York now knew the horrible story of the slaughters. It was a topic of conversation in every Deli and bar; and, of course, on the subway.

But Loretta Dyer was only the first.

Now three more bodies had been found in identical circumstances; though the work had clearly been interrupted on this occasion. Not all the bodies had been shaved, and the jugulars had not been severed to bleed them. There was another, more significant difference in the discovery: it was not a tourist who had stumbled on the sight, it was a reporter from *The New York Times*.

Kaufman surveyed the report that sprawled across the front page of the newspaper. He had no prurient interest in the story, unlike his elbow mate along the counter of the Deli. All he felt was a mild disgust, that made him push his plate of over-cooked eggs aside. It was simply further proof of his city's decadence. He could take no pleasure in her sickness.

Nevertheless, being human, he could not entirely ignore the gory details on the page in front of him. The article was unsensationally written, but the simple clarity of the style made the subject seem more appalling. He couldn't help wondering, too, about the man behind the atrocities. Was there one psychotic loose, or several, each inspired to copy the original murder? Perhaps this was only the beginning of the horror. Maybe more murders would follow, until at last the murderer, in his exhilaration or exhaustion, would step beyond caution and be taken. Until then the city, Kaufman's adored city, would live in a state somewhere between hysteria and ecstasy.

At his elbow a bearded man knocked over Kaufman's coffee.

'Shit!' he said.

Kaufman shifted on his stool to avoid the dribble of coffee running off the counter.

'Shit,' the man said again.

'No harm done,' said Kaufman.

He looked at the man with a slightly disdainful expression on his face. The clumsy bastard was attempting to soak up the coffee with a napkin, which was turning to mush as he did so.

Kaufman found himself wondering if this oaf, with his florid cheeks and his uncultivated beard, was capable of murder. Was there any sign on that over-fed face, any clue in the shape of his head or the turn of his small eyes that gave his true nature away?

The man spoke.

'Wannanother?'

Kaufman shook his head.

'Coffee. Regular. Dark,' the oaf said to the girl behind the counter. She looked up from cleaning the grill of cold fat.

'Huh?'

'Coffee. You deaf?'

The man grinned at Kaufman.

'Deaf,' he said.

Kaufman noticed he had three teeth missing from his lower jaw.

'Looks bad, huh?' he said.

What did he mean? The coffee? The absence of his teeth?

'Three people like that. Carved up.'

Kaufman nodded.

'Makes you think,' he said.

'Sure.'

'I mean, it's a cover-up isn't it? They know who did it.'

This conversation's ridiculous, thought Kaufman. He took off his spectacles and pocketed them: the bearded face was no longer in focus. That was some improvement at least.

'Bastards,' he said. 'Fucking bastards, all of them. I'll lay you anything it's a cover-up.'

'Of what?'

'They got the evidence: they're just keeping us in the fucking dark. There's something out there that's not human.'

Kaufman understood. It was a conspiracy theory the oaf was trotting out. He'd heard them so often; a panacea.

'See, they do all this cloning stuff and it gets out of hand. They could be growing fucking monsters for all we know. There's something down there they won't tell us about. Cover-up, like I say. Lay you anything.'

Kaufman found the man's certainty attractive. Monsters on the prowl. Six heads: a dozen eyes. Why not?

He knew why not. Because that excused his city: that let her off the hook. And Kaufman believed in his heart, that the monsters to be found in the tunnels were perfectly human.

The bearded man threw his money on the counter and got up, sliding his fat bottom off the stained plastic stool.

'Probably a fucking cop,' he said, as his parting shot. 'Tried to make a fucking hero, made a fucking monster instead.' He grinned grotesquely. 'Lay you anything,' he continued and lumbered out without another word.

Kaufman slowly exhaled through his nose, feeling the tension in his body abate.

He hated that sort of confrontation: it made him feel tongue-tied and ineffectual. Come to think of it, he hated that kind of man: the opinionated brute that New York bred so well.

It was coming up to six when Mahogany woke. The morning rain had turned into a light drizzle by twilight. The air was about as clear-smelling as it ever got in Manhattan. He stretched on his bed, threw off the dirty blanket and got up for work.

In the bathroom the rain was dripping on the box of the air-conditioner, filling the apartment with a rhythmical slapping sound. Mahogany turned on the television to cover the noise, disinterested in anything it had to offer.

He went to the window. The street six floors below was thick with traffic and people.

After a hard day's work New York was on its way home: to play, to make love. People were streaming out of their offices and into their automobiles. Some would be testy after a day's sweaty labour in a badly-aired office; others, benign as sheep, would be wandering home down the Avenues, ushered along by a ceaseless current of bodies. Still others would even now be cramming on to the subway, blind to the graffiti on every wall, deaf to the babble of their own voices, and to the cold thunder of the tunnels.

It pleased Mahogany to think of that. He was, after all, not one of the common herd. He could stand at his window and look down on a thousand heads below him, and know he was a chosen man.

He had deadlines to meet, of course, like the people in the street. But his work was not their senseless labour, it was more like a sacred duty.

He needed to live, and sleep, and shit like them, too. But it was not financial necessity that drove him, but the demands of history.

He was in a great tradition, that stretched further back than America. He was a night-stalker: like Jack the Ripper, like Gilles de Rais, a living embodiment of death, a wraith with a human face. He was a haunter of sleep, and an awakener of terrors.

The people below him could not know his face; nor would care to look twice at him. But his stare caught them, and weighed them

16

up, selecting only the ripest from the passing parade, choosing only the healthy and the young to fall under his sanctified knife.

Sometimes Mahogany longed to announce his identity to the world, but he had responsibilities and they bore on him heavily. He couldn't expect fame. His was a secret life, and it was merely pride that longed for recognition.

After all, he thought, does the beef salute the butcher as it throbs to its knees?

All in all, he was content. To be part of that great tradition was enough, would always have to remain enough.

Recently, however, there had been discoveries. They weren't his fault of course. Nobody could possibly blame him. But it was a bad time. Life was not as easy as it had been ten years ago. He was that much older, of course, and that made the job more exhausting; and more and more the obligations weighed on his shoulders. He was a chosen man, and that was a difficult privilege to live with.

He wondered, now and then, if it wasn't time to think about training a younger man for his duties. There would need to be consultations with the Fathers, but sooner or later a replacement would have to be found, and it would be, he felt, a criminal waste of his experience not to take on an apprentice.

There were so many felicities he could pass on. The tricks of his extraordinary trade. The best way to stalk, to cut, to strip, to bleed. The best meat for the purpose. The simplest way to dispose of the remains. So much detail, so much accumulated expertise.

Mahogany wandered into the bathroom and turned on the shower. As he stepped in he looked down at his body. The small paunch, the greying hairs on his sagging chest, the scars, and pimples that littered his pale skin. He was getting old. Still, tonight, like every other night, he had a job to do . . .

Kaufman hurried back into the lobby with his sandwich, turning down his collar and brushing rain off his hair. The clock above the elevator read seven-sixteen. He would work through until ten, no later.

The elevator took him up to the twelfth floor and to the Pappas offices. He traipsed unhappily through the maze of empty desks and hooded machines to his little territory, which was still illuminated. The women who cleaned the offices were chatting down the corridor: otherwise the place was lifeless.

He took off his coat, shook the rain off it as best he could, and hung it up.

Then he sat down in front of the piles of orders he had been tussling with for the best part of three days, and began work. It would only take one more night's labour, he felt sure, to break the back of the job, and he found it easier to concentrate without the incessant clatter of typists and typewriters on every side.

He unwrapped his ham on whole-wheat with extra mayonnaise and settled in for the evening.

It was nine now.

Mahogany was dressed for the nightshift. He had his usual sober suit on, with his brown tie neatly knotted, his silver cufflinks (a gift from his first wife) placed in the sleeves of his immaculately pressed shirt, his thinning hair gleaming with oil, his nails snipped and polished, his face flushed with cologne.

His bag was packed. The towels, the instruments, his chain-mail apron.

He checked his appearance in the mirror. He could, he thought, still be taken for a man of forty-five, fifty at the outside.

As he surveyed his face he reminded himself of his duty. Above all, he must be careful. There would be eyes on him every step of the way, watching his performance tonight, and judging it. He must walk out like an innocent, arousing no suspicion.

If they only knew, he thought. The people who walked, ran and skipped past him on the streets: who collided with him without apology: who met his gaze with contempt: who smiled at his bulk, looking uneasy in his ill-fitting suit. If only they knew what he did, what he was and what he carried.

Caution, he said to himself, and turned off the light. The apartment was dark. He went to the door and opened it, used to walking in blackness. Happy in it.

The rain clouds had cleared entirely. Mahogany made his way down Amsterdam towards the Subway at 145th Street. Tonight he'd take the AVENUE OF THE AMERICAS again, his favourite line, and often the most productive.

Down the Subway steps, token in hand. Through the automatic gates. The smell of the tunnels was in his nostrils now. Not the smell of the deep tunnels of course. They had a scent all of their own. But there was reassurance even in the stale electric air of this shallow line. The regurgitated breath of a million travellers circulated in this warren, mingling with the breath of creatures far older; things with voices soft like clay, whose appetites were abominable. How he loved it. The scent, the dark, the thunder.

He stood on the platform and scanned his fellow-travellers critically. There were one or two bodies he contemplated following, but there was so much dross amongst them: so few worth the chase. The physically wasted, the obese, the ill, the weary.

18

Bodies destroyed by excess and by indifference. As a professional it sickened him, though he understood the weakness that spoiled the best of men.

He lingered in the station for over an hour, wandering between platforms while the trains came and went, came and went, and the people with them. There was so little of quality around it was dispiriting. It seemed he had to wait longer and longer every day to find flesh worthy of use.

It was now almost half past ten and he had not seen a single creature who was really ideal for slaughter.

No matter, he told himself, there was time yet. Very soon the theatre crowd would be emerging. They were always good for a sturdy body or two. The well-fed intelligentsia, clutching their ticket-stubs and opining on the diversions of art – oh yes, there'd be something there.

If not, and there were nights when it seemed he would never find something suitable, he'd have to ride down-town and corner a couple of lovers out late, or find an athlete or two, fresh from one of the gyms. They were always sure to offer good material, except that with such healthy specimens there was always the risk of resistance.

He remembered catching two black bucks a year ago or more, with maybe forty years between them, father and son perhaps. They'd resisted with knives, and he'd been hospitalized for six weeks. It had been a close fought encounter and one that had set him doubting his skills. Worse, it had made him wonder what his masters would have done with him had he suffered a fatal injury. Would he have been delivered to his family in New Jersey, and given a decent Christian burial? Or would his carcass have been thrown into the dark, for their own use?

The headline of the *New York Post*, discarded on the seat across from him caught Mahogany's eye: 'Police All-Out to Catch Killer'. He couldn't resist a smile. Thoughts of failure, weakness and death evaporated. After all, he was that man, that killer, and tonight the thought of capture was laughable. After all, wasn't his career sanctioned by the highest possible authorities? No policeman could hold him, no court pass judgement on him. The very forces of law and order that made such a show of his pursuit served his masters no less than me; he almost wished some two-bit cop would catch him, take him in triumph before the judge, just to see the looks on their faces when the word came up from the dark that Mahogany was a protected man, above every law on the statute books.

It was now well after ten-thirty. The trickle of theatre-goers had begun, but there was nothing likely so far. He'd want to let the rush pass anyway: just follow one or two choice pieces to the end of the line. He bided his time, like any wise hunter.

Kaufman was not finished by eleven, an hour after he'd promised himself release. But exasperation and ennui were making the job more difficult, and the sheets of figures were beginning to blur in front of him. At ten past eleven he threw down his pen and admitted defeat. He rubbed his hot eyes with the cushions of his palms till his head filled with colours.

'Fuck it,' he said.

He never swore in company. But once in a while to say fuck it to himself was a great consolation. He made his way out of the office, damp coat over his arm, and headed for the elevator. His limbs felt drugged and his eyes would scarcely stay open.

It was colder outside than he had anticipated, and the air brought him out of his lethargy a little. He walked towards the Subway at 34th Street. Catch an Express to Far Rockaway. Home in an hour.

Neither Kaufman nor Mahogany knew it, but at 96th and Broadway the Police had arrested what they took to be the Subway Killer, having trapped him in one of the up-town trains. A small man of European extraction, wielding a hammer and a saw, had cornered a young woman in the second car and threatened to cut her in half in the name of Jehovah.

Whether he was capable of fulfilling his threat was doubtful. As it was, he didn't get the chance. While the rest of the passengers (including two Marines) looked on, the intended victim landed a kick to the man's testicles. He dropped the hammer. She picked it up and broke his lower jaw and right cheek-bone with it before the Marines stepped in.

When the train halted at 96th the Police were waiting to arrest the Subway Butcher. They rushed the car in a horde, yelling like banshees and scared as shit. The Butcher was lying in one corner of the car with his face in pieces. They carted him away, triumphant. The woman, after questioning, went home with the Marines.

It was to be a useful diversion, though Mahogany couldn't know it at the time. It took the Police the best part of the night to determine the identity of their prisoner, chiefly because he couldn't do more than drool through his shattered jaw. It wasn't until three-thirty in the morning that one Captain Davis, coming on duty, recognized the man as a retired flower salesman from the

Bronx called Hank Vasarely. Hank, it seemed, was regularly arrested for threatening behaviour and indecent exposure, all in the name of Jehovah. Appearances deceived: he was about as dangerous as the Easter Bunny. This was not the Subway Slaughterer. But by the time the cops had worked that out, Mahogany had been about his business a long while.

It was eleven-fifteen when Kaufman got on the Express through to Mott Avenue. He shared the car with two other travellers. One was a middle-aged black woman in a purple coat, the other a pale, acne-ridden adolescent who was staring at the 'Kiss My White Ass' graffiti on the ceiling with spaced-out eyes.

Kaufman was in the first car. He had a journey of thirty-five minutes' duration ahead of him. He let his eyes slide closed, reassured by the rhythmical rocking of the train. It was a tedious journey and he was tired. He didn't see the lights flicker off in the second car. He didn't see Mahogany's face, either, staring through the door between the cars, looking through for some more meat.

At 14th Street the black woman got out. Nobody got in.

Kaufman opened his eyes briefly, taking in the empty platform at 14th, then shut them again. The doors hissed closed. He was drifting in that warm somewhere between awareness and sleep and there was a fluttering of nascent dreams in his head. It was a good feeling. The train was off again, rattling down into the tunnels.

Maybe, at the back of his dozing mind, Kaufman half-registered that the doors between the second and first cars had been slid open. Maybe he smelt the sudden gush of tunnel-air, and registered that the noise of wheels was momentarily louder. But he chose to ignore it.

Maybe he even heard the scuffle as Mahogany subdued the youth with the spaced-out stare. But the sound was too distant and the promise of sleep was too tempting. He drowsed on.

For some reason his dreams were of his mother's kitchen. She was chopping turnips and smiling sweetly as she chopped. He was only small in his dream and was looking up at her radiant face while she worked. Chop. Chop. Chop.

His eyes jerked open. His mother vanished. The car was empty and the youth was gone.

How long had he been dozing? He hadn't remembered the train stopping at West 4th Street. He got up, his head full of slumber, and almost fell over as the train rocked violently. It seemed to have gathered quite a substantial head of speed. Maybe the driver was keen to be home, wrapped up in bed with his wife. They were going at a fair lick; in fact it was bloody terrifying.

21

There was a blind drawn down over the window between the cars which hadn't been down before as he remembered. A little concern crept into Kaufman's sober head. Suppose he'd been sleeping a long while, and the guard had overlooked him in the car. Perhaps they'd passed Far Rockaway and the train was now speeding on its way to wherever they took the trains for the night.

'Fuck it,' he said aloud.

Should he go forward and ask the driver? It was such a bloody idiot question to ask: where am I? At this time of night was he likely to get more than a stream of abuse by way of reply?

Then the train began to slow.

A station. Yes, a station. The train emereged from the tunnel and into the dirty light of the station at West 4th Street. He'd missed no stops.

So where had the boy gone?

He'd either ignored the warning on the car wall forbidding transfer between the cars while in transit, or else he'd gone into the driver's cabin up front. Probably between the driver's legs even now, Kaufman thought, his lip curling. It wasn't unheard of. This was the Palace of Delights, after all, and everyone had their right to a little love in the dark.

Kaufman shrugged to himself. What did he care where the boy had gone?

The doors closed. Nobody had boarded the train. It shunted off from the station, the lights flickering as it used a surge of power to pick up some speed again.

Kaufman felt the desire for sleep come over him afresh, but the sudden fear of being lost had pumped adrenalin into his system, and his limbs were tingling with nervous energy.

His senses were sharpened too.

Even over the clatter and the rumble of the wheels on the tracks, he heard the sound of tearing cloth coming from the next car. Was someone tearing their shirt off?

He stood up, grasping one of the straps for balance.

The window between the cars was completely curtained off, but he stared at it, frowning, as though he might suddenly discover X-ray vision. The car rocked and rolled. It was really travelling again.

Another ripping sound.

Was it rape?

With no more than a mild voyeuristic urge he moved down the see-sawing car towards the intersecting door, hoping there might be a chink in the curtain. His eyes were still fixed on the window, and he failed to notice the splatters of blood he was treading in.

22

Until –

– his heel slipped. He looked down. His stomach almost saw the blood before his brain and the ham on whole-wheat was half- way up his gullet catching in the back of his throat. Blood. He took several large gulps of stale air and looked away – back at the window.

His head was saying: blood. Nothing would make the word go away.

There was no more than a yard or two between him and the door now. He had to look. There was blood on his shoe, and a thin trail to the next car, but he still had to look.

He had to.

He took two more steps to the door and scanned the curtain looking for a flaw in the blind: a pulled thread in the weave would be sufficient. There was a tiny hole. He glued his eye to it.

His mind refused to accept what his eyes were seeing beyond the door. It rejected the spectacle as preposterous, as a dreamed sight. His reason said it couldn't be real, but his flesh knew it was. His body became rigid with terror. His eyes, unblinking, could not close off the appalling scene through the curtain. He stayed at the door while the train rattled on, while his blood drained from his extremities, and his brain reeled from lack of oxygen. Bright spots of light flashed in front of his vision, blotting out the atrocity.

Then he fainted.

He was unconscious when the train reached Jay Street. He was deaf to the driver's announcement that all travellers beyond that station would have to change trains. Had he heard this he would have questioned the sense of it. No trains disgorged all their passengers at Jay Street; the line ran to Mott Avenue, via the Aqueduct Race Track, past JFK Airport. He would have asked what kind of train this could be. Except that he already knew. The truth was hanging in the next car. It was smiling contentedly to itself from behind a bloody chain-mail apron.

This was the Midnight Meat Train.

There's no accounting for time in a dead faint. It could have been seconds or hours that passed before Kaufman's eyes flickered open again, and his mind focussed on his new-found situation.

He lay under one of the seats now, sprawled along the vibrating wall of the car, hidden from view. Fate was with him so far he thought: somehow the rocking of the car must have jockeyed his unconscious body out of sight.

He thought of the horror in Car Two, and swallowed back vomit. He was alone. Wherever the guard was (murdered perhaps), there was no way he could call for help. And the driver? Was he dead at his controls? Was the train even now hurtling through an unknown tunnel, a tunnel without a single station to identify it, towards its destruction?

And if there was no crash to be killed in, there was always the Butcher, still hacking away a door's thickness from where Kaufman lay.

Whichever way he turned, the name on the door was Death.

The noise was deafening, especially lying on the floor. Kaufman's teeth were shaking in their sockets and his face felt numb with the vibration; even his skull was aching.

Gradually he felt strength seeping back into his exhausted limbs. He cautiously stretched his fingers and clenched his fists, to set the blood flowing there again.

And as the feeling returned, so did the nausea. He kept seeing the grisly brutality of the next car. He'd seen photographs of murder victims before, of course, but these were no common murders. He was in the same train as the Subway Butcher, the monster who strung his victims up by the feet from the straps, hairless and naked.

How long would it be before the killer stepped through that door and claimed him? He was sure that if the slaughterer didn't finish him, expectation would.

He heard movement beyond the door.

Instinct took over. Kaufman thrust himself further under the seat and tucked himself up into a tiny ball, with his sick-white face to the wall. Then he covered his head with his hands and closed his eyes as tightly as any child in terror of the Bogeyman.

The door was slid open. Click. Whoosh. A rush of air up from the rails. It smelt stranger than any Kaufman had smelt before: and colder. This was somehow primal air in his nostrils, hostile and unfathomable air. It made him shudder.

The door closed. Click.

The Butcher was close, Kaufman knew it. He could be standing no more than a matter of inches from where he lay.

Was he even now looking down at Kaufman's back? Even now bending, knife in hand, to scoop Kaufman out of his hiding place, like a snail hooked from its shell?

Nothing happened. He felt no breath on his neck. His spine was not slit open.

There was simply a clatter of feet close to Kaufman's head; then that same sound receding.

Kaufman's breath, held in his lungs 'til they hurt, was expelled in a rasp between his teeth.

Mahogany was almost disappointed that the sleeping man had alighted at West 4th Street. He was hoping for one more job to do that night, to keep him occupied while they descended. But no: the man had gone. The potential victim hadn't looked that healthy anyway, he thought to himself, he was an anaemic Jewish accountant probably. The meat wouldn't have been of any quality. Mahogany walked the length of the car to the driver's cabin. He'd spend the rest of the journey there.

My Christ, thought Kaufman, he's going to kill the driver.

He heard the cabin door open. Then the voice of the Butcher: low and hoarse.

'Hi.'

'Hi.'

They knew each other.

'All done?'

'All done.'

Kaufman was shocked by the banality of the exchange. All done? What did that mean: all done?

He missed the next few words as the train hit a particularly noisy section of track.

Kaufman could resist looking no longer. Warily he uncurled himself and glanced over his shoulder down the length of the car. All he could see was the Butcher's legs, and the bottom of the open cabin door. Damn. He wanted to see the monster's face again.

There was laughter now.

Kaufman calculated the risks of his situation: the mathematics of panic. If he remained where he was, sooner or later the Butcher would glance down at him, and he'd be mincemeat. On the other hand, if he were to move from his hiding place he would risk being seen and pursued. Which was worse: stasis, and meeting his death trapped in a hole; or making a break for it and confronting his Maker in the middle of the car?

Kaufman surprised himself with his mettle: he'd move.

Infinitesimally slowly he crawled out from under the seat, watching the Butcher's back every minute as he did so. Once out, he began to crawl towards the door. Each step he took was a torment, but the Butcher seemed far too engrossed in his conversation to turn round.

Kaufman had reached the door. He began to stand up, trying all the while to prepare himself for the sight he would meet in Car Two. The handle was grasped; and he slid the door open.

The noise of the rails increased, and a wave of dank air, stinking of nothing on earth, came up at him. Surely the Butcher must hear, or smell? Surely he must turn –

25

But no. Kaufman skinned his way through the slit he had opened and so through into the bloody chamber beyond.

Relief made him careless. He failed to latch the door properly behind him and it began to slide open with the buffeting of the train.

Mahogany put his head out of the cabin and stared down the car towards the door.

'What the fuck's that?' said the driver.

'Didn't close the door properly. That's all.'

Kaufman heard The Butcher walking towards the door. He crouched, a ball of consternation, against the intersecting wall, suddenly aware of how full his bowels were. The door was pulled closed from the other side, and the footsteps receded again.

Safe, for another breath at least.

Kaufman opened his eyes, steeling himself for the slaughter-pen in front of him.

There was no avoiding it.

It filled every one of his senses: the smell of opened entrails, the sight of the bodies, the feel of fluid on the floor under his fingers, the sound of the straps creaking beneath the weight of the corpses, even the air, tasting salty with blood. He was with death absolutely in that cubby-hole, hurtling through the dark.

But there was no nausea now. There was no feeling left but a casual revulsion. He even found himself peering at the bodies with some curiosity.

The carcass closest to him was the remains of the pimply youth he'd seen in Car One. The body hung upside-down, swinging back and forth to the rhythm of the train, in unison with its three fellows; an obscene dance macabre. Its arms dangled loosely from the shoulder joints, into which gashes an inch or two deep had been made, so the bodies would hang more neatly.

Every part of the dead kid's anatomy was swaying hypnoti-cally. The tongue, hanging from the open mouth. The head, lolling on its slit neck. Even the youth's penis flapped from side to side on his plucked groin. The head wound and the open jugular still pulsed blood into a black bucket. There was an elegance about the whole sight: the sign of a job well-done.

Beyond that body were the strung-up corpses of two young white women and a darker skinned male. Kaufman turned his head on one side to look at their faces. They were quite blank. One of the girls was a beauty. He decided the male had been Puerto Rican. All were shorn of their head and body hair. In fact the air was still pungent with the smell of the shearing. Kaufman slid up the wall out of the crouching position, and as he did so one of the women's bodies turned around, presenting a dorsal view.

He was not prepared for this last horror.

The meat of her back had been entirely cleft open from neck to buttock and the muscle had been peeled back to expose the glistening vertebrae. It was the final triumph of The Butcher's craft. Here they hung, these shaved, bled, slit slabs of humanity, opened up like fish, and ripe for devouring.

Kaufman almost smiled at the perfection of its horror. He felt an offer of insanity tickling the base of his skull, tempting him into oblivion, promising a blank indifference to the world.

He began to shake, uncontrollably. He felt his vocal cords trying to form a scream. It was intolerable: and yet to scream was to become in a short while like the creatures in front of him.

'Fuck it,' he said, more loudly that he'd intended, then pushing himself off from the wall he began to walk down the car between the swaying corpses, observing the neat piles of clothes and belongings that sat on the seats beside their owners. Under his feet the floor was sticky with drying bile. Even with his eyes closed to cracks he could see the blood in the buckets too clearly: it was thick and heady, flecks of grit turning in it.

He was past the youth now and he could see the door into Car Three ahead. All he had to do was run this gauntlet of atrocities. He urged himself on, trying to ignore the horrors, and concentrate on the door that would lead him back into sanity.

He was past the first woman. A few more yards, he said to himself, ten steps at most, less if he walked with confidence.

Then the lights went out.

'Jesus Christ,' he said.

The train lurched, and Kaufman lost his balance.

In the utter blackness he reached out for support and his flailing arms encompassed the body beside him. Before he could prevent himself he felt his hands sinking into the lukewarm flesh, and his fingers grasping the open edge of muscle on the dead woman's back, his fingertips touching the bone of her spine. His cheek was laid against the bald flesh of the thigh.

He screamed; and even as he screamed, the lights flickered back on.

And as they flickered back on, and his scream died, he heard the noise of the Butcher's feet approaching down the length of Car One towards the intervening door.

He let go of the body he was embracing. His face was smeared with blood from her leg. He could feel it on his cheek, like warpaint.

27

The scream had cleared Kaufman's head and he suddenly felt released into a kind of strength. There would be no pursuit down the train, he knew that: there would be no cowardice, not now. This was going to be a primitive confrontation, two human beings, face to face. And there would be no trick – none – that he couldn't contemplate using to bring his enemy down. This was a matter of survival, pure and simple.

The door-handle rattled.

Kaufman looked around for a weapon, his eye steady and calculating. His gaze fell on the pile of clothes beside the Puerto Rican's body. There was a knife there, lying amongst the rhinestone rings and the imitation gold chains. A long-bladed, immaculately clean weapon, probably the man's pride and joy. Reaching past the well-muscled body, Kaufman plucked the knife from the heap. It felt good in his hand; in fact it felt positively thrilling.

The door was opening, and the face of the slaughterer came into view.

Kaufman looked down the abattoir at Mahogany. He was not terribly fearsome, just another balding, overweight man of fifty. His face was heavy and his eyes deep-set. His mouth was rather small and delicately lipped. In fact he had a woman's mouth.

Mahogany could not understand where this intruder had appeared from, but he was aware that it was another oversight, another sign of increasing incompetence. He must dispatch this ragged creature immediately. After all they could not be more than a mile or two from the end of the line. He must cut the little man down and have him hanging up by his heels before they reached their destination.

He moved into Car Two.

'You were asleep,' he said, recognizing Kaufman. 'I saw you.'

Kaufman said nothing.

'You should have left the train. What were you trying to do? Hide from me?'

Kaufman still kept his silence.

Mahogany grasped the hand of the cleaver hanging from his well-used leather belt. It was dirty with blood, as was his chain-mail apron, his hammer and his saw.

'As it is,' he said, 'I'll have to do away with you.'

Kaufman raised the knife. It looked a little small beside the Butcher's paraphernalia.

'Fuck it,' he said.

Mahogany grinned at the little man's pretensions to defence.

'You shouldn't have seen this: it's not for the likes of you,' he said, taking another step towards Kaufman. 'It's secret.'

Oh, so he's the divinely-inspired type is he? thought Kaufman. That explains something.

'Fuck it,' he said again.

The Butcher frowned. He didn't like the little man's indifference to his work, to his reputation.

'We all have to die some time,' he said. 'You should be well pleased: you're not going to be burnt up like most of them: I can use you. To feed the fathers.'

Kaufman's only response was a grin. He was past being terrorized by this gross, shambling hulk.

The Butcher unhooked the cleaver from his belt and brandished it.

'A dirty little Jew like you,' he said, 'should be thankful to be useful at all: meat's the best you can aspire to.'

Without warning, the Butcher swung. The cleaver divided the air at some speed, but Kaufman stepped back. The cleaver sliced his coat-arm and buried itself in the Puerto Rican's shank. The impact half-severed the leg and the weight of the body opened the gash even further. The exposed meat of the thigh was like prime steak, succulent and appetizing.

The Butcher started to drag the cleaver out of the wound, and in that moment Kaufman sprang. The knife sped towards Mahogany's eye, but an error of judgement buried it instead in his neck. It transfixed the column and appeared in a little gout of gore on the other side. Straight through. In one stroke. Straight through.

Mahogany felt the blade in his neck as a choking sensation, almost as though he had caught a chicken bone in this throat. He made a ridiculous, half-hearted coughing sound. Blood issued from his lips, painting them, like lipstick on his woman's mouth. The cleaver clattered to the floor.

Kaufman pulled out the knife. The two wounds spouted little arcs of blood.

Mahogany collapsed to his knees, staring at the knife that had killed him. The little man was watching him quite passively. He was saying something, but Mahogany's ears were deaf to the remarks, as though he was under water.

Mahogany suddenly went blind. He knew with a nostalgia for his senses that he would not see or hear again. This was death: it was on him for certain.

His hands still felt the weave of his trousers, however, and the hot splashes on his skin. His life seemed to totter on its tiptoes while his fingers grasped at one last sense . . . then his body collapsed, and his hands, and his life, and his sacred duty folded up under a weight of grey flesh.

The Butcher was dead.

Kaufman dragged gulps of stale air into his lungs and grabbed one of the straps to steady his reeling body. Tears blotted out the shambles he stood in. A time passed: he didn't know how long; he was lost in a dream of victory.

Then the train began to slow. He felt and heard the brakes being applied. The hanging bodies lurched forward as the careering train slowed, its wheels squealing on rails that were sweating slime.

Curiosity overtook Kaufman.

Would the train shunt into the Butcher's underground slaughterhouse, decorated with the meats he had gathered through his career? And the laughing driver, so indifferent to the massacre, what would he do once the train had stopped? Whatever happened now was academic. He could face anything at all; watch and see.

The tannoy crackled. The voice of the driver:

'We're here man. Better take your place eh?'

Take your place? What did that mean?

The train had slowed to a snail's pace. Outside the windows, everything was as dark as ever. The lights flickered, then went out. This time they didn't come back on.

Kaufman was left in total darkness.

'We'll be out in half-an-hour,' the tannoy announced, so like any station report.

The train had come to a stop. The sound of its wheels on the tracks, the rush of its passage, which Kaufman had grown so used to, were suddenly absent. All he could hear was the hum of the tannoy. He could still see nothing at all.

Then, a hiss. The doors were opening. A smell entered the car, a smell so caustic that Kaufman clapped his hand over his face to shut it out.

He stood in silence, hand to mouth, for what seemed a lifetime. See no evil. Hear no evil. Speak no evil.

Then, there was a flicker of light outside the window. It threw the door frame into silhouette, and it grew stronger by degrees. Soon there was sufficient light in the car for Kaufman to see the crumpled body of the Butcher at his feet, and the sallow sides of meat hanging on every side of him.

There was a whisper too, from the dark outside the train, a gathering of tiny noises like the voices of beetles. In the tunnel, shuffling towards the train, were human beings. Kaufman could see their outlines now. Some of them carried torches, which burned with a dead brown light. The noise was perhaps their feet on the damp earth, or perhaps their tongues clicking, or both.

Kaufman wasn't as naive as he'd been an hour before. Could

30

there be any doubt as to the intention these things had, coming out of the blackness towards the train? The Butcher had slaughtered the men and women as meat for these cannibals, they were coming, like diners at the dinner-gong, to eat in this restaurant car.

Kaufman bent down and picked up the cleaver the Butcher had dropped. The noise of the creatures' approach was louder every moment. He backed down the car away from the open doors, only to find that the doors behind him were also open, and there was the whisper of approach there too.

He shrank back against one of the seats, and was about to take refuge under them when a hand, thin and frail to the point of transparency appeared around the door.

He could not look away. Not that terror froze him as it had at the window. He simply wanted to watch.

The creature stepped into the car. The torches behind it threw its face into shadow, but its outline could be clearly seen.

There was nothing very remarkable about it.

It had two arms and two legs as he did; its head was not abnormally shaped. The body was small, and the effort of climbing into the train made its breath coarse. It seemed more geriatric than psychotic; generations of fictional man-eaters had not prepared him for its distressing vulnerability.

Behind it, similar creatures were appearing out of the darkness, shuffling into the train. In fact they were coming in at every door.

Kaufman was trapped. He weighed the cleaver in his hands, getting the balance of it, ready for the battle with these antique monsters. A torch had been brought into the car, and it illuminated the faces of the leaders.

They were completely bald. The tired flesh of their faces was pulled tight over their skulls, so that it shone with tension. There were stains of decay and disease on their skin, and in places the muscle had withered to a black pus, through which the bone of cheek or temple was showing. Some of them were naked as babies, their pulpy, syphilitic bodies scarcely sexed. What had been breasts were leathery bags hanging off the torso, the genitalia shrunken away.

Worse sights than the naked amongst them were those who wore a veil of clothes. It soon dawned on Kaufman that the rotting fabric slung around their shoulders, or knotted about their midriffs was made of human skins. Not one, but a dozen or more, heaped haphazardly on top of each other, like pathetic trophies.

The leaders of this grotesque meal-line had reached the bodies now, and the gracile hands were laid upon the shanks of meat, and were running up and down the shaved flesh in a manner that

31

suggested sensual pleasure. Tongues were dancing out of mouths, flecks of spittle landing on the meat. The eyes of the monsters were flickering back and forth with hunger and excitement.

Eventually one of them saw Kaufman.

Its eyes stopped flickering for a moment, and fixed on him. A look of enquiry came over the face, making a parody of puzzlement.

'You,' it said. The voice was as wasted as the lips it came from.

Kaufman raised the cleaver a little, calculating his chances. There were perhaps thirty of them in the car and many more outside. But they looked so weak, and they had no weapons, but their skin and bones.

The monster spoke again, its voice quite well-modulated, when it found itself, the piping of a once-cultured, once-charming man.

'You came after the other, yes?'

It glanced down at the body of Mahogany. It had clearly taken in the situation very quickly.

'Old anyway,' it said, its watery eyes back on Kaufman, studying him with care.

'Fuck you,' said Kaufman.

The creature attempted a wry smile, but it had almost forgotten the technique and the result was a grimace which exposed a mouthful of teeth that had been systematically filed into points.

'You must now do this for us,' it said through the bestial grin. 'We cannot survive without food.'

The hand patted the rump of human flesh. Kaufman had no reply to the idea. He just stared in disgust as the fingernails slid between the cleft in the buttocks, feeling the swell of tender muscle.

'It disgusts us no less than you,' said the creature. 'But we're bound to eat this meat, or we die. God knows, I have no appetite for it.'

The thing was drooling nevertheless.

Kaufman found his voice. It was small, more with a confusion of feelings than with fear.

'What are you?' He remembered the bearded man in the Deli. 'Are you accidents of some kind?'

'We are the City fathers,' the thing said. 'And mothers, and daughters and sons. The builders, the law-makers. We made this city.'

'New York?' said Kaufman. The Palace of Delights?

'Before you were born, before anyone living was born.'

As it spoke the creature's fingernails were running up under the skin of the split body, and were peeling the thin elastic layer off the

32

luscious brawn. Behind Kaufman, the other creatures had begun to unhook the bodies from the straps, their hands laid in that same delighting manner on the smooth breasts and flanks of flesh. These too had begun skinning the meat.

'You will bring us more,' the father said, 'More meat for us. The other one was weak.'

Kaufman stared in disbelief.

'Me?' he said, 'Feed you? What do you think I am?'

'You must do it for us, and for those older than us. For those born before the city was thought of, when America was a timberland and desert.'

The fragile hand gestured out of the train.

Kaufman's gaze followed the pointing finger into the gloom. There was something else outside the train which he'd failed to see before; much bigger than anything human.

The pack of creatures parted to let Kaufman through so that he could inspect more closely whatever it was that stood outside, but his feet would not move.

'Go on,' said the father.

Kaufman thought of the city he'd loved. Were these really its ancients, its philosophers, its creators? He had to believe it. Perhaps there were people on the surface – bureaucrats, politicians, authorities of every kind who knew this horrible secret and whose lives were dedicated to preserving these abominations, feeding them, as savages feed lambs to their gods. There was a horrible familiarity about this ritual. It rang a bell – not in Kaufman's conscious mind, but in his deeper, older self.

His feet, no longer obeying his mind, but his instinct to worship, moved. He walked through the corridor of bodies and stepped out of the train.

The light of the torches scarcely began to illuminate the limitless darkness outside. The air seemed solid, it was so thick with the smell of ancient earth. But Kaufman smelt nothing. His head bowed, it was all he could do to prevent himself from fainting again.

It was there; the precursor of man. The original American, whose homeland this was before Passamaquoddy or Cheyenne. Its eyes, if it had eyes, were on him.

His body shook. His teeth chattered.

He could hear the noise of its anatomy: ticking, crackling, sobbing.

It shifted a little in the dark.

The sound of its movement was awesome. Like a mountain sitting up.

Kaufman's face was raised to it, and without thinking about what he was doing or why, he fell to his knees in the shit in front of the Father of Fathers.

Every day of his life had been leading to this day, every moment quickening to this incalculable moment of holy terror.

Had there been sufficient light in that pit to see the whole, perhaps his tepid heart would have burst. As it was he felt it flutter in his chest as he saw what he saw.

It was a giant. Without head or limb. Without a feature that was analogous to human, without an organ that made sense, or senses. If it was like anything, it was like a shoal of fish. A thousand snouts all moving in unison, budding, blossoming and withering rhythmically. It was iridescent, like mother of pearl, but it was sometimes deeper than any colour Kaufman knew, or could put a name to.

That was all Kaufman could see, and it was more than he wanted to see. There was much more in the darkness, flickering and flapping.

But he could look no longer. He turned away, and as he did so a football was pitched out of the train and rolled to a halt in front of the Father.

At least he thought it was a football, until he peered more attentively at it, and recognized it as a human head, the head of the Butcher. The skin of the face had been peeled off in strips. It glistened with blood as it lay in front of its Lord.

Kaufman looked away, and walked back to the train. Every part of his body seemed to be weeping but his eyes. They were too hot with the sight behind him, they boiled his tears away.

Inside, the creatures had already set about their supper. One, he saw, was plucking the blue sweet morsel of a woman's eye out of the socket. Another had a hand in its mouth. At Kaufman's feet lay the Butcher's headless corpse, still bleeding profusely from where its neck had been bitten through.

The little father who had spoken earlier stood in front of Kaufman.

'Serve us?' it asked, gently, as you might ask a cow to follow you.

Kaufman was staring at the cleaver, the Butcher's symbol of office. The creatures were leaving the car now, dragging the half-eaten bodies after them. As the torches were taken out of the car, darkness was returning.

But before the lights had completely disappeared the father reached out and took hold of Kaufman's face, thrusting him round to look at himself in the filthy glass of the car window.

It was a thin reflection, but Kaufman could see quite well enough how changed he was. Whiter than any living man should be, covered in grime and blood.

The father's hand still gripped Kaufman's face, and its forefinger hooked into his mouth and down his gullet, the nail scoring the back of his throat. Kaufman gagged on the intruder, but had no will left to repel the attack.

'Serve,' said the creature. 'In silence.'

Too late, Kaufman realized the intention of the fingers –

Suddenly his tongue was seized tight and twisted on the root. Kaufman, in shock, dropped the cleaver. He tried to scream, but no sound came. Blood was in his throat, he heard his flesh tearing, and agonies convulsed him.

Then the hand was out of his mouth and the scarlet, spittle-covered fingers were in front of his face, with his tongue, held between thumb and forefinger.

Kaufman was speechless.

'Serve,' said the father, and stuffed the tongue into his own mouth, chewing on it with evident satisfaction. Kaufman fell to his knees, spewing up his sandwich.

The father was already shuffling away into the dark; the rest of the ancients had disappeared into their warren for another night.

The tannoy crackled.

'Home,' said the driver.

The doors hissed closed and the sound of power surged through the train. The lights flickered on, then off again, then on.

The train began to move.

Kaufman lay on the floor, tears pouring down his face, tears of discomfiture and of resignation. He would bleed to death, he decided, where he lay. It wouldn't matter if he died. It was a foul world anyway.

The driver woke him. He opened his eyes. The face that was looking down at him was black, and not unfriendly. It grinned. Kaufman tried to say something, but his mouth was sealed up with dried blood. He jerked his head around like a driveller trying to spit out a word. Nothing came but grunts.

He wasn't dead. He hadn't bled to death.

The driver pulled him to his knees, talking to him as though he were a three-year-old.

'You got a job to do, my man: they're very pleased with you.'

The driver had licked his fingers, and was rubbing Kaufman's swollen lips, trying to part them.

'Lots to learn before tomorrow night . . .'

Lots to learn. Lots to learn.

He led Kaufman out of the train. They were in no station he had ever seen before. It was white-tiled and absolutely pristine; a station-keeper's Nirvana. No graffiti disfigured the walls. There were no token-booths, but then there were no gates and no passengers either. This was a line that provided only one service: The Meat Train.

A morning shift of cleaners were already busy hosing the blood off the seats and the floor of the train. Somebody was stripping the Butcher's body, in preparation for dispatch to New Jersey. All around Kaufman people were at work.

A rain of dawn light was pouring through a grating in the roof of the station. Motes of dust hung in the beams, turning over and over. Kaufman watched them, entranced. He hadn't seen such a beautiful thing since he was a child. Lovely dust. Over and over, and over and over.

The driver had managed to separate Kaufman's lips. His mouth was too wounded for him to move it, but at least he could breathe easily. And the pain was already beginning to subside.

The driver smiled at him, then turned to the rest of the workers in the station.

'I'd like to introduce Mahogany's replacement. Our new butcher,' he announced.

The workers looked at Kaufman. There was a certain deference in their faces, which he found appealing.

Kaufman looked up at the sunlight, now falling all around him. He jerked his head, signifying that he wanted to go up, into the open air. The driver nodded, and led him up a steep flight of steps and through an alley-way and so out on to the sidewalk.

It was a beautiful day. The bright sky over New York was streaked with filaments of pale pink cloud, and the air smelt of morning.

The Streets and Avenues were practically empty. At a distance an occasional cab crossed an intersection, its engine a whisper; a runner sweated past on the other side of the street.

Very soon these same deserted sidewalks would be thronged with people. The city would go about its business in ignorance: never knowing what it was built upon, or what it owed its life to. Without hesitation, Kaufman fell to his knees and kissed the dirty concrete with his bloody lips, silently swearing his eternal loyalty to its continuance.

The Palace of Delights received the adoration without comment.

The Yattering and Jack

Why the powers (long may they hold court; long may they shit light on the heads of the damned) had sent it out from Hell to stalk Jack Polo, the Yattering couldn't discover. Whenever he passed a tentative enquiry along the system to his master, just asking the simple question, 'What am I doing here?' it was answered with a swift rebuke for its curiosity. None of its business, came the reply, its business was to do. Or die trying. And after six months of pursuing Polo, the Yattering was beginning to see extinction as an easy option. This endless game of hide and seek was to nobody's benefit, and to the Yattering's immense frustration. It feared ulcers, it feared psychosomatic leprosy (condition lower demons like itself were susceptible to), worst of all it feared losing its temper completely and killing the man outright in an uncontrollable fit of pique.

What was Jack Polo anyway?

A gherkin importer; by the balls of Leviticus, he was simply a gherkin importer. His life was worn out, his family was dull, his politics were simple-minded and his theology non-existent. The man was a no-account, one of nature's blankest little numbers – why bother with the likes of him? This wasn't a Faust: a pact-maker, a soul-seller. This one wouldn't look twice at the chance of divine inspiration: he'd sniff, shrug and get on with his gherkin importing.

Yet the Yattering was bound to that house, long night and longer day, until he had the man a lunatic, or as good as. It was going to be a lengthy job, if not interminable. Yes, there were times when even psychosomatic leprosy would be bearable if it meant being invalided off this impossible mission.

For his part, Jack J. Polo continued to be the most unknowing of men. He had always been that way; indeed his history was littered with the victims of his naïveté. When his late, lamented wife had cheated on him (he'd been in the house on at least two of the occasions, watching the television) he was the last one to find out. And the clues they'd left behind them! A blind, deaf and dumb man would have become suspicious. Not Jack. He pottered about his dull business and never noticed the tang of the adulterer's cologne, nor the abnormal regularity with which his wife changed the bed-linen.

37

He was no less disinterested in events when his younger daughter Amanda confessed her lesbianism to him. His response was a sigh and a puzzled look.

'Well, as long as you don't get pregnant, darling,' he replied, and sauntered off into the garden, blithe as ever.

What chance did a fury have with a man like that?

To a creature trained to put its meddling fingers into the wounds of the human psyche, Polo offered a surface so glacial, so utterly without distinguishing marks, as to deny malice any hold whatsoever.

Events seemed to make no dent in his perfect indifference. His life's disasters seemed not to scar his mind at all. When, eventually, he was confronted with the truth about his wife's infidelity (he found them screwing in the bath) he couldn't bring himself to be hurt or humiliated.

'These things happen,' he said to himself, backing out of the bathroom to let them finish what they'd started.

'*Che sera, sera.*'

Che sera, sera. The man muttered that damn phrase with monotonous regularity. He seemed to live by that philosophy of fatalism, letting attacks on his manhood, ambition and dignity slide off his ego like rain-water from his bald head.

The Yattering had heard Polo's wife confess all to her husband (it was hanging upside down from the light-fitting, invisible as ever) and the scene had made it wince. There was the distraught sinner, begging to be accused, bawled at, struck even, and instead of giving her the satisfaction of his hatred, Polo had just shrugged and let her say her piece without a word of interruption, until she had no more to unbosom. She'd left, at length, more out of frustration and sorrow than guilt; the Yattering had heard her tell the bathroom mirror how insulted she was at her husband's lack of righteous anger. A little while after she'd flung herself off the balcony of the Roxy Cinema.

Her suicide was in some ways convenient for the fury. With the wife gone, and the daughters away from home, it could plan for more elaborate tricks to unnerve its victim, without ever having to concern itself with revealing its presence to creatures the powers had not marked for attack.

But the absence of the wife left the house empty during the days, and that soon became a burden of boredom the Yattering found scarcely supportable. The hours from nine to five, alone in the house, often seemed endless. It would mope and wander, planning bizarre and impractical revenges upon the Polo-man, pacing the rooms, heartsick, companioned only by the clicks and whirrs of the house as the radiators cooled, or the refrigerator switched itself on and off. The situation rapidly became so desperate that the arrival of the midday post became the high-point of the day, and an unshakeable melancholy would settle on the Yattering if the postman had nothing to deliver and passed by to the next house.

When Jack returned the games would begin in earnest. The usual warm-up routine: it would meet Jack at the door and prevent his key from turning in the lock. The contest would go on for a minute or two until Jack accidentally found the measure of the Yattering's resistance, and won the day. Once inside, it would start all the lampshades swinging. The man would usually ignore this performance, however violent the motion. Perhaps he might shrug and murmur: 'Subsidence,' under his breath, then, inevitably, 'Che sera, sera.'

In the bathroom, the Yattering would have squeezed toothpaste around the toilet-seat and have plugged up the shower-head with soggy toilet-paper. It would even share the shower with Jack, hanging unseen from the rail that held up the shower curtain and murmuring obscene suggestions in his ear. That was always successful, the demons were taught at the Academy. The obscenities in the ear routine never failed to distress clients, making them think they were conceiving of these pernicious acts themselves, and driving them to self-disgust, then to self-rejection and finally to madness. Of course, in a few cases the victims would be so inflamed by these whispered suggestions they'd go out on the streets and act upon them. Under such circumstances the victim would often be arrested and incarcerated. Prison would lead to further crimes, and a slow dwindling of moral reserves – and the victory was won by that route. One way or another insanity would out.

Except that for some reason this rule did not apply to Polo; he was unperturbable: a tower of propriety.

Indeed, the way things were going the Yattering would be the one to break. It was tired; so very tired. Endless days of tormenting the cat, reading the funnies in yesterday's newspaper, watching the game shows: they drained the fury. Lately, it had developed a passion for the woman who lived across the street from Polo. She was a young widow; and seemed to spend most of her life parading around the house stark naked. It was almost unbearable sometimes, in the middle of a day when the postman failed to call, watching the woman and knowing it could never cross the threshold of Polo's house.

This was the Law. The Yattering was a minor demon, and his

soul-catching was strictly confined to the perimeters of his victim's house. To step outside was to relinquish all powers over the victim: to put itself at the mercy of humanity.

All June, all July and most of August it sweated in its prison, and all through those bright, hot months Jack Polo maintained complete indifference to the Yattering's attacks.

It was deeply embarrassing, and it was gradually destroying the demon's self-confidence, seeing this bland victim survive every trial and trick attempted upon him.

The Yattering wept.

The Yattering screamed.

In a fit of uncontrollable anguish, it boiled the water in the aquarium, poaching the guppies.

Polo heard nothing. Saw nothing.

At last, in late September, the Yattering broke one of the first rules of its condition, and appealed directly to its masters.

Autumn is Hell's season; and the demons of the higher dominations were feeling benign. They condescended to speak to their creature.

'What do you want?' asked Beelzebub, his voice blackening the air in the lounge.

'This man . . .' the Yattering began nervously.

'Yes?'

'This Polo . . .'

'Yes?'

'I am without issue upon him. I can't get panic upon him, I can't breed fear or even mild concern upon him. I am sterile, Lord of the Flies, and I wish to be put out of my misery.'

For a moment Beelzebub's face formed in the mirror over the mantelpiece.

'You want *what?*'

Beelzebub was part elephant, part wasp. The Yattering was terrified.

'I – want to die.'

'You cannot die.'

'From this world. Just die from this world. Fade away. Be replaced.'

'*You will not die.*'

'But I can't break him!' the Yattering shrieked, tearful.

'You must.'

'Why?'

'Because we tell you to.' Beelzebub always used the Royal 'we', though unqualified to do so.

40

'Let me at least know why I'm in this house.' the Yattering appealed. 'What is he? Nothing! He's nothing!'

Beelzebub found this rich. He laughed, buzzed, trumpeted.

'Jack Johnson Polo is the child of a worshipper at the Church of Lost Salvation. He belongs to us.'

'But why should you want him? He's so dull.'

'We want him because his soul was promised to us, and his mother did not deliver it. Or herself come to that. She cheated us. She died in the arms of a priest, and was safely escorted to − '

The word that followed was anathema. The Lord of the Flies could barely bring himself to pronounce it.

' − Heaven,' said Beelzebub, with infinite loss in his voice.

'Heaven,' said the Yattering, not knowing quite what was meant by the word.

'Polo is to be hounded in the name of the Old One, and punished for his mother's crimes. No torment is too profound for a family that has cheated us.'

'I'm tired,' the Yattering pleaded, daring to approach the mirror, 'Please. I beg you.'

'Claim this man,' said Beelzebub, 'or you will suffer in his place.'

The figure in the mirror waved its black and yellow trunk and faded.

'Where is your pride?' said the master's voice as it shrivelled into distance. 'Pride, Yattering, pride.'

Then he was gone.

In its frustration the Yattering picked up the cat and threw it into the fire, where it was rapidly cremated. If only the law allowed such easy cruelty to be visited upon human flesh, it thought. If only. If only. Then it'd make Polo suffer such torments. But no. The Yattering knew the laws as well as the back of its hand; they had been flayed on to its exposed cortex as a fledgling demon by its teachers. And Law One stated: 'Thou shalt not lay palm upon thy victims.'

It had never been told why this law pertained, but it did.

'Thou shalt not . . .'

So the whole painful process continued. Day in, day out, and still the man showed no sign of yielding. Over the next few weeks the Yattering killed two more cats that Polo brought home to replace his treasured Freddy (now ash).

The first of these poor victims was drowned in the toilet bowl one idle Friday afternoon. It was a petty satisfaction to see the look of distaste register on Polo's face as he unzipped his fly and glanced down. But any pleasure the Yattering took in Jack's discomfiture

41

was cancelled out by the blithely efficient way in which the man dealt with the dead cat, hoisting the bundle of soaking fur out of the pan, wrapping it in a towel and burying it in the back garden with scarcely a murmur.

The third cat that Polo brought home was wise to the invisible presence of the demon from the start. There was indeed an entertaining week in mid-November when life for the Yattering became almost interesting while it played cat and mouse with Freddy the Third. Freddy played the mouse. Cats not being especially bright animals the game was scarcely a great intellectual challenge, but it made a change from the endless days of waiting, haunting and failing. At least the creature accepted the Yattering's presence. Eventually however, in a filthy mood (caused by the re-marriage of the Yattering's naked widow) the demon lost its temper with the cat. It was sharpening its nails on the nylon carpet, clawing and scratching at the pile for hours on end. The noise put the demon's metaphysical teeth on edge. It looked at the cat once, briefly, and it flew apart as though it had swallowed a live grenade.

The effect was spectacular. The results were gross. Cat-brain, cat-fur, cat-gut everywhere.

Polo got home that evening exhausted, and stood in the doorway of the dining-room, his face sickened, surveying the carnage that had been Freddy III.

'Damn dogs,' he said. 'Damn, damn dogs.'

There was anger in his voice. Yes, exulted the Yattering, anger. The man was upset: there was clear evidence of emotion on his face.

Elated, the demon raced through the house, determined to capitalize on its victory. It opened and slammed every door. It smashed vases. It set the lampshades swinging.

Polo just cleaned up the cat.

The Yattering threw itself downstairs, tore up a pillow. Impersonated a thing with a limp and an appetite for human flesh in the attic, and giggling.

Polo just buried Freddy III, beside the grave of Freddy II, and the ashes of Freddy I.

Then he retired to bed, without his pillow.

The demon was utterly stumped. If the man could not raise more than a flicker of concern when his cat was exploded in the dining-room, what chance had it got of ever breaking the bastard?

There was one last opportunity left.

It was approaching Christ's Mass, and Jack's children would be coming home to the bosom of the family. Perhaps they could convince him that all was not well with the world; perhaps they could get their fingernails under his flawless indifference, and begin to break him down. Hoping against hope, the Yattering sat out the weeks to late December, planning its attacks with all the imaginative malice it could muster.

Meanwhile, Jack's life sauntered on. He seemed to live apart from his experience, living his life as an author might write a preposterous story, never involving himself in the narrative too deeply. In several significant ways, however, he showed his enthusiasm for the coming holiday. He cleared his daughters' rooms immaculately. He made their beds up with sweet-smelling linen. He cleaned every speck of cat's blood out of the carpet. He even set up a Christmas tree in the lounge, hung with iridescent balls, tinsel and presents.

Once in a while, as he went about the preparations, Jack thought of the game he was playing, and quietly calculated the odds against him. In the days to come he would have to measure not only his own suffering, but that of his daughters, against the possible victory. And always, when he made these calculations, the chance of victory seemed to outweigh the risks.

So he continued to write his life, and waited.

Snow came, soft pats of it against the windows, against the door. Children arrived to sing carols, and he was generous to them. It was possible, for a brief time, to believe in peace on earth.

Late in the evening of the twenty-third of December the daughters arrived, in a flurry of cases and kisses. The youngest, Amanda, arrived home first. From its vantage point on the landing the Yattering viewed the young woman balefully. She didn't look like ideal material in which to induce a breakdown. In fact, she looked dangerous. Gina followed an hour or two later; a smoothly-polished woman of the world at twenty-four, she looked every bit as intimidating as her sister. They came into the house with their bustle and their laughter; they re-arranged the furniture; they threw out the junk-food in the freezer, they told each other (and their father) how much they had missed each other's company. Within the space of a few hours the drab house was repainted with light, and fun and love.

It made the Yattering sick.

Whimpering, it hid its head in the bedroom to block out the din of affection, but the shock-waves enveloped it. All it could do was sit, and listen, and refine its revenge.

Jack was pleased to have his beauties home. Amanda so full of opinions, and so strong, like her mother. Gina more like *his* mother: poised, perceptive. He was so happy in their presence he could have wept; and here was he, the proud father, putting them both at such risk. But what was the alternative? If he had cancelled the Christmas celebrations, it would have looked highly suspicious. It might even have spoiled his whole strategy, waking the enemy to the trick that was being played.

No; he must sit tight. Play dumb, the way the enemy had come to expect him to be.

The time would come for action.

At 3.15 a.m. on Christmas morning the Yattering opened hostilities by throwing Amanda out of bed. A paltry performance at best, but it had the intended effect. Sleepily rubbing her bruised head, she climbed back into bed, only to have the bed buck and shake and fling her off again like an unbroken colt.

The noise woke the rest of the house. Gina was first in her sister's room.

'What's going on?'

'There's somebody under the bed.'

'What?'

Gina picked up a paperweight from the dresser and demanded the assailant come out. The Yattering, invisible, sat on the windowseat and made obscene gestures at the women, tying knots in its genitalia.

Gina peered under the bed. The Yattering was clinging to the light fixture now, persuading it to swing backwards and forwards, making the room reel.

'There's nothing there – '

'There is.'

Amanda knew. Oh yes, she knew.

'There's something here, Gina,' she said. 'Something in the room with us, I'm sure of it.'

'No.' Gina was absolute. 'It's empty.'

Amanda was searching behind the wardrobe when Polo came in.

'What's all the din?'

'There's something in the house Daddy. I was thrown out of bed.'

Jack looked at the crumpled sheets, the dislodged mattress, then at Amanda. This was the first test: he must lie as casually as possible.

'Looks like you've been having nightmares, beauty,' he said, affecting an innocent smile.

'There was something under the bed,' Amanda insisted.

'There's nobody here now.'

'But I felt it.'

'Well I'll check the rest of the house,' he offered, without enthusiasm for the task. 'You two stay here, just in case.'

As Polo left the room, the Yattering rocked the light a little more.

44

'Subsidence,' said Gina.

It was cold downstairs, and Polo could have done without padding around barefoot on the kitchen tiles, but he was quietly satisfied that the battle had been joined in such a petty manner. He'd half-feared that the enemy would turn savage with such tender victims at hand. But no: he'd judged the mind of the creature quite accurately. It was one of the lower orders. Powerful, but slow. Capable of being inveigled beyond the limits of its control. Carefully does it, he told himself, carefully does it.

He traipsed through the entire house, dutifully opening cupboards and peering behind the furniture, then returned to his daughters, who were sitting at the top of the stairs. Amanda looked small and pale, not the twenty-two-year-old woman she was, but a child again.

'Nothing doing,' he told her with a smile. 'It's Christmas morning and all through the house – '

Gina finished the rhyme.

'Nothing is stirring; not even a mouse.'

'Not even a mouse, beauty.'

At that moment the Yattering took its cue to fling a vase off the lounge mantelpiece.

Even Jack jumped.

'Shit,' he said. He needed some sleep, but quite clearly the Yattering had no intention of letting them alone just yet.

'*Che sera, sera*,' he murmured, scooping up the pieces of the Chinese vase, and putting them in a piece of newspaper. 'The house is sinking a little on the left side, you know,' he said more loudly. 'It has been for years.'

'Subsidence,' said Amanda with quiet certainty, 'would not throw me out of my bed.'

Gina said nothing. The options were limited. The alternatives unattractive.

'Well maybe it was Santa Claus,' said Polo, attempting levity. He parcelled up the pieces of the vase and wandered through into the kitchen, certain that he was being shadowed every step of the way. 'What else can it be?' He threw the question over his shoulder as he stuffed the newspaper into the wastebin. 'The only other explanation – ' here he became almost elated by his skimming so close to the truth, 'the only other possible explanation is too preposterous for words.'

It was an exquisite irony, denying the existence of the invisible world in the full knowledge that it even now it breathed vengefully down his neck.

'You mean poltergeists?' said Gina.

45

'I mean anything that goes bang in the night. But, we're grown-up people aren't we? We don't believe in Bogeymen.'

'No,' said Gina flatly, 'I don't, but I don't believe the house is subsiding either.'

'Well, it'll have to do for now,' said Jack with nonchalant finality. 'Christmas starts here. We don't want to spoil it talking about gremlins, now do we.'

They laughed together.

Gremlins. That surely bit deep. To call the Hell-spawn a gremlin.

The Yattering, weak with frustration, acid tears boiling on its intangible cheeks, ground its teeth and kept its peace.

There would be time yet to beat that atheistic smile off Jack Polo's smooth, fat face. Time aplenty. No half-measures from now on. No subtlety. It would be an all out attack.

Let there be blood. Let there be agony.

They'd all break.

Amanda was in the kitchen, preparing Christmas dinner, when the Yattering mounted its next attack. Through the house drifted the sound of King's College Choir, 'O Little Town of Bethlehem, how still we see thee lie . . .'

The presents had been opened, the G and T's were being downed, the house was one warm embrace from roof to cellar.

In the kitchen a sudden chill permeated the heat and the steam, making Amanda shiver; she crossed to the window, which was ajar to clear the air, and closed it. Maybe she was catching something.

The Yattering watched her back as she busied herself about the kitchen, enjoying the domesticity for a day. Amanda felt the stare quite clearly. She turned round. Nobody, nothing. She continued to wash the Brussels sprouts, cutting into one with a worm curled in the middle. She drowned it.

The Choir sang on.

In the lounge, Jack was laughing with Gina about something.

Then, a noise. A rattling at first, followed by a beating of somebody's fists against a door. Amanda dropped the knife into the bowl of sprouts, and turned from the sink, following the sound. It was getting louder all the time. Like something locked in one of the cupboards, desperate to escape. A cat caught in the box, or a –

Bird.

It was coming from the oven.

Amanda's stomach turned, as she began to imagine the worst. Had she locked something in the oven when she'd put in the turkey? She called for her father, as she snatched up the oven cloth and stepped towards the cooker, which was rocking with the panic of its prisoner. She had visions of a basted cat leaping out at her, its fur burned off, its flesh half-cooked.

Jack was at the kitchen door.

'There's something in the oven,' she said to him, as though he needed telling. The cooker was in a frenzy; its thrashing contents had all but beaten off the door.

He took the oven cloth from her. This is a new one, he thought. You're better than I judged you to be. This is clever. This is original.

Gina was in the kitchen now.

'What's cooking?' she quipped.

But the joke was lost as the cooker began to dance, and the pans of boiling water were twitched off the burners on to the floor. Scalding water seared Jack's leg. He yelled, stumbling back into Gina, before diving at the cooker with a yell that wouldn't have shamed a Samurai.

The oven handle was slippery with heat and grease, but he seized it and flung the door down.

A wave of steam and blistering heat rolled out of the oven, smelling of succulent turkey-fat. But the bird inside had apparently no intentions of being eaten. It was flinging itself from side to side on the roasting tray, tossing gouts of gravy in all directions. Its crisp brown wings pitifully flailed and flapped, its legs beat a tattoo on the roof of the oven.

Then it seemed to sense the open door. Its wings stretched themselves out to either side of its stuffed bulk and it half hopped, half fell on to the oven door, in a mockery of its living self. Headless, oozing stuffing and onions, it flopped around as though nobody had told the damn thing it was dead, while the fat still bubbled on its bacon-strewn back.

Amanda screamed.

Jack dived for the door as the bird lurched into the air, blind but vengeful. What it intended to do once it reached its three cowering victims was never discovered. Gina dragged Amanda into the hallway with her father in hot pursuit, and the door was slammed closed as the blind bird flung itself against the pannelling, beating on it with all its strength. Gravy seeped through the gap at the bottom of the door, dark and fatty.

The door had no lock, but Jack reasoned that the bird was not capable of turning the handle. As he backed away, breathless he cursed his confidence. The opposition had more up its sleeve than he'd guessed.

47

Amanda was leaning against the wall sobbing, her face stained with splotches of turkey grease. All she seemed able to do was deny what she'd seen, shaking her head and repeating the word 'no' like a talisman against the ridiculous horror that was still throwing itself against the door. Jack escorted her through to the lounge. The radio was still crooning carols which blotted out the din of the bird, but their promises of goodwill seemed small comfort.

Gina poured a hefty brandy for her sister and sat beside her on the sofa, plying her with spirits and reassurance in about equal measure. They made little impression on Amanda.

'What *was* that?' Gina asked her father, in a tone that demanded an answer.

'I don't know what it was,' Jack replied.

'Mass hysteria?' Gina's displeasure was plain. Her father had a secret: he knew what was going on in the house, but he was refusing to cough up for some reason.

'What do I call: the police or an exorcist?'

'Neither.'

'For God's sake – '

'There's *nothing* going on, Gina. Really.'

Her father turned from the window and looked at her. His eyes spoke what his mouth refused to say, that this was war.

Jack was afraid.

The house was suddenly a prison. The game was suddenly lethal. The enemy, instead of playing foolish games, meant harm, real harm to them all.

In the kitchen the turkey had at last conceded defeat. The carols on the radio had withered into a sermon on God's benedictions.

What had been sweet was sour and dangerous. He looked across the room at Amanda and Gina. Both for their own reasons, were trembling. Polo wanted to tell them, wanted to explain what was going on. But the thing must be there, he knew, gloating.

He was wrong. The Yattering had retired to the attic, well-satisfied with its endeavours. The bird, it felt, had been a stroke of genius. Now it could rest a while: recuperate. Let the enemy's nerves tatter themselves in anticipation. Then, in its own good time, it would deliver the coup de grâce.

Idly, it wondered if any of the inspectors had seen his work with the turkey. Maybe they would be impressed enough by the Yattering's originality to improve its job-prospects. Surely it hadn't gone through all those years of training simply to chase half-witted imbeciles like Polo. There must be something more challenging available than that. It felt victory in its invisible bones: and it was a good feeling.

48

The pursuit of Polo would surely gain momentum now. His daughters would convince him (if he wasn't now quite convinced) that there was something terrible afoot. He would crack. He would crumble. Maybe he'd go classically mad: tear out his hair, rip off his clothes; smear himself with his own excrement.

Oh yes, victory was close. And wouldn't his masters be loving then? Wouldn't it be showered with praise, and power?

One more manifestation was all that was required. One final, inspired intervention, and Polo would be so much blubbering flesh.

Tired, but confident, Yattering descended into the lounge.

Amanda was lying full-length on the sofa, asleep. She was obviously dreaming about the turkey. Her eyes rolled beneath her gossamer lids, her lower lip trembled. Gina sat beside the radio, which was silenced now. She had a book open on her lap, but she wasn't reading it.

The gherkin importer wasn't in the room. Wasn't that his footstep on the stair? Yes, he was going upstairs to relieve his brandy-full bladder.

Ideal timing.

The Yattering crossed the room. In her sleep Amanda dreamt something dark flitting across her vision, something malign, something that tasted bitter in her mouth.

Gina looked up from her book.

The silver balls on the tree were rocking, gently. Not just the balls. The tinsel and the branches too.

In fact, the tree. The whole tree was rocking as though someone had just seized hold of it.

Gina had a very bad feeling about this. She stood up. The book slid to the floor.

The tree began to spin.

'Christ,' she said. 'Jesus Christ.'

Amanda slept on.

The tree picked up momentum.

Gina walked as steadily as she could across to the sofa and tried to shake her sister awake. Amanda, locked in her dreams, resisted for a moment.

'Father,' said Gina. Her voice was strong, and carried through into the hall. It also woke Amanda.

Downstairs, Polo heard a noise like a whining dog. No, like two whining dogs. As he ran down the stairs, the duet became a trio. He burst into the lounge half expecting all the hosts of Hell to be in there, dog-headed, dancing on his beauties.

But no. It was the Christmas tree that was whining, whining like a pack of dogs, as it spun and spun.

The lights had long since been pulled from their sockets. The air stank of singed plastic and pine-sap. The tree itself was spinning like a top, flinging decorations and presents off its tortured branches with the largesse of a mad king.

Jack tore his eyes from the spectacle of the tree and found Gina and Amanda crouching, terrified, behind the sofa.

'Get out of here,' he yelled.

Even as he spoke the television sat up impertinently on one leg and began to spin like the tree, gathering momentum quickly. The clock on the mantelpiece joined the pirouetting. The pokers beside the fire. The cushions. The ornaments. Each object added its own singular note to the orchestration of whines which were building up, second by second, to a deafening pitch. The air began to brim with the smell of burning wood, as friction heated the spinning tops to flash-point. Smoke swirled across the room.

Gina had Amanda by the arm, and was dragging her towards the door, shielding her face against the hail of pine needles that the still-accelerating tree was throwing off.

Now the lights were spinning.

The books, having flung themselves off the shelves, had joined the tarantella.

Jack could see the enemy, in his mind's eye, racing between the objects like a juggler spinning plates on sticks, trying to keep them all moving at once. It must be exhausting work, he thought. The demon was probably close to collapse. It couldn't be thinking straight. Over-excited. Impulsive. Vulnerable. This must be the moment, if ever there was a moment, to join battle at last. To face the thing, defy it, and trap it.

For its part, the Yattering was enjoying this orgy of destruction. It flung every movable object into the fray, setting everything spinning.

It watched with satisfaction as the daughter twitched and scurried; it laughed to see the old man stare, pop-eyed, at this preposterous ballet.

Surely he was nearly mad, wasn't he?

The beauties had reached the door, their hair and skin full of needles. Polo didn't see them leave. He ran across the room, dodging a rain of ornaments to do so, and picked up a brass toasting fork which the enemy had overlooked. Bric-a-brac filled the air around his head, dancing around with sickening speed. His flesh was bruised and punctured. But the exhilaration of joining battle had overtaken him, and he set about beating the books, and the clocks, and the china to smithereens. Like a man in a cloud of locusts he ran around the room, bringing down his favourite books in a welter of fluttering pages, smashing whirling Dresden, shattering the lamps. A litter of broken possessions swamped the floor, some of it still twitching as the life went out of the fragments. But for every object brought low, there were a dozen still spinning, still whining.

He could hear Gina at the door, yelling to him to get out, to leave it alone.

But it was so enjoyable, playing against the enemy more directly than he'd ever allowed himself before. He didn't want to give up. He wanted the demon to show itself, to be known, to be recognized.

He wanted confrontation with the Old One's emissary once and for all.

Without warning the tree gave way to the dictates of centrifugal force, and exploded. The noise was like a howl of death. Branches, twigs, needles, balls, lights, wire, ribbons, flew across the room. Jack, his back to the explosion, felt a gust of energy hit him hard, and he was flung to the ground. The back of his neck and his scalp were shot full of pine-needles. A branch, naked of greenery, shot past his head and impaled the sofa. Fragments of tree pattered to the carpet around him.

Now other objects around the room, spun beyond the tolerance of their structures, were exploding like the tree. The television blew up, sending a lethal wave of glass across the room, much of which buried itself in the opposite wall. Fragments of the television's innards, so hot they singed the skin, fell on Jack, as he elbowed himself towards the door like a soldier under bombardment.

The room was so thick with a barrage of shards it was like a fog. The cushions had lent their down to the scene, snowing on the carpet. Porcelain pieces: a beautifully-glazed arm, a courtesan's head, bounced on the floor in front of his nose.

Gina was crouching at the door, urging him to hurry, her eyes narrowed against the hail. As Jack reached the door, and felt her arms around him, he swore he could hear laughter from the lounge. Tangible, audible laughter, rich and satisfied.

Amanda was standing in the hall, her hair full of pine-needles, staring down at him. He pulled his legs through the doorway and Gina slammed the door shut on the demolition.

'What is it?' she demanded. 'Poltergeist? Ghost? Mother's ghost?'

The thought of his dead wife being responsible for such wholesale destruction struck Jack as funny.

Amanda was half smiling. Good, he thought, she's coming out

of it. Then he met the vacant look in her eyes and the truth dawned. She'd broken, her sanity had taken refuge where this fantastique couldn't get at it.

'*What's in there?*' Gina was asking, her grip on his arm so strong it stopped the blood.

'I don't know,' he lied. 'Amanda?'

Amanda's smile didn't decay. She just stared on at him, through him.

'You do know.'

'No.'

'You're lying.'

'I think . . .'

He picked himself off the floor, brushing the pieces of porcelain, the feathers, the glass, off his shirt and trousers.

'I think . . . I shall go for a walk.'

Behind him, in the lounge, the last vestiges of whining had stopped. The air in the hallway was electric with unseen presences. It was very close to him, invisible as ever, but so close. This was the most dangerous time. He mustn't lose his nerve now. He must stand up as though nothing had happened; he must leave Amanda be, leave explanations and recriminations until it was all over and done with.

'Walk?' Gina said, disbelievingly.

'Yes . . . walk . . . I need some fresh air.'

'You can't leave us here.'

'I'll find somebody to help us clear up.'

'But Mandy.'

'She'll get over it. Leave her be.'

That was hard. That was almost unforgivable. But it was said now.

He walked unsteadily towards the front door, feeling nauseous after so much spinning. At his back Gina was raging.

'You can't just leave! Are you out of your mind?'

'I need the air,' he said, as casually as his thumping heart and his parched throat would permit. 'So I'll just go out for a moment.'

No, the Yattering said. No, no, no.

It was behind him, Polo could feel it. So angry now, so ready to twist off his head. Except that it wasn't allowed, *ever* to touch him. But he could feel its resentment like a physical presence.

He took another step towards the front door.

It was with him still, dogging his every step. His shadow, his fetch; unshakable. Gina shrieked at him, 'You sonofabitch, look at Mandy! She's lost her mind!'

No, he mustn't look at Mandy. If he looked at Mandy he might weep, he might break down as the thing wanted him to, then everything would be lost.

'She'll be all right,' he said, barely above a whisper.

He reached for the front door handle. The demon bolted the door, quickly, loudly. No temper left for pretence now.

Jack, keeping his movements as even as possible, unbolted the door, top and bottom. It bolted again.

It was thrilling, this game; it was also terrifying. If he pushed too far surely the demon's frustration would override its lessons?

Gently, smoothly, he unbolted the door again. Just as gently, just as smoothly, the Yattering bolted it.

Jack wondered how long he could keep this up for. Somehow he had to get outside: he had to coax it over the threshold. One step was all that the law required, according to his researches. One simple step.

Unbolted. Bolted. Unbolted. Bolted.

Gina was standing two or three yards behind her father. She didn't understand what she was seeing, but it was obvious her father was doing battle with someone, or something.

'Daddy – ' she began.

'Shut up,' he said benignly, grinning as he unbolted the door for the seventh time. There was a shiver of lunacy in the grin, it was too wide and too easy.

Inexplicably, she returned the smile. It was grim, but genuine. Whatever was at issue here, she loved him.

Polo made a break for the back door. The demon was three paces ahead of him, scooting through the house like a sprinter, and bolting the door before Jack could even reach the handle. The key was turned in the lock by invisible hands, then crushed to dust in the air.

Jack feigned a move towards the window beside the back door but the blinds were pulled down and the shutters slammed. The Yattering, too concerned with the window to watch Jack closely, missed his doubling back through the house.

When it saw the trick that was being played it let out a little screech, and gave chase, almost sliding into Jack on the smoothly-polished floor. It avoided the collision only by the most balletic of manoeuvres. That would be fatal indeed: to touch the man in the heat of the moment.

Polo was again, at the front door and Gina wise, to her father's strategy, had unbolted it while the Yattering and Jack fought at the back door. Jack had prayed she'd take the opportunity to open it. She had. It stood slightly ajar: the icy air of the crisp afternoon curled its way into the hallway.

Jack covered the last yards to the door in a flash, feeling without hearing the howl of complaint the Yattering loosed as it saw its victim escaping into the outside world.

It was not an ambitious creature. All it wanted at that moment, beyond any other dream, was to take this human's skull between its palms and make a nonsense of it. Crush it to smithereens, and pour the hot thought out on to the snow. To be done with Jack J. Polo, forever and forever.

Was that so much to ask?

Polo had stepped into the squeaky-fresh snow, his slippers and trouser-bottoms buried in chill. By the time the fury reached the step Jack was already three or four yards away, marching up the path towards the gate. Escaping. Escaping.

The Yattering howled again, forgetting its years of training. Every lesson it had learned, every rule of battle engraved on its skull was submerged by the simple desire to have Polo's life.

It stepped over the threshold and gave chase. It was an unpardonable transgression. Somewhere in Hell, the powers (long may they hold court; long may they shit light on the heads of the damned) felt the sin, and knew the war for Jack Polo's soul was lost.

Jack felt it too. He heard the sound of boiling water, as the demon's footsteps melted to steam the snow on the path. It was coming after him! The thing had broken the first rule of its existence. It was forfeit. He felt the victory in his spine, and his stomach.

The demon overtook him at the gate. Its breath could clearly be seen in the air, though the body it emanated from had not yet become visible.

Jack tried to open the gate, but the Yattering slammed it shut.

'*Che sera, sera,*' said Jack.

The Yattering could bear it no longer. He took Jack's head in his hands, intending to crush the fragile bone to dust.

The touch was its second sin; and it agonized the Yattering beyond endurance. It bayed like a banshee and reeled away from the contact, sliding in the snow and falling on its back.

It knew its mistake. The lessons it had had beaten into it came hurtling back. It knew the punishment too, for leaving the house, for touching the man. It was bound to a new lord, enslaved to this idiot-creature standing over it.

Polo had won.

He was laughing, watching the way the outline of the demon formed in the snow on the path. Like a photograph developing on a sheet of paper, the image of the fury came clear. The law was

54

taking its toll. The Yattering could never hide from its master again. There it was, plain to Polo's eyes, in all its charmless glory. Maroon flesh and bright lidless eye, arms flailing, tail thrashing the snow to slush.

'You bastard,' it said. Its accent had an Australian lilt.

'You will not speak unless spoken to,' said Polo, with quiet, but absolute, authority. 'Understood?'

The lidless eye clouded with humility.

'Yes.' The Yattering said.

'Yes, Mister Polo.'

'Yes, Mister Polo.'

Its tail slipped between its legs like that of a whipped dog.

'You may stand.'

'Thank you, Mr Polo.'

It stood. Not a pleasant sight, but one Jack rejoiced in nevertheless.

'They'll have you yet,' said the Yattering.

'Who will?'

'You know,' it said, hesitantly.

'Name them.'

'Beelzebub,' it answered, proud to name its old master. 'The powers. Hell itself.'

'I don't think so,' Polo mused. 'Not with you bound to me as proof of my skills. Aren't I the better of them?'

The eye looked sullen.

'*Aren't I?*'

'Yes,' it conceded bitterly. 'Yes. You are the better of them.'

It had begun to shiver.

'Are you cold?' asked Polo.

It nodded, affecting the look of a lost child.

'Then you need some exercise,' he said, 'You'd better go back into the house and start tidying up.'

The fury looked bewildered, even disappointed, by this instruction.

'Nothing more?' it asked incredulously. 'No miracles? No Helen of Troy? No flying?'

The thought of flying on a snow-spattered afternoon like this left Polo cold. He was essentially a man of simple tastes: all he asked for in life was the love of his children, a pleasant home, and a good trading price for gherkins.

'No flying,' he said.

As the Yattering slouched down the path towards the door it seemed to alight upon a new piece of mischief. It turned back to Polo, obsequious, but unmistakably smug.

55

'Could I just say something?' it said.

'Speak.'

'It's only fair that I inform you that it's considered ungodly to have any contact with the likes of me. Heretical even.'

'Is that so?'

'Oh yes,' said the Yattering, warming to its prophecy. 'People have been burned for less.'

'Not in this day and age,' Polo replied.

'But the Seraphim will see,' it said. 'And that means you'll never go to that place.'

'What place?'

The Yattering fumbled for the special word it had heard Beelzebub use.

'Heaven,' it said, triumphant. An ugly grin had come on to its face; this was the cleverest manoeuvre it had ever attempted; it was juggling theology here.

Jack nodded slowly, nibbling at his bottom lip.

The creature was probably telling the truth: association with it or its like would not be looked upon benignly by the Host of Saints and Angels. He probably *was* forbidden access to the plains of paradise.

'Well,' he said, 'You know what I have to say about that, don't you?'

The Yattering stared at him, frowning. No, it didn't know. Then the grin of satisfaction it had been wearing died, as it saw just what Polo was driving at.

'What do I say?' Polo asked it.

Defeated, the Yattering murmured the phrase.

'*Che sera, sera.*'

Polo smiled. 'There's a chance for you yet,' he said, and led the way over the threshold, closing the door with something very like serenity on his face.

Pig Blood Blues

You could smell the kids before you could see them, their young sweat turned stale in corridors with barred windows, their bolted breath sour, their heads musty. Then their voices, subdued by the rules of confinement.

Don't run. Don't shout. Don't whistle. Don't fight.

They called it a Remand Centre for Adolescent Offenders, but it was near as damn it a prison. There were locks and keys and warders. The gestures of liberalism were few and far between and they didn't disguise the truth too well; Tetherdowne was a prison by sweeter name, and the inmates knew it.

Not that Redman had any illusions about his pupils-to-be. They were hard, and they were locked away for a reason. Most of them would rob you blind as soon as look at you; cripple you if it suited them, no sweat. He had too many years in the force to believe the sociological lie. He knew the victims, and he knew the kids. They weren't misunderstood morons, they were quick and sharp and amoral, like the razors they hid under their tongues. They had no use for sentiment, they just wanted out.

'Welcome to Tetherdowne.'

Was the woman's name Leverton, or Leverfall, or –

'I'm Doctor Leverthal.'

Leverthal. Yes. Hard-bitten bitch he'd met at –

'We met at the interview.'

'Yes.'

'We're glad to see you, Mr Redman.'

'Neil; please call me Neil.'

'We try not to go on a first name basis in front of the boys, we find they think they've got a finger into your private life. So I'd prefer you to keep Christian names purely for off-duty hours.'

She didn't offer hers. Probably something flinty. Yvonne. Lydia. He'd invent something appropriate. She looked fifty, and was probably ten years younger. No make-up, hair tied back so severely he wondered her eyes didn't pop.

'You'll be beginning classes the day after tomorrow. The Governor asked me to welcome you to the Centre on his behalf, and apologise to you that he can't be here himself. There are funding problems.'

'Aren't there always?'

'Regrettably yes. I'm afraid we're swimming against the tide here; the general mood of the country is very Law and Order orientated.'

What was that a nice way of saying? Beat the shit out of any kid caught so much as jay-walking? Yes, he'd been that way himself in his time, and it was a nasty little cul-de-sac, every bit as bad as being sentimental.

'The fact is, we may lose Tetherdowne altogether,' she said, 'which would be a shame. I know it doesn't look like much . . .'

' – but it's home,' he laughed. The joke fell among thieves. She didn't even seem to hear it.

'You,' her tone hardened, 'you have a solid (did she say sullied?) background in the Police Force. Our hope is that your appointment here will be welcomed by the funding authorities.'

So that was it. Token ex-policeman brought in to appease the powers that be, to show willing in the discipline department. They didn't really want him here. They wanted some sociologist who'd write up reports on the effect of the class-system on brutality amongst teenagers. She was quietly telling him that he was the odd man out.

'I told you why I left the force.'

'You mentioned it. Invalided out.'

'I wouldn't take a desk job, it was as simple as that; and they wouldn't let me do what I did best. Danger to myself according to some of them.'

She seemed a little embarrassed by his explanation. Her a psychologist too; she should have been devouring this stuff, it was his private hurt he was making public here. He was coming clean, for Christ's sake.

'So I was out on my backside, after twenty-four years.' He hesitated, then said his piece. 'I'm not a token policeman; I'm not any kind of policeman. The force and I parted company. Understand what I'm saying?'

'Good, good.' She didn't understand a bloody word. He tried another approach.

'I'd like to know what the boys have been told.'

'Been told?'

'About me.'

'Well, something of your background.'

'I see.' They'd been warned. Here come the pigs.

'It seemed important.'

He grunted.

'You see, so many of these boys have real aggression problems.

58

That's a source of difficulty for so very many of them. They can't control themselves, and consequently they suffer.'

He didn't argue, but she looked at him severely, as though he had.

'Oh yes, they suffer. That's why we're at such pains to show some appreciation of their situation; to teach them that there are alternatives.'

She walked across to the window. From the second storey there was an adequate view of the grounds. Tetherdowne had been some kind of estate, and there was a good deal of land attached to the main house. A playing-field, its grass sere in the midsummer drought. Beyond it a cluster of out-houses, some exhausted trees, shrubbery, and then rough wasteland off to the wall. He'd seen the wall from the other side. Alcatraz would have been proud of it.

'We try to give them a little freedom, a little education and a little sympathy. There's a popular notion, isn't there, that delinquents enjoy their criminal activities? This isn't my experience at all. They come to me guilty, broken . . .'

One broken victim flicked a vee at Leverthal's back as he sauntered along the corridor. Hair slicked down and parted in three places. A couple of home-grown tattoos on his fore-arm, unfinished.

'They have committed criminal acts, however,' Redman pointed out.

'Yes, but – '

'And must, presumably, be reminded of the fact.'

'I don't think they need any reminding, Mr Redman. I think they burn with guilt.'

She was hot on guilt, which didn't surprise him. They'd taken over the pulpit, these analysts. They were up where the Bible-thumpers used to stand, with the threadbare sermons on the fires below, but with a slightly less colourful vocabulary. It was fundamentally the same story though, complete with the promises of healing, if the rituals were observed. And behold, the righteous shall inherit the Kingdom of Heaven.

There was a pursuit on the playing field, he noticed. Pursuit, and now a capture. One victim was laying into another smaller victim with his boot; it was a fairly merciless display.

Leverthal caught the scene at the same time as Redman.

'Excuse me. I must – '

She started down the stairs.

'Your workshop is third door on the left if you want to take a look,' she called over her shoulder, 'I'll be right back.'

Like hell she would. Judging by the way the scene on the field was progressing, it would be a three crowbar job to prize them apart.

Redman wandered along to his workshop. The door was locked, but through the wired glass he could see the benches, the vices, the tools. Not bad at all. He might even teach them some wood-work, if he was left alone long enough to do it.

A bit frustrated not to be able to get in, he doubled back along the corridor, and followed Leverthal downstairs, finding his way out easily on to the sun-lit playing field. A little knot of spectators had grown around the fight, or the massacre, which had now ceased. Leverthal was standing, staring down at the boy on the ground. One of the warders was kneeling at the boy's head; the injuries looked bad.

A number of the spectators looked up and stared at the new face as Redman approached. There were whispers amongst them, some smiles.

Redman looked at the boy. Perhaps sixteen, he lay with his cheek to the ground, as if listening for something in the earth.

'Lacey', Leverthal named the boy for Redman.

'Is he badly hurt?'

The man kneeling beside Lacey shook his head.

'Not too bad. Bit of a fall. Nothing broken.'

There was blood on the boy's face from his mashed nose. His eyes were closed. Peaceful. He could have been dead.

'Where's the bloody stretcher?' said the warder. He was clearly uncomfortable on the drought-hardened ground.

'They're coming, Sir,' said someone. Redman thought it was the aggressor. A thin lad: about nineteen. The sort of eyes that could sour milk at twenty paces.

Indeed a small posse of boys was emerging from the main building, carrying a stretcher and a red blanket. They were all grinning from ear to ear.

The band of spectators had begun to disperse, now that the best of it was over. Not much fun picking up the pieces.

'Wait, wait,' said Redman, 'don't we need some witnesses here? Who did this?'

There were a few casual shrugs, but most of them played deaf. They sauntered away as if nothing had been said.

Redman said: 'We saw it. From the window.'

Leverthal was offering no support.

'Didn't we?' he demanded of her.

'It was too far to lay any blame, I think. But I don't want to see any more of this kind of bullying, do you all understand me?'

She'd seen Lacey, and recognized him easily from that distance.

Why not the attacker too? Redman kicked himself for not concentrating; without names and personalities to go with the faces, it was difficult to distinguish between them. The risk of making a misplaced accusation was high, even though he was almost sure of the curdling-eyed boy. This was no time to make mistakes, he decided; this time he'd have to let the issue drop.

Leverthal seemed unmoved by the whole thing.

'Lacey,' she said quietly, 'it's always Lacey.'

'He asks for it,' said one of the boys with the stretcher, brushing a sheaf of blond-white hair from his eyes, 'he doesn't know no better.'

Ignoring the observation, Leverthal supervised Lacey's transfer to the stretcher, and started to walk back to the main building, with Redman in tow. It was all so casual.

'Not exactly wholesome, Lacey,' she said cryptically, almost by way of explanation; and that was all. So much for compassion.

Redman glanced back as they tucked the red blanket around Lacey's still form. Two things happened, almost simultaneously.

The first: Somebody in the group said, 'That's the pig'.

The second: Lacey's eyes opened and looked straight into Redman, wide, clear and true.

Redman spent a good deal of the next day putting his workshop in order. Many of the tools had been broken or rendered useless by untrained handling: saws without teeth, chisels that were chipped and edgeless, broken vices. He'd need money to resupply the shop with the basics of the trade, but now wasn't the time to start asking. Wiser to wait, and be seen to do a decent job. He was quite used to the politics of institutions; the force was full of it.

About four-thirty a bell started to ring, a good way from the workshop. He ignored it, but after a time his instincts got the better of him. Bells were alarms, and alarms were sounded to alert people. He left his tidying, locked the workshop door behind him, and followed his ears.

The bell was ringing in what was laughingly called the Hospital Unit, two or three rooms closed off from the main block and prettied up with a few pictures and curtains at the windows. There was no sign of smoke in the air, so it clearly wasn't a fire. There was shouting though. More than shouting. A howl.

He quickened his pace along the interminable corridors, and as he turned a corner towards the Unit a small figure ran straight into him. The impact winded both of them, but Redman grabbed the lad by the arm before he could make off again. The captive was quick to respond, lashing out with his shoeless feet against Redman's shin. But he had him fast.

'Let me go you fucking – '

'Calm down! Calm down!'

His pursuers were almost there.

'Hold him!'

'Fucker! Fucker! Fucker! Fucker!'

'Hold him!'

It was like wrestling a crocodile: the kid had all the strength of fear. But the best of his fury was spent. Tears were springing into his bruised eyes as he spat in Redman's face. It was Lacey in his arms, unwholesome Lacey.

'OK. We got him.'

Redman stepped back as the warder took over, putting Lacey in a hold that looked fit to break the boy's arm. Two or three others were appearing round the corner. Two boys, and a nurse, a very unlovely creature.

'Let me go . . . Let me go . . .' Lacey was yelling, but any stomach for the fight had gone out of him. A pout came to his face in defeat, and still the cow-like eyes turned up accusingly at Redman, big and brown. He looked younger than his sixteen years, almost prepubescent. There was a whisper of bum-fluff on his cheek and a few spots amongst the bruises and a badly-applied dressing across his nose. But quite a girlish face, a virgin's face, from an age when there were still virgins. And still the eyes.

Leverthal had appeared, too late to be of use.

'What's going on?'

The warder piped up. The chase had taken his breath, and his temper.

'He locked himself in the lavatories. Tried to get out through the window.'

'Why?'

The question was addressed to the warder, not to the child. A telling confusion. The warder, confounded, shrugged.

'Why?' Redman repeated the question to Lacey.

The boy just stared, as though he'd never been asked a question before.

'You the pig?' he said suddenly, snot running from his nose.

'Pig?'

'He means policeman,' said one of the boys. The noun was spoken with a mocking precision, as though he was addressing an imbecile.

'I know what he means, lad,' said Redman, still determined to out-stare Lacey, 'I know very well what he means.'

'Are you?'

62

'Be quiet, Lacey,' said Leverthal, 'you're in enough trouble as it is.'

'Yes, son. I'm the pig.'

The war of looks went on, a private battle between boy and man.

'You don't know nothing,' said Lacey. It wasn't a snide remark, the boy was simply telling his version of the truth; his gaze didn't flicker.

'All right, Lacey, that's enough.' The warder was trying to haul him away; his belly stuck out between pyjama top and bottom, a smooth dome of milk skin.

'Let him speak,' said Redman, 'What don't I know?'

'He can give his side of the story to the Governor,' said Leverthal before Lacey could reply, 'It's not your concern.'

But it was very much his concern. The stare made it his concern; so cutting, so damned. The stare demanded that it become his concern.

'Let him speak,' said Redman, the authority in his voice overriding Leverthal. The warder loosened his hold just a little.

'Why did you try and escape, Lacey?'

''Cause he came back.'

'Who came back? A name, Lacey. Who are you talking about?'

For several seconds Redman sensed the boy fighting a pact with silence; then Lacey shook his head, breaking the electric exchange between them. He seemed to lose his way somewhere; a kind of puzzlement gagged him.

'No harm's going to come to you.'

Lacey stared at his feet, frowning. 'I want to go back to bed now,' he said. A virgin's request.

'No harm, Lacey. I promise.'

The promise seemed to have precious little effect; Lacey was struck dumb. But it was a promise nevertheless, and he hoped Lacey realised that. The kid looked exhausted by the effort of his failed escape, of the pursuit, of staring. His face was ashen. He let the warder turn him and take him back. Before he rounded the corner again, he seemed to change his mind; he struggled to loose himself, failed, but managed to twist himself round to face his interrogator.

'Henessey,' he said, meeting Redman's eyes once more. That was all. He was shunted out of sight before he could say anything more.

'Henessey?' said Redman, feeling like a stranger suddenly, 'Who's Henessey?'

Leverthal was lighting a cigarette. Her hands were shaking ever so slightly as she did it. He hadn't noticed that yesterday, but he wasn't surprised. He'd yet to meet a head shrinker who didn't have problems of their own.

'The boy's lying,' she said, 'Henessey's no longer with us.'

A little pause. Redman didn't prompt, it would only make her jumpy.

'Lacey's clever,' she went on, putting the cigarette to her colourless lips. 'He knows just the spot.'

'Eh?'

'You're new here, and he wants to give you the impression that he's got a mystery all of his own.'

'It isn't a mystery then?'

'Henessey?' she snorted, 'Good God no. He escaped custody in early May. He and Lacey . . .' She hesitated, without wanting to. 'He and Lacey had something between them. Drugs perhaps, we never found out. Glue-sniffing, mutual masturbation, God knows what.'

She really did find the whole subject unpleasant. Distaste was written over her face in a dozen tight places.

'How did Henessey escape?'

'We still don't know,' she said, 'He just didn't turn up for roll-call one morning. The place was searched from top to bottom. But he'd gone.'

'Is it possible he'd come back?'

A genuine laugh.

'Jesus no. He hated the place. Besides, how could he get in?'

'He got out.'

Leverthal conceded the point with a murmur. 'He wasn't especially bright, but he was cunning. I wasn't altogether surprised when he went missing. The few weeks before his escape he'd really sunk into himself. I couldn't get anything out of him, and up until then he'd been quite talkative.'

'And Lacey?'

'Under his thumb. It often happens. Younger boy idolizes an older, more experienced individual. Lacey had a very unsettled family background.'

Neat, thought Redman. So neat he didn't believe a word of it. Minds weren't pictures at an exhibition, all numbered, and hung in order of influence, one marked 'Cunning', the next, 'Impressionable'. They were scrawls; they were sprawling splashes of graffiti, unpredictable, unconfinable.

And little boy Lacey? He was written on water.

Classes began the next day, in a heat so oppressive it turned the workshop into an oven by eleven. But the boys responded quickly

64

to Redman's straight dealing. They recognized in him a man they could respect without liking. They expected no favours, and received none. It was a stable arrangement.

Redman found the staff on the whole less communicative than the boys. An odd-ball bunch, all in all. Not a strong heart amongst them he decided. The routine of Tetherdowne, its rituals of classification, of humiliation, seemed to grind them into a common gravel. Increasingly he found himself avoiding conversation with his peers. The workshop became a sanctuary, a home from home, smelling of newly cut wood and bodies.

It was not until the following Monday that one of the boys mentioned the farm.

Nobody had told him there was a farm in the grounds of the Centre, and the idea struck Redman as absurd.

'Nobody much goes down there,' said Creeley, one of the worst woodworkers on God's earth, 'It stinks.'

General laughter.

'All right, lads, settle down.'

The laughter subsided, laced with a few whispered jibes.

'Where is this farm, Creeley?'

'It's not even a farm really, sir,' said Creeley, chewing his tongue (an incessant routine). 'It's just a few huts. Stink, they do sir. Especially now.'

He pointed out of the window to the wilderness beyond the playing field. Since he'd last looked out at the sight, that first day with Leverthal, the wasteland had ripened in the sweaty heat, ranker with weeds than ever. Creeley pointed out a distant brick wall, all but hidden behind a shield of shrubs.

'See it, sir?'

'Yes, I see it.'

'That's the sty, sir.'

Another round of sniggers.

'What's so funny?' he wheeled on the class. A dozen heads snapped down to their work.

'I wouldn't go down there sir. It's high as a fucking kite.'

Creeley wasn't exaggerating. Even in the relative cool of the late afternoon the smell wafting off the farm was stomach turning. Redman just followed his nose across the field and past the out-houses. The buildings he glimpsed from the workshop window were coming out of hiding. A few ramshackle huts thrown up out of corrugated iron and rotting wood, a chicken run, and the brick-built sty were all the farm could offer. As Creeley had said, it wasn't really a farm at all. It was a tiny domesticated Dachau;

filthy and forlorn. Somebody obviously fed the few prisoners: the hens, the half dozen geese, the pigs, but nobody seemed bothered to clean them out. Hence that rotten smell. The pigs particularly were living in a bed of their own ordure, islands of dung cooked to perfection in the sun, peopled with thousands of flies.

The sty itself was divided into two separate compartments, divided by a high brick wall. In the forecourt of one a small, mottled pig lay on its side in the filth, its flank alive with ticks and bugs. Another, smaller, pig could be glimpsed in the gloom of the interior, lying on shit-thick straw. Neither showed any interest in Redman.

The other compartment seemed empty.

There was no excrement in the forecourt, and far fewer flies amongst the straw. The accumulated smell of old faecal matter was no less acute however and Redman was about to turn away when there was a noise from inside, and a great bulk righted itself. He leaned over the padlocked wooden gate, blotting out the stench by an act of will, and peered through the doorway of the sty.

The pig came out to look at him. It was three times the size of its companions, a vast sow that might well have mothered the pigs in the adjacent pen. But where her farrow were filthy-flanked, the sow was pristine, her blushing pink frame radiant with good health. Her sheer size impressed Redman. She must have weighed twice what he weighed, he guessed: an altogether formidable creature. A glamorous animal in her gross way, with her curling blonde lashes and the delicate down on her shiny snout that coarsened to bristles around her lolling ears, and the oily, fetching look in her dark brown eyes.

Redman, a city boy, had seldom seen the living truth behind, or previous to, the meat on his plate. This wonderful porker came as a revelation. The bad press that he'd always believed about pigs, the reputation that made the very name a synonym for foulness, all that was given the lie.

The sow was beautiful, from her snuffling snout to the delicate corkscrew of her tail, a seductress on trotters.

Her eyes regarded Redman as an equal, he had no doubt of that, admiring him rather less than he admired her.

She was safe in her head, he in his. They were equal under a glittering sky.

Close to, her body smelt sweet. Somebody had clearly been there that very morning, sluicing her down, and feeding her. Her trough, Redman now noticed, still brimmed with a mush of slops, the remains of yesterday's meal. She hadn't touched it; she was no glutton.

Soon she seemed to have the sum of him, and grunting quietly she turned around on her nimble feet and returned to the cool of the interior. The audience was over.

That night he went to find Lacey. The boy had been removed from the Hospital Unit and put in a shabby room of his own. He was apparently still being bullied by the other boys in his dormitory, and the alternative was this solitary confinement. Redman found him sitting on a carpet of old comic books, staring at the wall. The lurid covers of the comics made his face look milkier than ever. The bandage had gone from his nose, and the bruise on the bridge was yellowing.

He shook Lacey's hand, and the boy gazed up at him. There was a real turn about since their last meeting. Lacey was calm, even docile. The handshake, a ritual Redman had introduced whenever he met boys out of the workshop, was weak.

'Are you well?'

The boy nodded.

'Do you like being alone?'

'Yes, sir.'

'You'll have to go back to the dormitory eventually.'

Lacey shook his head.

'You can't stay here forever, you know.'

'Oh, I know that, sir.'

'You'll have to go back.'

Lacey nodded. Somehow the logic didn't seem to have got through to the boy. He turned up the corner of a Superman comic and stared at the splash-page without scanning it.

'Listen to me Lacey. I want you and I to understand each other. Yes?'

'Yes, sir.'

'I can't help you if you lie to me. Can I?'

'No.'

'Why did you mention Kevin Henessey's name to me last week? I know that he isn't here any longer. He escaped, didn't he?'

Lacey stared at the three-colour hero on the page.

'Didn't he?'

'He's here,' said Lacey, very quietly. The kid was suddenly distraught,. It was in his voice, and in the way his face folded up on itself.

'If he escaped, why should he come back? That doesn't really make much sense to me, does it make much sense to you?'

Lacey shook his head. There were tears in his nose, that muffled his words, but they were clear enough.

'He never went away.'

67

'What? You mean he never escaped?'

'He's clever sir. You don't know Kevin. He's clever.'

He closed the comic, and looked up at Redman.

'In what way clever?'

'He planned everything, sir. All of it.'

'You have to be clear.'

'You won't believe me. Then that's the end, because you won't believe me. He hears you know, he's everywhere. He doesn't care about walls. Dead people don't care about nothing like that.'

Dead. A smaller word than alive; but it took the breath away.

'He can come and go,' said Lacey, 'any time he wants.'

'Are you saying Henessey is dead?' said Redman. 'Be careful, Lacey.'

The boy hesitated: he was aware that he was walking a tight rope, very close to losing his protector.

'You promised,' he said suddenly, cold as ice.

'Promised no harm would come to you. It won't. I said that and I meant it. But that doesn't mean you can tell me lies, Lacey.'

'What lies, sir?'

'Henessey isn't dead.'

'He is, sir. They all know he is. He hanged himself. With the pigs.'

Redman had been lied to many times, by experts, and he felt he'd become a good judge of liars. He knew all the tell-tale signs. But the boy exhibited none of them. He was telling the truth. Redman felt it in his bones.

The truth; the whole truth; nothing but.

That didn't mean that what the boy was saying was true. He was simply telling the truth as he understood it. He *believed* Henessey was deceased. That proved nothing.

'If Henessey were dead –'

'He *is*, sir.'

'If he were, how could he be here?'

The boy looked at Redman without a trace of guile in his face.

'Don't you believe in ghosts, sir?'

So transparent a solution, it flummoxed Redman. Henessey was dead, yet Henessey was here. Hence, Henessey was a ghost.

'Don't you sir?'

The boy wasn't asking a rhetorical question. He wanted, no, he demanded, a reasonable answer to his reasonable question.

'No, boy,' said Redman, 'No I don't.'

Lacey seemed unruffled by this conflict of opinion.

'You'll see,' he said simply, 'You'll see.'

* * *

68

In the sty at the perimeter of the grounds the great, nameless sow was hungry.

She judged the rhythm of the days, and with their progression her desires grew. She knew that the time for stale slops in a trough was past. Other appetites had taken the place of those piggy pleasures.

She had a taste, since the first time, for food with a certain texture, a certain resonance. It wasn't food she would demand all the time, only when the need came on her. Not a great demand: once in a while, to gobble at the hand that fed her.

She stood at the gate of her prison, listless with anticipation, waiting and waiting. She snaffled, she snorted, her impatience becoming a dull anger. In the adjacent pen her castrated sons, sensing her distress, became agitated in their turn. They knew her nature, and it was dangerous. She had, after all, eaten two of their brothers, living, fresh and wet from her own womb.

Then there were noises through the blue veil of twilight, the soft brushing sound of passage through the nettles, accompanied by the murmur of voices.

Two boys were approaching the sty, respect and caution in every step. She made them nervous, and understandably so. The tales of her tricks were legion.

Didn't she speak, when angered, in that possessed voice, bending her fat, porky mouth to talk with a stolen tongue? Wouldn't she stand on her back trotters sometimes, pink and imperial, and demand that the smallest boys be sent into her shadow to suckle her, naked like her farrow? And wouldn't she beat her vicious heels upon the ground, until the food they brought for her was cut into *petit* pieces and delivered into her maw between trembling finger and thumb? All these things she did.

And worse.

Tonight, the boys knew, they had not brought what she wanted. It was not the meat she was due that lay on the plate they carried. Not the sweet, white meat that she had asked for in that other voice of hers, the meat she could, if she desired, take by force. Tonight the meal was simply stale bacon, filched from the kitchens. The nourishment she really craved, the meat that had been pursued and terrified to engorge the muscle, then bruised like a hammered steak for her delectation, that meat was under special protection. It would take a while to coax it to the slaughter.

Meanwhile they hoped she would accept their apologies and their tears, and not devour them in her anger.

One of the boys had shat his pants by the time he reached the sty-wall, and the sow smelt him. Her voice took on a different

69

timbre, enjoying the piquancy of their fear. Instead of the low snort there was a higher, hotter note out of her. It said: I know, I know. Come and be judged. I know, I know.

She watched them through the slats of the gate, her eyes glinting like jewels in the murky night, brighter than the night because living, purer than the night because wanting.

The boys knelt at the gate, their heads bowed in supplication, the plate they both held lightly covered with a piece of stained muslin.

'Well?' she said. The voice was unmistakable in their ears. His voice, out of the mouth of the pig.

The elder boy, a black kid with a cleft palate, spoke quietly to the shining eyes, making the best of his fear:

'It's not what you wanted. We're sorry.'

The other boy, uncomfortable in his crowded trousers, murmured his apology too.

'We'll get him for you though. We will, really. We'll bring him to you very soon, as soon as we possibly can.'

'Why not tonight?' said the pig.

'He's being protected.'

'A new teacher. Mr Redman.'

The sow seemed to know it all already. She remembered the confrontation across the wall, the way he'd stared at her as though she was a zoological specimen. So that was her enemy, that old man. She'd have him. Oh yes.

The boys heard her promise of revenge, and seemed content to have the matter taken out of their hands.

'Give her the meat,' said the black boy.

The other one stood up, removing the muslin cloth. The bacon smelt bad, but the sow nevertheless made wet noises of enthusiasm. Maybe she had forgiven them.

'Go on, quickly.'

The boy took the first strip of bacon between finger and thumb and proffered it. The sow turned her mouth sideways up to it and ate, showing her yellowish teeth. It was gone quickly. The second, the third, fourth, fifth the same.

The sixth and last piece she took with his fingers, snatched with such elegance and speed the boy could only cry out as her teeth champed through the thin digits and swallowed them. He withdrew his hand from over the sty wall, and gawped at this mutilation. She had done only a little damage, considering. The top of his thumb and half his index finger had gone. The wounds bled quickly, fully, splashing on to his shirt and his shoes. She grunted and snorted and seemed satisfied.

The boy yelped and ran.

'Tomorrow,' said the sow to the remaining supplicant. 'Not this old pig-meat. It must be white. White and . . . lacy.' She thought that was a fine joke.

'Yes,' the boy said, 'Yes, of course.'

'Without fail,' she ordered.

'Yes.'

'Or I come for him myself. Do you hear me?'

'Yes.'

'I come for him myself, wherever he's hiding. I will eat him in his bed if I wish. In his sleep I will eat off his feet, then his legs, then his balls, then his hips – '

'Yes, yes.'

'*I want him,*' said the sow, grinding her trotter in the straw, 'He's mine.'

'Henessey dead?' said Leverthal, head still down as she wrote one of her interminable reports, 'It's another fabrication. One minute the child says he's in the Centre, the next he's dead. The boy can't even get his story straight.'

It was difficult to argue with the contradictions unless one accepted the idea of ghosts as readily as Lacey. There was no way Redman was going to try and argue that point with the woman. That part was a nonsense. Ghosts were foolishness; just fears made visible. But the possibility of Henessey's suicide made more sense to Redman. He pressed on with his argument.

'So where did Lacey get this story from, about Henessey's death? It's a funny thing to invent.'

She deigned to look up, her face drawn up into itself like a snail in its shell.

'Fertile imaginations are par for the course here. If you heard the tales I've got on tape: the exoticism of some of them would blow your head open.'

'Have there been suicides here?'

'In my time?' She thought for a moment, pen poised. 'Two attempts. Neither, I think, intended to succeed. Cries for help.'

'Was Henessey one?'

She allowed herself a little sneer as she shook her head.

'Henessey was unstable in a completely different direction. He thought he was going to live forever. That was his little dream: Henessey the Nietzchean Superman. He had something close to contempt for the common herd. As far as he was concerned, he was a breed apart. As far beyond the rest of us mere mortals as he was beyond that wretched – '

He knew she was going to say pig, but she stopped just short of the word.

'Those wretched animals on the farm,' she said, looking back down at her report.

'Henessey spent time at the farm?'

'No more than any other boy,' she lied, 'None of them like farm duties, but it's part of the work rota. Mucking out isn't a very pleasant occupation. I can testify to that.'

The lie he knew she'd told made Redman keep back Lacey's final detail: that Henessey's death had taken place in the pig-sty. He shrugged, and took an entirely different tack.

'Is Lacey under any medication?'

'Some sedatives.'

'Are the boys always sedated when they've been in a fight?'

'Only if they try to make escapes. We haven't got enough staff to supervize the likes of Lacey. I don't see why you're so concerned.'

'I want him to trust me. I promised him. I don't want him let down.'

'Frankly, all this sounds suspiciously like special pleading. The boy's one of many. No unique problems, and no particular hope of redemption.'

'Redemption?' It was a strange word.

'Rehabilitation, whatever you choose to call it. Look Redman, I'll be frank. There's a general feeling that you're not really playing ball here.'

'Oh?'

'We all feel, I think this includes the Governor, that you should let us go about our business the way we're used to. Learn the ropes before you start – '

'Interfering.'

She nodded. 'It's as good a word as any. You're making enemies.'

'Thank you for the warning.'

'This job's difficult enough without enemies, believe me.'

She attempted a conciliatory look, which Redman ignored. Enemies he could live with, liars he couldn't.

The Governor's room was locked, as it had been for a full week now. Explanations differed as to where he was. Meetings with funding bodies was a favourite reason touted amongst the staff, though the Secretary claimed she didn't exactly know. There were Seminars at the University he was running, somebody said, to bring some research to bear on the problems of Remand Centres. Maybe the Governor was at one of those. If Mr Redman wanted, he could leave a message, the Governor would get it.

Back in the workshop, Lacey was waiting for him. It was almost seven-fifteen: classes were well over.

'What are you doing here?'

'Waiting, sir.'

'What for?'

'You sir. I wanted to give you a letter, sir. For me mam. Will you get it to her?'

'You can send it through the usual channels, can't you? Give it to the Secretary, she'll forward it. You're allowed two letters a week.'

Lacey's face fell.

'They read them sir: in case you write something you shouldn't. And if you do, they burn them.'

'And you've written something you shouldn't?'

He nodded.

'What?'

'About Kevin. I told her all about Kevin, about what happened to him.'

'I'm not sure you've got your facts right about Henessey.'

The boy shrugged. 'It's true sir,' he said quietly, apparently no longer caring if he convinced Redman or not 'It's true. He's there, sir. In her.'

'In who? What are you talking about?'

Maybe Lacey was speaking, as Leverthal had suggested, simply out of his fear. There had to be a limit to his patience with the boy, and this was just about it.

A knock on the door, and a spotty individual called Slape was staring at him through the wired glass.

'Come in.'

'Urgent telephone call for you sir. In the Secretary's Office.'

Redman hated the telephone. Unsavoury machine: it never brought good tidings.

'Urgent. Who from?'

Slape shrugged and picked at his face.

'Stay with Lacey, will you?'

Slape looked unhappy with the prospect.

'Here, sir?' he asked.

'Here.'

'Yes, sir.'

'I'm relying on you, so don't let me down.'

'No, sir.'

Redman turned to Lacey. The bruised look was a wound now. Open, as he wept.

'Give me your letter. I'll take it to the Office.'

Lacey had thrust the envelope into his pocket. He retrieved it unwillingly, and handed it across to Redman.

'Say thank you.'

'Thank you, sir.'

The corridors were empty.

It was television time, and the nightly worship of the box had begun. They would be glued to the black and white set that dominated the Recreation Room, sitting through the pap of Cop Shows and Game Shows and Wars from the World Shows with their jaws open and their minds closed. A hypnotized silence would fall on the assembled company until a promise of violence or a hint of sex. Then the room would erupt in whistles, obscenities, and shouts of encouragement, only to subside again into sullen silence during the dialogue, as they waited for another gun, another breast. He could hear gunfire and music, even now, echoing down the corridor.

The Office was open, but the Secretary wasn't there. Gone home presumably. The clock in the Office said eight-nineteen. Redman amended his watch.

The telephone was on the hook. Whoever had called him had tired of waiting, leaving no message. Relieved as he was that the call wasn't urgent enough to keep the caller hanging on, he now felt disappointed not to be speaking to the outside world. Like Crusoe seeing a sail, only to have it sweep by his island.

Ridiculous: this wasn't his prison. He could walk out whenever he liked. He would walk out that very night: and be Crusoe no longer.

He contemplated leaving Lacey's letter on the desk, but thought better of it. He had promised to protect the boy's interests, and that he would do. If necessary, he'd post the letter himself.

Thinking of nothing in particular, he started back towards the workshop. Vague wisps of unease floated in his system, clogging his responses. Sighs sat in his throat, scowls on his face. This damn place, he said aloud, not meaning the walls and the floors, but the trap they represented. He felt he could die here with his good intentions arrayed around him like flowers round a stiff, and nobody would know, or care, or mourn. Idealism was weakness here, compassion an indulgence. Unease was all: unease and –

Silence.

That was what was wrong. Though the television still popped and screamed down the corridor, there was silence accompanying it. No wolf-whistles, no cat-calls.

Redman darted back to the vestibule and down the corridor to

74

the Recreation Room. Smoking was allowed in this section of the building, and the area stank of stale cigarettes. Ahead, the noise of mayhem continued unabated. A woman screamed somebody's name. A man answered and was cut off by a blast of gunfire. Stories, half-told, hung in the air.

He reached the room, and opened the door.

The television spoke to him. 'Get down!'

'*He's got a gun!*'

Another shot.

The woman, blonde, big-breasted, took the bullet in her heart, and died on the sidewalk beside the man she'd loved.

The tragedy went unwatched. The Recreation Room was empty, the old armchairs and graffiti-carved stools placed around the television set for an audience who had better entertainment for the evening. Redman wove between the seats and turned the television off. As the silver-blue fluorescence died, and the insistent beat of the music was cut dead, he became aware, in the gloom, in the hush, of somebody at the door.

'Who is it?'

'Slape, sir.'

'I told you to stay with Lacey.'

'He had to go, sir.'

'Go?'

'He ran off, sir. I couldn't stop him.'

'Damn you. What do you mean, you couldn't stop him?'

Redman started to re-cross the room, catching his foot on a stool. It scraped on the linoleum, a little protest.

Slape twitched.

'I'm sorry sir,' he said, 'I couldn't catch him. I've got a bad foot.'

Yes, Slape did limp.

'Which way did he go?'

Slape shrugged.

'Not sure sir.'

'Well remember.'

'No need to lose your temper, sir.'

The 'sir' was slurred: a parody of respect. Redman found his hand itching to hit this pus-filled adolescent. He was within a couple of feet of the door. Slape didn't move aside.

'Out of my way, Slape.'

'Really, sir, there's no way you can help him now. He's gone.'

'I said, out of my way.'

As he stepped forward to push Slape aside there was a click at navel-level and the bastard had a flick-knife pressed to Redman's belly. The point bit the fat of his stomach.

75

'There's really no need to go after him, sir.'

'What in God's name are you doing, Slape?'

'We're just playing a game,' he said through teeth gone grey. 'There's no real harm in it. Best leave well alone.'

The point of the knife had drawn blood. Warmly, it wended its way down into Redman's groin. Slape was prepared to kill him; no doubt of that. Whatever this game was, Slape was having a little fun all of his own. Killing teacher, it was called. The knife was still being pressed, infinitesimally slowly, through the wall of Redman's flesh. The little rivulet of blood had thickened into a stream.

'Kevin likes to come out and play once in a while,' said Slape.

'Henessey?'

'Yes, you like to call us by our second names, don't you? That's more manly isn't it? That means we're not children, that means we're men. Kevin isn't quite a man though, you see sir. He's never wanted to be a man. In fact, I think he hated the idea. You know why? (The knife divided muscle now, just gently). He thought once you were a man, you started to die: and Kevin used to say he'd never die.'

'Never die.'

'Never.'

'I want to meet him.'

'Everybody does, sir. He's charismatic. That's the Doctor's word for him: Charismatic.'

'I want to meet this charismatic fellow.'

'Soon.'

'Now.'

'I said soon.'

Redman took the knife-hand at the wrist so quickly Slape had no chance to press the weapon home. The adolescent's response was slow, doped perhaps, and Redman had the better of him. The knife dropped from his hand as Redman's grip tightened, the other hand took Slape in a strangle-hold, easily rounding his emaciated neck. Redman's palm pressed on his assailant's Adam's apple, making him gargle.

'Where's Henessey? You take me to him.'

The eyes that looked down at Redman were slurred as his words, the irises pin-pricks.

'Take me to him!' Redman demanded.

Slape's hand found Redman's cut belly, and his fist jabbed the wound. Redman cursed, letting his hold slip, and Slape almost slid out of his grasp, but Redman drove his knee into the other's groin, fast and sharp. Slape wanted to double up in agony, but the neck-hold prevented him. The knee rose again, harder. And again. Again.

Spontaneous tears ran down Slape's face, coursing through the minefield of his boils.

'I can hurt you twice as badly as you can hurt me,' Redman said, 'So if you want to go on doing this all night I'm happy as a sandboy.'

Slape shook his head, grabbing his breath through his constricted windpipe in short, painful gasps.

'You don't want any more?'

Slape shook his head again. Redman let go of him, and flung him across the corridor against the wall. Whimpering with pain, his face crimped, he slid down the wall into a foetal position, hands between his legs.

'Where's Lacey?'

Slape had begun to shake; the words tumbled out. 'Where d'you think? Kevin's got him.'

'Where's Kevin?'

Slape looked up at Redman, puzzled.

'Don't you know?'

'I wouldn't ask if I did, would I?'

Slape seemed to pitch forward as he spoke, letting out a sigh of pain. Redman's first thought was that the youth was collapsing, but Slape had other ideas. The knife was suddenly in his hand again, snatched from the floor, and Slape was driving it up towards Redman's groin. He side-stepped the cut with a hair's breadth to spare, and Slape was on his feet again, the pain forgotten. The knife slit the air back and forth, Slape hissing his intention through his teeth.

'Kill you, pig. Kill you, pig.'

Then his mouth was wide and he was yelling: 'Kevin! Kevin! Help me!'

The slashes were less and less accurate as Slape lost control of himself, tears, snot and sweat sliming his face as he stumbled towards his intended victim.

Redman chose his moment, and delivered a crippling blow to Slape's knee, the weak leg, he guessed. He guessed correctly. Slape screamed, and staggered back, reeling round and hitting the wall face on. Redman followed through, pressing Slape's back. Too late, he realized what he'd done. Slape's body relaxed as his knife hand, crushed between wall and body, slid out, bloody and weaponless. Slape exhaled death-air, and collapsed heavily against the wall, driving the knife still deeper into his own gut. He was dead before he touched the ground.

77

Redman turned him over. He'd never become used to the suddenness of death. To be gone so quickly, like the image on the television screen. Switched off and blank. No message.

The utter silence of the corridors became overwhelming as he walked back towards the vestibule. The cut on his stomach was not significant, and the blood had made its own scabby bandage of his shirt, knitting cotton to flesh and sealing the wound. It scarcely hurt at all. But the cut was the least of his problems: he had mysteries to unravel now, and he felt unable to face them. The used, exhausted atmosphere of the place made him feel, in his turn, used and exhausted. There was no health to be had here, no goodness, no reason.

He believed, suddenly, in ghosts.

In the vestibule there was a light burning, a bare bulb suspended over the dead space. By it, he read Lacey's crumpled letter. The smudged words on the paper were like matches set to the tinder of his panic.

Mama,
  They fed me to the pig. Don't believe them if they said I never loved you, or if they said I ran away. I never did. They fed me to the pig. I love you.
  Tommy.

He pocketed the letter and began to run out of the building and across the field. It was well dark now: a deep, starless dark, and the air was muggy. Even in daylight he wasn't sure of the route to the farm; it was worse by night. He was very soon lost, somewhere between the playing-field and the trees. It was too far to see the outline of the main building behind him, and the trees ahead all looked alike.

The night-air was foul; no wind to freshen tired limbs. It was as still outside as inside, as though the whole world had become an interior: a suffocating room bounded by a painted ceiling of cloud.

He stood in the dark, the blood thumping in his head, and tried to orient himself.

To his left, where he had guessed the out-houses to be, a light glimmered. Clearly he was completely mistaken about his position. The light was at the sty. It threw the ramshackle chicken run into silhouette as he stared at it. There were figures there, several; standing as if watching a spectacle he couldn't yet see.

He started towards the sty, not knowing what he would do once he reached it. If they were all armed like Slape, and shared his

78

murderous intentions, then that would be the end of him. The thought didn't worry him. Somehow tonight to get off of this closed-down world was an attractive option. Down and out.

And there was Lacey. There'd been a moment of doubt, after speaking to Leverthal, when he'd wondered why he cared so much about the boy. That accusation of special pleading, it had a certain truth to it. Was there something in him that wanted Thomas Lacey naked beside him? Wasn't that the sub-text of Leverthal's remark? Even now, running uncertainly towards the lights, all he could think of was the boy's eyes, huge and demanding, looking deep into his.

Ahead there were figures in the night, wandering away from the farm. He could see them against the lights of the sty. Was it all over already? He made a long curve around to the left of the buildings to avoid the spectators as they left the scene. They made no noise: there was no chatter or laughter amongst them. Like a congregation leaving a funeral they walked evenly in the dark, each apart from the other, heads bowed. It was eerie, to see these godless delinquents so subdued by reverence.

He reached the chicken-run without encountering any of them face to face.

There were still a few figures lingering around the pig-house. The wall of the sow's compartment was lined with candles, dozens and dozens of them. They burned steadily in the still air, throwing a rich warm light on to brick, and on to the faces of the few who still stared into the mysteries of the sty.

Leverthal was among them, as was the warder who'd knelt at Lacey's head that first day. Two or three boys were there too, whose faces he recognized but could put no name to.

There was a noise from the sty, the sound of the sow's feet on the straw as she accepted their stares. Somebody was speaking, but he couldn't make out who. An adolescent's voice, with a lilt to it. As the voice halted in its monologue, the warder and another of the boys broke rank, as if dismissed, and turned away into the dark. Redman crept a little closer. Time was of the essence now. Soon the first of the congregation would have crossed the field and be back in the Main Building. They'd see Slape's corpse: raise the alarm. He must find Lacey now, if indeed Lacey was still to be found.

Leverthal saw him first. She looked up from the sty and nodded a greeting, apparently unconcerned by his arrival. It was as if his appearance at this place was inevitable, as if all routes led back to the farm, to the straw house and the smell of excrement. It made a kind of sense that she'd believe that. He almost believed it himself.

'Leverthal,' he said.

She smiled at him, openly. The boy beside her raised his head and smiled too.

'Are you Henessey?' he asked, looking at the boy.

The youth laughed, and so did Leverthal.

'No,' she said, 'No. No. No. Henessey is here.'

She pointed into the sty.

Redman walked the few remaining yards to the wall of the sty, expecting and not daring to expect, the straw and the blood and the pig and Lacey.

But Lacey wasn't there. Just the sow, big and beady as ever, standing amongst pats of her own ordure, her huge, ridiculous ears flapping over her eyes.

'Where's Henessey?' asked Redman, meeting the sow's gaze.

'Here,' said the boy.

'This is a pig.'

'She ate him,' said the youth, still smiling. He obviously thought the idea delightful, 'She ate him: and he speaks out of her.'

Redman wanted to laugh. This made Lacey's tales of ghosts seem almost plausible by comparison. They were telling him the pig was possessed.

'Did Henessey hang himself, as Tommy said?'

Leverthal nodded.

'In the sty?'

Another nod.

Suddenly the pig took on a different aspect. In his imagination he saw her reaching up to sniff at the feet of Henessey's twitching body, sensing the death coming over it, salivating at the thought of its flesh. He saw her licking the dew that oozed from its skin as it rotted, lapping at it, nibbling daintly at first, then devouring it. It wasn't too difficult to understand how the boys could have made a mythology of that atrocity: inventing hymns to it, attending upon the pig like a god. The candles, the reverence, the intended sacrifice of Lacey: it was evidence of sickness, but it was no more strange than a thousand other customs of faith. He even began to understand Lacey's lassitude, his inability to fight the powers that overtook him.

Mama, they fed me to the pig.

Not Mama, help me, save me. Just: they gave me to the pig.

All this he could understand: they were children, many of them under-educated, some verging on mental instability, all susceptible to superstition. But that didn't explain Leverthal. She was staring into the sty again, and Redman registered for the first time that her hair was unclipped, and lay on her shoulders, honey-coloured in the candlelight.

'It looks like a pig to me, plain and simple,' he said.

'She speaks with his voice,' Leverthal said, quietly. 'Speaks in tongues, you might say. You'll hear him in a while. My darling boy.'

Then he understood. 'You and Henessey?'

'Don't look so horrified,' she said, 'He was eighteen: hair blacker than you've ever seen. And he loved me.'

'Why did he hang himself?'

'To live forever,' she said, 'so he'd never be a man, and die.'

'We didn't find him for six days,' said the youth, almost whispering it in Redman's ear, 'And even then she wouldn't let anybody near him, once she had him to herself. The pig, I mean. Not the Doctor. Everyone loved Kevin, you see,' he whispered intimately. 'He was beautiful.'

'And where's Lacey?'

Leverthal's loving smile decayed.

'With Kevin,' said the youth, 'Where Kevin wants him.'

He pointed through the door of the sty. There was a body lying on the straw, back to the door.

'If you want him, you'll have to go and get him,' said the boy, and the next moment he had the back of Redman's neck in a vice-like grip.

The sow responded to the sudden action. She started to stamp the straw, showing the whites of her eyes.

Redman tried to shrug off the boy's grip, at the same time delivering an elbow to his belly. The boy backed off, winded, and cursing, only to be replaced by Leverthal.

'Go to him,' she said as she snatched at Redman's hair. 'Go to him if you want him.' Her nails raked across his temple and nose, just missing his eyes.

'Get off me!' he said, trying to shake the woman off, but she clung, her head lashing back and forth as she tried to press him over the wall.

The rest happened with horrid speed. Her long hair brushed through a candle flame and her head caught fire, the flames climbing quickly. Shrieking for help she stumbled heavily against the gate. It failed to support her weight, and gave inward. Redman watched helplessly as the burning woman fell amongst the straw. The flames spread enthusiastically across the forecourt towards the sow, lapping up the kindling.

Even now, in extremis, the pig was still a pig. No miracles here: no speaking, or pleading, in tongues. The animal panicked as the

81

blaze surrounded her, cornering her stamping bulk and licking at her flanks. The air was filled with the stench of singeing bacon as the flames ran up her sides and over her head, chasing through her bristles like a grass-fire.

Her voice was a pig's voice, her complaints a pig's complaints. Hysterical grunts escaped her lips and she hurtled across the forecourt of the sty and out of the broken gate, trampling Leverthal.

The sow's body, still burning, was a magic thing in the night as she careered across the field, weaving about in her pain. Her cries did not diminish as the dark ate her up, they seemed just to echo back and forth across the field, unable to find a way out of the locked room.

Redman stepped over Leverthal's fire-ridden corpse and into the sty. The straw was burning on every side, and the fire was creeping towards the door. He half-shut his eyes against the stinging smoke and ducked into the pig-house.

Lacey was lying as he had been all along, back to the door. Redman turned the boy over. He was alive. He was awake. His face, bloated with tears and terror, stared up off his straw pillow, eyes so wide they looked fit to leap from his head.

'Get up,' said Redman, leaning over the boy.

His small body was rigid, and it was all Redman could do to prize his limbs apart. With little words of care, he coaxed the boy to his feet as the smoke began to swirl into the pig-house.

'Come on, it's all right, come on.'

He stood upright and something brushed his hair. Redman felt a little rain of worms across his face and glanced up to see Henessey, or what was left of him, still suspended from the crossbeam of the pig-house. His features were incomprehensible, blackened to a drooping mush. His body was raggedly gnawed off at the hip, and his innards hung from the foetid carcass, dangling in wormy loops in front of Redman's face.

Had it not been for the thick smoke the smell of the body would have been overpowering. As it was Redman was simply revolted, and his revulsion gave strength to his arm. He hauled Lacey out of the shadow of the body and pushed him through the door.

Outside the straw was no longer blazing as brightly, but the light of fire and candles and burning body still made him squint after the dark interior.

'Come on lad,' he said, lifting the kid through the flames. The boy's eyes were button-bright, lunatic-bright. They said futility.

They crossed the sty to the gate, skipping Leverthal's corpse, and headed into the darkness of the open field.

The boy seemed to be stirring from his stricken state with every step they took away from the farm. Behind them the sty was already a blazing memory. Ahead, the night was as still and impenetrable as ever.

Redman tried not to think of the pig. It must be dead by now, surely.

But as they ran, there seemed to be a noise in the earth as something huge kept pace with them, content to keep its distance, wary now but relentless in its pursuit.

He dragged on Lacey's arm, and hurried on, the ground sunbaked beneath their feet. Lacey was whimpering now, no words as yet, but sound at least. It was a good sign, a sign Redman needed. He'd had about his fill of insanity.

They reached the building without incident. The corridors were as empty as they'd been when he'd left an hour ago. Perhaps nobody had found Slape's corpse yet. It was possible. None of the boys had seemed in a fit mood for recreation. Perhaps they had slipped silently to their dormitories, to sleep off their worship.

It was time to find a phone and call the Police.

Man and boy walked down the corridor towards the Governor's Office hand in hand. Lacey had fallen silent again, but his expression was no longer so manic; it looked as though cleansing tears might be close. He sniffed; made noises in his throat.

His grip on Redman's hand tightened, then relaxed completely.

Ahead, the vestibule was in darkness. Somebody had smashed the bulb recently. It still rocked gently on its cable, illuminated by a seepage of dull light from the window.

'Come on. There's nothing to be afraid of. Come on, boy.'

Lacey bent to Redman's hand and bit the flesh. The trick was so quick he let the boy go before he could prevent himself, and Lacey was showing his heels as he scooted away down the corridor away from the vestibule.

No matter. He couldn't get far. For once Redman was glad the place had walls and bars.

Redman crossed the darkened vestibule to the Secretary's Office. Nothing moved. Whoever had broken the bulb was keeping very quiet, very still.

The telephone had been smashed too. Not just broken, smashed to smithereens.

Redman doubled back to the Governor's room. There was a telephone there; he'd not be stopped by vandals.

The door was locked, of course, but Redman was prepared for that. He smashed the frosted glass in the window of the door with his elbow, and reached through to the other side. No key there.

To hell with it, he thought, and put his shoulder to the door. It was sturdy, strong wood, and the lock was good quality. His shoulder ached and the wound in his stomach had reopened by the time the lock gave, and he gained access to the room.

The floor was littered with straw; the smell inside made the sty seem sweet. The Governor was lying behind his desk, his heart eaten out.

'The pig,' said Redman. 'The pig. The pig.' And saying, 'the pig', he reached for the phone.

A sound. He turned, and met the blow full-face. It broke his cheek-bone and his nose. The room mottled, and went white.

The vestibule was no longer dark. Candles were burning, it seemed hundreds of them, in every corner, on every edge. But then his head was swimming, his eyesight blurred with concussion. It could have been a single candle, multiplied by senses that could no longer be trusted to tell the truth.

He stood in the middle of the arena of the vestibule, not quite knowing how he could be standing, for his legs felt numb and useless beneath him. At the periphery of his vision, beyond the light of the candles, he could hear people talking. No, not really talking. They weren't proper words. They were nonsense sounds, made by people who may or may not have been there.

Then he heard the grunt, the low, asthmatic grunt of the sow, and straight ahead she emerged from the swimming light of the candles. She was bright and beautiful no longer. Her flanks were charred, her beady eyes withered, her snout somehow twisted out of true. She hobbled towards him very slowly, and very slowly the figure astride her became apparent. It was Tommy Lacey of course, naked as the day he was born, his body as pink and as hairless as one of her farrow, his face as innocent of human feeling. His eyes were now her eyes, as he guided the great sow by her ears. And the noise of the sow, the snaffling sound, was not out of the pig's mouth, but out of his. His was the voice of the pig.

Redman said his name, quietly. Not Lacey, but Tommy. The boy seemed not to hear. Only then, as the pig and her rider approached, did Redman register why he hadn't fallen on his face. There was a rope around his neck.

Even as he thought the thought, the noose tightened, and he was hauled off his feet into the air.

No pain, but a terrible horror, worse, so much worse than pain, opened in him, a gorge of loss and regret, and all he was sank away into it.

Below him, the sow and the boy had come to a halt, beneath his jangling feet. The boy, still grunting, had climbed off the pig and was squatting down beside the beast. Through the greying air Redman could see the curve of the boy's spine, the flawless skin of his back. He saw too the knotted rope that protruded from between his pale buttocks, the end frayed. For all the world like the tail of a pig.

The sow put its head up, though its eyes were beyond seeing. He liked to think that she suffered, and would suffer now until she died. It was almost sufficient, to think of that. Then the sow's mouth opened, and she spoke. He wasn't certain how the words came, but they came. A boy's voice, lilting.

'This is the state of the beast,' it said, 'to eat and be eaten.'

Then the sow smiled, and Redman felt, though he had believed himself numb, the first shock of pain as Lacey's teeth bit off a piece from his foot, and the boy clambered, snorting, up his saviour's body to kiss out his life.

Sex, Death and Starshine

Diane ran her scented fingers through the two days' growth of ginger stubble on Terry's chin.

'I love it,' she said, 'Even the grey bits.'

She loved everything about him, or at least that's what she claimed.

When he kissed her: I love it.

When he undressed her: I love it.

When he slid his briefs off: I love it, I love it, I love it.

She'd go down on him with such unalloyed enthusiasm, all he could do was watch the top of her ash-blonde head bobbing at his groin, and hope to God nobody chanced to walk into the dressing-room. She was a married woman, after all, even if she was an actress. He had a wife himself, somewhere. This tête-à-tête would make some juicy copy for one of the local rags, and here he was trying to garner a reputation as a serious-minded director; no gimmicks, no gossip; just art.

Then, even thoughts of ambition would be dissolved on her tongue, as she played havoc with his nerve-endings. She wasn't much of an actress, but by God she was quite a performer. Faultless technique; immaculate timing: she knew either by instinct or by rehearsal just when to pick up the rhythm and bring the whole scene to a satisfying conclusion.

When she'd finished milking the moment dry, he almost wanted to applaud.

The whole cast of Calloway's production of *Twelfth Night* knew about the affair, of course. There'd be the occasional snide comment passed if actress and director were both late for rehearsals, or if she arrived looking full, and he flushed. He tried to persuade her to control the cat-with-the-cream look that crept over her face, but she just wasn't that good a deceiver. Which was rich, considering her profession.

But then La Duvall, as Edward insisted on calling her, didn't need to be a great player, she was famous. So what if she spoke Shakespeare like it was Hiawatha, dum de dum de dum de dum? So what if her grasp of psychology was dubious, her logic faulty, her projection inadaquate? So what if she had as much sense of poetry as she did propriety? She was a star, and that meant business.

There was no taking that away from her: her name was money. The Elysium Theatre publicity announced her claim to fame in three inch Roman Bold, black on yellow:

'Diane Duvall: star of *The Love Child*.'

The Love Child. Possibly the worst soap opera to cavort across the screens of the nation in the history of that genre, two solid hours a week of under-written characters and mind-numbing dialogue, as a result of which it consistently drew high ratings, and its performers became, almost overnight, brilliant stars in television's rhinestone heaven. Glittering there, the brightest of the bright, was Diane Duvall.

Maybe she wasn't born to play the classics, but Jesus was she good box-office. And in this day and age, with theatres deserted, all that mattered was the number of punters on seats.

Calloway had resigned himself to the fact that this would not be the definitive *Twelfth Night*, but if the production were successful, and with Diane in the role of Viola it had every chance, and it might open a few doors to him in the West End. Besides, working with the ever-adoring, ever-demanding Miss D. Duvall had its compensations.

Calloway pulled up his serge trousers, and looked down at her. She was giving him that winsome smile of hers, the one she used in the letter scene. Expression Five in the Duvall repertoire, somewhere between Virginal and Motherly.

He acknowledged the smile with one from his own stock, a small, loving look that passed for genuine at a yard's distance. Then he consulted his watch.

'God, we're late, sweetie.'

She licked her lips. Did she really like the taste that much?

'I'd better fix my hair,' she said, standing up and glancing in the long mirror beside the shower.

'Yes.'

'Are you OK?'

'Couldn't be better,' he replied. He kissed her lightly on the nose and left her to her teasing.

On his way to the stage he ducked into the Men's Dressing Room to adjust his clothing, and dowse his burning cheeks with cold water. Sex always induced a giveaway mottling on his face and upper chest. Bending to splash water on himself Calloway studied his features critically in the mirror over the sink. After thirty-six years of holding the signs of age at bay, he was beginning to look the part. He was no more the juvenile lead. There was an indisputable puffiness beneath his eyes, which was nothing to do with sleeplessness and there were lines too, on his forehead, and round his mouth. He didn't look the *wunderkind* any longer; the secrets of his debauchery were written all over his face. The excess of sex, booze and ambition, the frustration of aspiring and just missing the main chance so many times. What would he look like now, he thought bitterly, if he'd been content to be some unenterprising nobody working in a minor rep, guaranteed a house of ten aficionados every night, and devoted to Brecht? Face as smooth as a baby's bottom probably, most of the people in the socially-committed theatre had that look. Vacant and content, poor cows.

'Well, you pays your money and you takes your choice,' he told himself. He took one last look at the haggard cherub in the mirror, reflecting that, crow's feet or not, women still couldn't resist him, and went out to face the trials and tribulations of Act III.

On stage there was a heated debate in progress. The carpenter, his name was Jake, had built two hedges for Olivia's garden. They still had to be covered with leaves, but they looked quite impressive, running the depth of the stage to the cyclorama, where the rest of the garden would be painted. None of this symbolic stuff. A garden was a garden: green grass, blue sky. That's the way the audience liked it North of Birmingham, and Terry had some sympathy for their plain tastes.

'Terry, love.'

Eddie Cunningham had him by the hand and elbow, escorting him into the fray.

'What's the problem?'

'Terry, love, you cannot be serious about these fucking (it came trippingly off the tongue: fuck-ing) hedges. Tell Uncle Eddie you're not serious before I throw a fit.' Eddie pointed towards the offending hedges. 'I mean look at them.' As he spoke a thin plume of spittle fizzed in the air.

'What's the problem?' Terry asked again.

'Problem? Blocking, love, blocking. *Think* about it. We've rehearsed this whole scene with me bobbing up and down like a March hare. Up right, down left – but it doesn't work if I haven't got access round the back. And look! These fuck-ing things are flush with the backdrop.'

'Well they have to be, for the illusion, Eddie.'

'I can't get round though, Terry. You must see my point.'

He appealed to the few others on stage: the carpenters, two technicians, three actors.

'I mean – there's just not enough time.'

'Eddie, we'll re-block.'

'Oh.'

That took the wind out of his sails.

'No?'

'Um.'

'I mean it seems easiest, doesn't it?'

'Yes . . . I just liked . . .'

'I know.'

'Well. Needs must. What about the croquet?'

'We'll cut that too.'

'All that business with the croquet mallets? The bawdy stuff?'

'It'll all have to go. I'm sorry, I haven't thought this through. I wasn't thinking straight.'

Eddie flounced.

'That's all you ever do, love, think straight . . .'

Titters. Terry let it pass. Eddie had a genuine point of criticism; he had failed to consider the problems of the hedge-design.

'I'm sorry about the business; but there's no way we can accommodate it.'

'You won't be cutting anybody else's business, I'm sure,' said Eddie. He threw a glance over Calloway's shoulder at Diane, then headed for the dressing-room. Exit enraged actor, stage left. Calloway made no attempt to stop him. It would have worsened the situation considerably to spoil his departure. He just breathed out a quiet 'oh Jesus', and dragged a wide hand down over his face. That was the fatal flaw of this profession: actors.

'Will somebody fetch him back?' he said.

Silence.

'Where's Ryan?'

The Stage Manager showed his bespectacled face over the offending hedge.

'Sorry?'

'Ryan, love – will you please take a cup of coffee to Eddie and coax him back into the bosom of the family?'

Ryan pulled a face that said: you offended him, you fetch him. But Calloway had passed this particular buck before: he was a past master at it. He just stared at Ryan, defying him to contradict his request, until the other man dropped his eyes and nodded his acquiescence.

'Sure,' he said glumly.

'Good man.'

Ryan cast him an accusatory look, and disappeared in pursuit of Ed Cunningham.

'No show without Belch,' said Calloway, trying to warm up the atmosphere a little. Someone grunted: and the small half-circle of onlookers began to disperse. Show over.

'OK, OK,' said Calloway picking up the pieces, 'Let's get to work. We'll run through from the top of the scene. Diane, are you ready?'

'Yes.'

'OK. Shall we run it?'

He turned away from Olivia's garden and the waiting actors just to gather his thoughts. Only the stage working lights were on, the auditorium was in darkness. It yawned at him insolently, row upon row of empty seats, defying him to entertain them. Ah, the loneliness of the long-distance director. There were days in this business when the thought of life as an accountant seemed a consummation devoutedly to be wished, to paraphrase the Prince of Denmark.

In the Gods of the Elysium, somebody moved. Calloway looked up from his doubts and stared through the swarthy air. Had Eddie taken residence on the very back row? No, surely not. For one thing, he hadn't had time to get all the way up there.

'Eddie?' Calloway ventured, capping his hand over his eyes. 'Is that you?'

He could just make the figure out. No, not a figure, figures. Two people, edging their way along the back row, making for the exit. Whoever it was, it certainly wasn't Eddie.

'That isn't Eddie, is it?' said Calloway, turning back into the fake garden.

'No,' someone replied.

It was Eddie speaking. He was back on stage, leaning on one of the hedges, cigarette clamped between his lips.

'Eddie . . .'

'It's all right,' said the actor good-humouredly, 'Don't grovel. I can't bear to see a pretty man grovel.'

'We'll see if we can slot the mallet-business in somewhere,' said Calloway, eager to be conciliatory.

Eddie shook his head, and flicked ash off his cigarette.

'No need.'

'Really – '

'It didn't work too well anyhow.'

The Grand Circle door creaked a little as it closed behind the visitors. Calloway didn't bother to look round. They'd gone, whoever they were.

'There was somebody in the house this afternoon.'

Hammersmith looked up from the sheets of figures he was poring over.

'Oh?' his eyebrows were eruptions of wire-thick hair that seemed ambitious beyond their calling. They were raised high above Hammersmith's tiny eyes in patently fake surprise. He plucked at his bottom lip with nicotine stained fingers.

'Any idea who it was?'

He plucked on, still staring up at the younger man; undisguised contempt on his face.

'Is it a problem?'

'I just want to know who was in looking at the rehearsal that's all. I think I've got a perfect right to ask.'

'Perfect right,' said Hammersmith, nodding slightly and making his lips into a pale bow.

'There was talk of somebody coming up from the National,' said Calloway. 'My agents were arranging something. I just don't want somebody coming in without me knowing about it. Especially if they're important.'

Hammersmith was already studying the figures again. His voice was tired.

'Terry: if there's someone in from the South Bank to look your opus over, I promise you, you'll be the first to be informed. All right?'

The inflexion was so bloody rude. So run-along-little-boy. Calloway itched to hit him.

'I don't want people watching rehearsals unless I authorize it, Hammersmith. Hear me? And I want to know who was in today.'

The Manager sighed heavily.

'Believe me, Terry,' he said, 'I don't know myself. I suggest you ask Tallulah – she was front of house this afternoon. If somebody came in, presumably she saw them.'

He sighed again.

'All right . . . Terry?'

Calloway left it at that. He had his suspicions about Hammersmith. The man couldn't give a shit about theatre, he never failed to make that absolutely plain; he affected an exhausted tone whenever anything but money was mentioned, as though matters of aesthetics were beneath his notice. And he had a word, loudly administered, for actors and directors alike: butterflies. One day wonders. In Hammersmith's world only money was forever, and the Elysium Theatre stood on prime land, land a wise man could turn a tidy profit on if he played his cards right.

Calloway was certain he'd sell off the place tomorrow if he could manoeuvre it. A satellite town like Redditch, growing as Birmingham grew, didn't need theatres, it needed offices, hypermarkets, warehouses: it needed, to quote the councillors, growth through investment in new industry. It also needed prime sites to build that industry upon. No mere art could survive such pragmatism.

Tallulah was not in the box, nor in the foyer, nor in the Green Room.

Irritated both by Hammersmith's incivility and Tallulah's disappearance, Calloway went back into the auditorium to pick up his jacket and go to get drunk. The rehearsal was over and the actors long gone. The bare hedges looked somewhat small from the back row of the stalls. Maybe they needed an extra few inches. He made a note on the back of a show bill he found in his pocket: Hedges, bigger?

A footfall made him look up, and a figure had appeared on stage. A smooth entrance, up-stage centre, where the hedges converged. Calloway didn't recognize the man.

'Mr Calloway? Mr Terence Calloway?'

'Yes?'

The visitor walked down stage to where, in an earlier age, the footlights would have been, and stood looking out into the auditorium.

'My apologies for interrupting your train of thought.'

'No problem.'

'I wanted a word.'

'With me?'

'If you would.'

Calloway wandered down to the front of the stalls, appraising the stranger.

He was dressed in shades of grey from head to foot. A grey worsted suit, grey shoes, a grey cravat. Piss-elegant, was Calloway's first, uncharitable summation. But the man cut an impressive figure nevertheless. His face beneath the shadow of his brim was difficult to discern.

'Allow me to introduce myself.'

The voice was persuasive, cultured. Ideal for advertisement voice-overs: soap commercials, maybe. After Hammersmith's bad manners, the voice came as a breath of good breeding.

'My name is Lichfield. Not that I expect that means much to a man of your tender years.'

Tender years: well, well. Maybe there was still something of the *wunderkind* in his face.

'Are you a critic?' Calloway inquired.

The laugh that emanated from beneath the immaculately-swept brim was ripely ironical.

'In the name of Jesus, no,' Lichfield replied.

'I'm sorry, then, you have me at a loss.'

'No need for an apology.'

'Were you in the house this afternoon?'

Lichfield ignored the question. 'I realize you're a busy man, Mr Calloway, and I don't want to waste your time. The theatre is my business, as it is yours. I think we must consider ourselves allies, though we have never met.'

Ah, the great brotherhood. It made Calloway want to spit, the familiar claims of sentiment. When he thought of the number of so-called allies that had cheerfully stabbed him in the back; and in return the playwrights whose work he'd smilingly slanged, the actors he'd crushed with a casual quip. Brotherhood be damned, it was dog eat dog, same as any over-subscribed profession.

'I have,' Lichfield was saying, 'an abiding interest in the Elysium.' There was a curious emphasis on the word abiding. It sounded positively funereal from Lichfield's lips. Abide with me.

'Oh?'

'Yes, I've spent many happy hours in this theatre, down the years, and frankly it pains me to carry this burden of news.'

'What news?'

'Mr Calloway, I have to inform you that your *Twelfth Night* will be the last production the Elysium will see.'

The statement didn't come as much of a surprise, but it still hurt, and the internal wince must have registered on Calloway's face.

'Ah . . . so you didn't know. I thought not. They always keep the artists in ignorance don't they? It's a satisfaction the Apolloians will never relinquish. The accountant's revenge.'

'Hammersmith,' said Calloway.

'Hammersmith.'

'Bastard.'

'His clan are never to be trusted, but then I hardly need to tell you that.'

'Are you sure about the closure?'

'Certainly. He'd do it tomorrow if he could.'

'But why? I've done Stoppard here, Tenessee Williams – always played to good houses. It doesn't make sense.'

'It makes admirable financial sense, I'm afraid, and if you think in figures, as Hammersmith does, there's no riposte to simple arithmetic. The Elysium's getting old. We're *all* getting old. We creak. We feel our age in our joints: our instinct is to lie down and be gone away.'

Gone away: the voice became melodramatically thin, a whisper of longing.

'How do you know about this?'

'I was, for many years, a trustee of the theatre, and since my retirement I've made it my business to – what's the phrase? – keep my ear to the ground. It's difficult, in this day and age, to evoke the triumph this stage has seen . . .'

His voice trailed away, in a reverie. It seemed true, not an effect.

Then, business-like once more: 'This theatre is about to die, Mr Calloway. You will be present at the last rites, through no fault of your own. I felt you ought to be . . . warned.'

'Thank you. I appreciate that. Tell me, were you ever an actor yourself?'

'What makes you think that?'

'The voice.'

'Too rhetorical by half, I know. My curse, I'm afraid. I can scarcely ask for a cup of coffee without sounding like Lear in the storm.'

He laughed, heartily, at his own expense. Calloway began to warm to the fellow. Maybe he was a little archaic-looking, perhaps even slightly absurd, but there was a full-bloodedness about his manner that caught Calloway's imagination. Lichfield wasn't apologetic about his love of theatre, like so many in the profession, people who trod the boards as a second-best, their souls sold to the movies.

'I have, I will confess, dabbled in the craft a little,' Lichfield confided, 'but I just don't have the stamina for it, I'm afraid. Now my wife – '

Wife? Calloway was surprised Lichfield had a heterosexual bone in his body.

' – My wife Constantia has played here on a number of occasions, and I may say very successfully. Before the war of course.'

'It's a pity to close the place.'

'Indeed. But there are no last act miracles to be performed, I'm afraid. The Elysium will be rubble in six weeks' time, and there's an end to it. I just wanted you to know that interests other than the crassly commercial are watching over this closing production. Think of us as guardian angels. We wish you well, Terence, we all wish you well.'

It was a genuine sentiment, simply stated. Calloway was touched by this man's concern, and a little chastened by it. It put his own stepping-stone ambitions in an unflattering perspective. Lichfield went on: 'We care to see this theatre end its days in suitable style, then die a good death.'

'Damn shame.'

94

'Too late for regrets by a long chalk. We should never have given up Dionysus for Apollo.'

'What?'

'Sold ourselves to the accountants, to legitimacy, to the likes of Mr Hammersmith, whose soul, if he has one, must be the size of my fingernail, and grey as a louse's back. We should have had the courage of our depictions, I think. Served poetry and lived under the stars.'

Calloway didn't quite follow the allusions, but he got the general drift, and respected the viewpoint.

Off stage left, Diane's voice cut the solemn atmosphere like a plastic knife.

'Terry? Are you there?'

The spell was broken: Calloway hadn't been aware how hypnotic Lichfield's presence was until that other voice came between them. Listening to him was like being rocked in familiar arms. Lichfield stepped to the edge of the stage, lowering his voice to a conspiratorial rasp.

'One last thing, Terence – '

'Yes?'

'Your Viola. She lacks, if you'll forgive my pointing it out, the special qualities required for the role.'

Calloway hung fire.

'I know,' Lichfield continued, 'personal loyalties prevent honesty in these matters.'

'No,' Calloway replied, 'you're right. But she's popular.'

'So was bear-baiting, Terence.'

A luminous smile spread beneath the brim, hanging in the shadow like the grin of the Cheshire Cat.

'I'm only joking,' said Lichfield, his rasp a chuckle now, 'Bears can be charming.'

'Terry, there you are.'

Diane appeared, over-dressed as usual, from behind the tabs. There was surely an embarrassing confrontation in the air. But Lichfield was walking away down the false perspective of the hedges towards the backdrop.

'Here I am,' said Terry.

'Who are you talking to?'

But Lichfield had exited, as smoothly and as quietly as he had entered. Diane hadn't even seen him go.

'Oh, just an angel,' said Calloway.

The first Dress Rehearsal wasn't, all things considered, as bad as Calloway had anticipated: it was immeasurably worse. Cues were

95

lost, props mislaid, entrances missed; the comic business seemed ill-contrived and laborious; the performances either hopelessly overwrought or trifling. This was a *Twelfth Night* that seemed to last a year. Halfway through the third act Calloway glanced at his watch, and realized an uncut performance of *Macbeth* (with interval) would now be over.

He sat in the stalls with his head buried in his hands, contemplating the work that he still had to do if he was to bring this production up to scratch. Not for the first time on this show he felt helpless in the face of the casting problems. Cues could be tightened, props rehearsed with, entrances practised until they were engraved on the memory. But a bad actor is a bad actor is a bad actor. He could labour 'til doomsday neatening and sharpening, but he could not make a silk purse of the sow's ear that was Diane Duvall.

With all the skill of an acrobat she contrived to skirt every significance, to ignore every opportunity to move the audience, to avoid every nuance the playwright would insist on putting in her way. It was a performance heroic in its ineptitude, reducing the delicate characterization Calloway had been at pains to create to a single-note whine. This Viola was soap-opera pap, less human than the hedges, and about as green.

The critics would slaughter her.

Worse than that, Lichfield would be disappointed. To his considerable surprise the impact of Lichfield's appearance hadn't dwindled; Calloway couldn't forget his actorly projection, his posing, his rhetoric. It had moved him more deeply than he was prepared to admit, and the thought of this *Twelfth Night*, with this Viola, becoming the swan-song of Lichfield's beloved Elysium perturbed and embarrassed him. It seemed somehow ungrateful.

He'd been warned often enough about a directors' burdens, long before he became seriously embroiled in the profession. His dear departed guru at the Actor's Centre, Wellbeloved (he of the glass eye) had told Calloway from the beginning:

'A director is the loneliest creature on God's earth. He knows what's good and bad in a show, or he should if he's worth his salt, and he has to carry that information around with him and keep smiling.'

It hadn't seemed so difficult at the time.

'This job isn't about succeeding,' Wellbeloved used to say, 'it's about learning not to fall on your sodding face.'

Good advice as it turned out. He could still see Wellbeloved handing out that wisdom on a plate, his bald head shiny, his living eye glittering with cynical delight. No man on earth, Calloway had thought, loved theatre with more passion than Wellbeloved, and surely no man could have been more scathing about its pretensions.

It was almost one in the morning by the time they'd finished the wretched run-through, gone through the notes, and separated, glum and mutually resentful, into the night. Calloway wanted none of their company tonight: no late drinking in one or others' digs, no mutual ego-massage. He had a cloud of gloom all to himself, and neither wine, women nor song would disperse it. He could barely bring himself to look Diane in the face. His notes to her, broadcast in front of the rest of the cast, had been acidic. Not that it would do much good.

In the foyer, he met Tallulah, still spry though it was long after an old lady's bedtime.

'Are you locking up tonight?' he asked her, more for something to say than because he was actually curious.

'I always lock up,' she said. She was well over seventy: too old for her job in the box office, and too tenacious to be easily removed. But then that was all academic now, wasn't it? He wondered what her response would be when she heard the news of the closure. It would probably break her brittle heart. Hadn't Hammersmith once told him Tallulah had been at the theatre since she was a girl of fifteen?

'Well, goodnight Tallulah.'

She gave him a tiny nod, as always. Then she reached out and took Calloway's arm.

'Yes?'

'Mr Lichfield . . .' she began.

'What about Mr Lichfield?'

'He didn't like the rehearsal.'

'He was in tonight?'

'Oh yes,' she replied, as though Calloway was an imbecile for thinking otherwise, 'of course he was in.'

'I didn't see him.'

'Well . . . no matter. He wasn't very pleased.'

Calloway tried to sound indifferent.

'It can't be helped.'

'Your show is very close to his heart.'

'I realize that, said Calloway, avoiding Tallulah's accusing looks. He had quite enough to keep him awake tonight, without her disappointed tones ringing in his ears.

He loosed his arm, and made for the door. Tallulah made no attempt to stop him. She just said: 'You should have seen Constantia.'

Constantia? Where had he heard that name? Of course, Lichfield's wife.

'She was a wonderful Viola.'

He was too tired for this mooning over dead actresses; she was dead wasn't she? He had said she was dead, hadn't he?

'Wonderful,' said Tallulah again.

'Goodnight, Tallulah. I'll see you tomorrow.'

The old crone didn't answer. If she was offended by his brusque manner, then so be it. He left her to her complaints and faced the street.

It was late November, and chilly. No balm in the night-air, just the smell of tar from a freshly laid road, and grit in the wind. Calloway pulled his jacket collar up around the back of his neck, and hurried off to the questionable refuge of Murphy's Bed and Breakfast.

In the foyer Tallulah turned her back on the cold and dark of the outside world, and shuffled back into the temple of dreams. It smelt so weary now: stale with use and age, like her own body. It was time to let natural processes take their toll; there was no point in letting things run beyond their allotted span. That was as true of buildings as of people. But the Elysium had to die as it had lived, in glory.

Respectfully, she drew back the red curtains that covered the portraits in the corridor that led from foyer to stalls. Barrymore, Irving: great names and great actors. Stained and faded pictures perhaps, but the memories were as sharp and as refreshing as spring water. And in pride of place, the last of the line to be unveiled, a portrait of Constantia Lichfield. A face of transcendent beauty; a bone structure to make an anatomist weep.

She had been far too young for Lichfield of course, and that had been part of the tragedy of it. Lichfield the Svengali, a man twice her age, had been capable of giving his brilliant beauty everything she desired; fame, money, companionship. Everything but the gift she most required: life itself.

She'd died before she was yet twenty, a cancer in the breast. Taken so suddenly it was still difficult to believe she'd gone.

Tears brimmed in Tallulah's eyes as she remembered that lost and wasted genius. So many parts Constantia would have illuminated had she been spared. Cleopatra, Hedda, Rosalind, Electra . . .

But it wasn't to be. She'd gone, extinguished like a candle in a hurricane, and for those who were left behind life was a slow and joyless march through a cold land. There were mornings now, stirring to another dawn, when she would turn over and pray to die in her sleep.

98

The tears were quite blinding her now, she was awash. And oh dear, there was somebody behind her, probably Mr Calloway back for something, and here was she, sobbing fit to burst, behaving like the silly old woman she knew he thought her to be. A young man like him, what did he understand about the pain of the years, the deep ache of irretrievable loss? That wouldn't come to him for a while yet. Sooner than he thought, but a while nevertheless.

'Tallie,' somebody said.

She knew who it was. Richard Walden Lichfield. She turned round and he was standing no more than six feet from her, as fine a figure of a man as ever she remembered him to be. He must be twenty years older than she was, but age didn't seem to bow him. She felt ashamed of her tears.

'Tallie,' he said kindly, 'I know it's a little late, but I felt you'd surely want to say hello.'

'Hello?'

The tears were clearing, and now she saw Lichfield's companion, standing a respectful foot or two behind him, partially obscured. The figure stepped out of Lichfield's shadow and there was a luminous, fine-boned beauty Tallulah recognized as easily as her own reflection. Time broke in pieces, and reason deserted the world. Longed-for faces were suddenly back to fill the empty nights, and offer fresh hope to a life grown weary. Why should she argue with the evidence of her eyes?

It was Constantia, the radiant Constantia, who was looping her arm through Lichfield's and nodding gravely at Tallulah in greeting.

Dear, dead Constantia.

The rehearsal was called for nine-thirty the following morning. Diane Duvall made an entrance her customary half hour late. She looked as though she hadn't slept all night.

'Sorry I'm late,' she said, her open vowels oozing down the aisle towards the stage.

Calloway was in no mood for foot-kissing.

'We've got an opening tomorrow,' he snapped, 'and everybody's been kept waiting by you.'

'Oh really?' she fluttered, trying to be devastating. It was too early in the morning, and the effect fell on stony ground.

'OK, we're going from the top,' Calloway announced, 'and everybody please have your copies and a pen. I've got a list of cuts here and I want them rehearsed in by lunchtime. Ryan, have you got the prompt copy?'

There was a hurried exchange with the ASM and an apologetic negative from Ryan.

'Well get it. And I don't want any complaints from anyone, it's too late in the day. Last night's run was a wake, not a performance. The cues took forever; the business was ragged. I'm going to cut, and it's not going to be very palatable.'

It wasn't. The complaints came, warning or no, the arguments, the compromises, the sour faces and muttered insults. Calloway would have rather been hanging by his toes from a trapeze than manoeuvering fourteen highly-strung people through a play two-thirds of them scarcely understood, and the other third couldn't give a monkey's about. It was nerve-wracking.

It was made worse because all the time he had the prickly sense of being watched, though the auditorium was empty from Gods to front stalls. Maybe Lichfield had a spyhole somewhere, he thought, then condemned the idea as the first signs of budding paranoia.

At last, lunch.

Calloway knew where he'd find Diane, and he was prepared for the scene he had to play with her. Accusations, tears, reassurance, tears again, reconciliation. Standard format.

He knocked on the Star's door.

'Who is it?'

Was she crying already, or talking through a glass of something comforting.

'It's me.'

'Oh.'

'Can I come in?'

'Yes.'

She had a bottle of vodka, good vodka, and a glass. No tears as yet.

'I'm useless, aren't I?' she said, almost as soon as he'd closed the door. Her eyes begged for contradiction.

'Don't be silly,' he hedged.

'I could never get the hang of Shakespeare,' she pouted, as though it were the Bard's fault, 'All those bloody words.' The squall was on the horizon, he could see it mustering.

'It's all right,' he lied, putting his arm around her, 'You just need a little time.'

Her face clouded.

'We open tomorrow,' she said flatly. The point was difficult to refute.

'They'll tear me apart, won't they?'

He wanted to say no, but his tongue had a fit of honesty.

100

'Yes. Unless – '

'I'll never work again, will I? Harry talked me into this, that damn half-witted Jew: good for my reputation, he said. Bound to give me a bit more clout, he said. What does he know? Takes his ten bloody per cent and leaves me holding the baby. I'm the one who looks the damn fool aren't I?'

At the thought of looking a fool, the storm broke. No light shower this: it was a cloudburst or nothing. He did what he could, but it was difficult. She was sobbing so loudly his pearls of wisdom were drowned out. So he kissed her a little, as any decent director was bound to do, and (miracle upon miracle) that seemed to do the trick. He applied the technique with a little more gusto, his hands straying to her breasts, ferreting under her blouse for her nipples and teasing them between thumb and forefinger.

It worked wonders. There were hints of sun between the clouds now; she sniffed and unbuckled his belt, letting his heat dry out the last of the rain. His fingers were finding the lacy edge of her panties, and she was sighing as he investigated her, gently but not too gently, insistent but never too insistent. Somewhere along the line she knocked over the vodka bottle but neither of them cared to stop and right it, so it sloshed on to the floor off the edge of the table, counterpointing her instructions, his gasps.

Then the bloody door opened, and a draught blew up between them, cooling the point at issue.

Calloway almost turned round, then realized he was unbuckled, and stared instead into the mirror behind Diane to see the intruder's face. It was Lichfield. He was looking straight at Calloway, his face impassive.

'I'm sorry, I should have knocked.'

His voice was as smooth as whipped cream, betraying nary a tremor of embarrassment. Calloway wedged himself away, buckled up his belt and turned to Lichfield, silently cursing his burning cheeks.

'Yes . . . it would have been polite,' he said.

'Again my apologies. I wanted a word with – ' His eyes, so deep-set they were unfathomable, were on Diane. ' – your star,' he said.

Calloway could practically feel Diane's ego expand at the word. The approach confounded him: had Lichfield undergone a volte-face? Was he coming here, the repentant admirer, to kneel at the feet of greatness?

'I would appreciate a word with the lady in private, if that were possible,' the mellow voice went on.

'Well, we were just – '

'Of course,' Diane interrupted, 'Just allow me a moment, would you?'

She was immediately on top of the situation, tears forgotten.

'I'll be just outside,' said Lichfield, already taking his leave.

Before he had closed the door behind him Diane was in front of the mirror, tissue-wrapped finger skirting her eye to divert a rivulet of mascara.

'Well,' she was cooing, 'how lovely to have a well-wisher. Do you know who he is?'

'His name's Lichfield,' Calloway told her, 'He used to be a trustee of the theatre.'

'Maybe he wants to offer me something.'

'I doubt it.'

'Oh don't be such a drag Terence,' she snarled, 'You just can't bear to have anyone else get any attention, can you?'

'My mistake.'

She peered at her eyes.

'How do I look?' she asked.

'Fine.'

'I'm sorry about before.'

'Before?'

'You know.'

'Oh . . . yes.'

'I'll see you in the pub, eh?'

He was summarily dismissed apparently, his function as lover or confidante no longer required.

In the chilly corridor outside the dressing room Lichfield was waiting patiently. Though the lights were better here than on the ill-lit stage, and he was closer now than he'd been the night before, Calloway could still not quite make out the face under the wide brim. There was something – what was the idea buzzing in his head? – something artificial about Lichfield's features. The flesh of his face didn't move as interlocking system of muscle and tendon, it was too stiff, too pink, almost like scar-tissue.

'She's not quite ready,' Calloway told him.

'She's a lovely woman,' Lichfield purred.

'Yes.'

'I don't blame you . . .'

'Um.'

'She's no actress though.'

'You're not going to interfere are you, Lichfield? I won't let you.'

'Perish the thought.'

The voyeuristic pleasure Lichfield had plainly taken in his embarrassment made Calloway less respectful than he'd been.

'I won't have you upsetting her – '

'My interests are your interests, Terence. All I want to do is see this production prosper, believe me. Am I likely, under those circumstances, to alarm your Leading Lady? I'll be as meek as a lamb, Terence.'

'Whatever you are,' came the testy reply, 'you're no lamb.'

The smile appeared again on Lichfield's face, the tissue round his mouth barely stretching to accommodate his expression.

Calloway retired to the pub with that predatory sickle of teeth fixed in his mind, anxious for no reason he could focus upon.

In the mirrored cell of her dressing-room Diane Duvall was just about ready to play her scene.

'You may come in now, Mr Lichfield,' she announced.

He was in the doorway before the last syllable of his name had died on her lips.

'Miss Duvall,' he bowed slightly in deference to her. She smiled; so courteous. 'Will you please forgive my blundering in earlier on?'

She looked coy; it always melted men.

'Mr Calloway – ' she began.

'A very insistent young man, I think.'

'Yes.'

'Not above pressing his attentions on his Leading Lady, perhaps?'

She frowned a little, a dancing pucker where the plucked arches of her brows converged.

'I'm afraid so.'

'Most unprofessional of him,' Lichfield said, 'But forgive me – an understandable ardour.'

She moved upstage of him, towards the lights of her mirror, and turned, knowing they would back-light her hair more flatteringly.

'Well, Mr Lichfield, what can I do for you?'

'This is frankly a delicate matter,' said Lichfield. 'The bitter fact is – how shall I put this? – your talents are not ideally suited to this production. Your style lacks delicacy.'

There was a silence for two beats. She sniffed, thought about the inference of the remark, and then moved out of centre-stage towards the door. She didn't like the way this scene had begun. She was expecting an admirer, and instead she had a critic on her hands.

'Get out!' she said, her voice like slate.

'Miss Duvall – '

'You heard me.'

'You're not comfortable as Viola, are you?' Lichfield continued, as though the star had said nothing.

103

'None of your bloody business,' she spat back.

'But it is. I saw the rehearsals. You were bland, unpersuasive. The comedy is flat, the reunion scene – it should break our hearts – is leaden.'

'I don't need your opinion, thank you.'

'You have no style – '

'Piss off.'

'No presence and no style. I'm sure on the television you are radiance itself, but the stage requires a special truth, a soulfulness you, frankly, lack.'

The scene was hotting up. She wanted to hit him, but she couldn't find the proper motivation. She couldn't take this faded poseur seriously. He was more musical comedy than melodrama, with his neat grey gloves, and his neat grey cravat. Stupid, waspish queen, what did he know about acting?

'Get out before I call the Stage Manager,' she said, but he stepped between her and the door.

A rape scene? Was that what they were playing? Had he got the hots for her? God forbid.

'My wife,' he was saying, 'has played Viola – '

'Good for her.'

' – and she feels she could breathe a little more life into the role than you.'

'We open tomorrow,' she found herself replying, as though defending her presence. Why the hell was she trying to reason with him; barging in here and making these terrible remarks. Maybe because she was just a little afraid. His breath, close to her now, smelt of expensive chocolate.

'She knows the role by heart.'

'The part's mine. And I'm doing it. I'm doing it even if I'm the worst Viola in theatrical history, all right?'

She was trying to keep her composure, but it was difficult. Something about him made her nervous. It wasn't violence she feared from him: but she feared something.

'I'm afraid I have already promised the part to my wife.'

'What?' she goggled at his arrogance.

'And Constantia will play the role.'

She laughed at the name. Maybe this was high comedy after all. Something from Sheridan or Wilde, arch, catty stuff. But he spoke with such absolute certainty. *Constantia will play the role*; as if it was all cut and dried.

'I'm not discussing this any longer, Buster, so if your wife wants to play Viola she'll have to do it in the fucking street. All right?'

'She opens tomorrow.'

'Are you deaf, or stupid, or both?'

Control, an inner voice told her, you're overplaying, losing your grip on the scene. Whatever scene this is.

He stepped towards her, and the mirror lights caught the face beneath the brim full on. She hadn't looked carefully enough when he first made his appearance: now she saw the deeply-etched lines, the gougings around his eyes and his mouth. It wasn't flesh, she was sure of it. He was wearing latex appliances, and they were badly glued in place. Her hand all but twitched with the desire to snatch at it and uncover his real face.

Of course. That was it. The scene she was playing: the Unmasking.

'Let's see what you look like,' she said, and her hand was at his cheek before he could stop her, his smile spreading wider as she attacked. This is what he wants, she thought, but it was too late for regrets or apologies. Her fingertips had found the line of the mask at the edge of his eye-socket, and curled round to take a better hold. She yanked.

The thin veil of latex came away, and his true physiognomy was exposed for the world to see. Diane tried to back away, but his hand was in her hair. All she could do was look up into that all-but fleshless face. A few withered strands of muscle curled here and there, and a hint of a beard hung from a leathery flap at his throat, but all living tissue had long since decayed. Most of his face was simply bone: stained and worn.

'I was not,' said the skull, 'enbalmed. Unlike Constantia.'

The explanation escaped Diane. She made no sound of protest, which the scene would surely have justified. All she could summon was a whimper as his hand-hold tightened, and he hauled her head back.

'We must make a choice, sooner or later,' said Lichfield, his breath smelling less like chocolate than profound putresence, 'between serving ourselves and serving our art.'

She didn't quite understand.

'The dead must choose more carefully than the living. We cannot waste our breath, if you'll excuse the phrase, on less than the purest delights. You don't want art, I think. Do you?'

She shook her head, hoping to God that was the expected response.

'You want the life of the body, not the life of the imagination. And you may have it.'

'Thank . . . you.'

'If you want it enough, you may have it.'

Suddenly his hand, which had been pulling on her hair so

105

painfully, was cupped behind her head, and bringing her lips up to meet his. She would have screamed then, as his rotting mouth fastened itself on to hers, but his greeting was so insistent it quite took her breath away.

Ryan found Diane on the floor of her dressing-room a few minutes before two. It was difficult to work out what had happened. There was no sign of a wound of any kind on her head or body, nor was she quite dead. She seemed to be in a coma of some kind. She had perhaps slipped, and struck her head as she fell. Whatever the cause, she was out for the count.

They were hours away from a Final Dress Rehearsal and Viola was in an ambulance, being taken into Intensive Care.

'The sooner they knock this place down, the better,' said Hammersmith. He'd been drinking during office hours, something Calloway had never seen him do before. The whisky bottle stood on his desk beside a half-full glass. There were glass-marks ringing his accounts, and his hand had a bad dose of the shakes.

'What's the news from the hospital?'

'She's a beautiful woman,' he said, staring at the glass. Calloway could have sworn he was on the verge of tears.

'Hammersmith? How is she?'

'She's in a coma. But her condition is stable.'

'That's something, I suppose.'

Hammersmith stared up at Calloway, his erupting brows knitted in anger.

'You runt,' he said, 'you were screwing her, weren't you? Fancy yourself like that, don't you? Well, let me tell you something, Diane Duvall is worth a dozen of you. A dozen!'

'Is that why you let this last production go on, Hammersmith? Because you'd seen her, and you wanted to get your hot little hands on her?'

'You wouldn't understand. You've got your brain in your pants.' He seemed genuinely offended by the interpretation Calloway had put on his admiration for Miss Duvall.

'All right, have it your way. We still have no Viola.'

'That's why I'm cancelling,' said Hammersmith, slowing down to savour the moment.

It had to come. Without Diane Duvall, there would be no *Twelfth Night*; and maybe it was better that way.

A knock on the door.

'Who the fuck's that?' said Hammersmith softly, 'Come.'

It was Lichfield. Calloway was almost glad to see that strange, scarred face. Though he had a lot of questions to ask of Lichfield, about the state he'd left Diane in, about their conversation together, it wasn't an interview he was willing to conduct in front of Hammersmith. Besides, any half-formed accusations he might have had were countered by the man's presence here. If Lichfield had attempted violence on Diane, for whatever reason, was it likely that he would come back so soon, so smilingly?

'Who are you?' Hammersmith demanded.

'Richard Walden Lichfield.'

'I'm none the wiser.'

'I used to be a trustee of the Elysium.'

'Oh.'

'I make it my business – '

'What do you want?' Hammersmith broke in, irritated by Lichfield's poise.

'I hear the production is in jeopardy,' Lichfield replied, unruffled.

'No jeopardy,' said Hammersmith, allowing himself a twitch at the corner of his mouth, 'No jeopardy at all, because there's no show. It's been cancelled.'

'Oh?' Lichfield looked at Calloway.

'Is this with your consent?' he asked.

'He has no say in the matter; I have sole right of cancellation if circumstances dictate it; its in his contract. The theatre is closed as of today: it will not reopen.'

'Yes it will,' said Lichfield.

'What?' Hammersmith stood up behind his desk, and Calloway realized he'd never seen the man standing before. He was very short.

'We will play *Twelfth Night* as advertized,' Lichfield purred. 'My wife has kindly agreed to understudy the part of Viola in place of Miss Duvall.'

Hammersmith laughed, a coarse, butcher's laugh. It died on his lips however, as the office was suffused with lavender, and Constantia Lichfield made her entrance, shimmering in silk and fur. She looked as perfect as the day she died: even Hammersmith held his breath and his silence at the sight of her.

'Our new Viola,' Lichfield announced.

After a moment Hammersmith found his voice. 'This woman can't step in at half a day's notice.'

'Why not?' said Calloway, not taking his eyes off the woman. Lichfield was a lucky man; Constantia was an extraordinary beauty. He scarcely dared draw breath in her presence for fear she'd vanish.

107

Then she spoke. The lines were from Act V, Scene I:

'If nothing lets to make us happy both
But this my masculine usurp'd attire,
Do not embrace me till each circumstance
Of place, time, fortune, do cohere and jump
That I am Viola.'

The voice was light and musical, but it seemed to resound in her body, filling each phrase with an undercurrent of suppressed passion.

And that face. It was wonderfully alive, the features playing the story of her speech with delicate economy.

She was enchanting.

'I'm sorry,' said Hammersmith, 'But there are rules and regulations about this sort of thing. Is she Equity?'

'No,' said Lichfield.

'Well you see, it's impossible. The union strictly precludes this kind of thing. They'd flay us alive.'

'What's it to you, Hammersmith?' said Calloway. 'What the fuck do you care? You'll never need set foot in a theatre again once this place is demolished.'

'My wife has watched the rehearsals. She is word perfect.'

'It could be magic,' said Calloway, his enthusiasm firing up with every moment he looked at Constantia.

'You're risking the Union, Calloway,' Hammersmith chided.

'I'll take that risk.'

'As you say, it's nothing to me. But if a little bird was to tell them, you'd have egg on your face.'

'Hammersmith: give her a chance. Give all of us a chance. If Equity blacks me, that's my look-out.' Hammersmith sat down again.

'Nobody'll come, you know that, don't you? Diane Duvall was a star; they would have sat through your turgid production to see her, Calloway. But an unknown . . . ? Well, it's your funeral. Go ahead and do it, I wash my hands of the whole thing. It's on your head Calloway, remember that. I hope they flay you for it.'

'Thank you,' said Lichfield. 'Most kind.'

Hammersmith began to rearrange his desk, to give more prominence to the bottle and the glass. The interview was over: he wasn't interested in these butterflies any longer.

'Go away,' he said, 'Just go away.'

'I have one or two requests to make,' Lichfield told Calloway as they left the office. 'Alterations to the production which would enhance my wife's performance.'

'What are they?'

'For Constantia's comfort, I would ask that the lighting levels be taken down substantially. She's simply not accustomed to performing under such hot, bright lights.'

'Very well.'

'I'd also request that we install a row of footlights.'

'Footlights?'

'An odd requirement, I realize, but she feels much happier with footlights.'

'They tend to dazzle the actors,' said Calloway, 'It becomes difficult to see the audience.'

'Nevertheless . . . I have to stipulate their installation.'

'OK.'

'Thirdly – I would ask that all scenes involving kissing, embracing or otherwise touching Constantia be re-directed to remove every instance of physical contact whatsoever.'

'Everything?'

'Everything.'

'For God's sake why?'

'My wife needs no business to dramatize the working of the heart, Terence.'

That curious intonation on the word 'heart'. Working of the *heart*.

Calloway caught Constantia's eye for the merest of moments. It was like being blessed.

'Shall we introduce our new Viola to the company?' Lichfield suggested.

'Why not?'

The trio went into the theatre.

The re-arranging of the blocking and the business to exclude any physical contact was simple. And though the rest of the cast were initially wary of their new colleague, her unaffected manner and her natural grace soon had them at her feet. Besides, her presence meant that the show would go on.

At six, Calloway called a break, announcing that they'd begin the Dress at eight, and telling them to go out and enjoy themselves for an hour or so. The company went their ways, buzzing with a new-found enthusiasm for the production. What had looked like a shambles half a day earlier now seemed to be shaping up quite well. There were a thousand things to be sniped at, of course: technical shortcomings, costumes that fitted badly, directorial foibles. All par for the course. In fact, the actors were happier than they'd been in a good while. Even Ed Cunningham was not above passing a compliment or two.

Lichfield found Tallulah in the Green Room, tidying.

'Tonight . . .'

'Yes, sir.'

'You must not be afraid.'

'I'm not afraid,' Tallulah replied. What a thought. As if – '

'There may be some pain, which I regret. For you, indeed for all of us.'

'I understand.'

'Of course you do. You love the theatre as I love it: you know the paradox of this profession. To play life . . . ah, Tallulah, to play life . . . what a curious thing it is. Sometimes I wonder, you know, how long I can keep up the illusion.'

'It's a wonderful performance,' she said.

'Do you think so? Do you really think so?' He was encouraged by her favourable review. It was so galling, to have to pretend all the time; to fake the flesh, the breath, the look of life. Grateful for Tallulah's opinion, he reached for her.

'Would you like to die, Tallulah?'

'Does it hurt?'

'Scarcely at all.'

'It would make me very happy.'

'And so it should.'

His mouth covered her mouth, and she was dead in less than a minute, conceding happily to his inquiring tongue. He laid her out on the threadbare couch and locked the door of the Green Room with her own key. She'd cool easily in the chill of the room, and be up and about again by the time the audience arrived.

At six-fifteen Diane Duvall got out of a taxi at the front of the Elysium. It was well dark, a windy November night, but she felt fine; nothing could depress tonight. Not the dark, not the cold.

Unseen, she made her way past the posters that bore her face and name, and through the empty auditorium to her dressing-room. There, smoking his way through a pack of cigarettes, she found the object of her affection.

'Terry.'

She posed in the doorway for a moment, letting the fact of her reappearance sink in. He went quite white at the sight of her, so she pouted a little. It wasn't easy to pout. There was a stiffness in the muscles of her face but she carried off the effect to her satisfaction.

Calloway was lost for words. Diane looked ill, no two ways about it, and if she'd left the hospital to take up her part in the Dress Rehearsal he was going to have to convince her otherwise. She was wearing no make-up, and her ash-blonde hair needed a wash.

'What are you doing here?' he asked, as she closed the door behind her.

'Unfinished business,' she said.

'Listen . . . I've got something to tell you . . .'

God, this was going to be messy. 'We've found a replacement, in the show.' She looked at him blankly. He hurried on, tripping over his own words, 'We thought you were out of commission, I mean, not permanently, but, you know, for the opening at least . . .'

'Don't worry,' she said.

His jaw dropped a little.

'Don't worry?'

'What's it to me?'

'You said you came back to finish – '

He stopped. She was unbuttoning the top of her dress. She's not serious, he thought, she can't be serious. Sex? Now?

'I've done a lot of thinking in the last few hours,' she said as she shimmied the crumpled dress over her hips, let it fall, and stepped out of it. She was wearing a white bra, which she tried, unsuccessfully, to unhook. 'I've decided I don't care about the theatre. Help me, will you?'

She turned round and presented her back to him. Automatically he unhooked the bra, not really analysing whether he wanted this or not. It seemed to be a *fait accompli*. She'd come back to finish what they'd been interrupted doing, simple as that. And despite the bizarre noises she was making in the back of her throat, and the glassy look in her eyes, she was still an attractive woman. She turned again, and Calloway stared at the fullness of her breasts, paler than he'd remembered them, but lovely. His trousers were becoming uncomfortably tight, and her performance was only worsening his situation, the way she was grinding her hips like the rawest of Soho strippers, running her hands between her legs.

'Don't worry about me,' she said, 'I've made up my mind. All I really want . . .'

She put her hands, so recently at her groin, on his face. They were icy cold.

'All I really want is you. I can't have sex *and* the stage . . . There comes a time in everyone's life when decisions have to be made.'

She licked her lips. There was no film of moisture left on her mouth when her tongue had passed over it.

'The accident made me think, made me analyse what it is I really care about. And frankly – ' She was unbuckling his belt. ' – I don't give a shit – '

Now the zip.

' – about this, or any other fucking play.'

His trousers fell down.

' – I'll show you what I care about.'

She reached into his briefs, and clasped him. Her cold hand somehow made the touch sexier. He laughed, closing his eyes as she pulled his briefs down to the middle of his thigh and knelt at his feet.

She was as expert as ever, her throat open like a drain. Her mouth was somewhat drier than usual, her tongue scouring him, but the sensations drove him wild. It was so good, he scarcely noticed the ease with which she devoured him, taking him deeper than she'd ever managed previously, using every trick she knew to goad him higher and higher. Slow and deep, then picking up speed until he almost came, then slowing again until the need passed. He was completely at her mercy.

He opened his eyes to watch her at work. She was skewering herself upon him, face in rapture.

'God,' he gasped, 'That is *so* good. Oh yes, oh yes.'

Her face didn't even flicker in response to his words, she just continued to work at him soundlessly. She wasn't making her usual noises, the small grunts of satisfaction, the heavy breathing through the nose. She just ate his flesh in absolute silence.

He held his breath a moment, while an idea was born in his belly. The bobbing head bobbed on, eyes closed, lips clamped around his member, utterly engrossed. Half a minute passed; a minute; a minute and a half. And now his belly was full of terrors.

She wasn't breathing. She was giving this matchless blow-job because she wasn't stopping, even for a moment, to inhale or exhale.

Calloway felt his body go rigid, while his erection wilted in her throat. She didn't falter in her labour; the relentless pumping continued at his groin even as his mind formed the unthinkable thought:

She's dead.

She has me in her mouth, in her cold mouth, and she's dead. That's why she'd come back, got up off her mortuary slab and come back. She was eager to finish what she'd started, no longer caring about the play, or her usurper. It was this act she valued, this act alone. She'd chosen to perform it for eternity.

Calloway could do nothing with the realization but stare down like a damn fool while this corpse gave him head.

Then it seemed she sensed his horror. She opened her eyes and

112

looked up at him. How could he ever have mistaken that dead stare for life? Gently, she withdrew his shrunken manhood from between her lips.

'What is it?' she asked, her fluting voice still affecting life.

'You . . . you're not . . . breathing.'

Her face fell. She let him go.

'Oh darling,' she said, letting all pretence to life disappear, 'I'm not so good at playing the part, am I?'

Her voice was a ghost's voice: thin, forlorn. Her skin, which he had thought so flatteringly pale was, on second view, a waxen white.

'You are dead?' he said.

'I'm afraid so. Two hours ago: in my sleep. But I had to come, Terry; so much unfinished business. I made my choice. You should be flattered. You are flattered, aren't you?'

She stood up and reached into her handbag, which she'd left beside the mirror. Calloway looked at the door, trying to make his limbs work, but they were inert. Besides, he had his trousers round his ankles. Two steps and he'd fall flat on his face.

She turned back on him, with something silver and sharp in her hand. Try as he might, he couldn't get a focus on it. But whatever it was, she meant it for him.

Since the building of the new Crematorium in 1934, one humiliation had come after another for the cemetery. The tombs had been raided for lead coffin-linings, the stones overturned and smashed; it was fouled by dogs and graffiti. Very few mourners now came to tend the graves. The generations had dwindled, and the small number of people who might still have had a loved one buried there were too infirm to risk the throttled walkways, or too tender to bear looking at such vandalism.

It had not always been so. There were illustrious and influential families interred behind the marble façades of the Victorian mausoleums. Founder fathers, local industrialists and dignitaries, any and all who had done the town proud by their efforts. The body of the actress Constantia Lichfield had been buried here ('Until the Day Break and the Shadows Flee Away'), though her grave was almost unique in the attention some secret admirer still paid to it.

Nobody was watching that night, it was too bitter for lovers. Nobody saw Charlotte Hancock open the door of her sepulchre, with the beating wings of pigeons applauding her vigour as she shambled out to meet the moon. Her husband Gerard was with her, he less fresh than she, having been dead thirteen years longer.

113

Joseph Jardine, *en famille*, was not far behind the Hancocks, as was Marriott Fletcher, and Anne Snell, and the Peacock Brothers; the list went on and on. In one corner, Alfred Crawshaw (Captain in the 17th Lancers), was helping his lovely wife Emma from the rot of their bed. Everywhere faces pressed at the cracks of the tomblids – was that not Kezia Reynolds with her child, who'd lived just a day, in her arms? and Martin van de Linde (the Memory of the Just is Blessed) whose wife had never been found; Rosa and Selina Goldfinch: upstanding women both; and Thomas Jerrey, and –

Too many names to mention. Too many states of decay to describe. Sufficient to say they rose: their burial finery flyborn, their faces stripped of all but the foundation of beauty. Still they came, swinging open the back gate of the cemetery and threading their way across the wasteland towards the Elysium. In the distance, the sound of traffic. Above, a jet roared in to land. One of the Peacock brothers, staring up at the winking giant as it passed over, missed his footing and fell on his face, shattering his jaw. They picked him up fondly, and escorted him on his way. There was no harm done; and what would a Resurrection be without a few laughs?

So the show went on.

'If music be the food of love, play on,
Give me excess of it; that, surfeiting,
The appetite may sicken and so die – '

Calloway could not be found at Curtain; but Ryan had instructions from Hammersmith (through the ubiquitous Mr Lichfield) to take the show up with or without the Director.

'He'll be upstairs, in the Gods,' said Lichfield. 'In fact, I think I can see him from here.'

'Is he smiling?' asked Eddie.

'Grinning from ear to ear.'

'Then he's pissed.'

The actors laughed. There was a good deal of laughter that night. The show was running smoothly, and though they couldn't see the audience over the glare of the newly-installed footlights they could feel the waves of love and delight pouring out of the auditorium. The actors were coming off stage elated.

'They're all sitting in the Gods,' said Eddie, 'but your friends, Mr Lichfield, do an old ham good. They're quiet of course, but such big smiles on their faces.'

Act I, Scene II; and the first entrance of Constantia Lichfield as Viola was met with spontaneous applause. Such applause. Like the hollow roll of snare drums, like the brittle beating of a thousand sticks on a thousand stretched skins. Lavish, wanton applause.

And, my God, she rose to the occasion. She began the play as she meant to go on, giving her whole heart to the role, not needing physicality to communicate the depth of her feelings, but speaking the poetry with such intelligence and passion the merest flutter of her hand was worth more than a hundred grander gestures. After that first scene her every entrance was met with the same applause from the audience, followed by almost reverential silence.

Backstage, a kind of buoyant confidence had set in. The whole company sniffed the success; a success which had been snatched miraculously from the jaws of disaster.

There again! Applause! Applause!

In his office, Hammersmith dimly registered the brittle din of adulation through a haze of booze.

He was in the act of pouring his eighth drink when the door opened. He glanced up for a moment and registered that the visitor was that upstart Calloway. Come to gloat I daresay, Hammersmith thought, come to tell me how wrong I was.

'What do you want?'

The punk didn't answer. From the corner of his eye Hammersmith had an impression of a broad, bright smile on Calloway's face. Self-satisfied half-wit, coming in here when a man was in mourning.

'I suppose you've heard?'

The other grunted.

'She died,' said Hammersmith, beginning to cry. 'She died a few hours ago, without regaining consciousness. I haven't told the actors. Didn't seem worth it.'

Calloway said nothing in reply to this news. Didn't the bastard care? Couldn't he see that this was the end of the world? The woman was dead. She'd died in the bowels of the Elysium. There'd be official enquiries made, the insurance would be examined, a post-mortem, an inquest: it would reveal too much.

He drank deeply from his glass, not bothering to look at Calloway again.

'Your career'll take a dive after this, son. It won't just be me: oh dear no.'

Still Calloway kept his silence.

'Don't you care?' Hammersmith demanded.

There was silence for a moment, then Calloway responded. 'I don't give a shit.'

'Jumped up little stage-manager, that's all you are. That's all *any*

115

of you fucking directors are! One good review and you're God's gift to art. Well let me set you straight about that – '

He looked at Calloway, his eyes, swimming in alcohol, having difficulty focussing. But he got there eventually.

Calloway, the dirty bugger, was naked from the waist down. He was wearing his shoes and his socks, but no trousers or briefs. His self-exposure would have been comical, but for the expression on his face. The man had gone mad: his eyes were rolling around uncontrollably, saliva and snot ran from mouth and nose, his tongue hung out like the tongue of a panting dog.

Hammersmith put his glass down on his blotting pad, and looked at the worst part. There was blood on Calloway's shirt, a trail of it which led up his neck to his left ear, from which protruded the end of Diane Duvall's nail-file. It had been driven deep into Calloway's brain. The man was surely dead.

But he stood, spoke, walked.

From the theatre, there rose another round of applause, muted by distance. It wasn't a real sound somehow; it came from another world, a place where emotions ruled. It was a world Hammersmith had always felt excluded from. He'd never been much of an actor, though God knows he'd tried, and the two plays he'd penned were, he knew, execrable. Book-keeping was his forte, and he'd used it to stay as close to the stage as he could, hating his own lack of art as much as he resented that skill in others.

The applause died, and as if taking a cue from an unseen prompter, Calloway came at him. The mask he wore was neither comic nor tragic, it was blood and laughter together. Cowering, Hammersmith was cornered behind his desk. Calloway leapt on to it (he looked so ridiculous, shirt-tails and balls flip-flapping) and siezed Hammersmith by the tie.

'Philistine,' said Calloway, never now to know Hammersmith's heart, and broke the man's neck – snap! – while below the applause began again.

'Do not embrace me till each circumstance
Of place, time, fortune, do cohere and jump
That I am Viola.'

From Constantia's mouth the lines were a revelation. It was almost as though this *Twelfth Night* were a new play, and the part of Viola had been written for Constantia Lichfield alone. The actors who shared the stage with her felt their egos shrivelling in the face of such a gift.

The last act continued to its bitter-sweet conclusion, the audience as enthralled as ever to judge by their breathless attention.

116

The Duke spoke: 'Give me thy hand;
And let me see thee in thy woman's weeds.'

In the rehearsal the invitation in the line had been ignored: no-one was to touch this Viola, much less take her hand. But in the heat of the performance such taboos were forgotten. Possessed by the passion of the moment the actor reached for Constantia. She, forgetting the taboo in her turn, reached to answer his touch.

In the wings Lichfield breathed 'no' under his breath, but his order wasn't heard. The Duke grasped Viola's hand in his, life and death holding court together under this painted sky.

It was a chilly hand, a hand without blood in its veins, or a blush in its skin.

But here it was as good as alive.

They were equals, the living and the dead, and nobody could find just cause to part them.

In the wings, Lichfield sighed, and allowed himself a smile. He'd feared that touch, feared it would break the spell. But Dionysus was with them tonight. All would be well; he felt it in his bones.

The act drew to a close, and Malvolio, still trumpeting his threats, even in defeat, was carted off. One by one the company exited, leaving the clown to wrap up the play.

'A great while ago the world began,
With hey, ho, the wind and the rain,
But that's all one, our play is done
And we'll strive to please you every day.'

The scene darkened to blackout, and the curtain descended. From the gods rapturous applause erupted, that same rattling, hollow applause. The company, their faces shining with the success of the Dress Rehearsal, formed behind the curtain for the bow. The curtain rose: the applause mounted.

In the wings, Calloway joined Lichfield. He was dressed now: and he'd washed the blood off his neck.

'Well, we have a brilliant success,' said the skull, 'It does seem a pity that this company should be dissolved so soon.'

'It does,' said the corpse.

The actors were shouting into the wings now, calling for Calloway to join them. They were applauding him, encouraging him to show his face.

He put a hand on Lichfield's shoulder.

'We'll go together, sir,' he said.

'No, no, I couldn't.'

'You must. It's your triumph as much as mine.' Lichfield

117

nodded, and they went out together to take their bows beside the company.

In the wings Tallulah was at work. She felt restored after her sleep in the Green Room. So much unpleasantness had gone, taken with her life. She no longer suffered the aches in her hip, or the creeping neuralgia in her scalp. There was no longer the necessity to draw breath through pipes encrusted with seventy years' muck, or to rub the backs of her hands to get the circulation going; not even the need to blink. She laid the fires with a new strength, pressing the detritus of past productions into use: old backdrops, props, costuming. When she had enough combustibles heaped, she struck a match and set the flame to them. The Elysium began to burn.

Over the applause, somebody was shouting:
    'Marvellous, sweethearts, marvellous.'
    It was Diane's voice, they all recognized it even though they couldn't quite see her. She was staggering down the centre aisle towards the stage, making quite a fool of herself.
    'Silly bitch,' said Eddie.
    'Whoops,' said Calloway.
    She was at the edge of the stage now, haranguing him.
    'Got all you wanted now, have you? This your new lady-love is it? Is it?'
    She was trying to clamber up, her hands gripping the hot metal hoods of the footlights. Her skin began to singe: the fat was well and truly in the fire.
    'For God's sake, somebody stop her,' said Eddie. But she didn't seem to feel the searing of her hands; she just laughed in his face. The smell of burning flesh wafted up from the footlights. The company broke rank, triumph forgotten.
    Somebody yelled: 'Kill the lights!'
    A beat, and then the stage lights were extinguished. Diane fell back, her hands smoking. One of the cast fainted, another ran into the wings to be sick. Somewhere behind them, they could hear the faint crackle of flames, but they had other calls on their attention.
    With the footlights gone, they could see the auditorium more clearly. The stalls were empty, but the Balcony and the gods were full to bursting with eager admirers. Every row was packed, and every available inch of aisle space thronged with audience. Somebody up there started clapping again, alone for a few moments before the wave of applause began afresh. But now few of the company took pride in it.

Even from the stage, even with exhausted and light-dazzled eyes, it was obvious that no man, woman or child in that adoring crowd was alive. They waved fine silk handkerchiefs at the players in rotted fists, some of them beat a tattoo on the seats in front of them, most just clapped, bone on bone.

Calloway smiled, bowed deeply, and received their admiration with gratitude. In all his fifteen years of work in the theatre he had never found an audience so appreciative.

Bathing in the love of their admirers, Constantia and Richard Lichfield joined hands and walked down-stage to take another bow, while the living actors retreated in horror.

They began to yell and pray, they let out howls, they ran about like discovered adulterers in a farce. But, like the farce, there was no way out of the situation. There were bright flames tickling the roof-joists, and billows of canvas cascaded down to right and left as the flies caught fire. In front, the dead: behind, death. Smoke was beginning to thicken the air, it was impossible to see where one was going. Somebody was wearing a toga of burning canvas, and reciting screams. Someone else was wielding a fire extinguisher against the inferno. All useless: all tired business, badly managed. As the roof began to give, lethal falls of timber and girder silenced most.

In the Gods, the audience had more or less departed. They were ambling back to their graves long before the fire department appeared, their cerements and their faces lit by the glow of the fire as they glanced over their shoulders to watch the Elysium perish. It had been a fine show, and they were happy to go home, content for another while to gossip in the dark.

The fire burned through the night, despite the never less than gallant efforts of the fire department to put it out. By four in the morning the fight was given up as lost, and the conflagration allowed its head. It had done with the Elysium by dawn.

In the ruins the remains of several persons was discovered, most of the bodies in states that defied easy identification. Dental records were consulted, and one corpse was found to be that of Giles Hammersmith (Administrator), another that of Ryan Xavier (Stage Manager) and, most shockingly, a third that of Diane Duvall. 'Star of *The Love Child* burned to death', read the tabloids. She was forgotten in a week.

There were no survivors. Several bodies were simply never found.

They stood at the side of the motorway, and watched the cars careering through the night.

Lichfield was there of course, and Constantia, radiant as ever. Calloway had chosen to go with them, so had Eddie, and Tallulah. Three or four others had also joined the troupe.

It was the first night of their freedom, and here they were on the open road, travelling players. The smoke alone had killed Eddie, but there were a few more serious injuries amongst their number, sustained in the fire. Burned bodies, broken limbs. But the audience they would play for in the future would forgive them their petty mutilations.

'There are lives lived for love,' said Lichfield to his new company, 'and lives lived for art. We happy band have chosen the latter persuasion.'

There was a ripple of applause amongst the actors.

'To you, who have never died, may I say: welcome to the world!'

Laughter: further applause.

The lights of the cars racing north along the motorway threw the company into silhouette. They looked, to all intents and purposes, like living men and women. But then wasn't that the trick of their craft? To imitate life so well the illusion was indistinguishable from the real thing? And their new public, awaiting them in mortuaries, churchyards and chapels of rest, would appreciate that skill more than most. Who better to applaud the sham of passion and pain they would perform than the dead, who had experienced such feelings, and thrown them off at last?

The dead. They needed entertainment no less than the living; and they were a sorely neglected market.

Not that this company would perform for money, they would play for the love of their art, Lichfield had made that clear from the outset. No more service would be done to Apollo.

'Now,' he said, 'which road shall we take, north or south?'

'North,' said Eddie. 'My mother's buried in Glasgow, she died before I ever played professionally. I'd like her to see me.'

'North it is, then,' said Lichfield, 'Shall we go and find ourselves some transport?'

He led the way towards the motorway restaurant, its neon flickering fitfully, keeping the night at light's length. The colours were theatrically bright: scarlet, lime, cobalt, and a wash of white that splashed out of the windows on to the car park where they stood. The automatic doors hissed as a traveller emerged, bearing gifts of hamburgers and cake to the child in the back of his car.

'Surely some friendly driver will find a niche for us,' said Lichfield.

'All of us?' said Calloway.

'A truck will do; beggars can't be too demanding,' said

Lichfield. 'And we are beggars now: subject to the whim of our patrons.'

'We can always steal a car,' said Tallulah.

'No need for theft, except in extremity,' Lichfield said. 'Constantia and I will go ahead and find a chauffeur.'

He took his wife's hand.

'Nobody refuses beauty,' he said.

'What do we do if anyone asks us what we're doing here?' asked Eddie nervously. He wasn't used to this role; he needed reassurance.

Lichfield turned towards the company, his voice booming in the night:

'What do you do?' he said, 'Play life, of course! And smile!'

In the Hills, The Cities

It wasn't until the first week of the Yugoslavian trip that Mick discovered what a political bigot he'd chosen as a lover. Certainly, he'd been warned. One of the queens at the Baths had told him Judd was to the Right of Attila the Hun, but the man had been one of Judd's ex-affairs, and Mick had presumed there was more spite than perception in the character assassination.

If only he'd listened. Then he wouldn't be driving along an interminable road in a Volkswagen that suddenly seemed the size of a coffin, listening to Judd's views on Soviet expansionism. Jesus, he was so boring. He didn't converse, he lectured, and endlessly. In Italy the sermon had been on the way the Communists had exploited the peasant vote. Now, in Yugoslavia, Judd had really warmed to his theme, and Mick was just about ready to take a hammer to his self-opinionated head.

It wasn't that he disagreed with everything Judd said. Some of the arguments (the ones Mick understood) seemed quite sensible. But then, what did he know? He was a dance teacher. Judd was a journalist, a professional pundit. He felt, like most journalists Mick had encountered, that he was obliged to have an opinion on everything under the sun. Especially politics; that was the best trough to wallow in. You could get your snout, eyes, head and front hooves in that mess of muck and have a fine old time splashing around. It was an inexhaustible subject to devour, a swill with a little of everything in it, because everything, according to Judd, was political. The arts were political. Sex was political. Religion, commerce, gardening, eating, drinking and farting – all political.

Jesus, it was mind-blowingly boring; killingly, love-deadeningly boring.

Worse still, Judd didn't seem to notice how bored Mick had become, or if he noticed, he didn't care. He just rambled on, his arguments getting windier and windier, his sentences lengthening with every mile they drove.

Judd, Mick had decided, was a selfish bastard, and as soon as their honeymoon was over he'd part with the guy.

It was not until their trip, that endless, motiveless caravan through the graveyards of mid-European culture, that Judd realized what a political lightweight he had in Mick. The guy showed precious little interest in the economics or the politics of the countries they passed through. He registered indifference to the full facts behind the Italian situation, and yawned, yes, yawned when he tried (and failed) to debate the Russian threat to world peace. He had to face the bitter truth: Mick was a queen; there was no other word for him; All right, perhaps he didn't mince or wear jewellery to excess, but he was a queen nevertheless, happy to wallow in a dream-world of early Renaissance frescoes and Yugoslavian icons. The complexities, the contradictions, even the agonies that made those cultures blossom and wither were just tiresome to him. His mind was no deeper than his looks; he was a well-groomed nobody.

Some honeymoon.

The road south from Belgrade to Novi Pazar was, by Yugoslavian standards, a good one. There were fewer pot-holes than on many of the roads they'd travelled, and it was relatively straight. The town of Novi Pazar lay in the valley of the River Raska, south of the city named after the river. It wasn't an area particularly popular with the tourists. Despite the good road it was still inaccessible, and lacked sophisticated amenities; but Mick was determined to see the monastery at Sopocani, to the west of the town and after some bitter argument, he'd won.

The journey had proved uninspiring. On either side of the road the cultivated fields looked parched and dusty. The summer had been unusually hot, and droughts were affecting many of the villages. Crops had failed, and livestock had been prematurely slaughtered to prevent them dying of malnutrition. There was a defeated look about the few faces they glimpsed at the roadside. Even the children had dour expressions; brows as heavy as the stale heat that hung over the valley.

Now, with the cards on the table after a row at Belgrade, they drove in silence most of the time; but the straight road, like most straight roads, invited dispute. When the driving was easy, the mind rooted for something to keep it engaged. What better than a fight?

'Why the hell do you want to see this damn monastery?' Judd demanded.

It was an unmistakable invitation.

'We've come all this way . . .' Mick tried to keep the tone conversational. He wasn't in the mood for an argument.

'More fucking Virgins, is it?'

Keeping his voice as even as he could, Mick picked up the Guide and read aloud from it: '. . . there, some of the greatest works of Serbian painting can still be seen and enjoyed, including what many commentators agree to be the enduring masterpiece of the Raska school: "The Dormition of the Virgin."'

Silence.

Then Judd: 'I'm up to here with churches.'

'It's a masterpiece.'

'They're all masterpieces according to that bloody book.'

Mick felt his control slipping.

'Two and a half hours at most – '

'I told you, I don't want to see another church; the smell of the places makes me sick. Stale incense, old sweat and lies . . .'

'It's a short detour; then we can get back on to the road and you can give me another lecture on farming subsidies in the Sandzak.'

'I'm just trying to get some decent conversation going instead of this endless tripe about Serbian fucking masterpieces – '

'Stop the car!'

'What?'

'Stop the car!'

Judd pulled the Volkswagen into the side of the road. Mick got out.

The road was hot, but there was a slight breeze. He took a deep breath, and wandered into the middle of the road. Empty of traffic and of pedestrians in both directions. In every direction, empty. The hills shimmered in the heat off the fields. There were wild poppies growing in the ditches. Mick crossed the road, squatted on his haunches and picked one.

Behind him he heard the VW's door slam.

'What did you stop us for?' Judd said. His voice was edgy, still hoping for that argument, begging for it.

Mick stood up, playing with the poppy. It was close to seeding, late in the season. The petals fell from the receptacle as soon as he touched them, little splashes of red fluttering down on to the grey tarmac.

'I asked you a question,' Judd said again.

Mick looked round. Judd was standing the far side of the car, his brows a knitted line of burgeoning anger. But handsome; oh yes; a face that made women weep with frustration that he was gay. A heavy black moustache (perfectly trimmed) and eyes you could watch forever, and never see the same light in them twice. Why in God's name, thought Mick, does a man as fine as that have to be such an insensitive little shit?

Judd returned the look of contemptuous appraisal, staring at the pouting pretty boy across the road. It made him want to puke, seeing the little act Mick was performing for his benefit. It might just have been plausible in a sixteen-year-old virgin. In a twenty-five-year-old, it lacked credibility.

Mick dropped the flower, and untucked his T-shirt from his jeans. A tight stomach, then a slim, smooth chest were revealed as he pulled it off. His hair was ruffled when his head re-appeared, and his face wore a broad grin. Judd looked at the torso. Neat, not too muscular. An appendix scar peering over his faded jeans. A gold chain, small but catching the sun, dipped in the hollow of his throat. Without meaning to, he returned Mick's grin, and a kind of peace was made between them.

Mick was unbuckling his belt.

'Want to fuck?' he said, the grin not faltering.

'It's no use,' came an answer, though not to that question.

'What isn't?'

'We're not compatible.'

'Want a bet?'

Now he was unzipped, and turning away towards the wheat-field that bordered the road.

Judd watched as Mick cut a swathe through the swaying sea, his back the colour of the grain, so that he was almost camouflaged by it. It was a dangerous game, screwing in the open air – this wasn't San Francisco, or even Hampstead Heath. Nervously, Judd glanced along the road. Still empty in both directions. And Mick was turning, deep in the field, turning and smiling and waving like a swimmer buoyed up in a golden surf. What the hell . . . there was nobody to see, nobody to know. Just the hills, liquid in the heat-haze, their forested backs bent to the business of the earth, and a lost dog, sitting at the edge of the road, waiting for some lost master.

Judd followed Mick's path through the wheat, unbuttoning his shirt as he walked. Field-mice ran ahead of him, scurrying through the stalks as the giant came their way, his feet like thunder. Judd saw their panic, and smiled. He meant no harm to them, but then how were they to know that? Maybe he'd put out a hundred lives, mice, beetles, worms, before he reached the spot where Mick was lying, stark bollock naked, on a bed of trampled grain, still grinning.

It was good love they made, good, strong love, equal in pleasure for both; there was a precision to their passion, sensing the moment when effortless delight became urgent, when desire became necessity. They locked together, limb around limb, tongue around tongue, in a knot only orgasm could untie, their backs alternately scorched and scratched as they rolled around exchanging blows and kisses. In the thick of it, creaming together, they heard the phut-phut-phut of a tractor passing by; but they were past caring.

They made their way back to the Volkswagen with body-threshed wheat in their hair and their ears, in their socks and between their toes. Their grins had been replaced with easy smiles: the truce, if not permanent, would last a few hours at least.

The car was baking hot, and they had to open all the windows and doors to let the breeze cool it before they started towards Novi Pazar. It was four o'clock, and there was still an hour's driving ahead.

As they got into the car Mick said, 'We'll forget the monastery, eh?'

Judd gaped.

'I thought – '

'I couldn't bear another fucking Virgin – '

They laughed lightly together, then kissed, tasting each other and themselves, a mingling of saliva, and the aftertaste of salt semen.

The following day was bright, but not particularly warm. No blue skies: just an even layer of white cloud. The morning air was sharp in the lining of the nostrils, like ether, or peppermint.

Vaslav Jelovsek watched the pigeons in the main square of Popolac courting death as they skipped and fluttered ahead of the vehicles that were buzzing around. Some about military business, some civilian. An air of sober intention barely suppressed the excitement he felt on this day, an excitement he knew was shared by every man, woman and child in Popolac. Shared by the pigeons too for all he knew. Maybe that was why they played under the wheels with such dexterity, knowing that on this day of days no harm could come to them.

He scanned the sky again, that same white sky he'd been peering at since dawn. The cloud-layer was low; not ideal for the celebrations. A phrase passed through his mind, an English phrase he'd heard from a friend, 'to have your head in the clouds'. It meant, he gathered, to be lost in a reverie, in a white, sightless dream. That, he thought wryly, was all the West knew about clouds, that they stood for dreams. It took a vision they lacked to make a truth out of that casual turn of phrase. Here, in these secret hills, wouldn't they create a spectacular reality from those idle words? A living proverb.

A head in the clouds.

Already the first contingent was assembling in the square. There were one or two absentees owing to illness, but the auxiliaries were ready and waiting to take their places. Such eagerness! Such wide smiles when an auxiliary heard his or her name and number called and was taken out of line to join the limb that was already taking shape. On every side, miracles of organization. Everyone with a job to do and a place to go. There was no shouting or pushing: indeed, voices were scarcely raised above an eager whisper. He watched in admiration as the work of positioning and buckling and roping went on.

It was going to be a long and arduous day. Vaslav had been in the square since an hour before dawn, drinking coffee from imported plastic cups, discussing the half-hourly meteorological reports coming in from Pristina and Mitrovica, and watching the starless sky as the grey light of morning crept across it. Now he was drinking his sixth coffee of the day, and it was still barely seven o'clock. Across the square Metzinger looked as tired and as anxious as Vaslav felt.

They'd watched the dawn seep out of the east together, Metzinger and he. But now they had separated, forgetting previous companionship, and would not speak until the contest was over. After all Metzinger was from Podujevo. He had his own city to support in the coming battle. Tomorrow they'd exchange tales of their adventures, but for today they must behave as if they didn't know each other, not even to exchange a smile. For today they had to be utterly partisan, caring only for the victory of their own city over the opposition.

Now the first leg of Popolac was erected, to the mutual satisfaction of Metzinger and Vaslav. All the safety checks had been meticulously made, and the leg left the square, its shadow falling hugely across the face of the Town Hall.

Vaslav sipped his sweet, sweet coffee and allowed himself a little grunt of satisfaction. Such days, such days. Days filled with glory, with snapping flags and high, stomach-turning sights, enough to last a man a lifetime. It was a golden foretaste of Heaven.

Let America have its simple pleasures, its cartoon mice, its candy-coated castles, its cults and its technologies, he wanted none of it. The greatest wonder of the world was here, hidden in the hills.

Ah, such days.

In the main square of Podujevo the scene was no less animated, and no less inspiring. Perhaps there was a muted sense of sadness underlying this year's celebration, but that was understandable. Nita Obrenovic, Podujevo's loved and respected organizer, was no longer living. The previous winter had claimed her at the age of

127

ninety-four, leaving the city bereft of her fierce opinions and her fiercer proportions. For sixty years Nita had worked with the citizens of Podujevo, always planning for the next contest and improving on the designs, her energies spent on making the next creation more ambitious and more life-like than the last.

Now she was dead, and sorely missed. There was no disorganization in the streets without her, the people were far too disciplined for that, but they were already falling behind schedule, and it was almost seven-twenty-five. Nita's daughter had taken over in her mother's stead, but she lacked Nita's power to galvanize the people into action. She was, in a word, too gentle for the job in hand. It required a leader who was part prophet and part ringmaster, to coax and bully and inspire the citizens into their places. Maybe, after two or three decades, and with a few more contests under her belt, Nita Obrenovic's daughter would make the grade. But for today Podujevo was behindhand; safety- checks were being overlooked; nervous looks replaced the confidence of earlier years.

Nevertheless, at six minutes before eight the first limb of Podujevo made its way out of the city to the assembly point, to wait for its fellow.

By that time the flanks were already lashed together in Popolac, and armed contingents were awaiting orders in the Town Square.

Mick woke promptly at seven, though there was no alarm clock in their simply furnished room at the Hotel Beograd. He lay in his bed and listened to Judd's regular breathing from the twin bed across the room. A dull morning light whimpered through the thin curtains, not encouraging an early departure. After a few minutes' staring at the cracked paintwork on the ceiling, and a while longer at the crudely carved crucifix on the opposite wall, Mick got up and went to the window. It was a dull day, as he had guessed. The sky was overcast, and the roofs of Novi Pazar were grey and featureless in the flat morning light. But beyond the roofs, to the east, he could see the hills. There was sun there. He could see shafts of light catching the blue-green of the forest, inviting a visit to their slopes.

Today maybe they would go south to Kosovska Mitrovica. There was a market there, wasn't there, and a museum? And they could drive down the valley of the Ibar, following the road beside the river, where the hills rose wild and shining on either side. The hills, yes; today he decided they would see the hills.

It was eight-fifteen.

* * *

By nine the main bodies of Popolac and Podujevo were substantially assembled. In their allotted districts the limbs of both cities were ready and waiting to join their expectant torsos.

Vaslav Jelovsek capped his gloved hands over his eyes and surveyed the sky. The cloud-base had risen in the last hour, no doubt of it, and there were breaks in the clouds to the west; even, on occasion, a few glimpses of the sun. It wouldn't be a perfect day for the contest perhaps, but certainly adequate.

Mick and Judd breakfasted late on hemendeks – roughly translated as ham and eggs – and several cups of good black coffee. It was brightening up, even in Novi Pazar, and their ambitions were set high. Kosovska Mitrovica by lunchtime, and maybe a visit to the hill-castle of Zvecan in the afternoon.

About nine-thirty they motored out of Novi Pazar and took the Srbovac road south to the Ibar valley. Not a good road, but the bumps and pot-holes couldn't spoil the new day.

The road was empty, except for the occasional pedestrian; and in place of the maize and corn fields they'd passed on the previous day the road was flanked by undulating hills, whose sides were thickly and darkly forested. Apart from a few birds, they saw no wildlife. Even their infrequent travelling companions petered out altogether after a few miles, and the occasional farmhouse they drove by appeared locked and shuttered up. Black pigs ran unattended in the yard, with no child to feed them. Washing snapped and billowed on a sagging line, with no washerwoman in sight.

At first this solitary journey through the hills was refreshing in its lack of human contact, but as the morning drew on, an uneasiness grew on them.

'Shouldn't we have seen a signpost to Mitrovica, Mick?'

He peered at the map.

'Maybe . . .'

' – we've taken the wrong road.'

'If there'd been a sign, I'd have seen it. I think we should try and get off this road, bear south a bit more – meet the valley closer to Mitrovica than we'd planned.'

'How do we get off this bloody road?'

'There've been a couple of turnings . . .'

'Dirt-tracks.'

'Well it's either that or going on the way we are.'

Judd pursed his lips.

'Cigarette?' he asked.

'Finished them miles back.'

In front of them, the hills formed an impenetrable line. There was no sign of life ahead; no frail wisp of chimney smoke, no sound of voice or vehicle.

'All right,' said Judd, 'we take the next turning. Anything's better than this.'

They drove on. The road was deteriorating rapidly, the pot-holes becoming craters, the hummocks feeling like bodies beneath the wheels.

Then:

'There!'

A turning: a palpable turning. Not a major road, certainly. In fact barely the dirt-track Judd had described the other roads as being, but it was an escape from the endless perspective of the road they were trapped on.

'This is becoming a bloody safari,' said Judd as the VW began to bump and grind its way along the doleful little track.

'Where's your sense of adventure?'

'I forgot to pack it.'

They were beginning to climb now, as the track wound its way up into the hills. The forest closed over them, blotting out the sky, so a shifting patchwork of light and shadow scooted over the bonnet as they drove. There was birdsong suddenly, vacuous and optimistic, and a smell of new pine and undug earth. A fox crossed the track, up ahead, and watched a long moment as the car grumbled up towards it. Then, with the leisurely stride of a fearless prince, it sauntered away into the trees.

Wherever they were going, Mick thought, this was better than the road they'd left. Soon maybe they'd stop, and walk a while, to find a promontory from which they could see the valley, even Novi Pazar, nestled behind them.

The two men were still an hour's drive from Popolac when the head of the contingent at last marched out of the Town Square and took up its position with the main body.

This last exit left the city completely deserted. Not even the sick or the old were neglected on this day; no-one was to be denied the spectacle and the triumph of the contest. Every single citizen, however young or infirm, the blind, the crippled, babes in arms, pregnant women – all made their way up from their proud city to the stamping ground. It was the law that they should attend: but it needed no enforcing. No citizen of either city would have missed the chance to see that sight – to experience the thrill of that contest.

The confrontation had to be total, city against city. This was the way it had always been.

130

So the cities went up into the hills. By noon they were gathered, the citizens of Popolac and Podujevo, in the secret well of the hills, hidden from civilized eyes, to do ancient and ceremonial battle.

Tens of thousands of hearts beat faster. Tens of thousands of bodies stretched and strained and sweated as the twin cities took their positions. The shadows of the bodies darkened tracts of land the size of small towns; the weight of their feet trampled the grass to a green milk; their movement killed animals, crushed bushes and threw down trees. The earth literally reverberated with their passage, the hills echoing with the booming din of their steps.

In the towering body of Podujevo, a few technical hitches were becoming apparent. A slight flaw in the knitting of the left flank had resulted in a weakness there: and there were consequent problems in the swivelling mechanism of the hips. It was stiffer than it should be, and the movements were not smooth. As a result there was considerable strain being put upon that region of the city. It was being dealt with bravely; after all, the contest was intended to press the contestants to their limits. But breaking point was closer than anyone would have dared to admit. The citizens were not as resilient as they had been in previous contests. A bad decade for crops had produced bodies less well-nourished, spines less supple, wills less resolute. The badly knitted flank might not have caused an accident in itself, but further weakened by the frailty of the competitors it set a scene for death on an unprecedented scale.

They stopped the car.

'Hear that?'

Mick shook his head. His hearing hadn't been good since he was an adolescent. Too many rock shows had blown his eardrums to hell.

Judd got out of the car.

The birds were quieter now. The noise he'd heard as they drove came again. It wasn't simply a noise: it was almost a motion in the earth, a roar that seemed seated in the substance of the hills.

Thunder, was it?

No, too rhythmical. It came again, through the soles of the feet. –

Boom.

Mick heard it this time. He leaned out of the car window.

'It's up ahead somewhere. I hear it now.'

Judd nodded.

Boom.

The earth-thunder sounded again.

'What the hell is it?' said Mick.

'Whatever it is, I want to see it – '

Judd got back into the Volkswagen, smiling.

'Sounds almost like guns,' he said, starting the car. 'Big guns.'

Through his Russian-made binoculars Vaslav Jelovsek watched the starting-official raise his pistol. He saw the feather of white smoke rise from the barrel, and a second later heard the sound of the shot across the valley.

The contest had begun.

He looked up at twin towers of Popolac and Podujevo. Heads in the clouds – well almost. They practically stretched to touch the sky. It was an awesome sight, a breath-stopping, sleep-stabbing sight. Two cities swaying and writhing and preparing to take their first steps towards each other in this ritual battle.

Of the two, Podujevo seemed the less stable. There was a slight hesitation as the city raised its left leg to begin its march. Nothing serious, just a little difficulty in co-ordinating hip and thigh muscles. A couple of steps and the city would find its rhythm; a couple more and its inhabitants would be moving as one creature, one perfect giant set to match its grace and power against its mirror-image.

The gunshot had sent flurries of birds up from the trees that banked the hidden valley. They rose up in celebration of the great contest, chattering their excitement as they swooped over the stamping-ground.

'Did you hear a shot?' asked Judd.

Mick nodded.

'Military exercises . . .?' Judd's smile had broadened. He could see the headlines already – exclusive reports of secret manouevres in the depths of the Yugoslavian countryside. Russian tanks perhaps, tactical exercises being held out of the West's prying sight. With luck, he would be the carrier of this news.

Boom.

Boom.

There were birds in the air. The thunder was louder now.

It did sound like guns.

'It's over the next ridge . . .' said Judd.

'I don't think we should go any further.'

'I have to see.'

'I don't. We're not supposed to be here.'

'I don't see any signs.'

'They'll cart us away; deport us – I don't know – I just think – '

Boom.

'I've got to see.'

The words were scarcely out of his mouth when the screaming started.

Podujevo was screaming: a death-cry. Someone buried in the weak flank had died of the strain, and had begun a chain of decay in the system. One man loosed his neighbour and that neighbour loosed his, spreading a cancer of chaos through the body of the city. The coherence of the towering structure deteriorated with terrifying rapidity as the failure of one part of the anatomy put unendurable pressure on the other.

The masterpiece that the good citizens of Podujevo had constructed of their own flesh and blood tottered and then – a dynamited skyscraper, it began to fall.

The broken flank spewed citizens like a slashed artery spitting blood. Then, with a graceful sloth that made the agonies of the citizens all the more horrible, it bowed towards the earth, all its limbs dissembling as it fell.

The huge head, that had brushed the clouds so recently, was flung back on its thick neck. Ten thousand mouths spoke a single scream for its vast mouth, a wordless, infinitely pitiable appeal to the sky. A howl of loss, a howl of anticipation, a howl of puzzlement. How, that scream demanded, could the day of days end like this, in a welter of falling bodies?

'Did you hear that?'

It was unmistakably human, though almost deafeningly loud. Judd's stomach convulsed. He looked across at Mick, who was as white as a sheet.

Judd stopped the car.

'No,' said Mick.

'Listen – for Christ's sake – '

The din of dying moans, appeals and imprecations flooded the air. It was very close.

'We've got to go on now,' Mick implored.

Judd shook his head. He was prepared for some military spectacle – all the Russian army massed over the next hill – but that noise in his ears was the noise of human flesh – too human for words. It reminded him of his childhood imaginings of Hell; the endless, unspeakable torments his mother had threatened him with if he failed to embrace Christ. It was a terror he'd forgotten for twenty years. But suddenly, here it was again, freshfaced. Maybe the pit itself gaped just over the next horizon, with

133

his mother standing at its lip, inviting him to taste its punishments.

'If you won't drive, I will.'

Mick got out of the car and crossed in front of it, glancing up the track as he did so. There was a moment's hesitation, no more than a moment's, when his eyes flickered with disbelief, before he turned towards the windscreen, his face even paler than it had been previously and said: 'Jesus Christ . . .' in a voice that was thick with suppressed nausea.

His lover was still sitting behind the wheel, his head in his hands, trying to blot out memories.

'Judd . . .'

Judd looked up, slowly. Mick was staring at him like a wildman, his face shining with a sudden, icy sweat. Judd looked past him. A few metres ahead the track had mysteriously darkened, as a tide edged towards the car, a thick, deep tide of blood. Judd's reason twisted and turned to make any other sense of the sight than that inevitable conclusion. But there was no saner explanation. It was blood, in unendurable abundance, blood without end –

And now, in the breeze, there was the flavour of freshly-opened carcasses: the smell out of the depths of the human body, part sweet, part savoury.

Mick stumbled back to the passenger's side of the VW and fumbled weakly at the handle. The door opened suddenly and he lurched inside, his eyes glazed.

'Back up,' he said.

Judd reached for the ignition. The tide of blood was already sloshing against the front wheels. Ahead, the world had been painted red.

'Drive, for fuck's sake, drive!'

Judd was making no attempt to start the car.

'We must look,' he said, without conviction, 'we have to.'

'We don't have to do anything,' said Mick, 'but get the hell out of here. It's not our business . . .'

'Plane-crash – '

'There's no smoke.'

'Those are human voices.'

Mick's instinct was to leave well alone. He could read about the tragedy in a newspaper – he could see the pictures tomorrow when they were grey and grainy. Today it was too fresh, too unpredictable –

Anything could be at the end of that track, bleeding –

'We must – '

Judd started the car, while beside him Mick began to moan

quietly. The VW began to edge forward, nosing through the river of blood, its wheels spinning in the queasy, foaming tide.

'No,' said Mick, very quietly, 'Please, no . . .'

'We must,' was Judd's reply. 'We must. We must.'

Only a few yards away the surviving city of Popolac was recovering from its first convulsions. It stared, with a thousand eyes, at the ruins of its ritual enemy, now spread in a tangle of rope and bodies over the impacted ground, shattered forever. Popolac staggered back from the sight, its vast legs flattening the forest that bounded the stamping-ground, its arms flailing the air. But it kept its balance, even as a common insanity, woken by the horror at its feet, surged through its sinews and curdled its brain. The order went out: the body thrashed and twisted and turned from the grisly carpet of Podujevo, and fled into the hills.

As it headed into oblivion, its towering form passed between the car and the sun, throwing its cold shadow over the bloody road. Mick saw nothing through his tears, and Judd, his eyes narrowed against the sight he feared seeing around the next bend, only dimly registered that something had blotted the light for a minute. A cloud, perhaps. A flock of birds.

Had he looked up at that moment, just stolen a glance out towards the north-east, he would have seen Popolac's head, the vast, swarming head of a maddened city, disappearing below his line of vision, as it marched into the hills. He would have known that this territory was beyond his comprehension; and that there was no healing to be done in this corner of Hell. But he didn't see the city, and he and Mick's last turning-point had passed. From now on, like Popolac and its dead twin, they were lost to sanity, and to all hope of life.

They rounded the bend, and the ruins of Podujevo came into sight.

Their domesticated imaginations had never conceived of a sight so unspeakably brutal.

Perhaps in the battlefields of Europe as many corpses had been heaped together: but had so many of them been women and children, locked together with the corpses of men? There had been piles of dead as high, but ever so many so recently abundant with life? There had been cities laid waste as quickly, but ever an entire city lost to the simple dictate of gravity?

It was a sight beyond sickness. In the face of it the mind slowed to a snail's pace, the forces of reason picked over the evidence with meticulous hands, searching for a flaw in it, a place where it could say:

135

This is not happening. This is a dream of death, not death itself.

But reason could find no weakness in the wall. This was true. It was death indeed.

Podujevo had fallen.

Thirty-eight thousand, seven hundred and sixty-five citizens were spread on the ground, or rather flung in ungainly, seeping piles. Those who had not died of the fall, or of suffocation, were dying. There would be no survivors from that city except that bundle of onlookers that had traipsed out of their homes to watch the contest. Those few Podujevians, the crippled, the sick, the ancient few, were now staring, like Mick and Judd, at the carnage, trying not to believe.

Judd was first out of the car. The ground beneath his suedes was sticky with coagulating gore. He surveyed the carnage. There was no wreckage: no sign of a plane crash, no fire, no smell of fuel. Just tens of thousands of fresh bodies, all either naked or dressed in an identical grey serge, men, women and children alike. Some of them, he could see, wore leather harnesses, tightly buckled around their upper chests, and snaking out from these contraptions were lengths of rope, miles and miles of it. The closer he looked, the more he saw of the extraordinary system of knots and lashings that still held the bodies together. For some reason these people had been tied together, side by side. Some were yoked on their neighbours' shoulders, straddling them like boys playing at horse back riding. Others were locked arm in arm, knitted together with threads of rope in a wall of muscle and bone. Yet others were trussed in a ball, with their heads tucked between their knees. All were in some way connected up with their fellows, tied together as though in some insane collective bondage game.

Another shot.

Mick looked up.

Across the field a solitary man, dressed in a drab overcoat, was walking amongst the bodies with a revolver, dispatching the dying. It was a pitifully inadequate act of mercy, but he went on nevertheless, choosing the suffering children first. Emptying the revolver, filling it again, emptying it, filling it, emptying it –

Mick let go.

He yelled at the top of his voice over the moans of the injured.

'*What is this?*'

The man looked up from his appalling duty, his face as dead-grey as his coat.

'Uh?' he grunted, frowning at the two interlopers through his thick spectacles.

'What's happened here?' Mick shouted across at him. It felt

good to shout, it felt good to sound angry at the man. Maybe he was to blame. It would be a fine thing, just to have someone to blame.

'Tell us – ' Mick said. He could hear the tears throbbing in his voice. 'Tell us, for God's sake. Explain.'

Grey-coat shook his head. He didn't understand a word this young idiot was saying. It was English he spoke, but that's all he knew. Mick began to walk towards him, feeling all the time the eyes of the dead on him. Eyes like black, shining gems set in broken faces: eyes looking at him upside down, on heads severed from their seating. Eyes in heads that had solid howls for voices. Eyes in heads beyond howls, beyond breath.

Thousands of eyes.

He reached Grey-coat, whose gun was almost empty. He had taken off his spectacles and thrown them aside. He too was weeping, little jerks ran through his big, ungainly body.

At Mick's feet, somebody was reaching for him. He didn't want to look, but the hand touched his shoe and he had no choice but to see its owner. A young man, lying like a flesh swastika, every joint smashed. A child lay under him, her bloody legs poking out like two pink sticks.

He wanted the man's revolver, to stop the hand from touching him. Better still he wanted a machine-gun, a flame-thrower, anything to wipe the agony away.

As he looked up from the broken body, Mick saw Grey-coat raise the revolver.

'Judd – ' he said, but as the word left his lips the muzzle of the revolver was slipped into Grey-coat's mouth and the trigger was pulled.

Grey-coat had saved the last bullet for himself. The back of his head opened like a dropped egg, the shell of his skull flying off. His body went limp and sank to the ground, the revolver still between his lips.

'We must – ' began Mick, saying the words to nobody. 'We must . . .'

What was the imperative? In this situation, what *must* they do? 'We must – '

Judd was behind him.

'Help – ' he said to Mick.

'Yes. We must get help. We must – '

'Go.'

Go! That was what they must do. On any pretext, for any fragile, cowardly reason, they must go. Get out of the battlefield, get out of the reach of a dying hand with a wound in place of a body.

'We have to tell the authorities. Find a town. Get help – '

'Priests,' said Mick. 'They need priests.'

It was absurd, to think of giving the Last Rites to so many people. It would take an army of priests, a water cannon filled with holy water, a loudspeaker to pronounce the benedictions.

They turned away, together, from the horror, and wrapped their arms around each other, then picked their way through the carnage to the car.

It was occupied.

Vaslav Jelovsek was sitting behind the wheel, and trying to start the Volkswagen. He turned the ignition key once. Twice. Third time the engine caught and the wheels span in the crimson mud as he put her into reverse and backed down the track. Vaslav saw the Englishmen running towards the car, cursing him. There was no help for it – he didn't want to steal the vehicle, but he had work to do. He had been a referee, he had been responsible for the contest, and the safety of the contestants. One of the heroic cities had already fallen. He must do everything in his power to prevent Popolac from following its twin. He must chase Popolac, and reason with it. Talk it down out of its terrors with quiet words and promises. If he failed there would be another disaster the equal of the one in front of him, and his conscience was already broken enough.

Mick was still chasing the VW, shouting at Jelovsek. The thief took no notice, concentrating on manouevering the car back down the narrow, slippery track. Mick was losing the chase rapidly. The car had begun to pick up speed. Furious, but without the breath to speak his fury, Mick stood in the road, hands on his knees, heaving and sobbing.

'Bastard!' said Judd.

Mick looked down the track. Their car had already disappeared.

'Fucker couldn't even drive properly.'

'We have . . . we have . . . to catch . . . up . . .' said Mick through gulps of breath.

'How?'

'On foot . . .'

'We haven't even got a map . . . it's in the car.'

'Jesus . . . Christ . . . Almighty.'

They walked down the track together, away from the field.

After a few metres the tide of blood began to peter out. Just a few congealing rivulets dribbled on towards the main road. Mick and Judd followed the bloody tyremarks to the junction.

The Srbovac road was empty in both directions. The tyremarks showed a left turn. 'He's gone deeper into the hills,' said Judd, staring along the lovely road towards the blue-green distance. 'He's out of his mind!'

'Do we go back the way we came?'

'It'll take us all night on foot.'

'We'll hop a lift.'

Judd shook his head: his face was slack and his look lost. 'Don't you see, Mick, they all knew this was happening. The people in the farms – they got the hell out while those people went crazy up there. There'll be no cars along this road, I'll lay you anything – except maybe a couple of shit-dumb tourists like us – and no tourist would stop for the likes of us.'

He was right. They looked like butchers – splattered with blood. Their faces were shining with grease, their eyes maddened.

'We'll have to walk,' said Judd, 'the way he went.'

He pointed along the road. The hills were darker now; the sun had suddenly gone out on their slopes.

Mick shrugged. Either way he could see they had a night on the road ahead of them. But he wanted to walk somewhere – anywhere – as long as he put distance between him and the dead.

In Popolac a kind of peace reigned. Instead of a frenzy of panic there was a numbness, a sheep-like acceptance of the world as it was. Locked in their positions, strapped, roped and harnessed to each other in a living system that allowed for no single voice to be louder than any other, nor any back to labour less than its neighbour's, they let an insane consensus replace the tranquil voice of reason. They were convulsed into one mind, one thought, one ambition. They became, in the space of a few moments, the single-minded giant whose image they had so brilliantly re-created. The illusion of petty individuality was swept away in an irresistible tide of collective feeling – not a mob's passion, but a telepathic surge that dissolved the voices of thousands into one irresistible command.

And the voice said: Go!

The voice said: take this horrible sight away, where I need never see it again.

Popolac turned away into the hills, its legs taking strides half a mile long. Each man, woman and child in that seething tower was sightless. They saw only through the eyes of the city. They were thoughtless, but to think the city's thoughts. And they believed themselves deathless, in their lumbering, relentless strength. Vast and mad and deathless.

Two miles along the road Mick and Judd smelt petrol in the air, and a little further along they came upon the VW. It had overturned in the reed-clogged drainage ditch at the side of the road. It had not caught fire.

The driver's door was open, and the body of Vaslav Jelovsek had tumbled out. His face was calm in unconsciousness. There seemed to be no sign of injury, except for a small cut or two on his sober face. They gently pulled the thief out of the wreckage and up out of the filth of the ditch on to the road. He moaned a little as they fussed about him, rolling Mick's sweater up to pillow his head and removing the man's jacket and tie.

Quite suddenly, he opened his eyes.

He stared at them both.

'Are you all right?' Mick asked.

The man said nothing for a moment. He seemed not to understand.

Then:

'English?' he said. His accent was thick, but the question was quite clear.

'Yes.'

'I heard your voices. English.'

He frowned and winced.

'Are you in pain?' said Judd.

The man seemed to find this amusing.

'Am I in pain?' he repeated, his face screwed up in a mixture of agony and delight.

'I shall die,' he said, through gritted teeth.

'No,' said Mick, 'You're all right – '

The man shook his head, his authority absolute.

'I shall die,' he said again, the voice full of determination, 'I want to die.'

Judd crouched closer to him. His voice was weaker by the moment.

'Tell us what to do,' he said. The man had closed his eyes. Judd shook him awake, roughly.

'Tell us,' he said again, his show of compassion rapidly disappearing. 'Tell us what this is all about.'

'About?' said the man, his eyes still closed. 'It was a fall, that's all. Just a fall . . .'

'What fell?'

'The city. Podujevo. My city.'

'What did it fall from?'

'Itself, of course.'

The man was explaining nothing; just answering one riddle with another.

'Where were you going?' Mick inquired, trying to sound as unaggressive as possible.

'After Popolac,' said the man.

'Popolac?' said Judd.

Mick began to see some sense in the story.

'Popolac is another city. Like Podujevo. Twin cities. They're on the map – '

'Where's the city now?' said Judd.

Vaslav Jelovsek seemed to choose to tell the truth. There was a moment when he hovered between dying with a riddle on his lips, and living long enough to unburden his story. What did it matter if the tale was told now? There could never be another contest: all that was over.

'They came to fight,' he said, his voice now very soft, 'Popolac and Podujevo. They come every ten years – '

'Fight?' said Judd, 'You mean all those people were slaughtered?'

Vaslav shook his head.

'No, no. They fell. I told you.'

'Well how do they fight?' Mick said.

'Go into the hills,' was the only reply.

Vaslav opened his eyes a little. The faces that loomed over him were exhausted and sick. They had suffered, these innocents. They deserved some explanation.

'As giants,' he said. 'They fought as giants. They made a body out of their bodies, do you understand? The frame, the muscles, the bone, the eyes, nose, teeth all made of men and women.'

'He's delirious,' said Judd.

'You go into the hills,' the man repeated. 'See for yourselves how true it is.'

'Even supposing – ' Mick began.

Vaslav interrupted him, eager to be finished. 'They were good at the game of giants. It took many centuries of practice: every ten years making the figure larger and larger. One always ambitious to be larger than the other. Ropes to tie them all together, flawlessly. Sinews . . . ligaments . . . There was food in its belly . . . there were pipes from the loins, to take away the waste. The best-sighted sat in the eye-sockets, the best voiced in the mouth and throat. You wouldn't believe the engineering of it.'

'I don't,' said Judd, and stood up.

'It is the body of the state,' said Vaslav, so softly his voice was barely above a whisper, 'it is the shape of our lives.'

There was a silence. Small clouds passed over the road, soundlessly shedding their mass to the air.

'It was a miracle,' he said. It was as if he realized the true enormity of the fact for the first time. 'It was a miracle.'

It was enough. Yes. It was quite enough.

His mouth closed, the words said, and he died.

Mick felt this death more acutely than the thousands they had fled from; or rather this death was the key to unlock the anguish he felt for them all.

Whether the man had chosen to tell a fantastic lie as he died, or whether this story was in some way true, Mick felt useless in the face of it. His imagination was too narrow to encompass the idea. His brain ached with the thought of it, and his compassion cracked under the weight of misery he felt.

They stood on the road, while the clouds scudded by, their vague, grey shadows passing over them towards the enigmatic hills.

It was twilight.

Popolac could stride no further. It felt exhaustion in every muscle. Here and there in its huge anatomy deaths had occurred; but there was no grieving in the city for its deceased cells. If the dead were in the interior, the corpses were allowed to hang from their harnesses. If they formed the skin of the city they were unbuckled from their positions and released, to plunge into the forest below.

The giant was not capable of pity. It had no ambition but to continue until it ceased.

As the sun slunk out of sight Popolac rested, sitting on a small hillock, nursing its huge head in its huge hands.

The stars were coming out, with their familiar caution. Night was approaching, mercifully bandaging up the wounds of the day, blinding eyes that had seen too much.

Popolac rose to its feet again, and began to move, step by booming step. It would not be long surely, before fatigue overcame it: before it could lie down in the tomb of some lost valley and die.

But for a space yet it must walk on, each step more agonizingly slow than the last, while the night bloomed black around its head.

Mick wanted to bury the car-thief, somewhere on the edge of the forest. Judd, however, pointed out that burying a body might seem, in tomorrow's saner light, a little suspicious. And besides, wasn't it absurd to concern themselves with one corpse when there were literally thousands of them lying a few miles from where they stood?

The body was left to lie, therefore, and the car to sink deeper into the ditch.

They began to walk again.

It was cold, and colder by the moment, and they were hungry.

But the few houses they passed were all deserted, locked and shuttered, every one.

'What did he mean?' said Mick, as they stood looking at another locked door.

'He was talking metaphor – '

'All that stuff about giants?'

'It was some Trotskyist tripe – ' Judd insisted.

'I don't think so.'

'I know so. It was his deathbed speech, he'd probably been preparing for years.'

'I don't think so,' Mick said again, and began walking back towards the road.

'Oh, how's that?' Judd was at his back.

'He wasn't towing some party line.'

'Are you saying you think there's some giant around here someplace? For God's sake!'

Mick turned to Judd. His face was difficult to see the twilight. But his voice was sober with belief.

'Yes. I think he was telling the truth.'

'That's absurd. That's ridiculous. No.'

Judd hated Mick that moment. Hated his naïvete, his passion to believe any half-witted story if it had a whiff of romance about it. And this? This was the worst, the most preposterous . . .

'No,' he said again. 'No. No. No.'

The sky was porcelain smooth, and the outline of the hills black as pitch.

'I'm fucking freezing,' said Mick out of the ink. 'Are you staying here or walking with me?'

Judd shouted: 'We're not going to find anything this way.'

'Well it's a long way back.'

'We're just going deeper into the hills.'

'Do what you like – I'm walking.'

His footsteps receded: the dark encased him.

After a minute, Judd followed.

The night was cloudless and bitter. They walked on, their collars up against the chill, their feet swollen in their shoes. Above them the whole sky had become a parade of stars. A triumph of spilled light, from which the eye could make as many patterns as it had patience for. After a while, they slung their tired arms around each other, for comfort and warmth.

About eleven o'clock, they saw the glow of a window in the distance.

The woman at the door of the stone cottage didn't smile, but she understood their condition, and let them in. There seemed to be no purpose in trying to explain to either the woman or her crippled husband what they had seen. The cottage had no telephone, and there was no sign of a vehicle, so even had they found some way to express themselves, nothing could be done.

With mimes and face-pullings they explained that they were hungry and exhausted. They tried further to explain they were lost, cursing themselves for leaving their phrasebook in the VW. She didn't seem to understand very much of what they said, but sat them down beside a blazing fire and put a pan of food on the stove to heat.

They ate thick unsalted pea soup and eggs, and occasionally smiled their thanks at the woman. Her husband sat beside the fire, making no attempt to talk, or even look at the visitors.

The food was good. It buoyed their spirits.

They would sleep until morning and then begin the long trek back. By dawn the bodies in the field would be being quantified, identified, parcelled up and dispatched to their families. The air would be full of reassuring noises, cancelling out the moans that still rang in their ears. There would be helicopters, lorry loads of men organizing the clearing-up operations. All the rites and paraphernalia of a civilized disaster.

And in a while, it would be palatable. It would become part of their history: a tragedy, of course, but one they could explain, classify and learn to live with. All would be well, yes, all would be well. Come morning.

The sleep of sheer fatigue came on them suddenly. They lay where they had fallen, still sitting at the table, their heads on their crossed arms. A litter of empty bowls and bread crusts surrounded them.

They knew nothing. Dreamt nothing. Felt nothing.

Then the thunder began.

In the earth, in the deep earth, a rhythmical tread, as of a titan, that came, by degrees, closer and closer.

The woman woke her husband. She blew out the lamp and went to the door. The night sky was luminous with stars: the hills black on every side.

The thunder still sounded: a full half minute between every boom, but louder now. And louder with every new step.

They stood at the door together, husband and wife, and listened to the night-hills echo back and forth with the sound. There was no lightning to accompany the thunder.

Just the boom –

Boom –

Boom –

It made the ground shake: it threw dust down from the door-lintel, and rattled the window-latches.

Boom –

Boom –

They didn't know what approached, but whatever shape it took, and whatever it intended, there seemed no sense in running from it. Where they stood, in the pitiful shelter of their cottage, was as safe as any nook of the forest. How could they choose, out of a hundred thousand trees, which would be standing when the thunder had passed? Better to wait: and watch.

The wife's eyes were not good, and she doubted what she saw when the blackness of the hill changed shape and reared up to block the stars. But her husband had seen it too: the unimaginably huge head, vaster in the deceiving darkness, looming up and up, dwarfing the hills themselves with its ambition.

He fell to his knees, babbling a prayer, his arthritic legs twisted beneath him.

His wife screamed: no words she knew could keep this monster at bay – no prayer, no plea, had power over it.

In the cottage, Mick woke and his outstretched arm, twitching with a sudden cramp, wiped the plate and the lamp off the table.

They smashed.

Judd woke.

The screaming outside had stopped. The woman had disappeared from the doorway into the forest. Any tree, any tree at all, was better than this sight. Her husband still let a string of prayers dribble from his slack mouth, as the great leg of the giant rose to take another step –

Boom –

The cottage shook. Plates danced and smashed off the dresser. A clay pipe rolled from the mantelpiece and shattered in the ashes of the hearth.

The lovers knew the noise that sounded in their substance: that earth-thunder.

Mick reached for Judd, and took him by the shoulder.

'You see,' he said, his teeth blue-grey in the darkness of the cottage. 'See? See?'

There was a kind of hysteria bubbling behind his words. He ran to the door, stumbling over a chair in the dark. Cursing and bruised he staggered out into the night –

Boom –

The thunder was deafening. This time it broke all the windows

145

in the cottage. In the bedroom one of the roof-joists cracked and flung debris downstairs.

Judd joined his lover at the door. The old man was now face down on the ground, his sick and swollen fingers curled, his begging lips pressed to the damp soil.

Mick was looking up, towards the sky. Judd followed his gaze.

There was a place that showed no stars. It was a darkness in the shape of a man, a vast, broad human frame, a colossus that soared up to meet heaven. It was not quite a perfect giant. Its outline was not tidy; it seethed and swarmed.

He seemed broader too, this giant, than any real man. His legs were abnormally thick and stumpy, and his arms were not long. The hands, as they clenched and unclenched, seemed oddly-jointed and over-delicate for its torso.

Then it raised one huge, flat foot and placed it on the earth, taking a stride towards them.

Boom –

The step brought the roof collapsing in on the cottage. Everything that the car-thief had said was true. Popolac was a city and a giant; and it had gone into the hills . . .

Now their eyes were becoming accustomed to the night light. They could see in ever more horrible detail the way this monster was constructed. It was a masterpiece of human engineering: a man made entirely of men. Or rather, a sexless giant, made of men and women and children. All the citizens of Popolac writhed and strained in the body of this flesh-knitted giant, their muscles stretched to breaking point, their bones close to snapping.

They could see how the architects of Popolac had subtly altered the proportions of the human body; how the thing had been made squatter to lower its centre of gravity; how its legs had been made elephantine to bear the weight of the torso; how the head was sunk low on to the wide shoulders, so that the problems of a weak neck had been minimized.

Despite these malformations, it was horribly life-like. The bodies that were bound together to make its surface were naked but for their harnesses, so that its surface glistened in the starlight, like one vast human torso. Even the muscles were well copied, though simplified. They could see the way the roped bodies pushed and pulled against each other in solid cords of flesh and bone. They could see the intertwined people that made up the body: the backs like turtles packed together to offer the sweep of the pectorals; the lashed and knotted acrobats at the joints of the arms and the legs alike, rolling and unwinding to articulate the city.

But surely the most amazing sight of all was the face.

Cheeks of bodies; cavenous eye-sockets in which heads stared, five bound together for each eyeball; a broad, flat nose and a mouth that opened and closed, as the muscles of the jaw bunched and hollowed rhythmically. And from that mouth, lined with teeth of bald children, the voice of the giant, now only a weak copy of its former powers, spoke a single note of idiot music.

Popolac walked and Popolac sang.

Was there ever a sight in Europe the equal of it?

They watched, Mick and Judd, as it took another step towards them.

The old man had wet his pants. Blubbering and begging, he dragged himself away from the ruined cottage into the surrounding trees, dragging his dead legs after him.

The Englishmen remained where they stood, watching the spectacle as it approached. Neither dread nor horror touched them now, just an awe that rooted them to the spot. They knew this was a sight they could never hope to see again; this was the apex – after this there was only common experience. Better to stay then, though every step brought death nearer, better to stay and see the sight while it was still there to be seen. And if it killed them, this monster, then at least they would have glimpsed a miracle, known this terrible majesty for a brief moment. It seemed a fair exchange.

Popolac was within two steps of the cottage. They could see the complexities of its structure quite clearly. The faces of the citizens were becoming detailed: white, sweat-wet, and content in their weariness. Some hung dead from their harnesses, their legs swinging back and forth like the hanged. Others, children particularly, had ceased to obey their training, and had relaxed their positions, so that the form of the body was degenerating, beginning to seethe with the boils of rebellious cells.

Yet it still walked, each step an incalculable effort of co-ordination and strength.

Boom –

The step that trod the cottage came sooner than they thought.

Mick saw the leg raised; saw the faces of the people in the shin and ankle and foot – they were as big as he was now – all huge men chosen to take the full weight of this great creation. Many were dead. The bottom of the foot, he could see, was a jigsaw of crushed and bloody bodies, pressed to death under the weight of their fellow citizens.

The foot descended with a roar.

In a matter of seconds the cottage was reduced to splinters and dust.

Popolac blotted the sky utterly. It was, for a moment, the whole world, heaven and earth, its presence filled the senses to overflowing. At this proximity one look could not encompass it, the eye had to range backwards and forwards over its mass to take it all in, and even then the mind refused to accept the whole truth.

A whirling fragment of stone, flung off from the cottage as it collapsed, struck Judd full in the face. In his head he heard the killing stroke like a ball hitting a wall: a play-yard death. No pain: no remorse. Out like a light, a tiny, insignificant light; his death-cry lost in the pandemonium, his body hidden in the smoke and darkness. Mick neither saw nor heard Judd die.

He was too busy staring at the foot as it settled for a moment in the ruins of the cottage, while the other leg mustered the will to move.

Mick took his chance. Howling like a banshee, he ran towards the leg, longing to embrace the monster. He stumbled in the wreckage, and stood again, bloodied, to reach for the foot before it was lifted and he was left behind. There was a clamour of agonized breath as the message came to the foot that it must move; Mick saw the muscles of the shin bunch and marry as the leg began to lift. He made one last lunge at the limb as it began to leave the ground, snatching a harness or a rope, or human hair, or flesh itself – anything to catch this passing miracle and be part of it. Better to go with it wherever it was going, serve it in its purpose, whatever that might be; better to die with it than live without it.

He caught the foot, and found a safe purchase on its ankle. Screaming his sheer ecstasy at his success he felt the great leg raised, and glanced down through the swirling dust to the spot where he had stood, already receding as the limb climbed.

The earth was gone from beneath him. He was a hitchhiker with a god: the mere life he had left was nothing to him now, or ever. He would live with this thing, yes, he would live with it – seeing it and seeing it and eating it with his eyes until he died of sheer gluttony.

He screamed and howled and swang on the ropes, drinking up his triumph. Below, far below, he glimpsed Judd's body, curled up pale on the dark ground, irretrievable. Love and life and sanity were gone, gone like the memory of his name, or his sex, or his ambition.

It all meant nothing. Nothing at all.

Boom –

Boom –

Popolac walked, the noise of its steps receding to the east. Popolac walked, the hum of its voice lost in the night.

* * *

148

After a day, birds came, foxes came, flies, butterflies, wasps came. Judd moved, Judd shifted, Judd gave birth. In his belly maggots warmed themselves, in a vixen's den the good flesh of his thigh was fought over. After that, it was quick. The bones yellowing, the bones crumbling: soon, an empty space which he had once filled with breath and opinions.

Darkness, light, darkness, light. He interrupted neither with his name.

BOOKS OF BLOOD
VOLUME 2

To Johnny

CONTENTS

Dread

There is no delight the equal of dread. If it were possible to sit, invisible, between two people on any train, in any waiting room or office, the conversation overheard would time and again circle on that subject. Certainly the debate might appear to be about something entirely different; the state of the nation, idle chat about death on the roads, the rising price of dental care; but strip away the metaphor, the innuendo, and there, nestling at the heart of the discourse, is dread. While the nature of God, and the possibility of eternal life go undiscussed, we happily chew over the minutiae of misery. The syndrome recognizes no boundaries; in bath-house and seminar-room alike, the same ritual is repeated. With the inevitability of a tongue returning to probe a painful tooth, we come back and back and back again to our fears, sitting to talk them over with the eagerness of a hungry man before a full and steaming plate.

While he was still at university, and afraid to speak, Stephen Grace was taught to speak of why he was afraid. In fact not simply to talk about it, but to analyse and dissect his every nerve-ending, looking for tiny terrors.

In this investigation, he had a teacher: Quaid.

It was an age of gurus; it was their season. In universities up and down England young men and women were looking east and west for people to follow like lambs; Steve Grace was just one of many. It was his bad luck that Quaid was the Messiah he found.

They'd met in the Student Common Room.

'The name's Quaid,' said the man at Steve's elbow at the bar.

'Oh.'

'You're – ?'

'Steve Grace.'

'Yes. You're in the Ethics class, right?'

'Right.'

'I don't see you in any of the other Philosophy seminars or lectures.'

'It's my extra subject for the year. I'm on the English

1

Literature course. I just couldn't bear the idea of a year in the Old Norse classes.'

'So you plumped for Ethics.'

'Yes.'

Quaid ordered a double brandy. He didn't look that well off, and a double brandy would have just about crippled Steve's finances for the next week. Quaid downed it quickly, and ordered another.

'What are you having?'

Steve was nursing half a pint of luke-warm lager, determined to make it last an hour.

'Nothing for me.'

'Yes you will.'

'I'm fine.'

'Another brandy and a pint of lager for my friend.'

Steve didn't resist Quaid's generosity. A pint and a half of lager in his unfed system would help no end in dulling the tedium of his oncoming seminars on 'Charles Dickens as a Social Analyst'. He yawned just to think of it.

'Somebody ought to write a thesis on drinking as a social activity.'

Quaid studied his brandy a moment, then downed it.

'Or as oblivion,' he said.

Steve looked at the man. Perhaps five years older than Steve's twenty. The mixture of clothes he wore was confusing. Tattered running shoes, cords, a grey-white shirt that had seen better days: and over it a very expensive black leather jacket that hung badly on his tall, thin frame. The face was long and unremarkable; the eyes milky-blue, and so pale that the colour seemed to seep into the whites, leaving just the pin-pricks of his irises visible behind his heavy glasses. Lips full, like a Jagger, but pale, dry and unsensual. Hair, a dirty blond.

Quaid, Steve decided, could have passed for a Dutch dope-pusher.

He wore no badges. They were the common currency of a student's obsessions, and Quaid looked naked without something to imply how he took his pleasures. Was he a gay, feminist, save-the-whale campaigner; or a fascist vegetarian? What was he into, for God's sake?

'You should have been doing Old Norse,' said Quaid.

'Why?'

'They don't even bother to mark the papers on that course,' said Quaid.

2

Steve hadn't heard about this. Quaid droned on.

'They just throw them all up into the air. Face up, an A. Face down, a B.'

Oh, it was a joke. Quaid was being witty. Steve attempted a laugh, but Quaid's face remained unmoved by his own attempt at humour.

'You should be in Old Norse,' he said again. 'Who needs Bishop Berkeley anyhow. Or Plato. Or – '

'Or?'

'It's all shit.'

'Yes.'

'I've watched you, in the Philosophy Class – '

Steve began to wonder about Quaid.

' – You never take notes do you?'

'No.'

'I thought you were either sublimely confident, or you simply couldn't care less.'

'Neither. I'm just completely lost.'

Quaid grunted, and pulled out a pack of cheap cigarettes. Again, that was not the done thing. You either smoked Gauloises,Camel or nothing at all.

'It's not true philosophy they teach you here,' said Quaid, with unmistakable contempt.

'Oh?'

'We get spoonfed a bit of Plato, or a bit of Bentham – no real analysis. It's got all the right markings of course. It looks like the beast: it even smells a bit like the beast to the uninitiated.'

'What beast?'

'Philosophy. *True* Philosophy. It's a beast, Stephen. Don't you think?'

'I hadn't – '

'It's wild. It bites.'

He grinned, suddenly vulpine.

'Yes. It bites,' he replied.

Oh, that pleased him. Again, for luck: 'Bites.'

Stephen nodded. The metaphor was beyond him.

'I think we should feel mauled by our subject.' Quaid was warming to the whole subject of mutilation by education. 'We should be frightened to juggle the ideas we should talk about.'

'Why?'

'Because if we were philosophers worth we wouldn't be

3

exchanging academic pleasantries. We wouldn't be talking semantics; using linguistic trickery to cover the real concerns.'

'What would we be doing?'

Steve was beginning to feel like Quaid's straight-man. Except that Quaid wasn't in a joking mood. His face was set: his pin-prick irises had closed down to tiny dots.

'We should be walking close to the beast, Steve, don't you think? Reaching out to stroke it, pet it, milk it – '

'What . . . er . . . what is the beast?'

Quaid was clearly a little exasperated by the pragmatism of the enquiry.

'It's the subject of any worthwhile philosophy, Stephen. It's the things we fear, because we don't understand them. It's the dark behind the door.'

Steve thought of a door. Thought of the dark. He began to see what Quaid was driving at in his labyrinthine fashion. Philosophy was a way to talk about fear.

'We should discuss what's intimate to our psyches,' said Quaid. 'If we don't . . . we risk . . .'

Quaid's loquaciousness deserted him suddenly.

'What?'

Quaid was staring at his empty brandy glass, seeming to will it to be full again.

'Want another?' said Steve, praying that the answer would be no.

'What do we risk?' Quaid repeated the question. 'Well, I think if we don't go out and find the beast – '

Steve could see the punchline coming.

' – sooner or later the beast will come and find us.'

There is no delight the equal of dread. As long as it's someone else's.

Casually, in the following week or two, Steve made some enquiries about the curious Mr Quaid.

Nobody knew his first name.

Nobody was certain of his age; but one of the secretaries thought he was over thirty, which came as a surprise.

His parents, Cheryl had heard him say, were dead. Killed, she thought.

That appeared to be the sum of human knowledge where Quaid was concerned.

* * *

4

'I owe you a drink,' said Steve, touching Quaid on the shoulder. He looked as though he'd been bitten.

'Brandy?'

'Thank you.'

Steve ordered the drinks.

'Did I startle you?'

'I was thinking.'

'No philosopher should be without one.'

'One what?'

'Brain.'

They fell to talking. Steve didn't know why he'd approached Quaid again. The man was ten years his senior and in a different intellectual league. He probably intimidated Steve, if he was to be honest about it. Quaid's relentless talk of beasts confused him. Yet he wanted more of the same: more metaphors: more of that humourless voice telling him how useless the tutors were, how weak the students.

In Quaid's world there were no certainties. He had no secular gurus and certainly no religion. He seemed incapable of viewing any system, whether it was political or philosophical, without cynicism.

Though he seldom laughed out loud, Steve knew there was a bitter humour in his vision of the world. People were lambs and sheep, all looking for shepherds. Of course these shepherds were fictions, in Quaid's opinion. All that existed, in the darkness outside the sheep-fold were the fears that fixed on the innocent mutton: waiting, patient as stone, for their moment.

Everything was to be doubted, but the fact that dread existed.

Quaid's intellectual arrogance was exhilarating. Steve soon came to love the iconoclastic ease with which he demolished belief after belief. Sometimes it was painful when Quaid formulated a water-tight argument against one of Steve's dogma. But after a few weeks, even the sound of the demolition seemed to excite. Quaid was clearing the undergrowth, felling the trees, razing the stubble. Steve felt free.

Nation, family, Church, law. All ash. All useless. All cheats, and chains and suffocation.

There was only dread.

'I fear, you fear, we fear,' Quaid was fond of saying. 'He, she or it fears. There's no conscious thing on the face of the world that doesn't know dread more intimately than its own heartbeat.'

One of Quaid's favourite baiting-victims was another Philosophy and Eng. Lit. student, Cheryl Fromm. She would rise to his more outrageous remarks like fish to rain, and while the two of them took knives to each other's arguments Steve would sit back and watch the spectacle. Cheryl was, in Quaid's phrase, a pathological optimist.

'And you're full of shit,' she'd say when the debate had warmed up a little. 'So who cares if you're afraid of your own shadow? I'm not. I feel fine.'

She certainly looked it. Cheryl Fromm was wet dream material, but too bright for anyone to try making a move on her.

'We all taste dread once in a while,' Quaid would reply to her, and his milky eyes would study her face intently, watching for her reaction, trying, Steve knew, to find a flaw in her conviction.

'I don't.'

'No fears? No nightmares?'

'No way. I've got a good family; I don't have any skeletons in my closet. I don't even eat meat, so I don't feel bad when I drive past a slaughterhouse. I don't have any shit to put on show. Does that mean I'm not real?'

'It means,' Quaid's eyes were snake-slits, 'it means your confidence has something big to cover.'

'Back to nightmares.'

'Big nightmares.'

'Be specific: define your terms.'

'I can't tell you what you fear.'

'Tell me what you fear then.'

Quaid hesitated. 'Finally,' he said, 'it's beyond analysis.'

'Beyond analysis, my ass!'

That brought an involuntary smile to Steve's lips. Cheryl's ass was indeed beyond analysis. The only response was to kneel down and worship.

Quaid was back on his soap-box.

'What I fear is personal to me. It makes no sense in a larger context. The signs of my dread, the images my brain uses, if you like, to *illustrate* my fear, those signs are mild stuff by comparison with the real horror that's at the root of my personality.'

'I've got images,' said Steve. Pictures from childhood that make me think of – ' He stopped, regretting this confessional already.

What?' said Cheryl. 'You mean things to do with bad experiences? Falling off your bike, or something like that?'

'Perhaps,' Steve said. 'I find myself, sometimes, thinking of those pictures. Not deliberately, just when my concentration's idling. It's almost as though my mind went to them automatically.'

6

Quaid gave a little grunt of satisfaction. 'Precisely,' he said.

'Freud writes on that,' said Cheryl.

'What?'

'Freud,' Cheryl repeated, this time making a performance of it, as though she were speaking to a child. 'Sigmund Freud: you may have heard of him.'

Quaid's lip curled with unrestrained contempt. 'Mother fixations don't answer the problem. The real terrors in me, in all of us, are pre-personality. Dread's there before we have any notion of ourselves as individuals. The thumb-nail, curled up on itself in the womb, feels fear.'

'You remember do you?' said Cheryl.

'Maybe,' Quaid replied, deadly serious.

'The womb?'

Quaid gave a sort of half-smile. Steve thought the smile said: 'I have knowledge you don't.'

It was a weird, unpleasant smile; one Steve wanted to wash off his eyes.

'You're a liar,' said Cheryl, getting up from her seat, and looking down her nose at Quaid.

'Perhaps I am,' he said, suddenly the perfect gentleman.

After that the debates stopped.

No more talking about nightmares, no more debating the things that go bump in the night. Steve saw Quaid irregularly for the next month, and when he did Quaid was invariably in the company of Cheryl Fromm. Quaid was polite with her, even deferential. He no longer wore his leather jacket, because she hated the smell of dead animal matter. This sudden change in their relationship confounded Stephen; but he put it down to his primitive understanding of sexual matters. He wasn't a virgin, but women were still a mystery to him: contradictory and puzzling.

He was also jealous, though he wouldn't entirely admit that to himself. He resented the fact that the wet dream genius was taking up so much of Quaid's time.

There was another feeling; a curious sense he had that Quaid was courting Cheryl for his own strange reasons. Sex was not Quaid's motive, he felt sure. Nor was it respect for Cheryl's intelligence that made him so attentive. No, he was cornering her somehow; that was Steve's instinct. Cheryl Fromm was being rounded up for the kill.

Then, after a month, Quaid let a remark about Cheryl drop in conversation.

'She's a vegetarian,' he said.

'Cheryl?'

'Of course, Cheryl.'

'I know. She mentioned it before.'

'Yes, but it isn't a fad with her. She's passionate about it. Can't even bear to look in a butcher's window. She won't touch meat, smell meat – '

'Oh.' Steve was stumped. Where was this leading?

'Dread, Steve.'

'Of meat?'

'The signs are different from person to person. *She fears meat.* She says she's so healthy, so balanced. Shit! I'll find it – '

'Find what?'

'The fear, Steve.'

'You're not going to . . . ?' Steve didn't know how to voice his anxiety without sounding accusatory.

'Harm her?' said Quaid. 'No, I'm not going to harm her in any way. Any damage done to her will be strictly self-inflicted.'

Quaid was staring at him almost hypnotically.

'It's about time we learnt to trust one another,' Quaid went on. He leaned closer. 'Between the two of us – '

'Listen, I don't think I want to hear.'

'We have to touch the beast, Stephen.'

'Damn the beast! I don't want to hear!'

Steve got up, as much to break the oppression of Quaid's stare as to finish the conversation.

'We're friends, Stephen.'

'Yes . . .'

'Then respect that.'

'What?'

'Silence. Not a word.'

Steve nodded. That wasn't a difficult promise to keep. There was nobody he could tell his anxieties to without being laughed at.

Quaid looked satisfied. He hurried away, leaving Steve feeling as though he had unwillingly joined some secret society, for what purpose he couldn't begin to tell. Quaid had made a pact with him and it was unnerving.

For the next week he cut all his lectures and most of his seminars. Notes went uncopied, books unread, essays unwritten. On the two occasions he actually went into the university building he crept around like a cautious mouse, praying he wouldn't collide with Quaid.

8

He needn't have feared. The one occasion he did see Quaid's stooping shoulders across the quadrangle he was involved in a smiling exchange with Cheryl Fromm. She laughed, musically, her pleasure echoing off the wall of the History Department. The jealousy had left Steve altogether. He wouldn't have been paid to be so near to Quaid, so intimate with him.

The time he spent alone, away from the bustle of lectures and overfull corridors, gave Steve's mind time to idle. His thoughts returned, like tongue to tooth, like fingernail to scab, to his fears.

And so to his childhood.

At the age of six, Steve had been struck by a car. The injuries were not particularly bad, but concussion left him partially deaf. It was a profoundly distressing experience for him; not understanding why he was suddenly cut off from the world. It was an inexplicable torment, and the child assumed it was eternal.

One moment his life had been real, full of shouts and laughter. The next he was cut off from it, and the external world became an aquarium, full of gaping fish with grotesque smiles. Worse still, there were times when he suffered what the doctors called tinnitus, a roaring or ringing sound in the ears. His head would fill with the most outlandish noises, whoops and whistlings, that played like sound-effects to the flailings of the outside world. At those times his stomach would churn, and a band of iron would be wrapped around his forehead, crushing his thoughts into fragments, dissociating head from hand, intention from practice. He would be swept away in a tide of panic, completely unable to make sense of the world while his head sang and rattled.

But at night came the worst terrors. He would wake, sometimes, in what had been (before the accident) the reassuring womb of his bedroom, to find the ringing had begun in his sleep.

His eyes would jerk open. His body would be wet with sweat. His mind would be filled with the most raucous din, which he was locked in with, beyond hope of reprieve. Nothing could silence his head, and nothing, it seemed, could bring the world, the speaking, laughing, crying world back to him.

He was alone.

That was the beginning, middle and end of the dread. He was absolutely alone with his cacophony. Locked in this house, in this room, in this body, in this head, a prisoner of deaf, blind flesh.

It was almost unbearable. In the night the boy would sometimes cry out, not knowing he was making any sound, and the fish who had been his parents would turn on the light and come to try and help him, bending over his bed making faces, their

9

soundless mouths forming ugly shapes in their attempts to help. Their touches would calm him at last; with time his mother learned the trick of soothing away the panic that swept over him.

A week before his seventh birthday his hearing returned, not perfectly, but well enough for it to seem like a miracle. The world snapped back into focus; and life began afresh.

It took several months for the boy to trust his senses again. He would still wake in the night, half-anticipating the head-noises.

But though his ears would ring at the slightest volume of sound, preventing Steve from going to rock concerts with the rest of the students, he now scarcely ever noticed his slight deafness.

He remembered, of course. Very well. He could bring back the taste of his panic; the feel of the iron band around his head. And there was a residue of fear there; of the dark, of being alone.

But then, wasn't everyone afraid to be alone? To be utterly alone.

Steve had another fear now, far more difficult to pin down.

Quaid.

In a drunken revelation session he had told Quaid about his childhood, about the deafness, about the night terrors.

Quaid knew about his weakness: the clear route into the heart of Steve's dread. He had a weapon, a stick to beat Steve with, should it ever come to that. Maybe that was why he chose not to speak to Cheryl (warn her, was that what he wanted to do?) and certainly that was why he avoided Quaid.

The man had a look, in certain moods, of malice. Nothing more or less. He looked like a man with malice deep, deep in him.

Maybe those four months of watching people with the sound turned down had sensitized Steve to the tiny glances, sneers and smiles that flit across people's faces. He knew Quaid's life was a labyrinth; a map of its complexities was etched on his face in a thousand tiny expressions.

The next phase of Steve's initiation into Quaid's secret world didn't come for almost three and a half months. The university broke for the summer recess, and the students went their ways. Steve took his usual vacation job at his father's printing works; it was long hours, and physically exhausting, but an undeniable relief for him. Academe had overstuffed his mind, he felt force-fed with words and ideas. The print work sweated all of that out of him rapidly, sorting out the jumble in his mind.

It was a good time: he scarcely thought of Quaid at all.

10

He returned to campus in the late September. The students were still thin on the ground. Most of the courses didn't start for another week; and there was a melancholy air about the place without its usual mêlée of complaining, flirting, arguing kids.

Steve was in the library, cornering a few important books before others on his course had their hands on them. Books were pure gold at the beginning of term, with reading lists to be checked off, and the university book shop forever claiming the necessary titles were on order. They would invariably arrive, those vital books, two days after the seminar in which the author was to be discussed. This final year Steve was determined to be ahead of the rush for the few copies of seminal works the library possessed.

The familiar voice spoke.

'Early to work.'

Steve looked up to meet Quaid's pin-prick eyes.

'I'm impressed, Steve.'

'What with?'

'Your enthusiasm for the job.'

'Oh.'

Quaid smiled. 'What are you looking for?'

'Something on Bentham.'

'I've got "Principles of Morals and Legislation." Will that do?'

It was a trap. No: that was absurd. He was offering a book; how could that simple gesture be construed as a trap?

'Come to think of it,' the smile broadened, 'I think it's the library copy I've got. I'll give it to you.'

'Thanks.'

'Good holiday?'

'Yes. Thank you. You?'

'Very rewarding.'

The smile had decayed into a thin line beneath his –

'You've grown a moustache.'

It was an unhealthy example of the species. Thin, patchy, and dirty-blond, it wandered back and forth under Quaid's nose as if looking for a way off his face. Quaid looked faintly embarrassed.

'Was it for Cheryl?'

He was definitely embarrassed now.

'Well . . .'

'Sounds like you had a good vacation.'

The embarrassment was surmounted by something else.

'I've got some wonderful photographs,' Quaid said.

'What of?'

'Holiday snaps.'

Steve couldn't believe his ears. Had C. Fromm tamed the Quaid? Holiday snaps?

'You won't believe some of them.'

There was something of the Arab selling dirty postcards about Quaid's manner. What the hell were these photographs? Split beaver shots of Cheryl, caught reading Kant?

'I don't think of you as being a photographer.'

'It's become a passion of mine.'

He grinned as he said 'passion'. There was a barely-suppressed excitement in his manner. He was positively gleaming with pleasure.

'You've got to come and see them.'

'I –'

'Tonight. And pick up the Bentham at the same time.'

'Thanks.'

'I've got a house for myself these days. Round the corner from the Maternity Hospital, in Pilgrim Street. Number sixty-four. Some time after nine?'

'Right. Thanks. Pilgrim Street.'

Quaid nodded.

'I didn't know there were any habitable houses in Pilgrim Street.'

'Number sixty-four.'

Pilgrim Street was on its knees. Most of the houses were already rubble. A few were in the process of being knocked down. Their inside walls were unnaturally exposed; pink and pale green wallpapers, fireplaces on upper storeys hanging over chasms of smoking brick. Stairs leading from nowhere to nowhere, and back again.

Number sixty-four stood on its own. The houses in the terrace to either side had been demolished and bull-dozed away, leaving a desert of impacted brick-dust which a few hardy, and fool-hardy, weeds had tried to populate.

A three-legged white dog was patrolling its territory along the side of sixty-four, leaving little piss-marks at regular intervals as signs of its ownership.

Quaid's house, though scarcely palatial, was more welcoming than the surrounding wasteland.

They drank some bad red wine together, which Steve had brought with him, and they smoked some grass. Quaid was far more mellow than Steve had ever seen him before, quite happy to

12

talk trivia instead of dread; laughing occasionally; even telling a dirty joke. The interior of the house was bare to the point of being spartan. No pictures on the walls; no decoration of any kind. Quaid's books, and there were literally hundreds of them, were piled on the floor in no particular sequence that Steve could make out. The kitchen and bathroom were primitive. The whole atmosphere was almost monastic.

After a couple of easy hours, Steve's curiosity got the better of him.

'Where's the holiday snaps, then?' he said, aware that he was slurring his words a little, and no longer giving a shit.

'Oh yes. My experiment.'

'Experiment?'

'Tell you the truth, Steve, I'm not so sure I should show them to you.'

'Why not?'

'I'm into serious stuff, Steve.'

'And I'm not ready for serious stuff, is that what you're saying?'

Steve could feel Quaid's technique working on him, even though it was transparently obvious what he was doing.

'I didn't say you weren't ready – '

'What the hell is this stuff?'

'Pictures.'

'Of?'

'You remember Cheryl.'

Pictures of Cheryl. Ha.

'How could I forget?'

'She won't be coming back this term.'

'Oh.'

'She had a revelation.'

Quaid's stare was basilisk-like.

'What do you mean?'

'She was always so calm, wasn't she?' Quaid was talking about her as though she were dead. 'Calm, cool and collected.'

'Yes, I suppose she was.'

'Poor bitch. All she wanted was a good fuck.'

Steve smirked like a kid at Quaid's dirty talk. It was a little shocking; like seeing teacher with his dick hanging out of his trousers.

'She spent some of the vacation here.'

'Here?'

'In this house.'

'You like her then?'

'She's an ignorant cow. She's pretentious, she's weak, she's stupid. But she wouldn't *give*, she wouldn't give a fucking thing.'

'You mean she wouldn't screw?'

'Oh no, she'd strip off her knickers soon as look at you. It was her fears she wouldn't give – '

Same old song.

'But I persuaded her, in the fullness of time.'

Quaid pulled out a box from behind a pile of philosophy books. In it was a sheaf of black and white photographs, blown up to twice postcard size. He passed the first one of the series over to Steve.

'I locked her away you see, Steve.' Quaid was as unemotional as a newsreader. 'To see if I could needle her into showing her dread a little bit.'

'What do you mean, locked her away?'

'Upstairs.'

Steve felt strange. He could hear his ears singing, very quietly. Bad wine always made his head ring.

'I locked her away upstairs,' Quaid said again, 'as an experiment. That's why I took this house. No neighbours to hear.'

No neighbours to hear what?

Steve looked at the grainy image in his hand.

'Concealed camera,' said Quaid, 'she never knew I was photographing her.'

Photograph One was of a small, featureless room. A little plain furniture.

'That's the room. Top of the house. Warm. A bit stuffy even. No noise.'

No noise.

Quaid proffered Photograph Two.

Same room. Now most of the furniture had been removed. A sleeping bag was laid along one wall. A table. A chair. A bare light bulb.

'That's how I laid it out for her.'

'It looks like a cell.'

Quaid grunted.

Photograph Three. The same room. On the table a jug of water. In the corner of the room, a bucket, roughly covered with a towel.

'What's the bucket for?'

'She had to piss.'

'Yes.'

'All amenities provided,' said Quaid. 'I didn't intend to reduce her to an animal.'

Even in his drunken state, Steve took Quaid's inference. He didn't *intend* to reduce her to an animal. However . . .

Photograph Four. On the table, on an unpatterned plate, a slab of meat. A bone sticks out from it.

'Beef,' said Quaid.

'But she's a vegetarian.'

'So she is. It's slightly salted, well-cooked, good beef.'

Photograph Five. The same. Cheryl is in the room. The door is closed. She is kicking the door, her foot and fist and face a blur of fury.

'I put her in the room about five in the morning. She was sleeping: I carried her over the threshold myself. Very romantic. She didn't know what the hell was going on.'

'You locked her in there?'

'Of course. An experiment.'

'She knew nothing about it?'

'We'd talked about dread, you know me. She knew what I wanted to discover. Knew I wanted guinea-pigs. She soon caught on. Once she realized what I was up to she calmed down.'

Photograph Six. Cheryl sits in the corner of the room, thinking.

'I think she believed she could out-wait me.'

Photograph Seven. Cheryl looks at the leg of beef, glancing at it on the table.

'Nice photo, don't you think? Look at the expression of disgust on her face. She hated even the smell of cooked meat. She wasn't hungry then, of course.'

Eight: she sleeps.

Nine: she pisses. Steve felt uncomfortable, watching the girl squatting on the bucket, knickers round her ankles. Tearstains on her face.

Ten: she drinks water from the jug.

Eleven: she sleeps again, back to the room, curled up like a foetus.

'How long has she been in the room?'

'This was only fourteen hours in. She lost orientation as to time very quickly. No light change, you see. Her body-clock was fucked up pretty soon.'

'How long was she in here?'

'Till the point was proved.'

15

Twelve: Awake, she cruises the meat on the table, caught surreptitiously glancing down at it.

'This was taken the following morning. I was asleep: the camera just took pictures every quarter hour. Look at her eyes . . .'

Steve peered more closely at the photograph. There was a certain desperation on Cheryl's face: a haggard, wild look. The way she stared at the beef she could have been trying to hypnotize it.

'She looks sick.'

'She's tired, that's all. She slept a lot, as it happened, but it seemed just to make her more exhausted than ever. She doesn't know now if it's day or night. And she's hungry of course. It's been a day and a half. She's more than a little peckish.'

Thirteen: she sleeps again, curled into an even tighter ball, as though she wanted to swallow herself.

Fourteen: she drinks more water.

'I replaced the jug when she was asleep. She slept deeply: I could have done a jig in there and it wouldn't have woken her. Lost to the world.'

He grinned. Mad, thought Steve, the man's mad.

'God, it stank in there. You know how women smell sometimes; it's not sweat, it's something else. Heavy odour: meaty. Bloody. She came on towards the end of her time. Hadn't planned it that way.'

Fifteen: she touches the meat.

'This is where the cracks begin to show,' said Quaid, with quiet triumph in his voice. 'This is where the dread begins.'

Steve studied the photograph closely. The grain of the print blurred the detail, but the cool mama was in pain, that was for sure. Her face was knotted up, half in desire, half in repulsion, as she touched the food.

Sixteen: she was at the door again, throwing herself at it, every part of her body flailing. Her mouth a black blur of angst, screaming at the blank door.

'She always ended up haranguing me, whenever she'd had a confrontation with the meat.'

'How long is this?'

'Coming up for three days. You're looking at a hungry woman.'

It wasn't difficult to see that. The next photo she stood still in the middle of the room, averting her eyes from the temptation of the food, her entire body tensed with the dilemma.

'You're starving her.'

'She can go ten days without eating quite easily. Fasts are common in any civilized country, Steve. Sixty per cent of the British population is clinically obese at any one time. She was too fat anyhow.'

Eighteen: she sits, the fat girl, in her corner of the room, weeping.

'About now she began to hallucinate. Just little mental ticks. She thought she felt something in her hair, or on the back of her hand. I'd see her staring into mid-air sometimes watching nothing.'

Nineteen: she washes herself. She is stripped to the waist, her breasts are heavy, her face is drained of expression. The meat is a darker tone than in the previous photographs.

'She washed herself regularly. Never let twelve hours go by without washing from head to toe.'

'The meat looks . . .'

'Ripe?'

'Dark.'

'It's quite warm in her little room; and there's a few flies in there with her. They've found the meat: laid their eggs. Yes, it's ripening up quite nicely.'

'Is that part of the plan?'

'Sure. If the meat revolted when it was fresh, what about her disgust at rotted meat? That's the crux of her dilemma, isn't it? The longer she waits to eat, the more disgusted she becomes with what she's been given to feed on. She's trapped with her own horror of meat on the one hand, and her dread of dying on the other. Which is going to give first?'

Steve was no less trapped now.

On the one hand this joke had already gone too far, and Quaid's experiment had become an exercise in sadism. On the other hand he wanted to know how far this story ended. There was un undeniable fascination in watching the woman suffer.

The next seven photographs – twenty, twenty-one, two, three, four, five and six pictured the same circular routine. Sleeping, washing, pissing, meat-watching. Sleeping, washing, pissing –

Then twenty-seven.

'See?'

She picks up the meat.

Yes, she picks it up, her face full of horror. The haunch of the beef looks well-ripened now, speckled with flies' eggs. Gross.

'She bites it.'

17

The next photograph, and her face is buried in the meat.

Steve seemed to taste the rotten flesh in the back of his throat. His mind found a stench to imagine, and created a gravy of putresence to run over his tongue. How could she do it?

Twenty-nine: she is vomiting in the bucket in the corner of the room.

Thirty: she is sitting looking at the table. It is empty. The water-jug has been thrown against the wall. The plate has been smashed. The beef lies on the floor in a slime of degeneration.

Thirty-one: she sleeps. Her head is lost in a tangle of arms.

Thirty-two: she is standing up. She is looking at the meat again, defying it. The hunger she feels is plain on her face. So is the disgust.

Thirty-three. She sleeps.

'How long now?' asked Steve.

'Five days. No, six.'

Six days.

Thirty-four. She is a blurred figure, apparently flinging herself against a wall. Perhaps beating her head against it, Steve couldn't be sure. He was past asking. Part of him didn't want to know.

Thirty-five: she is again sleeping, this time beneath the table. The sleeping bag has been torn to pieces, shredded cloth and pieces of stuffing littering the room.

Thirty-six: she speaks to the door, through the door, knowing she will get no answer.

Thirty-seven: she eats the rancid meat.

Calmly she sits under the table, like a primitive in her cave, and pulls at the meat with her incisors. Her face is again expressionless; all her energy is bent to the purpose of the moment. To eat. To eat 'til the hunger disappears, 'til the agony in her belly, and the sickness in her head disappear.

Steve stared at the photograph.

'It startled me,' said Quaid, 'how suddenly she gave in. One moment she seemed to have as much resistance as ever. The monologue at the door was the same mixture of threats and apologies as she'd delivered day in, day out. Then she broke. Just like that. Squatted under the table and ate the beef down to the bone, as though it were a choice cut.'

Thirty-eight: she sleeps. The door is open. Light pours in.

Thirty-nine: the room is empty.

'Where did she go?'

'She wandered downstairs. She came into the kitchen, drank

18

several glasses of water, and sat in a chair for three or four hours without saying a word.'

'Did you speak to her?'

'Eventually. When she started to come out of her fugue state. The experiment was over. I didn't want to hurt her.'

'What did she say?'

'Nothing.'

'Nothing?'

'Nothing at all. For a long time I don't believe she was even aware of my presence in the room. Then I cooked some potatoes, which she ate.'

'She didn't try and call the police?'

'No.'

'No violence?'

'No. She knew what I'd done, and why I'd done it. It wasn't pre-planned, but we'd talked about such experiments, in abstract conversations. She hadn't come to any harm, you see. She'd lost a bit of weight perhaps, but that was about all.'

'Where is she now?'

'She left the day after. I don't know where she went.'

'And what did it all prove?'

'Nothing at all, perhaps. But it made an interesting start to my investigations.'

'Start? This was only a start?'

There was plain disgust for Quaid in Steve's voice.

'Stephen – '

'You could have killed her!'

'No.'

'She could have lost her mind. Unbalanced her permanently.'

'Possibly. But unlikely. She was a strong-willed woman.'

'But you broke her.'

'Yes. It was a journey she was ready to take. We'd talked of going to face her fear. So here was I, arranging for Cheryl to do just that. Nothing much really.'

'You forced her to do it. She wouldn't have gone otherwise.'

'True. It was an education for her.'

'So now you're a teacher?'

Steve wished he'd been able to keep the sarcasm out of his voice. But it was there. Sarcasm; anger; and a little fear.

'Yes, I'm a teacher,' Quaid replied, looking at Steve obliquely, his eyes not focussed. 'I'm teaching people dread.'

Steve stared at the floor. 'Are you satisfied with what you've taught?'

'And learned, Steve. I've learned too. It's a very exciting prospect: a world of fears to investigate. Especially with intelligent subjects. Even in the face of rationalization – '

Steve stood up. 'I don't want to hear any more.'

'Oh? OK.'

'I've got classes early tomorrow.'

'No.'

'What?'

A beat, faltering.

'No. Don't go yet.'

'Why?' His heart was racing. He feared Quaid, he'd never realized how profoundly.

'I've got some more books to give you.'

Steve felt his face flush. Slightly. What had he thought in that moment? That Quaid was going to bring him down with a rugby tackle and start experimenting on his fears?

No. Idiot thoughts.

'I've got a book on Kierkegaard you'll like. Upstairs. I'll be two minutes.'

Smiling, Quaid left the room.

Steve squatted on his haunches and began to sheaf through the photographs again. It was the moment when Cheryl first picked up the rotting meat that fascinated him most. Her face wore an expression completely uncharacteristic of the woman he had known. Doubt was written there, and confusion, and deep –

Dread.

It was Quaid's word. A dirty word. An obscene word, associated from this night on with Quaid's torture of an innocent girl.

For a moment Steve thought of the expression on his own face, as he stared down at the photograph. Was there not some of the same confusion on his face? And perhaps some of the dread too, waiting for release.

He heard a sound behind him, too soft to be Quaid.

Unless he was creeping.

Oh, God, unless he was –

A pad of chloroformed cloth was clamped over Steve's mouth and his nostrils. Involuntarily, he inhaled and the vapours stung his sinuses, made his eyes water.

A blob of blackness appeared at the corner of the world, just out of sight, and it started to grow, this stain, pulsing to the rhythm of his quickening heart.

In the centre of Steve's head he could see Quaid's voice as a veil. It said his name.

'Stephen.'

Again.

' – ephen.'

' – phen.'

' – hen.'

'en.'

The stain was the world. The world was dark, gone away. Out of sight, out of mind.

Steve fell clumsily amongst the photographs.

When he woke up he was unaware of his consciousness. There was darkness everywhere, on all sides. He lay awake for an hour with his eyes wide before he realized they were open.

Experimentally, he moved first his arms and his legs, then his head. He wasn't bound as he'd expected, except by his ankle. There was definitely a chain or something similar around his left ankle. It chafed his skin when he tried to move too far.

The floor beneath him was very uncomfortable, and when he investigated it more closely with the palm of his hand he realized he was lying on a huge grille or grid of some kind. It was metal, and its regular surface spread in every direction as far as his arms would reach. When he poked his arm down through the holes in this lattice he touched nothing. Just empty air falling away beneath him.

The first infra-red photographs Quaid took of Stephen's confinement pictured his exploration. As Quaid had expected the subject was being quite rational about his situation. No hysterics. No curses. No tears. That was the challenge of this particular subject. He knew precisely what was going on; and he would respond logically to his fears. That would surely make a more difficult mind to break than Cheryl's.

But how much more rewarding the results would be when he did crack. Would his soul not open up then, for Quaid to see and touch? There was so much there, in the man's interior, he wanted to study.

Gradually Steve's eyes became accustomed to the darkness.

He was imprisoned in what appeared to be some kind of shaft. It was, he estimated, about twenty feet wide, and completely round. Was it some kind of air-shaft, for a tunnel, or an underground factory? Steve's mind mapped the area around Pilgrim Street, trying to pinpoint the most likely place for Quaid to have taken him. He could think of nowhere.

Nowhere.

He was lost in a place he couldn't fix or recognize. The shaft had no corners to focus his eyes on; and the walls offered no crack or hole to hide his consciousness in.

Worse, he was lying spreadeagled on a grid that hung over this shaft. His eyes could make no impression on the darkness beneath him: it seemed that the shaft might be bottomless. And there was only the thin network of the grill, and the fragile chain that shackled his ankle to it, between him and falling.

He pictured himself poised under an empty black sky, and over an infinite darkness. The air was warm and stale. It dried up the tears that had suddenly sprung to his eyes, leaving them gummy. When he began to shout for help, which he did after the tears had passed, the darkness ate his words easily.

Having yelled himself hoarse, he lay back on the lattice. He couldn't help but imagine that beyond his frail bed, the darkness went on forever. It was absurd, of course. Nothing goes on forever, he said aloud.

Nothing goes on forever.

And yet, he'd never know. If he fell in the absolute blackness beneath him, he'd fall and fall and fall and not see the bottom of the shaft coming. Though he tried to think of brighter, more positive, images, his mind conjured his body cascading down this horrible shaft, with the bottom a foot from his hurtling body and his eyes not seeing it, his brain not predicting it.

Until he hit.

Would he see light as his head was dashed open on impact? Would he understand, in the moment that his body became offal, why he'd lived and died?

Then he thought: Quaid wouldn't dare. 'Wouldn't dare!' he screeched. 'Wouldn't dare!'

The dark was a glutton for words. As soon as he'd yelled into it, it was as though he'd never made a sound.

And then another thought: a real baddie. Suppose Quaid had found this circular hell to put him in because it would *never* be found, *never* be investigated? Maybe he wanted to take his experiment to the limits.

To the limits. Death was at the limits. And wouldn't that be the ultimate experiment for Quaid? Watching a man die: watching the fear of death, the motherlode of dread, approach. Sartre had written that no man could ever know his own death. But to know the deaths of others, intimately – to watch the acrobatics that the mind would surely perform to avoid the bitter truth –

that was a clue to death's nature, wasn't it? That might, in some small way, prepare a man for his own death. To live another's dread vicariously was the safest, cleverest way to touch the beast.

Yes, he thought, Quaid might kill me; out of his own terror.

Steve took a sour satisfaction in that thought. That Quaid, the impartial experimenter, the would-be educator, was obsessed with terrors because his own dread ran deepest.

That was why he had to watch others deal with their fears. He needed a solution, a way out for himself.

Thinking all this through took hours. In the darkness Steve's mind was quick-silver, but uncontrollable. He found it difficult to keep one train of argument for very long. His thoughts were like fish, small, fast fish, wriggling out of his grasp as soon as he took a hold of them.

But underlying every twist of thought was the knowledge that he must out-play Quaid. That was certain. He must be calm; prove himself a useless subject for Quaid's analysis.

The photographs of these hours showed Stephen lying with his eyes closed on the grid, with a slight frown on his face. Occasionally, paradoxically, a smile would flit across his lips. Sometimes it was impossible to know if he was sleeping or waking, thinking or dreaming.

Quaid waited.

Eventually Steve's eyes began to flicker under his lids, the unmistakable sign of dreaming. It was time, while the subject slept, to turn the wheel of the rack –

Steve woke with his hands cuffed together. He could see a bowl of water on a plate beside him; and a second bowl, full of luke-warm unsalted porridge, beside it. He ate and drank thankfully.

As he ate, two things registered. First, that the noise of his eating seemed very loud in his head; and second, that he felt a construction, a tightness, around his temples.

The photographs show Stephen clumsily reaching up to his head. A harness is strapped on to him, and locked in place. It clamps plugs deep into his ears, preventing any sound from getting in.

The photographs show puzzlement. Then anger. Then fear.

Steve was deaf.

All he could hear were the noises in his head. The clicking of his teeth. The slush and swallow of his palate. The sounds boomed between his ears like guns.

Tears sprang to his eyes. He kicked at the grid, not hearing the clatter of his heels on the metal bars. He screamed until his throat felt as if it was bleeding. He heard none of his cries.

Panic began in him.

The photographs showed its birth. His face was flushed. His eyes were wide, his teeth and gums exposed in a grimace.

He looked like a frightened monkey.

All the familiar, childhood feelings swept over him. He remembered them like the faces of old enemies; the chittering limbs, the sweat, the nausea. In desperation he picked up the bowl of water and upturned it over his face. The shock of the cold water diverted his mind momentarily from the panic-ladder it was climbing. He lay back down on the grid, his body a board, and told himself to breathe deeply and evenly.

Relax, relax, relax, he said aloud.

In his head, he could hear his tongue clicking. He could hear his mucus too, moving sluggishly in the panic-constricted passages of his nose, blocking and unblocking in his ears. Now he could detect the low, soft hiss that waited under all the other noises. The sound of his mind –

It was like the white noise between stations on the radio, this was the same whine that came to fetch him under anaesthetic, the same noise that would sound in his ears on the borders of sleep.

His limbs still twitched nervously, and he was only half-aware of the way he wrestled with his handcuffs, indifferent to their edges scouring the skin at his wrists.

The photographs recorded all these reactions precisely. His war with hysteria: his pathetic attempts to keep the fears from resurfacing. His tears. His bloody wrists.

Eventually, exhaustion won over panic; as it had so often as a child. How many times had he fallen asleep with the salt-taste of tears in his nose and mouth, unable to fight any longer?

The exertion had heightened the pitch of his head-noises. Now, instead of a lullaby, his brain whistled and whooped him to sleep.

Oblivion was good.

Quaid was disappointed. It was clear from the speed of his response that Stephen Grace was going to break very soon indeed. In fact, he was as good as broken, only a few hours into the experiment. And Quaid had been relying on Stephen. After months of preparing the ground, it seemed that this subject was going to lose his mind without giving up a single clue.

One word, one miserable word was all Quaid needed. A little sign as to the nature of the experience. Or better still, something to suggest a solution, a healing totem, a prayer even. Surely some Saviour comes to the lips, as the personality is swept away in madness? There must be *something*.

Quaid waited like a carrion bird at the site of some atrocity, counting the minutes left to the expiring soul, hoping for a morsel.

Steve woke face down on the grid. The air was much staler now, and the metal bars bit into the flesh of his cheek. He was hot and uncomfortable.

He lay still, letting his eyes become accustomed to his surroundings again. The lines of the grid ran off in perfect perspective to meet the wall of the shaft. The simple network of criss-crossed bars struck him as pretty. Yes, pretty. He traced the lines back and forth,' 'til he tired of the game. Bored, he rolled over onto his back, feeling the grid vibrate under his body. Was it less stable now? It seemed to rock a little as he moved.

Hot and sweaty, Steve unbuttoned his shirt. There was sleep-spittle on his chin but he didn't care to wipe it off. What if he drooled? Who was to see?

He half pulled off his shirt, and using one foot, kicked his shoe off the other.

Shoe: lattice: fall. Sluggishly, his mind made the connection. He sat up. Oh poor shoe. His shoe would fall. It would slip between the bars and be lost. But no. It was finely balanced across two sides of a lattice-hole; he could still save it if he tried.

He reached for his poor, poor shoe, and his movement shifted the grid.

The shoe began to slip.

'Please,' he begged it, 'don't fall.' He didn't want to lose his nice shoe, his pretty shoe. It mustn't fall. It mustn't fall.

As he stretched to snatch it, the shoe tipped, heel down, through the grid and fell into the darkness.

He let out a cry of loss that he couldn't hear.

Oh, if only he could listen to the shoe falling; to count the seconds of its descent. To hear it thud home at the bottom of the shaft. At least then he'd know how far he had to fall to his death.

He couldn't endure it any longer. He rolled over on to his stomach and thrust both arms through the grid, screaming:

'I'll go too! I'll go too!'

He couldn't bear waiting to fall, in the dark, in the whining silence, he just wanted to follow his shoe down, down, down the dark shaft to extinction, and have the whole game finished once and for all.

'I'll go! I'll go! I'll go!' he shrieked. He pleaded with gravity. Beneath him, the grid moved.

Something had broken. A pin, a chain, a rope that held the grid in position had snapped. He was no longer horizontal; already he was sliding across the bars as they tipped him off into the dark.

With shock he realized his limbs were no longer chained.

He would fall.

The man wanted him to fall. The bad man – what was his name? Quake? Quail? Quarrel –

Automatically he siezed the grid with both hands as it tipped even further over. Maybe he didn't want to fall after his shoe, after all? Maybe life, a little moment more of life, was worth holding on to –

The dark beyond the edge of the grid was so deep; and who could guess what lurked in it?

In his head the noises of his panic multiplied. The thumping of his bloody heart, the stutter of his mucus, the dry rasp of his palate. His palms, slick with sweat, were losing their grip. Gravity wanted him. It demanded its rights of his body's bulk: demanded that he fall. For a moment, glancing over his shoulder at the mouth that opened under him, he thought he saw monsters stirring below him. Ridiculous, loony things, crudely drawn, dark on dark. Vile graffiti leered up from his childhood and uncurled their claws to snatch at his legs.

'Mama,' he said, as his hands failed him, and he was delivered into dread.

'*Mama.*'

That was the word. Quaid heard it plainly, in all its banality.

'Mama!'

By the time Steve hit the bottom of the shaft, he was past judging how far he'd fallen. The moment his hands let go of the grid, and he knew the dark would have him, his mind snapped. The animal self survived to relax his body, saving him all but minor injury on impact. The rest of his life, all but the simplest responses, were shattered, the pieces flung into the recesses of his memory.

When the light came, at last, he looked up at the person in the Mickey Mouse mask at the door, and smiled at him. It was a child's smile, one of thankfulness for his comical rescuer. He let the man take him by the ankles and haul him out of the big round room in which he was lying. His pants were wet, and he knew he'd dirtied himself in his sleep. Still, the Funny Mouse would kiss him better.

His head lolled on his shoulders as he was dragged out of the torture-chamber. On the floor beside his head was a shoe. And seven or eight feet above him was the grid from which he had fallen.

It meant nothing at all.

He let the Mouse sit him down in a bright room. He let the Mouse give him his ears back, though he didn't really want them. It was funny watching the world without sound, it made him laugh.

He drank some water, and ate some sweet cake.

He was tired. He wanted to sleep. He wanted his Mama. But the Mouse didn't seem to understand, so he cried, and kicked the table and threw the plates and cups on the floor. Then he ran into the next room, and threw all the papers he could find in the air. It was nice watching them flutter up and flutter down. Some of them fell face down, some face up. Some were covered with writing. Some were pictures. Horrid pictures. Pictures that made him feel very strange.

They were all pictures of dead people, every one of them. Some of the pictures were of little children, others were of grown-up children. They were lying down, or half-sitting, and there were big cuts in their faces and their bodies, cuts that showed a mess underneath, a mish-mash of shiny bits and oozy bits. And all around the dead people: black paint. Not in neat puddles, but splashed all around, and finger-marked, and hand-printed and very messy.

In three or four of the pictures the thing that made the cuts was still there. He knew the word for it.

Axe.

There was an axe in a lady's face buried almost to the handle. There was an axe in a man's leg, and another lying on the floor of a kitchen beside a dead baby.

This man collected pictures of dead people and axes, which Stevie thought was strange.

That was his last thought before the too-familiar scent of chloroform filled his head and he lost consciousness.

The sordid doorway smelt of old urine and fresh vomit. It was his own vomit; it was all over the front of his shirt. He tried to stand up, but his legs felt wobbly. It was very cold. His throat hurt.

Then he heard footsteps. It sounded like the Mouse was coming back. Maybe he'd take him home.

'Get up, son.'

It wasn't the Mouse. It was a policeman.

'What are you doing down there? I said get up.'

Bracing himself against the crumbling brick of the doorway Steve got to his feet. The policeman shone his torch at him.

'Jesus Christ,' said the policeman, disgust written over his face. 'You're in a right fucking state. Where do you live?'

Steve shook his head, staring down at his vomit-soaked shirt like a shamed schoolboy.

'What's your name?'

He couldn't quite remember.

'Name, lad?'

He was trying. If only the policeman wouldn't shout.

'Come on, take a hold of yourself.'

The words didn't make much sense. Steve could feel tears pricking the backs of his eyes.

'Home.'

Now he was blubbering, sniffing snot, feeling utterly forsaken. He wanted to die: he wanted to lie down and die.

The policeman shook him.

'You high on something?' he demanded, pulling Steve into the glare of the streetlights and staring at his tear-stained face.

'You'd better move on.'

'Mama,' said Steve, 'I want my Mama.'

The words changed the encounter entirely.

Suddenly the policeman found the spectacle more than disgusting; more than pitiful. This little bastard, with his bloodshot eyes and his dinner down his shirt was really getting on his nerves. Too much money, too much dirt in his veins, too little discipline.

'Mama' was the last straw. He punched Steve in the stomach, a neat, sharp, functional blow. Steve doubled up, whimpering.

'Shut up, son.'

Another blow finished the job of crippling the child, and then he took a fistful of Steve's hair and pulled the little druggy's face up to meet his.

'You want to be a derelict, is that it?'

'No. No.'

Steve didn't know what a derelict was; he just wanted to make the policeman like him.

'Please,' he said, tears coming again, 'take me home.'

The policeman seemed confused. The kid hadn't started fighting back and calling for civil rights, the way most of them did. That was the way they usually ended up: on the ground, bloody-nosed, calling for a social worker. This one just wept. The policeman began to get a bad feeling about the kid. Like he was mental or something. And he'd beaten the shit out of the little snot. Fuck it. Now he felt responsible. He took hold of Steve by the arm and bundled him across the road to his car.

'Get in.'

'Take me – '

'I'll take you home, son. I'll take you home.'

At the Night Hostel they searched Steve's clothes for some kind of identification, found none, then scoured his body for fleas, his hair for nits. The policeman left him then, which Steve was relieved about. He hadn't liked the man.

The people at the Hostel talked about him as though he wasn't in the room. Talked about how young he was; discussed his mental-age; his clothes; his appearance. Then they gave him a bar of soap and showed him the showers. He stood under the cold water for ten minutes and dried himself with a stained towel. He didn't shave, though they'd lent him a razor. He'd forgotten how to do it.

Then they gave him some old clothes, which he liked. They weren't such bad people, even if they did talk about him as though he wasn't there. One of them even smiled at him; a burly man with a grizzled beard. Smiled as he would at a dog.

They were odd clothes he was given. Either too big or too small. All colours: yellow socks, dirty white shirt, pin-stripe trousers that had been made for a glutton, a thread-bare sweater, heavy boots. He liked dressing up, putting on two vests and two pairs of socks when they weren't looking. He felt reassured with several thicknesses of cotton and wool wrapped around him.

Then they left him with a ticket for his bed in his hand, to wait for the dormitories to be unlocked. He was not impatient, like some of the men in the corridors with him. They yelled incoherently, many of them, their accusations laced with obscenities, and they spat at each other. It frightened him. All he wanted was to sleep. To lie down and sleep.

At eleven o'clock one of the warders unlocked the gate to the dormitory, and all the lost men filed through to find themselves an iron bed for the night. The dormitory, which was large and badly-lit, stank of disinfectant and old people.

Avoiding the eyes and the flailing arms of the other derelicts, Steve found himself an ill-made bed, with one thin blanket tossed across it, and lay down to sleep. All around him men were

29

coughing and muttering and weeping. One was saying his prayers as he lay, staring at the ceiling, on his grey pillow. Steve thought that was a good idea. So he said his own child's prayer.

'Gentle Jesus, meek and mild,
Look upon this little child,
Pity my –
What was the word?
Pity my – *simplicity*,
Suffer me to come to thee.'

That made him feel better; and the sleep, a balm, was blue and deep.

Quaid sat in darkness. The terror was on him again, worse than ever. His body was rigid with fear; so much so that he couldn't even get out of bed and snap on the light. Besides, what if this time, this time of all times, the terror was true? What if the axe-man was at the door in flesh and blood? Grinning like a loon at him, dancing like the devil at the top of the stairs, as Quaid had seen him, in dreams, dancing and grinning, grinning and dancing.

Nothing moved. No creak of the stair, no giggle in the shadows. It wasn't him, after all. Quaid would live 'til morning.

His body had relaxed a little now. He swung his legs out of bed and switched on the light. The room was indeed empty. The house was silent. Through the open door he could see the top of the stairs. There was no axe-man, of course.

Steve woke to shouting. It was still dark. He didn't know how long he'd been asleep, but his limbs no longer ached so badly. Elbows on his pillow, he half-sat up and stared down the dormitory to see what all the commotion was about. Four bed-rows down from his, two men were fighting. The bone of contention was by no means clear. They just grappled with each other like girls (it made Steve laugh to watch them), screeching and pulling each other's hair. By moonlight the blood on their faces and hands was black. One of them, the older of the two, was thrust back across his bed, screaming: 'I will not go to the Finchley Road! You will not make me. Don't strike me! I'm not your man! I'm not!'

The other was beyond listening; he was too stupid, or too mad, to understand that the old man was begging to be left alone. Urged on by spectators on every side, the old man's assailant had taken off his shoe and was belabouring his victim with it. Steve could hear the crack, crack of his blows: heel on head. There were cheers accompanying each strike, and lessening cries from the old man.

Suddenly, the applause faltered, as somebody came into the dormitory. Steve couldn't see who it was; the mass of men crowded around the fight were between him and the door.

He did see the victor toss his shoe into the air however, with a final shout of 'Fucker!'

The shoe.

Steve couldn't take his eyes off the shoe. It rose in the air, turning as it rose, then plummeted to the bare boards like a shot bird. Steve saw it clearly, more clearly than he'd seen anything in many days.

It landed not far from him.

It landed with a loud thud.

It landed on its side. As his shoe had landed. His shoe. The one he kicked off. On the grid. In the room. In the house. In Pilgrim Street.

Quaid woke with the same dream. Always the stairway. Always him looking down the tunnel of the stairs, while that ridiculous sight, half-joke, half-horror, tip-toed up towards him, a laugh on every step.

He'd never dreamt twice in one night before. He swung his hand out over the edge of the bed and fumbled for the bottle he kept there. In the dark he swigged from it, deeply.

Steve walked past the knot of angry men, not caring about their shouts or the old man's groans and curses. The warders were having a hard time dealing with the disturbance. It was the last time Old Man Crowley would be let in: he always invited violence. This had all the marks of a near-riot; it would take hours to settle them down again.

Nobody questioned Steve as he wandered down the corridor, through the gate, and into the vestibule of the Night Hostel. The swing doors were closed, but the night air, bitter before dawn, smelt refreshing as it seeped in.

The pokey reception office was empty, and through the door Steve could see the fire-extinguisher hanging on the wall. It was red and bright. Beside it was a long black hose, curled up on a red drum like a sleeping snake. Beside that, sitting in two brackets on the wall, was an axe.

A very pretty axe.

Stephen walked into the office. A little distance away he heard running feet, shouts, a whistle. But nobody came to interrupt Steve, as he made friends with the axe.

First he smiled at it.

The curve of the blade of the axe smiled back.

Then he touched it.

The axe seemed to like being touched. It was dusty, and hadn't been used in a long while. Too long. It wanted to be picked up, and stroked, and smiled at. Steve took it out of its brackets very gently, and slid it under his jacket to keep warm. Then he walked back out of the reception office, through the swing-doors and out to find his other shoe.

Quaid woke again.

It took Steve a very short time to orient himself. There was a spring in his step as he began to make his way to Pilgrim Street. He felt like a clown, dressed in so many bright colours, in such floppy trousers, such silly boots. He was a comical fellow, wasn't he? He made himself laugh, he was so comical.

The wind began to get into him, whipping him up into a frenzy as it scooted through his hair and made his eye-balls as cold as two lumps of ice in his sockets.

He began to run, skip, dance, cavort through the streets, white under the lights, dark in between. Now you see me, now you don't. Now you see me, now you –

Quaid hadn't been woken by the dream this time. This time he had heard a noise. Definitely a noise.

The moon had risen high enough to throw its beams through the window, through the door and on to the top of the stairs. There was no need to put on the light. All he needed to see, he could see. The top of the stairs were empty, as ever.

Then the bottom stair creaked, a tiny noise as though a breath had landed on it.

Quaid knew dread then.

Another creak, as it came up the stairs towards him, the ridiculous dream. It had to be a dream. After all, he knew no clowns, no axe-killers. So how could that absurd image, the same image that woke him night after night, be anything but a dream?

Yet, perhaps there were some dreams so preposterous they could only be true.

No clowns, he said to himself, as he stood watching the door, and the stairway, and the spotlight of the moon. Quaid knew only fragile minds, so weak they couldn't give him a clue to the nature, to the origin, or to the cure for the panic that now held him in thrall. All they did was break, crumble into dust, when faced with the slightest sign of the dread at the heart of life.

He knew no clowns, never had, never would.

Then it appeared; the face of a fool. Pale to whiteness in the light of the moon, its young features bruised, unshaven and puffy, its smile open like a child's smile. It had bitten its lip in its excitement. Blood was smeared across its lower jaw, and its gums were almost black with blood. Still it was a clown. Indisputably a clown even to its ill-fitting clothes, so incongruous, so pathetic.

Only the axe didn't quite match the smile.

It caught the moonlight as the maniac made small, chopping motions with it, his tiny black eyes glinting with anticipation of the fun ahead.

Almost at the top of the stairs, he stopped, his smile not faltering for a moment as he gazed at Quaid's terror.

Quaid's legs gave out, and he stumbled to his knees.

The clown climbed another stair, skipping as he did so, his glittering eyes fixed on Quaid, filled with a sort of benign malice. The axe rocked back and forth in his white hands, in a petite version of the killing stroke.

Quaid knew him.

It was his pupil: his guinea-pig, transformed into the image of his own dread.

Him. Of all men. Him. The deaf boy.

The skipping was bigger now, and the clown was making a deep-throated noise, like the call of some fantastical bird. The axe was describing wider and wider sweeps in the air, each more lethal than the last.

'Stephen,' said Quaid.

The name meant nothing to Steve. All he saw was the mouth opening. The mouth closing. Perhaps a sound came out: perhaps not. It was irrelevant to him.

The throat of the clown gave out a screech, and the axe swung up over his head, two-handed. At the same moment the merry little dance became a run, as the axeman leapt the last two stairs and ran into the bedroom, full into the spotlight.

Quaid's body half turned to avoid the killing blow, but not quickly or elegantly enough. The blade slit the air and sliced through the back of Quaid's arm, sheering off most of his

33

triceps, shattering his humerus and opening the flesh of his lower arm in a gash that just missed his artery.

Quaid's scream could have been heard ten houses away, except that those houses were rubble. There was nobody to hear. Nobody to come and drag the clown off him.

The axe, eager to be about its business, was hacking at Quaid's thigh now, as though it was chopping a log. Yawning wounds four or five inches deep exposed the shiny steak of the philosopher's muscle, the bone, the marrow. With each stroke the clown would tug at the axe to pull it out, and Quaid's body would jerk like a puppet.

Quaid screamed. Quaid begged. Quaid cajoled.

The clown didn't hear a word.

All he heard was the noise in his head: the whistles, the whoops, the howls, the hums. He had taken refuge where no rational argument, not threat, would ever fetch him out again. Where the thump of his heart was law, and the whine of his blood was music.

How he danced, this deaf-boy, danced like a loon to see his tormentor gaping like a fish, the depravity of his intellect silenced forever. How the blood spurted! How it gushed and fountained!

The little clown laughed to see such fun. There was a night's entertainment to be had here, he thought. The axe was his friend forever, keen and wise. It could cut, and cross-cut, it could slice and amputate, yet still they could keep this man alive, if they were cunning enough, alive for a long, long while.

Steve was happy as a lamb. They had the rest of the night ahead of them, and all the music he could possibly want was sounding in his head.

And Quaid knew, meeting the clown's vacant stare through an air turned bloody, that there was worse in the world than dread. Worse than death itself.

There was pain without hope of healing. There was life that refused to end, long after the mind had begged the body to cease. And worst, there were dreams come true.

Hell's Event

Hell came up to the streets and squares of London that September, icy from the depths of the Ninth Circle, too frozen to be warmed even by the swelter of an Indian summer. It had laid its plans as carefully as ever, plans being what they were, and fragile. This time it was perhaps a little more finicky than usual, checking every last detail twice or three times, to be certain it had every chance of winning this vital game.

It had never lacked competitive spirit; it had matched fire against flesh a thousand thousand times down the centuries, sometimes winning, more often losing. Wagers were, after all, the stuff of its advancement. Without the human urge to compete, to bargain, and to bet, Pandemonium might well have fallen for want of citizens. Dancing, dog racing, fiddle-playing: it was all one to the gulfs; all a game in which it might, if it played with sufficient wit, garner a soul or two. That was why Hell came up to London that bright blue day: to run a race, and to win, if it could, enough souls to keep it busy with perdition another age.

Cameron tuned his radio; the voice of the commentator flared and faded as though he was speaking from the Pole instead of St Paul's Cathedral. It was still a good half-hour before the race began, but Cameron wanted to listen to the warm-up commentary, just to hear what they were saying about his boy.

'. . . atmosphere is electric . . . probably tens of thousands along the route . . .'

The voice disappeared: Cameron cursed, and toyed with the dial until the imbecilities reappeared.

'. . . been called the race of the year, and what a day it is! Isn't it, Jim?'

'It certainly is, Mike – '

'That's big Jim Delaney, who's up there in the Eye in the Sky, and he'll be following the race along the route, giving us a bird's eye view, won't you, Jim?'

'I certainly will, Mike – '

'Well, there's a lot of activity behind the line, the competitors are all loosening up for the start. I can see Nick Loyer there, he's wearing number three, and I must say he's looking very fit. He said to me when he arrived he didn't usually like to run on Sundays, but he's made an exception for this race, because of course it's a charity event, and all the proceeds will be going to Cancer Research. Joel Jones, our Gold Medallist in the 800 metres is here, and he'll be running against his great rival Frank McCloud. And besides the big boys we've got a smattering of new faces. Wearing number five, the South African, Malcolm Voight, and completing the field Lester Kinderman, who was of course the surprise winner of the marathon in Austria last year. And I must say they all look fresh as daisies on this superb September afternoon. Couldn't ask for a better day, could we Jim?'

Joel had woken with bad dreams.

'You'll be fine, stop fretting,' Cameron had told him.

But he didn't feel fine; he felt sick in the pit of his stomach. Not pre-race nerves; he was used to those, and he could deal with the feeling. Two fingers down the throat and throw up, that was the best remedy he'd found; get it over and done with. No, this wasn't pre-race nerves, or anything like them. It was deeper, for a start, as though his bowels, to his centre, to his source, were cooking.

Cameron had no sympathy.

'It's a charity race, not the Olympics,' he said, looking the boy over. 'Act your age.'

That was Cameron's technique. His mellow voice was made for coaxing, but was used to bully. Without that bullying there would have been no gold medal, no cheering crowds, no admiring girls. One of the tabloids had voted Joel the best loved black face in England. It was good to be greeted as a friend by people he'd never met; he liked the admiration, however short-lived it might turn out to be.

'They love you,' said Cameron. 'God knows why – they love you.'

Then he laughed, his little cruelty over.

'You'll be all right, son,' he said. 'Get out and run for your life.'

Now, in the broad daylight, Joel looked at the rest of the field and felt a little more buoyant. Kinderman had stamina, but he had no finishing power over middle-distance. Marathon technique was a different skill altogether. Besides he was so short-sighted he wore wire-rimmed glasses so thick they gave him the look of a bemused frog. No danger there. Loyer; he was good, but this wasn't really his distance either. He was a hurdler, and a sometime sprinter. 400 metres was his limit and even then he wasn't happy. Voight, the South African. Well, there was not much information on him. Obviously a fit man to judge by the look of him, and someone to watch out for just in case he sprung a surprise. But the real problem of the race was McCloud. Joel had run against Frank 'Flash' McCloud three times. Twice beaten him into second place, once (painfully) had the positions reversed. And Frankie boy had a few scores to settle: especially the Olympics defeat; he hadn't liked taking the silver. Frank was the man to watch. Charity race or no charity race McCloud would be running his best, for the crowd and for his pride. He was at the line already testing his starting position, his ears practically pricked. Flash was the man, no doubt of it.

For a moment Joel caught Voight staring at him. Unusual that. Competitors seldom even glanced at each other before a race, it was a kind of coyness. The man's face was pale, and his hair-line was receding. He looked to be in his early thirties, but had a younger, leaner physique. Long legs, big hands. A body somehow out of proportion to his head. When their eyes met, Voight looked away. The fine chain around his neck caught the sun and the crucifix he was wearing glinted gold as it swung gently beneath his chin.

Joel had his good-luck charm with him too. Tucked into the waistband of his shorts, a lock of his mother's hair, which she had plaited for him half a decade ago, before his first major race. She had returned to Barbados the following year, and died there. A great grief: an unforgettable loss. Without Cameron, he would have crumbled.

Cameron watched the preparations from the steps of the Cathedral; he planned to see the start, then ride his bike round the back of the Strand to catch the finish. He'd arrive well before the competitors, and he could keep up with the race on his radio. He felt good with the day. His boy was in fine shape, nausea or no nausea, and the race was an ideal way to keep the lad in a competitive mood without over-stretching him. It was quite a distance of course, across Ludgate Circus, along Fleet Street and past Temple Bar into the Strand, then cutting across the corner of Trafalgar and down Whitehall to the Houses of Parliament. Running on tarmac too. But it was good experience for Joel, and it would pressure him a little, which was useful. There was a distance runner in the boy, and Cameron knew it. He'd never been a sprinter, he couldn't pace himself accurately enough. He needed distance and time, to find his pulse, to settle down and to work out his tactics. Over 800 metres the boy was a natural: his stride was a model of economy, his rhythm damn-near perfect. But more, he had courage. Courage had won him the gold, and courage would take him first to the finish again and again. That's what made Joel different. Any number of technical whizz-kids came and went, but without courage to supplement those skills they went for almost nothing. To risk when it was worth risking, to run 'til the pain blinded you, that was special and Cameron knew it. He liked to think he'd had a little of it himself.

Today, the boy looked less than happy. Women trouble was Cameron's bet. There were always problems with women, especially with the golden boy reputation Joel had garnered. He'd tried to explain that there'd be plenty of time for bed and bawd when his career had run out of steam, but Joel wasn't interested in celibacy, and Cameron didn't altogether blame him.

The pistol was raised, and fired. A plume of blue-white smoke followed by a sound more pop than bang. The shot woke the pigeons from the dome of St Paul's and they rose in a chattering congregation, their worship interrupted.

Joel was off to a good start. Clean, neat and fast.

The crowd began to call his name immediately, their voices at his back, at his side, a gale of loving enthusiasm.

Cameron watched the first two dozen yards, as the field jockeyed for a running order. Loyer was at the front of the pack, though Cameron wasn't sure whether he'd got there by choice or chance. Joel was behind McCloud, who was behind Loyer. No hurry, boy, said Cameron, and slipped away from the starting line. His bicycle was chained up in Paternoster Row, a minute's walk from the square. He'd always hated cars: godless things, crippling, inhuman, unChristian things. With a bike you were your own master. Wasn't that all a man could ask?

' – And it's a superb start here, to what looks like a potentially marvellous race. They're already across the square and the crowd's going wild here: it really is more like the European Games than a Charity Race. What does it look like to you, Jim?'

'Well Mike, I can see crowds lining the route all the way along Fleet Street: and I've been asked by the police to tell people please not to try and drive down to see the race, because of course all these roads have been cleared for the event, and if you try and drive, really you'll get nowhere.'

'Who's got the lead at the moment?'

'Well, Nick Loyer is really setting the pace at this stage in the game, though of course as we know there's going to be a lot of tactical running over this kind of distance. It's more than a middle-distance, and it's less than a marathon, but these men are all tacticians, and they'll each be trying to let the other make the running in the early stages.'

Cameron always said: let the others be heroes.

That was a hard lesson to learn, Joel had found. When the pistol was fired it was difficult not to go for broke, unwind suddenly like a tight spring. All gone in the first two hundred yards and nothing left in reserve.

It's easy to be a hero, Cameron used to say. It's not clever, it's not clever at all. Don't waste your time showing off, just let the Supermen have their moment. Hang on to the pack, but hold back a little. Better to be cheered at the post because you won than have them call you a good-hearted loser.

Win. Win. Win.

At all costs. At *almost* all costs.

Win.

The man who doesn't want to win is no friend of mine, he'd say. If you want to do it for the love of it, for the sport of it, do it with somebody else. Only public schoolboys believe that crap about the joy of playing the game. There's no joy for losers, boy. What did I say?

There's no joy for losers.

Be barbaric. Play the rules, but play them to the limit. As far as you can push, push. Let no other sonofabitch tell you differently. You're here to win. What did I say?

Win.

In Paternoster Row the cheering was muted, and the shadows of the buildings blocked the sun. It was almost cold. The pigeons still passed over, unable to settle now they'd been roused from their roost. They were the only occupants of the back streets. The rest of the living world, it seemed, was watching this race.

Cameron unlocked his bicycle, pocketed the chain and pad-locks, and hopped on. Pretty healthy for a fifty year old he thought, despite the addiction to cheap cigars. He switched on the radio. Reception was bad, walled in by the buildings; all crackle. He stood astride his bike and tried to improve the tuning. It did a little good.

' – and Nick Loyer is falling behind already – '

That was quick. Mind you, Loyer was past his prime by two or three years. Time to throw in the spikes and let the younger men take over. He'd had to do it, though my God it had been painful. Cameron remembered acutely how he'd felt at thirty-three, when he realized that his best running years were over. It was like having one foot buried in the grave, a salutory reminder of how quickly the body blooms and begins to wither.

As he pedalled out of the shadows into a sunnier street a black Mercedes, chauffeur-driven, sailed past, so quietly it could have been wind-propelled. Cameron caught sight of the passengers only briefly. One he recognized as a man Voight had been talking with before the race, a thin faced individual of about forty, with a mouth so tight his lips might have been surgically removed.

Beside him sat Voight.

Impossible as it seemed it was Voight's face that glanced back out of the smoked glass windows; he was even dressed for the race.

Cameron didn't like the look of this at all. He'd seen the South African five minutes earlier, off and running. So who was this? A double obviously. It smelt of a fix, somehow; it stank to high heaven.

The Mercedes was already disappearing around a corner. Cameron turned off the radio and pedalled pell-mell after the car. The balmy sun made him sweat as he rode.

The Mercedes was threading its way through the narrow streets with some difficulty, ignoring all the One Way signs as it went. Its slow passage made it relatively easy for Cameron to keep the vehicle in view without being seen by its occupants, though the effort was beginning to light a fire in his lungs.

In a tiny, nameless alley just west of Fetter Lane, where the shadows were particularly dense, the Mercedes stopped. Cameron, hidden from view round a corner not twenty yards from the car, watched as the door was opened by the chauffeur and the lipless man, with the Voight lookalike close behind, stepped out and went into a nondescript building. When all three had disappeared Cameron propped his bike up against the wall and followed.

The street was pin-drop hushed. From this distance the roar of the crowd was only a murmur. It could have been another world, this street. The flitting shadows of birds, the windows of the buildings bricked up, the peeling paint, the rotten smell in the still air. A dead rabbit lay in the gutter, a black rabbit with a white collar, someone's lost pet. Flies rose and fell on it, alternately startled and ravenous.

Cameron crept towards the open door as quietly as he was able.

He had, as it turned out, nothing to fear. The trio had disappeared down the dark hallway of the house long since. The air was cool in the hall, and smelt of damp. Looking fearless, but feeling afraid, Cameron entered the blind building. The wallpaper in the hallway was shit-coloured, the paint the same. It was like walking into a bowel; a dead man's bowel, cold and shitty. Ahead, the stairway had collapsed, preventing access to the upper storey. They had not gone up, but down.

The door to the cellar was adjacent to the defunct staircase, and Cameron could hear voices from below.

No time like the present, he thought, and opened the door sufficiently to squeeze into the dark beyond. It was icy. Not just cold, not damp, but refrigerated. For a moment he thought he'd stepped into a cold storage room. His breath became a mist at his lips: his teeth wanted to chatter.

Can't turn back now, he thought, and started down the frost-slick steps. It wasn't impossibly dark. At the bottom of the flight, a long way down, a pale light flickered, its uninspired glow aspiring to the day. Cameron glanced longingly round at the open door behind him. It looked extremely tempting, but he was curious, so curious. There was nothing to do but descend.

In his nostrils the scent of the place teased. He had a lousy sense of smell, and a worse palate, as his wife was fond of reminding him. She'd say he couldn't distinguish between garlic and a rose, and it was probably true. But the smell in this deep meant something to him, something that stirred the acid in his belly into life.

Goats. It smelt, ha, he wanted to tell her then and there how he'd remembered, it smelt of goats.

He was almost at the bottom of the stairs, twenty, maybe thirty, feet underground. The voices were still some distance away, behind a second door.

He was standing in a little chamber, its walls badly white-washed and scrawled with obscene graffiti, mostly pictures of the sex-act. On the floor, a candelabra, seven forked. Only two of the dingy candles were lit, and they burned with a guttering flame that was almost blue. The goaty smell was stronger now: and mingled with a scent so sickly-sweet it belonged in a Turkish brothel.

Two doors led off the chamber, and from behind one Cameron heard the conversation continuing. With scrupulous caution he crossed the slippery floor to the door, straining to make sense of the murmuring voices. There was an urgency in them.

'– hurry –'
'– the right skills –'
'children, children –'
Laughter.
'I believe we – tomorrow – all of us –'
Laughter again.

Suddenly the voices seemed to change direction, as if the speakers were moving back towards the door. Cameron took three steps back across the icy floor, almost colliding with the candelabra. The flames spat and whispered in the chamber as he passed.

He had to choose either the stairs or the other door. The stairs represented utter retreat. If he climbed them he'd be safe, but he would never know. Never know why the cold, why the blue flames, why the smell of goats. The door was a chance. Back to it, his eyes on the door opposite, he fought with the bitingly cold brass handle. It turned with some tussling, and he ducked out of sight as the door opposite opened. The two movements were perfectly syncopated: God was with him.

Even as he closed the door he knew he'd made an error. God wasn't with him at all.

Needles of cold penetrated his head, his teeth, his eyes, his fingers. He felt as though he'd been thrown naked into the heart of an iceberg. His blood seemed to stand still in his veins: the spit on his tongue crystallized: the mucus on the lining of his nose pricked as it turned to ice. The cold seemed to cripple him: he couldn't even turn round.

Barely able to move his joints, he fumbled for his cigarette lighter with fingers so numb they could have been cut off without him feeling it.

The lighter was already glued to his hand, the sweat on his fingers had turned to frost. He tried to ignite it, against the dark, against the cold. Reluctantly it sparked into a spluttering half-life.

The room was large: an ice-cavern. Its walls, its encrusted roof, sparkled and shone. Stalactites of ice, lance-sharp, hung over his head. The floor on which he stood, poised uncertainly, was raked towards a hole in the middle of the room. Five or six feet across, its edges and walls were so lined with ice it seemed as though a river had been arrested as it poured down into the darkness.

He thought of *Xanadu*, a poem he knew by heart. Visions of another Albion –

> 'Where Alph the sacred river ran,
> Through caverns measureless to man,
> Down to a sunless sea.'

If there was indeed a sea down there, it was a frozen sea. It was death forever.

It was as much as he could do to keep upright, to prevent himself from sliding down the incline towards the unknown. The lighter flickered as an icy air blew it out.

'Shit,' said Cameron as he was plunged into darkness.

Whether the word alerted the trio outside, or whether God deserted him totally at that moment and invited them to open the door, he would never know. But as the door swung wide it pushed Cameron off his feet. Too numb and too frozen to prevent his fall he collapsed to the ice floor as the smell of the goat wafted into the room.

Cameron half turned. Voight's double was at the door, as was the chauffeur, and the third man in the Mercedes. He wore a coat apparently made of several goat-skins. The hooves and the horns still hung from it. The blood on its fur was brown and gummy.

'What are you doing here, Mr Cameron?' asked the goat-coated man.

Cameron could barely speak. The only feeling left in his head was a pin-point of agony in the middle of his forehead.

'What the hell is going on?' he said, through lips almost too frozen to move.

'Precisely that, Mr Cameron,' the man replied. 'Hell is going on.'

As they ran past St Mary-le-Strand, Loyer glanced behind him, and stumbled. Joel, a full three metres behind the leaders, knew the man was giving up. So quickly too; there was something amiss. He slackened his pace, letting McCloud and Voight pass him. No great hurry. Kinderman was quite a way behind, unable to compete with these fast boys. He was the tortoise in this race, for sure. Loyer was overtaken by McCloud, then Voight, and finally Jones and Kinderman. His breath had suddenly deserted him, and his legs felt like lead. Worse, he was seeing the tarmac under his running shoes creaking and cracking, and fingers, like loveless children, seeking up out of the ground to touch him. Nobody else was seeing them, it seemed. The crowds just roared on, while these illusory hands broke out of their tarmac graves and secured a hold on him. He collapsed into their dead arms exhausted, his youth broken and his strength spent. The enquiring fingers of the dead continued to pluck at him, long after the doctors had removed him from the track, examined him and sedated him.

He knew why, of course, lying there on the hot tarmac while they had their pricking way with him. He'd looked behind him. That's what had made them come. He'd looked –

'And after Loyer's sensational collapse, the race is open wide. Frank the Flash McCloud is setting the pace now, and he's really speeding away from the new boy, Voight. Joel Jones is even further behind, he doesn't seem to be keeping up with the leaders at all. What do you think, Jim?'

'Well he's either pooped already, or he's really taking a chance that they'll exhaust themselves. Remember he's new over this distance – '

'Yes, Jim – '

'And that might make him careless. Certainly he's going to have to do a lot of work to improve on his present position in third place.'

Joel felt giddy. For a moment, as he'd watched Loyer begin to lose his grip on the race, he'd heard the man praying out loud. Praying to God to save him. He'd been the only one who heard the words –

> 'Yea, though I walk through the
> shadows of the Valley of Death I shall
> fear no evil, for thou art with
> me, thy rod and thy staff they – '

The sun was hotter now, and Joel was beginning to feel the familiar voices of his tiring limbs. Running on tarmac was hard on the feet, hard on the joints. Not that that would make a man take to praying. He tried to put Loyer's desperation out of his mind, and concentrate on the matter in hand.

There was still a lot of running to do, the race was not even half over. Plenty of time to catch up with the heroes: plenty of time.

As he ran, his brain idly turned over the prayers his mother had taught him in case he should need one, but the years had eroded them: they were all but gone.

'My name,' said the goat-coated man, 'is Gregory Burgess. Member of Parliament. You wouldn't know me. I try to keep a low profile.'

'MP?' said Cameron.

'Yes. Independent. *Very* independent.'

'Is that Voight's brother?'

Burgess glanced at Voight's other self. He was not even shivering in the intense cold, despite the fact that he was only wearing a thin singlet and shorts.

'Brother?' Burgess said. 'No, no. He is my – what is the word? Familiar.'

The word rang a bell, but Cameron wasn't well-read. What was a familiar?

'Show him,' said Burgess magnanimously.

Voight's face shook, the skin seeming to shrivel, the lips curling back from the teeth, the teeth melting into a white wax that poured down a gullet that was itself transfiguring into a column of shimmering silver. The face was no longer human, no longer even mammalian. It had become a fan of knives, their blades glistening in the candlelight through the door. Even as this bizarrerie became fixed, it started to change again, the knives melting and darkening, fur sprouting, eyes appearing and swelling to balloon size. Antennae leapt from this new head, mandibles were extruded from the pulp of transfiguration, and the head of a bee, huge and perfectly intricate, now sat on Voight's neck.

Burgess obviously enjoyed the display; he applauded with gloved hands.

'Familiars both,' he said, gesturing to the chauffeur, who had removed the cap, and let a welter of auburn hair fall to her shoulders. She was ravishingly beautiful, a face to give your life for. But an illusion, like the other. No doubt capable of infinite personae.

'They're both mine, of course,' said Burgess proudly.

'What?' was all Cameron could manage; he hoped it stood for all the questions in his head.

'I serve Hell, Mr Cameron. And in its turn Hell serves me.'

'Hell?'

'Behind you, one of the entrances to the Ninth Circle. You know your Dante, I presume?

"Lo! Dis; and lo! the place
Where thou hast need to arm thy heart with strength."

'Why are you here?'

'To run this race. Or rather my third familiar is already running the race. He will not be beaten this time. This time it is Hell's event, Mr Cameron, and we shall not be cheated of the prize.'

45

'Hell,' said Cameron again.

'You believe don't you? You're a good church-goer. Still pray before you eat, like any God-fearing soul. Afraid of choking on your dinner.'

'How do you know I pray?'

'Your wife told me. Oh, your wife was very informative about you, Mr Cameron, she really opened up to me. Very accommodating. A confirmed analist, after my attentions. She gave me so much . . . information. You're a good Socialist, aren't you, like your father.'

'Politics now – '

'Oh, politics is the hub of the issue, Mr Cameron. Without politics we're lost in a wilderness, aren't we? Even Hell needs order. Nine great circles: a pecking order of punishments. Look down; see for yourself.'

Cameron could feel the hole at his back: he didn't need to look.

'We stand for order, you know. Not chaos. That's just heavenly propaganda. And you know what we'll win?'

'It's a charity race.'

'Charity is the least of it. We're not running this race to save the world from cancer. We're running it for government.'

Cameron half-grasped the point.

'Government,' he said.

'Once every century this race is run from St Paul's to the Palace of Westminster. Often it has been run at the dead of night, unheralded, unapplauded. Today it is run in full sunshine, watched by thousands. But whatever the circumstance, it is always the same race. Your athletes, against one of ours. If you win, another hundred years of democracy. If we win . . . as we will . . . the end of the world as you know it.'

At his back Cameron felt a vibration. The expression on Burgess' face had abruptly changed; the confidence had become clouded, the smugness was instantly replaced by a look of nervous excitement.

'Well, well,' he said, his hands flapping like birds. 'It seems we are about to be visited by higher powers. How flattering – '

Cameron turned, and peered over the edge of the hole. It didn't matter how curious he was now. They had him; he may as well see all there was to see.

A wave of icy air blew up from the sunless circle and in the darkness of the shaft he could see a shape approaching. Its movement was steady, and its face was thrown back to look at the world.

Cameron could hear its breathing, see the wound of its features open and close in the murk, oily bone locking and unlocking like the face of a crab.

Burgess was on his knees, the two familiars flat on the floor to either side of him, faces to the ground.

Cameron knew he would have no other chance. He stood up, his limbs hardly in his control, and blundered towards Burgess, whose eyes were closed in reverent prayer. More by accident than intention his knee caught Burgess under the jaw as he passed, and the man was sent sprawling. Cameron's soles slid on the floor out of the ice-cavern and into the candlelit chamber beyond.

Behind him, the room was filling with smoke and sighs, and Cameron, like Lot's wife fleeing from the destruction of Sodom, glanced back just once to see the forbidden sight behind him.

It was emerging from the shaft, its grey bulk filling the hole, lit by some radiance from below. Its eyes, deep-set in the naked bone of its elephantine head, met Cameron's through the open door. They seemed to touch him like a kiss, entering his thoughts through his eyes.

He was not turned to salt. Pulling his curious glance away from the face, he skated across the ante-chamber and started to climb the stairs two and three at a time, falling and climbing, falling and climbing. The door was still ajar. Beyond it, daylight and the world.

He flung the door open and collapsed into the hallway, feeling the warmth already beginning to wake his frozen nerves. There was no noise on the stairs behind him: clearly they were too in awe of their fleshless visitor to follow him. He hauled himself along the wall of the hallway, his body wracked with shivers and chatterings.

Still they didn't follow.

Outside the day was blindingly bright, and he began to feel the exhilaration of escape. It was like nothing he'd ever felt before. To have been so close, yet survived. God had been with him after all.

He staggered along the road back to his bicycle, determined to stop the race, to tell the world –

His bike was untouched, its handlebars warm as his wife's arms.

As he hooked his leg over, the look he had exchanged with Hell caught fire. His body, ignorant of the heat in his brain, continued about its business for a moment, putting its feet on the pedals and starting to ride away.

Cameron felt the ignition in his head and knew he was dead. The look, the glance behind him –

Lot's wife.

Like Lot's stupid wife –

The lightning leapt between his ears: faster than thought.

His skull cracked, and the lightning, white-hot, shot out from the furnace of his brain. His eyes withered to black nuts in his sockets, he belched light from mouth and nostrils. The combustion turned him into a column of black flesh in a matter of seconds, without a flame or a wisp of smoke.

Cameron's body was completely incinerated by the time the bicycle careered off the road and crashed through the tailor's shop window, where it lay like a dummy, face down amongst the ashen suits. He, too, had looked back.

The crowds at Trafalgar Square were a seething mass of enthusiasm. Cheers, tears and flags. It was as though this little race had become something special for these people: a ritual the significance of which they could not know. Yet somewhere in them they understood the day was laden with sulphur, they sensed their lives stood on tiptoe to reach heaven. Especially the children. They ran along the route, shouting incoherent blessings, their faces squeezed up with their fears. Some called his name.

'Joel! Joel!'

Or did he imagine that? Had he imagined, too, the prayer from Loyer's lips, and the signs in the radiant faces of the babies held high to watch the runners pass?

As they turned into Whitehall Frank McCloud glanced confidentially over his shoulder and Hell took him.

It was sudden: it was simple.

He stumbled, an icy hand in his chest crushing the life out of him. Joel slowed as he approached the man. His face was purple: his lips foamy.

'McCloud,' he said, and stopped to stare in his great rival's thin face.

McCloud looked up at him from behind a veil of smoke that had turned his grey eyes ochre. Joel reached down to help him.

'Don't touch me,' McCloud growled. The filament vessels in his eyes bulged and bled.

'Cramp?' asked Joel. 'Is it cramp?'

'Run you bastard, run,' McCloud was saying at him, as the hand in his innards seized his life out. He was oozing blood

48

through the pores on his face now, weeping red tears. 'Run. And don't look back. For Christ's sake, *don't look back.*'

'What is it?'

'Run for your life!'

The words weren't requests but imperatives.

Run.

Not for gold or glory. Just to live.

Joel glanced up, suddenly aware that there was some huge-headed thing at his back, cold breath on his neck.

He picked up his heels and *ran.*

' – Well, things aren't going so well for the runners here, Jim. After Loyer going down so sensationally, now Frank McCloud has stumbled too. I've never seen anything quite like it. But he seems to have had a few words with Joel Jones as he ran past, so he must be OK.'

McCloud was dead by the time they put him in the ambulance, and putrefied by the following morning.

Joel ran. Jesus, did he run. The sun had become ferocious in his face, washing the colour out of the cheering crowds, out of the faces, out of the flags. Everything was one sheet of noise, drained of humanity.

Joel knew the feeling that was coming over him, the sense of dislocation that accompanied fatigue and over-oxygenation. He was running in a bubble of his own consciousness, thinking, sweating, suffering by himself, for himself, in the name of himself.

And it wasn't so bad, this being alone. Songs began to fill his head: snatches of hymns, sweet phrases from love-songs, dirty rhymes. His self idled, and his dream-mind, unnamed and fearless, took over.

Ahead, washed by the same white rain of light, was Voight. That was the enemy, that was the thing to be surpassed. Voight, with his shining crucifix rocking in the sun. He could do it, as long as he didn't look, as long as he didn't look –

Behind him.

Burgess opened the door of the Mercedes and climbed in. Time had been wasted: valuable time. He should be at the Houses of Parliament, at the finishing line, ready to welcome the runners home. There was a scene to play, in which he would pretend the mild and smiling face of democracy. And tomorrow? Not so mild.

His hands were clammy with excitement, and his pinstripe suit smelt of the goat-skin coat he was obliged to wear in the room. Still, nobody would notice; and even if they did what Englishman would be so impolite to mention that he smelt goaty?

He hated the Lower Chamber, the perpetual ice, that damn yawning hole with its distant sound of loss. But all that was over now. He'd made his oblations, he'd shown his utter and ceaseless adoration of the pit; now it was time to reap the rewards.

As they drove, he thought of his many sacrifices to ambition. At first, minor stuff: kittens and cockerels. Later, he was to discover how ridiculous they thought such gestures were. But at the beginning he'd been innocent: not knowing what to give or how to give it. They began to make their requirements clear as the years went by, and he, in time, learnt to practice the etiquette of selling his soul. His self mortifications were studiously planned and immaculately staged, though they had left him without nipples or the hope of children. It was worth the pain, though: the power came to him by degrees. A triple first at Oxford, a wife endowed beyond the dreams of priapism, a seat in Parliament, and soon, soon enough, the country itself.

The cauterized stumps of his thumbs ached, as they often did when he was nervous. Idly, he sucked on one.

' – Well we're now in the closing stages of what really has been one hell of a race, eh, Jim?'

'Oh yes, it's really been a revelation, hasn't it? Voight is really the outsider of the field; and here he is streaking away from the competition without much effort. Of course, Jones made the unselfish gesture of checking with Frank McCloud that he was indeed all right after that bad fall of his, and that put him behind.'

'It's lost the race for Jones really, hasn't it?'

'I think that's right. I think it lost the race for him.'

'This is a charity race, of course.'

'Absolutely. And in a situation like this it's not whether you win or lose – '

'It's how you play the game.'

'Right.'

'Right.'

'Well they're both in sight of the Houses of Parliament now as they come round the bend of Whitehall. And the crowds are cheering their boy on, but I really think it's a lost cause – '

'Mind you, he brought something special out of the bag in Sweden.'

'He did. He did.'
'Maybe he'll do it again.'

Joel ran, and the gap between himself and Voight was beginning to close. He concentrated on the man's back, his eyes boring into his shirt, learning his rhythm, looking for weaknesses.

There was a slowing there. The man was not as fast as he had been. An unevenness had crept into his stride, a sure sign of fatigue.

He could take him. With courage, he could take him . . .

And Kinderman. He'd forgotten about Kinderman. Without thinking, Joel glanced over his shoulder and looked behind him.

Kinderman was way back, still keeping his steady. Marathon runner's pace unchanged. But there was something else behind Joel: another runner, almost on his heels; ghostly, vast.

He averted his eyes and stared ahead, cursing his stupidity.

He was gaining on Voight with every pace. The man was really running out of steam, quite clearly. Joel knew he could take him for certain, if he worked at it. Forget his pursuer, whatever it was, forget everything except overtaking Voight.

But the sight at his back wouldn't leave his head.

'*Don't look back*': McCloud's words. Too late, he'd done it. Better to know then who this phantom was.

He looked again.

At first he saw nothing, just Kinderman jogging along. And then the ghost runner appeared once more and he knew what had brought McCloud and Loyer down.

It was no runner, living or dead. It wasn't even human. A smoky body, and yawning darkness for its head, it was Hell itself that was pressing on him.

'*Don't look back.*'

Its mouth, if mouth it was, was open. Breath so cold it made Joel gasp swirled around him. That was why Loyer had muttered prayers as he ran. Much good it had done him; death had come anyway.

Joel looked away, not caring to see Hell so close, trying to ignore the sudden weakness in his knees.

Now Voight, too, was glancing behind him. The look on his face was dark and uneasy: and Joel knew somehow that he belonged to Hell, that the shadow behind him was Voight's master.

'Voight, Voight. Voight. Voight – ' Joel expelled the word with every stride.

51

Voight heard his name being spoken.

'Black bastard,' he said aloud.

Joel's stride lengthened a little. He was within two metres of Hell's runner.

'Look . . . Behind . . . You,' said Voight.

'I see it.'

'It's . . . come . . . for . . . you.'

The words were mere melodrama: two-dimensional. *He* was master of his body wasn't he? And he was not afraid of darkness, he was painted in it. Wasn't that what made him less than human as far as so many people were concerned? Or more, more than human; bloodier, sweatier, fleshier. More arm, more leg, more head. More strength, more appetite. What could Hell do? Eat him? He'd taste foul on the palate. Freeze him? He was too hot-blooded, too fast, too living.

Nothing would take him, he was a barbarian with the manners of a gentleman.

Neither night nor day entirely.

Voight was suffering: his pain was in his torn breath, in the gangling rags of his stride. They were just fifty metres from the steps and the finishing line, but Voight's lead was being steadily eroded; each step brought the runners closer.

Then the bargains began.

'Listen . . . to . . . me.'

'What are you?'

'Power . . . I'll get you power . . . just . . . let . . . us . . . win.'

Joel was almost at his side now.

'Too late.'

His legs elated: his mind span with pleasure. Hell behind him: Hell beside him, what did he care? He could run.

He passed Voight, joints fluent: an easy machine.

'Bastard. Bastard. Bastard – ' the familiar was saying, his face contorted with the agonies of stress. And didn't that face flicker as Joel passed it by? Didn't its features seem to lose, momentarily, the illusion of being human?

Then Voight was falling behind him, and the crowds were cheering, and the colours were flooding back into the world. It was victory ahead. He didn't know for what cause, but victory nevertheless.

There was Cameron, he saw him now, standing on the steps beside a man Joel didn't know, a man in a pinstripe suit. Cameron was smiling and shouting with uncharacteristic enthusiasm, beckoning to Joel from the steps.

He ran, if anything, a little faster towards the finishing line, his strength coaxed by Cameron's face.

Then the face seemed to change. Was it the heat haze that made his hair shimmer? No, the flesh of his cheeks was bubbling now, and there were dark patches growing darker still on his neck, at his forehead. Now his hair was rising from his head and cremating light was flickering up from his scalp. Cameron was burning. Cameron was burning, and still the smile, and still the beckoning hand.

Joel felt sudden despair.

Hell behind. Hell in front.

This wasn't Cameron. Cameron was nowhere to be seen: so Cameron was gone.

He knew it in his gut. Cameron was gone: and this black parody that smiled at him and welcomed him was his last moments, replayed for the delight of his admirers.

Joel's step faltered, the rhythm of his stride lost. At his back he heard Voight's breath, horridly thick, close, closer.

His whole body suddenly revolted. His stomach demanded to throw up its contents, his legs cried out to collapse, his head refused to think, only to fear.

'Run,' he said to himself. 'Run. Run. Run.'

But Hell was ahead. How could he run into the arms of such foulness?

Voight had closed the gap between them, and was at his shoulder, jostling him as he passed. The victory was being snatched from Joel easily: sweets from a babe.

The finishing line was a dozen strides away, and Voight had the lead again. Scarcely aware of what he was doing, Joel reached out and snatched at Voight as he ran, grabbing his singlet. It was a cheat, clear to everybody in the crowd. But what the Hell.

He pulled hard at Voight, and both men stumbled. The crowd parted as they veered off the track and fell heavily, Voight on top of Joel.

Joel's arm, flung out to prevent him falling too heavily, was crushed under the weight of both bodies. Caught badly, the bone of his forearm cracked. Joel heard it snap a moment before he felt the spasm; then the pain threw a cry out of his mouth.

On the steps, Burgess was screeching like a wild man. Quite a performance. Cameras were snapping, commentators commenting.

'Get up! Get up!' the man was yelling.

53

But Joel had snatched Voight with his one good arm, and nothing was going to make him let go.

The two rolled around in the gravel, every roll crushing Joel's arm and sending spurts of nausea through his gut.

The familiar playing Voight was exhausted. It had never been so tired: unprepared for the stress of the race its master had demanded it run. Its temper was short, its control perilously close to snapping. Joel could smell its breath on his face, and it was the smell of a goat.

'Show yourself,' he said.

The thing's eyes had lost their pupils: they were all white now. Joel hawked up a clot of phlegm from the back of his thick-spittled mouth and spat it in the familiar's face.

Its temper broke.

The face dissolved. What had seemed to be flesh sprouted into a new resemblance, a devouring trap without eyes or nose, or ears, or hair.

All around, the crowd shrank back. People shrieked: people fainted. Joel saw none of this: but heard the cries with satisfaction. This transformation was not just for his benefit: it was common knowledge. They were seeing it all, the truth, the filthy, gaping truth.

The mouth was huge, and lined with teeth like the maw of some deep-water fish, ridiculously large. Joel's one good arm was under its lower jaw, just managing to keep it at bay, as he cried for help.

Nobody stepped forward.

The crowd stood at a polite distance, still screaming, still staring, unwilling to interfere. It was purely a spectator sport, wrestling with the Devil. Nothing to do with them.

Joel felt the last of his strength falter: his arm could keep the mouth at bay no longer. Despairing, he felt the teeth at his brow and at his chin, felt them pierce his flesh and his bone, felt, finally, the white night invade him, as the mouth bit off his face.

The familiar rose up from the corpse with strands of Joel's head hanging out from between its teeth. It had taken off the features like a mask, leaving a mess of blood and jerking muscle. In the open hole of Joel's mouth the root of his tongue flapped and spurted, past speaking sorrow.

Burgess didn't care how he appeared to the world. The race was everything: a victory was a victory however it was won. And Jones had cheated after all.

'Here!' he yelled to the familiar. 'Heel!'

It turned its blood-strung face to him.

'Come here,' Burgess ordered it.

They were only a few yards apart: a few strides to the line and the race was won.

'Run to me!' Burgess screeched. 'Run! Run! Run!'

The familiar was weary, but it knew its master's voice. It loped towards the line, blindly following Burgess' calls.

Four paces. Three –

And Kinderman ran past it to the line. Short-sighted Kinderman, a pace ahead of Voight, took the race without knowing the victory he had won, without even seeing the horrors that were sprawled at his feet.

There were no cheers as he passed the line. No congratulations.

The air around the steps seemed to darken, and an unseasonal frost appeared in the air.

Shaking his head apologetically, Burgess fell to his knees.

'Our Father, who wert in Heaven, unhallowed be thy name – '

Such an old trick. Such a naïve response.

The crowd began to back away. Some people were already running. Children, knowing the nature of the dark having been so recently touched by it, were the least troubled. They took their parents' hands and led them away from the spot like lambs, telling them not to look behind them, and their parents half-remembered the womb, the first tunnel, the first aching exit from a hallowed place, the first terrible temptation to look behind and die. Remembering, they went with their children.

Only Kinderman seemed untouched. He sat on the steps and cleaned his glasses, smiling to have won, indifferent to the chill.

Burgess, knowing his prayers were insufficient, turned tail and disappeared into the Palace of Westminster.

The familiar, deserted, relinquished all claim to human appearance and became itself. Insolid, insipid, it spat out the foul-tasting flesh of Joel Jones. Half chewed, the runner's face lay on the gravel beside his body. The familiar folded itself into the air and went back to the Circle it called home.

It was stale in the corridors of power: no life, no help.

Burgess was out of condition, and his running soon became a walk. A steady step along the gloom-panelled corridors, his feet almost silent on the well trodden carpet.

He didn't quite know what to do. Clearly he would be blamed for his failure to plan against all eventualities, but he was confident he could argue his way out of that. He would give them whatever they required as recompense for his lack of foresight. An ear, a foot; he had nothing to lose but flesh and blood.

But he had to plan his defence carefully, because they hated bad logic. It was more than his life was worth to come before them with half-formed excuses.

There was a chill behind him; he knew what it was. Hell had followed him along these silent corridors, even into the very womb of democracy. He would survive though, as long as he didn't turn round: as long as he kept his eyes on the floor, or on his thumbless hands, no harm would come to him. That was one of the first lessons one learnt, dealing with the gulfs.

There was a frost in the air. Burgess' breath was visible in front of him, and his head was aching with cold.

'I'm sorry,' he said sincerely to his pursuer.

The voice that came back to him was milder than he'd expected.

'It wasn't your fault.'

'No,' said Burgess, taking confidence from its conciliatory tone. 'It was an error and I am contrite. I overlooked Kinderman.'

'That was a mistake. We all make them,' said Hell. 'Still, in another hundred years, we'll try again. Democracy is still a new cult: it's not lost its superficial glamour yet. We'll give it another century, and have the best of them then.'

'Yes.'

'But you – '

'I know.'

'No power for you, Gregory.'

'No.'

'It's not the end of the world. Look at me.'

'Not at the moment, if you don't mind.'

Burgess kept walking, steady step upon steady step. Keep it calm, keep it rational.

'Look at me, please,' Hell cooed.

'Later, sir.'

'I'm only asking you to look at me. A little respect would be appreciated.'

'I will. I will, really. Later.'

The corridor divided here. Burgess took the left-hand fork. He thought the symbolism might flatter. It was a cul-de-sac.

Burgess stood still facing the wall. The cold air was in his marrow, and the stumps of his thumbs were really giving him jip. He took off his gloves and sucked, hard.

'Look at me. Turn and look at me,' said the courteous voice.

What was he to do now? Back out of the corridor and find another way was best, presumably. He'd just have to walk around and around in circles until he'd argued his point sufficiently well for his pursuer to leave him be.

As he stood, juggling the alternatives available to him, he felt a slight ache in his neck.

'Look at me,' the voice said again.

And his throat was constricted. There was, strangely, a grinding in his head, the sound of bone rasping bone. It felt like a knife was lodged in the base of his skull.

'Look at me,' Hell said one final time, and Burgess' head turned.

Not his body. That stayed standing facing the blank wall of the cul-de-sac.

But his head cranked around on its slender axis, disregarding reason and anatomy. Burgess choked as his gullet twisted on itself like a flesh rope, his vertebrae screwed to powder, his cartilege to fibre mush. His eyes bled, his ears popped, and he died, looking at that sunless, unbegotten face.

'I told you to look at me,' said Hell, and went its bitter way, leaving him standing there, a fine paradox for the democrats to find when they came, bustling with words, into the Palace of Westminster.

Jacqueline Ess: Her Will and Testament

My God, she thought, this can't be living. Day in, day out: the boredom, the drudgery, the frustration.

My Christ, she prayed, let me out, set me free, crucify me if you must, but put me out of my misery.

In lieu of his euthanasian benediction, she took a blade from Ben's razor, one dull day in late March, locked herself in the bathroom, and slit her wrists.

Through the throbbing in her ears, she faintly heard Ben outside the bathroom door.

'Are you in there, darling?'

'Go away,' she thought she said.

'I'm back early, sweetheart. The traffic was light.'

'Please go away.'

The effort of trying to speak slid her off the toilet seat and on to the white-tiled floor, where pools of her blood were already cooling.

'Darling?'

'Go.'

'Darling.'

'Away.'

'Are you all right?'

Now he was rattling at the door, the rat. Didn't he realize she couldn't open it, wouldn't open it?

'Answer me, Jackie.'

She groaned. She couldn't stop herself. The pain wasn't as terrible as she'd expected, but there was an ugly feeling, as though she'd been kicked in the head. Still, he couldn't catch her in time, not now. Not even if he broke the door down.

He broke the door down.

She looked up at him through an air grown so thick with death you could have sliced it.

'Too late,' she thought she said.

But it wasn't.

My God, she thought, this can't be suicide. I haven't died.

The doctor Ben had hired for her was too perfectly benign.

Only the best, he'd promised, only the very best for my Jackie.

'It's nothing,' the doctor reassured her, 'that we can't put right with a little tinkering.'

Why doesn't he just come out with it? she thought. He doesn't give a damn. He doesn't know what it's like.

'I deal with a lot of these women's problems,' he confided, fairly oozing a practiced compassion. 'It's got to epidemic proportions among a certain age-bracket.'

She was barely thirty. What was he telling her? That she was prematurely menopausal?

'Depression, partial or total withdrawal, neuroses of every shape and size. You're not alone, believe me.'

Oh yes I am, she thought. I'm here in my head, on my own, and you can't know what it's like.

'We'll have you right in two shakes of a lamb's tail.'

I'm a lamb, am I? Does he think I'm a lamb?

Musing, he glanced up at his framed qualifications, then at his manicured nails, then at the pens on his desk and notepad. But he didn't look at Jacqueline. Anywhere but at Jacqueline.

'I know,' he was saying now, 'what you've been through, and it's been traumatic. Women have certain needs. If they go unanswered – '

What would he know about women's needs?

You're not a woman, she thought she thought.

'What?' he said.

Had she spoken? She shook her head: denying speech. He went on; finding his rhythm once more: 'I'm not going to put you through interminable therapy-sessions. You don't want that, do you? You want a little reassurance, and you want something to help you sleep at nights.'

He was irritating her badly now. His condescension was so profound it had no bottom. All-knowing, all-seeing Father; that was his performance. As if he were blessed with some miraculous insight into the nature of a woman's soul.

'Of course, I've tried therapy courses with patients in the past. But between you and me – '

He lightly patted her hand. Father's palm on the back of her hand. She was supposed to be flattered, reassured, maybe even seduced.

' – between you and me it's so much talk. Endless talk. Frankly, what good does it do? We've all got problems. You can't talk them away, can you?'

You're not a woman. You don't look like a woman, you don't feel like a woman –

'Did you say something?'

She shook her head.

'I thought you said something. Please feel free to be honest with me.'

She didn't reply, and he seemed to tire of pretending intimacy. He stood up and went to the window.

'I think the best thing for you – '

He stood against the light: darkening the room, obscuring the view of the cherry trees on the lawn through the window. She stared at his wide shoulders, at his narrow hips. A fine figure of a man, as Ben would have called him. No child-bearer he. Made to remake the world, a body like that. If not the world, remaking minds would have to do.

'I think the best thing for you – '

What did he know, with his hips, with his shoulders? He was too much a man to understand anything of her.

'I think the best thing for you would be a course of sedatives – '

Now her eyes were on his waist.

' – and a holiday.'

Her mind had focussed now on the body beneath the veneer of his clothes. The muscle, bone and blood beneath the elastic skin. She pictured it from all sides, sizing it up, judging its powers of resistance, then closing on it. She thought:

Be a woman.

Simply, as she thought that preposterous idea, it began to take shape. Not a fairy-tale transformation, unfortunately, his flesh resisted such magic. She willed his manly chest into making breasts of itself and it began to swell most fetchingly, until the skin burst and his sternum flew apart. His pelvis, teased to breaking point, fractured at its centre; unbalanced, he toppled over on to his desk and from there stared up at her, his face yellow with shock. He licked his lips, over and over again, to find some wetness to talk with. His mouth was dry: his words were still-born. It was from between his legs that all the noise was coming; the splashing of his blood; the thud of his bowel on the carpet.

She screamed at the absurd monstrosity she had made, and withdrew to the far corner of the room, where she was sick in the pot of the rubber plant.

My God, she thought, this can't be murder. I didn't so much as touch him.

* * *

What Jacqueline had done that afternoon, she kept to herself. No sense in giving people sleepless nights, thinking about such peculiar talent.

The police were very kind. They produced any number of explanations for the sudden departure of Dr Blandish, though none quite described how his chest had erupted in that extraordinary fashion, making two handsome (if hairy) domes of his pectorals.

It was assumed that some unknown psychotic, strong in his insanity, had broken in, done the deed with hands, hammers and saws, and exited, locking the innocent Jacqueline Ess in an appalled silence no interrogation could hope to penetrate.

Person or persons unknown had clearly dispatched the doctor to where neither sedatives nor therapy could help him.

She almost forgot for a while. But as the months passed it came back to her by degrees, like a memory of a secret adultery. It teased her with its forbidden delights. She forgot the nausea, and remembered the power. She forgot sordidity, and remembered strength. She forgot the guilt that had seized her afterwards and longed, longed to do it again.

Only better.

'Jacqueline.'

Is this my husband, she thought, actually calling me by my name? Usually it was Jackie, or Jack, or nothing at all.

'Jacqueline.'

He was looking at her with those big baby blues of his, like the college-boy she'd loved at first sight. But his mouth was harder now, and his kisses tasted like stale bread.

'Jacqueline.'

'Yes.'

'I've got something I want to speak to you about.'

A conversation? she thought, it must be a public holiday.

'I don't know how to tell you this.'

'Try me,' she suggested.

She knew that she could think his tongue into speaking if it pleased her. Make him tell her what she wanted to hear. Words of love, maybe, if she could remember what they sounded like. But what was the use of that? Better the truth.

'Darling, I've gone off the rails a bit.'

'What do you mean?' she said.

Have you, you bastard, she thought.

61

'It was while you weren't quite yourself. You know, when things had more or less stopped between us. Separate rooms . . . you wanted separate rooms . . . and I just went bananas with frustration. I didn't want to upset you, so I didn't say anything. But it's no use me trying to live two lives.'

'You can have an affair if you want to, Ben.'

'It's not an affair, Jackie. I love her – '

He was preparing one of his speeches, she could see it gathering momentum behind his teeth. The justifications that became accusations, those excuses that always turned into assaults on her character. Once he got into full flow there'd be no stopping him. She didn't want to hear.

' – she's not like you at all, Jackie. She's frivolous in her way. I suppose you'd call her shallow.'

It might be worth interrupting here, she thought, before he ties himself in his usual knots.

'She's not moody like you. You know, she's just a normal woman. I don't mean to say you're not normal: you can't help having depressions. But she's not so sensitive.'

'There's no need, Ben – '

'No, damn it, I want it all off my chest.'

On to me, she thought.

'You've never let me explain,' he was saying. 'You've always given me one of those damn looks of yours, as if you wished I'd –'

Die.

' – wished I'd shut up.'

Shut up.

'You don't care how I feel!' He was shouting now. 'Always in your own little world.'

Shut up, she thought.

His mouth was open. She seemed to wish it closed, and with the thought his jaws snapped together, severing the very tip of his pink tongue. It fell from between his lips and lodged in a fold of his shirt.

Shut up, she thought again.

The two perfect regiments of his teeth ground down into each other, cracking and splitting, nerve, calcium and spit making a pinkish foam on his chin as his mouth collapsed inwards.

Shut up, she was still thinking as his startled baby blues sank back into his skull and his nose wormed its way into his brain.

He was not Ben any longer, he was a man with a red lizard's head, flattening, battening down upon itself, and, thank God, he was past speech-making once and for all.

Now she had the knack of it, she began to take pleasure in the changes she was willing upon him.

She flipped him head over heels on to the floor and began to compress his arms and legs, telescoping flesh and resistant bone into a smaller and yet smaller space. His clothes were folded inwards, and the tissue of his stomach was plucked from his neatly packaged entrails and stretched around his body to wrap him up. His fingers were poking from his shoulder-blades now, and his feet, still thrashing with fury, were tripped up in his gut. She turned him over one final time to pressure his spine into a foot-long column of muck, and that was about the end of it.

As she came out of her ecstasy she saw Ben sitting on the floor, shut up into a space about the size of one of his fine leather suitcases, while blood, bile and lymphatic fluid pulsed weakly from his hushed body.

My God, she thought, this can't be my husband. He's never been as tidy as that.

This time she didn't wait for help. This time she knew what she'd done (guessed, even, how she'd done it) and she accepted her crime for the too-rough justice it was. She packed her bags and left the home.

I'm alive, she thought. For the first time in my whole, wretched life, I'm alive.

Vassi's Testimony (part one)

'To you who dream of sweet, strong women I leave this story. It is a promise, as surely as it is a confession, as surely as it's the last words of a lost man who wanted nothing but to love and be loved. I sit here trembling, waiting for the night, waiting for that whining pimp Koos to come to my door again, and take everything I own from me in exchange for the key to her room.

I am not a courageous man, and I never have been: so I'm afraid of what may happen to me tonight. But I cannot go through life dreaming all the time, existing through the darkness on only a glimpse of heaven. Sooner or later, one has to gird one's loins (that's appropriate) and get up and find it. Even if it means giving away the world in exchange.

I probably make no sense. You're thinking, you who chanced on this testimony, you're thinking, who was he, this imbecile?

My name was Oliver Vassi. I am now thirty-eight years old. I was a lawyer, until a year or more ago, when I began the search that ends tonight with that pimp and that key and that holy of holies.

But the story begins more than a year ago. It is many years since Jacqueline Ess first came to me.

She arrived out of the blue at my offices, claiming to be the widow of a friend of mine from Law School, one Benjamin Ess, and when I thought back, I remembered the face. A mutual friend who'd been at the wedding had shown me a photograph of Ben and his blushing bride. And here she was, every bit as elusive a beauty as her photograph promised.

I remember being acutely embarrassed at that first interview. She'd arrived at a busy time, and I was up to my neck in work. But I was so enthralled by her, I let all the day's interviews fall by the wayside, and when my secretary came in she gave me one of her steely glances as if to throw a bucket of cold water over me. I suppose I was enamoured from the start, and she sensed the electric atmosphere in my office. Me, I pretended I was merely being polite to the widow of an old friend. I didn't like to think about passion: it wasn't a part of my nature, or so I thought. How little we know – I mean *really* know – about our capabilities.

Jacqueline told me lies at that first meeting. About how Ben had died of cancer, of how often he had spoken of me, and how fondly. I suppose she could have told me the truth then and there, and I would have lapped it up – I believe I was utterly devoted from the beginning.

But it's difficult to remember quite how and when interest in another human being flares into something more committed, more passionate. It may be that I am inventing the impact she had on me at that first meeting, simply re-inventing history to justify my later excesses. I'm not sure. Anyway, wherever and whenever it happened, however quickly or slowly, I succumbed to her, and the affair began.

I'm not a particularly inquisitive man where my friends, or my bed-partners, are concerned. As a lawyer one spends one's time going through the dirt of other people's lives, and frankly, eight hours a day of that is quite enough for me. When I'm out of the office my pleasure is in letting people be. I don't pry, I don't dig, I just take them on face value.

Jacqueline was no exception to this rule. She was a woman I was glad to have in my life whatever the truth of her past. She possessed a marvellous *sang-froid*, she was witty, bawdy, oblique. I had never met a more enchanting woman. It was none of my business how she'd lived with Ben, what the marriage had been like etc., etc. That was her history. I was happy to live in the present, and let the past die its own death. I think I even flattered myself that whatever pain she had experienced, I could help her forget it.

Certainly her stories had holes in them. As a lawyer, I was trained to be eagle-eyed where fabrications were concerned, and however much I tried to put my perceptions aside I sensed that she wasn't quite coming clean with me. But everyone has secrets: I knew that. Let her have hers, I thought.

Only once did I challenge her on a detail of her pretended life-story. In talking about Ben's death, she let slip that he had got what he deserved. I asked her what she meant. She smiled, that Gioconda smile of hers, and told me that she felt there was a balance to be redressed between men and women. I let the observation pass. After all, I was obsessed by that time, past all hope of salvation; whatever argument she was putting, I was happy to concede it.

She was so beautiful, you see. Not in any two-dimensional sense: she wasn't young, she wasn't innocent, she didn't have that pristine symmetry so favoured by ad-men and photographers. Her face was plainly that of a woman in her early forties: it had been used to laugh and cry, and usage leaves its marks. But she had a power to transform herself, in the subtlest way, making that face as various as the sky. Early on, I thought it was a make-up trick. But as we slept together more and more, and I watched her in the mornings, sleep in her eyes, and in the evenings, heavy with fatigue, I soon realized she wore nothing on her skull but flesh and blood. What transformed her was internal: it was a trick of the will.

And, you know, that made me love her all the more.

Then one night I woke with her sleeping beside me. We slept often on the floor, which she preferred to the bed. Beds, she said, reminded her of marriage. Anyway, that night she was lying under a quilt on the carpet of my room, and I, simply out of adoration, was watching her face in sleep.

If one has given oneself utterly, watching the beloved sleep can be a vile experience. Perhaps some of you have known that paralysis, staring down at features closed to your enquiry, locked away from you where you can never, ever go, into the other's mind. As I say, for us who have given ourselves, that is a horror. One knows, in those moments, that one does not exist, except in relation to that face, that personality. Therefore, when that face is closed down, that personality is lost in its own unknowable world, one feels completely without purpose. A planet without a sun, revolving in darkness.

That's how I felt that night, looking down at her extraordinary features, and as I chewed on my soullessness, her face began to alter. She was clearly dreaming; but what dreams must she have been having. Her very fabric was on the move, her muscle, her hair, the down on her cheek moving to the dictates of some internal tide. Her lips bloomed from her bone, boiling up into a slavering tower of skin; her hair swirled around her head as though she were lying in water; the substance of her cheeks formed furrows and ridges like the ritual scars on a warrior; inflamed and throbbing patterns of tissue, swelling up and changing again even as a pattern formed. This fluxion was a terror to me, and I must have made some noise. She didn't wake, but came a little closer to the surface of sleep, leaving the deeper waters where these powers were sourced. The patterns sank away in an instant, and her face was again that of a gently sleeping woman.

That was, you can understand, a pivotal experience, even though I spent the next few days trying to convince myself that I hadn't seen it.

The effort was useless. I knew there was something wrong with her; and at that time I was certain she knew nothing about it. I was convinced that something in her system was awry, and that I was best to investigate her history before I told her what I had seen.

On reflection, of course, that seems laughably naïve. To think she wouldn't have known that she contained such a power. But it was easier for me to picture her as prey to such skill, than mistress of it. That's a man speaking of a woman; not just me, Oliver Vassi, of her, Jacqueline Ess. We cannot believe, we men, that power will ever reside happily in the body of a woman, unless that power is a male child. Not true power. The power must be in male hands, God-given. That's what our fathers tell us, idiots that they are.

Anyway, I investigated Jacqueline, as surreptitiously as I could. I had a contact in York where the couple had lived, and it wasn't difficult to get some enquiries moving. It took a week for my contact to get back to me, because he'd had to cut through a good deal of shit from the police to get a hint of the truth, but the news came, and it was bad.

Ben was dead, that much was true. But there was no way he had died of cancer. My contact had only got the vaguest clues as to the condition of Ben's corpse, but he gathered it had been spectacularly mutilated. And the prime suspect? My beloved

Jacqueline Ess. The same innocent woman who was occupying my flat, sleeping by my side every night.

So I put it to her that she was hiding something from me. I don't know what I was expecting in return. What I got was a demonstration of her power. She gave it freely, without malice, but I would have been a fool not to have read a warning into it. She told me first how she had discovered her unique control over the sum and substance of human beings. In her despair, she said, when she was on the verge of killing herself, she had found, in the very deep-water trenches of her nature, faculties she had never known existed. Powers which came up out of those regions as she recovered, like fish to the light.

Then she showed me the smallest measure of these powers, plucking hairs from my head, one by one. Only a dozen; just to demonstrate her formidable skills. I felt them going. She just said: one from behind your ear, and I'd feel my skin creep and then jump as fingers of her volition snatched a hair out. Then another, and another. It was an incredible display; she had this power down to a fine art, locating and withdrawing single hairs from my scalp with the precision of tweezers.

Frankly, I was sitting there rigid with fear, knowing that she was just toying with me. Sooner or later, I was certain the time would be right for her to silence me permanently.

But she had doubts about herself. She told me how the skill, though she had honed it, scared her. She needed, she said, someone to teach her how to use it best. And I was not that somebody. I was just a man who loved her, who had loved her before this revelation, and would love her still, in spite of it.

In fact, after that display I quickly came to accommodate a new vision of Jacqueline. Instead of fearing her, I became more devoted to this woman who tolerated my possession of her body.

My work became an irritation, a distraction that came between me and thinking of my beloved. What reputation I had began to deteriorate; I lost briefs, I lost credibility. In the space of two or three months my professional life dwindled away to almost nothing. Friends despaired of me, colleagues avoided me.

It wasn't that she was feeding on me. I want to be clear about that. She was no lamia, no succubus. What happened to me, my fall from grace with ordinary life if you like, was of my own making. She didn't bewitch me; that's a romantic lie to excuse rape. She was a sea: and I had to swim in her. Does that make any sense? I'd lived my life on the shore, in the solid world of law, and I was tired of it. She was liquid; a boundless sea in a single body, a deluge in a small room, and I will gladly drown in her, if she grants me the chance. But that was my decision. Understand that. This has always been my decision. I have decided to go to the room tonight, and be with her one final time. That is of my own free will.

And what man would not? She was (is) sublime.

For a month after that demonstration of power I lived in a permanent ecstasy of her. When I was with her she showed me ways to love beyond the limits of any other creature on God's earth. I say beyond the limits: with her there were no limits. And when I was away from her the reverie continued: because she seemed to have changed my world.

Then she left me.

I knew why: she'd gone to find someone to teach her how to use strength. But understanding her reasons made it no easier.

I broke down: lost my job, lost my identity, lost the few friends I had left in the world. I scarcely noticed. They were minor losses, beside the loss of Jacqueline . . .'

'Jacqueline.'

My God, she thought, can this really be the most influential man in the country? He looked so unprepossessing, so very unspectacular. His chin wasn't even strong.

But Titus Pettifer was power.

He ran more monopolies than he could count; his word in the financial world could break companies like sticks, destroying the ambitions of hundreds, the careers of thousands. Fortunes were made overnight in his shadow, entire corporations fell when he blew on them, casualties of his whim. This man knew power if any man knew it. He had to be learned from.

'You wouldn't mind if I called you J., would you?'

'No.'

'Have you been waiting long?'

'Long enough.'

'I don't normally leave beautiful women waiting.'

'Yes you do.'

She knew him already: two minutes in his presence was enough to find his measure. He would come quickest to her if she was quietly insolent.

'Do you always call women you've never met before by their initials?'

'It's convenient for filing; do you mind?'

'It depends.'

'On what?'

'What I get in return for giving you the privilege.'

'It's a privilege, is it, to know your name?'

'Yes.'

'Well . . . I'm flattered. Unless of course you grant that privilege widely?'

She shook her head. No, he could see she wasn't profligate with her affections.

'Why have you waited so long to see me?' he said. 'Why have I had reports of your wearing my secretaries down with your constant demands to meet with me? Do you want money? Because if you do you'll go away empty-handed. I became rich by being mean, and the richer I get, the meaner I become.'

The remark was truth; he spoke it plainly.

'I don't want money,' she said, equally plainly.

'That's refreshing.'

'There's richer than you.'

He raised his eyebrows in surprise. She could bite, this beauty.

'True,' he said. There were at least half a dozen richer men in the hemisphere.

'I'm not an adoring little nobody. I haven't come here to screw a name. I've come here because we can be together. We have a great deal to offer each other.'

'Such as?' he said.

'I have my body.'

He smiled. It was the straightest offer he'd heard in years.

'And what do I offer you in return for such largesse?'

'I want to learn – '

'Learn?'

' – how to use power.'

She was stranger and stranger, this one.

'What do you mean?' he replied, playing for time. He hadn't got the measure of her; she vexed him, confounded him.

'Shall I recite it for you again, in bourgeois?' she said, playing insolence with such a smile he almost felt attractive again.

'No need. You want to learn to use power. I suppose I could teach you – '

'I know you can.'

'You realize I'm a married man. Virginia and I have been together eighteen years.'

'You have three sons, four houses, a maid-servant called Mirabelle. You loathe New York, and you love Bangkok; your shirt collar is 16½, your favourite colour green.'

'Turquoise.'

'You're getting subtler in your old age.'

'I'm not old.'

'Eighteen years a married man. It ages you prematurely.'

'Not me.'

'Prove it.'

'How?'

'Take me.'

'What?'

'Take me.'

'Here?'

'Draw the blinds, lock the door, turn off the computer terminus, and take me. I dare you.'

'Dare?'

How long was it since anyone had *dared* him to do anything?

'Dare?'

He was excited. He hadn't been so excited in a dozen years. He drew the blinds, locked the door, turned off the video display of his fortunes.

My God, she thought, I've got him.

It wasn't an easy passion, not like that with Vassi. For one thing, Pettifer was a clumsy, uncultured lover. For another, he was too nervous of his wife to be a wholly successful adulterer. He thought he saw Virginia everywhere: in the lobbies of the hotels they took a room in for the afternoon, in cabs cruising the street outside their rendezvous, once even (he swore the likeness was exact) dressed as a waitress, and swabbing down a table in a restaurant. All fictional fears, but they dampened the spontaneity of the romance somewhat.

Still, she was learning from him. He was as brilliant a potentate as he was inept a lover. She learned how to be powerful without exercising power, how to keep one's self uncontaminated by the foulness all charisma stirs up in the uncharismatic; how to make the plain decisions plainly; how to be merciless. Not that she needed much education in that particular quarter. Perhaps it was more truthful to say he taught her never to regret her absence of instinctive compassion, but to judge with her intellect alone who deserved extinction and who might be numbered amongst the righteous.

Not once did she show herself to him, though she used her skills in the most secret of ways to tease pleasure out of his stale nerves.

In the fourth week of their affair they were lying side by side in a lilac room, while the mid-afternoon traffic growled in the street below. It had been a bad bout of sex; he was nervous, and no tricks would coax him out of himself. It was over quickly, almost without heat.

He was going to tell her something. She knew it: it was waiting, this revelation, somewhere at the back of his throat. Turning to him she massaged his temples with her mind, and soothed him into speech.

He was about to spoil the day.

He was about to spoil his career.

He was about, God help him, to spoil his life.

'I have to stop seeing you,' he said.

He wouldn't dare, she thought.

'I'm not sure what I know about you, or rather, what I *think* I know about you, but it makes me . . . cautious of you, J. Do you understand?'

'No.'

'I'm afraid I suspect you of . . . crimes.'

'Crimes?'

'You have a history.'

'Who's been rooting?' she asked. 'Surely not Virginia?'

'No, not Virginia, she's beyond curiosity.'

'Who then?'

'It's not your business.'

'Who?'

She pressed lightly on his temples. It hurt him and he winced.

'What's wrong?' she asked.

'My head's aching.'

'Tension, that's all, just tension. I can take it away, Titus.' She touched her fingers to his forehead, relaxing her hold on him. He sighed as relief came.

'Is that better?'

'Yes.'

'Who's been snooping, Titus?'

'I have a personal secretary. Lyndon. You've heard me speak of him. He knew about our relationship from the beginning. Indeed, he books the hotels, arranges my cover stories for Virginia.'

There was a sort of boyishness in this speech, that was rather touching. As though he was embarrassed to leave her, rather than heartbroken. 'Lyndon's quite a miracle-worker. He's manouevred a lot of things to make it easier between us. So he's got nothing against you. It's just that he happened to see one of the photographs I took of you. I gave them to him to shred.'

'Why?'

'I shouldn't have taken them; it was a mistake. Virginia might have . . .' He paused, began again. 'Anyhow, he recognized you, although he couldn't remember where he'd seen you before.'

'But he remembered eventually.'

'He used to work for one of my newspapers, as a gossip columnist. That's how he came to be my personal assistant. He remembered you from your previous incarnation, as it were. Jacqueline Ess, the wife of Benjamin Ess, deceased.'

'Deceased.'

'He brought me some other photographs, not as pretty as the ones of you.'

'Photographs of what?'

'Your home. And the body of your husband. They said it was a body, though in God's name there was precious little human being left in it.'

'There was precious little to start with,' she said simply, thinking of Ben's cold eyes, and colder hands. Fit only to be shut up, and forgotten.

'What happened?'

'To Ben? He was killed.'

'How?' Did his voice waver a little?

'Very easily.' She had risen from the bed, and was standing by the window. Strong summer light carved its way through the slats of the blind, ridges of shadow and sunlight charting the contours of her face.

'You did it.'

'Yes.' He had taught her to be plain. 'Yes, I did it.'

He had taught her an economy of threat too. 'Leave me, and I'll do the same again.'

He shook his head. 'Never. You wouldn't dare.'

He was standing in front of her now.

'We must understand each other, J. I am powerful and I am pure. Do you see? My public face isn't even touched by a glimmer of scandal. I could afford a mistress, a dozen mistresses, to be revealed. But a murderess? No, that would spoil my life.'

'Is he blackmailing you? This Lyndon?'

He stared at the day through the blinds, with a crippled look on his face. There was a twitch in the nerves of his cheek, under his left eye.

72

'Yes, if you must know,' he said in a dead voice. 'The bastard has me for all I'm worth.'

'I see.'

'And if he can guess, so can others. You understand?'

'I'm strong: you're strong. We can twist them around our little fingers.'

'No.'

'Yes! I have skills, Titus.'

'I don't want to know.'

'You *will* know,' she said.

She looked at him, taking hold of his hands without touching him. He watched, all astonished eyes, as his unwilling hands were raised to touch her face, to stroke her hair with the fondest of gestures. She made him run his trembling fingers across her breasts, taking them with more ardour than he could summon on his own initiative.

'You are always too tentative, Titus,' she said, making him paw her almost to the point of bruising. 'This is how I like it.' Now his hands were lower, fetching out a different look from her face. Tides were moving over it, she was all alive –

'Deeper – '

His finger intruded, his thumb stroked.

'I like that, Titus. Why can't you do that to me without me demanding?'

He blushed. He didn't like to talk about what they did together. She coaxed him deeper, whispering.

'I won't break, you know. Virginia may be Dresden china, I'm not. I want feeling; I want something that I can remember you by when I'm not with you. Nothing is everlasting, is it? But I want something to keep me warm through the night.'

He was sinking to his knees, his hands kept, by her design, on her and in her, still roving like two lustful crabs. His body was awash with sweat. It was, she thought, the first time she'd ever seen him sweat.

'Don't kill me,' he whimpered.

'I could wipe you out.' Wipe, she thought, then put the image out of her mind before she did him some harm.

'I know. I know,' he said. 'You can kill me easily.'

He was crying. My God, she thought, the great man is at my feet, sobbing like a baby. What can I learn of power from this puerile performance? She plucked the tears off his cheeks, using rather more strength than the task required. His skin reddened under her gaze.

'Let me be, J. I can't help you. I'm useless to you.'

It was true. He was absolutely useless. Contemptuously, she let his hands go. They fell limply by his sides.

'Don't ever try and find me, Titus. You understand? Don't ever send your minions after me to preserve your reputation, because I will be more merciless than you've ever been.'

He said nothing; just knelt there, facing the window, while she washed her face, drank the coffee they'd ordered, and left.

Lyndon was surprised to find the door of his office ajar. It was only seven-thirty-six. None of the secretaries would be in for another hour. Clearly one of the cleaners had been remiss, leaving the door unlocked. He'd find out who: sack her.

He pushed the door open.

Jacqueline was sitting with her back to the door. He recognized the back of her head, that fall of auburn hair. A sluttish display; too teased, too wild. His office, an annex to Mr Pettifer's, was kept meticulously ordered. He glanced over it: everything seemed to be in place.

'What are you doing here?'

She took a little breath, preparing herself.

This was the first time she had planned to do it. Before it had been a spur-of-the-moment decision.

He was approaching the desk, and putting down his briefcase and his neatly-folded copy of the *Financial Times*.

'You have no right to come in here without my permission,' he said.

She turned on the lazy swivel of his chair; the way he did when he had people in to discipline.

'Lyndon,' she said.

'Nothing you can say or do will change the facts, Mrs Ess,' he said, saving her the trouble of introducing the subject, 'you are a cold-blooded killer. It was my bounden duty to inform Mr Pettifer of the situation.'

'You did it for the good of Titus?'

'Of course.'

'And the blackmail, that was also for the good of Titus, was it?'

'Get out of my office — '

'Was it, Lyndon?'

'You're a whore! Whores know nothing: they are ignorant, diseased animals,' he spat. 'Oh, you're cunning, I grant you that — but then so's any slut with a living to make.'

She stood up. He expected a riposte. He got none; at least not verbally. But he felt a tautness across his face: as though someone was pressing on it.

'What . . . are . . . you . . . doing?' he said.

'Doing?'

His eyes were being forced into slits like a child imitating a monstrous Oriental, his mouth was hauled wide and tight, his smile brilliant. The words were difficult to say –

'Stop . . . it . . .'

She shook her head.

'Whore . . .' he said again, still defying her.

She just stared at him. His face was beginning to jerk and twitch under the pressure, the muscles going into spasm.

'The police . . .' he tried to say, 'if you lay a finger on me . . .'

'I won't,' she said, and pressed home her advantage.

Beneath his clothes he felt the same tension all over his body, pulling his skin, drawing him tighter and tighter. Something was going to give; he knew it. Some part of him would be weak, and tear under this relentless assault. And if he once began to break open, nothing would prevent her ripping him apart. He worked all this out quite coolly, while his body twitched and he swore at her through his enforced grin.

'Cunt,' he said. 'Syphilitic cunt.'

He didn't seem to be afraid, she thought.

In extremis he just unleashed so much hatred of her, the fear was entirely eclipsed. Now he was calling her a whore again; though his face was distorted almost beyond recognition.

And then he began to split.

The tear began at the bridge of his nose and ran up, across his brow, and down, bisecting his lips and his chin, then his neck and chest. In a matter of seconds his shirt was dyed red, his dark suit darkening further, his cuffs and trouser-legs pouring blood. The skin flew off his hands like gloves off a surgeon, and two rings of scarlet tissue lolled down to either side of his flayed face like the ears of an elephant.

His name-calling had stopped.

He had been dead of shock now for ten seconds, though she was still working him over vengefully, tugging his skin off his body and flinging the scraps around the room, until at last he stood, steaming, in his red suit, and his red shirt, and his shiny red shoes, and looked, to her eyes, a little more like a sensitive man. Content with the effect, she released him. He lay down quietly in a blood puddle and slept.

My God, she thought, as she calmly took the stairs out the back way, that was murder in the first degree.

She saw no reports of the death in any of the papers, and nothing on the news bulletins. Lyndon had apparently died as he had lived, hidden from public view.

But she knew wheels, so big their hubs could not be seen by insignificant individuals like herself, would be moving. What they would do, how they would change her life, she could only guess at. But the murder of Lyndon had not simply been spite, though that had been a part of it. No, she'd also wanted to stir them up, her enemies in the world, and bring them after her. Let them show their hands: let them show their contempt, their terror. She'd gone through her life, it seemed, looking for a sign of herself, only able to define her nature by the look in others' eyes. Now she wanted an end to that. It was time to deal with her pursuers.

Surely now everyone who had seen her, Pettifer first, then Vassi, would come after her, and she would close their eyes permanently: make them forgetful of her. Only then, the witnesses destroyed, would she be free.

Pettifer didn't come, of course, not in person. It was easy for him to find agents, men without scruple or compassion, but with a nose for pursuit that would shame a bloodhound.

A trap was being laid for her, though she couldn't yet see its jaws. There were signs of it everywhere. An eruption of birds from behind a wall, a peculiar light from a distant window, footsteps, whistles, dark-suited men reading the news at the limit of her vision. As the weeks passed they didn't come any closer to her, but then neither did they go away. They waited, like cats in a tree, their tails twitching, their eyes lazy.

But the pursuit had Pettifer's mark. She'd learned enough from him to recognize his circumspection and his guile. They would come for her eventually, not in her time, but in theirs. Perhaps not even in theirs: in his. And though she never saw his face, it was as though Titus was on her heels personally.

My God, she thought, I'm in danger of my life and I don't care.

It was useless, this power over flesh, if it had no direction behind it. She had used it for her own petty reasons, for the gratification of nervous pleasure and sheer anger. But these displays hadn't brought her any closer to other people: they just made her a freak in their eyes.

Sometimes she thought of Vassi, and wondered where he was, what he was doing. He hadn't been a strong man, but he'd had a little passion in his soul. More than Ben, more than Pettifer, certainly more than Lyndon. And, she remembered, fondly, he was the only man she'd ever known who had called her Jacqueline. All the rest had manufactured unendearing corruptions of her name: Jackie, or J., or, in Ben's more irritating moods, Ju-ju. Only Vassi had called her Jacqueline, plain and simple, accepting, in his formal way, the completeness of her, the totality of her. And when she thought of him, tried to picture how he might return to her, she feared for him.

Vassi's Testimony (part two)

Of course I searched for her. It's only when you've lost someone, you realize the nonsense of that phrase 'it's a small world'. It isn't. It's a vast, devouring world, especially if you're alone.

When I was a lawyer, locked in that incestuous coterie, I used to see the same faces day after day. Some I'd exchange words with, some smiles, some nods. We belonged, even if we were enemies at the Bar, to the same complacent circle. We ate at the same tables, we drank elbow to elbow. We even shared mistresses, though we didn't always know it at the time. In such circumstances, it's easy to believe the world means you no harm. Certainly you grow older, but then so does everyone else. You even believe, in your self-satisfied way, that the passage of years makes you a little wiser. Life is bearable; even the 3 a.m. sweats come more infrequently as the bank-balance swells.

But to think that the world is harmless is to lie to yourself, to believe in so-called certainties that are, in fact, simply shared delusions.

When she left, all the delusions fell away, and all the lies I had assiduously lived by became strikingly apparent.

It's not a small world, when there's only one face in it you can bear to look upon, and that face is lost somewhere in a maelstrom. It's not a small world when the few, vital memories of your object of affection are in danger of being trampled out by the thousands of moments that assail you every day, like children tugging at you, demanding your sole attention.

I was a broken man.

I would find myself (there's an apt phrase) sleeping in tiny bedrooms in forlorn hotels, drinking more often than eating, and writing her name, like a classic obsessive, over and over again. On the walls, on the pillow, on the palm of my hand. I broke the

77

skin of my palm with my pen, and the ink infected it. The mark's still there, I'm looking at it now. Jacqueline it says. Jacqueline.

Then one day, entirely by chance, I saw her. It sounds melodramatic, but I thought I was going to die at that moment. I'd imagined her for so long, keyed myself up for seeing her again, that when it happened I felt my limbs weaken, and I was sick in the middle of the street. Not a classic reunion. The lover, on seeing his beloved, throws up down his shirt. But then, nothing that happened between Jacqueline and myself was ever quite normal. Or natural.

I followed her, which was difficult. There were crowds, and she was walking fast. I didn't know whether to call out her name or not. I decided not. What would she have done anyway, seeing this unshaven lunatic shambling towards her, calling her name? She would have run probably. Or worse, she would have reached into my chest, seizing my heart in her will, and put me out of my misery before I could reveal her to the world.

So I was silent, and simply followed her, doggedly, to what I assumed was her apartment. And I stayed there, or in the vicinity, for the next two and a half days, not quite knowing what to do. It was a ridiculous dilemma. After all this time of watching for her, now that she was within speaking distance, touching distance, I didn't dare approach.

Maybe I feared death. But then, here I am, in this stinking room in Amsterdam, setting my testimony down and waiting for Koos to bring me her key, and I don't fear death now. Probably it was my vanity that prevented me from approaching her. I didn't want her to see me cracked and desolate; I wanted to come to her clean, her dream-lover.

While I waited, they came for her.

I don't know who they were. Two men, plainly dressed. I don't think policeman: too smooth. Cultured even. And she didn't resist. She went smilingly, as if to the opera.

At the first opportunity I returned to the building a little better dressed, located her apartment from the porter, and broke in. She had been living plainly. In one corner of the room she had set up a table, and had been writing her memoirs. I sat down and read, and eventually took the pages away with me. She had got no further than the first seven years of her life. I wondered, again in my vanity, if I would have been chronicled in the book. Probably not.

I took some of her clothes too; only items she had worn when I had known her. And nothing intimate: I'm not a fetishist. I wasn't going to go home and bury my face in the smell of her underwear. But I wanted something to remember her by; to picture her in. Though on reflection I never met a human being more fitted to dress purely in her skin.

So I lost her a second time, more the fault of my own cowardice than circumstance.

Pettifer didn't come near the house they were keeping Mrs Ess in for four weeks. She was given more or less everything she asked for, except her freedom, and she only asked for that in the most abstracted fashion. She wasn't interested in escape: though it would have been easy to achieve. Once or twice she wondered if Titus had told the two men and the woman who were keeping her a prisoner in the house exactly what she was capable of: she guessed not. They treated her as though she were simply a woman Titus had set eyes on and desired. They had procured her for his bed, simple as that.

With a room to herself, and an endless supply of paper, she began to write her memoirs again, from the beginning.

It was late summer, and the nights were getting chilly. Sometimes, to warm herself, she would lie on the floor, (she'd asked them to remove the bed) and will her body to ripple like the surface of a lake. Her body, without sex, became a mystery to her again; and she realized for the first time that physical love had been an exploration of that most intimate, and yet most unknown region of her being: her flesh. She had understood herself best embracing someone else: seen her own substance clearly only when another's lips were laid on it, adoring and gentle. She thought of Vassi again; and the lake, at the thought of him, was roused as if by a tempest. Her breasts shook into curling mountains, her belly ran with extraordinary tides, currents crossed and recrossed her flickering face, lapping at her mouth and leaving their mark like waves on sand. As she was fluid in his memory, so as she remembered him, she liquified.

She thought of the few times she had been at peace in her life; and physical love, discharging ambition and vanity, had always preceded those fragile moments. There were other ways presumably; but her experience had been limited. Her mother had always said that women, being more at peace with themselves than men needed fewer distractions from their hurts. But she'd not found it like that at all. She'd found her life full of hurts, but almost empty of ways to salve them.

She left off writing her memoirs when she reached her ninth

79

year. She despaired of telling her story from that point on, with the first realization of on-coming puberty. She burnt the papers on a bonfire she lit in the middle of her room the day that Pettifer arrived.

My God, she thought, this can't be power.

Pettifer looked sick; as physically changed as a friend she'd lost to cancer. One month seemingly healthy, the next sucked up from the inside, self-devoured. He looked like a husk of a man: his skin grey and mottled. Only his eyes glittered, and those like the eyes of a mad dog.

He was dressed immaculately, as though for a wedding. .

'J.'

'Titus.'

He looked her up and down.

'Are you well?'

'Thank you, yes.'

'They give you everything you ask for?'

'Perfect hosts.'

'You haven't resisted.'

'Resisted?'

'Being here. Locked up. I was prepared, after Lyndon, for another slaughter of the innocents.'

'Lyndon was not innocent, Titus. These people are. You didn't tell them.'

'I didn't deem it necessary. May I close the door?'

He was her captor: but he came like an emissary to the camp of a greater power. She liked the way he was with her, cowed but elated. He closed the door, and locked it.

'I love you, J. And I fear you. In fact, I think I love you because I fear you. Is that a sickness?'

'I would have thought so.'

'Yes, so would I.'

'Why did you take such a time to come?'

'I had to put my affairs in order. Otherwise there would have been chaos. When I was gone.'

'You're leaving?'

He looked into her, the muscles of his face ruffled by anticipation.

'I hope so.'

'Where to?'

Still she didn't guess what had brought him to the house, his affairs neatened, his wife unknowingly asked forgiveness of as she slept, all channels of escape closed, all contradictions laid to rest.

Still she didn't guess he'd come to die.

'I'm reduced by you, J. Reduced to nothing. And there is nowhere for me to go. Do you follow?'

'No.'

'I cannot live without you,' he said. The cliché was unpardonable. Could he not have found a better way to say it? She almost laughed, it was so trite.

But he hadn't finished.

' – and I certainly can't live *with* you.' Abruptly, the tone changed. 'Because you revolt me, woman, your whole being disgusts me.'

'So?' she asked, softly.

'So . . .' He was tender again and she began to understand. '. . . kill me.'

It was grotesque. The glittering eyes were steady on her.

'It's what I want,' he said. 'Believe me, it's all I want in the world. Kill me, however you please. I'll go without resistance, without complaint.'

She remembered the old joke. Masochist to Sadist: Hurt me! For God's sake, hurt me! Sadist to Masochist: No.

'And if I refuse?' she said.

'You can't refuse. I'm loathsome.'

'But I don't hate you, Titus.'

'You should. I'm weak. I'm useless to you. I taught you nothing.'

'You taught me a great deal. I can control myself now.'

'Lyndon's death was controlled, was it?'

'Certainly.'

'It looked a little excessive to me.'

'He got everything he deserved.'

'Give me what I deserve, then, in my turn. I've locked you up. I've rejected you when you needed me. Punish me for it.'

'I survived.'

'J!'

Even in this extremity he couldn't call her by her full name.

'Please to God. Please to God. I need only this one thing from you. Do it out of whatever motive you have in you. Compassion, or contempt, or love. But do it, please do it.'

'No,' she said.

He crossed the room suddenly, and slapped her, very hard.

'Lyndon said you were a whore. He was right; you are. Gutterslut, nothing better.'

He walked away, turned, walked back, hit her again, faster, harder, and again, six or seven times, backwards and forwards.

Then he stopped, panting.

'You want money?' Bargains now. Blows, then bargains.

She was seeing him twisted through tears of shock, which she was unable to prevent.

'Do you want money?' he said again.

'What do you think?'

He didn't hear her sarcasm, and began to scatter notes around her feet, dozens and dozens of them, like offerings around the Statue of the Virgin.

'Anything you want,' he said, '*Jacqueline*.'

In her belly she felt something close to pain as the urge to kill him found birth, but she resisted it. It was playing into his hands, becoming the instrument of his will: powerless. Usage again; that's all she ever got. She had been bred like a cow, to give a certain supply. Of care to husbands, of milk to babies, of death to old men. And, like a cow, she was expected to be compliant with every demand made of her, whenever the call came. Well, not this time.

She went to the door.

'Where are you going?'

She reached for the key.

'Your death is your own business, not mine,' she said.

He ran at her before she could unlock the door, and the blow – in its force, in its malice – was totally unexpected.

'Bitch!' he shrieked, a hail of blows coming fast upon the first.

In her stomach, the thing that wanted to kill grew a little larger.

He had his fingers tangled in her hair, and pulled her back into the room, shouting obscenities at her, an endless stream of them, as though he'd opened a dam full of sewer-water on her. This was just another way for him to get what he wanted she told herself, if you succumb to this you've lost: he's just manipulating you. Still the words came: the same dirty words that had been thrown at generations of unsubmissive women. Whore; heretic; cunt; bitch; monster.

Yes, she was that.

Yes, she thought: monster I am.

The thought made it easy. She turned. He knew what she intended even before she looked at him. He dropped his hands from her head. Her anger was already in her throat coming out of her – crossing the air between them.

Monster he calls me: monster I am.

I do this for myself, not for him. Never for him. For myself!

He gasped as her will touched him, and the glittering eyes stopped glittering for a moment, the will to die became the will to survive, all too late of course, and he roared. She heard answering shouts, steps, threats on the stairs. They would be in the room in a matter of moments.

'You are an animal,' she said.

'No,' he said, certain even now that his place was in command.

'You don't exist,' she said, advancing on him. 'They'll never find the part that was Titus. Titus is gone. The rest is just – '

The pain was terrible. It stopped even a voice coming out from him. Or was that her again, changing his throat, his palate, his very head? She was unlocking the plates of his skull, and reorganizing him.

No, he wanted to say, this isn't the subtle ritual I had planned. I wanted to die folded into you, I wanted to go with my mouth clamped to yours, cooling in you as I died. This is not the way I want it.

No. No. No.

They were at the door, the men who'd kept her here, beating on it. She had no fear of them, of course, except that they might spoil her handiwork before the final touches were added to it.

Someone was hurling themselves at the door now. Wood splintered: the door was flung open. Ths two men were both armed. They pointed their weapons at her, steady-handed.

'Mr Pettifer?' said the younger man. In the corner of the room, under the table, Pettifer's eyes shone.

'Mr Pettifer?' he said again, forgetting the woman.

Pettifer shook his snouted head. Don't come any closer, please, he thought.

The man crouched down and stared under the table at the disgusting beast that was squatting there; bloody from its transformation, but alive. She had killed his nerves: he felt no pain. He just survived, his hands knotted into paws, his legs scooped up around his back, knees broken so he had the look of a four-legged crab, his brain exposed, his eyes lidless, lower jaw broken and swept up over his top jaw like a bulldog, ears torn off, spine snapped, humanity bewitched into another state.

'You are an animal,' she'd said. It wasn't a bad facsimile of beasthood.

The man with the gun gagged as he recognized fragments of

his master. He stood up, greasy-chinned, and glanced around at the woman.

Jacqueline shrugged.

'You did this?' Awe mingled with the revulsion.

She nodded.

'Come Titus,' she said, clicking her fingers.

The beast shook its head, sobbing.

'Come Titus,' she said more forcefully, and Titus Pettifer waddled out of his hiding place, leaving a trail like a punctured meat-sack.

The man fired at Pettifer's remains out of sheer instinct. Anything, anything at all to prevent this disgusting creature from approaching him.

Titus stumbled two steps back on his bloody paws, shook himself as if to dislodge the death in him, and failing, died.

'Content?' she asked.

The gunman looked up from the execution. Was the power talking to him? No; Jacqueline was staring at Pettifer's corpse, asking the question of him.

Content?

The gunman dropped his weapon. The other man did the same.

'How did this happen?' asked the man at the door. A simple question: a child's question.

'He asked,' said Jacqueline. 'It was all I could give him.'

The gunman nodded, and fell to his knees.

Vassi's Testimony (final part)

Chance has played a worryingly large part in my romance with Jacqueline Ess. Sometimes it's seemed I've been subject to every tide that passes through the world, spun around by the merest flick of accident's wrist. Other times I've had the suspicion that she was masterminding my life, as she was the lives of a hundred others, a thousand others, arranging every fluke meeting, choreographing my victories and my defeats, escorting me, blindly, towards this last encounter.

I found her without knowing I'd found her, that was the irony of it. I'd traced her first to a house in Surrey, a house that had a year previous seen the murder of one Titus Pettifer, a billionaire shot by one of his own bodyguards. In the upstairs room, where the murder had taken place, all was serenity. If she had been there, they had removed any sign. But the house, now in virtual ruin, was prey to all manner of graffiti; and on the stained plaster wall of that room someone had scrawled a woman. She was obscenely over-endowed, her gaping sex blazing with what looked like lightning. And at her feet there was a creature of indeterminate species. Perhaps a crab, perhaps a dog, perhaps even a man. Whatever it was it had no power over itself. It sat in the light of her agonizing presence and counted itself amongst the fortunate. Looking at that wizened creature, with its eyes turned up to gaze on the burning Madonna, I knew the picture was a portrait of Jacqueline.

I don't know how long I stood looking at the graffiti, but I was interrupted by a man who looked to be in a worse condition than me. A beard that had never been trimmed or washed, a frame so wasted I wondered how he managed to stand upright, and a smell that would not have shamed a skunk.

I never knew his name: but he was, he told me, the maker of the picture on the wall. It was easy to believe that. His desperation, his hunger, his confusion were all marks of a man who had seen Jacqueline.

If I was rough in my interrogration of him I'm sure he forgave me. It was an unburdening for him, to tell everything he'd seen the day that Pettifer had been killed, and know that I believed it all. He told me his fellow bodyguard, the man who had fired the shots that had killed Pettifer, had committed suicide in prison.

His life, he said, was meaningless. She had destroyed it. I gave him what reassurances I could; that she meant no harm, and that he needn't fear that she would come for him. When I told him that, he cried, more, I think, out of loss than relief.

Finally I asked him if he knew where Jacqueline was now. I'd left that question to the end, though it had been the most pressing enquiry, because I suppose I didn't dare hope he'd know. But my God, he did. She had not left the house immediately after the shooting of Pettifer. She had sat down with this man, and talked to him quietly about his children, his tailor, his car. She'd asked him what his mother had been like, and he'd told her his mother had been a prostitute. Had she been happy? Jacqueline had asked. He'd said he didn't know. Did she ever cry, she'd asked. He'd said he never saw her laugh or cry in his life. And she'd nodded, and thanked him.

Later, before his suicide, the other gunman had told him Jacqueline had gone to Amsterdam. This he knew for a fact, from a man called Koos. And so the circle begins to close, yes?

I was in Amsterdam seven weeks, without finding a single clue to her whereabouts, until yesterday evening. Seven weeks of celibacy, which is unusual for me. Listless with frustration I went down to the red-light district, to find a woman. They sit there you know, in the windows, like mannequins, beside pink-fringed lamps. Some have miniature dogs on their laps; some read. Most just stare out at the street, as if mesmerized.

There were no faces there that interested me. They all seemed joyless, lightless, too much unlike her. Yet I couldn't leave. I was like a fat boy in a sweet shop, too nauseous to buy, too gluttonous to go.

Towards the middle of the night, I was spoken to out of the crowd by a young man who, on closer inspection, was not young at all, but heavily made up. He had no eyebrows, just pencil marks drawn on to his shiny skin. A cluster of gold earrings in his left ear, a half-eaten peach in his white-gloved hand, open sandals, lacquered toenails. He took hold of my sleeve, proprietorially.

I must have sneered at his sickening appearance, but he didn't seem at all upset by my contempt. You look like a man of discernment, he said. I looked nothing of the kind: you must be mistaken, I said. No, he replied, I am not mistaken. You are Oliver Vassi.

My first thought, absurdly, was that he intended to kill me. I tried to pull away; his grip on my cuff was relentless.

You want a woman, he said. Did I hesitate enough for him to know I meant yes, though I said no? I have a woman like no other, he went on, she's a miracle. I know you'll want to meet her in the flesh.

What made me know it was Jacqueline he was talking about? Perhaps the fact that he had known me from out of the crowd, as though she was up at a window somewhere, ordering her admirers to be brought to her like a diner ordering lobster from a tank. Perhaps too the way his eyes shone at me, meeting mine without fear because fear, like rapture, he felt only in the presence of one creature on God's cruel earth. Could I not also see myself reflected in his perilous look? He knew Jacqueline, I had no doubt of it.

He knew I was hooked, because once I hesitated he turned away from me with a mincing shrug, as if to say: you missed your chance. Where is she? I said, seizing his twig-thin arm. He cocked his head down the street and I followed him, suddenly as witless as an idiot, out of the throng. The road emptied as we walked; the red lights gave way to gloom, and then to darkness. If I asked him where we were going once I asked him a dozen times; he chose not to answer, until we reached a narrow door in a narrow house down some razor-thin street. We're here, he announced, as though the hovel were the Palace of Versailles.

Up two flights in the otherwise empty house there was a room with a black door. He pressed me to it. It was locked.

'See,' he invited, 'she's inside.'

'It's locked,' I replied. My heart was fit to burst: she was near, for certain, I knew she was near.

'See,' he said again, and pointed to a tiny hole in the panel of the door. I devoured the light through it, pushing my eye towards her through the tiny hole.

The squalid interior was empty, except for a mattress and Jacqueline. She lay spreadeagled, her wrists and ankles bound to rough posts set in the bare floor at the four corners of the mattress.

'Who did this?' I demanded, not taking my eye from her nakedness.

'She asks,' he replied. 'It is her desire. She asks.'

She had heard my voice; she cranked up her head with some difficulty and stared directly at the door. When she looked at me all the hairs rose on my head, I swear it, in welcome, and swayed at her command.

'Oliver,' she said.

'Jacqueline.' I pressed the word to the wood with a kiss.

Her body was seething, her shaved sex opening and closing like some exquisite plant, purple and lilac and rose.

'Let me in,' I said to Koos.

'You will not survive one night with her.'

'Let me in.'

'She is expensive,' he warned.

'How much do you want?'

'Everything you have. The shirt off your back, your money, your jewellery; then she is yours.'

I wanted to beat the door down, or break his nicotine-stained fingers one by one until he gave me the key. He knew what I was thinking.

'The key is hidden,' he said, 'And the door is strong. You must pay, Mr Vassi. You want to pay.'

It was true. I wanted to pay.

'You want to give me all you have ever owned, all you have ever been. You want to go to her with nothing to claim you back. I know this. It's how they all go to her.'

'All? Are there many?'

'She is insatiable,' he said, without relish. It wasn't a pimp's boast: it was his pain, I saw that clearly. 'I am always finding more for her, and burying them.'

Burying them.

That, I suppose, is Koos' function; he disposes of the dead. And he will get his lacquered hands on me after tonight; he will fetch me off her when I am dry and useless to her, and find some pit, some canal, some furnace to lose me in. The thought isn't particularly attractive.

Yet here I am with all the money I could raise from selling my few remaining possessions on the table in front of me, my dignity gone, my life hanging on a thread, waiting for a pimp and a key.

It's well dark now, and he's late. But I think he is obliged to come. Not for the money, he probably has few requirements beyond his heroin and his mascara. He will come to do business with me because she demands it and he is in thrall to her, every bit as much as I am. Oh, he will come. Of course he will come.

Well, I think that is sufficient.

This is my testimony. I have no time to re-read it now. His footsteps are on the stairs (he limps) and I must go with him. This I leave to whoever finds it, to use as they think fit. By morning I shall be dead, and happy. Believe it.

My God, she thought, Koos has cheated me.

Vassi had been outside the door, she'd felt his flesh with her mind and she'd embraced it. But Koos hadn't let him in, despite her explicit orders. Of all men, Vassi was to be allowed free access, Koos knew that. But he'd cheated her, the way they'd all cheated her except Vassi. With him (perhaps) it had been love.

She lay on the bed through the night, never sleeping. She seldom slept now for more than a few minutes: and only then with Koos watching her. She'd done herself harm in her sleep, mutilating herself without knowing it, waking up bleeding and screaming with every limb sprouting needles she'd made out of her own skin and muscle, like a flesh cactus.

It was dark again, she guessed, but it was difficult to be sure. In this heavily curtained, bare-bulb lit room, it was a perpetual day to the senses, perpetual night to the soul. She would lie, bed-sores on her back, on her buttocks, listening to the far sounds of the street, sometimes dozing for a while, sometimes eating from Koos' hand, being washed, being toileted, being used.

A key turned in the lock. She strained from the mattress to see who it was. The door was opening . . . opening . . . opened.

Vassi. Oh God, it was Vassi at last, she could see him crossing the room towards her.

Let this not be another memory, she prayed, please let it be him this time: true and real.

'Jacqueline.'

He said the name of her flesh, the whole name.

'Jacqueline.' It *was* him.

Behind him, Koos stared between her legs, fascinated by the dance of her labia.

'Koo . . .' she said, trying to smile.

'I brought him,' he grinned at her, not looking away from her sex.

'A day,' she whispered. 'I waited a day, Koos. You made me wait – '

'What's a day to you?' he said, still grinning.

She didn't need the pimp any longer, not that he knew that. In his innocence he thought Vassi was just another man she'd seduced along the way; to be drained and discarded like the others. Koos believed he would be needed tomorrow; that's why he played this fatal game so artlessly.

'Lock the door,' she suggested to him. 'Stay if you like.'

'Stay?' he said, leering. 'You mean, and watch?'

He watched anyway. She knew he watched through that hole he had bored in the door; she could hear him pant sometimes. But this time, let him stay forever.

Carefully, he took the key from the outside of the door, closed it, slipped the key into the inside and locked it. Even as the lock clicked she killed him, before he could even turn round and look at her again. Nothing spectacular in the execution; she just reached into his pigeon chest and crushed his lungs. He slumped against the door and slid down, smearing his face across the wood.

Vassi didn't even turn round to see him die; she was all he ever wanted to look at again.

He approached the mattress, crouched, and began to untie her ankles. The skin was chafed, the rope scabby with old blood. He worked at the knots systematically, finding a calm he thought he'd lost, a simple contentment in being here at the end, unable to go back, and knowing that the path ahead was deep in her.

When her ankles were free, he began on her wrists, interrupting her view of the ceiling as he bent over her. His voice was soft.

'Why did you let him do this to you?'

'I was afraid.'

'Of what?'

'To move; even to live. Every day, agony.'

'Yes.'

He understood so well that total incapacity to exist.

She felt him at her side, undressing, then laying a kiss on the sallow skin of the stomach of the body she occupied. It was marked with her workings; the skin had been stretched beyond its tolerance and was permanently criss-crossed.

He lay down beside her, and the feel of his body against hers was not unpleasant.

She touched his head. Her joints were stiff, the movements painful, but she wanted to draw his face up to hers. He came, smiling, into her sight, and they exchanged kisses.

My God, she thought, we are together.

And thinking they were together, her will was made flesh. Under his lips her features dissolved, becoming the red sea he'd dreamt of, and washing up over his face, that was itself dissolving: common waters made of thought and bone.

Her keen breasts pricked him like arrows; his erection, sharpened by her thought, killed her in return with his only thrust. Tangled in a wash of love they thought themselves extinguished, and were.

Outside, the hard world mourned on, the chatter of buyers and sellers continuing through the night. Eventually indifference and fatigue claimed even the eagerest merchant. Inside and out there was a healing silence: an end to losses and to gains.

The Skins of the Fathers

The car coughed, and choked, and died. Davidson was suddenly aware of the wind on the desert road, as it keened at the windows of his Mustang. He tried to revive the engine, but it refused life. Exasperated, Davidson let his sweating hands drop off the wheel and surveyed the territory. In every direction, hot air, hot rock, hot sand. This was Arizona.

He opened the door and stepped out on to the baking dust highway. In front and behind it stretched unswervingly to the pale horizon. If he narrowed his eyes he could just make out the mountains, but as soon as he attempted to fix his focus they were eaten up by the heat-haze. Already the sun was corroding the top of his head, where his blond hair was thinning. He threw up the hood of the car and peered hopelessly into the engine, regretting his lack of mechanical know-how. Jesus, he thought, why don't they make the damn things foolproof?

Then he heard the music.

It was so far off it sounded like a whistling in his ears at first: but it became louder.

It was music, of a sort.

How did it sound? Like the wind through telephone lines, a sourceless, rhythmless, heartless air-wave plucking at the hairs on the back of his neck and telling them to stand. He tried to ignore it, but it wouldn't go away.

He looked up out of the shade of the bonnet to find the players, but the road was empty in both directions. Only as he scanned the desert to the south-east did a line of tiny figures become visible to him, walking, or skipping, or dancing at the furthest edge of his sight, liquid in the heat off the earth. The procession, if that was its nature, was long, and making its way across the desert parallel to the highway. Their paths would not cross.

Davidson glanced down once more into the cooling entrails of his vehicle and then up again at the distant line of dancers.

He needed help: no doubt of it.

He started off across the desert towards them.

Once off the highway the dust, not impacted by the passage of cars, was loose: it flung itself up at his face with every step.

Progress was slow: he broke into a trot: but they were receding from him. He began to run.

Over the thunder of his blood, he could hear the music more loudly now. There was no melody apparent, but a constant rising and falling of many instruments; howls and hummings, whistlings, drummings and roarings.

The head of the procession had now disappeared, received into distance, but the celebrants (if that they were) still paraded past. He changed direction a little, to head them off, glancing over his shoulder briefly to check his way back. With a stomach-churning sense of loneliness he saw his vehicle, as small as a beetle on the road behind him, sitting weighed down by a boiling sky.

He ran on. A quarter of an hour, perhaps and he began to see the procession more clearly, though its leaders were well out of sight. It was, he began to believe, a carnival of some sort, extraordinary as that seemed out here in the middle of God's nowhere. The last dancers in the parade were definitely costumed, however. They wore headdresses and masks that tottered well above human height – there was the flutter of brightly-coloured feathers, and streamers coiling in the air behind them. Whatever the reason for the celebration they reeled like drunkards, loping one moment, leaping the next, squirming, some of them, on the ground, bellies to the hot sand.

Davidson's lungs were torn with exhaustion, and it was clear he was losing the pursuit. Having gained on the procession, it was now moving off faster than he had strength or willpower to follow.

He stopped, bracing his arms on his knees to support his aching torso, and looked under his sweat-sodden brow at his disappearing salvation. Then, summoning up all the energy he could muster, he yelled:

Stop!

At first there was no response. Then, through the slits of his eyes, he thought he saw one or two of the revellers halt. He straightened up. Yes, one or two were looking at him. He felt, rather than saw, their eyes upon him.

He began to walk towards them.

Some of the instruments had died away, as though word of his presence was spreading among them. They'd definitely seen him, no doubt of that.

He walked on, faster now, and out of the haze, the details of the procession began to come clear.

His pace slowed a little. His heart, already pounding with exertion, thudded in his chest.

– My Jesus, he said, and for the first time in his thirty-six godless years the words were a true prayer.

He stood off half a mile from them, but there was no mistaking what he saw. His aching eyes knew papier-mâché from flesh, illusion from misshapen reali·y.

The creatures at the end of the procession, the least of the least, the hangers-on, were monsters whose appearance beggared the nightmares of insanity.

One was perhaps eighteen or twenty feet tall. Its skin, that hung in folds on its muscle, was a sheath of spikes, its head a cone of exposed teeth, set in scarlet gums. Another was three-winged, its triple ended tail thrashing the dust with reptilian enthusiasm. A third and fourth were married together in a union of monstrosities the result of which was more disgusting than the sum of its parts. Through its length and breadth this symbiotic horror was locked in seeping marriage, its limbs thrust in and through wounds in its partners flesh. Though the tongues of its heads were wound together it managed a cacophonous howl.

Davidson took a step back, and glanced round at the car and the highway. As he did so one of the things, black and red, began to scream like a whistle. Even at a half mile's distance the noise cut into Davidson's head. He looked back at the procession.

The whistling monster had left its place in the parade, and its clawed feet were pounding the desert as it began to race towards him. Uncontrollable panic swept through Davidson, and he felt his trousers fill as his bowels failed him.

The thing was rushing towards him with the speed of a cheetah, growing with every second, so he could see more detail of its alien anatomy with every step. The thumbless hands with their toothed palms, the head that bore only a tri-coloured eye, the sinew of its shoulder and chest, even its genitals, erect with anger, or (God help me) lust, two-pronged and beating against its abdomen.

Davidson shrieked a shriek that was almost the equal of the monster's noise, and fled back the way he had come.

The car was a mile, two miles away, and he knew it offered no protection were he to reach it before the monster overcame him. In that moment he realized how close death was, how close it had always been, and he longed for a moment's comprehension of this idiot horror.

It was already close behind him as his shit-slimed legs buckled, and he fell, and crawled, and dragged himself towards the car. As he heard the thud of its feet at his back he instinctively huddled into a ball of whimpering flesh, and awaited the coup de grace.

He waited two heart-beats.

Three. Four. Still it didn't come.

The whistling voice had grown to an unbearable pitch, and was now fading a little. The gnashing palms did not connect with his body. Cautiously, expecting his head to be snapped from his neck at any moment, he peered through his fingers.

The creature had overtaken him.

Perhaps contemptuous of his frailty it had run on past him towards the highway.

Davidson smelt his excrement, and his fear. He felt curiously ignored. Behind him the parade had moved on. Only one or two inquisitive monsters still looked over their shoulders in his direction, as they receded into the dust.

The whistling now changed pitch. Davidson cautiously raised his head from ground level. The noise was all but outside his hearing-range, just a shrill whine at the back of his aching head.

He stood up.

The creature had leapt on to the top of his car. Its head was thrown back in a kind of ecstasy, its erection plainer than ever, the eye in its huge head glinting. With a final swoop to its voice, which took the whistle out of human hearing, it bent upon the car, smashing the windshield and curling its mouthed hands upon the roof. It then proceeded to tear the steel back like so much paper, its body twitching with glee, its head jerking about. Once the roof was torn up, it leapt on to the highway and threw the metal into the air. It turned in the sky and smashed down on the desert floor. Davidson briefly wondered what he could possibly put on the insurance form. Now the creature was tearing the vehicle apart. The doors were scattered. The engine was ripped out. The wheels slashed and wrenched off the axles.

To Davidson's nostrils there drifted the unmistakable stench of gasoline. No sooner had he registered the smell than a shard of metal glanced against another and the creature and the car were sheathed in a billowing column of fire, blackening into smoke as it balled over the highway.

The thing did not call out: or if it did its agonies were beyond hearing. It staggered out of the inferno with its flesh on fire, every inch of its body alight; its arms flailed wildly in a vain attempt to douse the fire, and it began to run off down the highway, fleeing from the source of its agony towards the mountains. Flames sprouted off its back and the air was tinged with the smell of its cooking flesh.

It didn't fall however, though the fire must have been devouring it. The run went on and on, until the heat dissolved the highway into the blue distance, and it was gone.

Davidson sank down on to his knees. The shit on his legs was already dry in the heat. The car continued to burn. The music had gone entirely, as had the procession.

It was the sun that drove him from the sand back towards his gutted car.

He was blank-eyed when the next vehicle along the highway stopped to pick him up.

Sheriff Josh Packard stared in disbelief at the claw prints on the ground at his feet. They were etched in slowly solidifying fat, the liquid flesh of the monster that had run through the main street (the only street) of Welcome minutes ago. It had then collapsed, breathing its last breath, and died in a writhing ball three trucks' length from the bank. The normal business of Welcome, the trading, the debating, the how do you do's, had halted. One or two nauseous individuals had been received into the lobby of the Hotel while the smell of fricassied flesh thickened the good desert air of the town.

The stench was something between over-cooked fish and an exhumation, and it offended Packard. This was his town, overlooked by him, protected by him. The intrusion of this fireball was not looked upon kindly.

Packard took out his gun and began to walk towards the corpse. The flames were all but out now, having eaten the best of their meal. Even so destroyed by fire, it was a sizeable bulk. What might once have been its limbs were gathered around what might have been its head. The rest was beyond recognition. All in all, Packard was glad of that small mercy. But even in the charnel-house confusion of rendered flesh and blackened bone he could make out enough inhuman forms to quicken his pulse.

This was a monster: no doubt of it.

A creature from earth: out of earth, indeed. Up from the underworld and on its way to the great bowl for a night of celebration. Once every generation or so, his father had told him, the desert spat out its demons and let them loose awhile. Being a child who thought for himself Packard had never believed the shit his father talked but was this not such a demon?

Whatever mischance had brought this burning monstrosity

into his town to die, there was pleasure for Packard in the proof of their vulnerability. His father had never mentioned that possibility.

Half-smiling at the thought of mastering such foulness, Packard stepped up to the smoking corpse and kicked it. The crowd, still lingering in the safety of the doorways, cooed with admiration at his bravery. The half-smile spread across his face. That kick alone would be worth a night of drinks, perhaps even a woman.

The thing was belly up. With the dispassionate gaze of a professional demon-kicker, Packard scrutinized the tangle of limbs across the head. It was quite dead, that was obvious. He sheathed his gun and bent towards the corpse.

'Get a camera out here, Jedediah,' he said, impressing even himself.

His deputy ran off towards the office.

'What we need,' he said, 'is a picture of this here beauty.'

Packard went down on his haunches and reached across to the blackened limbs of the thing. His gloves would be ruined, but it was worth the inconvenience for the good this gesture would be doing for his public image. He could almost feel the admiring looks as he touched the flesh, and began to shake a limb loose from the head of the monster.

The fire had welded the parts together, and he had to wrench the limb free. But it came, with a jellied sound, revealing the heat-withered eye on the face beneath.

He dropped the limb back where it had come with a look of disgust.

A beat.

Then the demon's arm was snaking up – suddenly – too suddenly for Packard to move, and in a moment sublime with terror the Sheriff saw the mouth open in the palm of its forefoot and close again around his own hand.

Whimpering he lost balance and sat in the fat, pulling away from the mouth, as his glove was chewed through, and the teeth connected with his hand, clipping off his fingers as the rasping maw drew digits, blood and stumps further into its gut.

Packard's bottom slid in the mess under him and he squirmed, howling now, to loose himself. It still had life in it, this thing from the underworld. Packard bellowed for mercy as he staggered to his feet, dragging the sordid bulk of the thing up off the ground as he did so.

A shot sounded, close to Packard's ear. Fluids, blood and pus spattered him as the limb was blown to smithereens at the shoulder, and the mouth loosed its grip on Packard. The wasted mass of devouring muscle fell to the ground, and Packard's hand, or what was left of it, was in the open air again. There were no fingers remaining on his right hand, and barely half a thumb; the shattered bone of his digits jutted awkwardly from a partially chewed palm.

Eleanor Kooker dropped the barrel of the shotgun she had just fired, and grunted with satisfaction.

'Your hand's gone,' she said, with brutal simplicity.

Monsters, Packard remembered his father telling him, never die. He'd remembered too late, and now he'd sacrificed his hand, his drinking, sexing hand. A wave of nostalgia for lost years with those fingers washed over him, while dots burst into darkness before his eyes. The last thing he saw as a dead faint carried him to the ground was his dutiful deputy raising a camera to record the whole scene.

The shack at the back of the house was Lucy's refuge and always had been. When Eugene came back drunk from Welcome, or a sudden fury took him because the stew was cold, Lucy retired into the shack where she could weep in peace. There was no pity to be had in Lucy's life. None from Eugene certainly, and precious little time to pity herself.

Today, the old source of irritation had got Eugene into a rage:

The child.

The nurtured and carefully cultivated child of their love; named after the brother of Moses, Aaron, which meant 'exalted one'. A sweet boy. The prettiest boy in the whole territory; five years old and already as charming and polite as any East Coast Momma could wish to raise.

Aaron.

Lucy's pride and joy, a child fit to blow bubbles in a picture book, fit to dance, fit to charm the Devil himself.

That was Eugene's objection.

'That fucking child's no more a boy than you are,' he said to Lucy. 'He's not even a half-boy. He's only fit for putting in fancy shoes and selling perfume. Or a preacher, he's fit for a preacher.'

He pointed a nail-bitten, crook-thumbed hand at the boy.

'You're a shame to your father.'

Aaron met his father's stare.

'You hear me, boy?'

Eugene looked away. The boy's big eyes made him sick to his stomach, more like a dog's eyes than anything human.

'I want him out of this house.'

'What's he done?'

'He doesn't need to do a thing. It's sufficient he's the way he is. They laugh at me, you know that? They laugh at me because of him.'

'Nobody laughs at you, Eugene.'

'Oh yes – '

'Not for the boy's sake.'

'Huh?'

'If they laugh, they don't laugh at the boy. They laugh at you.'

'Shut your mouth.'

'They know what you are, Eugene. They see you clear, clear as I see you.'

'I tell you, woman – '

'Sick as a dog in the street, talking about what you've seen and what you're scared of – '

He struck her as he had many times before. The blow drew blood, as similar blows had for five years, but though she reeled, her first thoughts were for the boy.

'Aaron,' she said through the tears the pain had brought. 'Come with me.'

'You let the bastard alone.' Eugene was trembling.

'Aaron.'

The child stood between father and mother, not knowing which to obey. The look of confusion on his face brought Lucy's tears more copiously.

'Mama,' said the child, very quietly. There was a grave look in his eyes, that went beyond confusion. Before Lucy could find a way to cool the situation, Eugene had hold of the boy by his hair and was dragging him closer.

'You listen to your father, boy.'

'Yes – '

'Yes, sir, we say to our father, don't we? We say, yes, sir.'

Aaron's face was thrust into the stinking crotch of his father's jeans.

'Yes, sir.'

'He stays with me woman. You're not taking him out into that fucking shack one more time. He stays with his father.'

The skirmish was lost and Lucy knew it. If she pressed the point any further, she only put the child at further risk.

'If you harm him – '

'I'm his father, woman,' Eugene grinned. 'What, do you think I'd hurt my own flesh and blood?'

The boy was locked to his father's hips in a position that was scarcely short of obscene. But Lucy knew her husband: and he was close to an outburst that would be uncontrollable. She no longer cared for herself – she'd had her joys – but the boy was so vulnerable.

'Get out of our sight, woman, why don't you? The boy and I want to be alone, don't we?'

Eugene dragged Aaron's face from his crotch and sneered down at his pale face.

'Don't we?'

'Yes, Papa.'

'Yes, Papa. Oh yes indeed, Papa.'

Lucy left the house and retired into the cool darkness of the shack, where she prayed for Aaron, named after the brother of Moses. Aaron, whose name meant 'exalted one'; she wondered how long he could survive the brutalities the future would provide.

The boy was stripped now. He stood white in front of his father. He wasn't afraid. The whipping that would be meted out to him would pain him, but this was not true fear.

'You're sickly, lad,' said Eugene, running a huge hand over his son's abdomen. 'Weak and sickly like a runty hog. If I was a farmer, and you were a hog, boy, you know what I'd do?'

Again, he took the boy by the hair. The other hand, between the legs.

'You know what I'd do, boy?'

'No, Papa. What would you do?'

The scored hand slid up over Aaron's body while his father made a slitting sound.

'Why, I'd cut you up and feed you to the rest of the litter. Nothing a hog likes better to eat, than hog-meat. How'd you like that?'

'No, Papa.'

'You wouldn't like that?'

'No thank you, Papa.'

Eugene's face hardened.

'Well I'd like to see that, Aaron. I'd like to see what you'd do if I was to open you up and have a look inside you.'

There was a new violence in his father's games, which Aaron couldn't understand: new threats, new intimacy. Uncomfortable as he was the boy knew the real fear was felt not by him but by his father; fear was Eugene's birthright, just as it was Aaron's to watch, and wait, and suffer, until the moment came. He knew (without understanding how or why), that he would be an instrument in the destruction of his father. Maybe more than an instrument.

Anger erupted in Eugene. He stared at the boy, his brown fists clenched so tight that the knuckles burned white. The boy was his ruin, somehow; he'd killed the good life they'd lived before he was born, as surely as if he'd shot his parents dead. Scarcely thinking of what he was doing, Eugene's hands closed around the back of the boy's frail neck.

Aaron made no sound.

'I could kill you boy.'

'Yes, sir.'

'What do you say to that?'

'Nothing, sir.'

'You should say thank you, sir.'

'Why?'

'Why, boy? 'Cause this life's not worth what a hog can shit, and I'd be doing you a loving service, as a father should a son.'

'Yes, sir.'

In the shack behind the house Lucy had stopped crying. There was no purpose in it; and besides, something in the sky she could see through the holes in the roof had brought memories to her that wiped the tears away. A certain sky: pure blue, sheeny-clear. Eugene wouldn't harm the boy. He wouldn't dare, ever dare, harm that child. He knew what the boy was, though he'd never admit to it.

She remembered the day, six years ago now, when the sky had been sheened like today, and the air had been livid with the heat. Eugene and she had been just about as hot as the air, they hadn't taken their eyes off each other all day. He was stronger then: in his prime. A soaring, splendid man, his body made heavy with work, and his legs so hard they felt like rock when she ran her hands over them. She had been quite a looker herself; the best damn backside in Welcome, firm and downy; a divide so softly haired Eugene couldn't keep from kissing her, even there, in the secret place. He'd pleasure her all day and all night sometimes; in the house they were building, or out on the sand in the late afternoon. The desert made a fine bed, and they could lie uninterrupted beneath the wide sky.

That day six years ago the sky had darkened too soon; long before night was due. It had seemed to blacken in a moment, and the lovers were suddenly cold in their hurried nakedness. She had seen, over his shoulder, the shapes the sky had taken: the vast and monumental creatures that were watching them. He, in his passion, still worked at her, thrust to his root and out the length again as he knew she delighted in, 'til a hand the colour of beets and the size of a man pinched his neck, and plucked him out of his wife's lap. She watched him lifted into the sky like a squirming jack-rabbit, spitting from two mouths, North and South, as he finished his thrusts on the air. Then his eyes opened for a moment, and he saw his wife twenty feet below him, still bare, still spread butterfly wide, with monsters on every side. Casually, without malice, they threw him away, out of their ring of admiration, and out of her sight.

She remembered so well the hour that followed. the embraces of the monsters. Not foul in any way, not gross or harmful, never less than loving. Even the machineries of reproduction that they pierced her with, one after the other, were not painful, though some were as large as Eugene's fisted arm, and hard as bone. How many of those strangers took her that afternoon – three, four, five? Mingling their semen in her body, fondly teasing joy from her with their patient thrusts. When they went away, and her skin was touched with sunlight again, she felt, though on reflection it seemed shameful, a loss; as though the zenith of her life was passed, and the rest of her days would be a cold ride down to death.

She had got up at last, and walked over to where Eugene was lying unconscious on the sand, one of his legs broken by the fall. She had kissed him, and then squatted to pass water. She hoped, and hope it was, that there would be fruit from the seed of that day's love, and it would be a keepsake of her joy.

In the house Eugene struck the boy. Aaron's nose bled, but he made no sound.

'Speak, boy.'

'What shall I say?'

'Am I your father or not?'

'Yes, father.'

'Liar!'

He struck again, without warning; this time the blow carried Aaron to the floor. As his small, uncalloused palms flattened against the kitchen tiles to raise himself he felt something through the floor. There was a music in the ground.

'Liar!' his father was saying still.

There would be more blows to come, the boy thought, more pain, more blood. But it was bearable; and the music was a promise, after a long wait, of an end to blows once and for all.

Davidson staggered into the main street of Welcome. It was the middle of the afternoon, he guessed (his watch had stopped, perhaps out of sympathy), but the town appeared to be empty, until his eye alighted on the dark, smoking mound in the middle of the street, a hundred yards from where he stood.

If such a thing had been possible, his blood would have run cold at the sight.

He recognized what that bundle of burned flesh had been, despite the distance, and his head spun with horror. It had all been real after all. He stumbled on a couple more steps, fighting the dizziness and losing, until he felt himself supported by strong arms, and heard, through a fuzz of head-noises, reassuring words being spoken to him. They made no sense, but at least they were soft and human: he could give up any pretense to consciousness. He fainted, but it seemed there was only a moment of respite before the world came back into view again, as odious as ever.

He had been carried inside and was lying on an uncomfortable sofa, a woman's face, that of Eleanor Kooker, staring down at him. She beamed as he came round.

'The man'll survive,' she said, her voice like cabbage going through a grater.

She leaned further forward.

'You seen the thing, did you?'

Davidson nodded.

'Better give us the low-down.'

A glass was thrust into his hand and Eleanor filled it generously with whisky.

'Drink,' she demanded, 'then tell us what you got to tell – '

He downed the whisky in two, and the glass was immediately refilled. He drank the second glass more slowly, and began to feel better.

The room was filled with people: it was as though all of Welcome was pressing into the Kooker front parlour. Quite an audience: but then it was quite a tale. Loosened by the whisky, he began to tell it as best he could, without embellishment, just letting the words come. In return Eleanor described the circumstances of Sherriff Packard's 'accident' with the body of the car-wrecker. Packard was in the room, looking the worse for consoling whiskies and pain killers, his mutilated hand bound up so well it looked more like a club than a limb.

'It's not the only devil out there,' said Packard when the stories were out.

'So's you say,' said Eleanor, her quick eyes less than convinced.

'My Papa said so,' Packard returned, staring down at his bandaged hand. 'And I believe it, sure as Hell I believe it.'

'Then we'd best do something about it.'

'Like what?' posed a sour looking individual leaning against the mantelpiece. 'What's to be done about the likes of a thing that eats automobiles?'

Eleanor straightened up and delivered a well-aimed sneer at the questioner.

'Well let's have the benefit of your wisdom, Lou,' she said. 'What do *you* think we should do?'

'I think we should lie low and let 'em pass.'

'I'm no ostrich,' said Eleanor, 'but if you want to go bury your head, I'll lend you a spade, Lou. I'll even dig you the hole.'

General laughter. The cynic, discomforted, fell silent and picked at his nails.

'We can't sit here and let them come running through,' said Packard's deputy, between blowing bubbles with his gum.

'They were going towards the mountains,' Davidson said. 'Away from Welcome.'

'So what's to stop them changing their goddam minds?' Eleanor countered. 'Well?'

No answer. A few nods, a few headshakings.

'Jedediah,' she said, 'you're deputy – what do you think about this?'

The young man with the badge and the gum flushed a little, and plucked at his thin moustache. He obviously hadn't a clue.

'I see the picture,' the woman snapped back before he could answer. 'Clear as a bell. You're all too shit-scared to go poking them divils out of their holes, that it?'

Murmurs of self-justification around the room, more headshaking.

'You're just planning to sit yourselves down and let the women folk be devoured.'

A good word: devoured. So much more emotive than eaten. Eleanor paused for effect. Then she said darkly: 'Or worse.'

Worse than devoured? Pity sakes, what was worse than devoured?

'You're not going to be touched by no divils,' said Packard, getting up from his seat with some difficulty. He swayed on his feet as he addressed the room.

'We're going to have them shit-eaters and lynch 'em.'

This rousing battle-cry left the males in the room unroused; the sheriff was low on credibility since his encounter in Main Street.

'Discretion's the better part of valour,' Davidson murmured under his breath.

'That's so much horse-shit,' said Eleanor.

Davidson shrugged, and finished off the whisky in his glass. It was not re-filled. He reflected ruefully that he should be thankful he was still alive. But his work-schedule was in ruins. He had to get to a telephone and hire a car; if necessary have someone drive out to pick him up. The 'divils', whatever they were, were not his problem. Perhaps he'd be interested to read a few column-inches on the subject in *Newsweek*, when he was back East and relaxing with Barbara; but now all he wanted to do was finish his business in Arizona and get home as soon as possible.

Packard, however, had other ideas.

'You're a witness,' he said, pointing at Davidson, 'and as Sheriff of this community I order you to stay in Welcome until you've answered to my satisfaction all inquiries I have to put to you.'

The formal language sounded odd from his slobbish mouth.

'I've got business – ' Davidson began.

'Then you just send a cable and cancel that business, Mr-fancy-Davidson.'

The man was scoring points off him, Davidson knew, bolstering his shattered reputation by taking pot-shots at the Easterner. Still, Packard was the law: there was nothing to be done about it. He nodded his assent with as much good grace as he could muster. There'd be time to lodge a formal complaint against this hick-town Mussolini when he was home, safe and sound. For now, better to send a cable, and let business go hang.

'So what's the plan?' Eleanor demanded of Packard.

The Sheriff puffed out his booze-brightened cheeks.

'We deal with the divils,' he said.

'How?'

'Guns, woman.'

'You'll need more than guns, if they're as big as he says they are – '

'They are – ' said Davidson, 'believe me, they are.'

Packard sneered.

'We'll take the whole fucking arsenal,' he said jerking his remaining thumb at Jedediah. 'Go break out the heavy-duty weapons, boy. Anti-tank stuff. Bazookas.'

General amazement.

'You got bazookas?' said Lou, the mantelpiece cynic.

Packard managed a leering smile.

'Military stuff,' he said, 'left over from the Big One.'

Davidson sighed inwardly. The man was a psychotic, with his own little arsenal of out-of-date weapons, which were probably more lethal to the user than to the victim. They were all going to die. God help him, they were all going to die.

'You may have lost your fingers,' said Eleanor Kooker, delighted by this show of bravado, 'but you're the only man in this room, Josh Packard.'

Packard beamed and rubbed his crotch absent-mindedly. Davidson couldn't take the atmosphere of hand-me-down machismo in the room any longer.

'Look,' he piped up 'I've told you all I know. Why don't I just let you folks get on with it.'

'You ain't leaving,' said Packard, 'if that's what you're rooting after.'

'I'm just saying – '

'We know what you're saying son, and I ain't listening. If I see you hitch up your britches to leave I'll string you up by your balls. If you've got any.'

The bastard would try it too, thought Davidson, even if he only had one hand to do it with. Just go with the flow, he told himself, trying to stop his lip curling. If Packard went out to find the monsters and his damn bazooka backfired, that was his business. Let it be.

'There's a whole tribe of them,' Lou was quietly pointing out. 'According to this man. So how do we take out so many of them?'

'Strategy,' said Packard.

'We don't know their positions.'

'Surveillance,' replied Packard.

'They could really fuck us up Sherriff,' Jedediah observed, picking a collapsed gum-bubble from his moustache.

'This is our territory,' said Eleanor. 'We got it: we keep it.'

Jedediah nodded.

'Yes, ma,' he said.

'Suppose they just disappeared? Suppose we can't find them no more?' Lou was arguing. 'Couldn't we just let 'em go to ground?'

'Sure,' said Packard. 'And then we're left waiting around for them to come out again and devour the women folk.'

'Maybe they mean no harm – ' Lou replied.

Packard's reply was to raise his bandaged hand.

'They done me harm.'

That was incontestable.

Packard continued, his voice hoarse with feeling.

'Shit, I want them come-bags so bad I'm going out there with or without help. But we've got to out-think them, out-manoeuvre them, so we don't get anybody hurt.'

The man talks some sense, thought Davidson. Indeed, the whole room seemed impressed. Murmurs of approval all round; even from the mantelpiece.

Packard rounded on the deputy again.

'You get your ass moving, son. I want you to call up that bastard Crumb out of Caution and get his boys down here with every goddam gun and grenade they've got. And if he asks what for you tell him Sherriff Packard's declaring a State of Emergency, and I'm requisitioning every asshole weapon in fifty miles, and the man on the other end of it. Move it, son.'

Now the room was positively glowing with admiration, and Packard knew it.

'We'll blow the fuckers apart,' he said.

For a moment the rhetoric seemed to work its magic on Davidson, and he half-believed it might be possible; then he remembered the details of the procession, tails, teeth and all, and his bravado sank without trace.

They came up to the house so quietly, not intending to creep, just so gentle with their tread nobody heard them.

Inside, Eugene's anger had subsided. He was sitting with his legs up on the table, an empty bottle of whisky in front of him. The silence in the room was so heavy it suffocated.

Aaron, his face puffed up with his father's blows, was sitting beside the window. He didn't need to look up to see them coming across the sand towards the house, their approach sounded in his veins. His bruised face wanted to light up with a smile of welcome, but he repressed the instinct and simply waited, slumped in beaten resignation, until they were almost upon the house. Only when their massive bodies blocked out the sunlight through the window did he stand up. The boy's movement woke Eugene from his trance.

'What is it, boy?'

The child had backed off from the window, and was standing in the middle of the room, sobbing quietly with anticipation. His tiny hands were spread like sun-rays, his fingers jittering and twitching in his excitement.

'What's wrong with the window, boy?'

Aaron heard one of his true father's voices eclipse Eugene's mumblings. Like a dog eager to greet his master after a long separation, the boy ran to the door and tried to claw it open. It was locked and bolted.

'What's that noise, boy?'

Eugene pushed his son aside and fumbled with the key in the lock, while Aaron's father called to his child through the door. His voice sounded like a rush of water, counterpointed by soft, piping sighs. It was an eager voice, a loving voice.

All at once, Eugene seemed to understand. He took hold of the boy's hair and hauled him away from the door.

Aaron squealed with pain.

'Papa!' he yelled.

Eugene took the cry as addressed to himself, but Aaron's true father also heard the boy's voice. His answering call was threaded with piercing notes of concern.

Outside the house Lucy had heard the exchange of voices. She came out of the protection of her shack, knowing what she'd see against that sheening sky, but no less dizzied by the monumental creatures that had gathered on every side of the house. An anguish went through her, remembering the lost joys of that day six years previous. They were all there, the unforgettable creatures, an incredible selection of forms –

Pyramidal heads on rose coloured, classically proportioned torsos, that umbrellaed into shifting skirts of lace flesh. A headless silver beauty whose six mother of pearl arms sprouted in a circle from around its purring, pulsating mouth. A creature like a ripple on a fast-running stream, constant but moving, giving out a sweet and even tone. Creatures too fantastic to be real, too real to be disbelieved; angels of the hearth and threshold. One had a head, moving back and forth on a gossamer neck, like some preposterous weather-vane, blue as the early night sky and shot with a dozen eyes like so many suns. Another father, with a body like a fan, opening and closing in his excitement, his orange flesh flushing deeper as the boy's voice was heard again.

'Papa!'

At the door of the house stood the creature Lucy remembered with greatest affection; the one who had first touched her, first soothed her fears, first entered her, infinitely gentle. It was perhaps twenty feet tall when standing at its full height. Now it was bowed towards the door, its mighty, hairless head, like that of a bird painted by a schizophrenic, bent close to the house as it spoke to the child. It was naked, and its broad, dark back sweated as it crouched.

Inside the house, Eugene drew the boy close to him, as a shield.

'What do you know, boy?'

'Papa?'

'I said what do you know?'

'*Papa!*'

Jubilation was in Aaron's voice. The waiting was over.

The front of the house was smashed inwards. A limb like a flesh hook curled under the lintel and hauled the door from its hinges. Bricks flew up and showered down again; wood-splinters and dust filled the air. Where there had once been safe darkness, cataracts of sunlight now poured onto the dwarfed human figures in the ruins.

Eugene peered up through the veil of dust. The roof was being peeled back by giant hands, and there was sky where there had been beams. Towering on every side he saw the limbs, bodies and faces of impossible beasts. They were teasing the remaining walls down, destroying his house as casually as he would break a bottle. He let the boy slip from his grasp without realizing what he'd done.

Aaron ran towards the creature on the threshold.

'Papa!'

It scooped him up like a father meeting a child out of school, and its head was thrown back in a wave of ecstasy. A long, indescribable noise of joy was uttered out of its length and breadth. The hymn was taken up by the other creatures, mounting in celebration. Eugene covered his ears and fell to his knees. His nose had begun to bleed at the first notes of the monster's music, and his eyes were full of stinging tears. He wasn't frightened. He knew they were not capable of doing him harm. He cried because he had ignored this eventuality for six years, and now, with their mystery and their glory in front of him, he sobbed not to have had the courage to face them and know them. Now it was too late. They'd taken the boy by force, and reduced his house, and his life, to ruins. Indifferent to his agonies, they were leaving, singing their jubilation, his boy in their arms forever.

In the township of Welcome organization was the by-word of the day. Davidson could only watch with admiration the way these foolish, hardy people were attempting to confront impossible odds. He was strangely enervated by the spectacle; like watching settlers, in some movie, preparing to muster paltry weaponry and simple faith to meet the pagan violence of the savage. But, unlike the movie, Davidson knew defeat was pre-ordained. He'd seen these monsters: awe-inspiring. Whatever the rightness of the cause, the purity of the faith, the savages trampled the settlers underfoot fairly often. The defeats just make it into the movies.

Eugene's nose ceased to bleed after half an hour or so, but he didn't notice. He was dragging, pulling, cajoling Lucy towards Welcome. He wanted to hear no explanations from the slut, even though her voice was babbling ceaselessly. He could only hear the sound of the monsters' churning tones, and Aaron's repeated call of 'Papa', that was answered by a house-wrecking limb.

Eugene knew he had been conspired against, though even in his most tortured imaginings he could not grasp the whole truth.

Aaron was mad, he knew that much. And somehow his wife, his ripe-bodied Lucy, who had been such a beauty and such a comfort, was instrumental in both the boy's insanity and his own grief.

She'd sold the boy: that was his half-formed belief. In some unspeakable way she had bargained with these things from the underworld, and had exchanged the life and sanity of his only son for some kind of gift. What had she gained, for this payment? Some trinket or other that she kept buried in her shack? My God, she would suffer for it. But before he made her suffer, before he wrenched her hair from its holes, and tarred her flashing breasts with pitch, she would confess. He'd make her confess; not to him but to the people of Welcome – the men and women who scoffed at his drunken ramblings, laughed when he wept into his beer. They would hear, from Lucy's own lips, the truth behind the nightmares he had endured, and learn, to their horror, that demons he talked about were real. Then he would be exonerated, utterly, and the town would take him back into its bosom asking for his forgiveness, while the feathered body of his bitch-wife swung from a telephone pole outside the town's limits.

They were two miles outside Welcome when Eugene stopped. 'Something's coming.'

A cloud of dust, and at its swirling heart a multitude of burning eyes.

He feared the worst.

'My Christ!'

He loosed his wife. Were they coming to fetch her too? Yes, that was probably another part of the bargain she'd made.

'They've taken the town,' he said. The air was full of their voices; it was too much to bear.

They were coming at him down the road in a whining horde, driving straight at him – Eugene turned to run, letting the slut go. They could have her, as long as they left him alone; Lucy was smiling in to the dust.

'It's Packard,' she said.

Eugene glanced back along the road and narrowed his eyes. The cloud of divils was resolving itself. The eyes at its heart were headlights, the voices were sirens; there was an army of cars and motorcycles, led by Packard's howling vehicle, careering down the road from Welcome.

Eugene was confounded. What was this, a mass exodus?

Lucy, for the first time that glorious day, felt a twinge of doubt.

As it approached, the convoy slowed, and came to a halt; the dust settled, revealing the extent of Packard's kamikaze squad. There were about a dozen cars and half a dozen bikes, all of them loaded with police and weapons. A smattering of Welcome citizens made up the army, among them Eleanor Kooker. An impressive array of mean-minded, well-armed people.

Packard leant out of his car, spat, and spoke.

'Got problems, Eugene?' he asked.

'I'm no fool, Packard,' said Eugene.

'Not saying you are.'

'I seen these things. Lucy'll tell you.'

'I know you have, Eugene; I know you have. There's no denying that there's divils in them hills, sure as shit. What'd you think I've got this posse together for, if it ain't divils?'

Packard grinned across to Jedediah at the wheel.

'Sure as shit,' he said again. 'We're going to blow them all to Kingdom Come.'

From the back of the car, Miss Kooker leaned out the window; she was smoking a cigar.

'Seems we owe you an apology, Gene,' she said, offering an

apology for a smile. He's still a sot, she thought; marrying that fat-bottomed whore was the death of him. What a waste of a man.

Eugene's face tightened with satisfaction.

'Seems you do.'

'Get in one of them cars behind,' said Packard, 'you and Lucy both; and we'll fetch them out of their holes like snakes – '

'They've gone towards the hills,' said Eugene.

'That so?'

'Took my boy. Threw my house down.'

'Many of them?'

'Dozen or so.'

'OK Eugene, you'd best get in with us.' Packard ordered a cop out of the back. 'You're going to be hot for them bastards, eh?'

Eugene turned to where Lucy had been standing.

'And I want her tried – ' he said.

But Lucy was gone, running off across the desert: doll-sized already.

'She's headed off the road,' said Eleanor. 'She'll kill herself.'

'Killing's too good for her,' said Eugene, as he climbed into the car. 'That woman's meaner than the Devil himself.'

'How's that, Gene?'

'Sold my only son to Hell, that woman – '

Lucy was erased by the heat-haze.

' – to Hell.'

'Then let her be,' said Packard. 'Hell'll take her back, sooner or later.'

Lucy had known they wouldn't bother to follow her. From the moment she'd seen the car lights in the dust-cloud, seen the guns, and the helmets, she knew she had little place in the events ahead. At best, she would be a spectator. At worst, she'd die of heatstroke crossing the desert, and never know the upshot of the oncoming battle. She'd often mused about the existence of the creatures who were collectively Aaron's father. Where they lived, why they'd chosen, in their wisdom, to make love to her. She'd wondered also whether anyone else in Welcome had knowledge of them. How many human eyes, other than her own, had snatched glimpses of their secret anatomies, down the passage of years? And of course she'd wondered if there would one day come a reckoning time, a confrontation between one species and the other. Now it seemed to be here, without warning, and against the background of such a reckoning her life was as nothing.

Once the cars and bikes had disappeared out of sight, she

doubled back, tracing her footmarks in the sand, 'til she met the road again. There was no way of regaining Aaron, she realized that. She had, in a sense, merely been a guardian of the child, though she'd borne him. He belonged, in some strange way, to the creatures that had married their seeds in her body to make him. Maybe she'd been a vessel for some experiment in fertility, and now the doctors had returned to examine the resulting child. Maybe they had simply taken him out of love. Whatever the reasons she only hoped she would see the outcome of the battle. Deep in her, in a place touched only by monsters, she hoped for their victory, even though many of the species she called her own would perish as a result.

In the foothills there hung a great silence. Aaron had been set down amongst the rocks, and they gathered around him eagerly to examine his clothes, his hair, his eyes, his smile.

It was towards evening, but Aaron didn't feel cold. The breaths of his fathers were warm, and smelt, he thought, like the interior of the General Supplies Emporium in Welcome, a mingling of toffee and hemp, fresh cheese and iron. His skin was tawny in the light of the diminishing sun, and at his zenith stars were appearing. He was not happier at his mother's nipple than in that ring of demons.

At the toe of the foothills Packard brought the convoy to a halt. Had he known who Napoleon Bonaparte was, no doubt he would have felt like that conqueror. Had he known that conqueror's life-story, he might have sensed that this was his Waterloo: but Josh Packard lived and died bereft of heroes.

He summoned his men from their cars and went amongst them, his mutilated hand tucked in his shirt for support. It was not the most encouraging parade in military history. There were more than a few white and sickly-pale faces amongst his soldiers, more than a few eyes that avoided his stare as he gave his orders.

'Men,' he bawled.

(It occurred to both Kooker and Davidson that as sneak-attacks went this would not be amongst the quietest.)

'Men – we've arrived, we're organized, and we've got God on our side. We've got the best of the brutes already, understand?'

Silence; baleful looks; more sweat.

'I don't want to see one jack man of you turn your heel and run, 'cause if you do and I set my eyes on you, you'll crawl home with your backside shot to Hell!'

Eleanor thought of applauding; but the speech wasn't over.

'And remember, men,' here Packard's voice dropped to a conspiratorial whisper, 'these divils took Eugene's boy Aaron not four hours past. Took him fairly off his mother's tit, while she was rocking him to sleep. They ain't nothing but savages, whatever they may look like. They don't give a mind to a mother, or a child, or nothing. So when you get up close to one you just think how you'd have felt if you'd been taken from your mother's tit – '

He liked the phrase 'mother's tit'. It said so much, so simply. Momma's tit had a good deal more power to move these men than her apple pie.

'You've nothing to fear but seeming less than men, men.'

Good line to finish on.

'Get on with it.'

He got back into the car. Someone down the line began to applaud, and the clapping was taken up by the rest of them. Packard's wide red face was cleft with a hard, yellow smile.

'Wagon's roll!' he grinned, and the convoy moved off into the hills.

Aaron felt the air change. It wasn't that he was cold: the breaths that warmed him remained as embracing as ever. But there was nevertheless an alteration in the atmosphere: some kind of intrusion. Fascinated, he watched his fathers respond to the change: their substance glinting with new colours, graver, warier colours. One or two even lifted their heads as if to sniff the air.

Something was wrong. Something, someone, was coming to interfere with this night of festival, unplanned and uninvited. The demons knew the signs and they were not unprepared for the eventuality. Was it not inevitable that the heroes of Welcome would come after the boy? Didn't the men believe, in their pitiable way, that their species was born out of earth's necessity to know itself, nurtured from mammal to mammal until it blossomed as humanity?

Natural then to treat the fathers as the enemy, to root them out and try to destroy them. A tragedy really: when the only thought the fathers had was of unity through marriage, that their children should blunder in and spoil the celebration.

Still, men would be men. Maybe Aaron would be different, though perhaps he too would go back in time into the human world and forget what he was learning here. The creatures who were his fathers were also men's fathers: and the marriage of

113

semen in Lucy's body was the same mix that made the first males. Women had always existed: they had lived, a species to themselves, with the demons. But they had wanted playmates: and together they had made men.

What an error, what a cataclysmic miscalculation. Within mere eons, the worst rooted out the best; the women were made slaves, the demons killed or driven underground, leaving only a few pockets of survivors to attempt again that first experiment, and make men, like Aaron, who would be wiser to their histories. Only by infiltrating humanity with new male children could the master race be made milder. That chance was slim enough, without the interference of more angry children, their fat white fists hot with guns.

Aaron scented Packard and his stepfather, and smelling them, knew them to be alien. After tonight they would be known dispassionately, like animals of a different species. It was the gorgeous array of demons around him he felt closest to, and he knew he would protect them, if necessary, with his life.

Packard's car led the attack. The wave of vehicles appeared out of the darkness, their sirens blaring, their headlights on, and drove straight towards the knot of celebrants. From one or two of the cars terrified cops let out spontaneous howls of terror when the full spectacle came into view, but by that time the attack force was committed. Shots were fired. Aaron felt his fathers close around him protectively, their flesh now darkening with anger and fear.

Packard knew instinctively that these things were capable of fear, he could smell it off them. It was part of his job to recognize fear, to play on it, to use it against the miscreant. He screeched his orders into his microphone and led the cars into the circle of demons. In the back of one of the following cars Davidson closed his eyes and offered up a prayer to Yahweh, Buddha and Groucho Marx. Grant me power, grant me indifference, grant me a sense of humour. But nothing came to assist him: his bladder still bubbled, and his throat still throbbed.

Ahead, the shriek of brakes. Davidson opened his eyes (just a slit) and caught sight of one of the creatures wrapping its purple-black arm around Packard's car and lifting it into the air. One of the back doors flung open and a figure he recognized as Eleanor Kooker fell the few feet to the ground followed closely by Eugene. Leaderless, the cars were in a frenzy of collisions – the whole scene partially eclipsed by smoke and dust. There was the sound of breaking windscreens as cops took the quick way out of their cars; the shrieks of crumpling hoods and sheered off doors. The dying howl of a crushed siren; the dying plea of a crushed cop.

Packard's voice was clear enough, however, howling orders from his car even as it was lifted higher into the air, its engine revving, its wheels spinning foolishly in space. The demon was shaking the car as a child might a toy until the driver's door opened and Jedediah fell to the ground at the creature's skirt of skin. Davidson saw the skirt envelop the broken-backed deputy and appear to suck him into its folds. He could see too how Eleanor was standing up to the towering demon as it devoured her son.

'Jedediah, come out of there!' she shrieked, and fired shot after shot into his devourer's featureless, cylindrical head.

Davidson got out of the car to see better. Across a clutter of crashed vehicles and blood-splattered hoods he could make the whole scene out more plainly. The demons were sloping away from the battle, leaving this one extraodinary monster to hold the bridgehead. Quietly Davidson offered up a prayer of thanks to any passing deity. The divils were disappearing. There'd be no pitched battle: no hand-to-tentacle fight. The boy would be simply eaten alive, or whatever they planned for the poor little bastard. Indeed, couldn't he see Aaron from where he stood? Wasn't that his frail form the retreating demons were holding so high, like a trophy?

With Eleanor's curses and accusations in their ears the sheltering cops began to emerge from their hiding-places to surround the remaining demon. There was, after all, only one left to face, and it had their Napoleon in its slimy grip. They let off volley upon volley into its creases and tucks, and against the impartial geometry of its head, but the divil seemed unconcerned. Only when it had shaken Packard's car until the Sherriff rattled like a dead frog in a tin can did it lose interest and drop the vehicle. A smell of gasoline filled the air, and turned Davidson's stomach.

Then a cry: 'Heads down!'

A grenade? Surely not; not with so much gasoline on the –

Davidson fell to the floor. A sudden silence, in which an injured man could be heard whimpering somewhere in the chaos, then the dull, earth-rocking thud of the erupting grenade.

Somebody said Jesus Christ – with a kind of victory in his voice.

Jesus Christ. In the name of . . . for the glory of . . .

The demon was ablaze. The thin tissue of its gasoline-soaked

115

skirt was burning; one of its limbs had been blown off by the blast, another partially destroyed; thick, colourless blood splashed from the wounds and the stump. There was a smell in the air like burnt candy: the creature was clearly in an agony of cremation. Its body reeled and shuddered as the flames licked up to ignite its empty face, and it stumbled away from its tormentors, not sounding its pain. Davidson got a kick out of seeing it burn: like the simple pleasure he had from putting the heel of his boot in the centre of a jelly-fish. Favourite summer-time occupation of his childhood. In Maine: hot afternoons: spiking men-o'-war.

Packard was being dragged out of the wreckage of his car. My God, that man was made of steel: he was standing upright and calling his men to advance on the enemy. Even in his finest hour, a flake of fire dropped from the flowering demon, and touched the lake of gasoline Packard was standing in. A moment later he, the car, and two of his saviours were enveloped in a billowing cloud of white fire. They stood no chance of survival: the flames just washed them away. Davidson could see their dark forms being wasted in the heart of the inferno, wrapped in folds of fire, curling in on themselves as they perished.

Almost before Packard's body had hit the ground Davidson could hear Eugene's voice over the flames.

'See what they've done? See what they've done?'

The accusation was greeted by feral howls from the cops.

'Waste them!' Eugene was screaming. 'Waste them!'

Lucy could hear the noise of the battle, but she made no attempt to go in the direction of the foothills. Something about the way the moon was suspended in the sky, and the smell on the breeze, had taken all desire to move out of her. Exhausted, and enchanted, she stood in the open desert, and watched the sky.

When, after an age, she brought her gaze back down to fix on the horizon, she saw two things that were of mild interest. Out of the hills, a dirty smudge of smoke, and the edge of her vision in the gentle night light, a line of creatures, hurrying away from the hills. She suddenly began to run.

It occurred to her, as she ran, that her gait was sprightly as a young girl's, and that she had a young girl's motive: that is, she was in pursuit of her lover.

In an empty stretch of desert, the convocation of demons simply disappeared from sight. From where Lucy was standing, panting in the middle of nowhere, they seemed to have been swallowed up by the earth. She broke into a run again. Surely she could see her son and his fathers once more before they left forever? Or was she, after all her years of anticipation, to be denied even that?

In the lead car Davidson was driving, commandeered to do so by Eugene, who was not at present a man to be argued with. Something about the way he carried his rifle suggested he'd shoot first and ask questions later; his orders to the straggling army that followed him were two parts incoherent obscenities to one part sense. His eyes gleamed with hysteria: his mouth dribbled a little. He was a wild man, and he terrified Davidson. But it was too late now to turn back: he was in cahoots with the man for this last, apocalyptic pursuit.

'See, them black-eyed sons of bitches don't have no fucking heads,' Eugene was screaming over the tortured roar of the engine. 'Why you taking this track so slow, boy?'

He jabbed the rifle in Davidson's crotch.

'Drive, or I'll blow your brains out.'

'I don't know which way they've gone,' Davidson yelled back at Eugene.

'What you mean? Show me!'

'I can't show you if they've disappeared.'

Eugene just about appreciated the sense of the response.

'Slow down, boy.' He waved out of the car window to slow the rest of the army.

'Stop the car – stop the car!'

Packard brought the car to a halt.

'And put those fucking lights out. All of you!'

The headlights were quenched. Behind, the rest of the entourage followed suit.

A sudden dark. A sudden silence. There was nothing to be seen or heard in any direction. They'd disappeared, the whole cacophonous tribe of demons had simply vanished into the air, chimerical.

The desert vista brightened as their eyes became accustomed to the gleam of the moonlight. Eugene got out of the car, rifle still at the ready, and stared at the sand, willing it to explain.

'Fuckers,' he said, very softly.

Lucy had stopped running. Now she was walking towards the line of cars. It was all over by now. They had all been tricked: the disappearing act was a trump card no-one could have anticipated.

Then, she heard Aaron.

She couldn't see him, but his voice was as clear as a bell; and like a bell, it summoned. Like a bell, it rang out: this is a time of festival: celebrate with us.

Eugene heard it too; he smiled. They were near after all.

'Hey!' the boy's voice said.

'Where is he? You see him, Davidson?'

Davidson shook his head. Then –

'Wait! Wait! I see a light – look, straight ahead awhile.'

'I see it.'

With exaggerated caution, Eugene motioned Davidson back into the driver's seat.

'Drive, boy. But slowly. And no lights.'

Davidson nodded. More jelly-fish for the spiking, he thought; they were going to get the bastards after all, and wasn't that worth a little risk? The convoy started up again, creeping forward at a snail's pace.

Lucy began to run once more: she could see the tiny figure of Aaron now, standing on the lip of a slope that led under the sand. The cars were moving towards it.

Seeing them approaching, Aaron stopped his calls and began to walk away, back down the slope. There was no need to wait any longer, they were following for certain. His naked feet made scarcely a mark in the soft-sanded incline that led away from the idiocies of the world. In the shadows of the earth at the end of that slope, fluttering and smiling at him, he could see his family.

'He's going in,' said Davidson.

'Then follow the little bastard,' said Eugene. 'Maybe the kid doesn't know what he's doing. And get some light on him.'

The headlights illuminated Aaron. His clothes were in tatters, and his body was slumped with exhaustion as he walked.

A few yards off to the right of the slope Lucy watched as the lead car drove over the lip of the earth and followed the boy down, into –

'No,' she said to herself, 'don't.'

Davidson was suddenly scared. He began to slow the car.

'Get on with it, boy.' Eugene jabbed the rifle into his crotch again. 'We've got them cornered. We've got a whole nest of them here. The boy's leading us right to them.'

The cars were all on the slope now, following the leader, their wheels slipping in the sand.

Aaron turned. Behind him, illuminated only by the phosphorescence of their own matter, the demons stood; a mass of impossible geometries. All the attributes of Lucifer were spread among the bodies of the fathers. The extraordinary anatomies, the dreaming spires of heads, the scales, the skirts, the claws, the clippers.

Eugene brought the convoy to a halt, got out of the car and began to walk towards Aaron.

'Thank you boy,' he said. 'Come here – we'll look after you now. We've got them. You're safe.'

Aaron stared at his father, uncomprehending.

The army was disgorging from the cars behind Eugene, readying their weapons. A bazooka was being hurriedly assembled; a cocking of rifles, a weighing-up of grenades.

'Come to Papa, boy,' Eugene coaxed.

Aaron didn't move, so Eugene followed him a few yards deeper into the ground. Davidson was out of the car now, shaking from head to foot.

'Maybe you should put down the rifle. Maybe he's scared,' he suggested.

Eugene grunted, and let the muzzle of the rifle drop a few inches.

'You're safe,' said Davidson. 'It's all right.'

'Walk towards us, boy. Slowly.'

Aaron's face began to flush. Even in the deceptive light of the headlamps it was clearly changing colour. His cheeks were blowing up like balloons, and the skin on his forehead was wriggling as though his flesh was full of maggots. His head seemed to liquify, to become a soup of shapes, shifting and blossoming like a cloud, the façade of boyhood broken as the father inside the son showed its vast and unimaginable face.

Even as Aaron became his father's son, the slope began to soften. Davidson felt it first: a slight shift in the texture of the sand, as though an order had passed through it, subtle but all-pervasive.

Eugene could only gape as Aaron's transformation continued, his entire body now overtaken by the tremors of change. His belly had become distended and a harvest of cones budded from it, which even now flowered into dozens of coiled legs; the change was marvellous in its complexity, as out of the cradle of the boy's substance came new glories.

Without warning Eugene raised his rifle and fired at his son.

The bullet struck the boy-demon in the middle of his face. Aaron fell back, his transformation still taking its course even as his blood, a stream part scarlet, part silver, ran from his wound into the liquefying earth.

The geometries in the darkness moved out of hiding to help

the child. The intricacy of their forms was simplified in the glare of the headlamps but they seemed, even as they appeared, to be changing again: bodies becoming thin in their grief, a whine of mourning like a solid wall of sound from their hearts.

Eugene raised his rifle a second time, whooping at his victory. He had them . . . My God, he had them. Dirty, stinking, faceless fuckers.

But the mud beneath his feet was like warm treacle as it rose around his shins, and when he fired he lost balance. He yelled for assistance, but Davidson was already staggering back up the slope out of the gully fighting a losing battle against the rising mire. The rest of the army were similarly trapped, as the desert liquified beneath them, and glutinous mud began to creep up the slope.

The demons had gone: retreated into the dark, their lament sunk away.

Eugene, flat on his back in the sinking sand, fired off two useless, vehement shots into the darkness beyond Aaron's corpse. He was kicking like a hog with its throat cut, and with every kick his body sunk deeper. As his face disappeared beneath the mud, he just glimpsed Lucy, standing at the edge of the slope, staring down towards Aaron's body. Then the mire covered his face, and blotted him out.

The desert was upon them with lightning speed.

One or two of the cars were already entirely submerged, and the tide of sand climbing the slope was relentlessly catching up with the escapees. Feeble cries for assistance ended with choking silences as mouths were filled with desert; somebody was shooting at the ground in an hysterical attempt to dam the flow, but it reached up swiftly to snatch every last one of them. Even Eleanor Kooker wasn't to be let free: she struggled, cursing and pressing the thrashing body of a cop deeper into the sand in her frantic attempts to step out of the gully.

There were universal howls now, as panicking men groped and grasped at each other for support, desperately trying to keep their heads afloat in the sea of sand.

Davidson was buried up to his waist. The ground that eddied about his lower half was hot and curiously inviting. The intimacy of its pressure had given him an erection. A few yards behind him a cop was screaming blue murder as the desert ate him up. Further still from him he could see a face peering out from the seething ground like a living mask thrown on the earth. There was an arm close by, still waving, as it sank; a pair of fat buttocks was poking up from the silt sea like two watermelons, a policeman's farewell.

Lucy took one step backwards as the mud slightly overran the lip of the gully, but it didn't reach her feet. Nor, curiously, did it dissipate itself, as a water-wave might have done.

Like concrete, it hardened, fixing its living trophies like flies in amber. From the lips of every face that still took air came a fresh cry of terror, as they felt the desert floor stiffen around their struggling limbs.

Davidson saw Eleanor Kooker, buried to breast-level. Tears were pouring down her cheeks; she was sobbing like a little girl. He scarcely thought of himself. Of the East, of Barbara, of the children, he thought not at all.

The men whose faces were buried but whose limbs, or parts of bodies, still broke surface, were dead of asphyxiation by now. Only Eleanor Kooker, Davidson and two other men survived. One was locked in the earth up to his chin, Eleanor was buried so that her breasts sat on the ground, her arms were free to beat uselessly at the ground that held her fast. Davidson himself was held from his hips down. And most horribly, one pathetic victim was seen only by his nose and mouth. His head was tipped back into the ground, blinded by rock. Still he breathed, still he screamed.

Eleanor Kooker was scrabbling at the ground with torn nails, but this was not loose sand. It was immovable.

'Get help,' she demanded of Lucy, hands bleeding.

The two women stared at each other.

'Jesus God!' screamed the Mouth.

The Head was silent: by his glazed look it was apparent that he'd lost his mind.

'Please help us . . .' pleaded Davidson's Torso. 'Fetch help.'

Lucy nodded.

'Go!' demanded Eleanor Kooker. 'Go!'

Numbly, Lucy obeyed. Already there was a glimmer of dawn in the east. The air would soon be blistering. In Welcome, three hours walk away, she would find only old men, hysterical women and children. She would have to summon help from perhaps fifty miles distance. Even assuming she found her way back. Even assuming she didn't collapse exhausted to the sand and die.

It would be noon before she could fetch help to the woman, to the Torso, to the Head, to the Mouth. By that time the wilderness would have had the best of them. The sun would have boiled their brain-pans dry, snakes would have nested in their hair, the buzzards would have hooked out their helpless eyes.

She glanced round once more at their trivial forms, dwarfed by the bloody sweep of the dawn sky. Little dots and commas of human pain on a blank sheet of sand; she didn't care to think of the pen that wrote them there. That was for tomorrow.

After a while, she began to run.

New Murders in the Rue Morgue

Winter, Lewis decided, was no season for old men. The snow that lay five inches thick on the streets of Paris froze him to the marrow. What had been a joy to him as a child was now a curse. He hated it with all his heart; hated the snowballing children (squeals, howls, tears); hated, too, the young lovers, eager to be caught in a flurry together (squeals, kisses, tears). It was uncomfortable and tiresome, and he wished he was in Fort Lauderdale, where the sun would be shining.

But Catherine's telegram, though not explicit, had been urgent, and the ties of friendship between them had been unbroken for the best part of fifty years. He was here for her, and for her brother Phillipe. However thin his blood felt in this ice land, it was foolish to complain. He'd come at a summons from the past, and he would have come as swiftly, and as willingly, if Paris had been burning.

Besides, it was his mother's city. She'd been born on the Boulevard Diderot, back in a time when the city was untrammelled by free-thinking architects and social engineers. Now every time Lewis returned to Paris he steeled himself for another desecration. It was happening less of late, he'd noticed. The recession in Europe made governments less eager with their bulldozers. But still, year after year, more fine houses found themselves rubble. Whole streets sometimes, gone to ground.

Even the Rue Morgue.

There was, of course, some doubt as to whether that infamous street had ever existed in the first place, but as his years advanced Lewis had seen less and less purpose in distinguishing between fact and fiction. That great divide was for young men, who still had to deal with life. For the old (Lewis was 73), the distinction was academic. What did it matter what was true and what was false, what real and what invented? In his head all of it, the half-lies and the truths, were one continuum of personal history.

Maybe the Rue Morgue had existed, as it had been described in Edgar Allan Poe's immortal story; maybe it was pure invention. Whichever, the notorious street was no longer to be found on a map of Paris.

Perhaps Lewis was a little disappointed not to have found the Rue Morgue. After all, it was part of his heritage. If the stories he had been told as a young boy were correct, the events described in the *Murders in the Rue Morgue* had been narrated to Poe by Lewis' grandfather. It was his mother's pride that her father had met Poe, while travelling in America. Apparently his grandfather had been a globe-trotter, unhappy unless he visited a new town every week. And in the winter of 1835 he had been in Richmond, Virginia. It was a bitter winter, perhaps not unlike the one Lewis was presently suffering, and one night the grandfather had taken refuge in a bar in Richmond. There, with a blizzard raging outside, he had met a small, dark, melancholy young man called Eddie. He was something of a local celebrity apparently, having written a tale that had won a competition in the *Baltimore Saturday Visitor*. The tale was 'MS found in a bottle' and (the haunted young man was Edgar Allan Poe.

The two had spent the evening together, drinking, and (this is how the story went, anyway) Poe had gently pumped Lewis' grandfather for stories of the bizarre, of the occult and of the morbid. The worldly-wise traveller was glad to oblige, pouring out believe-it-or-not fragments that the writer later turned into *The Mystery of Marie Roget*' *and* 'The Murders in the Rue Morgue*. In both those stories, peering out from between the atrocities, was the peculiar genius of C. Auguste Dupin.

C. Auguste Dupin. Poe's vision of the perfect detective: calm, rational and brilliantly perceptive. The narratives in which he appeared rapidly became well-known, and through them Dupin became a fictional celebrity, without anyone in America knowing that Dupin was a real person.

He was the brother of Lewis' grandfather. Lewis' great uncle was C. Auguste Dupin.

And his greatest case – the Murders in the Rue Morgue – they too were based on fact. The slaughters that occurred in the story had actually taken place. Two women had indeed been brutally killed in the Rue Morgue. They were, as Poe had written, Madame L'Espanaye and her daughter Mademoiselle Camille L'Espanaye. Both women of good reputation, who lived quiet and unsensational lives. So much more horrible then to find those lives so brutally cut short. The daughter's body had been thrust up the chimney; the body of the mother was discovered in the yard at the back of the house, her throat cut with such savagery that her head was all but sawn off. No apparent motive could be found for the murders, and the mystery further deepened when all the occupants of the house claimed to have heard the voice of the murderer speaking in a different language. The Frenchman was certain the voice had spoken Spanish, the Englishman had heard German, the Dutchman thought it was French. Dupin, in his investigations, noted that none of the witnesses actually spoke the language they claimed to have heard from the lips of the unseen murderer. He concluded that the language was no language at all, but the wordless voice of a wild beast.

An ape in fact, a monstrous orang-outang from the East Indian Islands. Its tawny hairs had been found in the grip of the slain Madame L'Espanaye. Only its strength and agility made the appalling fate of Mademoiselle L'Espanaye plausible. The beast had belonged to a Maltese sailor, had escaped, and run riot in the bloody apartment on the Rue Morgue.

That was the bones of the story.

Whether true or not the tale held a great romantic appeal for Lewis. He liked to think of his great uncle logically pacing his way through the mystery, undistressed by the hysteria and horror around him. He thought of that calm as essentially European; belonging to a lost age in which the light of reason was still valued, and the worst horror that could be conceived of was a beast with a cut-throat razor.

Now, as the twentieth century ground through its last quarter, there were far greater atrocities to be accounted for, all committed by human beings. The humble orang-outang had been investigated by anthropologists and found to be a solitary herbivore; quiet and philosophical. The true monsters were far less apparent, and far more powerful. Their weapons made razors look pitiful; their crimes were vast. In some ways Lewis was almost glad to be old and close to leaving the century to its own devices. Yes, the snow froze his marrow. Yes, to see a young girl with a face of a goddess uselessly stirred his desires. Yes, he felt like an observer now instead of a participator.

But it had not always been that way.

In 1937, in the very room at number eleven, Quai de Bourbon, where he now sat, there had been experience enough. Paris was still a pleasure-dome in those days, studiously ignoring rumours of war, and preserving, though at times the strain told, an air of sweet naïveté. They had been careless then; in both senses of the word, living endless lives of perfect leisure.

It wasn't so of course. The lives had not been perfect, or endless. But for a time – a summer, a month, a day – it had seemed nothing in the world would change.

In half a decade Paris would burn, and its playful guilt, which was true innocence, would be soiled permanently. They had spent many days (and nights) in the apartment Lewis now occupied, wonderful times; when he thought of them his stomach seemed to ache with the loss.

His thoughts turned to more recent events. To his New York exhibition, in which his series of paintings chronicling the damnation of Europe had been a brilliant critical success. At the age of seventy-three Lewis Fox was a fêted man. Articles were being written in every art periodical. Admirers and buyers had sprung up like mushrooms overnight, eager to purchase his work, to talk with him, to touch his hand. All too late, of course. The agonies of creation were long over, and he'd put down his brushes for the last time five years ago. Now, when he was merely a spectator, his critical triumph seemed like a parody: he viewed the circus from a distance with something approaching distaste.

When the telegram had come from Paris, begging for his assistance, he had been more than pleased to slip away from the ring of imbeciles mouthing his praise.

Now he waited in the darkening apartment, watching the steady flow of cars across the Pont Louis-Phillipe, as tired Parisians began the trek home through the snow. Their horns blared; their engines coughed and growled; their yellow foglamps made a ribbon of light across the bridge.

Still Catherine didn't come.

The snow, which had held off for most of the day, was beginning to fall again, whispering against the window. The traffic flowed across the Seine, the Seine flowed under the traffic. Night fell. At last, he heard footsteps in the hall; exchanged whispers with the housekeeper.

It was Catherine. At last, it was Catherine.

He stood up and stared at the door, imagining it opening before it opened, imagining her in the doorway.

'Lewis, my darling – '

She smiled at him; a pale smile on a paler face. She looked older than he'd expected. How long was it since he'd seen her? Four years or five? Her fragrance was the same as she always wore: and it reassured Lewis with its permanence. He kissed her cold cheeks lightly.

'You look well,' he lied.

'No I don't,' she said. 'If I look well it's an insult to Phillipe. How can I be well when he's in such trouble?'

126

Her manner was brisk, and forbidding, as always.

She was three years his senior, but she treated him as a teacher would a recalcitrant child. She always had: it was her way of being fond.

Greetings over, she sat down beside the window, staring out over the Seine. Small grey ice-floes floated under the bridge, rocking and revolving in the current. The water looked deadly, as though its bitterness could crush the breath out of you.

'What trouble is Phillipe in?'

'He's accused of – '

A tiny hesitation. A flicker of an eyelid.

' – murder.'

Lewis wanted to laugh; the very thought was preposterous. Phillipe was sixty-nine years old, and as mild-mannered as a lamb.

'It's true, Lewis. I couldn't tell you by telegram, you understand. I had to say it myself. Murder. He's accused of murder.'

'Who?'

'A girl, of course. One of his fancy women.'

'He still gets around, does he?'

'We used to joke he'd die on a woman, remember?'

Lewis half-nodded.

'She was nineteen. Natalie Perec. Quite an educated girl, apparently. And lovely. Long red hair. You remember how Phillipe loved redheads?'

'Nineteen? He has nineteen year olds?'

She didn't reply. Lewis sat down, knowing his pacing of the room irritated her. In profile she was still beautiful, and the wash of yellow-blue through the window softened the lines on her face, magically erasing fifty years of living.

'Where is he?'

'They locked him up. They say he's dangerous. They say he could kill again.'

Lewis shook his head. There was a pain at his temples, which might go if he could only close his eyes.

'He needs to see you. Very badly.'

But maybe sleep was just an escape. Here was something even he couldn't be a spectator to.

Phillipe Laborteaux stared at Lewis across the bare, scored table, his face weary and lost. They had greeted each other only with handshakes; all other physical contact was strictly forbidden.

'I am in despair,' he said. 'She's dead. My Natalie is dead.'

'Tell me what happened.'

'I have a little apartment in Montmartre. In the Rue des Martyrs. Just a room really, to entertain friends. Catherine always keeps number 11 so neat, you know, a man can't spread himself out. Natalie used to spend a lot of time with me there: everyone in the house knew her. She was so good natured, so beautiful. She was studying to go into Medical School. Bright. And she loved me.'

Phillipe was still handsome. In fact, as the fashion in looks came full circle his elegance, his almost dashing face, his unhurried charm were the order of the day. A breath of a lost age, perhaps.

'I went out on Sunday morning: to the patisserie. And when I came back . . .'

The words failed him for a moment.

'Lewis . . .'

His eyes filled with tears of frustration. This was so difficult for him his mouth refused to make the necessary sounds.

'Don't – ' Lewis began.

'I want to tell you, Lewis. I want you to know, I want you to see her as I saw her – so you know what there is . . . there is . . . what there is in the world.'

The tears ran down his face in two graceful rivulets. He gripped Lewis' hand in his, so tightly it ached.

'She was covered in blood. In wounds. Skin torn off . . . hair torn out. Her tongue was on the pillow Lewis. Imagine that. She'd bitten it off in her terror. It was just lying on the pillow. And her eyes, all swimming in blood, like she'd wept blood. She was the dearest thing in all creation, Lewis. She was beautiful.'

'No more.'

'I want to die, Lewis.'

'No.'

'I don't want to live now. There's no point.'

'They won't find you guilty.'

'I don't care, Lewis. You must look after Catherine now. I read about the exhibition – '

He almost smiled.

' – Wonderful for you. We always said, didn't we? before the war, you'd be the one to be famous, I'd be – '

The smile had gone.

' – notorious. They say terrible things about me now, in the newspapers. An old man going with young girls, you see, that doesn't make me very wholesome. They probably think I lost my temper because I couldn't perform with her. That's what they think, I'm certain.' He lost his way, halted, began again. 'You must look after Catherine. She's got money, but no friends. She's too cool, you see. Too hurt inside; and that makes people wary of her. You have to stay with her.'

'I shall.'

'I know. I know. That's why I feel happy, really, to just . . .'

'No, Phillipe.'

'Just die. There's nothing left for us, Lewis. The world's too hard.'

Lewis thought of the snow, and the ice-floes, and saw the sense in dying.

The officer in charge of the investigation was less than helpful, though Lewis introduced himself as a relative of the esteemed Detective Dupin. Lewis' contempt for the shoddily-dressed weasel, sitting in his cluttered hole of an office, made the interview crackle with suppressed anger.

'Your friend,' the Inspector said, picking at the raw cuticle of his thumb, 'is a murderer, Monsieur Fox. It is as simple as that. The evidence is overwhelming.'

'I can't believe that.'

'Believe what you like to believe, that's your prerogative. We have all the evidence we need to convict Phillipe Laborteaux of murder in the first degree. It was a cold-blooded killing and he will be punished to the full extent of the law. This is my promise.'

'What evidence do you have against him?'

'Monsieur Fox; I am not beholden to you. What evidence we have is our business. Suffice it to say that no other person was seen in the house during the time that the accused claims he was at some fictional patisserie; and as access to the room in which the deceased was found is only possible by the stairs – '

'What about a window?'

'A plain wall: three flights up. Maybe an acrobat: an acrobat might do it.'

'And the state of the body?'

The Inspector made a face. Disgust.

'Horrible. Skin and muscle stripped from the bone. All the spine exposed. Blood; much blood.'

'Phillipe is seventy.'

'So?'

'An old man would not be capable – '

'In other respects,' the Inspector interrupted, 'he seems to have been quite capable, *oui*? The lover, yes? The passionate lover: he was capable of that.'

'And what motive would you claim he had?'

His mouth scalloped, his eyes rolled and he tapped his chest.

'*Le coeur humain*,' he said, as if despairing of reason in affairs of the heart. '*Le coeur humain, quel mystère, n'est-ce pas?*' and exhaling the stench of his ulcer at Lewis, he proffered the open door.

'Merci, Monsieur Fox. I understand your confusion, *oui*? But you are wasting your time. A crime is a crime. It is real; not like your paintings.'

He saw the surprise on Lewis' face.

'Oh, I am not so uncivilized as not to know your reputation, Monsieur Fox. But I ask you, make your fictions as best you can; that is your genius, *oui*? Mine; to investigate the truth.'

Lewis couldn't bear the weasel's cant any longer.

'Truth?' he snapped back at the Inspector. 'You wouldn't know the truth if you tripped over it.'

The weasel looked as though he'd been slapped with a wet fish.

It was precious little satisfaction; but it made Lewis feel better for at least five minutes.

The house on the Rue des Martyrs was not in good condition, and Lewis could smell the damp as he climbed to the little room on the third floor. Doors opened as he passed, and inquiring whispers ushered him up the stairs, but nobody tried to stop him. The room where the atrocity had happened was locked. Frustrated, but not knowing how or why it would help Phillipe's case to see the interior of the room, he made his way back down the stairs and into the bitter air.

Catherine was back at the Quai de Bourbon. As soon as Lewis saw her he knew there was something new to hear. Her grey hair was loosed from the bun she favoured wearing, and hung unbraided at her shoulders. Her face was a sickly yellow-grey by the lamplight. She shivered, even in the clogged air of the centrally-heated apartment.

'What's wrong?' he asked.

'I went to Phillipe's apartment.'

'So did I. It was locked.'

'I have the key: Phillipe's spare key. I just wanted to pick up a few clothes for him.'

Lewis nodded.

'And?'

'Somebody else was there.'

'Police?'

'No.'

'Who?'

'I couldn't see. I don't know exactly. He was dressed in a big coat, scarf over his face. Hat. Gloves.' She paused. Then, 'he had a razor, Lewis.'

'A razor?'

'An open razor, like a barber.'

Something jangled in the back of Lewis Fox's mind. An open razor; a man dressed so well he couldn't be recognized.

'I was terrified.'

'Did he hurt you?'

She shook her head.

'I screamed and he ran away.'

'Didn't say anything to you?'

'No.'

'Maybe a friend of Phillipe's?'

'I know Phillipe's friends.'

'Then of the girl. A brother.'

'Perhaps. But – '

'What?'

'There was something odd about him. He smelt of perfume, stank of it, and he walked with such mincing little steps, even though he was huge.'

Lewis put his arm around her.

'Whoever it was, you scared them off. You just mustn't go back there. If we have to fetch clothes for Phillipe, I'll gladly go.'

'Thank you. I feel a fool: he may have just stumbled in. Come to look at the murder-chamber. People do that, don't they? Out of some morbid fascination . . .'

'Tomorrow I'll speak to the Weasel.'

'Weasel?'

'Inspector Marais. Have him search the place.'

'Did you see Phillipe?'

'Yes.'

'Is he well?'

Lewis said nothing for a long moment.

'He wants to die, Catherine. He's given up fighting already, before he goes to trial.'

'But he didn't do anything.'

'We can't prove that.'

'You're always boasting about your ancestors. Your blessed Dupin. You prove it . . .'

'Where do I start?'

'Speak to some of his friends, Lewis. *Please*. Maybe the woman had enemies.'

Jacques Solal stared at Lewis through his round-bellied spectacles, his irises huge and distorted through the glass. He was the worse for too much cognac.

'She hadn't got any enemies,' he said, 'not her. Oh maybe a few women jealous of her beauty . . .'

Lewis toyed with the wrapped cubes of sugar that had come with his coffee. Solal was as uninformative as he was drunk; but unlikely as it seemed Catherine had described the runt across the table at Phillipe's closest friend.

'Do you think Phillipe murdered her?'

Solal pursed his lips.

'Who knows?'

'What's your instinct?'

'Ah; he was my friend. If I knew who had killed her I would say so.'

It seemed to be the truth. Maybe the little man was simply drowning his sorrows in cognac.

'He was a gentlemen,' Solal said, his eyes drifting towards the street. Through the steamed glass of the Brasserie window brave Parisians were struggling through the fury of another blizzard, vainly attempting to keep their dignity and their posture in the teeth of a gale.

'A gentleman,' he said again.

'And the girl?'

'She was beautiful, and he was in love with her. She had other admirers, of course. A woman like her – '

'Jealous admirers?'

'Who knows?'

Again: who knows? The inquiry hung on the air like a shrug. Who knows? Who knows? Lewis began to understand the Inspector's passion for truth. For the first time in ten years perhaps a goal appeared in his life; an ambition to shoot this indifferent 'who knows?' out of the air. To discover what had happened in that room on the Rue des Martyrs. Not an approximation, not a fictionalized account, but the truth, the absolute, unquestionable truth.

'Do you remember if there were any particular men who fancied her?' he asked.

Solal grinned. He only had two teeth in his lower jaw.

'Oh yes. There was one.'

'Who?'

'I never knew his name. A big man: I saw him outside the house three or four times. Though to smell him you'd have thought – '

He made an unmistakable face that implied he thought the man was homosexual. The arched eyebrows and the pursed lips made him look doubly ridiculous behind the thick spectacles.

'He smelt?'

'Oh yes.'

'Of what?'

'Perfume, Lewis. Perfume.'

Somewhere in Paris there was man who had known the girl Phillipe loved. Jealous rage had overcome him. In a fit of uncontrollable anger he had broken into Phillipe's apartment and slaughtered the girl. It was as clear as that.

Somewhere in Paris.

'Another cognac?'

Solal shook his head.

'Already I'm sick,' he said.

Lewis called the waiter across, and as he did so his eye alighted on a cluster of newspaper clippings pinned behind the bar.

Solal followed his gaze.

'Phillipe: he liked the pictures,' he said.

Lewis stood up.

'He came here, sometimes, to see them.'

The cuttings were old, stained and fading. Some were presumably of purely local interest. Accounts of a fireball seen in a nearby street. Another about a boy of two burned to death in his cot. One concerned an escaped puma; one, an unpublished manuscript by Rimbaud; a third (accompanied by a photograph) detailed casualties in a plane crash at Orleans airport. But there were other cuttings too; some far older than others. Atrocities, bizarre murders, ritual rapes, an advertisement for 'Fantomas', another for Cocteau's 'La Belle et La Bete'. And almost buried under this embarrassment of bizarreries, was a sepia photograph so absurd it could have come from the hand of Max Ernst. A half-ring of well-dressed gentlemen, many sporting the thick moustaches popular in the eighteen-nineties, were grouped around the vast, bleeding bulk of an ape, which was suspended by its feet from a lamppost. The faces in the picture bore expressions of mute pride; of absolute authority over the dead beast, which Lewis clearly recognized as a gorilla. Its inverted head had an almost noble tilt in death. Its brow was deep and furrowed, its jaw, though shattered by a fearsome wound, was thinly bearded like that of a patrician, and its eyes, rolled back in its head, seemed full of concern for this merciless world. They reminded Lewis, those rolling eyes, of the Weasel in his hole, tapping his chest.

'*Le coeur humain.*'

Pitiful.

'What is that?' he asked the acne-ridden barman, pointing at the picture of the dead gorilla.

A shrug was the reply: indifferent to the fate of men and apes.

'Who knows?' said Solal at his back. 'Who knows?'

It was not the ape of Poe's story, that was certain. That tale had been told in 1835, and the photograph was far more recent. Besides, the ape in the picture was a gorilla: clearly a gorilla.

Had history repeated itself? Had another ape, a different species but an ape nevertheless, been loosed on the streets of Paris at the turn of the century?

And if so, if the story of the ape could repeat itself once . . . why not twice?

As Lewis walked through the freezing night back to the apartment at the Quai de Bourbon, the imagined repetition of events became more attractive; and now further symmetry presented itself to him. Was it possible that he, the great nephew of C. Auguste Dupin, might become involved in another pursuit, not entirely dissimilar from the first?

The key to Phillipe's room at the Rue des Martyrs was icy in Lewis' hand, and though it was now well past midnight he couldn't help but turn off at the bridge and make his way up the Boulevard de Sebastopol, west on to Boulevard Bonne-Nouvelle, then north again towards the Place Pigalle. It was a long, exhausting trudge, but he felt in need of the cold air, to keep his head clear of emotionalism. It took him an hour and a half to reach the Rue des Martyrs.

It was Saturday night, and there was still a lot of noise in a number of the rooms. Lewis made his way up the two flights as quietly as he could, his presence masked by the din. The key turned easily, and the door swung open.

Street lights illuminated the room. The bed, which dominated the space, was bare. Presumably sheets and blankets had been taken away for forensic tests. The eruption of blood onto the mattress was a mulberry colour in the gloom. Otherwise, there was no sign of the violence the room had witnessed.

Lewis reached for the lightswitch, and snapped it on. Nothing happened. He stepped deeply into the room and stared up at the light fixture. The bulb was shattered.

He half thought of retreating, of leaving the room to darkness, and returning in the morning when there were fewer shadows. But as he stood under the broken bulb his eyes began to pierce the gloom a little better, and he began to make out the shape of a large teak chest of drawers along the far wall. Surely it was a matter of a few minutes work to find a change of clothes for Phillipe. Otherwise he would have to return the next day; another long journey through the snow. Better to do it now, and save his bones.

The room was large, and had been left in chaos by the police. Lewis stumbled and cursed as he crossed to the chest of drawers, tripping over a fallen lamp, and a shattered vase. Downstairs the howls and shrieks of a well-advanced party drowned any noise he made. Was it an orgy or a fight? The noise could have been either.

He struggled with the top drawer of the teak chest, and eventually wrenched it open, ferreting in the depths for the bare essentials of Phillipe's comfort: a clean undershirt, a pair of socks, initialled handkerchiefs, beautifully pressed.

He sneezed. The chilly weather had thickened the catarrh on his chest and the mucus in his sinuses. A handkerchief was to hand, and he blew his nose, clearing his blocked nostrils. For the first time the smell of the room came to him.

One odour predominated, above the damp, and the stale vegetables. Perfume, the lingering scent of perfume.

He turned into the darkened room, hearing his bones creak, and his eyes fell on the shadow behind the bed. A huge shadow, a bulk that swelled as it rose into view.

It was, he saw at once, the razor-yielding stranger. He was here: in waiting.

Curiously, Lewis wasn't frightened.

'What are you doing?' he demanded, in a loud, strong voice.

As he emerged from his hiding place the face of the stranger came into the watery light from the street; a broad, flat-featured, flayed face. His eyes were deep-set, but without malice; and he was smiling, smiling generously, at Lewis.

'Who are you?' Lewis asked again.

The man shook his head; shook his body, in fact, his gloved hands gesturing around his mouth. Was he dumb? The shaking of the head was more violent now, as though he was about to have a fit.

'Are you all right?'

Suddenly, the shaking stopped, and to his surprise Lewis saw tears, large, syrupy tears well up in the stranger's eyes and roll down his rough cheeks and into the bush of his beard.

As if ashamed of his display of feelings, the man turned away from the light, making a thick noise of sobbing in his throat, and exited. Lewis followed, more curious about this stranger than nervous of his intentions.

'Wait!'

The man was already half-way down the first flight of stairs, nimble despite his build.

'Please wait, I want to talk to you,' Lewis began down the stairs after him, but the pursuit was lost before it was started. Lewis' joints were stiff with age and the cold, and it was late. No time to be running after a much younger man, along a pavement made lethal with ice and snow. He chased the stranger as far as the door and then watched him run off down the street; his gait was mincing as Catherine had said. Almost a waddle, ridiculous in a man so big.

The smell of his perfume was already snatched away by the north-east wind. Breathless, Lewis climbed the stairs again, past the din of the party, to claim a set of clothes for Phillipe.

The next day Paris woke to a blizzard of unprecedented ferocity. The calls to Mass went unrequited, the hot Sunday croissants went unbought, the newspapers lay unread on the vendor's stalls. Few people had either the nerve or the motive to step outside into the howling gale. They sat by their fires, hugging their knees, and dreamt of spring.

Catherine wanted to go to the prison to visit Phillipe, but Lewis insisted that he go alone. It was not simply the cold weather that made him cautious on her behalf; he had difficult words to say to Phillipe, delicate questions to ask him. After the previous night's encounter in his room, he had no doubt that Phillipe had a rival, probably a murderous rival. The only way to save Phillipe's life, it seemed, was to trace the man. And if that meant delving into Phillipe's sexual arrangements, then so be it. But it wasn't a conversation he, or Phillipe, would have wanted to conduct in Catherine's presence.

The fresh clothes Lewis had brought were searched, then given to Phillipe, who took them with a nod of thanks.

'I went to the house last night to fetch these for you.'

'Oh.'

'There was somebody in the room already.'

Phillipe's jaw muscle began to churn, as he ground his teeth together. He was avoiding Lewis' eyes.

'A big man, with a beard. Do you know him, or *of* him?'

'No.'

'Phillipe – '

'*No!*'

'The same man attacked Catherine,' Lewis said.

'What?' Phillipe had begun to tremble.

'With a razor.'

'Attacked her?' Phillipe said. 'Are you sure?'

'Or was going to.'

'No! He would never have touched her. Never!'

'Who is it Phillipe? Do you know?'

'Tell her not to go there again; please, Lewis – ' His eyes implored. 'Please, for God's sake tell her never to go there again. Will you do that? Or you. Not you either.'

'Who is it?'

'*Tell her.*'

'I will. But you must tell me who this man is, Phillipe.'

He shook his head, grinding his teeth together audibly now.

'You wouldn't understand, Lewis. I couldn't expect you to understand.'

'Tell me; I want to help.'

'Just let me die.'

'*Who is he?*'

'Just let me die . . . I want to forget, why do you try to make me remember? I want to – '

He looked up again: his eyes were bloodshot, and red-rimmed from nights of tears. But now it seemed there were no more tears left in him; just an arid place where there had been an honest fear of death, a love of love, and an appetite for life. What met Lewis' eyes was a universal indifference: to continuation, to self-preservation, to feeling.

'She was a whore,' he suddenly exclaimed. His hands were fists. Lewis had never seen Phillipe make a fist in his life. Now his nails bit into the soft flesh of his palm until blood began to flow.

'Whore,' he said again, his voice too loud in the little cell.

'Keep your row down,' snapped the guard.

'A whore!' This time Phillipe hissed the accusation through teeth exposed like those of an angry baboon.

Lewis could make no sense of the transformation.

'You began all this – ' Phillipe said, looking straight at Lewis, meeting his eyes fully for the first time. It was a bitter accusation, though Lewis didn't understand its significance.

'Me?'

'With your stories. With your damn Dupin.'

'Dupin?'

'It was all a lie: all stupid lies. Women, murder – '

'You mean the Rue Morgue story?'

'You were so proud of that, weren't you? All those silly lies. None of it was true.'

'Yes it was.'

'No. It never was, Lewis: it was a story, that's all. Dupin, the Rue Morgue, the murders . . .'

His voice trailed away, as though the next words were unsayable.

'. . . the ape.'

Those were the words: the apparently unspeakable was spoken as though each syllable had been cut from his throat.

'. . . the ape.'

'What about the ape?'

'There are beasts, Lewis. Some of them are pitiful; circus animals. They have no brains; they are born victims. Then there are others.'

'What others?'

'*Natalie was a whore!*' he screamed again, his eyes big as saucers. He took hold of Lewis' lapels, and began to shake him. Everybody else in the little room turned to look at the two old men as they wrestled over the table. Convicts and their sweethearts grinned as Phillipe was dragged off his friend, his words descending into incoherence and obscenity as he thrashed in the warder's grip.

'Whore! Whore! Whore!' was all he could say as they hauled him back to his cell.

Catherine met Lewis at the door of her apartment. She was shaking and tearful. Beyond her, the room was wrecked.

She sobbed against his chest as he comforted her, but she was inconsolable. It was many years since he'd comforted a woman, and he'd lost the knack of it. He was embarrassed instead of soothing, and she knew it. She broke away from his embrace, happier untouched.

'He was here,' she said.

He didn't need to ask who. The stranger, the tearful, razor-wielding stranger.

'What did he want?'

'He kept saying "Phillipe" to me. Almost saying it; grunting it more than saying it: and when I didn't answer he just destroyed the furniture, the vases. He wasn't even looking for anything: he just wanted to make a mess.'

It made her furious: the uselessness of the attack.

The apartment was in ruins. Lewis wandered through the fragments of porcelain and shredded fabric, shaking his head. In his mind a confusion of tearful faces: Catherine, Phillipe, the stranger. Everyone in his narrow world, it seemed, was hurt and broken. Everyone was suffering; and yet the source, the heart of the suffering, was nowhere to be found.

Only Phillipe had pointed an accusing finger: at Lewis himself.

'You began all this.' Weren't those his words? 'you began all this.'

But how?

Lewis stood at the window. Three of the small panes had been cracked by flying debris, and a wind was insinuating itself into the apartment, with frost in its teeth. He looked across at the ice-thickened waters of the Seine; then a movement caught his eye. His stomach turned.

The full face of the stranger was turned up to the window, his expression wild. The clothes he had always worn so impeccably were in disarray, and the look on his face was of utter, utter despair, so pitiful as to be almost tragic. Or rather, a performance of tragedy: an actor's pain. Even as Lewis stared down at him the stranger raised his arms to the window in a gesture that seemed to beg either forgiveness or understanding, or both.

Lewis backed away from the appeal. It was too much; all too much. The next moment the stranger was walking across the courtyard away from the apartment. The mincing walk had deteriorated into a rolling lope. Lewis uttered a long, low moan of recognition as the ill-dressed bulk disappeared from view.

'Lewis?'

It wasn't a man's walk, that roll, that swagger. It was the gait of an upright beast who'd been taught to walk, and now, without its master, was losing the trick of it.

It was an ape.

Oh God, oh God, it was an ape.

'I have to see Phillipe Laborteaux.'

   'I'm sorry, Monsieur; but prison visitors – '

   'This is a matter of life and death, officer.'

   'Easily said, Monsieur.'

Lewis risked a lie.

   'His sister is dying. I beg you to have some compassion.'

   'Oh . . . well . . .'

A little doubt. Lewis levered a little further.

   'A few minutes only; to settle arrangements.'

   'Can't it wait until tomorrow?'

   'She'll be dead by morning.'

Lewis hated talking about Catherine in such a way, even for the purpose of this deception, but it was necessary; he had to see Phillipe. If his theory was correct, history might repeat itself before the night was out.

Phillipe had been woken from a sedated sleep. His eyes were circled with darkness.

   'What do you want?'

Lewis didn't even attempt to proceed any further with his lie; Phillipe was drugged as it was, and probably confused. Best to confront him with the truth, and see what came of it.

   'You kept an ape, didn't you?'

A look of terror crossed Phillipe's face, slowed by the drugs in his blood, but plain enough.

   'Didn't you?'

   'Lewis . . .' Phillipe looked so very old.

   'Answer me, Phillipe, I beg you: before it's too late. Did you keep an ape?'

   'It was an experiment, that's all it was. An experiment.'

   'Why?'

   'Your stories. Your damn stories: I wanted to see if it was true that they were wild. I wanted to make a man of it.'

   'Make a man of it,'

   'And that whore . . .'

   'Natalie.'

   'She seduced it.'

Lewis felt sick. This was a convolution he hadn't anticipated.

   'Seduced it?'

   'Whore,' Phillipe said, with infinite regret.

   'Where is this ape of yours?'

   'You'll kill it.'

'It broke into the apartment, while Catherine was there. Destroyed everything, Phillipe. It's dangerous now that it has no master. Don't you understand?'

'Catherine?'

'No, she's all right.'

'It's trained: it wouldn't harm her. It's watched her, in hiding. Come and gone. Quiet as a mouse.'

'And the girl?'

'It was jealous.'

'So it murdered her?'

'Perhaps. I don't know. I don't want to think about it.'

'Why haven't you told them; had the thing destroyed?'

'I don't know if it's true. It's probably all a fiction, one of your damn fictions, just another story.'

A sour, wily smile crossed his exhausted face.

'You must know what I mean, Lewis. It could be a story, couldn't it? Like your tales of Dupin. Except that maybe I made it true for a while; did you ever think of that? Maybe I made it true.'

Lewis stood up. It was a tired debate: reality and illusion. Either a thing was, or was not. Life was not a dream.

'Where is the ape?' he demanded.

Phillipe pointed to his temple.

'Here; where you can never find him,' he said, and spat in Lewis' face. The spittle hit his lip, like a kiss.

'You don't know what you did. You'll never know.'

Lewis wiped his lip as the warders escorted the prisoner out of the room and back to his happy drugged oblivion. All he could think of now, left alone in the cold interview room, was that Phillipe had it easy. He'd taken refuge in pretended guilt, and locked himself away where memory, and revenge, and the truth, the wild, marauding truth, could never touch him again. He hated Phillipe at that moment, with all his heart. Hated him for the dilettante and the coward he'd always known him to be. It wasn't a more gentle world Phillipe had created around him; it was a hiding place, as much a lie as that summer of 1937 had been. No life could be lived the way he'd lived it without a reckoning coming sooner or later; and here it was.

That night, in the safety of his cell, Phillipe woke. It was warm, but he was cold. In the utter dark he chewed at his wrists until a pulse of blood bubbled into his mouth. He lay back on his bed, and quietly splashed and fountained away to death, out of sight and out of mind.

* * *

141

The suicide was reported in a small article on the second page of *Le Monde*. The big news of the following day however was the sensational murder of a redheaded prostitute in a little house off the Rue de Rochechquant. Monique Zevaco had been found at three o'clock in the morning by her flatmate, her body in a state so horrible as to 'defy description'.

Despite the alleged impossibility of the task, the media set about describing the indescribable with a morbid will. Every last scratch, tear and gouging on Monique's partially nude body – tattooed, drooled *Le-Monde*, with a map of France – was chronicled in detail. As indeed was the appearance of her well-dressed, over-perfumed murderer, who had apparently watched her at her toilet through a small back window, then broken in and attacked Mademoiselle Zevaco in her bathroom. The murderer had then fled down the stairs, bumping into the flatmate who would minutes after discover Mademoiselle Zevaco's mutilated corpse. Only one commentator made any connection between the murder at the Rue des Martyrs and the slaughter of Mme Zevaco; and he failed to pick up on the curious coincidence that the accused Phillipe Laborteaux had that same night taken his own life.

The funeral took place in a storm, the cortège edging its pitiful way through the abandoned streets towards Montparnasse with the lashing snow entirely blotting out the road ahead. Lewis sat with Catherine and Jacques Solal as they laid Phillipe to rest. Every one of his circle had deserted him, unwilling to attend the funeral of a suicide and of a suspected murderer. His wit, his good looks, his infinite capacity to charm went for nothing at the end.

He was not, as it turned out, entirely unmourned by strangers. As they stood at the graveside, the cold cutting into them, Solal sidled up to Lewis and nudged him.

'What?'

'Over there. Under the tree.' Solal nodded beyond the praying priest.

The stranger was standing at a distance, almost hidden by the marble mausoleums. A heavy black scarf was wrapped across his face, and a wide-brimmed hat pulled down over his brow, but his bulk was unmistakable. Catherine had seen him too. She was shaking as she stood, wrapped round by Lewis' embrace, not just with cold, but with fear. It was as though the creature was some morbid angel, come to hover a while, and enjoy the grief. It was

142

grotesque, and eerie, that this thing should come to see Phillipe consigned to the frozen earth. What did it feel? Anguish? Guilt?

Yes, did it feel guilt?

It knew it had been seen, and it turned its back, shambling away. Without a word to Lewis, Jacques Solal slipped away from the grave in pursuit. In a short while both the stranger and his pursuer were erased by the snow.

Back at the Quai de Bourbon Catherine and Lewis said nothing of the incident. A kind of barrier had appeared between them, forbidding contact on any level but the most trivial. There was no purpose in analysis, and none in regrets. Phillipe was dead. The past, their past together, was dead. This final chapter in their joint lives soured utterly everything that preceded it, so that no shared memory could be enjoyed without the pleasure being spoilt. Phillipe had died horribly, devouring his own flesh and blood, perhaps driven mad by a knowledge he possessed of his own guilt and depravity. No innocence, no history of joy could remain unstained by that fact. Silently they mourned the loss, not only of Phillipe, but of their own past. Lewis understood now Phillipe's reluctance to live when there was such loss in the world.

Solal rang. Breathless after his chase, but elated, he spoke in whispers to Lewis, clearly enjoying the excitement.

'I'm at the Gare du Nord, and I've found out where our friend lives. I've found him Lewis!'

'Excellent. I'll come straight away. I'll meet you on the steps of the Gare du Nord. I'll take a cab: ten minutes.'

'It's in the basement of number sixteen, Rue des Fleurs. I'll see you there – '

'Don't go in, Jacques. Wait for me. Don't – '

The telephone clicked and Solal was gone. Lewis reached for his coat.

'Who was that?'

She asked, but she didn't want to know. Lewis shrugged on his overcoat and said: 'Nobody at all. Don't worry. I won't be long.'

'Take your scarf,' she said, not glancing over her shoulder.

'Yes. Thank you.'

'You'll catch a chill.'

He left her gazing over the night-clad Seine, watching the ice-floes dance together on the black water.

* * *

143

When he arrived at the house on the Rue des Fleurs, Solal was not to be seen, but fresh footprints in the powdery snow led to the front door of number sixteen and then, foiled, went around the back of the house. Lewis followed them. As he stepped into the yard behind the house, through a rotted gate that had been crudely forced by Solal, he realized he had come without a weapon. Best to go back, perhaps, find a crowbar, a knife; something. Even as he was debating with himself, the back door opened, and the stranger appeared, dressed in his now familiar overcoat. Lewis flattened himself against the wall of the yard, where the shadows were deepest, certain that he would be seen. But the beast was about other business. He stood in the doorway with his face fully exposed, and for the first time, in the reflected moonlight off the snow, Lewis could see the creature's physiognomy plainly. Its face was freshly shaved; and the scent of cologne was strong, even in the open air. Its skin was pink as a peach, though nicked in one or two places by a careless blade. Lewis thought of the open-razor it had apparently threatened Catherine with. Was that what its business had been in Phillipe's room, the purloining of a good razor? It was pulling its leather gloves on over its wide, shaved hands, making small coughing noises in its throat that sounded almost like grunts of satisfaction. Lewis had the impression that it was preparing itself for the outside world; and the sight was touching as much as intimidating. All this thing wanted was to be human. It was aspiring, in its way, to the model Phillipe had given it, had nurtured in it. Now, deprived of its mentor, confused-and unhappy, it was attempting to face the world as it had been taught to do. There was no way back for it. Its days of innocence had gone: it could never be an unambitious beast again. Trapped in its new persona, it had no choice but to continue in the life its master had awoken its taste for. Without glancing in Lewis' direction, it gently closed the door behind it and crossed the yard, its walk transforming in those few steps from a simian roll to the mincing waddle that it used to simulate humanity.

Then it was gone.

Lewis waited a moment in the shadows, breathing shallowly. Every bone in his body ached with cold now, and his feet were numb. The beast showed no sign of returning; so he ventured out of his hiding place and tried the door. It was not locked. As he stepped inside a stench struck him: the sickly sweet smell of rotten fruit mingled with the cloying cologne: the zoo and the boudoir.

He edged down a flight of slimy stone steps, and along a short, tiled corridor towards a door. It too was unlocked; and the bare bulb inside illuminated a bizarre scene.

On the floor, a large, somewhat thread-bare Persian carpet; sparse furnishings; a bed, roughly covered with blankets and stained hessian; a wardrobe, bulging with oversize clothes; discarded fruit in abundance, some trodden into the floor; a bucket, filled with straw and stinking of droppings. On the wall, a large crucifix. On the mantelpiece a photograph of Catherine, Lewis and Phillipe together in a sunlit past, smiling. At the sink, the creature's shaving kit. Soap, brush, razor. Fresh suds. On the dresser a pile of money, left in careless abundance beside a pile of hypodermics and a collection of small bottles. It was warm in the beast's garret; perhaps the furnace for the house roared in an adjacent cellar. Solal was not there.

Suddenly, a noise.

Lewis turned to the door, expecting the ape to be filling it, teeth bared, eyes demonic. But he had lost all orientation; the noise was not from the door but from the wardrobe. Behind the pile of clothes there was a movement.

'Solal?'

Jacques Solal half fell out of the wardrobe, and sprawled across the Persian carpet. His face was disfigured by one foul wound, so that it was all but impossible to find any part of his features that was still Jacques.

The creature had taken hold of his lip and pulled his muscle off his bone, as though removing a balaclava. His exposed teeth chattered away in nervous response to oncoming death; his limbs jangled and shook. But Jacques was already gone. These shudders and jerks were not signs of thought or personality, just the din of passing. Lewis knelt at Solal's side; his stomach was strong. During the war, being a conscientious objector, he had volunteered to serve in the Military Hospital, and there were few transformations of the human body he had not seen in one combination or another. Tenderly, he cradled the body, not noticing the blood. He hadn't loved this man, scarcely cared for him at all, but now all he wanted was to take him away, out of the ape's cage, and find him a human grave. He'd take the photograph too. That was too much, giving the beast a photograph of the three friends together. It made him hate Phillipe more than ever.

He hauled the body off the carpet. It required a gargantuan effort, and the sultry heat in the room, after the chill of the outside world, made him dizzy. He could feel a jittering nervousness in his limbs. His body was close to betraying him, he knew it; close to failing, to losing its coherence and collapsing.

Not here. In God's name, not here.

Maybe he should go now, and find a phone. That would be wise. Call the police, yes . . . call Catherine, yes . . . even find somebody in the house to help him. But that would mean leaving Jacques in the lair, for the beast to assault again, and he had become strangely protective of the corpse; he was unwilling to leave it alone. In an anguish of confused feelings, unable to leave Jacques yet unable to move him far, he stood in the middle of the room and did nothing at all. That was best; yes. Nothing at all. Too tired, too weak. Nothing at all was best.

The reverie went on interminably; the old man fixed beyond movement at the crux of his feelings, unable to go forward into the future, or back into the soiled past. Unable to remember. Unable to forget.

Waiting, in a dreamy half-life, for the end of the world.

It came home noisily like a drunken man, and the sound of its opening the outer door stirred Lewis into a slow response. With some difficulty he hauled Jacques into the wardrobe, and hid there himself, with the faceless head in his lap.

There was a voice in the room, a woman's voice. Maybe it wasn't the beast, after all. But no: through the crack of the wardrobe door Lewis could see the beast, and a red-haired young woman with him. She was talking incessantly, the perpetual trivia of a spaced-out mind.

'You've got more; oh you sweetie, oh you dear man, that's wonderful. Look at all this stuff.'

She had pills in her hands and was swallowing them like sweets, gleeful as a child at Christmas.

'Where did you get all this? OK, if you don't want to tell me, it's fine by me.'

Was this Phillipe's doing too, or had the ape stolen the stuff for his own purposes? Did he regularly seduce redheaded prostitutes with drugs?

The girl's grating babble was calming now, as the pills took effect, sedating her, transporting her to a private world. Lewis watched, entranced, as she began to undress.

'It's so . . . hot . . . in here.'

The ape watched, his back to Lewis. What expression did that shaved face wear? Was there lust in its eyes, or doubt?

The girl's breasts were beautiful, though her body was rather

146

too thin. The young skin was white, the nipples flower-pink. She raised her arms over her head and as she stretched the perfect globes rose and flattened slightly. The ape reached a wide hand to her body and tenderly plucked at one of her nipples, rolling it between dark-meat fingers. The girl sighed.

'Shall I . . . take everything off?'

The monkey grunted.

'You don't say much, do you?'

She shimmied out of her red skirt. Now she was naked but for a pair of knickers. She lay on the bed stretching again, luxuriating in her body and the welcome heat of the room, not even bothering to look at her admirer.

Wedged underneath Solal's body, Lewis began to feel dizzy again. His lower limbs were now completely numb, and he had no feeling in his right arm, which was pressed against the back of the wardrobe, yet he didn't dare move. The ape was capable of anything, he knew that. If he was discovered what might it not choose to do, to him and to the girl?

Every part of his body was now either nerveless, or wracked with pain. In his lap Solal's seeping body seemed to become heavier with every moment. His spine was screaming, and the back of his neck pained him as though pierced with hot knitting-needles. The agony was becoming unbearable; he began to think he would die in this pathetic hiding place, while the ape made love.

The girl sighed, and Lewis looked again at the bed. The ape had its hand between her legs, and she squirmed beneath its ministrations.

'Yes, oh yes,' she said again and again, as her lover stripped her completely.

It was too much. The dizziness throbbed through Lewis' cortex. Was this death? The lights in the head, and the whine in the ears?

He closed his eyes, blotting out the sight of the lovers, but unable to shut out the noise. It seemed to go on forever, invading his head. Sighs, laughter, little shrieks.

At last, darkness.

Lewis woke on an invisible rack; his body had been wrenched out of shape by the limitations of his hiding-place. He looked up. The door of the wardrobe was open, and the ape was staring down at him, its mouth attempting a grin. It was naked; and its body was almost entirely shaved. In the cleft of its immense chest a small gold crucifix glinted. Lewis recognized the jewellery immediately. He had bought it for Phillipe in the Champs Elysees just before the war. Now it nestled in a tuft of reddish-orange hair. The beast proffered a hand to Lewis, and he automatically took it. The coarse-palmed grip hauled him from under Solal's body. He couldn't stand straight. His legs were rubbery, his ankles wouldn't support him. The beast took hold of him, and steadied him. His head spinning, Lewis looked down into the wardrobe, where Solal was lying, tucked up like a baby in its womb, face to the wall.

The beast closed the door on the corpse, and helped Lewis to the sink, where he was sick.

'Phillipe?' He dimly realized that the woman was still here: in the bed: just woken after a night of love.

'Phillipe: who's this?' She was scrabbling for pills on the table beside the bed. The beast sauntered across and snatched them from her hands.

'Ah . . . Phillipe . . . please. Do you want me to go with this one as well? I will if you want. Just give me back the pills.'

She gestured towards Lewis.

'I don't usually go with old men.'

The ape growled at her. The expression on her face changed, as though for the first time she had an inkling of what this john was. But the thought was too difficult for her drugged mind, and she let it go.

'Please, Phillipe . . .' she whimpered.

Lewis was looking at the ape. It had taken the photograph from the mantelpiece. Its dark nail was on Lewis' picture. It was smiling. It recognized him, even though forty-odd years had drained so much life from him.

'Lewis,' it said, finding the word quite easy to say.

The old man had nothing in his stomach to vomit, and no harm left to feel. This was the end of the century, he should be ready for anything. Even to be greeted as a friend of a friend by the shaved beast that loomed in front of him. It would not harm him, he knew that. Probably Phillipe had told the ape about their lives together; made the creature love Catherine and himself as much as it had adored Phillipe.

'Lewis,' it said again, and gestured to the woman, (now sitting open-legged on the bed) offering her for his pleasure.

Lewis shook his head.

In and out, in and out, part fiction, part fact.

It had come to this; offered a human woman by this naked ape.

148

It was the last, God help him, the very last chapter in the fiction his great uncle had begun. From love to murder back to love again. The love of an ape for a man. He had caused it, with his dreams of fictional heroes, steeped in absolute reason. He had coaxed Phillipe into making real the stories of a lost youth. He *was* to blame. Not this poor strutting ape, lost between the jungle and the Stock Exchange; not Phillipe, wanting to be young forever; certainly not cold Catherine, who after tonight would be completely alone. It was him. His the crime, his the guilt, his the punishment.

His legs had regained a little feeling, and he began to stagger to the door.

'Aren't you staying?' said the red-haired woman.

'This thing . . .' he couldn't bring himself to name the animal.

'You mean Phillipe?'

'He isn't called Phillipe,' Lewis said. 'He's not even human.'

'Please yourself,' she said, and shrugged.

To his back, the ape spoke, saying his name. But this time, instead of it coming out as a sort of grunt-word, its simian palate caught Phillipe's inflexion with unnerving accuracy, better than the most skilful of parrots. It was Phillipe's voice, perfectly.

'Lewis,' it said.

Not pleading. Not demanding. Simply naming, for the pleasure of naming, an equal.

The passers-by who saw the old man clamber on to the parapet of the Pont du Carrousel stared, but made no attempt to stop him jumping. He teetered a moment as he stood up straight, then pitched over into the threshing, churning ice-water.

One or two people wandered to the other side of the bridge to see if the current had caught him: it had. He rose to the surface, his face blue-white and blank as a baby's, then some intricate eddy snatched at his feet and pulled him under. The thick water closed over his head and churned on.

'Who was that?' somebody asked.

'Who knows?'

It was a clear-heaven day; the last of the winter's snow had fallen, and the thaw would begin by noon. Birds, exulting in the sudden sun, swooped over the Sacré Coeur. Paris began to undress for spring, its virgin white too spoiled to be worn for long.

149

In mid-morning, a young woman with red hair, her arm linked in that of a large ugly man, took a leisurely stroll to the steps of the Sacre1 Coeur. The sun blessed them. Bells rang.

It was a new day.

BOOKS OF BLOOD
VOLUME 3

To Roy and Lynne

CONTENTS

Son of Celluloid

ONE: TRAILER

Barberio felt fine, despite the bullet. Sure, there was a catch in his chest if he breathed too hard, and the wound in his thigh wasn't too pretty to look at, but he'd been holed before and come up smiling. At least he was free: that was the main thing. Nobody, he swore, nobody would ever lock him up again, he'd kill himself rather than be taken back into custody. If he was unlucky and they cornered him, he'd stick the gun in his mouth and blow off the top of his head. No way would they drag him back to that cell alive.

Life was too long if you were locked away and counting it in seconds. It had only taken him a couple of months to learn that lesson. Life was long, and repetitive and debilitating, and if you weren't careful you were soon thinking it would be better to die than go on existing in the shit-hole they'd put you in. Better to string yourself up by your belt in the middle of the night rather than face the tedium of another twenty-four hours, all eighty-six thousand four hundred seconds of it.

So he went for broke.

First he bought a gun on the prison black market. It cost him everything he had and a handful of IOUs he'd have to make good on the outside if he wanted to stay alive. Then he made the most obvious move in the book: he climbed the wall. And whatever god looked after the liquor-store muggers of this world was looking after him that night, because hot damn if he didn't scoot right over that wall and away without so much as a dog sniffing at his heels.

And the cops? Why they screwed it up every which way from Sunday, looking for him where he'd never gone, pulling in his brother and his sister-in-law on suspicion of harbouring him when they didn't even know he'd escaped, putting out an All-Points Bulletin with a description of his pre-prison self, twenty pounds heavier than he was now. All this he'd heard from

1

Geraldine, a lady he'd courted in the good old days, who'd given him a dressing for his leg and the bottle of Southern Comfort that was now almost empty in his pocket. He'd taken the booze and sympathy and gone on his way, trusting to the legendary idiocy of the law and the god who'd got him so far already.

Sing-Sing he called this god. Pictured him as a fat guy with a grin that hooked from one ear to the other, a prime salami in one hand, and a cup of dark coffee in the other. In Barberio's mind Sing-Sing smelt like a full belly at Mama's house, back in the days when Mama was still well in the head, and he'd been her pride and joy.

Unfortunately Sing-Sing had been looking the other way when the one eagle-eye cop in the whole city saw Barberio draining his snake in a back alley, and recognised him from that obsolete APB. Young cop, couldn't have been more than twenty-five, out to be a hero. He was too dumb to learn the lesson of Barberio's warning shot. Instead of taking cover, and letting Barberio make a break, he'd forced the issue by coming straight down the alley at him.

Barberio had no choice. He fired.

The cop fired back. Sing-Sing must have stepped in there somewhere, spoiling the cop's aim so that the bullet that should have found Barberio's heart hit his leg, and guiding the returning shot straight into the cop's nose. Eagle-eye went down as if he'd just remembered an appointment with the ground, and Barberio was away, cursing, bleeding and scared. He'd never shot a man before, and he'd started with a cop. Quite an introduction to the craft.

Sing-Sing was still with him though. The bullet in his leg ached, but Geraldine's ministrations had stopped the blood, the liquor had done wonders for the pain, and here he was half a day later, tired but alive, having hopped half-way across a city so thick with vengeful cops it was like a psycho's parade at the Policemen's Ball. Now all he asked of his protector was a place to rest up awhile. Not for long, just enough time to catch his breath and plan his future movements. An hour or two of shut-eye wouldn't go amiss either.

Thing was, he'd got that belly-ache, the deep, gnawing pain he got more and more these days. Maybe he'd find a phone, when he'd rested for a time, and call Geraldine again, get her to sweet-talk a doctor into seeing him. He'd been planning to get out of the city before midnight, but that didn't look like a plausible option now. Dangerous as it was, he would have to stay in the locality a night and maybe the best part of the next day; make his break for the open country when he'd recouped a little energy and had the bullet taken out of his leg.

Jeez, but that belly griped. His guess was it was an ulcer, brought on by the filthy slop they called food at the penitentiary. Lots of guys had belly and shit-chute problems in there. He'd be better after a few days of pizzas and beers, he was damn sure of that.

The word *cancer* wasn't in Barberio's vocabulary. He never thought about terminal disease, especially in reference to himself. That'd be like a piece of slaughterhouse beef fretting about an ingrowing hoof as it stepped up to meet the gun. A man in his trade, surrounded by lethal tools, doesn't expect to perish from a malignancy in his belly. But that's what that ache was.

The lot at the back of the Movie Palace cinema had been a restaurant, but a fire had gutted it three years back, and the ground had never been cleared.

It wasn't a good spec for rebuilding, and no-one had shown much interest in the site. The neighbourhood had once been buzzing, but that was in the sixties, early seventies. For a heady decade places of entertainment – restaurants, bars, cinemas – had flourished. Then came the inevitable slump. Fewer and fewer kids came this way to spend their money: there were new spots to hit, new places to be seen in. The bars closed up, the restaurants followed. Only the Movie Palace remained as a token reminder of more innocent days in a district that was becoming tackier and more dangerous every year.

The jungle of convolvulus and rotted timbers that throttled the vacant lot suited Barberio just fine. His leg was giving him jip, he was stumbling from sheer fatigue, and the pain in his belly was worsening. A spot to lay down his clammy head was needed, and damn quick. Finish off the Southern Comfort, and think about Geraldine.

It was one-thirty am; the lot was a trysting-ground for cats. They ran, startled, through the man-high weeds as he pushed aside some of the fencing timbers and slid into the shadows. The refuge stank of piss, human and cat, of garbage, of old fires, but it felt like a sanctuary.

3

Seeking the support of the back wall of the Movie Palace, Barberio leaned on his forearm and threw up a bellyful of Southern Comfort and acid. Along the wall a little way some kids had built a makeshift den of girders, fire-blackened planks and corrugated iron. Ideal, he thought, a sanctuary within a sanctuary. Sing-Sing was smiling at him, all greasy chops. Groaning a little (the belly was really bad tonight) he staggered along the wall to the lean-to den, and ducked through the door.

Somebody else had used this place to sleep in: he could feel damp sacking under his hand as he sat down, and a bottle clinked against a brick somewhere to his left. There was a smell close by he didn't want to think too much about, like the sewers were backing up. All in all, it was squalid: but it was safer than the street. He sat with his back against the wall of the Movie Palace and exhaled his fears in a long, slow breath.

No more than a block away, perhaps half a block, the babe-in-the-night wail of a cop-car began, and his newly acquired sense of security sank without trace. They were closing in for the kill, he knew it. They'd just been playing him along, letting him think he was away, all the time cruising him like sharks, sleek and silent, until he was too tired to put up any resistance. Jeez: he'd killed a cop, what they wouldn't do to him once they had him alone. They'd crucify him.

OK Sing-Sing, what now? Take that surprised look off your face, and get me out of this.

For a moment, nothing. Then the god smiled in his mind's eye, and quite coincidentally he felt the hinges pressing into his back.

Shit! A door. He was leaning against a door.

Grunting with pain he turned and ran his fingers around this escape hatch at his back. To judge by touch it was a small ventilation grille no more than three feet square. Maybe it let on to a crawlspace or maybe into someone's kitchen – what the hell? It was safer inside than out: that was the first lesson any newborn kid got slapped into him.

The siren-song wailed on, making Barberio's skin creep. Foul sound. It quickened his heart hearing it.

His thick fingers fumbled down the side of the grille feeling for a lock of some kind, and sure as shit there was a padlock, as gritty with rust as the rest of the metalwork.

Come on Sing-Sing, he prayed, one more break is all I'm asking, let me in, and I swear I'm yours forever.

4

He pulled at the lock, but damn it, it wasn't about to give so easily. Either it was stronger than it felt, or he was weaker. Maybe a little of both.

The car was slinking closer with every second. The wail drowned out the sound of his own panicking breath.

He pulled the gun, the cop-killer, out of his jacket-pocket and pressed it into service as a snub-nosed crowbar. He couldn't get much leverage on the thing, it was too short, but a couple of cursing heaves did the trick. The lock gave, a shower of rust scales peppered his face. He only just silenced a whoop of triumph.

Now to open the grille, to get out of this wretched world into the dark.

He insinuated his fingers through the lattice and pulled. Pain, a continuum of pain that ran from his belly to his bowel to his leg, made his head spin. Open, damn you, he said to the grille, open sesame.

The door conceded.

It opened suddenly, and he fell back on to the sodden sacking. A moment and he was up again, peering into the darkness within this darkness that was the interior of the Movie Palace.

Let the cop-car come, he thought buoyantly, I've got my hidey-hole to keep me warm. And warm it was: almost hot in fact. The air out of the hole smelt like it had been simmering in there for a good long while.

His leg had gone into a cramp and it hurt like fuck as he dragged himself through the door and into the solid black beyond. Even as he did so the siren turned a corner nearby and the baby wail died. Wasn't that the patter of lawlike feet he could hear on the sidewalk?

He turned clumsily in the blackness, his leg a dead-weight, his foot feeling about the size of a watermelon, and pulled the grille-door to after him. The satisfaction was that of pulling up a drawbridge and leaving the enemy on the other side of the moat, somehow it didn't matter that they could open the door just as easily as he had, and follow him in. Childlike, he felt sure nobody could possibly find him here. As long as he couldn't see his pursuers, his pursuers couldn't see him.

If the cops did indeed duck into the lot to look for him, he didn't hear them. Maybe he'd been mistaken, maybe they were after some other poor punk on the street, and not him. Well OK,

5

whatever. He had found himself a nice niche to rest up awhile, and that was fine and dandy.

Funny, the air wasn't so bad in here after all. It wasn't the stagnant air of a crawlspace or an attic, the atmosphere in the hidey-hole was alive. Not fresh air, no it wasn't that, it smelt old and trapped sure enough, but it was buzzing nevertheless. It fairly sang in his ears, it made his skin tingle like a cold shower, it wormed its way up his nose and put the weirdest things in his head. It was like being high on something: he felt that good. His leg didn't hurt anymore, or if it did he was too distracted by the pictures in his head. He was filling up to overflowing with pictures: dancing girls and kissing couples, farewells at stations, old dark houses, comedians, cowboys, undersea adventures – scenes he'd never lived in a million years, but that moved him now like raw experience, true and incontestable. He wanted to cry at the farewells, except that he wanted to laugh at the comedians, except that the girls needed ogling, the cowboys needed hollering for.

What kind of place was this anyhow? He peered through the glamour of the pictures which were damn close to getting the better of his eyes. He was in a space no more than four feet wide, but tall, and lit by a flickering light that chanced through cracks in the inner wall. Barberio was too befuddled to recognise the origins of the light, and his murmuring ears couldn't make sense of the dialogue from the screen on the other side of the wall. It was 'Satyricon', the second of the two Fellini movies the Palace was showing as their late-night double feature that Saturday.

Barberio had never seen the movie, never even heard of Fellini. It would have disgusted him (faggot film, Italian crap). He preferred undersea adventures, war movies. Oh, and dancing girls. Anything with dancing girls.

Funny, though he was all alone in his hidey-hole, he had the weird sensation of being watched. Through the kaleidoscope of Busby Berkeley routines that was playing on the inside of his skull he felt eyes, not a few – thousands – watching him. The feeling wasn't so bad you'd want to take a drink for it, but they were always there, staring away at him like he was something worth looking at, laughing at him sometimes, crying sometimes, but mostly just gawping with hungry eyes.

Truth was, there was nothing he could do about them anyhow. His limbs had given up the ghost; he couldn't feel his hands or

6

feet at all. He didn't know, and it was probably better that he didn't, that he'd torn open his wound getting into this place, and he was bleeding to death.

About two-fifty-five am, as Fellini's 'Satyricon' came to its ambiguous end, Barberio died in the space between the back of the building proper and the back wall of the cinema.

The Movie Palace had once been a Mission Hall, and if he'd looked up as he died he might have glimpsed the inept fresco depicting an Angelic Host that was still to be seen through the grime, and assumed his own Assumption. But he died watching the dancing girls, and that was fine by him.

The false wall, the one that let through the light from the back of the screen, had been erected as a makeshift partition to cover the fresco of the Host. It had seem more respectful to do that than paint the Angels out permanently, and besides the man who had ordered the alterations half-suspected that the movie house bubble would burst sooner or later. If so, he could simply demolish the wall, and he'd be back in business for the worship of God instead of Garbo.

It never happened. The bubble, though fragile, never burst, and the movies carried on. The Doubting Thomas (his name was Harry Cleveland) died, and the space was forgotten. Nobody now living even knew it existed. If he'd searched the city from top to bottom Barberio couldn't have found a more secret place to perish.

The space however, the air itself, had lived a life of its own in that fifty years. Like a reservoir, it had received the electric stares of thousands of eyes, of tens of thousands of eyes. Half a century of movie-goers had lived vicariously through the screen of the Movie Palace, pressing their sympathies and their passions on to the flickering illusion, the energy of their emotions gathering strength like a neglected cognac in that hidden passage of air. Sooner or later, it must discharge itself. All it lacked was a catalyst.

Until Barberio's cancer.

TWO: THE MAIN FEATURE

After loitering in the cramped foyer of the Movie Palace for twenty minutes or so, the young girl in the cerise and lemon print dress began to look distinctly agitated. It was almost three in the morning, and the late-night movies were well over.

Eight months had passed since Barberio had died in the back of the cinema, eight slow months in which business had been at best patchy. Still, the late-night double bill on Fridays and Saturdays always packed in the punters. Tonight it had been two Eastwood movies: spaghetti westerns. The girl in the cerise dress didn't look like much of a western fan to Birdy; it wasn't really a women's genre. Maybe she'd come for Eastwood rather than the violence, though Birdy had never seen the attraction of that eternally squinting face.

'Can I help you?' Birdy asked.

The girl looked nervously at Birdy.

'I'm waiting for my boyfriend,' she said. 'Dean.'

'Have you lost him?'

'He went to the rest-room at the end of the movie and he hasn't come out yet.'

'Was he feeling . . . er . . . ill?'

'Oh no,' said the girl quickly, protecting her date from this slight on his sobriety.

'I'll get someone to go and look for him,' said Birdy. It was late, she was tired, and the speed was wearing off. The idea of spending any more time than she strictly needed to in this fleapit was not particularly appealing. She wanted home; bed and sleep. Just sleep. At thirty-four, she'd decided she'd grown out of sex. Bed was for sleep, especially for fat girls.

She pushed the swing door, and poked her head into the cinema. A ripe smell of cigarettes, popcorn and people enveloped her; it was a few degrees hotter in here than in the foyer.

'Ricky?'

Ricky was locking up the back exit, at the far end of the cinema.

'That smell's completely gone,' he called to her.

'Good.' A few months back there'd been a hell of a stench at the screen-end of the cinema.

'Something dead in the lot next door,' he said.

'Can you help me a minute?' she called back.

'What'd you want?'

He sauntered up the red-carpeted aisle towards her, keys jangling at his belt. His tee-shirt proclaimed 'Only the Young Die Good'.

'Problem?' he said, blowing his nose.

'There's a girl out here. She says she lost her boyfriend in the john.'

8

Ricky looked pained.

'In the john?'

'Right. Will you take a look? You don't mind, do you?'

And she could cut out the wisecracks for a start, he thought, giving her a sickly smile. They were hardly on speaking terms these days. Too many high times together: it always dealt a crippling blow to a friendship in the long run. Besides, Birdy'd made some very uncharitable (accurate) remarks about his associates and he'd returned the salvo with all guns blazing. They hadn't spoken for three and a half weeks after that. Now there was an uncomfortable truce, more for sanity's sake than anything. It was not meticulously observed.

He about turned, wandered back down the aisle, and took row E across the cinema to the john, pushing up seats as he went. They'd seen better days, those seats: sometime around 'Now Voyager'. Now they looked thoroughly shot at: in need of refurbishing, or replacing altogether. In row E alone four of the seats had been slashed beyond repair, now he counted a fifth mutilation which was new tonight. Some mindless kid bored with the movie and/or his girlfriend, and too stoned to leave. Time was he'd done that kind of thing himself: and counted it a blow for freedom against the capitalists who ran these joints. Time was he'd done a lot of damn-fool things.

Birdy watched him duck into the Men's Room. He'll get a kick out of that, she thought with a sly smile, just his sort of occupaion. And to think, she'd once had the hots for him, back in the old days (six months ago) when razor-thin men with noses like Durante and an encyclopaedic knowledge of de Niro movies had really been her style. Now she saw him for what he was, flotsam from a lost ship of hope. Still a pill-freak, still a theoretical bisexual, still devoted to early Polanski movies and symbolic pacifism. What kind of dope did he have between his ears anyhow? The same as she'd had, she chided herself, thinking there was something sexy about the bum.

She waited for a few seconds, watching the door. When he failed to re-emerge she went back into the foyer for a moment, to see how the girl was going on. She was smoking a cigarette like an amateur actress who's failed to get the knack of it, leaning against the rail, her skirt hitched up as she scratched her leg.

'Tights,' she explained.

'The Manager's gone to find Dean.'

'Thanks,' she scratched on. 'They bring me out in a rash, I'm allergic to them.'

There were blotches on the girl's pretty legs, which rather spoiled the effect.

'It's because I'm hot and bothered,' she ventured. 'Whenever I get hot and bothered, I get allergic.'

'Oh.'

'Dean's probably run off, you know, when I had my back turned. He'd do that. He doesn't give a f – . He doesn't care.'

Birdy could see she was on her way to tears, which was a drag. She was bad with tears. Shouting matches, even fights, OK. Tears, no go.

'It'll be OK' was all she could find to say to keep the tears from coming.

'No it's not,' said the girl. 'It won't be OK, because he's a bastard. He treats everyone like dirt.' She ground out the half-smoked cigarette with the pointed toe of her cerise shoes, taking particular care to extinguish every glowing fragment of tobacco.

'Men don't care, do they?' she said looking up at Birdy with heart-melting directness. Under the expert make-up, she was perhaps seventeen, certainly not much more. Her mascara was a little smeared, and there were arcs of tiredness under her eyes.

'No,' replied Birdy, speaking from painful experience. 'No they don't.'

Birdy thought ruefully that she'd never looked as attractive as this tired nymphet. Her eyes were too small, and her arms were fat. (Be honest, girl, you're fat all over.) But the arms were her worst feature, she'd convinced herself of that. There were men, a lot of them, who got off on big breasts, on a sizeable ass, but no man she'd ever known liked fat arms. They always wanted to be able to encircle the wrist of their girlfriend between thumb and index finger, it was a primitive way to measure attachment. Her wrists, however, if she was brutal with herself, were practically undiscernible. Her fat hands became her fat fore-arms, which became, after a podgy time, her fat upper arms. Men couldn't encircle her wrists because she had no wrists, and that alienated them. Well, that was one of the reasons anyhow. She was also very bright: and that was always a drawback if you wanted men at your feet. But of the options as to why she'd never been successful in love, she plumped for the fat arms as the likeliest explanation.

Whereas this girl had arms as slender as a Balinese dancer's, her wrists looked thin as glass, and about as fragile.

Sickening, really. She was probably a lousy conversationalist to boot. God, the girl had all the advantages.

'What's your name?' she asked.

'Lindi Lee,' the girl replied.

It would be.

Ricky thought he'd made a mistake. This can't be the toilet, he said to himself.

He was standing in what appeared to be the main street of a frontier town he'd seen in two hundred westerns. A dust storm seemed to be raging, forcing him to narrow his eyes against the stinging sand. Through the swirl of the ochre-grey air he could pick out, he thought, the General Stores, the Sheriff's Office and the Saloon. They stood in lieu of the toilet cubicles. Optional tumble-weed danced by him on the hot desert wind. The ground beneath his feet was impacted sand: no sign of tiles. No sign of anything that was faintly toilet-like.

Ricky looked to his right, down the street. Where the far wall of the john should have been the street receded, in forced perspective, towards a painted distance. It was a lie, of course, the whole thing was a lie. Surely if he concentrated he'd begin to see through the mirage to find out how it had been achieved; the projections, the concealed lighting effects, the backcloths, the miniatures; all the tricks of the trade. But though he concentrated as hard as his slightly spaced-out condition would allow, he just couldn't seem to get his fingers under the edge of the illusion to strip it back.

The wind just went on blowing, the tumble-weed tumbled on. Somewhere in the storm a barn-door was slamming, opening and slamming again in the gusts. He could even smell horse-shit. The effect was so damn perfect, he was breathless with admiration.

But whoever had created this extraordinary set had proved their point. He was impressed: now it was time to stop the game.

He turned back to the toilet door. It was gone. A wall of dust had erased it, and suddenly he was lost and alone.

The barn-door kept slamming. Voices called to each other in the worsening storm. Where was the Saloon and the Sheriff's office? They too had been obscured. Ricky tasted something he hadn't experienced since childhood: the panic of losing the hand of a guardian. In this case the lost parent was his sanity.

11

Somewhere to his left a shot sounded in the depths of the storm, and he heard something whistle in his ear, then felt a sharp pain. Gingerly he raised his hand to his ear-lobe and touched the place that hurt. Part of his ear had been shot away, a neat nick in his lobe. His ear-stud was gone, and there was blood, real blood, on his fingers. Someone had either just missed blowing off his head or was really playing silly fuckers.

'Hey, man,' he appealed into the teeth of this wretched fiction, whirling around on his heel to see if he could locate the aggressor. But he could see no one. The dust had totally enclosed him: he couldn't move backwards or forwards with any safety. The gunman might be very close, waiting for him to step in his direction.

'I don't like this,' he said aloud, hoping the real world would hear him somehow, and step in to salvage his tattered mind. He rummaged in his jeans pocket for a pill or two, anything to improve the situation, but he was all out of instant sunshine, not even a lowly Valium was to be found lurking in the seam of his pocket. He felt naked. What a time to be lost in the middle of Zane Grey's nightmares.

A second shot sounded, but this time there was no whistling. Ricky was certain this meant he'd been shot, but as there was neither pain nor blood it was difficult to be sure.

Then he heard the unmistakable flap of the saloon door, and the groan of another human being somewhere near. A tear opened up in the storm for a moment. Did he see the saloon through it, and a young man stumbling out, leaving behind him a painted world of tables, mirrors, and gunslingers? Before he could focus properly the tear was sewn up with sand, and he doubted the sight. Then, shockingly, the young man he'd come looking for was there, a foot away, blue-lipped with death, and falling forward into Ricky's arms. He wasn't dressed for a part in this movie anymore than Ricky was. His bomber jacket was a fair copy of a fifties style, his tee-shirt bore the smiling face of Mickey Mouse.

Mickey's left eye was bloodshot, and still bleeding. The bullet had unerringly found the young man's heart.

He used his last breath to ask: 'What the fuck is going on?' and died.

As last words went, it lacked style, but it was deeply felt. Ricky stared into the young man's frozen face for a moment, then the dead weight in his arms became too much, and he had no choice but to drop him. As the body hit the ground the dust seemed to turn into piss-stained tiling for an instant. Then the fiction took precedence again, and the dust swirled, and the tumble-weed tumbled, and he was standing in the middle of Main Street, Deadwood Gulch, with a body at his feet.

Ricky felt something very like cold turkey in his system. His limbs began a St Vitus' dance, and the urge to piss came on him, very strong. Another half-minute, he'd wet his pants.

Somewhere, he thought, somewhere in this wild world, there is a urinal. There is a graffiti-covered wall, with numbers for the sex-crazed to call, with 'This is not a fallout shelter' scrawled on the tiles, and a cluster of obscene drawings. There are water-tanks and paperless toilet-roll holders and broken seats. There is the squalid smell of piss and old farts. Find it! in God's name find the real thing before the fiction does you some permanent damage.

If, for the sake of argument, the Saloon and the General Stores are the toilet cubicles, then the urinal must be behind me, he reasoned. So step back. It can't do you any more harm than staying here in the middle of the street while someone takes pot-shots at you.

Two steps, two cautious steps, and he found only air. But on the third – well, well, what have we here? – his hand touched a cold tile surface.

'Whoo-ee!' he said. It was the urinal: and touching it was like finding gold in a pan of trash. Wasn't that the sickly smell of disinfectant wafting up from the gutter? It was, oh boy, it was.

Still whooping, he unzipped and started to relieve the ache in his bladder, splashing his feet in his haste. What the hell: he had this illusion beat. If he turned round now he'd find the fantasy dispersed, surely. The saloon, the dead boy, the storm, all would be gone. It was some chemical throw-back, bad dope lingering in his system and playing dumb-ass games with his imagination. As he shook the last drops on to his blue suedes, he heard the hero of this movie speak.

'What you doin' pissin' in mah street, boy?'

It was John Wayne's voice, accurate to the last slurred syllable, and it was just behind him. Ricky couldn't even contemplate turning round. The guy would blow off his head for sure. It was in the voice, that threatful ease that warned: I'm ready to draw, so do your worst. The cowboy was armed, and all Ricky had in his hand was his dick, which was no match for a gun even if he'd been better hung.

Very cautiously he tucked his weapon away and zipped himself up, then raised his hands. In front of him the wavering image of the toilet wall had disappeared again. The storm howled: his ear bled down his neck.

'OK boy, I want you to take off that gunbelt and drop it to the ground. You hear me?' said Wayne.

'Yes.'

'Take it nice and slow, and keep those hands where I can see them.'

Boy, this guy was really into it.

Nice and slow, like the man said, Ricky unbuckled his belt, pulled it through the loops in his jeans and dropped it to the floor. The keys should have jangled as they hit the tiles, he hoped to God they would. No such luck. There was a clinking thud that was the sound of metal on sand.

'OK,' said Wayne. 'Now you're beginning to behave. What have you got to say for yourself?'

'I'm sorry?' said Ricky lamely.

'Sorry?'

'For pissing in the street.'

'I don't reckon sorry is sufficient penitence,' said Wayne.

'But really I am. It was all a mistake.'

'We've had about enough of you strangers around these parts. Found that kid with his trousers round his ankles takin' a dump in the middle of the saloon. Well I call that uncouth! Where's you sons of bitches been educated anyhow? It that what they're teaching you in them fancy schools out East?'

'I can't apologise enough.'

'Damn right you can't' Wayne drawled. 'You with the kid?'

'In a manner of speaking.'

'What kind of fancy-talk is that?' he jabbed his gun in Rick's back: it felt very real indeed. 'Are you with him or not?'

'I just meant – '

'You don't mean nothing in this territory, mister, you take that from me.'

He cocked the gun, audibly.

'Why don't you turn round, son and let's us see what you're made of?'

Ricky had seen this routine before. The man turns, he goes for a concealed gun, and Wayne shoots him. No debate, no time to discuss the ethics of it, a bullet would do the job better than words.

'Turn round I said.'

Very slowly, Ricky turned to face the survivor of a thousand shootouts, and there was the man himself, or rather a brilliant impersonation of him. A middle period Wayne, before he'd grown fat and sick-looking. A Rio Grande Wayne, dusty from the long trail and squinting from a lifetime of looking at the horizon. Ricky had never had a taste for Westerns. He hated all the forced machismo, the glorification of dirt and cheap heroism. His generation had put flowers in rifle-barrels, and he'd thought that was a nice thing to do at the time; still did, in fact.

This face, so mock-manly, so uncompromising, personified a handful of lethal lies – about the glory of America's frontier origins, the morality of swift justice, the tenderness in the heart of brutes. Ricky hated the face. His hands just itched to hit it.

Fuck it, if the actor, whoever he was, was going to shoot him anyway, what was to be lost by putting his fist in the bastard's face? The thought became the act: Ricky made a fist, swung and his knuckles connected with Wayne's chin. The actor was slower than his screen image. He failed to dodge the blow, and Ricky took the opportunity to knock the gun out of Wayne's hand. He then followed through with a barrage of punches to the body, just as he'd seen in the movies. It was a spectacular display.

The bigger man reeled backwards under the blows, and tripped, his spur catching in the dead boy's hair. He lost his balance and fell in the dust, bested.

The bastard was down! Ricky felt a thrill he'd never tasted before; the exhilaration of physical triumph. My God! he'd brought down the greatest cowboy in the world. His critical faculties were overwhelmed by the victory.

The dust-storm suddenly thickened. Wayne was still on the floor, splattered with blood from a smashed nose and a broken lip. The sand was already obscuring him, a curtain drawn across the shame of his defeat.

'Get up,' Ricky demanded, trying to capitalise on the situation before the opportunity was lost entirely.

Wayne seemed to grin as the storm covered him.

'Well boy,' he leered, rubbing his chin, 'we'll make a man of you yet . . .'

15

Then his body was eroded by the driving dust, and momentarily something else was there in its place, a form Ricky could make no real sense of. A shape that was and was not Wayne, which deteriorated rapidly towards inhumanity.

The dust was already a furious bombardment, filling ears and eyes. Ricky stumbled away from the scene of the fight, choking, and miraculously he found a wall, a door, and before he could make sense of where he was the roaring storm had spat him out into the silence of the Movie Palace.

There, though he'd promised himself to butch it up since he'd grown a moustache, he gave a small cry that would not have shamed Fay Wray, and collapsed.

In the foyer Lindi Lee was telling Birdy why she didn't like films very much.

'I mean, Dean likes cowboy movies. I don't really like any of that stuff. I guess I shouldn't say that to you – '

'No, that's OK.'

' – But I mean you must really love movies, I guess. 'Cause you work here.'

'I like some movies. Not everything.'

'Oh.' She seemed surprised. A lot of things seemed to surprise her. 'I like wild-life movies, you know.'

'Yes . . .'

'You know? Animals . . . and stuff.'

'Yes . . .' Birdy remembered her guess about Lindi Lee, that she wasn't much of a conversationalist. Got it in one.

'I wonder what's keeping them?' said Lindi.

The lifetime Ricky had been living in the dust-storm had lasted no more than two minutes in real time. But then in the movies time was elastic.

'I'll go look,' Birdy ventured.

'He's probably left without me,' Lindi said again.

'We'll find out.'

'Thanks.'

'Don't fret,' said Birdy, lightly putting her hand on the girl's thin arm as she passed. 'I'm sure everything's OK.'

She disappeared through the swing doors into the cinema, leaving Lindi Lee alone in the foyer. Lindi sighed. Dean wasn't the first boy who'd run out on her, just because she wouldn't produce the goods. Lindi had her own ideas about when and how she'd go all the way with a boy; this wasn't the time and Dean wasn't the boy. He was too slick, too shifty, and his hair smelt of diesel oil. If he had run out on her, she wasn't going to weep buckets over the loss. As her mother always said, there were plenty more fish in the sea.

She was staring at the poster for next week's attraction when she heard a thump behind her, and there was a pie-bald rabbit, a fat, dozy sweetheart of a thing, sitting in the middle of the foyer staring up at her.

'Hello,' she said to the rabbit.

The rabbit licked itself adorably.

Lindi Lee loved animals; she loved True Life Adventure Movies in which creatures were filmed in their native habitat to tunes from Rossini, and scorpions did square-dances while mating, and every bear-cub was lovingly called a little scamp. She lapped up that stuff. But most of all she loved rabbits.

The rabbit took a couple of hops towards her. She knelt to stroke it. It was warm and its eyes were round and pink. It hopped past her up the stairs.

'Oh I don't think you should go up there,' she said.

For one thing it was dark at the top of the stairs. For another there was a sign that read 'Private. Staff only' on the wall. But the rabbit seemed determined, and the clever mite kept well ahead of her as she followed it up the stairs.

At the top it was pitch black, and the rabbit had gone.

Something else was sitting there in the rabbit's place, its eyes burning bright.

With Lindi Lee illusions could be simple. No need to seduce her into a complete fiction like the boy, this one was already dreaming. Easy meat.

'Hello,' Lindi Lee said, scared a little by the presence ahead of her. She looked into the dark, trying to sort out some outline, a hint of a face. But there was none. Not even a breath.

She took one step back down the stairs but it reached for her suddenly, and caught her before she toppled, silencing her quickly, intimately.

This one might not have much passion to steal, but it sensed another use here. The tender body was still budding: the orifices unused to invasions. It took Lindi up the few remaining stairs and sealed her away for future investigation.

* * *

17

'Ricky? Oh God, Ricky!'

Birdy knelt beside Ricky's body and shook him. At least he was still breathing, that was something, and though at first sight there seemed to be a great deal of blood, in fact the wound was merely a nick in his ear.

She shook him again, more roughly, but there was no response. After a frantic search she found his pulse: it was strong and regular. Obviously he'd been attacked by somebody, possibly Lindi Lee's absent boyfriend. In which case, where was he? Still in the john perhaps, armed and dangerous. There was no way she was going to be damn fool enough to step in there and have a look, she'd seen that routine too many times. Woman in Peril: standard stuff. The darkened room, the stalking beast. Well, instead of walking bang into that cliché she was going to do what she silently exhorted heroines to do time and again: defy her curiosity and call the cops.

Leaving Ricky where he lay, she walked up the aisle, and back into the foyer.

It was empty. Lindi Lee had either given up on her boyfriend altogether, or found somebody else on the street outside to take her home. Whichever, she'd closed the front door behind her as she left, leaving only a hint of Johnson's Baby Powder on the air behind her. OK, that certainly made things easier, Birdy thought, as she stepped into the Ticket Office to dial the cops. She was rather pleased to think that the girl had found the commonsense to give up on her lousy date.

She picked up the receiver, and immediately somebody spoke.

'Hello there,' said the voice, nasal and ingratiating, 'it's a little late at night to be using the phone, isn't it?'

It wasn't the operator, she was sure. She hadn't even punched a number.

Besides, it sounded like Peter Lorre.

'Who is this?'

'Don't you recognise me?'

'I want to speak to the police.'

'I'd like to oblige, really I would.'

'Get off the line, will you? This is an emergency! I need the police.'

'I heard you first time,' the whine went on.

'Who are you?'

'You already played that line.'

'There's somebody hurt in here. Will you *please* – '

'Poor Rick.'

He knew the name. Poor Rick, he said, as though he was a loving friend.

She felt the sweat begin in her brow: felt it sprout out of her pores. He knew Ricky's name.

'Poor, poor Rick,' the voice said again. 'Still I'm sure we'll have a happy ending. Aren't you?'

'This is a matter of life and death,' Birdy insisted, impressed by how controlled she felt sure she was sounding.

'I know,' said Lorre. 'Isn't it exciting?'

'Damn you! Get off this phone! Or so help me – '

'So help you what? What can a fat girl like you hope to do in a situation like this, except blubber?'

'You fucking creep.'

'My pleasure.'

'Do I know you?'

'Yes and no,' the tone of the voice was wavering.

'You're a friend of Ricky's, is that it?' One of the dope-fiends he used to hang out with. Kind of idiot-game they'd get up to. All right, you've had your stupid little joke,' she said, 'now get off the line before you do some serious harm.'

'You're harassed,' the voice said, softening. 'I understand . . .' it was changing magically, sliding up an octave, 'you're trying to help the man you love . . .' its tone was feminine now, the accent altering, the slime becoming a purr. And suddenly it was Garbo.

'Poor Richard,' she said to Birdy. 'He's tried so hard, hasn't he?' She was gentle as a lamb.

Birdy was speechless: the impersonation was as faultless as that of Lorre, as female as the first had been male.

'All right, I'm impressed,' said Birdy, 'now let me speak to the cops.'

'Wouldn't this be a fine and lovely night to go out walking, Birdy? Just we two girls together.'

'You know my name.'

'Of course I know your name. I'm very close to you.'

'What do you mean, close to me?'

The reply was throaty laughter, Garbo's lovely laughter.

Birdy couldn't take it any more. The trick was too clever; she could feel herself succumbing to the impersonation, as though she were speaking to the star herself.

'No,' she said down the phone, 'you don't convince me, you hear?' Then her temper snapped. She yelled: 'You're a fake!' into the mouthpiece of the phone so loudly she felt the receiver tremble, and then slammed it down. She opened the Office and went to the outer door. Lindi Lee had not simply slammed the door behind her. It was locked and bolted from the inside.

'Shit,' Birdy said quietly.

Suddenly the foyer seemed smaller than she'd previously thought it, and so did her reserve of cool. She mentally slapped herself across the face, the standard response for a heroine verging on hysteria. Think this through, she instructed herself. One: the door was locked. Lindi Lee hadn't done it, Ricky couldn't have done it, she certainly hadn't done it. Which implied –

Two: There was a weirdo in here. Maybe the same he, she or it that was on the phone. Which implied –

Three: He, she or it must have access to another line, somewhere in the building. The only one she knew of was upstairs, in the storeroom. But there was no way she was going up there. For reasons see Heroine in Peril. Which implied –

Four: She had to open this door with Ricky's keys.

Right, there was the imperative: get the keys from Ricky.

She stepped back into the cinema. For some reason the house-lights were jumpy, or was that just panic in her optic nerve? No, they were flickering slightly; the whole interior seemed to be fluctuating, as though it were breathing.

Ignore it: fetch the keys.

She raced down the aisle, aware, as she always was when she ran, that her breasts were doing a jig, her buttocks too. A right sight I look, she thought for anyone with the eyes to see. Ricky, was moaning in his faint. Birdy looked for the keys, but his belt had disappeared.

'Ricky . . .' she said close to his face. The moans multiplied.

'Ricky, can you hear me? It's Birdy, Rick. *Birdy.*'

'Birdy?'

'We're locked in, Ricky. Where are the keys?'

' . . . keys?'

'You're not wearing your belt, Ricky,' she spoke slowly, as if to an idiot, 'where-are-your-keys?'

The jigsaw Ricky was doing in his aching head was suddenly solved, and he sat up.

'Boy!' he said.

'What boy?'

'In the john. Dead in the john.'

'Dead? Oh Christ. Dead? Are you sure?'

Ricky was in some sort of trance, it seemed. He didn't look at her, he just stared into middle-distance, seeing something she couldn't.

'Where are the keys?' she asked again. '*Ricky*. It's important. Concentrate.'

'Keys?'

She wanted to slap him now, but his face was already bloody and it seemed sadistic.

'On the floor,' he said after a time.

'In the john? On the floor in the john?'

Ricky nodded. The movement of his head seemed to dislodge some terrible thoughts: suddenly he looked as though he was going to cry.

'It's all going to be all right,' said Birdy.

Ricky's hands had found his face, and he was feeling his features, a ritual of reassurance.

'Am I here?' he inquired quietly. Birdy didn't hear him, she was steeling herself for the john. She had to go in there, no doubt about that, body or no body. Get in, fetch the keys, get out again. Do it *now*.

She stepped through the door. It occurred to her as she did so that she'd never been in a men's toilet before, and she sincerely hoped this would be the first and only occasion.

The toilet was almost in darkness. The light was flickering in the same fitful way as the lights in the cinema, but at a lower level. She stood at the door, letting her eyes accommodate the gloom, and scanned the place.

The toilet was empty. There was no boy on the floor, dead or alive.

The keys were there though. Ricky's belt was lying in the gutter of the urinal. She fished it out, the oppressive smell of the disinfectant block making her sinuses ache. Disengaging the keys from their ring she stepped out of the toilet into the comparative freshness of the cinema. And it was all over, simple as that.

Ricky had hoisted himself on to one of the seats, and was slumped in it, looking sicker and sorrier for himself than ever. He looked up as he heard Birdy emerge.

'I've got the keys,' she said.

He grunted: God, he looked ill, she thought. Some of her sympathy had evaporated however. He was obviously having hallucinations, and they probably had chemical origins. It was his own damn fault.

'There's no boy in there, Ricky.'

'What?'

'There's no body in the john; nobody at all. What are you on anyhow?'

Ricky looked down at his shaking hands.

'I'm not on anything. Honestly.'

'Damn stupid,' she said. She half-suspected that he'd set her up for this somehow, except that practical jokes weren't his style. Ricky was quite a puritan in his way: that had been one of his attractions.

'Do you need a doctor?'

He shook his head sulkily.

'Are you sure?'

'I said no,' he snapped.

'OK, I offered.' She was already marching up the rake of the aisle, muttering something under her breath. At the foyer door she stopped and called across to him.

'I think we've got an intruder. There was somebody on the extension line. Do you want to stand watch by the front door while I fetch a cop?'

'In a minute.'

Ricky sat in the flickering light and examined his sanity. If Birdy said the boy wasn't in there, then presumably she was telling the truth. The best way to verify that was to see for himself. Then he'd be certain he'd suffered a minor reality crisis brought on by some bad dope, and he'd go home, lay his head down to sleep and wake tomorrow afternoon healed. Except that he didn't want to put his head in that evil-smelling room. Suppose she was wrong, and *she* was the one having the crisis? Weren't there such things as hallucinations of normality?

Shakily, he hauled himself up, crossed the aisle and pushed open the door. It was murky inside, but he could see enough to know that there were no sand-storms, or dead boys, no gun-toting cowboys, nor even a solitary tumble-weed. It's quite a thing, he thought, this mind of mine. To have created an alternative world so eerily well. It was a wonderful trick. Pity it couldn't be turned to better use than scaring him shitless. You win some, you lose some.

And then he saw the blood. On the tiles. A smear of blood that hadn't come from his nicked ear, there was too much of it. Ha! He didn't imagine it at all. There was blood, heel marks, every sign that what he thought he'd seen, he'd seen. But Jesus in Heaven, which was worse? To see, or not to see? Wouldn't it have been better to be wrong, and just a little spaced-out tonight, than right, and in the hands of a power that could literally change the world?

Ricky stared at the trail of blood, and followed it across the floor of the toilet to the cubicle on the left of his vision. Its door was closed: it had been open before. The murderer, whoever he was, had put the boy in there, Ricky knew it without looking.

'OK,' he said, 'now I've got you.'

He pushed on the door. It swung open and there was the boy, propped up on the toilet seat, legs spread, arms hanging.

His eyes had been scooped out of his head. Not neatly: no surgeon's job. They'd been wrenched out, leaving a trail of mechanics down his cheek.

Ricky put his hand over his mouth and told himself he wasn't going to throw up. His stomach churned, but obeyed, and he ran to the toilet door as though any moment the body was going to get up and demand its ticket-money back.

'Birdy . . . Birdy . . .'

The fat bitch had been wrong, all wrong. There was death here, and worse.

Ricky flung himself out of the john into the body of the cinema.

The wall-lights were fairly dancing behind their Deco shades, guttering like candles on the verge of extinction. Darkness would be too much; he'd lose his mind.

There was, it occurred to him, something familiar about the way the lights flickered, something he couldn't quite put his finger on. He stood in the aisle for a moment, hopelessly lost.

Then the voice came; and though he guessed it was death this time, he looked up.

'Hello Ricky,' she was saying as she came along Row E towards him. Not Birdy. No, Birdy never wore a white gossamer dress, never had bruise-full lips, or hair so fine, or eyes so sweetly

23

promising. It was Monroe who was walking towards him, the blasted rose of America.

'Aren't you going to say hello?' she gently chided.

'. . . er . . .'

'Ricky. Ricky. Ricky. After all this time.'

All this time? What did she mean: all this time?

'Who are you?'

She smiled radiantly at him.

'As if you didn't know.'

'You're not Marilyn. Marilyn's dead.'

'Nobody dies in the movies, Ricky. You know that as well as I do. You can always thread the celluloid up again – '

– that was what the flickering reminded him of, the flicker of celluloid through the gate of a projector, one image hot on the next, the illusion of life created from a perfect sequence of little deaths.

' – and we're there again, all-talking, all-singing.' She laughed: ice-in-a-glass laughter, 'We never fluff our lines, never age, never lose our timing – '

'You're not real,' said Ricky.

She looked faintly bored by the observation, as if he was being pedantic.

By now sh̲ ̲ come to the end of the row and was standing no more than three feet away from him. At this distance the illusion was as ravishing and as complete as ever. He suddenly wanted to take her, there, in the aisle. What the hell if she was just a fiction: fictions are fuckable if you don't want marriage.

'I want you,' he said, surprised by his own bluntness.

'I want *you*,' she replied, which surprised him even more. 'In fact I need you. I'm very weak.'

'Weak?'

'It's not easy, being the centre of attraction, you know. You find you need it, more and more. Need people to look at you. All the night, all the day.'

'I'm looking.'

'Am I beautiful?'

'You're a goddess: whoever you are.'

'I'm yours: that's who I am.'

It was a perfect answer. She was defining herself through him. I am a function of you; made for you out of you. The perfect fantasy.

24

'Keep looking at me; looking *forever*, Ricky. I need your loving looks. I can't live without them.'

The more he stared at her the stronger her image seemed to become. The flickering had almost stopped; a calm had settled over the place.

'Do you want to touch me?'

He thought she'd never ask.

'Yes,' he said.

'Good.' She smiled coaxingly at him, and he reached to make contact. She elegantly avoided his fingertips at the last possible moment, and ran, laughing, down the aisle towards the screen. He followed, eager. She wanted a game: that was fine by him.

She'd run into a cul-de-sac. There was no way out from this end of the cinema, and judging by the come-ons she was giving him, she knew it. She turned and flattened herself against the wall, feet spread a little.

He was within a couple of yards of her when a breeze out of nowhere billowed her skirt up around her waist. She laughed, half-closing her eyes, as the surf of silk rose and exposed her. She was naked underneath.

Ricky reached for her again and this time she didn't avoid his touch. The dress billowed up a little higher and he stared, fixated, at the part of Marilyn he had never seen, the fur divide that had been the dream of millions.

There was blood there. Not much, a few fingermarks on her inner thighs. The faultless gloss of her flesh was spoiled slightly. Still he stared; and the lips parted a little as she moved her hips, and he realised the glint of wetness in her interior was not the juice of her body, but something else altogether. As her muscles moved the bloody eyes she'd buried in her body shifted, and came to rest on him.

She knew by the look on his face that she hadn't hidden them deep enough, but where was a girl with barely a veil of cloth covering her nakedness to hide the fruits of her labour?

'You killed him,' said Ricky, still looking at the lips, and the eyes that peeked out between. The image was so engrossing, so pristine, it all but cancelled out the horror in his belly. Perversely, his disgust fed his lust instead of killing it. So what if she *was* a murderer: she was legend.

'Love me,' she said. 'Love me forever.'

He came to her, knowing now full well that it was death to do so. But death was a relative matter, wasn't it? Marilyn was dead in the flesh, but alive here, either in his brain, or in the buzzing matrix of the air or both; and he could be with her.

He embraced her, and she him. They kissed. It was easy. Her lips were softer than he'd imagined, and he felt something close to pain at his crotch he wanted to be in her so much.

The willow-thin arms slipped around his waist, and he was in the lap of luxury.

'You make me strong,' she said. 'Looking at me that way. I need to be looked at, or I die. It's the natural state of illusions.'

Her embrace was tightening; the arms at his back no longer seemed quite so willow-like. He struggled a little against the discomfort.

'No use,' she cooed in his ear. 'You're mine.'

He wrenched his head around to look at her grip and to his amazement the arms weren't arms any longer, just a loop of something round his back, without hands or fingers or wrists.

'Jesus Christ!' he said.

'Look at me, boy,' she said. The words had lost their delicacy. It wasn't Marilyn that had him in its arms any more: nothing like her. The embrace tightened again, and the breath was forced from Ricky's body, breath the tightness of the hold prevented him from recapturing. His spine creaked under the pressure, and pain shot through his body like flares, exploding in his eyes, all colours.

'You should have got out of town,' said Marilyn, as Wayne's face blossomed under the sweep of her perfect cheek-bones. His look was contemptuous, but Ricky had only a moment to register it before that image cracked too, and something else came into focus behind this façade of famous faces. For the last time in his life, Ricky asked the question:

'Who are you?'

His captor didn't answer. It was feeding on his fascination; even as he stared twin organs erupted out of its body like the horns of a slug, antennae perhaps, forming themselves into probes and crossing the space between its head and Ricky's.

'I need you,' it said, its voice now neither Wayne nor Monroe, but a crude, uncultivated voice, a thug's voice. 'I'm so fucking weak; it uses me up, being in the world.'

It was mainlining on him, feeding itself, whatever it was, on his stares, once adoring – now horrified. He could feel it draining

26

out his life through his eyes, luxuriating in the soul-looks he was giving it as he perished.

He knew he must be nearly dead, because he hadn't taken a breath in a long while. It seemed like minutes, but he couldn't be sure.

Just as he was listening for the sound of his heart, the horns divided around his head and pressed themselves into his ears. Even in this reverie, the sensation was disgusting, and he wanted to cry out for it to stop. But the fingers were working their way into his head, bursting his ear-drums, and passing on like inquisitive tapeworms through brain and skull. He was alive, even now, still staring at his tormentor, and he knew that the fingers were finding his eyeballs, and pressing on them now from behind.

His eyes bulged suddenly and broke from their housing, splashing from his sockets. Momentarily he saw the world from a different angle as his sense of sight cascaded down his cheek. There was his lip, his chin –

It was an appalling experience, and mercifully short. Then the feature Ricky'd lived for thirty-seven years snapped in mid-reel, and he slumped in the arms of fiction.

Ricky's seduction and death had occupied less than three minutes. In that time Birdy had tried every key on Ricky's ring, and could get none of the damn things to open the door. Had she not persisted she might have gone back into the cinema and asked for some help. But things mechanical, even locks and keys, were a challenge to her womanhood. She despised the way men felt some instinctive superiority over her sex when it came to engines, systems and logical processes, and she was damned if she was going to go whining back to Ricky to tell him she couldn't open the damn door.

By the time she'd given up the job, so had Ricky. He was dead and gone. She swore, colourfully, at the keys, and admitted defeat. Ricky clearly had a knack with these wretched things that she'd never quite grasp. Good luck to him. All she wanted now was out of this place. It was getting claustrophobic. She didn't like being locked in, not knowing who was lurking around upstairs.

And now to cap it all, the lights in the foyer were on the blink, dying away flicker by flicker.

What the hell was going on in this place anyhow?

Without warning the lights went out altogether, and beyond the doors into the cinema she was sure she heard movement. A light spilled through from the other side, stronger than torchlight, twitching, colourful.

'Ricky?' she chanced into the dark. It seemed to swallow her words. Either that or she didn't believe it was Ricky at all, and something was telling her to make her appeal, if she had to, in a whisper.

'Ricky . . .?'

The lips of the swing-doors smacked together gently as something pressed on them from the other side.

'. . . is that you?'

The air was electric: static was crackling off her shoes as she walked towards the door, the hairs on her arms were rigid. The light on the other side was growing brighter with every step.

She stopped advancing, thinking better of her enquiries. It wasn't Ricky, she knew that. Maybe it was the man or woman on the phone, some pebble-eyed lunatic who got off on stalking fat women.

She stook two steps back towards the Ticket Office, her feet sparking, and reached under the counter for the Motherfucker, an iron bar which she'd kept there since she'd been trapped in the Office by three would-be thieves with shaved heads and electric drills. She'd screamed blue murder and they'd fled, but next time she swore she'd beat one (or all of them) senseless rather than be terrorised. And the Motherfucker, all three feet of it, was her chosen weapon.

Armed now, she faced the doors.

They blew open suddenly, and a roar of white noise filled her head, and a voice through the roar said:

'Here's looking at you, kid.'

An eye, a single vast eye, was filling the doorway. The noise deafened her; the eye blinked, huge and wet and lazy, scanning the doll in front of it with the insolence of the One True God, the maker of celluloid Earth and celluloid Heaven.

Birdy was terrified, no other word for it. This wasn't a look-behind-you thrill, there was no delicious anticipation, no pleasurable fright. It was real fear, bowel-fear, unadorned and ugly as shit.

She could hear herself whimpering under the relentless gaze of the eye, her legs were weakening. Soon she'd fall on the carpet in front of the door, and that would be the end of her, surely.

Then she remembered Motherfucker. Dear Motherfucker, bless his phallic heart. She raised the bar in a two-handed grip and ran at the eye, swinging.

Before she made contact the eye closed, the light went out, and she was in darkness again, her retina burning from the sight.

In the darkness, somebody said: 'Ricky's dead.'

Just that. It was worse than the eye, worse than all the dead voices of Hollywood, because she knew somehow it was true. The cinema had become a slaughterhouse. Lindi Lee's Dean had died as Ricky had said he had, and now Ricky was dead as well. The doors were all locked, the game was down to two. Her and it.

She made a dash for the stairs, not sure of her plan of action, but certain that remaining in the foyer was suicidal. As her foot touched the bottom stair the swing-doors sighed open again behind her and something came after her, fast and flickering. It was a step or two behind her as she breathlessly mounted the stairs, cursing her bulk. Spasms of brilliant light shot by her from its body like the first igniting flashes of a Roman Candle. It was preparing another trick, she was certain of it.

She reached the top of the stairs with her admirer still on her heels. Ahead, the corridor, lit by a single greasy bulb, promised very little comfort. It ran the full length of the cinema, and there were a few storerooms off it, piled with crap: posters, 3-D spectacles, mildewed stills. In one of the storerooms there was a fire-door, she was sure. But which? She'd only been up here once, and that two years ago.

'Shit. Shit. Shit,' she said. She ran to the first storeroom. The door was locked. She beat on it, protesting. It stayed locked. The next the same. The third the same. Even if she could remember which storeroom contained the escape route the doors were too heavy to break down. Given ten minutes and Motherfucker's help she might do it. But the Eye was at her back: she didn't have ten seconds, never mind ten minutes.

There was nothing for it but confrontation. She spun on her heel, a prayer on her lips, to face the staircase and her pursuer. The landing was empty.

She stared at the forlorn arrangement of dead bulbs and peeling paint as if to discover the invisible, but the thing wasn't in front of her at all, it was behind. The brightness flared again at her back, and this time the Roman Candle caught, fire became light, light became image, and glories she'd almost forgotten were spilling down the corridor towards her. Unleashed scenes from a thousand movies: each with its unique association. She began, for the first time, to understand the origins of this remarkable species. It was a ghost in the machine of the cinema: a son of celluloid.

'Give your soul to me,' a thousand stars.' said.

'I don't believe in souls,' she replied truthfully.

'Then give me what you give to the screen, what everybody gives. *Give me some love.*'

That's why all those scenes were playing, and replaying, and playing again, in front of her. They were all moments when an audience was magically united with the screen, bleeding through its eyes, looking and looking and looking. She'd done it herself, often. Seen a film and felt it move her so deeply it was almost a physical pain when the end credits rolled and the illusion was broken, because she felt she'd left something of herself behind, a part of her inner being lost up there amongst her heroes and her heroines. Maybe she had. Maybe the air carried the cargo of her desires and deposited them somewhere, intermingled with the cargo of other hearts, all gathering together in some niche, until –

Until this. This child of their collective passions: this technicolour seducer; trite, crass and utterly bewitching.

Very well, she thought, it's one thing to understand your executioner: another thing altogether to talk it out of its professional obligations.

Even as she sorted the enigma out she was lapping up the pictures in the thing: she couldn't help herself. Teasing glimpses of lives she'd lived, faces she'd loved. Mickey Mouse, dancing with a broom, Gish in 'Broken Blossoms', Garland (with Toto at her side) watching the twister louring over Kansas, Astaire in 'Top Hat', Welles in 'Kane', Brando and Crawford, Tracy and Hepburn – people so engraved on our hearts they need no Christian names. And so much better to be teased by these moments, to be shown only the pre-kiss melt, not the kiss itself; the slap, not the reconciliation; the shadow, not the monster; the wound, not death.

It had her in thrall, no doubt of it. She was held by her eyes as surely as if it had them out on their stalks, and chained.

'Am I beautiful?' it said.

Yes it was beautiful.

'Why don't you give yourself to me?'

She wasn't thinking any more, her powers of analysis had drained from her, until something appeared in the muddle of images that slapped her back into herself. 'Dumbo'. The fat elephant. *Her* fat elephant: no more than that, the fat elephant she'd thought *was* her.

The spell broke. She looked away from the creature. For a moment, out of the corner of her eye, she saw something sickly and fly-blown beneath the glamour. They'd called her Dumbo as a child, all the kids on her block. She'd lived with that ridiculous grey horror for twenty years, never able to shake it off. Its fat body reminded her of her fat, its lost look of her isolation. She thought of it cradled in the trunk of its mother, condemned as a Mad Elephant, and she wanted to beat the sentimental thing senseless.

'It's a fucking lie!' she spat at it.

'I don't know what you mean,' it protested.

'What's under all the pizzazz then? Something very nasty I think.'

The light began to flicker, the parade of trailers faltering. She could see another shape, small and dark, lurking behind the curtains of light. Doubt was in it. Doubt and fear of dying. She was sure she could smell the fear off it, at ten paces.

'What are you, under there?'

She took a step towards it.

'What are you hiding? Eh?'

It found a voice. A frightened, human voice. 'You've no business with me.'

'You tried to kill me.'

'I want to live.'

'So do I.'

It was getting dark this end of the corridor, and there was an old, bad smell here, of rot. She knew rot, and this was something animal. Only last spring, when the snow had melted, she'd found something very dead in the yard behind her apartment. Small dog, large cat, it was difficult to be sure. Something domestic that had died of cold in the sudden snows the December before. Now it was besieged with maggots: yellowish, greyish, pinkish: a pastel fly-machine with a thousand moving parts.

It had around it the same stink that lingered here. Maybe that was somehow the flesh behind the fantasy.

31

Taking courage, her eyes still stinging with 'Dumbo', she advanced on the wavering mirage, Motherfucker raised in case the thing tried any funny business.

The boards beneath her feet were creaking, but she was too interested in her quarry to listen to their warnings. It was time she got a hold of this killer, shook it and made it spit its secret.

They'd almost gone the length of the corridor now, her advancing, it retreating. There was nowhere left for the thing to go.

Suddenly the floorboards folded up into dusty fragments under her weight and she was falling through the floor in a cloud of dust. She dropped Motherfucker as she threw out her hands to catch hold of something, but it was all worm-ridden, and crumbled in her grasp.

She fell awkwardly and landed hard on something soft. Here the smell of rot was incalculably stronger, it coaxed the stomach into the throat. She reached out her hand to right herself in the darkness, and on every side there was slime and cold. She felt as though she'd been dumped in a case of partially-gutted fish. Above her, the anxious light shone through the boards as it fell on her bed. She looked, though God knows she didn't want to, and she was lying in the remains of a man, his body spread by his devourers over quite an area. She wanted to howl. Her instinct was to tear off her skirt and blouse, both of which were gluey with matter; but she couldn't go naked, not in front of the son of celluloid.

It still looked down at her.

'Now you know,' it said, lost.

'This is you – '

'This is the body I once occupied, yes. His name was Barberio. A criminal; nothing spectacular. He never aspired to greatness.'

'And you?'

'His cancer. I'm the piece of him which did aspire, that did long to be more than a humble cell. I am a dreaming disease. No wonder I love the movies.'

The son of celluloid was weeping over the edge of the broken floor, its true body exposed now it had no reason to fabricate a glory.

It was a filthy thing, a tumour grown fat on wasted passion. A parasite with the shape of a slug, and the texture of raw liver. For a moment a toothless mouth, badly moulded, formed at its

32

head-end and said: 'I'm going to have to find a new way to eat your soul.'

It flopped down into the crawlspace beside Birdy. Without its shimmering coat of many technicolours it was the size of a small child. She backed away as it stretched a sensor to touch her, but avoidance was a limited option. The crawlspace was narrow, and further along it was blocked with what looked to be broken chairs and discarded prayer-books. There was no way out but the way she'd come, and that was fifteen feet above her head.

Tentatively, the cancer touched her foot, and she was sick. She couldn't help it, even though she was ashamed to be giving in to such primitive responses. It revolted her as nothing ever had before; it brought to mind something aborted, a bucket-case.

'Go to hell,' she said to it, kicking at its head, but it kept coming, its diarrhoeal mass trapping her legs. She could feel the churning motion of its innards as it rose up to her.

Its bulk on her belly and groin was almost sexual, and revolted as she was by her own train of thought she wondered dimly if such a thing aspired to sex. Something about the insistence of its forming and reforming feelers against her skin, probing tenderly beneath her blouse, stretching to touch her lips, only made sense as desire. Let it come then, she thought, let it come if it has to.

She let it crawl up her until it was entirely perched on her body, fighting every moment the urge to throw it off – and then she sprang her trap.

She rolled over.

She'd weighed 225 pounds at the last count, and she was probably more now. The thing was beneath her before it could work out how or why this had happened, and its pores were oozing the sick sap of tumours.

It fought, but it couldn't get out from under, however much it squirmed. Birdy dug her nails into it and began to tear at its sides, taking cobs out of it, spongey cobs that set more fluids gushing. Its howls of anger turned into howls of pain. After a short while, the dreaming disease stopped fighting.

Birdy lay still for a moment. Underneath her, nothing moved.

At last, she got up. It was impossible to know if the tumour was dead. It hadn't, by any standards that she understood, lived. Besides, she wasn't touching it again. She'd wrestle the Devil himself rather than embrace Barberio's cancer a second time.

She looked up at the corridor above her and despaired. Was

33

she now to die in here, like Barberio before her? Then, as she glanced down at her adversary, she noticed the grille. It hadn't been visible while it was still night outside. Now dawn was breaking, and columns of dishwater light were creeping through the lattice.

She bent to the grille, pushed it hard, and suddenly the day was in the crawlspace with her, all around her. It was a squeeze to get through the small door, and she kept thinking every moment that she felt the thing crawling across her legs, but she hauled herself into the world with only bruised breasts to complain of.

The abandoned lot hadn't changed substantially since Barberio's visit there. It was merely more nettle-thronged. She stood for a while breathing in draughts of fresh air, then made for the fence and the street beyond it.

The fat woman with the haggard look and the stinking clothes was given a wide berth by newsboys and dogs alike as she made her way home.

THREE: CENSORED SCENES

It wasn't the end.

The police went to the Movie Palace just after nine-thirty. Birdy went with them. The search revealed the mutilated bodies of Dean and Ricky, as well as the remains of 'Sonny' Barberio. Upstairs, in the corner of the corridor, they found a cerise shoe.

Birdy said nothing, but she knew. Lindi Lee had never left.

She was put on trial for a double murder nobody really thought she'd committed, and acquitted for lack of evidence. It was the order of the court that she be put under psychiatric observation for a period of not less than two years. The woman might not have committed murder, but it was clear she was a raving lunatic. Tales of walking cancers do nobody's reputation much good.

In the early summer of the following year Birdy gave up eating for a week. Most of the weight-loss in that time was water, but it was sufficient to encourage her friends that she was at last going to tackle the Big Problem.

That weekend, she went missing for twenty-four hours.

Birdy found Lindi Lee in a deserted house in Seattle. She hadn't been so difficult to trace: it was hard for poor Lindi to keep

34

control of herself these days, never mind avoid would-be pursuers. As it happened her parents had given up on her several months previous. Only Birdy had continued to look, paying for an investigator to trace the girl, and finally her patience was rewarded with the sight of the frail beauty, frailer than ever but still beautiful sitting in this bare room. Flies roamed the air. A turd, perhaps human, sat in the middle of the floor.

Birdy had a gun out before she opened the door. Lindi Lee looked up from her thoughts, or maybe *its* thoughts, and smiled at her. The greeting lasted a moment only before the parasite in Lindi Lee recognised Birdy's face, saw the gun in her hand and knew exactly what she'd come to do.

'Well,' it said, getting up to meet its visitor.

Lindi Lee's eyes burst, her mouth burst, her cunt and ass, her ears and nose all burst, and the tumour poured out of her in shocking pink rivers. It came worming out of her milkless breasts, out of a cut in her thumb, from an abrasion on her thigh. Wherever Lindi Lee was open, it came.

Birdy raised the gun and fired three times. The cancer stretched once towards her, fell back, staggered and collapsed. Once it was still, Birdy calmly took the acid-bottle out of her pocket, unscrewed the top and emptied the scalding contents on human limb and tumour alike. It made no shout as it dissolved, and she left it there, in a patch of sun, a pungent smoke rising from the confusion.

She stepped out into the street, her duty done, and went her way, confidently planning to live long after the credits for this particular comedy had rolled.

Rawhead Rex

Of all the conquering armies that had tramped the streets of Zeal down the centuries, it was finally the mild tread of the Sunday tripper that brought the village to its knees. It had suffered Roman legions, and the Norman conquest, it had survived the agonies of Civil War, all without losing its identity to the occupying forces. But after centuries of boot and blade it was to be the tourists – the new barbarians – that bested Zeal, their weapons courtesy and hard cash.

It was ideally suited for the invasion. Forty miles south-east of London, amongst the orchards and hop-fields of the Kentish Weald, it was far enough from the city to make the trip an adventure, yet close enough to beat a quick retreat if the weather turned foul. Every weekend between May and October Zeal was a watering-hole for parched Londoners. They would swarm through the village on each Saturday that promised sun, bringing their dogs, their plastic balls, their litters of children, and their children's litter, disgorging them in bawling hordes on to the village green, then returning to 'The Tall Man' to compare traffic stories over glasses of warm beer.

For their part the Zealots weren't unduly distressed by the Sunday trippers; at least they didn't spill blood. But their very lack of aggression made the invasion all the more insidious.

Gradually these city-weary people began to work a gentle but permanent change on the village. Many of them set their hearts on a home in the country; they were charmed by stone cottages set amongst churning oaks, they were enchanted by doves in the churchyard yews. Even the air, they'd say as they inhaled deeply, even the air smells fresher here. It smells of England.

At first a few, then many, began to make bids for the empty barns and deserted houses that littered Zeal and its outskirts. They could be seen every fine weekend, standing in the nettles and rubble, planning how to have a kitchen extension built, and where to install the jacuzzi. And although many of them, once back in the comfort of Kilburn or St John's Wood, chose to stay there, every year one or two of them would strike a reasonable bargain with one of the villagers, and buy themselves an acre of the good life.

So, as the years passed and the natives of Zeal were picked off by old age, the civil savages took over in their stead. The occupation was subtle, but the change was plain to the knowing eye. It was there in the newspapers the Post Office began to stock – what native of Zeal had ever purchased a copy of 'Harpers and Queen' magazine, or leafed through 'The Times Literary Supplement'? It was there, that change, in the bright new cars that clogged the one narrow street, laughingly called the High Road, that was Zeal's backbone. It was there too in the buzz of gossip at 'The Tall Man', a sure sign that the affairs of the foreigners had become fit subject for debate and mockery.

Indeed, as time went by the invaders found a yet more permanent place in the heart of Zeal, as the perennial demons of their hectic lives, Cancer and Heart Disease, took their toll, following their victims even into this newfound-land. Like the Romans before them, like the Normans, like all invaders, the commuters made their profoundest mark upon this usurped turf not by building on it, but by being buried under it.

It was clammy the middle of that September; Zeal's last September.

Thomas Garrow, the only son of the late Thomas Garrow, was sweating up a healthy thirst as he dug in the corner of the Three Acre Field. There'd been a violent rainstorm the previous day, Thursday, and the earth was sodden. Clearing the ground for sowing next year hadn't been the easy job Thomas thought it'd be, but he'd sworn blind he'd have the field finished by the end of the week. It was heavy labour, clearing stones, and sorting out the detritus of out-of-date machinery his father, lazy bastard, had left to rust where it lay. Must have been some good years, Thomas thought, some pretty fine damn years, that his father could afford to let good machinery waste away. Come to think of it, that he could have afforded to leave the best part of three acres unploughed; good healthy soil too. This was the Garden of England after all: land was money. Leaving three acres fallow was a luxury nobody could afford in these straitened times. But Jesus, it was hard work: the kind of work his father had put him to in his youth, and he'd hated with a vengeance ever since.

37

Still, it had to be done.

And the day had begun well. The tractor was healthier after its overhaul, and the morning sky was rife with gulls, across from the coast for a meal of freshly turned worms. They'd kept him raucous company as he worked, their insolence and their short tempers always entertaining. But then, when he came back to the field after a liquid lunch in 'The Tall Man, things began to go wrong. The engine started to cut out for one, the same problem that he'd just spent £200 having seen to; and then, when he'd only been back at work a few minutes, he'd found the stone.

It was an unspectacular lump of stuff: poking out of the soil perhaps a foot, its visible diameter a few inches short of a yard, its surface smooth and bare. No lichen even; just a few grooves in its face that might have once been words. A love-letter perhaps, a 'Kilroy was here' more likely, a date and a name likeliest of all. Whatever it had once been, monument or milestone, it was in the way now. He'd have to dig it up, or next year he'd lose a good three yards of ploughable land. There was no way a plough could skirt around a boulder that size.

Thomas was surprised that the damn thing had been left in the field for so long without anyone bothering to remove it. But then it was a long spell since the Three Acre Field had been planted: certainly not in his thirty-six years. And maybe, now he came to think of it, not in his father's lifetime either. For some reason (if he'd ever known the reason he'd forgotten it) this stretch of Garrow land had been left fallow for a good many seasons, maybe even for generations. In fact there was a suspicion tickling the back of his skull that someone, probably his father, had said no crop would ever grow in that particular spot. But that was plain nonsense. If anything plant life, albeit nettles and convolvulus, grew thicker and ranker in this forsaken three acres than in any other plot in the district. So there was no reason on earth why hops shouldn't flourish here. Maybe even an orchard: though that took more patience and love than Thomas suspected he possessed. Whatever he chose to plant, it would surely spring up from such rich ground with a rare enthusiasm, and he'd have reclaimed three acres of good land to bolster his shaky finances.

If he could just dig out that bloody stone.

He'd half thought of hiring in one of the earth movers from the building site at the North End of the village, just to haul itself across here and get its mechanical jaws working on the problem.

Have the stone out and away in two seconds flat. But his pride resisted the idea of running for help at the first sign of a blister. The job was too small anyhow. He'd dig it out himself, the way his father would have done. That's what he'd decided. Now, two and a half hours later, he was regretting his haste.

The ripening warmth of the afternoon had soured in that time, and the air, without much of a breeze to stir it around, had become stifling. Over from the Downs came a stuttering roll of thunder, and Thomas could feel the static crawling at the nape of his neck, making the short hairs there stand up. The sky above the field was empty now: the gulls, too fickle to hang around once the fun was over, had taken some salt-smelling thermal.

Even the earth, that had given up a sweet-sharp flavour as the blades turned it that morning, now smelt joyless; and as he dug the black soil out from around the stone his mind returned helplessly to the putrefaction that made it so very rich. His thoughts circled vacuously on the countless little deaths on every spadeful of soil he dug. This wasn't the way he was used to thinking, and the morbidity of it distressed him. He stopped for a moment, leaning on his spade, and regretting the fourth pint of Guinness he'd downed at lunch. That was normally a harmless enough ration, but today it swilled around in his belly, he could hear it, as dark as the soil on his spade, working up a scum of stomach-acid and half-digested food.

Think of something else, he told himself, or you'll get to puking. To take his mind off his belly, he looked at the field. It was nothing out of the ordinary; just a rough square of land bounded by an untrimmed hawthorn hedge. One or two dead animals lying in the shadow of the hawthorn: a starling; something else, too far gone to be recognisable. There was a sense of absence, but that wasn't so unusual. It would soon be autumn, and the summer had been too long, too hot for comfort.

Looking up higher than the hedge he watched the mongol-headed cloud discharge a flicker of lightning to the hills. What had been the brightness of the afternoon was now pressed into a thin line of blue at the horizon. Rain soon, he thought, and the thought was welcome. Cool rain; perhaps a downpour like the previous day. Maybe this time it would clear the air good and proper.

Thomas stared back down at the unyielding stone, and struck it with his spade. A tiny arc of white flame flew off.

He cursed, loudly and inventively: the stone, himself, the

field. The stone just sat there in the moat he'd dug around it, defying him. He'd almost run out of options: the earth around the thing had been dug out two feet down; he'd hammered stakes under it, chained it and then got the tractor going to haul it out. No joy. Obviously he'd have to dig the moat deeper, drive the stakes further down. He wasn't going to let the damn thing beat him.

Grunting his determination he set to digging again. A fleck of rain hit the back of his hand, but he scarcely noticed it. He knew by experience that labour like this took singularity of purpose: head down, ignore all distractions. He made his mind blank. There was just the earth, the spade, the stone and his body.

Push down, scoop up. Push down, scoop up, a hypnotic rhythm of effort. The trance was so total he wasn't sure how long he worked before the stone began to shift.

The movement woke him. He stood upright, his vertebrae clicking, not quite certain that the shift was anything more than a twitch in his eye. Putting his heel against the stone, he pushed. Yes, it rocked in its grave. He was too drained to smile, but he felt victory close. He had the bugger.

The rain was starting to come on heavier now, and it felt fine on his face. He drove a couple more stakes in around the stone to unseat it a little further: he was going to get the better of the thing. You'll see, he said, you'll see. The third stake went deeper than the first two, and it seemed to puncture a bubble of gas beneath the stone, a yellowish cloud smelling so foul he stepped away from the hole to snatch a breath of purer air. There was none to be had. All he could do was hawk up a wad of phlegm to clear his throat and lungs. Whatever was under the stone, and there was something animal in the stench, it was very rotten.

He forced himself back down to the work, taking gasps of the air into his mouth, not through his nostrils. His head felt tight, as though his brain was swelling and straining against the dome of his skull, pushing to be let out.

'Fuck you,' he said and beat another stake under the stone. His back felt as though it was about to break. On his right hand a blister had bust. A cleg sat on his arm and feasted itself, unswatted.

'Do it. Do it. Do it.' He beat the last stake in without knowing he was doing it.

And then, the stone began to roll.

He wasn't even touching it. The stone was being pushed out of its seating from beneath. He reached for his spade, which was still wedged beneath the stone. He suddenly felt possessive of it; it was his, a part of him, and he didn't want it near the hole. Not now; not with the stone rocking like it had a geyser under it about to blow. Not with the air yellow, and his brain swelling up like a marrow in August.

He pulled hard on his spade: it wouldn't come.

He cursed it, and took two hands to the job, keeping at arm's length from the hole as he hauled, the increasing motion of the stone slinging up showers of soil, lice, and pebbles.

He heaved at the spade again, but it wouldn't give. He didn't stop to analyse the situation. The work had sickened him, all he wanted was to get his spade, *his* spade, out of the hole and get the hell out of there.

The stone bucked, but still he wouldn't let go of the spade, it had become fixed in his head that he had to have it before he could leave. Only when it was back in his hands, safe and sound, would he obey his bowels, and run.

Beneath his feet the ground began to erupt. The stone rolled away from the tomb as if feather-light, a second cloud of gas, more obnoxious than the first, seemed to blow it on its way. At the same time the spade came out of the hole, and Thomas saw what had hold of it.

Suddenly there was no sense in heaven or earth.

There was a hand, a living hand, clutching the spade, a hand so wide it could grasp the blade with ease.

Thomas knew the moment well. The splitting earth: the hand: the stench. He knew it from some nightmare he'd heard at his father's knee.

Now he wanted to let go of the spade, but he no longer had the will. All he could do was obey some imperative from underground, to haul until his ligaments tore and his sinews bled.

Beneath the thin crust of earth, Rawhead smelt the sky. It was pure ether to his dulled senses, making him sick with pleasure. Kingdoms for the taking, just a few inches away. After so many years, after the endless suffocation, there was light on his eyes again, and the taste of human terror on his tongue.

His head was breaking surface now, his black hair wreathed with worms, his scalp seething with tiny red spiders. They'd irritated him a hundred years, those spiders burrowing into his

41

marrow, and he longed to crush them out. Pull, pull, he willed the human, and Thomas Garrow pulled until his pitiful body had no strength left, and inch by inch Rawhead was hoisted out of his grave in a shroud of prayers.

The stone that had pressed on him for so long had been removed, and he was dragging himself up easily now, sloughing off the grave-earth like a snake its skin. His torso was free. Shoulders twice as broad as a man's; lean, scarred arms stronger than any human. His limbs were pumping with blood like a butterfly's wings, juicing with resurrection. His long, lethal fingers rhythmically clawed the ground as they gained strength.

Thomas Garrow just stood and watched. There was nothing in him but awe. Fear was for those who still had a chance of life: he had none.

Rawhead was out of his grave completely. He began to stand upright for the first time in centuries. Clods of damp soil fell from his torso as he stretched to his full height, a yard above Garrow's six feet.

Thomas Garrow stood in Rawhead's shadow with his eyes still fixed on the gaping hole the King had risen from. In his right hand he still clutched his spade. Rawhead picked him up by the hair. His scalp tore under the weight of his body, so Rawhead seized Garrow round the neck, his vast hand easily enclosing it.

Blood ran down Garrow's face from his scalp, and the sensation stirred him. Death was imminent, and he knew it. He looked down at his legs, thrashing uselessly below him, then he looked up and stared directly into Rawhead's pitiless face.

It was huge, like the harvest moon, huge and amber. But this moon had eyes that burned in its pallid, pitted face. They were for all the world like wounds, those eyes, as though somebody had gouged them in the flesh of Rawhead's face then set two candles to flicker in the holes.

Garrow was entranced by the vastness of this moon. He looked from eye to eye, and then to the wet slits that were its nose, and finally, in a childish terror, down to the mouth. God, that mouth. It was so wide, so cavernous it seemed to split the head in two as it opened. That was Thomas Garrow's last thought. That the moon was splitting in two, and falling out of the sky on top of him.

Then the King inverted the body, as had always been his way with his dead enemies, and drove Thomas head first into the hole, winding him down into the very grave his forefathers had intended to bury Rawhead in forever.

By the time the thunderstorm proper broke over Zeal, the King was a mile away from the Three Acre Field, sheltering in the Nicholson barn. In the village everyone went about their business, rain or no rain. Ignorance was bliss. There was no Cassandra amongst them, nor had 'Your Future in the Stars' in that week's 'Gazette' even hinted at the sudden deaths to come to a Gemini, three Leos, a Sagittarian and a minor star-system of others in the next few days.

The rain had come with the thunder, fat cool spots of it, which rapidly turned into a downpour of monsoonal ferocity. Only when the gutters became torrents did people begin to take shelter.

On the building site the earth-mover that had been roughly landscaping Ronnie Milton's back garden sat idling in the rain, receiving a second washdown in two days. The driver had taken the downpour as a signal to retire into the hut to talk race-horses and women.

In the doorway of the Post Office three of the villagers watched the drains backing up, and tutted that this always happened when it rained, and in half an hour there'd be a pool of water in the dip at the bottom of the High Street so deep you could sail a boat on it.

And down in the dip itself, in the vestry of St Peter's, Declan Ewan, the Verger, watched the rain pelting down the hill in eager rivulets, and gathering into a little sea outside the vestry gate. Soon be deep enough to drown in, he thought, and then, puzzled by why he imagined drowning, he turned away from the window and went back to the business of folding vestments. A strange excitement was in him today: and he couldn't, wouldn't, didn't want to suppress it. It was nothing to do with the thunderstorm, though he'd always loved them since he was a child. No: there was something else stirring him up, and he was damned if he knew what. It was like being a child again. As if it was Christmas, and any minute Santa, the first Lord he'd ever believed in, would be at the door. The very idea made him want to laugh out loud, but the vestry was too sober a place for laughter, and he stopped himself, letting the smile curl inside him, a secret hope.

* * *

43

While everyone else took refuge from the rain, Gwen Nicholson was getting thoroughly drenched. She was still in the yard behind the house, coaxing Amelia's pony towards the barn. The thunder had made the stupid beast jittery, and it didn't want to budge. Now Gwen was soaked and angry.

'Will you come on, you brute?' she yelled at it over the noise of the storm. The rain lashed the yard, and pummelled the top of her head. Her hair was flattened. *'Come on! Come on!'*

The pony refused to budge. Its eyes showed crescents of white in its fear. And the more the thunder rolled and crackled around the yard the less it wanted to move. Angrily, Gwen slapped it across the backside, harder than she strictly needed to. It took a couple of steps in response to the blow, dropping steaming turds as it went, and Gwen took the advantage. Once she had it moving she could drag it the rest of the way.

'Warm barn,' she promised it; 'Come on, it's wet out here, you don't want to stay out here.'

The barn-door was slightly ajar. Surely it must look like an inviting prospect, she thought, even to a pea-brained pony. She dragged it to within spitting distance of the barn, and one more slap got it through the door.

As she'd promised the damn thing, the interior of the barn was sweet and dry, though the air smelt metallic with the storm. Gwen tied the pony to the crossbar in its stall and roughly threw a blanket over its glistening hide. She was damned if she was going to swab the creature down, that was Amelia's job. That was the bargain she'd made with her daughter when they'd agreed to buy the pony: that all the grooming and clearing out would be Amelia's responsibility, and to be fair to her, she'd done what she promised, more or less.

The pony was still panicking. It stamped and rolled its eyes like a bad tragedian. There were flecks of foam on its lips. A little apologetically Gwen patted its flank. She'd lost her temper. Time of the month. Now she regretted it. She only hoped Amelia hadn't been at her bedroom window watching.

A gust of wind caught the barn-door and it swung closed. The sound of rain on the yard outside was abruptly muted. It was suddenly dark.

The pony stopped stamping. Gwen stopped stroking its side. Everything stopped: her heart too, it seemed.

Behind her a figure that was almost twice her size rose from beyond the bales of hay. Gwen didn't see the giant, but her innards churned. Damn periods, she thought, rubbing her lower belly in a slow circle. She was normally as regular as clockwork, but this month she'd come on a day early. She should go back to the house, get changed, get clean.

Rawhead stood and looked at the nape of Gwen Nicholson's neck, where a single nip would easily kill. But there was no way he could bring himself to touch this woman; not today. She had the blood-cycle on her, he could taste its tang, and it sickened him. It was taboo, that blood, and he had never taken a woman poisoned by its presence.

Feeling the damp between her legs, Gwen hurried out of the barn without looking behind her, and ran through the downpour back to the house, leaving the fretting pony in the darkness of the barn.

Rawhead heard the woman's feet recede, heard the housedoor slam.

He waited, to be sure she wouldn't come back, then he padded across to the animal, reached down and took hold of it. The pony kicked and complained, but Rawhead had in his time taken animals far bigger and far better armed than this.

He opened his mouth. The gums were suffused with blood as the teeth emerged from them, like claws unsheathed from a cat's paw. There were two rows on each jaw, two dozen needle-sharp points. They gleamed as they closed around the meat of the pony's neck. Thick, fresh blood poured down Rawhead's throat; he gulped it greedily. The hot taste of the world. It made him feel strong and wise. This was only the first of many meals he would take, he'd gorge on anything that took his fancy and nobody would stop him, not this time. And when he was ready he'd throw those pretenders off his throne, he'd cremate them in their houses, he'd slaughter their children and wear their infants' bowels as necklaces. *This place was his*. Just because they'd tamed the wilderness for a while didn't mean they owned the earth. It was his, and nobody would take it from him, not even the holiness. He was wise to that too. They'd never subdue him again.

He sat cross-legged on the floor of the barn, the grey-pink intestines of the pony coiled around him, planning his tactics as best he could. He'd never been a great thinker. Too much appetite: it overwhelmed his reason. He lived in the eternal

45

present of his hunger and his strength, feeling only the crude territorial instinct that would sooner or later blossom into carnage.

The rain didn't let up for over an hour.

Ron Milton was becoming impatient: a flaw in his nature that had given him an ulcer and a top-flight job in Design Consultancy. What Milton could get done for you, couldn't be done quicker. He was the best: and he hated sloth in other people as much as in himself. Take this damn house, for instance. They'd promised it would be finished by mid-July, garden landscaped, driveway laid, everything, and here he was, two months after that date, looking at a house that was still far from habitable. Half the windows without glass, the front door missing, the garden an assault-course, the driveway a mire.

This was to be his castle: his retreat from a world that made him dyspeptic and rich. A haven away from the hassles of the city, where Maggie could grow roses, and the children could breathe clean air. Except that it wasn't ready. Damn it, at this rate he wouldn't be in until next spring. Another winter in London: the thought made his heart sink.

Maggie joined him, sheltering him under her red umbrella.

'Where are the kids?' he asked.

She grimaced. 'Back at the hotel, driving Mrs Blatter crazy.'

Enid Blatter had borne their cavortings for half a dozen weekends through the summer. She'd had kids of her own, and she handled Debbie and Ian with aplomb. But there was a limit, even to her fund of mirth and merriment.

'We'd better get back to town.'

'No. Please let's stay another day or two. We can go back on Sunday evening. I want us all to go to the Harvest Festival Service on Sunday.'

Now it was Ron's turn to grimace.

'Oh hell.'

'It's all part of village life, Ronnie. If we're going to live here, we have to become part of the community.'

He whined like a little boy when he was in this kind of mood. She knew him so well she could hear his next words before he said them.

'I don't want to.'

'Well we've no choice.'

46

'We can go back tonight.'

'Ronnie – '

'There's nothing we can do here. The kids are bored, you're miserable . . .'

Maggie had set her features in concrete; she wasn't going to budge an inch. He knew that face as well as she knew his whining.

He studied the puddles that were forming in what might one day be their front garden, unable to imagine grass there, roses there. It all suddenly seemed impossible.

'You go back to town if you like, Ronnie. Take the kids. I'll stay here. Train it home on Sunday night.'

Clever, he thought, to give him a get-out that's more unattractive than staying put. Two days in town looking after the kids alone? No thank you.

'OK. You win. We'll go to the Harvest-bloody-Festival.'

'Martyr.'

'As long as I don't have to pray.'

Amelia Nicholson ran into the kitchen, her round face white, and collapsed in front of her mother. There was greasy vomit on her green plastic mackintosh, and blood on her green plastic wellingtons.

Gwen yelled for Denny. Their little girl was shivering in her faint, her mouth chewing at a word, or words, that wouldn't come.

'What is it?'

'Denny was thundering down the stairs.

'For Christ's sake – '

Amelia was vomiting again. Her face was practically blue.

'What's wrong with her?'

'She just came in. You'd better ring for an ambulance.'

'Denny put his hand on her cheek.

'She's in shock.'

'Ambulance, Denny . . .' Gwen was taking off the green mackintosh, and loosening the child's blouse. Slowly, Denny stood up. Through the rain-laced window he could see into the yard: the barn door flapped open and closed in the wind. Somebody was inside; he glimpsed movement.

'For Christ's sake – ambulance!' Gwen said again.

Denny wasn't listening. There was somebody in his barn, on his property, and he had a strict ritual for trespassers.

The barn door opened again, teasing. Yes! Retreating into the dark. Interloper.

He picked up the rifle beside the door, keeping his eyes on the yard as much as he could. Behind him, Gwen had left Amelia on the kitchen floor and was dialling for help. The girl was moaning now: she was going to be OK. Just some filthy trespasser scaring her, that's all. On his land.

He opened the door and stepped into the yard. He was in his shirt-sleeves and the wind was bitingly cold, but the rain had stopped. Underfoot the ground glistened, and drips fell from every eave and portico, a fidgety percussion that accompanied him across the yard.

The barn door swung listlessly ajar again, and this time stayed open. He could see nothing inside. Half wondered if a trick of the light had –

But no. He'd seen someone moving in here. The barn wasn't empty. Something (not the pony) was watching him even now. They'd see the rifle in his hands, and they'd sweat. Let them. Come into his place like that. Let them think he was going to blow their balls off.

He covered the distance in a half a dozen confident strides and stepped into the barn.

The pony's stomach was beneath his shoe, one of its legs to his right, the upper shank gnawed to the bone. Pools of thickening blood reflected the holes in the roof. The mutilation made him want to heave.

'All right,' he challenged the shadows. 'Come out.' He raised his rifle. 'You hear me you bastard? Out I said, or I'll blow you to Kingdom Come.'

He meant it too.

At the far end of the barn something stirred amongst the bales.

Now I've got the son of a bitch, thought Denny. The trespasser got up, all nine feet of him, and stared at Denny.

'Jee-sus.'

And without warning it was coming at him, coming like a locomotive smooth and efficient. He fired into it, and the bullet struck its upper chest, but the wound hardly slowed it.

Nicholson turned and ran. The stones of the yard were slippery beneath his shoes, and he had no turn of speed to outrun it. It was at his back in two beats, and on him in another.

Gwen dropped the phone when she heard the shot. She raced

48

to the window in time to see her sweet Denny eclipsed by a gargantuan form. It howled as it took him, and threw him up into the air like a sack of feathers. She watched helplessly as his body twisted at the apex of its journey before plummetting back down to earth again. It hit the yard with a thud she felt in her every bone, and the giant was at his body like a shot, treading his loving face to muck.

She screamed; trying to silence herself with her hand. Too late. The sound was out and the giant was looking at her, straight at her, its malice piercing the window. Oh God, it had seen her, and now it was coming for her, loping across the yard, a naked engine, and grinning a promise at her as it came.

Gwen snatched Amelia off the floor and hugged her close, pressing the girl's face against her neck. Maybe she wouldn't see: she mustn't see. The sound of its feet slapping on the wet yard got louder. Its shadow filled the kitchen.

'Jesus help me.'

It was pressing at the window, its body so wide that it cancelled out the light, its lewd, revolting face smeared on the watery pane. Then it was smashing through, ignoring the glass that bit into its flesh. It smelled child-meat. It wanted child-meat. It would *have* child-meat.

Its teeth were spilling into view, widening that smile into an obscene laugh. Ropes of saliva hung from its jaw as it clawed the air, like a cat after a mouse in a cage, pressing further and further in, each swipe closer to the morsel.

Gwen flung open the door into the hall as the thing lost patience with snatching and began to demolish the window-frame and clamber through. She locked the door after her while crockery smashed and wood splintered on the other side, then she began to load all the hall furniture against it. Tables, chairs, coat-stand, knowing even as she did it, that it would be matchwood in two seconds flat. Amelia was kneeling on the hall floor where Gwen had set her down. Her face was a thankful blank.

All right, that was all she could do. Now, upstairs. She picked up her daughter, who was suddenly air-light, and took the stairs two at a time. Halfway up, the noise in the kitchen below stopped utterly.

She suddenly had a reality crisis. On the landing where she stood all was peace and calm. Dust gathered minutely on the window-sills, flowers wilted; all the infinitesimal domestic procedures went on as though nothing had happened.

'Dreaming it,' she said. God, yes: dreaming it.

She sat down on the bed Denny and she had slept in together for eight years, and tried to think straight.

Some vile menstrual nightmare, that's what it was, some rape-fantasy out of all control. She lay Amelia on the pink eiderdown (Denny hated pink, but suffered it for her sake) and stroked the girl's clammy forehead.

'Dreaming it.'

Then the room darkened, and she looked up knowing what she'd see.

It was there, the nightmare, all over the upper windows, its spidery arms spanning the width of the glass, clinging like an acrobat to the frame, its repellent teeth sheathing and unsheathing as it gawped at her terror.

In one swooping movement she snatched Amelia up from the bed and dived towards the door. Behind her, glass shattered, and a gust of cold air swept into the bedroom. It was coming.

She ran across the landing to the top of the stairs but it was after her in a heart's beat, ducking through the bedroom door, its mouth a tunnel. It whooped as it reached to steal the mute parcel in her arms, huge in the confined space of the landing.

She couldn't out-run it, she couldn't out-fight it. Its hands fixed on Amelia with insolent ease, and tugged.

The child screamed as it took her, her fingernails raking four furrows across her mother's face as she left her arms.

Gwen stumbled back, dizzied by the unthinkable sight in front of her, and lost balance at the top of the stairs. As she fell backwards she saw Amelia's tear-stained face, doll-stiff, being fed between those rows of teeth. Then her head hit the bannister, and her neck broke. She bounced down the last six steps a corpse.

The rain-water had drained away a little by early evening, but the artificial lake at the bottom of the dip still flooded the road to a depth of several inches. Serenely, it reflected the sky. Pretty, but inconvenient. Reverend Coot quietly reminded Declan Ewan to report the blocked drains to the County Council. It was the third time of asking, and Declan blushed at the request.

'Sorry, I'll . . .'

'All right. No problem, Declan. But we really must get them cleared.'

A vacant look. A beat. A thought.

'Autumn fall always clogs them again, of course.'

Coot made a roughly cyclical gesture, intending a sort of observation about how it really wouldn't make that much difference when or if the Council cleared the drains, then the thought disappeared. There were more pressing issues. For one, the Sunday Sermon. For a second, the reason why he couldn't make much sense of sermon writing this evening. There was an unease in the air today, that made every reassuring word he committed to paper curdle as he wrote it. Coot went to the window, back to Declan, and scratched his palms. They itched: maybe an attack of eczema again. If he could only speak; find some words to shape his distress. Never, in his forty-five years, had he felt so incapable of communication; and never in those years had it been so vital that he talk.

'Shall I go now?' Declan asked.

Coot shook his head.

'A moment longer. If you would.'

He turned to the Verger. Declan Ewan was twenty-nine, though he had the face of a much older man. Bland, pale features: his hair receding prematurely.

What will this egg-face make of my revelation? thought Coot. He'll probably laugh. That's why I can't find the words, because I don't want to. I'm afraid of looking stupid. Here I am, a man of the cloth, dedicated to the Christian Mysteries. For the first time in forty odd years I've had a real glimpse of something, a vision maybe, and I'm scared of being laughed at. Stupid man, Coot, stupid, stupid man.

He took off his glasses. Declan's empty features became a blur. Now at least he didn't have to look at the smirking.

'Declan, this morning I had what I can only describe as a . . . as a . . . visitation.'

Declan said nothing, nor did the blur move.

'I don't quite know how to say this . . . our vocabulary's impoverished when it comes to these sorts of things . . . but frankly I've never had such a direct, such an unequivocal, manifestation of – '

Coot stopped. Did he mean God?

'God,' he said, not sure that he did.

51

Declan said nothing for a moment. Coot risked returning his glasses to their place. The egg hadn't cracked.

'Can you say what it was like?' Declan asked, his equilibrium absolutely unspoiled.

Coot shook his head; he'd been trying to find the words all day, but the phrases all seemed so predictable.

'What was it like?' Declan insisted.

Why didn't he understand that there were no words? I must try, thought Coot, I *must*.

'I was at the Altar after Morning Prayer . . .' he began, 'and I felt something going through me. Like electricity almost. It made my hair stand on end. Literally on end.'

Coot's hand was running through his short-cropped hair as he remembered the sensation. The hair standing bolt upright, like a field of grey-ginger corn. And that buzzing at the temples, in his lungs, at his groin. It had actually given him a hard-on; not that he was going to be able to tell Declan that. But he'd stood there at the Altar with an erection so powerful it was like discovering the joy of lust all over again.

'I won't claim . . . I *can't* claim it was our Lord God – '

(Though he wanted to believe that; that his God was the Lord of the Hard-on.) ' – I can't even claim it was Christian. But something happened today. I felt it.'

Declan's face was still impenetrable. Coot watched it for several seconds, impatient for its disdain.

'Well?' he demanded.

'Well what?'

'Nothing to say?'

The egg frowned for a moment, a furrow in its shell. Then it said:

'God help us,' almost in a whisper.

'What?'

'I felt it too. Not quite as you describe: not quite an electric shock. But something.'

'Why God help us, Declan? Are you afraid of something?'

He made no reply.

'If you know something about these experiences that I don't . . . please tell me. I want to know, to understand. God, I *have* to understand.'

Declan pursed his lips. 'Well . . .' his eyes became more indecipherable than ever; and for the first time Coot caught a glimpse of a ghost behind Declan's eyes. Was it despair, perhaps?

'There's a lot of history to this place you know,' he said, 'a history of things . . . on this site.'

Coot knew Declan had been delving into Zeal's history. Harmless enough pastime: the past was the past.

'There's been a settlement here for centuries, stretches back well before Roman occupation. No one knows how long. There's probably always been a temple on this site.'

'Nothing odd about that.' Coot offered up a smile, inviting Declan to reassure him. A part of him wanted to be told everything was well with his world: even if it was a lie.

Declan's face darkened. He had no reassurance to give. 'And there was a forest here. Huge. The Wild Woods.' Was it still despair behind the eyes? Or was it nostalgia? 'Not some tame little orchard. A forest you could lose a city in; full of beasts . . .'

'Wolves you mean? Bears?'

Declan shook his head.

'There were things that owned this land. Before Christ. Before civilisation. Most of them didn't survive the destruction of their natural habitat: too primitive I suppose. But strong. Not like us; not human. Something else altogether.'

'So what?'

'One of them survived as late as the fourteen hundreds. There's a carving of it being buried. It's on the Altar.'

'On the Altar?'

'Underneath the cloth. I found it a while ago: never thought much of it. Till today. Today I . . . tried to touch it.'

He produced his fist, and unclenched it. The flesh of his palm was blistered. Pus ran from the broken skin.

'It doesn't hurt,' he said. 'In fact it's quite numb. Serves me right, really. I should have known.'

Coot's first thought was that the man was lying. His second was that there was some logical explanation. His third was his father's dictum: 'Logic is the last refuge of a coward.'

Declan was speaking again. This time he was seeping excitement.

'They called it Rawhead.'

'What?'

'The beast they buried. It's in the history books. Rawhead it was called, because its head was huge, and the colour of the moon, and raw, like meat.'

53

Declan couldn't stop himself now. He was beginning to smile.

'It ate children,' he said, and beamed like a baby about to receive its mother's tit.

It wasn't until early on the Saturday morning that the atrocity at the Nicholson Farm was discovered. Mick Glossop had been driving up to London, and he'd taken the road that ran beside the farm, ('Don't know why. Don't usually. Funny really.') and Nicholson's Friesian herd was kicking up a row at the gate, their udders distended. They'd clearly not been milked in twenty-four hours. Glossop had stopped his jeep on the road and gone into the yard.

The body of Denny Nicholson was already crawling with flies, though the sun had barely been up an hour. Inside the house the only remains of Amelia Nicholson were shreds of a dress and a casually discarded foot. Gwen Nicholson's unmutilated body lay at the bottom of the stairs. There was no sign of a wound or any sexual interference with the corpse.

By nine-thirty Zeal was swarming with police, and the shock of the incident registered on every face in the street. Though there were conflicting reports as to the state of the bodies there was no doubt of the brutality of the murders. Especially the child, dismembered presumably. Her body taken away by her killer for God knows what purpose.

The Murder Squad set up a Unit at 'The Tall Man', while house to house interviews were conducted throughout the village. Nothing came immediately to light. No strangers seen in the locality; no more suspicious behaviour from anyone than was normal for a poacher or a bent building merchant. It was Enid Blatter, she of the ample bust and the motherly manner, who mentioned that she hadn't seen Thom Garrow for over twenty-four hours.

They found him where his killer had left him, the worse for a few hours of picking. Worms at his head and gulls at his legs. The flesh of his shins, where his trousers had slid out of his boots, was pecked to the bone. When he was dug up families of refugee lice scurried from his ears.

The atmosphere in the hotel that night was subdued. In the bar Detective Sergeant Gissing, down from London to head the investigation, had found a willing ear in Ron Milton. He was

54

glad to be conversing with a fellow Londoner, and Milton kept them both in Scotch and water for the best part of three hours.

'Twenty years in the force,' Gissing kept repeating, 'and I've never seen anything like it.'

Which wasn't strictly true. There'd been that whore (or selected highlights thereof) he'd found in a suitcase at Euston's left luggage department, a good decade ago. And the addict who'd taken it upon himself to hypnotise a polar bear at London Zoo: he'd been a sight for sore eyes when they dredged him out of the pool. He'd seen a good deal, had Stanley Gissing –

'But this . . . never seen anything like it,' he insisted. 'Fair made me want to puke.'

Ron wasn't quite sure why he listened to Gissing; it was just something to while the night away. Ron, who'd been a radical in his younger days, had never liked policemen much, and there was some quirky satisfaction to be had from getting this self-satisfied prat pissed out of his tiny skull.

'He's a fucking lunatic,' Gissing said, 'you can take my word for it. We'll have him easy. A man like that isn't in control, you see. Doesn't bother to cover his tracks, doesn't even care if he lives or dies. God knows, any man who can tear a seven-year-old girl to shreds like that, he's on the verge of going bang. Seen 'em.'

'Yes?'

'Oh yes. Seen 'em weep like children, blood all over 'em like they was just out of the abattoir, and tears on their faces. Pathetic.'

'So, you'll have him.'

'Like that,' said Gissing, and snapped his fingers. He got to his feet, a little unsteadily, 'Sure as God made little apples, we'll have him.' He glanced at his watch and then at the empty glass.

Ron made no further offers of refills.

'Well,' said Gissing,' I must be getting back to town. Put in my report.'

He swayed to the door and left Milton to the bill.

Rawhead watched Gissing's car crawl out of the village and along the north road, the headlights making very little impression on the night. The noise of the engine made Rawhead nervous though, as it over-revved up the hill past the Nicholson Farm. It roared and coughed like no beast he had encountered before, and somehow the homo sapiens had control of it. If the Kingdom was to be taken back from the usurpers, sooner or later he would have to best one of these beasts. Rawhead swallowed his fear and prepared for the confrontation.

The moon grew teeth.

In the back of the car Stanley was near as damnit asleep, dreaming of little girls. In his dreams these charming nymphettes were climbing a ladder on their way to bed, and he was on duty beside the ladder watching them climb, catching glimpses of their slightly soiled knickers as they disappeared into the sky. It was a familiar dream, one that he would never have admitted to, not even drunk. Not that he was ashamed exactly; he knew for a fact many of his colleagues entertained peccadilloes every bit as off-beatas, and some a good deal less savoury than, his. But he was possessive of it: it was his particular dream, and he wasn't about to share it with anyone.

In the driving seat the young officer who had been chauffeuring Gissing around for the best part of six months was waiting for the old man to fall well and truly asleep. Then and only then could he risk turning the radio on to catch up with the cricket scores. Australia were well down in the Test: a late rally seemed unlikely. Ah, now there was a career, he thought as he drove. Beats this routine into a cocked hat.

Both lost in their reveries, driver and passenger, neither caught sight of Rawhead. He was stalking the car now, his giant's stride easily keeping pace with it as it navigated the winding, unlit road.

All at once his anger flared, and roaring, he left the field for the tarmac.

The driver swerved to avoid the immense form that skipped into the burning headlights, its mouth issuing a howl like a pack of rabid dogs.

The car skidded on the wet ground, its left wing grazing the bushes that ran along the side of the road, a tangle of branches lashing the windscreen as it careered on its way. On the back seat Gissing fell off the ladder he was climbing, just as the car came to the end of its hedgerow tour and met an iron gate. Gissing was flung against the front seat, winded but uninjured. The impact took the driver over the wheel and through the window in two short seconds. His feet, now in Gissing's face, twitched.

From the road Rawhead watched the death of the metal box. Its tortured voice, the howl of its wrenched flank, the shattering of its face, frightened him. But it was dead.

He waited a few cautious moments before advancing up the road to sniff the crumpled body. There was an aromatic smell in the air, which pricked his sinuses, and the cause of it, the blood of the box, was dribbling out of of its broken torso, and running away down the road. Certain now that it must be finished, he approached.

There was someone alive in the box. None of the sweet child-flesh he savoured so much, just tough male-meat. It was a comical face that peered at him. Round, wild eyes. Its silly mouth opened and closed like a fish's. He kicked the box to make it open, and when that didn't work he wrenched off the doors. Then he reached and drew the whimpering male out of his refuge. Was this one of the species that had subdued him? This fearful mite, with its jelly-lips? He laughed at its pleas, then turned Gissing on his head, and held him upside down by one foot. He waited until the cries died down, then reached between the twitching legs and found the mite's manhood. Not large. Quite shrunk, in fact, by fear. Gissing was blathering all kinds of stuff: none of it made any sense. The only sound Rawhead understood from the mouth of the man was this sound he was hearing now, this high-pitched shriek that always attended a gelding. Once finished, he dropped Gissing beside the car.

A fire had begun in the smashed engine, he could smell it. He was not so much a beast that he feared fire. Respected it yes: but not feared. Fire was a tool, he'd used it many times: to burn out enemies, to cremate them in their beds.

Now he stepped back from the car as the flame found the petrol and fire erupted into the air. Heat balled towards him, and he smelt the hair on the front of his body crisp, but he was too entranced by the spectacle not to look. The fire followed the blood of the beast, consuming Gissing, and licking along the rivers of petrol like an eager dog after a trail of piss. Rawhead watched, and learned a new and lethal lesson.

In the chaos of his study Coot was unsuccessfully fighting off sleep. He'd spent a good deal of the evening at the Altar, some of it with Declan. Tonight there'd be no praying, just sketching. Now he had a copy of the Altar carving on his desk in front of him, and he'd spent an hour just staring at it. The exercise had been fruitless. Either the carving was too ambiguous, or his imagination lacked breadth. Whichever, he could make very little sense of the image. It pictured a burial certainly, but that was about all he was able to work out. Maybe the body was a little bigger than that of the mourners, but nothing exceptional. He thought of Zeal's pub, 'The Tall Man', and smiled. It might well have pleased some Mediaeval wit to picture the burial of a brewer under the Altar cloth.

In the hall, the sick clock struck twelve-fifteen, which meant it was almost one. Coot got up from his desk, stretched, and switched off the lamp. He was surprised by the brilliance of the moonlight streaming through the crack in the curtain. It was a full, harvest moon, and the light, though cold, was luxuriant.

He put the guard in front of the fire, and stepped into the darkened hallway, closing the door behind him. The clock ticked loudly. Somewhere over towards Goudhurst, he heard the sound of an ambulance siren.

What's happening? he wondered, and opened the front door to see what he could see. There were car headlights on the hill, and the distant throb of blue police lights, more rhythmical than the ticking at his back. Accident on the north road. Early for ice, and surely not cold enough. He watched the lights, set on the hill like jewels on the back of a whale, winking away. It was quite chilly, come to think of it. No weather to be standing in the –

He frowned; something caught his eye, a movement in the far corner of the churchyard, underneath the trees. The moonlight etched the scene in monochrome. Black yews, grey stones, a white chrysanthemum strewing its petals on a grave. And black in the shadow of the yews, but outlined clearly against the slab of a marble tomb beyond, a giant.

Coot stepped out of the house in slippered feet.

The giant was not alone. Somebody was kneeling in front of it, a smaller, more human shape, its face raised and clear in the light. It was Declan. Even from a distance it was clear that he was smiling up at his master.

Coot wanted to get closer; a better look at the nightmare. As he took his third step his foot crunched on a piece of gravel.

The giant seemed to shift in the shadows. Was it turning to look at him? Coot chewed on his heart. No, let it be deaf; please God, let it not see me, make me invisible.

The prayer was apparently answered. The giant made no sign of having seen his approach. Taking courage Coot advanced across the pavement of gravestones, dodging from tomb to tomb

58

for cover, barely daring to breathe. He was within a few feet of the tableau now and he could see the way the creature's head was bowed towards Declan; he could hear the sound like sandpaper on stone it was making at the back of its throat. But there was more to the scene.

Declan's vestments were torn and dirtied, his thin chest bare. Moonlight caught his sternum, his ribs. His state, and his position, were unequivocal. This was adoration – pure and simple. Then Coot heard the splashing; he stepped closer and saw that the giant was directing a glistening rope of its urine onto Declan's upturned face. It splashed into his slackly opened mouth, it ran over his torso. The gleam of joy didn't leave Declan's eyes for a moment as he received this baptism, indeed he turned his head from side to side in his eagerness to be totally defiled.

The smell of the creature's discharge wafted across to Coot. It was acidic, vile. How could Declan bear to have a drop of it on him, much less bathe in it? Coot wanted to cry out, stop the depravity, but even in the shadow of the yew the shape of the beast was terrifying. It was too tall and too broad to be human.

This was surely the Beast of the Wild Woods Declan had been trying to describe; this was the child-devourer. Had Declan guessed, when he eulogised about this monster, what power it would have over his imagination? Had he known all along that if the beast were to come sniffing for him he'd kneel in front of it, call it Lord (before Christ, before Civilisation, he'd said), let it discharge its bladder on to him, and smile?

Yes. Oh yes.

And so let him have his moment. Don't risk your neck for him, Coot thought, he's where he wants to be. Very slowly he backed off towards the Vestry, his eyes still fixed on the degradation in front of him. The baptism dribbled to a halt, but Declan's hands, cupped in front of him, still held a quantity of fluid. He put the heels of his hands to his mouth, and drank.

Coot gagged, unable to prevent himself. For an instant he closed his eyes to shut out the sight, and opened them again to see that the shadowy head had turned towards him and was looking at him with eyes that burned in the blackness.

'Christ Almighty.'

It saw him. For certain this time, it saw him. It roared, and its head changed shape in the shadow, its mouth opened so horribly wide.

'Sweet Jesus.'

Already it was charging towards him, antelope-lithe, leaving its acolyte slumped beneath the tree. Coot turned and ran, ran as he hadn't in many a long year, hurdling the graves aş he fled. It was just a few yards: the door, some kind of safety. Not for long maybe, but time to think, to find a weapon. Run, you old bastard. Christ the race, Christ the prize. Four yards.

Run.

The door was open.

Almost there; a yard to go —

He crossed the threshold and swung round to slam the door on his pursuer. But no! Rawhead had shot his hand through the door, a hand three times the size of a human hand. It was snatching at the empty air, trying to find Coot, the roars relentless.

Coot threw his full weight against the oak door. The door stile, edged with iron, bit into Rawhead's forearm. The roar became a howl: venom and agony mingled in a din that was heard from one end of Zeal to the other.

It stained the night up as far as the north road, where the remains of Gissing and his driver were being scraped up and parcelled in plastic. It echoed round the icy walls of the Chapel of Rest where Denny and Gwen Nicholson were already beginning to degenerate. It was heard too in the bedrooms of Zeal, where living couples lay side by side, maybe an arm numbed under the other's body; where the old lay awake working out the geography of the ceiling; where children dreamt of the womb, and babies mourned it. It was heard again and again and again as Rawhead raged at the door.

The howl made Coot's head swim. His mouth babbled prayers, but the much needed support from on high showed no sign of coming. He felt his strength ebbing away. The giant was steadily gaining access, pressing the door open inch by inch. Coot's feet slid on the too-well-polished floor, his muscles were fluttering as they faltered. This was a contest he had no chance of winning, not if he tried to match his strength to that of the beast, sinew for sinew. If he was to see tomorrow morning, he needed some strategy.

Coot pressed harder against the wood, his eyes darting around the hallway looking for a weapon. It mustn't get in: it mustn't have mastery over him. A bitter smell was in his nostrils. For a moment he saw himself naked and kneeling in front of the giant, with its piss beating on his skull. Hard on the heels of that picture, came another flurry of depravities. It was all he could do not to let it in, let the obscenities get a permanent hold. Its mind was working its way into his, a thick wedge of filth pressing its way through his memories, encouraging buried thoughts to the surface. Wouldn't it ask for worship, just like any God? And wouldn't its demands be plain, and real? Not ambiguous, like those of the Lord he'd served up 'til now. That was a fine thought: to give himself up to this certainty that beat on the other side of the door, and lie open in front of it, and let it ravage him.

Rawhead. Its name was a pulse in his ear – Raw. Head.

In desperation, knowing his fragile mental defences were within an ace of collapsing, his eyes alighted on the clothes stand to the left of the door.

Raw. Head. Raw. Head. The name was an imperative. Raw. Head. Raw. Head. It evoked a skinned head, its defences peeled back, a thing close to bursting, no telling if it was pain or pleasure. But easy to find out –

It almost had possession of him, he knew it: it was now or never. He took one arm from the door and stretched towards the rack for a walking-stick. There was one amongst them he wanted in particular. He called it his cross-country stick, a yard and a half of stripped ash, well used and resilient. His fingers coaxed it towards him.

Rawhead had taken advantage of the lack of force behind the door; its leathery arm was working its way in, indifferent to the way the door jamb scored the skin. The hand, its fingers strong as steel, had caught the folds of Coot's jacket.

Coot raised the ash stick and brought it down on Rawhead's elbow, where the bone was vulnerably close to the surface. The weapon splintered on impact, but it did its job. On the other side of the door the howl began again, and Rawhead's arm was rapidly withdrawn. As the fingers slid out Coot slammed the door and bolted it. There was a short hiatus, seconds only, before the attack began again, this time a two-fisted beating on the door. The hinges began to buckle; the wood groaned. It would be a short time, a very short time, before it gained access. It was strong; and now it was furious too.

Coot crossed the hall and picked up the phone. Police, he said, and began to dial. How long before it put two and two together, gave up on the door, and moved to the windows? They were leaded, but that wouldn't keep it out for long. He had minutes at the most, probably seconds, depending on its brain power.

His mind, loosed from Rawhead's grasp, was a chorus of fragmented prayers and demands. If I die, he found himself thinking, will I be rewarded in Heaven for dying more brutally than any country vicar might reasonably expect? Is there compensation in paradise for being disembowelled in the front hall of your own Vestry?

There was only one officer left on duty at the Police Station: the rest were up on the north road, clearing up after Gissing's party. The poor man could make very little sense of Reverend Coot's pleas, but there was no mistaking the sound of splintering wood that accompanied the babbles, nor the howling in the background.

The officer put the phone down and radioed for help. The patrol on the north road took twenty, maybe twenty-five seconds to answer. In that time Rawhead had smashed the central panel of the Vestry door, and was now demolishing the rest. Not that the patrol knew that. After the sights they'd faced up there, the chauffeur's charred body, Gissing's missing manhood, they had become insolent with experience, like hour-old war veterans. It took the officer at the Station a good minute to convince them of the urgency in Coot's voice. In that time Rawhead had gained access.

In the hotel Ron Milton watched the parade of lights blinking on the hill, heard the sirens, and Rawhead's howls, and was besieged by doubts. Was this really the quiet country village he had intended to settle himself and his family in? He looked down at Maggie, who had been woken by the noise but was now asleep again, her bottle of sleeping tablets almost empty on the bedside cabinet. He felt, though she would have laughed at him for it, protective towards her: he wanted to be her hero. She was the one who took the self-defence night classes however, while he grew overweight on expense account lunches. It made him inexplicably sad to watch her sleep, knowing he had so little power over life and death.

Rawhead stood in the hall of the Vestry in a confetti of shattered wood. His torso was pin-pricked with splinters, and dozens of tiny wounds bled down his heaving bulk. His sour sweat permeated the hail like incense.

He sniffed the air for the man, but he was nowhere near.

62

Rawhead bared his teeth in frustration, expelling a thin whistle of air from the back of his throat, and loped down the hall towards the study. There was warmth there, his nerves could feel it at twenty yards, and there was comfort too. He overturned the desk and shattered two of the chairs, partly to make more room for himself, mostly out of sheer destructiveness, then threw away the fire guard and sat down. Warmth surrounded him: healing, living warmth. He luxuriated in the sensation as it embraced his face, his lean belly, his limbs. He felt it heat his blood too, and so stir memories of other fires, fires he'd set in fields of burgeoning wheat.

And he recalled another fire, the memory of which his mind tried to dodge and duck, but he couldn't avoid thinking about it: the humiliation of that night would be with him forever. They'd picked their season so carefully: high summer, and no rain in two months. The undergrowth of the Wild Woods was tinder dry, even the living tree caught the flame easily. He had been flushed out of his fortress with streaming eyes, confused and fearful, to be met with spikes and nets on every side, and that . . . *thing* they had, that sight that could subdue him.

Of course they weren't courageous enough to kill him; they were too superstitious for that. Besides, didn't they recognise his authority, even as they wounded him, their terror a homage to it? So they buried him alive: and that was worse than death. Wasn't that the very worst? Because he could live an age, ages, and never die, not even locked in the earth. Just left to wait a hundred years, and suffer, and another hundred and another, while the generations walked the ground above his head and lived and died and forgot him. Perhaps the women didn't forget him: he could smell them even through the earth, when they came close to his grave, and though they might not have known it they felt anxious, they persuaded their men to abandon the place altogether, so he was left absolutely alone, with not even a gleaner for company. Loneliness was their revenge on him, he thought, for the times he and his brothers had taken women into the woods, spread them out, spiked and loosed them again, bleeding but fertile. They would die having the children of those rapes; no woman's anatomy could survive the thrashing of a hybrid, its teeth, its anguish. That was the only revenge he and his brothers ever had on the big-bellied sex.

Rawhead stroked himself and looked up at the gilded reproduction of 'The Light of the World' that hung above Coot's mantelpiece. The image woke no tremors of fear or remorse in him: it was a picture of a sexless martyr, doe-eyed and woebegone. No challenge there. The true power, the only power that could defeat him, was apparently gone: lost beyond recall, its place usurped by a virgin shepherd. He ejaculated, silently, his thin semen hissing on the hearth. The world was his to rule unchallenged. He would have warmth, and food in abundance. Babies even. Yes, baby-meat, that was the best. Just dropped mites, still blind from the womb.

He stretched, sighing in anticipation of that delicacy, his brain awash with atrocities.

From his refuge in the crypt Coot heard the police cars squealing to a halt outside the Vestry, then the sound of feet on the gravel path. He judged there to be at least half a dozen. It would be enough, surely.

Cautiously he moved through the darkness towards the stairs.

Something touched him: he almost yelled, biting his tongue a moment before the cry escaped.

'Don't go now,' a voice said from behind him. It was Declan, and he was speaking altogether too loudly for comfort. The thing was above them, somewhere, it would hear them if he wasn't careful. Oh God, it mustn't hear.

'It's up above us,' said Coot in a whisper.

'I know.'

The voice seemed to come from his bowels not from his throat; it was bubbled through filth.

'Let's have him come down here shall we? He wants you, you know. He wants me to – '

'What's happened to you?'

Declan's face was just visible in the dark. It grinned; lunatic.

'I think he might want to baptise you too. How'd you like that? Like that would you? He pissed on me: you see him? And that wasn't all. Oh no, he wants more than that. He wants everything. Hear me? Everything.'

Declan grabbed hold of Coot, a bear-hug that stank of the creature's urine.

'Come with me?' he leered in Coot's face.

'I put my trust in God.'

Declan laughed. Not a hollow laugh; there was genuine compassion in it for this lost soul.

'He *is* God,' he said. 'He was here before this fucking shit-house was built, you know that.'

'So were dogs.'

'Uh?'

'Doesn't mean I'd let them cock their legs on me.'

'Clever old fucker aren't you?' said Declan, the smile inverted. 'He'll show you. You'll change.'

'No, Declan. Let go of me – '

The embrace was too strong.

'Come on up the stairs, fuck-face. Mustn't keep God waiting.'

He pulled Coot up the stairs, arms still locked round him. Words, all logical argument, eluded Coot: was there nothing he could say to make the man see his degradation? They made an ungainly entrance into the Church, and Coot automatically looked towards the altar, hoping for some reassurance, but he got none. The altar had been desecrated. The cloths had been torn and smeared with excrement, the cross and candlesticks were in the middle of a fire of prayer-books that burned healthily on the altar steps. Smuts floated around the Church, the air was grimy with smoke.

'You did this?'

Declan grunted.

'He wants me to destroy it all. Take it apart stone by stone if I have to.'

'He wouldn't dare.'

'Oh he'd dare. He's not scared of Jesus, he's not scared of . . .'

The certainty lapsed for a telling instant, and Coot leapt on the hesitation.

'There's something here he *is* scared of, though, isn't there, or he'd have come in here himself, done it all himself . . .'

Declan wasn't looking at Coot. His eyes had glazed.

'What is it, Declan? What is it he doesn't like? You can tell me –'

Declan spat in Coot's face, a wad of thick phlegm that hung on his cheek like a slug.

'None of your business.'

'In the name of Christ, Declan, look at what he's done to you.'

'I know my master when I see him – '

Declan was shaking

65

'– and so will you.'

He turned Coot round to face the south door. It was open, and the creature was there on the threshold, stooping gracefully to duck under the porch. For the first time Coot saw Rawhead in a good light, and the terrors began in earnest. He had avoided thinking too much of its size, its stare, its origins. Now, as it came towards him with slow, even stately steps, his heart conceded its mastery. It was no mere beast, despite its mane, and its awesome array of teeth; its eyes lanced him through and through, gleaming with a depth of contempt no animal could ever muster. Its mouth opened wider and wider, the teeth gliding from the gums, two, three inches long, and still the mouth was gaping wider. When there was nowhere to run, Declan let Coot go. Not that Coot could have moved anyway: the stare was too insistent. Rawhead reached out and picked Coot up. The world turned on its head –

There were seven officers, not six as Coot had guessed. Three of them were armed, their weapons brought down from London on the order of Detective Sergeant Gissing. The late, soon to be decorated posthumously, Detective Sergeant Gissing. They were led, these seven good men and true, by Sergeant Ivanhoe Baker. Ivanhoe was not an heroic man, either by inclination or education. His voice, which he had prayed would give the appropriate orders when the time came without betraying him, came out as a strangled yelp as Rawhead appeared from the interior of the Church.

'I can see it!' he said. Everybody could: it was nine feet tall, covered in blood, and it looked like Hell on legs. Nobody needed it pointed out. The guns were raised without Ivanhoe's instruction: and the unarmed men, suddenly feeling naked, kissed their truncheons and prayed. One of them ran.

'Hold your ground!' Ivanhoe shrieked; if those sons of bitches turned tail he'd be left on his own. They hadn't issued him with a gun, just authority, and that was not much comfort.

Rawhead was still holding Coot up, at arm's length, by the neck. The Reverend's legs dangled a foot above the ground, his head lolled back, his eyes were closed. The monster displayed the body for his enemies, proof of power.

'Shall we . . . please . . . can we . . . shoot the bastard?' One of the gunmen inquired.

Ivanhoe swallowed before answering. 'We'll hit the vicar.'

'He's dead already.' said the gunman.

'We don't know that.'

'He must be dead. Look at him – '

Rawhead was shaking Coot like an eiderdown, and his stuffing was falling out, much to Ivanhoe's intense disgust. Then, almost lazily, Rawhead flung Coot at the police. The body hit the gravel a little way from the gate and lay still. Ivanhoe found his voice –

'Shoot!'

The gunmen needed no encouragement; their fingers were depressing the triggers before the syllable was out of his mouth. Rawhead was hit by three, four, five bullets in quick succession, most of them in the chest. They stung him and he put up an arm to protect his face, covering his balls with the other hand. This was a pain he hadn't anticipated. The wound he'd received from Nicholson's rifle had been forgotten in the bliss of the blood-letting that came soon after, but these barbs hurt him, and they kept coming. He felt a twinge of fear. His instinct was to fly in the face of these popping, flashing rods, but the pain was too much. Instead, he turned and made his retreat, leaping over the tombs as he fled towards the safety of the hills. There were copses he knew, burrows and caves, where he could hide and find time to think this new problem through. But first he had to elude them.

They were after him quickly, flushed with the ease of their victory, leaving Ivanhoe to find a vase on one of the graves, empty it of chrysanthemums, and be sick.

Out of the dip there were no lights along the road, and Rawhead began to feel safer. He could melt into the darkness, into the earth, he'd done it a thousand times. He cut across a field. The barley was still unharvested, and heavy with its grain. He trampled it as he ran, grinding seed and stalk. At his back his pursuers were already losing the chase. The car they'd piled into had stopped in the road, he could see its lights, one blue, two white, way behind him. The enemy was shouting a confusion of orders, words Rawhead didn't understand. No matter; he knew men. They were easily frightened. They would not look far for him tonight; they'd use the dark as an excuse to call off the search, telling themselves that his wounds were probably fatal anyhow. Trusting children that they were.

He climbed to the top of the hill and looked down into the

valley. Below the snake of the road, its eyes the headlights of the enemy's car, the village was a wheel of warm light, with flashing blues and reds at its hub. Beyond, in every direction, the impenetrable black of the hills, over which the stars hung in loops and clusters. By day this would seem a counterpane valley, toytown small. By night it was fathomless, more his than theirs.

His enemies were already returning to their hovels, as he'd known they would. The chase was over for the night.

He lay down on the earth and watched a meteor burn up as it fell to the south-west. It was a brief, bright streak, which edge-lit a cloud, then went out. Morning was many long, healing hours in the future. He would soon be strong again: and then, then – he'd burn them all away.

Coot was not dead: but so close to death it scarcely made any difference. Eighty per cent of the bones in his body were fractured or broken: his face and neck were a maze of lacerations: one of his hands was crushed almost beyond recognition. He would certainly die. It was purely a matter of time and inclination.

In the village those who had glimpsed so much as a fragment of the events in the dip were already elaborating on their stories: and the evidence of the naked eye lent credence to the most fantastic inventions. The chaos in the churchyard, the smashed door of the Vestry: the cordoned-off car on the north road, Whatever had happened that Saturday night it was going to take a long time to forget.

There was no harvest festival service, which came as no surprise to anyone.

Maggie was insistent: 'I want us all to go back to London.'

'A day ago you wanted us to stay here. Get to be part of the community.'

'That was on Friday, before all this . . . this . . . There's a maniac loose, Ron.'

'If we go now, we won't come back.'

'What are you talking about; of course we'll come back.'

'If we leave once the place is threatened, we give up on it altogether.'

'That's ridiculous.'

'You were the one who was so keen on us being visible, being seen to join in village life. Well, we'll have to join in the deaths too. And I'm going to stay – see it through. You can go back to London. Take the kids.'

'No.'

He sighed, heavily.

'I want to see him caught: whoever he is. I want to know it's all been cleared up, see it with my own eyes. That's the only way we'll ever feel safe here.'

Reluctantly, she nodded.

'At least let's get out of the hotel for a while. Mrs Blatter's going loopy. Can't we go for a drive? Get some air – '

'Yes, why not?'

It was a balmy September day: the countryside, always willing to spring a surprise, was gleaming with life. Late flowers shone in the roadside hedges, birds dipped over the road as they drove. The sky was azure, the clouds a fantasia in cream. A few miles outside the village all the horrors of the previous night began to evaporate and the sheer exuberance of the day began to raise the family's spirits. With every mile they drove out of Zeal Ron's fears diminished. Soon, he was singing.

On the back seat Debbie was being difficult. One moment 'I'm hot Daddy', the next: 'I want an orange juice Daddy'; the next: 'I have to pee'.

Ron stopped the car on an empty stretch of road, and played the indulgent father. The kids had been through a lot; today they could be spoiled.

'All right, darling, you can have a pee here, then we'll go and find an ice-cream for you.'

'Where's the la-la?' she said. Damn stupid phrase; mother-in-law's euphemism.

Maggie chipped in. She was better with Debbie in these moods than Ron. 'You can go behind the hedge,' she said.

Debbie looked horrified. Ron exchanged a half-smile with Ian. The boy had a put-upon look on his face. Grimacing, he went back to his dog-eared comic.

'Hurry up, can't you?' he muttered. 'Then we can go somewhere proper.'

Somewhere proper, thought Ron. He means a town. He's a city kid: its going to take a while to convince him that a hill with a view *is* somewhere proper. Debbie was still being difficult.

'I can't go here Mummy – '

'Why not?'

'Somebody might see me.'

'Nobody's going to see you darling,' Ron reassured her. 'Now do as your Mummy says.' He turned to Maggie, 'Go with her, love.'

Maggie wasn't budging.

'She's OK.'

'She can't climb over the gate on her own.'

'Well you go, then.'

Ron was determined not to argue; he forced a smile. 'Come on,' he said.

Debbie got out of the car and Ron helped her over the iron gate into the field beyond. It was already harvested. It smelt . . . earthy.

'Don't look,' she admonished him, wide-eyed, 'you *mustn't* look.'

She was already a manipulator, at the ripe old age of nine. She could play him better than the piano she was taking lessons on. He knew it, and so did she. He smiled at her and closed his eyes.

'All right. See? I've got my eyes closed. Now hurry up, Debbie. Please.'

'Promise you won't peek.'

'I won't peek'. My God, he thought, she's certainly making a production number out of this. 'Hurry up.'

He glanced back towards the car. Ian was sitting in the back, still reading, engrossed in some cheap heroics, his face set as he stared into the adventure. The boy was so serious: the occasional half-smile was all Ron could ever win from him. It wasn't a put-on, it wasn't a fake air of mystery. He seemed content to leave all the performing to his sister.

Behind the hedge Debbie pulled down her Sunday knickers and squatted, but after all the fuss her pee wouldn't come. She concentrated but that just made it worse.

Ron looked up the field towards the horizon. There were gulls up there, squabbling over a tit-bit. He watched them awhile, impatience growing.

'Come on love,' he said.

He looked back at the car, and Ian was watching him now, his face slack with boredom; or something like it. Was there something else there: a deep resignation? Ron thought. The boy looked back to his comic book 'Utopia' without acknowledging his father's gaze.

Then Debbie screamed: an ear-piercing shriek.

'Christ!' Ron was clambering over the gate in an instant, and Maggie wasn't far behind him.

'Debbie!'

Ron found her standing against the hedge, staring at the ground, blubbering, face red. 'What's wrong, for God's sake?'

She was yabbering incoherently. Ron followed her eye.

'What's happened?' Maggie was having difficulty getting over the gate.

'It's all right . . . it's all right.'

There was a dead mole almost buried in the tangle at the edge of the field, its eyes pecked out, its rotting hide crawling with flies.

'Oh God, Ron.' Maggie looked at him accusingly, as though he'd put the damn thing there with malice aforethought.

'It's all right, sweetheart,' she said, elbowing past her husband and wrapping Debbie up in her arms.

Her sobs quietened a bit. City kids, thought Ron. They're going to have to get used to that sort of thing if they're going to live in the country. No road-sweepers here to brush up the run-over cats every morning. Maggie was rocking her, and the worst of the tears were apparently over.

'She'll be all right,' Ron said.

'Of course she will, won't you, darling?' Maggie helped her pull up her knickers. She was still snivelling, her need for privacy forgotten in her unhappiness.

In the back of the car Ian listened to his sister's caterwauling and tried to concentrate on his comic. Anything for attention, he thought. Well, she's welcome.

Suddenly, it went dark.

He looked up from the page, his heart loud. At his shoulder, six inches away from him, something stooped to peer into the car, its face like Hell. He couldn't scream, his tongue refused to move. All he could do was flood the seat and kick uselessly as the long, scarred arms reached through the window towards him. The nails of the beast gouged his ankles, tore his sock. One of his new shoes fell off in the struggle. Now it had his foot and he was being dragged across the wet seat towards the window. He found his voice. Not quite *his* voice, it was a pathetic, a silly-sounding voice, not the equal of the mortal terror he felt. And all too late anyway; it was dragging his legs through the window, and his bottom was almost through now. He looked through the back window as it hauled his torso into the open air and in a dream he saw Daddy at the gate, his face looking so, so ridiculous. He was climbing the gate, coming to help, coming to save him but he was far too slow. Ian knew he was beyond salvation from the beginning, because he'd died this way in his sleep on a hundred occasions and Daddy never got there in time. The mouth was wider even than he'd dreamed it, a hole which he was being delivered into, head first. It smelt like the dustbins at the back of the school canteen, times a million. He was sick down its throat, as it bit the top of his head off.

Ron had never screamed in his life. The scream had always belonged to the other sex, until that instant. Then, watching the monster stand up and close its jaws around his son's head, there was no sound appropriate but a scream.

Rawhead heard the cry, and turned, without a trace of fear on his face, to look at the source. Their eyes met. The King's glance penetrated Milton like a spike, freezing him to the road and to the marrow. It was Maggie who broke its hold, her voice a dirge.

'Oh . . . please . . . no.'

Ron shook Rawhead's look from his head, and started towards the car, towards his son. But the hesitation had given Rawhead a moment's grace he scarcely needed anyway, and he was already away, his catch clamped between his jaws, spilling out to right and left. The breeze carried motes of Ian's blood back down the road towards Ron; he felt them spot his face in a gentle shower.

Declan stood in the chancel of St Peter's and listened for the hum. It was still there. Sooner or later he'd have to go to the source of that sound and destroy it, even if it meant, as it well might, his own death. His new master would demand it. But that was par for the course; and the thought of death didn't distress him; far from it. In the last few days he'd realised ambitions that he'd nurtured (unspoken, even unthought) for years.

Looking up at the black bulk of the monster as it rained piss on him he'd found the purest joy. If that experience, which would once have disgusted him, could be so consummate, what might death be like? rarer still. And if he could contrive to die by Rawhead's hand, by that wide hand that smelt so rank, wouldn't that be the rarest of the rare?

He looked up at the altar, and at the remains of the fire the police had extinguished. They'd searched for him after Coot's death, but he had a dozen hiding places they would never find, and they'd soon given up. Bigger fish to fry. He collected a fresh armful of *Songs of Praise* and threw them down amongst the damp ashes. The candlesticks were warped, but still recognisable. The cross had disappeared, either shrivelled away or removed by some light-fingered officer of the law. He tore a few handfuls of hymns from the books, and lit a match. The old songs caught easily.

Ron Milton was tasting tears, and it was a taste he'd forgotten. It was many years since he'd wept, especially in front of other males. But he didn't care any longer: these bastard policemen weren't human anyway. They just looked at him while he poured out his story, and nodded like idiots.

'We've drafted men in from every division within fifty miles, Mr Milton,' said the bland face with the understanding eyes. 'The hills are being scoured. We'll have it, whatever it is.'

'It took my child, you understand me? It killed him, in front of me – '

They didn't seem to appreciate the horror of it all.

'We're doing what we can.'

'It's not enough. This thing . . . it's not human.'

Ivanhoe, with the understanding eyes, knew bloody well how unhuman it was.

'There's people coming from the Ministry of Defence: we can't do much more 'til they've had a look at the evidence,' he said. Then added, as a sop: 'It's all public money sir.'

'You fucking idiot! What does it matter what it costs to kill it? It's not human. It's out of Hell.'

Ivanhoe's look lost compassion.

'If it came out of Hell, sir,' he said, 'I don't think it would have found the Reverend Coot such easy pickings.'

Coot: that was his man. Why hadn't he thought of that before? Coot.

Ron had never been much of a man of God. But he was

prepared to be open-minded, and now that he'd seen the opposition, or one of its troops, he was ready to reform his opinions. He'd believe anything, anything at all, if it gave him a weapon against the Devil.

He must get to Coot.

'What about your wife?' the officer called after him. Maggie was sitting in one of the side-offices, dumb with sedation, Debbie asleep beside her. There was nothing he could do for them. They were as safe here as anywhere.

He must get to Coot, before he died.

He'd know, whatever Reverends know; and he'd understand the pain better than these monkeys. Dead sons were the crux of the Church after all.

As he got into the car it seemed for a moment he smelt his son: the boy who would have carried his name (Ian Ronald Milton he'd been christened), the boy who was his sperm made flesh, who he'd had circumcised like himself. The quiet child who'd looked out of the car at him with such resignation in his eyes.

This time the tears didn't begin. This time there was just an anger that was almost wonderful.

It was half past eleven at night. Rawhead Rex lay under the moon in one of the harvested fields to the south-west of the Nicholson Farm. The stubble was darkening now, and there was a tantalising smell of rotting vegetable matter off the earth. Beside him lay his dinner, Ian Ronald Milton, face up on the field, his midriff torn open. Occasionally the beast would lean up on one elbow and paddle its fingers in the cooling soup of the boy-child's body, fishing for a delicacy.

Here, under the full moon, bathing in silver, stretching his limbs and eating the flesh of human kind, he felt irresistible. His fingers drew a kidney off the plate beside him and he swallowed it whole.

Sweet.

Coot was awake, despite the sedation. He knew he was dying, and the time was too precious to doze through. He didn't know the name of the face that was interrogating him in the yellow gloom of his room, but the voice was so politely insistent he had to listen, even though it interrupted his peace-making with

74

God. Besides, they had questions in common: and they all circled, those questions, on the beast that had reduced him to this pulp.

'It took my son,' the man said. 'What do you know about the thing? Please tell me. I'll believe whatever you tell me – ' Now *there* was desperation – 'Just explain – '

Time and again, as he'd lain on that hot pillow, confused thoughts had raced through Coot's mind. Declan's baptism; the embrace of the beast; the altar; his hair rising and his flesh too. Maybe there was something he could tell the father at his bedside.

'. . . in the church . . .'

Ron leaned closer to Coot; he smelt of earth already.

'. . . the altar . . . it's afraid . . . the altar . . .'

'You mean the cross? It's afraid of the cross?'

'No . . . not – '

'Not – '

The body creaked once, and stopped. Ron watched death come over the face: the saliva dry on Coot's lips, the iris of his remaining eye contract. He watched a long while before he rang for the nurse, then quietly made his escape.

There was somebody in the Church. The door, which had been padlocked by the police, was ajar, the lock smashed. Ron pushed it open a few inches and slid inside. There were no lights on in the Church, the only illumination was a bonfire on the altar steps. It was being tended by a young man Ron had seen on and off in the village. He looked up from his fire-watching, but kept feeding the flames the guts of books.

'What can I do for you?' he asked, without interest.

'I came to – ' Ron hesitated. What to tell this man: the truth? No, there was something wrong here.

'I asked you a frigging question,' said the man. 'What do you want?'

As he walked down the aisle towards the fire Ron began to see the questioner in more detail. There were stains, like mud, on his clothes, and his eyes had sunk in their orbits as if his brain had sucked them in.

'You've got no right to be in here – '

'I thought anyone could come into a church,' said Ron, staring at the burning pages as they blackened.

'Not tonight. You get the fuck out of here.' Ron kept walking towards the altar.

'You get the fuck out, I said!'

The face in front of Ron was alive with leers and grimaces: there was lunacy in it.

'I came to see the altar; I'll go when I've seen it, and not before.'

'You've been talking to Coot. That it?'

'Coot?'

'What did the old wanker tell you? It's all a lie, whatever it was; he never told the truth in his frigging life, you know that? You take it from he. He used to get up there – ' he threw a prayer-book at the pulpit ' – and tell fucking lies!'

'I want to see the altar for myself. We'll see if he was telling lies –'

'*No you won't!*'

The man threw another handful of books on to the fire and stepped down to block Ron's path. He smelt not of mud but of shit. Without warning, he pounced. His hands seized Ron's neck, and the two of them toppled over. Declan's fingers reaching to gouge at Ron's eyes: his teeth snapping at his nose.

Ron was surprised at the weakness of his own arms; why hadn't he played squash the way Maggie had suggested, why were his muscles so ineffectual? If he wasn't careful this man was going to kill him.

Suddenly a light, so bright it could have been a midnight dawn, splashed through the west window. A cloud of screams followed close on it. Firelight, dwarfing the bonfire on the altar steps, dyed the air. The stained glass danced.

Declan forgot his victim for an instant, and Ron rallied. He pushed the man's chin back, and got a knee under his torso, then he kicked hard. The enemy went reeling, and Ron was up and after him, a fistful of hair securing the target while the ball of his other hand hammered at the lunatic's face 'til it broke. It wasn't enough to see the bastard's nose bleed, or to hear the cartilage mashed; Ron kept beating and beating until his fist bled. Only then did he let Declan drop.

Outside, Zeal was ablaze.

Rawhead had made fires before, many fires. But petrol was a new weapon, and he was still getting the hang of it. It didn't take him long to learn. The trick was to wound the wheeled boxes, that was easy. Open their flanks and out their blood would pour, blood that made his head ache. The boxes were easy prey, lined up on the pavement like bullocks to be slaughtered. He went amongst them demented with death, splashing their blood down the High Street and igniting it. Streams of liquid fire poured into gardens, over thresholds. Thatches caught; wood-beamed cottages went up. In minutes Zeal was burning from end to end.

In St Peter's, Ron dragged the filthied cloth off the altar, trying to block out all thoughts of Debbie and Margaret. The police would move them to a place of safety, for certain. The issue at hand must take precedence.

Beneath the cloth was a large box, its front panel roughly carved. He took no notice of the design; there were more urgent matters to attend to. Outside, the beast was loose. He could hear its triumphant roars, and he felt eager, yes eager, to go to it. To kill it or be killed. But first, the box. It contained power, no doubt about that; a power that was even now raising the hairs on his head, that was working at his cock, giving him an aching hard-on. His flesh seemed to seethe with it, it elated him like love. Hungry, he put his hands on the box, and a shock that seemed to cook his joints ran up both his arms. He fell back, and for a moment he wondered if he was going to remain conscious, the pain was so bad, but it subsided, in moments. He cast around for a tool, something to get him into the box without laying flesh to it.

In desperation he wrapped his hand with a piece of the altar cloth and snatched one of the brass candleholders from the edge of the fire. The cloth began to smoulder as the heat worked its way through to his hand. He stepped back to the altar and beat at the wood like a madman until it began to splinter. His hands were numb now; if the heated candlesticks were burning his palms he couldn't feel it. What did it matter anyhow? There was a weapon here: a few inches away from him, if only he could get to it, to wield it. His erection throbbed, his balls tingled.

'Come to me,' he found himself saying, 'come on, come on. Come to me. Come to me.' Like he was willing it into his embrace, this treasure, like it was a girl he wanted, his hard-on wanted, and he was hypnotising her into his bed.

'Come to me, come to me – '

The wood façade was breaking. Panting now, he used the corners of the candlestick base to lever larger chunks of timber away. The altar was hollow, as he'd known it would be. And empty.

Empty.

Except for a ball of stone, the size of a small football. Was this his prize? He couldn't believe how insignificant it looked: and yet the air was still electric around him; his blood still danced. He reached through the hole he'd made in the altar and picked the relic up.

Outside, Rawhead was jubilating.

Images flashed before Ron's eyes as he weighed the stone in his deadened hand. A corpse with its feet burning. A flaming cot. A dog, running along the street, a living ball of fire. It was all outside, waiting to unfold.

Against the perpetrator, he had this stone.

He'd trusted God, just for half a day, and he got shat on. It was just a stone: just a fucking *stone*. He turned the football over and over in his hand, trying to make some sense of its furrows and its mounds. Was it meant to *be* something, perhaps; was he missing its deeper significance?

There was a knot of noise at the other end of the church; a crash, a cry, from beyond the door a whoosh of flame.

Two people staggered in, followed by smoke and pleas.

'He's burning the village,' said a voice Ron knew. It was that benign policeman who hadn't believed in Hell; he was trying to keep his act together, perhaps for the benefit of his companion, Mrs Blatter from the hotel. The nightdress she'd run into the street wearing was torn. Her breasts were exposed; they shook with her sobs; she didn't seem to know she was naked, didn't even know where she was.

'Christ in Heaven help us,' said Ivanhoe.

'There's no fucking Christ in here,' came Declan's voice. He was standing up, and reeling towards the intruders. Ron couldn't see his face from where he stood, but he knew it must be near as damn it unrecognisable. Mrs Blatter avoided him as he staggered towards the door, and she ran towards the altar. She'd been married here: on the very spot he'd built the fire.

Ron stared at her body entranced.

She was considerably overweight, her breasts sagging, her belly overshadowing her cunt so he doubted if she could even see it. But it was for this his cock-head throbbed, for this his head reeled –

Her image was in his hand. God yes, she was there in his hand, she was the living equivalent of what he held. A woman. The stone was the statue of a woman, a Venus grosser than Mrs Blatter, her belly swelling with children, tits like mountains, cunt a valley that began at her navel and gaped to the world. All this time, under the cloth and the cross, they'd bowed their heads to a goddess.

Ron stepped off the altar and began to run down the aisle, pushing Mrs Blatter, the policeman and the lunatic aside.

'Don't go out,' said Ivanhoe, 'It's right outside.'

Ron held the Venus tight, feeling her weight in his hands and taking security from her. Behind him, the Verger was screeching a warning to his Lord. Yes, it was a warning for sure.

Ron kicked open the door. On every side, fire. A flaming cot, a corpse (it was the postmaster) with its feet burning, a dog skinned by fire, hurtling past. And Rawhead, of course, silhouetted against a panorama of flames. It looked round, perhaps because it heard the warnings the Verger was yelling, but more likely, he thought, because it knew, knew without being told, that the woman had been found.

'Here!' Ron yelled, 'I'm here! I'm here!'

It was coming for him now, with the steady gait of a victor closing in to claim its final and absolute victory. Doubt surged up in Ron. Why did it come so surely to meet him, not seeming to care about the weapon he carried in his hands?

Hadn't it seen, hadn't it heard the warning?

Unless –

Oh God in Heaven.

– Unless Coot had been wrong. Unless it *was* only a stone he held in his hand, a useless, meaningless lump of stone.

Then a pair of hands grabbed him around the neck.

The lunatic.

A low voice spat the word 'Fucker' in his ear.

Ron watched Rawhead approaching, heard the lunatic screeching now: 'Here he is. Fetch him. Kill him. Here he is.'

Without warning the grip slackened, and Ron half-turned to see Ivanhoe dragging the lunatic back against the Church wall. The mouth in the Verger's broken face continued to screech.

'He's here! Here!

Ron looked back at Rawhead: the beast was almost on him, and he was too slow to raise the stone in self-defence. But Rawhead had no intention of taking him. It was Declan he was smelling and hearing. Ivanhoe released Declan as Rawhead's huge hands veered past Ron and fumbled for the lunatic. What followed was unwatchable. Ron couldn't bear to see the hands take Declan apart: but he heard the gabble of pleas become whoops of disbelieving grief. When he next looked round there was nothing recognisably human on ground or wall –

– And Rawhead was coming for him now, coming to do the same or worse. The huge head craned round to fix on Ron, its maw gaping, and Ron saw how the fire had wounded Rawhead. The beast had been careless in the enthusiasm for destruction: fire had caught its face and upper torso. Its body hair was crisped, its mane was stubble, and the flesh on the left hand side of its face was black and blistered. The flames had roasted its eyeballs, they were swimming in a gum of mucus and tears. That was why it had followed Declan's voice and bypassed Ron; it could scarcely see.

But it must see now. It must.

'Here . . . here . . .' said Ron, 'Here I am!' Rawhead heard. He looked without seeing, his eyes trying to focus.

'Here! I'm here!'

Rawhead growled in his chest. His burned face pained him; he wanted to be away from here, away in the cool of a birch-thicket, moon-washed.

His dimmed eyes found the stone; the homo sapien was nursing it like a baby. It was difficult for Rawhead to see clearly, but he knew. It ached in his mind, that image. It pricked him, it teased him.

It was just a symbol of course, a sign of the power, not the power itself, but his mind made no such distinction. To him the stone was the thing he feared most: the bleeding woman, her gaping hole eating seed and spitting children. It was life, that hole, that woman, it was endless fecundity. It terrified him.

Rawhead stepped back, his own shit running freely down his leg. The fear on his face gave Ron strength. He pressed home his advantage, closing in after the retreating beast, dimly aware that Ivanhoe was rallying allies around him, armed figures waiting at the corners of his vision, eager to bring the fire-raiser down.

His own strength was failing him. The stone, lifted high above his head so Rawhead could see it plainly, seemed heavier by the moment.

'Go on,' he said quietly to the gathering Zealots. 'Go on, take him. Take him . . .'

They began to close in, even before he finished speaking.

Rawhead smelt them more than saw them: his hurting eyes were fixed on the woman.

His teeth slid from their sheaths in preparation for the attack. The stench of humanity closed in around him from every direction.

Panic overcame his superstitions for one moment and he snatched down towards Ron, steeling himself against the stone. The attack took Ron by surprise. The claws sank in his scalp, blood poured down over his face.

Then the crowd closed in. Human hands, weak, white human hands were laid on Rawhead's body. Fists beat on his spine, nails raked his skin.

He let Ron go as somebody took a knife to the backs of his legs and hamstrung him. The agony made him howl the sky down, or so it seemed. In Rawhead's roasted eyes the stars reeled as he fell backwards on to the road, his back cracking under him. They took the advantage immediately, overpowering him by sheer weight of numbers. He snapped off a finger here, a face there, but they would not be stopped now. Their hatred was old; in their bones, did they but know it.

He thrashed under their assaults for as long as he could, but he knew death was certain. There would be no resurrection this time, no waiting in the earth for an age until their descendants forgot him. He'd be snuffed out absolutely, and there would be nothingness.

He became quieter at the thought, and looked up as best he could to where the little father was standing. Their eyes met, as they had on the road when he'd taken the boy. But now Rawhead's look had lost its power to transfix. His face was empty and sterile as the moon, defeated long before Ron slammed the stone down between his eyes. The skull was soft: it buckled inwards and a slop of brain splattered the road.

The King went out. It was suddenly over, without ceremony or celebration. Out, once and for all. There was no cry.

Ron left the stone where it lay, half buried in the face of the beast. He stood up groggily, and felt his head. His scalp was

81

loose, his fingertips touched his skull, blood came and came. But there were arms to support him, and nothing to fear if he slept.

It went unnoticed, but in death Rawhead's bladder was emptying. A stream of urine pulsed from the corpse and ran down the road. The rivulet steamed in the chilling air, its scummy nose sniffing left and right as it looked for a place to drain. After a few feet it found the gutter and ran along it awhile to a crack in the tarmac; there it drained off into the welcoming earth.

Confessions of a (Pornographer's) Shroud

He had been flesh once. Flesh, and bone, and ambition. But that was an age ago, or so it seemed, and the memory of that blessed state was fading fast.

Some traces of his former life remained; time and exhaustion couldn't take everything from him. He could picture clearly and painfully the faces of those he'd loved and hated. They stared through at him from the past, clear and luminous. He could still see the sweet, goodnight expressions in his children's eyes. And the same look, less sweet but no less goodnight, in the eyes of the brutes he had murdered.

Some of those memories made him want to cry, except that there were no tears to be wrong out of his starched eyes. Besides, it was far too late for regret. Regret was a luxury reserved for the living, who still had the time, the breath and the energy to act.

He was beyond all that. He, his mother's little Ronnie (oh, if she could see him now), he was almost three weeks dead. Too late for regrets by a long chalk.

He'd done all he could do to correct the errors he'd made. He'd spun out his span to its limits and beyond, stealing himself precious time to sew up the loose ends of his frayed existence. Mother's little Ronnie had always been tidy: a paragon of neatness. That was one of the reasons he'd enjoyed accountancy. The pursuit of a few misplaced pence through hundreds of figures was a game he relished; and how satisfying, at the end of the day, to balance the books. Unfortunately life was not so perfectable, as now, too late in the day, he realized. Still, he'd done his best, and that, as Mother used to say, was all anybody could hope to do. There was nothing left but to confess, and having confessed, go to his Judgement empty-handed and contrite. As he sat, draped over the use-shined seat in the Confessional Box of St Mary Magdalene's, he fretted that the shape of his usurped body would not hold out long enough for him to unburden himself of all the sins that languished in his linen heart. He concentrated, trying to keep body and soul together for these last, vital few minutes.

Soon Father Rooney would come. He would sit behind the lattice-divide of the Confessional and offer words of consolation, of understanding, of forgiveness; then, in the remaining minutes of his stolen existence, Ronnie Glass would tell his story.

He would begin by denying that most terrible stain on his character: the accusation of pornographer.

Pornographer.

The thought was absurd. There wasn't a pornographer's bone in his body. Anyone who had known him in his thirty-two years would have testified to that. My Christ, he didn't even like sex very much. That was the irony. Of all the people to be accused of peddling filth, he was about the most unlikely. When it had seemed everyone about him was parading their adulteries like third legs, he had lived a blameless existence. The forbidden life of the body happened, like car accidents, to other people; not to him. Sex was simply a roller-coaster ride that one might indulge in once every year or so. Twice might be tolerable; three times nauseating. Was it any surprise then, that in nine years of marriage to a good Catholic girl this good Catholic boy only fathered two children?

But he'd been a loving man in his lustless way, and his wife Bernadette had shared his indifference to sex, so his unenthusiastic member had never been a bone of contention between them. And the children were a joy. Samantha was already growing into a model of politeness and tidiness, and Imogen (though scarcely two) had her mother's smile.

Life had been fine, all in all. He had almost owned a featureless semi-detached house in the leafier suburbs of South London. He had possessed a small garden, Sunday-tended: a soul the same. It had been, as far as he could judge, a model life, unassuming and dirt-free.

And it would have remained so, had it not been for that worm of greed in his nature. Greed had undone him, no doubt.

If he hadn't been greedy, he wouldn't have looked twice at the job that Maguire had offered him. He would have trusted his instinct, taken one look around the pokey smoke-filled office above the Hungarian pastry-shop in Soho, and turned tail. But his itch for wealth diverted him from the plain truth – that he was using all his skills as an accountant to give a gloss of credibility to an operation that stank of corruption. He'd known that in his heart, of course. Known that despite Maguire's ceaseless talk of

Moral Rearmament, his fondness for his children, his obsession with the gentlemanly art of Bonsai, the man was a louse. The lowest of the low. But he'd successfully shut out that knowledge, and contented himself with the job in hand: balancing the books. Maguire was generous: and that made the blindness easier to induce. He even began to like the man and his associates. He'd got used to seeing the shambling bulk that was Dennis 'Dork' Luzzati, a fresh cream pastry perpetually hovering at his fat lips; got used, too, to little three-fingered Henry B. Henry, with his card tricks and his patter, a new routine every day. They weren't the most sophisticated of conversationalists, and they certainly wouldn't have been welcome at the Tennis Club, but they seemed harmless enough.

It was a shock then, a terrible shock, when he eventually drew back the veil and saw Dork, Henry and Maguire for the beasts they really were.

The revelation had occurred by accident.

One night, finishing some tax-work late, Ronnie had caught a cab down to the warehouse, planning to deliver his report to Maguire by hand. He'd never actually visited the warehouse, though he'd heard it mentioned between them often enough. Maguire had been stock-piling his supplies of books there for some months. Mostly cookery books, from Europe, or so Ronnie had been told. That night, that last night of cleanliness, he walked into the truth, in all its full-colour glory.

Maguire was there, in one of the plain-brick rooms, sitting on a chair surrounded by packages and boxes. An unshaded bulb threw a halo on to his thinning scalp; it glistened, pinkly. Dork was there too, engrossed in a cake. Henry B. was playing Patience. Piled high on every side of the trio there were magazines, thousand upon thousand of them, their covers shining, virginal, and somehow fleshy.

Maguire looked up from his calculations.

'Glassy,' he said. He always used that nickname.

Ronnie stared into the room, guessing, even from a distance, what these heaped treasures were.

'Come on in,' said Henry B. 'Good for a game?'

'Don't look so serious,' soothed Maguire, 'this is just merchandise.'

A kind of numb horror drew Ronnie to approach one of the stacks of magazines, and open the top copy.

85

Climax Erotica, the cover read, *Full Colour Pornography for the Discriminating Adult. Text in English, German and French.* Unable to prevent himself he began to look through the magazine, his face stinging with embarrassment, only half-hearing the barrage of jokes and threats that Maguire was shooting off.

Swarms of obscene images flew out of the pages, horribly abundant. He'd never seen anything like it in his life. Every sexual act possible between consenting adults (and a few only doped acrobats would consent to) were chronicled in glorious detail. The performers of these unspeakable acts smiled, glassy-eyed, at Ronnie as they swarmed up out of a grease of sex, neither shame nor apology on their lust-puffed faces. Every slit, every slot, every pucker and pimple of their bodies was exposed, naked beyond nakedness. The pouting, panting excess of it turned Ronnie's stomach to ash.

He closed the magazine and glanced at another pile beside it. Different faces, same furious coupling. Every depravity was catered for somewhere. The titles alone testified to the delights to be found inside. *Bizarre Women in Chains*, one read. *Enslaved by Rubber*, another promised. *Labrador Lover*, a third portrayed, in perfect focus down to the last wet whisker.

Slowly Michael Maguire's cigarette-worn voice filtered through into Ronnie's reeling brain. It cajoled, or tried to; and worse it mocked him, in its subtle way, for his naïveté.

'You had to find out sooner or later,' he said. 'I suppose it may as well be sooner, eh? No harm in it. All a bit of fun.'

Ronnie shook his head violently, trying to dislodge the images that had taken root behind his eyes. They were multiplying already, invading a territory that had been so innocent of such possibilities. In his imagination, labradors scampered around in leather, drinking from the bodies of bound whores. It was frightening the way these pictures flowed out into his eyes, each page a new abomination. He felt he'd choke on them unless he acted.

'Horrible,' was all he could say. 'Horrible. Horrible. Horrible.'

He kicked a pile of *Bizarre Women in Chains*, and they toppled over, the repeated images of the cover sprawling across the dirty floor.

'Don't do that,' said Maguire, very quietly.

'Horrible,' said Ronnie. 'They're all horrible.'

'There's a big market for them.'

'Not me!' he said, as though Maguire was suggesting he had some personal interest in them.

'All right, so you don't like them. He doesn't like them, Dork.'

Dork was wiping cream off his short fingers with a dainty handkerchief.

'Why not?'

'Too dirty for him.'

'Horrible,' said Ronnie again.

'Well you're in this up to your neck, my son,' said Maguire. His voice was the Devil's voice, wasn't it? Surely the Devil's voice, 'You may as well grin and bear it.'

Dork guffawed, 'Grin and bare it; I like it Mick, I like it.'

Ronnie looked up at Maguire. The man was forty-five, maybe fifty; but his face had a fretted, cracked look, old before its years. The charm was gone; it was scarcely human, the face he locked eyes with. Its sweat, its bristles, its puckered mouth made it resemble, in Ronnie's mind, the proffered backside of one of the red-raw sluts in the magazines.

'We're all- known villains here,' the organ was saying, 'and we've got nothing to lose if we're caught again.'

'Nothing,' said Dork.

'Whereas you, my son, you're a spit-clean professional. Way I see it, if you want to go gabbing about this dirty business, you're going to lose your reputation as a nice, honest accountant. In fact I'd venture to suggest you'll never work again. Do you take my meaning?'

Ronnie wanted to hit Maguire, so he did; hard too. There was a satisfying snap as Maguire's teeth met at speed, and blood came quickly from between his lips. It was the first time Ronnie had fought since his schooldays, and he was slow to avoid the inevitable retaliation. The blow that Maguire returned sent him sprawling, bloodied, amongst the Bizarre Women. Before he could clamber to his feet Dork had slammed his heel into Ronnie's face, grinding the gristle in his nose. While Ronnie blinked back the blood Dork hoisted him to his feet, and held him up as a captive target for Maguire. The ringed hand became a fist, and for the next five minutes Maguire used Ronnie as a punchbag, starting below the belt and working up.

Ronnie found the pain curiously reassuring; it seemed to heal his guilty psyche better than a string of Hail Marys. When the beating was over, and Dork had let him out, defaced, into the dark, there wasn't any anger left in him, only a need to finish the cleansing Maguire had begun.

He went home to Bernadette that night and told her a lie about being mugged in the steet. She was so consoling, it made him sick to be deceiving her, but he had no choice. That night, and the night after, were sleepless. He lay in his own bed, just a few feet from that of his trusting spouse, and tried to make sense of his feelings. He knew in his bones the truth would sooner or later become public knowledge. Better surely to go to the police, come clean. But that took courage, and his heart had never felt weaker. So he prevaricated through the Thursday night and the Friday, letting the bruises yellow and the confusion settle.

Then on Sunday, the shit hit the fan.

The lowest of the Sunday filth-sheets had his face on the front cover: complete with the banner headline: 'The Sex Empire of Ronald Glass'. Inside, were photographs, snatched from innocent circumstance and construed as guilt. Glass appearing to look pursued. Glass appearing to look devious. His natural hirsuteness made him seem ill-shaven; his neat hair-cut suggested the prison aesthetic favoured by some of the criminal fraternity. Being short-sighted he squinted; photographed squinting he looked like a lustful rat.

He stood in the newsagents, staring at his own face, and knew his personal Armageddon was on the horizon. Shaking, he read the terrible lies inside.

Somebody, he never exactly worked out who, had told the whole story. The pornography, the brothels, the sex-shops, the cinemas. The secret world of smut that Maguire had masterminded was here detailed in every sordid particular. Except that Maguire's name did not appear. Neither did Dork's, nor Henry's. It was Glass, Glass all the way: his guilt was transparent. He had been framed, neat as anything. A corrupter of children, the leader called him, Little Boy Blue grown fat and horny.

It was too late to deny anything. By the time he got back to the house Bernadette had gone, with the children in tow. Somebody had got to her with the news, probably salivating down the phone, delighting in the sheer dirt of it.

He stood in the kitchen, where the table was laid for a breakfast the family hadn't yet eaten, and would now never eat, and he cried. Not a great deal: his supply of tears was strictly limited, but enough to feel the duty done. Then, having finished with his gesture of remorse, he sat down, like any decent man who has been deeply wronged, and planned murder.

In many ways getting the gun was more difficult than anything that followed. It required some careful thought, some soft words, and a good deal of hard cash. It took him a day and a half to locate the weapon he wanted, and to learn how to use it.

Then, in his own good time, he went about his business.

Henry B. died first. Ronnie shot him in his own stripped pinewood kitchen in up-and-coming Islington. He had a cup of freshly-brewed coffee in his three-fingered hand and a look of almost pitiable terror on his face. The first shot struck him in the side, denting his shirt, and causing a little blood to come. Far less than Ronnie had been steeling himself for however. More confident, he fired again. The second shot hit his intended in the neck: and that seemed to be the killer. Henry B. pitched forward like a comedian in a silent movie, not relinquishing the coffee cup until the moment before he hit the floor. The cup spun in the mingled dregs of coffee and life, and rattled, at last, to a halt.

Ronnie stepped over to the body and fired a third shot straight through the back of Henry B.'s neck. This last bullet was almost casual; swift and accurate. Then he escaped easily out of the back gate, almost elated by the ease of the act. He felt as though he'd cornered and killed a rat in his cellar; an unpleasant duty that needed to be done.

The frisson lasted five minutes. Then he was profoundly sick.

Anyway, that was Henry. All out of tricks.

Dork's death was rather more sensational. He ran out of time at the Dog Track; indeed, he was showing Ronnie his winning ticket when he felt the long-bladed knife insinuate itself between his fourth and fifth ribs. He could scarcely believe he was being murdered, the expression on his pastry-fattened face was one of complete amazement. He kept looking from side to side at the punters milling around as though at any moment one of them would point, and laugh, and tell him that this was all a joke, a premature birthday game.

Then Ronnie twisted the blade in the wound (he'd read that this was surely lethal) and Dork realised that, winning ticket or not, this wasn't his lucky day.

His heavy body was carried along in the crush of the crowd for a good ten yards until it became wedged in the teeth of the turnstile. Only then did someone feel the hot gush from Dork, and scream.

By then Ronnie was well away.

Content, feeling cleaner by the hour, he went back to the house. Bernadette had been in, collecting clothes and favourite ornaments. He wanted to say to her: take everything, it means nothing to me, but she'd slipped in and gone again, like a ghost of a housewife. In the kitchen the table was still set for that final Sunday breakfast. There was dust on the cornflakes in the children's bowls; the rancid butter was beginning to grease the air. Ronnie sat through the late afternoon, through the dusk, through until the early hours of the following morning, and tasted his new found power over life and death. Then he went to bed in his clothes, no longer caring to be tidy, and slept the sleep of the almost good.

It wasn't so hard for Maguire to guess who'd wasted Dork and Henry B. Henry, though the idea of that particular worm turning was hard to swallow. Many of the criminal community had known Ronald Glass, had laughed with Maguire over the little deception that was being played upon the innocent. But no-one had believed him capable of such extreme sanctions against his enemies. In some seedier quarters he was now being saluted for his sheer bloody-mindedness; others, Maguire included, felt he had gone too far to be welcomed into the fold like a strayed sheep. The general opinion was that he be dispatched, before he did any more damage to the fragile balance of power.

So Ronnie's days became numbered. They could have been counted on the three fingers of Henry B.'s hand.

They came for him on the Saturday afternoon and took him quickly, without him having time to wield a weapon in his defence. They escorted him to a Salami and Cooked Meats warehouse, and in the icy white safety of the cold storage room they hung him from a hook and tortured him. Anyone with any claim to Dork's or Henry B.'s affections was given an opportunity to work out their grief on him. With knives, with hammers, with oxyacetylene torches. They shattered his knees and his elbows. They put out his eardrums, burned the flesh off the soles of his feet.

Finally, about eleven or so, they began to lose interest. The clubs were just getting into their rhythm, the gaming tables were beginning to simmer, it was time to be done with justice and get out on the town.

That was when Micky Maguire arrived, dressed to kill in his best bib and tucker. Ronnie knew he was there somewhere in the haze, but his senses were all but out, and he only half-saw the gun levelled at his head, half felt the noise of the blast bounce around the white-tiled room.

A single bullet, immaculately placed, entered his brain through the middle of his forehead. As neat as even he could have wished, like a third eye.

His body twitched on its hook a moment, and died.

Maguire took his applause like a man, kissed the ladies, thanked his dear friends who had seen this deed done with him, and went to play. The body was dumped in a black plastic bag on the edge of Epping Forest, early on Sunday morning, just as the dawn chorus was tuning up in the ash trees and the sycamores. And that, to all intents and purposes, was the end of that. Except that it was the beginning.

Ronnie's body was found by a jogger, out before seven on the following Monday. In the day between his being dumped and being found his corpse had already begun to deteriorate.

But the pathologist had seen far, far worse. He watched dispassionately while the two mortuary technicians stripped the body, folded the clothes and placed them in tagged plastic bags. He waited patiently and attentively while the wife of the deceased was ushered into his echoing domain, her face ashen, her eyes swelled to bursting with too many tears. She looked down at her husband without love, staring at the wounds and at the marks of torture quite unflinchingly. The pathologist had a whole story written behind this last confrontation between Sex-King and untroubled wife. Their loveless marriage, their arguments over his despicable way of life, her despair, his brutality, and now, her relief that the torment was finally over and she was released to start a new life without him. The pathologist made a mental note to look up the pretty widow's address. She was delicious in her indifference to mutilation; it made his mouth wet to think of her.

Ronnie knew Bernadette had come and gone; he could sense too the other faces that popped into the mortuary just to peer down at the Sex-King. He was an object of fascination, even in death, and it was a horror he hadn't predicted, buzzing around in the cool coils of his brain, like a tenant who refuses to be ousted by the bailiffs, still seeing the world hovering around him, and not being able to act upon it.

In the days since his death there had been no hint of escape from this condition. He had sat here, in his own dead skull, unable to find a way out into the living world, and unwilling, somehow, to relinquish life entirely and leave himself to Heaven. There was still a will to revenge in him. A part of his mind, unforgiving of trespasses, was prepared to postpone Paradise in order to finish the job he had started. The books needed balancing; and until Michael Maguire was dead Ronnie could not go to his atonement.

In his round bone prison he watched the curious come and go, and knotted up his will.

The pathologist did his work on Ronnie's corpse with all the respect of an efficient fish-gutter, carelessly digging the bullet out of his cranium, and nosing around in the stews of smashed bone and cartilage that had formerly been his knees and elbows. Ronnie didn't like the man. He'd leered at Bernadette in a highly unprofessional way; and now, when he was playing the professional, his callousness was positively shameful. Oh for a voice; for a fist, for a body to use for a time. Then he'd show this meat-merchant how bodies should be treated. The will was not enough though: it needed a focus, and a means of escape.

The pathologist finished his report and his rough sewing, flung his juice-shiny gloves and his stained instruments on to the trolley beside the swabs and the alcohol, and left the body to the assistants.

Ronnie heard the swing-doors close behind him as the man departed. Water was running somewhere, splashing into the sink; the sound irritated him.

Standing beside the table on which he lay, the two technicians discussed their shoes. Of all things, shoes. The banality of it, thought Ronnie, the life-decaying banality of it.

'You know them new heels, Lenny? The ones I got to put on my brown suedes? Useless. No bleeding good at all.'

'I'm not surprised.'

'And the price I paid for them. Look at that; just look at that. Worn through in a month.'

'Paper-thin.'

'They are, Lenny, they're paper-thin. I'm going to take them back.'

'I would.'

'I am.'

'I would.'

This mindless conversation, after those hours of torture, of sudden death, of the post-mortem that he'd so recently endured, was almost beyond endurance. Ronnie's spirit began to buzz round and round in his brain like an angry bee trapped in an upturned jam-jar, determined to get out and start stinging –

Round and round; like the conversation.

'Paper-bloody-thin.'

'I'm not surprised.'

'Bloody foreign. These soles. Made in fucking Korea.'

'Korea?'

'That's why they're paper-thin.'

It was unforgivable: the trudging stupidity of these people. That they should live and act and *be:* while he buzzed on and on, boiling with frustration. Was that fair?

'Neat-shot, eh Lenny?'

'What?'

'The stiff. Old what's his name the Sex-King. Bang in the middle of the forehead. See that? Pop goes the weasel.'

Lenny's companion, it seemed, was still preoccupied with his paper-thin sole. He didn't reply. Lenny inquisitively inched back the shroud from Ronnie's forehead. The lines of sawn and scalped flesh were inelegantly sewn, but the bullet hole itself was neat.

'Look at it.'

The other glanced round at the dead face. The head-wound had been cleaned after the probing pincers had worked at it. The edges were white and puckered.

'I thought they usually went for the heart,' said the sole-searcher.

'This wasn't any street-fight. It was an execution; formal like,' said Lenny, poking his little finger into the wound. 'It's a perfect shot. Bang in the middle of the forehead. Like he had three eyes.'

'Yeah . . .'

The shroud was tossed back over Ronnie's face. The bee buzzed on; round and round.

'You hear about third eyes, don't you?'

'Do you?'

'Stella read me something about it being the centre of the body.'

'That's your navel. How can your forehead be the centre of your body?'

'Well . . .'

'That's your navel.'

'No, it's more your spiritual centre.'

The other didn't deign to respond.

'Just about where this bullet-hole is,' said Lenny, still lost in admiration for Ronnie's killer.

The bee listened. The bullet-hole was just one of many holes in his life. Holes where his wife and children should have been. Holes winking up at him like sightless eyes from the pages of the magazines, pink and brown and hair-lipped. Holes to the right of him, holes to the left –

Could it be, at last, that he had found here a hole that he could profit by? Why not leave by the wound?

His spirit braced itself, and made for his brow, creeping through his cortex with a mixture of trepidation and excitement. Ahead, he could sense the exit door like the light at the end of a long tunnel. Beyond the hole, the warp and weft of his shroud glittered like a promised land. His sense of direction was good; the light grew as he crept, the voices became louder. Without fanfare Ronnie's spirit spat itself into the outside world: a tiny seepage of soul. The motes of fluid that carried his will and his consciousness were soaked up by his shroud like tears by tissues.

His flesh and blood body was utterly deserted now; an icy bulk fit for nothing but the flames.

Ronnie Glass existed in a new world: a white linen world like no state he had lived or dreamed before.

Ronnie Glass was his shroud.

Had Ronnie's pathologist not been forgetful he wouldn't have come back into the mortuary at that moment, trying to locate the diary he'd written the Widow Glass' number in; and, had he not come in, he would have lived. As it was –

'Haven't you started on this one yet?' he snapped at the technicians.

They murmured some apology or other. He was always testy at this time of night; they were used to his tantrums.

'Get on with it,' he said, stripping the shroud off the body and flinging it to the floor in irritation, 'before the fucker walks out of here in disgust. Don't want to get our little hotel a bad reputation, do we?'

'Yes, sir. I mean, no sir.'

'Well don't stand there: parcel it up. There's a widow wants him dispatched as soon as possible. I've seen all I need to see of him.'

Ronnie lay on the floor in a crumpled heap, slowly spreading his influence through this new-found land. It felt good to have a body, even if it was sterile and rectangular. Bringing a power of will to bear he hadn't known he possessed, Ronnie took full control of the shroud.

At first it refused life. It had always been passive: that was its condition. It wasn't use to occupation by spirits. But Ronnie wasn't to be beaten now. His will was an imperative. Against all rules of natural behaviour it stretched and knotted the sullen linen into a semblance of life.

The shroud rose.

The pathologist had located his little black book, and was in the act of pocketing it when this white curtain spread itself in his path, stretching like a man who has just woken from a deep sleep.

Ronnie tried to speak; but the only voice he could find was a whisper of the cloth on the air, too light, too insubstantial to be heard over the complaints of frightened men. And frightened they were. Despite the pathologist's call for assistance, none was forthcoming. Lenny and his companion were sliding away towards the swing-doors, gaping mouths babbling entreaties to any local god who would listen.

The pathologist backed off against the post-mortem table, quite out of gods.

'Get out of my sight,' he said.

Ronnie embraced him, tightly.

'Help,' said the pathologist, almost to himself. But help was gone. It was running down the corridors, still babbling, keeping its back to the miracle that was taking place in the mortuary. The pathologist was alone, wrapped up in this starched embrace, murmuring, at the last, some apologies he had found beneath his pride.

'I'm sorry, whoever you are. Whatever you are. I'm sorry.'

But there was an anger in Ronnie that would not have any truck with late converts; no pardons or reprieves were available. This fish-eyed bastard, this son of the scalpel had cut and

95

examined his old body as though it was a side of beef. It made Ronnie livid to think of this creep's oh-so-cool appraisal of life, death and Bernadette. The bastard would die, here, amongst his remains, and let that be an end to his callous profession.

The corners of the shroud were forming into crude arms now, as Ronnie's memory shaped them. It seemed natural to recreate his old appearance in this new medium. He made hands first: then digits: even a rudimentary thumb. He was like a morbid Adam raised out of linen.

Even as they formed, the hands had the pathologist about the neck. As yet they had no sense of touch in them, and it was difficult to judge how hard to press on the throbbing skin, so he simply used all the strength he could muster. The man's face blackened, and his tongue, the colour of a plum, stuck out from his mouth like a spear-head, sharp and hard. In his enthusiasm, Ronnie broke his neck. It snapped suddenly, and the head fell backwards at a horrid angle. The vain apologies had long since stopped.

Ronnie dropped him to the polished floor, and stared down at the hands he had made, with eyes that were still two pin-pricks in a sheet of stained cloth.

He felt certain of himself in this body, and God, he was strong; he'd broken the bastard's neck without exerting himself at all. Occupying this strange, bloodless physique he had a new freedom from the constraints of humanity. He was alive suddenly to the life of the air, feeling it now fill and billow him. Surely he could fly, like a sheet in the wind, or if it suited him knot himself into a fist and beat the world into submission. The prospects seemed endless.

And yet ... he sensed that this possession was at best temporary. Sooner or later the shroud would want to resume its former life as an idle piece of cloth, and its true, passive nature would be restored. This body had not been given to him, merely loaned; it was up to him to use it to the best of his vengeful abilities. He knew the priorities. First and foremost to find Michael Maguire and dispatch him. Then, if he still had the time left, he would see the children. But it wasn't wise to go visiting as a flying shroud. Better by far to work at this illusion of humanity, and see if he could sophisticate the effect.

He'd seen what freak creases could do, making faces appear in a crumpled pillow, or in the folds of a jacket hanging on the back of the door. More extraordinary still, there was the Shroud of Turin, in which the face and body of Jesus Christ had been miraculously imprinted. Bernadette had been sent a postcard of the Shroud, with every wound of lance and nail in place. Why couldn't he make the same miracle, by force of will? Wasn't he resurrected too?

He went to the sink in the morgue and turned off the running tap, then stared into the mirror to watch his will take shape. The surface of the shroud was already twitching and scurrying as he demanded new forms of it. At first there was only the primitive outline of his head, roughly shaped, like that of a snowman. Two pits for eyes: a lumpen nose. But he concentrated, willing the linen to stretch itself to the limits of its elasticity. And behold! it worked, it really worked! The threads complained, but acquiesced to his demands, forming in exquisite reproduction the nostrils, and then the eyelids; the upper lip: now the lower. He traced from memory the contours of his lost face like an adoring lover, and remade them in every detail. Now he began to make a column for the neck, filled with air, but looking deceptively solid. Below that the shroud swelled into a manly torso. The arms were already formed; the legs followed quickly on. And it was done.

He was re-made, in his own image.

The illusion was not perfect. For one thing, he was pure white, except for the stains, and his flesh had the texture of cloth. The creases of his face were perhaps too severe, almost cubist in appearance, and it was impossible to coax the cloth to make a semblance of either hair or nails. But he was as ready for the world as any living shroud could hope to be.

It was time to go out and meet his public.

'Your game, Micky.'

Maguire seldom lost at poker. He was too clever, and that used face too unreadable; his tired, bloodshot eyes never let anything out. Yet, despite his formidable reputation as a winner, he never cheated. That was his bond with himself. There was no lift in winning if there was a cheat involved. It was just stealing then; and that was for the criminal classes. He was a businessman, pure and simple.

Tonight, in the space of two and a half hours, he'd pocketed a tidy sum. Life was good. Since the deaths of Dork, Henry B.

Henry and Glass, the police had been too concerned with Murder to take much notice of the lower orders of Vice. Besides, their palms were well crossed with silver; they had nothing to complain about. Inspector Wall, a drinking companion of many years' standing, had even offered Maguire protection from the lunatic killer who was apparently on the loose. The irony of the idea pleased Maguire mightily.

It was almost three am. Time for bad girls and boys to be in their beds, dreaming of crimes for the morrow. Maguire rose from the table, signifying the end of the night's gambling. He buttoned up his waistcoat and carefully reknotted his lemon water-ice silk tie.

'Another game next week?' he suggested.

The defeated players agreed. They were used to losing money to their boss, but there were no hard feelings amongst the quartet. There was a tinge of sadness perhaps: they missed Henry B. and Dork. Saturday nights had been such joyous affairs. Now there was a muted tone over the proceedings.

Perlgut was the first to leave, stubbing out his cheroot in the brimming ashtray.

'Night, Mick.'

'Night, Frank. Give the kids a kiss from their Uncle Mick, eh?'

'Will do.'

Perlgut shuffled off, with his stuttering brother in tow.

'G-g-g-goodnight.'

'Night, Ernest.'

The brothers clattered down the stairs.

Norton was the last to go, as always.

'Shipment tomorrow?' he asked.

'Tomorrow's Sunday,' said Maguire. He never worked on Sundays; it was a day for the family.

'Not, today's Sunday,' said Norton, not trying to be pedantic, just letting it come naturally. 'Tomorrow's Monday.'

'Yes.'

'Shipment Monday?'

'I hope so.'

'You going to the warehouse?'

'Probably.'

'I'll pick you up then: we can run down together.'

'Fine.'

Norton was a good man. Humourless, but reliable.

'Night then.'

'Night.'

His three-inch heels were steel-tipped; they sounded like a woman's stilettos on the stairs. The door slammed below.

Maguire counted his profits, drained his glass of Cointreau, and switched out the light in the gaming room. The smoke was already staling. Tomorrow he'd have to get somebody to come up and open the window, let some fresh Soho smells in there. Salami and coffee beans, commerce and sleaze. He loved it, loved it with a passion, like a babe loves a tit.

As he descended the stairs into the darkened sex shop he heard the exchange of farewells in the street outside, followed by the slamming of car doors and the purring departure of expensive cars. A good night with good friends, what more could any man reasonably ask?

At the bottom of the stairs he stopped for a moment. The blinking street-sign lights opposite illuminated the shop sufficiently for him to make out the rows of magazines. Their plastic-bound faces glinted; siliconed breasts and spanked buttocks swelled from the covers like over-ripe fruit. Faces dripping mascara pouted at him, offering every lonely satisfaction paper could promise. But he was unmoved; the time had long since passed when he found any of that stuff of interest. It was simply currency to him; he was neither disgusted nor aroused by it. He was a happily married man after all, with a wife whose imagination barely stretched beyond page two of the *Kama Sutra*, and whose children were slapped soundly if they spoke one questionable word.

In the corner of the shop, where the Bondage and Domination material was displayed, something rose from the floor. Maguire found it hard to focus in the intermittent light. Red, blue. Red, blue. But it wasn't Norton, nor one of the Perlguts.

It was a face he knew however, smiling at him against the background of 'Roped and Raped' magazines. Now he saw: it was Glass, clear as day, and, despite the coloured lights, white as a sheet.

He didn't try to reason how a dead man could be staring at him, he just dropped his coat and his jaw, and ran.

The door was locked, and the key was one of two dozen on his ring. Oh Jesus, why did he have so many keys? Keys to the warehouse, keys to the greenhouse, keys to the whorehouse. And only that twitching light to see them by. Red, blue. Red, blue.

He rummaged amongst the keys and by some magical chance the first he tried slotted easily in the lock and turned like a finger in hot grease. The door was open, the street ahead.

But Glass glided up behind him soundlessly, and before he could step over the threshold he had thrown something around Maguire's face, a cloth of some kind. It smelt of hospitals, of ether or disinfectant or both. Magure tried to cry out but a fist of cloth was being thrust down his throat. He gagged on it, the vomit-reflex making his system revolt. In response the assassin just tightened his grip.

In the street opposite a girl Maguire knew only as Natalie (Model: seeks interesting position with strict disciplinarian) was watching the struggle in the doorway of the shop with a doped look on her vapid face. She'd seen murder once or twice; she'd seen rape aplenty, and she wasn't about to get involved. Besides, it was late, and the insides of her thighs ached. Casually she turned away down the pink-lit corridor, leaving the violence to take its course. Maguire made a mental note to have the girl's face carved up one of these days. If he survived; which seemed less likely by the moment. The red, blue, red, blue was unfixable now, as his airless brain went colourblind, and though he seemed to snatch a grip on his would-be assassin, the hold seemed to evaporate, leaving cloth, empty cloth, running through his sweating hands like silk.

Then someone spoke. Not behind him, not the voice of his assassin, but in front. In the street. Norton. It was Norton. He'd returned for some reason, God love him, and he was getting out of his car ten yards down the street, shouting Maguire's name.

The assassin's choke-hold faltered and gravity claimed Maguire. He fell heavily, the world spinning, to the pavement, his face purple in the lurid light.

Norton ran towards his boss, fumbling for his gun amongst the bric-à-brac in his pocket. The white-suited assassin was already backing off down the street, unprepared to take on another man. He looked, thought Norton, for all the world like a failed member of the Klu Klux Klan; a hood, a robe, a cloak. Norton dropped to one knee, took a double-handed aim at the man and fired. The result was startling. The figure seemed to balloon up, his body losing its shape, becoming a flapping mass of white cloth, with a face loosely imprinted on it. There was a noise like the snapping of Monday-washed sheets on a line, a sound that was out of place in this grimy back-street. Norton's confusion left him responseless for a moment, and the man-sheet seemed to rise in the air, illusory.

At Norton's feet, Maguire was coming round, groaning. He was trying to speak but having difficulty making himself understood through his bruised larynx and throat. Norton bent closer to him. He smelt of vomit and fear.

'Glass,' he seemed to be saying.

It was enough. Norton nodded, said hush. That was the face, of course, on the sheet. Glass, the imprudent accountant. He'd watched the man's feet fried, watched the whole vicious ritual; not to his taste at all.

Well, well: Ronnie Glass had some friends apparently, friends not above revenge.

Norton looked up, but the wind had lifted the ghost above the rooftops and away.

That had been a bad experience; the first taste of failure. Ronnie remembered it still, the desolation of that night. He'd lain, heaped in a rat-run corner of a derelict factory south of the river, and calmed the panic in his fibres. What good was this trick he'd mastered if he lost control of it the instant he was threatened? He must plan more carefully, and wind his will up until it would brook no resistance. Already he sensed that his energy was ebbing: and there was a hint of difficulty in restructuring his body this second time round. He had no time to waste with fumbled failures. He must corner the man where he could not possibly escape.

Police investigations at the mortuary had led round in circles for half a day; and now into the night. Inspector Wall of the Yard had tried every technique he knew. Soft words, hard words, promises, threats, seductions, surprises, even blows. Still Lenny told the same story; a ridiculous story he swore would be corroborated when his fellow technician came out of the catatonic state he'd now taken refuge in. But there was no way the Inspector could take the story seriously. A shroud that walked?

How could he put that in his report? No, he wanted something concrete, even if it was a lie.

'Can I have a cigarette?' asked Lenny for the umpteenth time. Wall shook his head.

'Hey, Fresco – ' Wall addressed his right-hand man, Al Kincaid. 'I think it's time you searched the lad again.'

Lenny knew what another search implied; it was a euphemism for a beating. Up against the wall, legs spread, hands on head: wham! His stomach jumped at the thought.

'Listen . . .' he implored.

'What, Lenny?'

'I didn't do it.'

'Of course you did it,' said Wall, picking his nose. 'We just want to know why. Didn't you like the old fucker? Make dirty remarks about your lady-friends, did he? He had a bit of a reputation for that, I understand.'

Al Fresco smirked.

'Was that why you nobbled him?'

'For God's sake,' said Lenny, 'you think I'd tell you a fucking story like that if I didn't see it with my own fucking eyes.'

'Language,' chided Fresco.

'Shrouds don't fly,' said Wall, with understandable conviction.

'Then where is the shroud, eh?' reasoned Lenny.

'You incinerated it, you ate it, how the fuck should I know?'

'Lauguage,' said Lenny quietly.

The phone rang before Fresco could hit him. He picked it up, spoke and handed it to Wall. Then he hit Lenny, a friendly slap that drew a little blood.

'Listen,' said Fresco, beathing with lethal proximity to Lenny as if to suck the air out of his mouth, 'We know you did it, see? You were the only one in the morgue *alive* to do it, see? We just want to know why. That's all. Just why.'

'Fresco.' Wall had covered the receiver as he spoke to the muscle-man.

'Yes, sir.'

'It's Mr Maguire.'

'Mr Maguire?'

'Micky Maguire.'

Fresco nodded.

'He's very upset.'

'Oh yeah? Why's that?'

'He thinks he's been attacked, by the man in the morgue. The pornographer.'

'Glass,' said Lenny, 'Ronnie Glass.'

'Ronald Glass, like the man says,' said Wall, grinning at Lenny.

'That's ridiculous,' said Fresco.

'Well I think we ought to do our duty to an upstanding member of the community, don't you? Duck in to the morgue will you, make sure – '

'Make sure?'

'That the bastard's still down there – '

'Oh.'

Fresco exited, confused but obedient.

Lenny didn't understand any of this: but he was past caring. What the hell was it to him anyway? He started to play with his balls through a hole in his left-hand pocket. Wall watched him with disdain.

'Don't do that,' he said. 'You can play with yourself as much as you like once we've got you tucked up in a nice, warm cell.'

Lenny shook his head slowly, and removed his hand from his pocket. Just wasn't his day.

Fresco was already back from down the hall, a little breathless.

'He's there,' he said, visibly brightened by the simplicity of the task.

'Of course he is,' said Wall.

'Dead as a Dodo,' said Fresco.

'What's a Dodo?' asked Lenny.

Fresco looked blank.

'Turn of phrase,' he said testily.

Wall of the Yard was back on the line, talking to Maguire. The man at the other end sounded well spooked; and his reassurances seemed to do little good.

'He's all present and correct, Micky. You must have been mistaken.'

Maguire's fear ran back through the phone line like a mild electric charge.

'I saw him, damn you.'

'Well, he's lying down there with a hole in the middle of his head, Micky. So tell me how *can* you have seen him?'

'I don't know,' said Maguire.

'Well then.'

'Listen . . . if you get the chance, drop by will you? Same arrangement as usual. I could put some nice work your way.'

Wall didn't like talking business on the phone, it made him uneasy.

'Later, Micky.'

'OK. Call by?'

'I will.'

'Promise?'

'Yes.'

Wall put down the receiver and stared at the suspect. Lenny was back to pocket billiards again. Crass little animal; another search was clearly called for.

'Fresco,' said Wall in dove-like tones, 'will you please teach Lenny not to play with himself in front of police officers?'

In his fortress in Richmond, Maguire cried like a baby.

He'd seen Glass, no doubt of it. Whatever Wall believed about the body being at the mortuary, he knew otherwise. Glass was out, on the street, foot-loose and fancy-free, despite the fact that he'd blown a hole in the bastard's head.

Maguire was a God-fearing man, and he believed in life after death, though until now he'd never questioned how it would come about. This was the answer, this blank-faced son of a whore stinking of ether: this was the way the afterlife would be. It made him weep, fearing to live, and fearing to die.

It was well past dawn now; a peaceful Sunday morning. Nothing would happen to him in the safety of the 'Ponderosa', and in full daylight. This was his castle, built with his hard-won thievings. Norton was here, armed to the teeth. There were dogs at every gate. No-one, living or dead, would dare challenge his supremacy in this territory. Here, amongst the portraits of his heroes: Louis B. Mayer, Dillinger, Churchill; amongst his family; amidst his good taste, his money, his *objets d'art*, here he was his own man. If the mad accountant came for him he'd be blasted in his tracks, ghost or no ghost. *Finis*.

After all, wasn't he Michael Roscoe Maguire, an empire builder? Born with nothing, he'd risen by virtue of his stock-broker's face and his maverick's heart. Once in a while, maybe, and only under very controlled conditions, he might let his darker appetites show; as at the execution of Glass. He'd taken genuine pleasure in that little scenario; *his* the *coup de grâce*, *his* the infinite compassion of the killing stroke. But his life of violence was all but behind him now. Now he was a bourgeois, secure in his fortress.

Raquel woke at eight, and busied herself with preparing breakfast.

'You want anything to eat?' she asked Maguire.

He shook his head. His throat hurt too much.

'Coffee?'

'Yes.'

'You want it in here?'

He nodded. He liked sitting in front of the window that overlooked the lawn and the greenhouse. The day was brightening; fat, fleecy clouds bucked the wind, their shadows passing over the perfect green. Maybe he'd take up painting, he thought, like Winston. Commit his favourite landscapes to canvas; maybe a view of the garden, even a nude of Raquel, immortalised in oils before her tits sagged beyond all hope of support.

She was back purring at his side, with the coffee.

'You, OK?' she asked.

Dumb bitch. Of course he wasn't OK.

'Sure,' he said.

'You've got a visitor.'

'What?' He sat up straight in the leather chair. 'Who?'

She was smiling at him.

'Tracy,' she said. 'She wants to come in and cuddle.'

He expelled a hiss of air from the sides of his mouth. Dumb, dumb bitch.

'You want to see Tracy?'

'Sure.'

The little accident, as he was fond of calling her, was at the door, still in her dressing gown.

'Hi, Daddy.'

'Hello, sweetheart.'

She sashayed across the room towards him, her mother's walk in embryo.

'Mummy says you're ill.'

'I'm getting better.'

'I'm glad.'

'So am I.'

'Shall we go out today?'

105

'Maybe.'

'See the fair?'

'Maybe.'

She pouted fetchingly, perfectly in control of the effect. Raquel's tricks all over again. He just hoped to God she wasn't going to grow up as dumb as her mother.

'We'll see,' he said, hoping to imply yes, but knowing he meant no.

She hoisted herself on to his knee and he indulged her tales of a five year old's mischiefs for a while, then sent her packing. Talking made his throat hurt, and he didn't feel too much like the loving father today.

Alone again, he watched the shadows waltz on the lawn.

The dogs began to bark just after eleven. Then, after a short while, they fell silent. He got up to find Norton, who was in the kitchen doing a jigsaw with Tracy. 'The Hay-Wain' in two thousand pieces. One of Raquel's favourites.

'You check the dogs, Norton?'

'No, boss.'

'Well fucking do it.'

He didn't often swear in front of the child; but he felt ready to go bang. Norton snapped to it. As he opened the back door Maguire could smell the day. It was tempting to step outside the house. But the dogs barked in a way that set his head thumping and his palms prickling. Tracy had her head down to the business of the jigsaw, her body tense with anticipation of her father's anger. He said nothing, but went straight back into the lounge.

From his chair he could see Norton striding across the lawn. The dogs weren't making a sound now. Norton disappeared from sight behind the greenhouse. A long wait. Maguire was just beginning to get agitated, when Norton appeared again, and looked up at the house, shrugging at Maguire, and speaking. Maguire unlocked the sliding door, opened it and stepped on to the patio. The day met him: balmy.

'What are you saying?' he called to Norton.

'The dogs are fine,' Norton returned.

Maguire felt his body relax. Of course the dogs were OK; why shouldn't they bark a bit, what else were they for? He was damn near making a fool of himself, pissing his pants just because the

106

dogs barked. He nodded to Norton and stepped off the patio on to the lawn. Beautiful day, he thought. Quickening his pace he crossed the lawn to the greenhouse, where his carefully nurtured Bonsai trees bloomed. At the door of the greenhouse Norton was waiting dutifully, going through his pockets, looking for mints.

'You want me here, sir?'

'No.'

'Sure?'

'Sure,' he said magnanimously, 'you go back up and play with the kid.'

Norton nodded.

'Dogs are fine,' he said again.

'Yeah.'

'Must have been the wind stirred them up.'

There was a wind. Warm, but strong. It stirred the line of copper beeches that bounded the garden. They shimmered, and showed the paler undersides of their leaves to the sky, their movement reassuring in its ease and gentility.

Maguire unlocked the greenhouse and stepped into his haven. Here in this artificial Eden were his true loves, nurtured on coos and cuttlefish manure. His Sargent's Juniper, that had survived the rigours of Mount Ishizuchi; his flowering quince, his Yeddo Spruce (Picea Jesoensis), his favourite dwarf, that he'd trained, after several failed attempts, to cling to a stone. All beauties: all minor miracles of winding trunk and cascading needles, worthy of his fondest attention.

Content, mindless for a while of the outside world, he pottered amongst his flora.

The dogs had fought over possession of Ronnie as though he were a plaything. They'd caught him breaching the wall and surrounded him before he could make his escape, grinning as they seized him, tore him and spat him out. He escaped only because Norton had approached, and distracted them from their fury for a moment.

His body was torn in several places after their attack. Confused, concentrating to try and keep his shape coherent, he had narrowly avoided being spotted by Norton.

Now he crept out of hiding. The fight had sapped him of energy, and the shroud gaped, so that the illusion of substance was spoiled. His belly was torn open; his left leg all but severed. The stains had multiplied; mucus and dog-shit joining the blood.

But the will, the will was all. He had come so close; this was not the time to relinquish his grip and let nature take its course. He existed in mutiny against nature, that was his state; and for the first time in his life (and death) he felt an elation. To be unnatural: to be in defiance of system and sanity, was that so bad? He was shitty, bloody, dead and resurrected in a piece of stained cloth; he was a nonsense. *Yet he was.* No-one could deny him being, as long as he had the will to be. The thought was delicious: like finding a new sense in a blind, deaf world.

He saw Maguire in the greenhouse and watched him awhile. The enemy was totally absorbed in his hobby; he was even whistling the National Anthem as he tended his flowering charges. Ronnie moved closer to the glass, and closer, his voice an oh-so-gentle moan in the failing weave.

Maguire didn't hear the sigh of cloth on the window, until Ronnie's face pressed flat to the glass, the features smeared and misshapen. He dropped the Yeddo Spruce. It shattered on the floor, its branches broken.

Maguire tried to yell, but all he could squeeze from his vocal cords was a strangled yelp. He broke for the door, as the face, huge with greed for revenge, broke the glass. Maguire didn't quite comprehend what happened next. The way the head and the body seemed to flow through the broken pane, defying physics, and reassembled in his sanctum, taking on the shape of a human being.

No, it wasn't quite human. It had the look of a stroke-victim, its white mask and its white body sagged down the right side, and it dragged its torn leg after it as it lunged at him.

He opened the door and retreated into the garden. The thing followed, speaking now, arms extended towards him.

'Maguire . . .'

It said his name in a voice so soft he might have imagined it. But no, it spoke again.

'Recognise me, Maguire?' it said.

And of course he did, even with its stroke-stricken, billowing features it was clearly Ronnie Glass.

'Glass,' he said.

'Yes,' said the ghost.

'I don't want – ' Maguire began, then faltered. What didn't he want? To speak with this horror, certainly. To know that it existed; that too. To die, most of all.

'I don't want to die.'

'You will,' said the ghost.

Maguire felt the gust of the sheet as it flew in his face, or perhaps it was the wind that caught this insubstantial monster and threw it around him.

Whichever, the embrace stank of ether, and disinfectant, and death. Arms of linen tightened around him, the gaping face was pressed on to his, as though the thing wanted to kiss him.

Instinctively Maguire reached round his attacker, and his hands found the rent the dogs had made in the shroud. His fingers gripped the open edge of the cloth, and he pulled. He was satisfied to hear the linen tearing along its weave, and the bear-hug fell away from him. The shroud bucked in his hand, the liquefied mouth wide in a silent scream.

Ronnie was feeling an agony he thought he'd left behind him with flesh and bone. But here it was again: pain, pain, pain.

He fluttered away from his mutilator, letting out what cry he could, while Maguire stumbled away up the lawn, his eyes huge. The man was close to madness, surely his mind was as good as broken. But that wasn't enough. He had to kill the bastard; that was his promise to himself and he intended to keep it.

The pain didn't disappear, but he tried to ignore it, putting all his energy into pursuing Maguire up the garden towards the house. But he was so weak now: the wind almost had mastery of him; gusting through his form and catching the frayed entrails of his body. He looked like a war-torn flag, fouled so it was scarcely recognisable, and just about ready to call it a day.

Except, except . . . Maguire.

Maguire reached the house, and slammed the door. The sheet pressed itself against the window, flapping ludicrously, its linen hands raking the glass, its almost-lost face demanding vengeance.

'Let me in,' it said, 'I *will* come in.'

Maguire stumbled backwards across the room into the hall.

'Raquel . . .'

Where was the woman?

'Raquel . . . ?'

'Raquel . . .'

She wasn't in the kitchen. From the den, the sound of Tracy's singing. He peered in. The little girl was alone. She was sitting in the middle of the floor, headphones clamped over her ears, singing along to some favourite song.

'Mummy?' he mimed at her.

'Upstairs,' she replied, without taking off the headphones.

Upstairs. As he climbed the stairs he heard the dogs barking down the garden. What was it doing? What was the fucker doing?

'Raquel . . . ? His voice was so quiet he could barely hear it himself. It was as though he'd prematurely become a ghost in his own house.

There was no noise on the landing.

He stumbled into the brown-tiled bathroom and snapped on the light. It was flattering, and he had always liked to look at himself in it. The mellow radiance dulled the edge of age. But now it refused to lie. His face was that of an old and haunted man.

He flung open the airing cupboard and fumbled amongst the warm towels. There! a gun, nestling in scented comfort, hidden away for emergencies only. The contact made him salivate. He snatched the gun and checked it. All in working order. This weapon had brought Glass down once, and it could do it again. And again. And again.

He opened the bedroom door.

'Raquel – '

She was sitting on the edge of the bed, with Norton inserted between her legs. Both still dressed, one of Raquel's sumptuous breasts teased from her bra and pressed into Norton's accommodating mouth. She looked round, dumb as ever, not knowing what she'd done.

Without thinking, he fired.

The bullet found her open-mouthed, gormless as ever, and blew a sizeable hole in her neck. Norton pulled himself out, no necrophiliac he, and ran towards the window. Quite what he intended wasn't clear. Flight was impossible.

The next bullet caught Norton in the middle of the back, and passed through his body, puncturing the window.

Only then, with her lover dead, did Raquel topple back across the bed, her breast spattered, her legs splayed wide. Maguire watched her fall. The domestic obscenity didn't disgust him; it was quite tolerable. Tit and blood and mouth and lost love and all; it was quite, quite tolerable. Maybe he was becoming insensitive.

He dropped the gun.

The dogs had stopped barking.

He slipped out of the room on to the landing, closing the door quietly, so as not to disturb the child.

Mustn't disturb the child. As he walked to the top of the stairs he saw his daughter's winsome face staring up at him from the bottom.

'Daddy.'

He stared at her with a puzzled expression.

'There was someone at the door. I saw them passing the window.'

He started to walk unsteadily down the stairs, one at a time. Slowly does it, he thought.

'I opened the door, but there was nobody there.'

Wall. It must be Wall. He would know what to do for the best.

'Was it a tall man?'

'I didn't see him properly, Daddy. Just his face. He was even whiter than you.'

The door! Oh Jesus, the door! If she'd left it open. Too late.

The stranger came into the hall and his face crinkled into a kind of smile, which Maguire thought was about the worst thing he'd ever seen.

It wasn't Wall.

Wall was flesh and blood: the visitor was a rag-doll. Wall was a grim man; this one smiled. Wall was life and law and order. This thing wasn't.

It was Glass of course.

Maguire shook his head. The child, not seeing the thing wavering on the air behind her, misunderstood.

'What did I do wrong?' she asked.

Ronnie sailed past her up the stairs, more a shadow now than anything remotely manlike, shreds of cloth trailing behind him. Maguire had no time to resist, nor will left to do so. He opened his mouth to say something in defence of his life, and Ronnie thrust his remaining arm, wound into a rope of linen, down Maguire's throat. Maguire choked on it, but Ronnie snaked on, past his protesting epiglottis, forging a rough way down his oesophagus into Maguire's stomach. Maguire felt it there, a fullness that was like overeating, except that it squirmed in the middle of his body, raking his stomach wall and catching hold of the lining. It was all so quick, Maguire had no time to die of suffocation. In the event, he might have wished to go that way,

111

horrid as it would have been. Instead, he felt Ronnie's hand convulse in his belly, digging deeper for a decent grip on his colon, on his duodenum. And when the hand had all it could hold, the fuckhead pulled out his arm.

The exit was swift, but for Maguire the moment would seemingly have no end. He doubled up as the disembowelling began, feeling his viscera surge up his throat, turning him inside out. His lights went out through his throat in a welter of fluids, coffee, blood, acid.

Ronnie pulled on the guts and hauled Maguire, his emptied torso collapsing on itself, towards the top of the stairs. Led by a length of his own entrails Maguire reached the top stair and pitched forward. Ronnie relinquished his hold and Maguire fell, head swathed in gut, to the bottom of the stairs, where his daughter still stood.

She seemed, by her expression, not the least alarmed; but then Ronnie knew children could deceive so easily.

The job completed, he began to totter down the stairs, uncoiling his arm, and shaking his head as he tried to recover a smidgen of human appearance. The effort worked. By the time he reached the child at the bottom of the stairs he was able to offer her something very like a human touch. She didn't respond, and all he could do was leave and hope that in time she'd come to forget.

Once he'd gone Tracy went upstairs to find her mother. Raquel was unresponsive to her questions, as was the man on the carpet by the window. But there was something about him that fascinated her. A fat, red snake pressing out from his trousers. It made her laugh, it was such a silly little thing.

The girl was still laughing when Wall of the Yard appeared, late as usual. Though viewing the death-dances the house had jumped to he was, on the whole, glad he'd been a late arrival at that particular party.

In the confessional of St Mary Magdalene's the shroud of Ronnie Glass was now corrupted beyond recognition. He had very little feeling left in him, just the desire, so strong he knew he couldn't resist for very much longer, to let go of this wounded body. It had served him well; he had no complaints to make of it. But now he was out of breath. He could animate the inanimate no longer.

He wanted to confess though, wanted to confess so very badly.

112

To tell the Father, to tell the Son, to tell the Holy Ghost what sins he'd performed, dreamt, longed for. There was only one thing for it: if Father Rooney wouldn't come to him then he'd go to Father Rooney.

He opened the door of the Confessional. The church was almost empty. It was evening now, he guessed, and who had the time for the lighting of candles when there was food to be cooked, love to be bought, life to be had? Only a Greek florist, praying in the aisle for his sons to be acquited, saw the shroud stagger from the Confessional towards the door of the Vestry. It looked like some damn-fool adolescent with a filthy sheet slung over his head. The florist hated that kind of Godless behaviour – look where it had got his children – he wanted to beat the kid around a bit, and teach him not to play silly beggars in the House of the Lord.

'Hey, you!' he said, too loudly.

The shroud turned to look at the florist, its eyes like two holes pressed in warm dough. The face of the ghost was so woebegone it froze the words on the florist's lips.

Ronnie tried the handle of the Vestry door. The rattling got him nowhere. The door was locked.

From inside, a breathless voice said:

'Who is it?' It was Father Rooney speaking.

Ronnie tried to reply, but no words would come. All he could do was rattle, like any worthy ghost.

'Who is it?' asked the good Father again, a little impatiently.

Confess me, Ronnie wanted to say, confess me, for I have sinned.

The door stayed shut. Inside, Father Rooney was busy. He was taking photographs for his private collection; his subject a favourite lady of his by the name of Natalie. A daughter of vice somebody had told him, but he couldn't believe that. She was too obliging, too cherubic, and she wound a rosary around her pert bosom as though she was barely out of a convent.

The jiggling of the handle had stopped now. Good, thought Father Rooney. They'd come back, whoever they were. Nothing was that urgent. Father Rooney grinned at the woman. Natalie's lips pouted back.

In the church Ronnie hauled himself to the altar, and genuflected.

Three rows back the florist rose from his prayers, incensed by

113

this desecration. The boy was obviously drunk, the way he was reeling, the man wasn't about to be frightened by a tuppenny-coloured death-mask. Cursing the desecrator in ripe Greek, he snatched at the ghost as it knelt in front of the altar.

There was nothing under the sheet: nothing at all.

The florist felt the living cloth twitch in his hand, and dropped it with a tiny cry. Then he backed off down the aisle, crossing himself back and forth, back and forth, like a demented widow. A few yards from the door of the church he turned tail and ran.

The shroud lay where the florist had dropped it. Ronnie, lingering in the creases, looked up from the crumpled heap at the splendour of the altar. It was radiant, even in the gloom of the candlelit interior, and moved by its beauty, he was content to put the illusion behind him. Unconfessed, but unfearful of judgment, his spirit crept away.

After an hour or so Father Rooney unbolted the Vestry, escorted the chaste Natalie out of the church, and locked the front door. He peered into the Confessional on his way back, to check for hiding children. Empty, the entire church was empty. St Mary Magdalene was a forgotten woman.

As he meandered, whistling, back to the Vestry he caught sight of Ronnie Glass' shroud. It lay sprawled on the altar steps, a forlorn pile of shabby cloth. Ideal, he thought, picking it up. There were some indiscreet stains on the Vestry floor. Just the job to wipe them up.

He sniffed the cloth, he loved to sniff. It smelt of a thousand things. Ether, sweat, dogs, entrails, blood, disinfectant, empty rooms, broken hearts, flowers and loss. Fascinating. This was the thrill of the Parish of Soho, he thought. Something new every day. Mysteries on the doorstep, on the altar-step. Crimes so numerous they would need an ocean of Holy Water to wash them out. Vice for sale on every corner, if you knew where to look.

He tucked the shroud under his arm.

'I bet you've got a tale to tell,' he said, snuffing out the votive candles with fingers too hot to feel the flame.

Scape-goats

It wasn't a real island the tide had carried us on to, it was a lifeless mound of stones. Calling a hunch-backed shit-pile like this an island is flattery. Islands are oases in the sea: green and abundant. This is a forsaken place: no seals in the water around it, no birds in the air above it. I can think of no use for a place like this, except that you could say of it: I saw the heart of nothing, and survived.

'It's not on any of the charts,' said Ray, poring over the map of the Inner Hebrides, his nail at the spot where he'd calculated that we should be. It was, as he'd said, an empty space on the map, just pale blue sea without the merest speck to sign the existence of this rock. It wasn't just the seals and the birds that ignored it then, the chart-makers had too. There were one or two arrows in the vicinity of Ray's finger, marking the currents that should have been taking us north: tiny red darts on a paper ocean. The rest, like the world outside, was deserted.

Jonathan was jubilant of course, once he discovered that the place wasn't even to be found on the map; he seemed to feel instantly exonerated. The blame for our being here wasn't his any longer, it was the map-makers': he wasn't going to be held responsible for our being beached if the mound wasn't even marked on the charts. The apologetic expression he'd worn since our unscheduled arrival was replaced with a look of self-satisfaction.

'You can't avoid a place that doesn't exist, can you?' he crowed. 'I mean, can you?'

'You could have used the eyes God gave you,' Ray flung back at him; but Jonathan wasn't about to be cowed by reasonable criticism.

'It was so sudden, Raymond,' he said. 'I mean, in this mist I didn't have a chance. It was on top of us before I knew it.'

It had been sudden, no two ways about that. I'd been in the galley preparing breakfast, which had become my responsibility since neither Angela nor Jonathan showed any enthusiasm for the task, when the hull of the 'Emmanuelle' grated on shingle, then ploughed her way, juddering, up on to the stony beach. There was a moment's silence: then the shouting began. I climbed up out of the galley to find Jonathan standing on deck, grinning sheepishly and waving his arms around to semaphore his innocence.

'Before you ask,' he said, 'I don't know how it happened. One minute we were just coasting along – '

'Oh Jesus Christ all-fucking Mighty,' Ray was clambering out of the cabin, hauling a pair of jeans on as he did so, and looking much the worse for a night in a bunk with Angela. I'd had the questionable honour of listening to her orgasms all night; she was certainly demanding. Jonathan began his defence-speech again from the beginning: 'Before you ask – ', but Ray silenced him with a few choice insults. I retreated into the confines of the galley while the argument raged on deck. It gave me no small satisfaction to hear Jonathan slanged; I even hoped Ray would lose his cool enough to bloody that perfect hook nose.

The galley was a slop bucket. The breakfast I'd been preparing was all over the floor and I left it there, the yolks of the eggs, the gammon and the french toasts all congealing in pools of spilt fat. It was Jonathan's fault; let him clear it up. I poured myself a glass of grapefruit juice, waited until the recriminations died down, and went back up.

It was barely two hours after dawn, and the mist that had shrouded this island from Jonathan's view still covered the sun. If today was anything like the week that we'd had so far, by noon the deck would be too hot to step on barefoot, but now, with the mist still thick, I felt cold wearing just the bottom of my bikini. It didn't matter much, sailing amongst the islands, what you wore. There was no one to see you. I'd got the best all over tan I'd ever had. But this morning the chill drove me back below to find a sweater. There was no wind: the cold was coming up out of the sea. It's still night down there, I thought, just a few yards off the beach; limitless night.

I pulled on a sweater, and went back on deck. The maps were out, and Ray was bending over them. His bare back was peeling from an excess of sun, and I could see the bald patch he tried to hide in his dirty-yellow curls. Jonathan was staring at the beach and stroking his nose.

'Christ, what a place,' I said.

He glanced at me, trying a smile. He had this illusion, poor Jonathan, that his face could charm a tortoise out of its shell, and to be fair to him there were a few women who melted if he so much as looked at them. I wasn't one of them, and it irritated him. I'd always thought his Jewish good looks too bland to be beautiful. My indifference was a red rag to him.

A voice, sleepy and pouting, drifted up from below deck. Our Lady of the Bunk was awake at last: time to make her late entrance, coyly wrapping a towel around her nakedness as she emerged. Her face was puffed up with too much red wine, and her hair needed a comb through it. Still she turned on the radiance, eyes wide, Shirley Temple with cleavage.

'What's happening, Ray? Where are we?'

Ray didn't look up from his computations, which earned him a frown.

'We've got a bloody awful navigator, that's all,' he said.

'I don't even know what happened,' Jonathan protested, clearly hoping for a show of sympathy from Angela. None was forthcoming.

'But where are we?' she asked again.

'Good morning, Angela,' I said; I too was ignored.

'Is it an island?' she said.

'Of course it's an island: I just don't know which one yet,' Ray replied.

'Perhaps it's Barra,' she suggested.

Ray pulled a face. 'We're nowhere near Barra,' he said. 'If you'll just let me retrace our steps – '

Retrace our steps, in the sea? Just Ray's Jesus fixation, I thought, looking back at the beach. It was impossible to guess how big the place was, the mist erased the landscape after a hundred yards. Perhaps somewhere in that grey wall there was human habitation.

Ray, having located the blank spot on the map where we were supposedly stranded, climbed down on to the beach and took a critical look at the bow. More to be out of Angela's way than anything else I climbed down to join him. The round stones of the beach were cold and slippery on the bare soles of my feet. Ray smoothed his palm down the side of the 'Emmanuelle', almost a caress, then crouched to look at the damage to the bow.

'I don't think we're holed,' he said, 'but I can't be sure.'

'We'll float off come high tide,' said Jonathan, posing on the bow, hands on hips, 'no sweat,' he winked at me, 'no sweat at all.'

'Will we shit float off!', Ray snapped. 'Take a look for yourself.'

'Then we'll get some help to haul us off.' Jonathan's confidence was unscathed.

'And you can damn well fetch someone, you asshole.'

'Sure, why not? Give it an hour or so for the fog to shift and I'll take a walk, find some help.'

He sauntered away.

'I'll put on some coffee,' Angela volunteered.

Knowing her, that'd take an hour to brew. There was time for a stroll.

I started along the beach.

'Don't go too far, love,' Ray called.

'No.'

Love, he said. Easy word; he meant nothing by it.

The sun was warmer now, and as I walked I stripped off the sweater. My bare breasts were already brown as two nuts, and, I thought, about as big. Still, you can't have everything. At least I'd got two neurons in my head to rub together, which was more than could be said for Angela; she had tits like melons and a brain that'd shame a mule.

The sun still wasn't getting through the mist properly. It was filtering down on the island fitfully, and its light flattened everything out, draining the place of colour or weight, reducing the sea and the rocks and the rubbish on the beach to one bleached-out grey, the colour of over-boiled meat.

After only a hundred yards something about the place began to depress me, so I turned back. On my right tiny, lisping waves crept up to the shore and collapsed with a weary slopping sound on the stones. No majestic rollers here: just the rhythmical slop, slop, slop of an exhausted tide.

I hated the place already.

Back at the boat, Ray was trying the radio, but for some reason all he could get was a blanket of white noise on every frequency. He cursed it awhile, then gave up. After half an hour, breakfast was served, though we had to make do with sardines, tinned mushrooms and the remains of the French toast. Angela served this feast with her usual aplomb, looking as though she was performing a second miracle with loaves and fishes. It was all but impossible to enjoy the food anyway; the air seemed to drain all the taste away.

'Funny isn't it – ' began Jonathan.

'Hilarious,' said Ray.

' – there's no fog-horns. Mist, but no horns. Not even the sound of a motor; weird.'

He was right. Total silence wrapped us up, a damp and smothering hush. Except for the apologetic slop of the waves and the sound of our voices, we might as well have been deaf.

I sat at the stern and looked into the empty sea. It was still grey, but the sun was beginning to strike other colours in it now: a sombre green, and, deeper, a hint of blue-purple. Below the boat I could see strands of kelp and Maiden's Hair, toys to the tide, swaying. It looked inviting: and anything was better than the sour atmosphere on the 'Emmanuelle'.

'I'm going for a swim,' I said.

'I wouldn't, love,' Ray replied.

'Why not?'

'The current that threw us up here must be pretty strong, you don't want to get caught in it.'

'But the tide's still coming in: I'd only be swept back to the beach.'

'You don't know what cross-currents there are out there. Whirlpools even: they're quite common. Suck you down in a flash.'

I looked out to sea again. It looked harmless enough, but then I'd read that these were treacherous waters, and thought better of it.

Angela had started a little sulking session because nobody had finished her immaculately prepared breakfast. Ray was playing up to it. He loved babying her, letting her play damn stupid games. It made me sick.

I went below to do the washing-up, tossing the slops out of the porthole into the sea. They didn't sink immediately. They floated in an oily patch, half-eaten mushrooms and slivers of sardines bobbing around on the surface, as though someone had thrown up on the sea. Food for crabs, if any self-respecting crab condescended to live here.

Jonathan joined me in the galley, obviously still feeling a little foolish, despite the bravado. He stood in the doorway, trying to catch my eye, while I pumped up some cold water into the bowl and half-heartedly rinsed the greasy plastic plates. All he wanted was to be told I didn't think this was his fault, and yes, of course he was a kosher Adonis. I said nothing.

'Do you mind if I lend a hand?' he said.

'There's not really room for two,' I told him, trying not to sound too dismissive. He flinched nevertheless: this whole episode had punctured his self-esteem more badly than I'd realized, despite his strutting around.

'Look,' I said gently, 'why don't you go back on deck: take in the sun before it gets too hot?'

'I feel like a shit,' he said.

'It was an accident.'

'An utter shit.'

'Like you said, we'll float off with the tide.'

He moved out of the doorway and down into the galley; his proximity made me feel almost claustrophobic. His body was too large for the space: too tanned, too assertive.

'I said there wasn't any room, Jonathan.'

He put his hand on the back of my neck, and instead of shrugging it off I let it stay there, gently massaging the muscles. I wanted to tell him to leave me alone, but the lassitude of the place seemed to have got into my system. His other hand was palm-down on my belly, moving up to my breast. I was indifferent to these ministrations: if he wanted this he could have it.

Above deck Angela was gasping in the middle of a giggling-fit, almost choking on her hysteria. I could see her in my mind's eye, throwing back her head, shaking her hair loose. Jonathan had unbuttoned his shorts, and had let them drop. The gift of his foreskin to God had been neatly made; his erection was so hygienic in its enthusiasm it seemed incapable of the least harm. I let his mouth stick to mine, let his tongue explore my gums, insistent as a dentist's finger. He slid my bikini down far enough to get access, fumbled to position himself, then pressed in.

Behind him, the stair creaked, and I looked over his shoulder in time to glimpse Ray, bending at the hatch and staring down at Jonathan's buttocks and at the tangle of our arms. Did he see, I wondered, that I felt nothing; did he understand that I did this dispassionately, and could only have felt a twinge of desire if I substituted his head, his back, his cock for Jonathan's? Soundlessly, he withdrew from the stairway; a moment passed, in which Jonathan said he loved me, then I heard Angela's laughter begin again as Ray described what he'd just witnessed. Let the bitch think whatever she pleased: I didn't care.

Jonathan was still working at me with deliberate but uninspired strokes , a frown on his face like that of a schoolboy trying to solve some impossible equation. Discharge came without warning, signalled only by a tightening of his hold on my shoulders, and a deepening of his frown. His thrusts slowed and stopped; his eyes found mine for a flustered moment. I wanted to kiss him, but he'd lost all interest. He withdrew still hard, wincing. 'I'm always sensitive when I've come,' he murmured, hauling his shorts up. 'Was it good for you?'

I nodded. It was laughable; the whole thing was laughable. Stuck in the middle of nowhere with this little boy of twenty-six, and Angela, and a man who didn't care if I lived or died. But then perhaps neither did I. I thought, for no reason, of the slops on the sea, bobbing around, waiting for the next wave to catch them.

Jonathan had already retreated up the stairs. I boiled up some coffee, standing staring out of the porthole and feeling his come dry to a corrugated pearliness on the inside of my thigh.

Ray and Angela had gone by the time I'd brewed the coffee, off for a walk on the island apparently, looking for help.

Jonathan was sitting in my place at the stern, gazing out at the mist. More to break the silence than anything I said:

'I think it's lifted a bit.'

'Has it?'

I put a mug of black coffee beside him.

'Thanks.'

'Where are the others?'

'Exploring.'

He looked round at me, confusion in his eyes. 'I still feel like a shit.'

I noticed the bottle of gin on the deck beside him.

'Bit early for drinking, isn't it?'

'Want some?'

'It's not even eleven.'

'Who cares?'

He pointed out to sea. 'Follow my finger,' he said.

I leaned over his shoulder and did as he asked.

'No, you're not looking at the right place. Follow my finger – see it?'

121

'Nothing.'

'At the edge of the mist. It appears and disappears. There! Again!'

I did see something in the water, twenty or thirty yards from the 'Emmanuelle's' stern. Brown-coloured, wrinkled, turning over.

'It's a seal,' I said.

'I don't think so.'

'The sun's warming up the sea. They're probably coming in to bask in the shallows.'

'It doesn't look like a seal. It rolls in a funny way – '

'Maybe a piece of flotsam – '

'Could be.'

He swigged deeply from the bottle.

'Leave some for tonight.'

'Yes, mother.'

We sat in silence for a few minutes. Just the waves on the beach. Slop. Slop. Slop.

Once in a while the seal, or whatever it was, broke surface, rolled, and disappeared again.

Another hour, I thought, and the tide will begin to turn. Float us off this little afterthought of creation.

'Hey!' Angela's voice, from a distance. 'Hey, you guys!'

You guys she called us.

Jonathan stood up, hand up to his face against the glare of sunlit rock. It was much brighter now: and getting hotter all the time.

'She's waving to us,' he said, disinterested.

'Let her wave.'

'You guys!' she screeched, her arms waving. Jonathan cupped his hands around his mouth and bawled a reply:

'What-do-you-want?'

'Come and see,' she replied.

'She wants us to come and see.'

'I heard.'

'Come on,' he said, 'nothing to lose.'

I didn't want to move, but he hauled me up by the arm. It wasn't worth arguing. His breath was inflammable.

It was difficult making our way up the beach. The stones were not wet with sea-water, but covered in a slick film of grey-green algae, like sweat on a skull.

Jonathan was having even more difficulty getting across the

beach than I was. Twice he lost his balance and fell heavily on his backside, cursing. The seat of his shorts was soon a filthy olive colour, and there was a tear where his buttocks showed.

I was no ballerina, but I managed to make it, step by slow step, trying to avoid the large rocks so that if I slipped I wouldn't have far to fall.

Every few yards we'd have to negotiate a line of stinking seaweed. I was able to jump them with reasonable elegance but Jonathan, pissed and uncertain of his balance, ploughed through them, his naked feet completely buried in the stuff. It wasn't just kelp: there was the usual detritus washed up on any beach: the broken bottles, the rusting Coke cans, the scum-stained cork, globs of tar, fragments of crabs, pale-yellow durex. And crawling over these stinking piles of dross were inch-long, fat-eyed blue flies. Hundreds of them, clambering over the shit, and over each other, buzzing to be alive, and alive to be buzzing.

It was the first life we'd seen.

I was doing my best not to fall flat on my face as I stepped across one of these lines of seaweed, when a little avalanche of pebbles began off to my left. Three, four, five stones were skipping over each other towards the sea, and setting another dozen stones moving as they jumped.

There was no visible cause for the effect.

Jonathan didn't even bother to look up; he was having too much trouble staying vertical.

The avalanche stopped: run out of energy. Then another: this time between us and the sea. Skipping stones: bigger this time than the last, and gaining more height as they leapt.

The sequence was longer than before: it knocked stone into stone until a few pebbles actually reached the sea at the end of the dance.

Plop.

Dead noise.

Plop. Plop.

Ray appeared from behind one of the big boulders at the height of the beach, beaming like a loon.

'There's life on Mars,' he yelled and ducked back the way he'd come.

A few more perilous moments and we reached him, the sweat sticking our hair to our foreheads like caps.

Jonathan looked a little sick.

'What's the big deal?' he demanded.

'Look what we've found,' said Ray, and led the way beyond the boulders.

The first shock.

Once we got to the height of the beach we were looking down on to the other side of the island. There was more of the same drab beach, and then sea. No inhabitants, no boats, no sign of human existence. The whole place couldn't have been more than half a mile across: barely the back of a whale.

But there was some life here; that was the second shock.

In the sheltering ring of the large, bald, boulders, which crowned the island was a fenced-in compound. The posts were rotting in the salt air, but a tangle of rusted barbed-wire had been wound around and between them to form a primitive pen. Inside the pen there was a patch of coarse grass, and on this pitiful lawn stood three sheep. And Angela.

She was standing in the penal colony, stroking one of the inmates and cooing in its blank face.

'Sheep,' she said, triumphantly.

Jonathan was there before me with his snapped remark: 'So what?'

'Well it's strange, isn't it?' said Ray. 'Three sheep in the middle of a little place like this?'

'They don't look well to me,' said Angela.

She was right. The animals were the worse for their exposure to the elements; their eyes were gummy with matter, and their fleeces hung off their hides in knotted clumps, exposing panting flanks. One of them had collapsed against the barbed-wire, and seemed unable to right itself again, either too depleted or too sick.

'It's cruel,' said Angela.

I had to agree: it seemed positively sadistic, locking up these creatures without more than a few blades of grass to chew on, and a battered tin bath of stagnant water, to quench their thirst.

'Odd isn't is?' said Ray.

'I've cut my foot.' Jonathan was squatting on the top of one of the flatter boulders, peering at the underside of his right foot.

'There's glass on the beach,' I said, exchanging a vacant stare with one of the sheep.

'They're so dead-pan,' said Ray. 'Nature's straight men.'

Curiously, they didn't look so unhappy with their condition, their stares were philosophical. Their eyes said: I'm just a sheep, I don't expect you to like me, care for me, preserve me, except for your stomach's sake. There were no angry baas, no stamping of a frustrated hoof.

Just three grey sheep, waiting to die.

Ray had lost interest in the business. He was wandering back down the beach, kicking a can ahead of him. It rattled and skipped, reminding me of the stones.

'We should let them free,' said Angela.

I ignored her; what was freedom in a place like this? She persisted, 'Don't you think we should?'

'No.'

'They'll die.'

'Somebody put them here for a reason.'

'But they'll *die*.'

'They'll die on the beach if we let them out. There's no food for them.'

'We'll feed them.'

'French toast and gin,' suggested Jonathan, picking a sliver of glass from his sole.

'We can't just leave them.'

'It's not our business,' I said. It was all getting boring. Three sheep. Who cared if they lived or –

I'd thought that about myself an hour earlier. We had something in common, the sheep and I.

My head was aching.

'They'll die,' whined Anglea, for the third time.

'You're a stupid bitch,' Jonathan told her. The remark was made without malice: he said it calmly, as a statement of plain fact.

I couldn't help grinning.

'What?' She looked as though she'd been bitten.

'Stupid bitch,' he said again. 'B-I-T-C-H.'

Angela flushed with anger and embarrassment, and turned on him. 'You got us stuck here,' she said, lip curling.

The inevitable accusation. Tears in her eyes. Stung by his words.

'I did it deliberately,' he said, spitting on his fingers and rubbing saliva into the cut. 'I wanted to see if we could leave you here.'

'You're drunk.'

'And you're stupid. But I'll be sober in the morning.'

The old lines still made their mark.

Outstripped, Angela started down the beach after Ray, trying to hold back her tears until she was out of sight. I almost felt some sympathy for her. She was, when it came down to verbal fisticuffs, easy meat.

'You're a bastard when you want to be,' I told Jonathan; he just looked at me, glassy-eyed.

'Better be friends. Then I won't be a bastard to you.'

'You don't scare me.'

'I know.'

The mutton was staring at me again. I stared back.

'Fucking sheep,' he said.

'They can't help it.'

'If they had any decency, they'd slit their ugly fucking throats.'

'I'm going back to the boat.'

'Ugly fuckers.'

'Coming?'

He took hold of my hand: fast, tight, and held it in his hand like he'd never let go. Eyes on me suddenly.

'Don't go.'

'It's too hot up here.'

'Stay. The stone's nice and warm. Lie down. They won't interrupt us this time.'

'You knew?' I said.

'You mean Ray? Of course I knew. I thought we put on quite a little performance.'

He drew me close, hand over hand up my arm, like he was hauling in a rope. The smell of him brought back the galley, his frown, his muttered profession ('Love you'), the quiet retreat.

Déja vu.

Still, what was there to do on a day like this but go round in the same dreary circle, like the sheep in the pen? Round and round. Breathe, sex, eat, shit.

The gin had gone to his groin. He tried his best but he hadn't got a hope. It was like trying to thread spaghetti.

Exasperated, he rolled off me.

'Fuck. Fuck. Fuck.'

Senseless word, once it was repeated, it had lost all its meaning, like everything else. Signifying nothing.

'It doesn't matter,' I said.

'Fuck off.'

'It really doesn't.'

He didn't look at me, just stared down at his cock. If he'd had a knife in his hand at that moment, I think he'd have cut it off and laid it on the warm rock, a shrine to sterility.

I left him studying himself, and walked back to the 'Emmanuelle'. Something odd struck me as I went, something I hadn't noticed before. The blue flies, instead of jumping ahead of me as I approached, just let themselves be trodden on. Positively lethargic; or suicidal. They sat on the hot stones and popped under my soles, their gaudy little lives going out like so many lights.

The mist was disappearing at last, and as the air warmed up, the island unveiled its next disgusting trick: the smell. The fragrance was as wholesome as a roomful of rotting peaches, thick and sickly. It came in through the pores as well as the nostrils, like a syrup. And under the sweetness, something else, rather less pleasant than peaches, fresh or rotten. A smell like an open drain clogged with old meat: like the gutters of a slaughter-house, caked with suet and black blood. It was the seaweed I assumed, although I'd never smelt anything to match the stench on any other beach.

I was half-way back to the 'Emmanuelle', holding my nose as I stepped over the bands of rotting weed, when I heard the noise of a little murder behind me. Jonathan's whoops of satanic glee almost drowned the pathetic voice of the sheep as it was killed, but I knew instinctively what the drunken bastard had done.

I turned back, my heel pivoting on the slime. It was almost certainly too late to save one of the beasts, but maybe I could prevent him massacring the other two. I couldn't see the pen; it was hidden behind the boulders, but I could hear Jonathan's triumphant yells, and the thud, thud of his strokes. I knew what I'd see before it came into sight.

The grey-green lawn had turned red. Jonathan was in the pen with the sheep. The two survivors were charging back and forth in a rhythmical trot of panic, baaing in terror, while Jonathan stood over the third sheep, erect now. The victim had partially collapsed, its stick-like front legs buckled beneath it, its back legs rigid with approaching death. Its bulk shuddered with nervous spasms, and its eyes showed more white than brown. The top of its skull had been almost entirely dashed to pieces, and the grey hash of its brain exposed, punctured by shards of its own bone, and pulped by the large round stone that Jonathan was still wielding. Even as I watched he brought the weapon down once more onto the sheep's brain-pan. Globs of tissue flew off in every direction, speckling me with hot mattter and blood. Jonathan looked like some nightmare lunatic (which for that moment, I suppose, he was). His naked body, so recently white, was stained as a butcher's apron after a hard day's hammering at the abattoir. His face was more sheep's gore than Jonathan –

The animal itself was dead. Its pathetic complaints had ceased completely. It keeled over, rather comically, like a cartoon character, one of its ears snagging the wire. Jonathan watched it fall: his face a grin under the blood. Oh that grin: it served so many purposes. Wasn't that the same smile he charmed women with? The same grin that spoke lechery and love? Now, at last, it was put to its true purpose: the gawping smile of the satisfied savage, standing over his prey with a stone in one hand and his manhood in the other.

Then, slowly, the smile decayed, as his senses returned.

'Jesus,' he said, and from his abdomen a wave of revulsion climbed up his body. I could see it quite clearly; the way his gut rolled as a throb of nausea threw his head forward, pitching half-digested gin and toast over the grass.

I didn't move. I didn't want to comfort him, calm him, console him – he was simply beyond my help.

I turned away.

'Frankie,' he said through a throat of bile.

I couldn't bring myself to look at him. There was nothing to be done for the sheep, it was dead and gone; all I wanted to do was run away from that little ring of stones, and put the sight out of my head.

'Frankie.'

I began to walk, as fast as I was able over such tricky terrain, back down towards the beach and the relative sanity of the 'Emmanuelle'.

The smell was stronger now: coming up out of the ground towards my face in filthy waves.

Horrible island. Vile, stinking, insane island.

All I thought was hate as I stumbled across the weed and the filth. The 'Emmanuelle' wasn't far off –

128

Then, a little pattering of pebbles like before. I stopped, balancing uneasily on the sleek dome of a stone, and looked to my left, where even now one of the pebbles was rolling to a halt. As it stopped another, larger pebble, fully six inches across, seemed to move spontaneously from its resting place, and roll down the beach, striking its neighbours and beginning another exodus towards the sea. I frowned: the frown made my head buzz.

Was there some sort of animal – a crab maybe – under the beach, moving the stones? Or was it the heat that in some way twitched them into life?

Again: a bigger stone –

I walked on, while behind the rattle and patter continued, one little sequence coming close upon another, to make an almost seamless percussion.

I began, without real focus or explanation, to be afraid.

Angela and Ray were sunning themselves on the deck of the 'Emmanuelle'.

'Another couple of hours before we can start to get the bitch off her backside,' he said, squinting as he looked up at me.

I thought he meant Angela at first, then realised he was talking about floating the boat out to sea again.

'May as well get some sun.' he smiled wanly at me.

'Yeah.'

Angela was either asleep or ignoring me. Whichever, it suited me fine.

I slumped down on the sun-deck at Ray's feet and let the sun soak into me. The specks of blood had dried on my skin, like tiny scabs. I picked them off idly, and listened to the noise of the stones, and the slop of the sea.

Behind me, pages were being turned. I glanced round. Ray, never able to lie still for very long, was flicking through a library book on the Hebrides he'd brought from home.

I looked back at the sun. My mother always said it burned a hole in the back of your eye, to look straight into the sun, but it was hot and alive up there; I wanted to look into its face. There was a chill in me – I don't know where it had come from – a chill in my gut and in between my legs – that wouldn't go away. Maybe I would have to burn it away by looking at the sun.

Some way along the beach I glimpsed Jonathan, tiptoeing down towards the sea. From that distance the mixture of blood and white skin made him look like some pie-bald freak. He'd stripped off his shorts and he was crouching at the sea's edge to wash off the sheep.

Then, Ray's voice, very quietly: 'Oh God,' he said, in such an understated way that I knew the news couldn't be brilliant.

'What is it?'

'I've found out where we are.'

'Good.'

'No, not good.'

'Why? What's wrong?' I sat upright, turning to him.

'It's here, in the book. There's a paragraph on this place.'

Angela opened one eye. 'Well?' she said.

'It's not just an island. It's a burial mound.'

The chill in between my legs fed upon itself, and grew gross. The sun wasn't hot enough to warm me that deep, where I should be hottest.

I looked away from Ray along the beach again. Jonathan was still washing, splashing water up on to his chest. The shadows of the stones suddenly seemed very black and heavy, their edges pressed down on the upturned faces of –

Seeing me looking his way Jonathan waved.

Can it be there are corpses under those stones? Buried face up to the sun, like holiday-makers laid out on a Blackpool beach?

The world is monochrome. Sun and shadow. The white tops of stones and their black underbellies. Life on top, death underneath.

'Burial?' said Angela. 'What sort of burial?'

'War dead,' Ray answered.

Angela: 'What, you mean Vikings or something?'

'World War 1, World War 11. Soldiers from torpedoed troop-ships, sailors washed up. Brought down here by the Gulf Stream; apparently the current funnels them through the straits and washes them up on the beaches of the islands around here.'

'Washes them up?' said Angela.

'That's what it says.'

'Not any longer though.'

'I'm sure the occasional fisherman gets buried here still,' Ray replied.

Jonathan had stood up, staring out to sea, the blood off his body. His hand shaded his eyes as he looked out over the blue-grey water, and I followed his gaze as I had followed his finger. A hundred yards out that seal, or whale, or whatever it was, had returned, lolling in the water. Sometimes, as it turned, it threw up a fin, like a swimmer's arm, beckoning.

'How many people were buried?' asked Angela, nonchalantly. She seemed completely unperturbed by the fact that we were sitting on a grave.

'Hundreds probably.'

'Hundreds?'

'It just says "many dead", in the book.'

'And do they put them in coffins?'

'How should I know?'

What else could it be, this God-forsaken mound – but a cemetery? I looked at the island with new eyes, as though I'd just recognised it for what it was. Now I had a reason to despise its humpy back, its sordid beach, the smell of peaches.

'I wonder if they buried them all over,' mused Angela, 'or just at the top of the hill, where we found the sheep? Probably just at the top; out of the way of the water.'

Yes, they'd probably had too much of water: their poor green faces picked by fish, their uniforms rotted, their dog-tags encrusted with algae. What deaths; and worse, what journeys after death, in squads of fellow corpses, along the Gulf Stream to this bleak landfall. I saw them, in my mind's eye, the bodies of the soldiers, subject to every whim of the tide, borne backwards and forwards in a slush of rollers until a casual limb snagged on a rock, and the sea lost possession of them. With each receding wave uncovered; sodden and jellied brine, spat out by the sea to stink a while and be stripped by gulls.

I had a sudden, morbid desire to walk on the beach again, armed with this knowledge, kicking over the pebbles in the hope of turning up a bone or two.

As the thought formed, my body made the decision for me. I was standing: I was climbing off the 'Emmanuelle'.

'Where are you off to?' said Angela.

'Jonathan,' I murmured, and set foot on the mound.

The stench was clearer now: that was the accrued odour of the dead. Maybe drowned men got buried here still, as Ray had suggested, slotted under the pile of stones. The unwary yachtsman, the careless swimmer, their faces wiped off with water. At the feet the beach flies were less sluggish than they'd been:

instead of waiting to be killed they jumped and buzzed ahead of my steps, with a new enthusiasm for life.

Jonathan was not to be seen. His shorts were still on the stones at the water's edge, but he'd disappeared. I looked out to sea: nothing: no bobbing head: no lolling, beckoning something.

I called his name.

My voice seemed to excite the flies, they rose in seething clouds. Jonathan didn't reply.

I began to walk along the margin of the sea, my feet sometimes caught by an idle wave, as often as not left untouched. I realised I hadn't told Angela and Ray about the dead sheep. Maybe that was a secret between us four. Jonathan, myself, and the two survivors in the pen.

Then I saw him: a few yards ahead – his chest white, wide and clean, every speck of blood washed off. A secret it is then,' I thought.

'Where have you been?' I called to him.

'Walking it off,' he called back.

'What off?'

'Too much gin,' he grinned.

I returned the smile, spontaneously; he'd said he loved me in the galley; that counted for something.

Behind him, a rattle of skipping stones. He was no more than ten yards from me now, shamelessly naked as he walked; his gait was sober.

The rattle of stones suddenly seemed rhythmical. It was no longer a random series of notes as one pebble struck another – it was a beat, a sequence of repeated sounds, a tick-tap pulse.

No accident: intention.

Not chance: purpose.

Not stone: thought. Behind stone, with stone, carrying stone –

Jonathan, now close, was bright. His skin was almost luminous with sun on it, thrown into relief by the darkness behind him.

Wait –

– What darkness?

The stone mounted the air like a bird, defying gravity. A blank black stone, disengaged from the earth. It was the size of a baby: a whistling baby, and it grew behind Jonathan's head as it shimmered down the air towards him.

The beach had been flexing its muscles, tossing small pebbles down to the sea, all the time strengthening its will to raise this boulder off the ground and fling it at Jonathan.

It swelled behind him, murderous in its intention, but my throat had no sound to make worthy of my fright.

Was he deaf? His grin broke open again; he thought the horror on my face was a jibe at his nakedness, I realized. He doesn't understand –

The stone sheered off the top of his head, from the middle of his nose upwards, leaving his mouth still wide, his tongue rooted in blood, and flinging the rest of his beauty towards me in a cloud of wet red dust. The upper part of his head was spilt on to the face of the stone, its expression intact as it swooped towards me. I half fell, and it screamed past me, veering off towards the sea. Once over the water the assassin seemed to lose its will somehow, and faltered in the air before plunging into the waves.

At my feet, blood. A trail that led to where Jonathan's body lay, the open edge of his head towards me, its machinery plain for the sky to see.

I was still not screaming, though for sanity's sake I had to unleash the terror suffocating me. Somebody must hear me, hold me, take me away and explain to me, before the skipping pebbles found their rhythm again. Or worse, before the minds below the beach, unsatisfied with murder by proxy, rolled away their grave stones and rose to kiss me themselves.

But the scream would not come.

All I could hear was the patter of stones to my right and left. They intend to kill us all for invading their sacred ground. Stoned to death, like heretics.

Then, a voice.

'For Christ's sake – '

A man's voice; but not Ray's.

He seemed to have appeared from out of thin air: a short, broad man, standing at the sea's edge. In one hand a bucket and under his arm a bundle of coarsely-cut hay. Food for the sheep, I thought, through a jumble of half-formed words. Food for sheep.

He stared at me, then down at Jonathan's body, his old eyes wild.

'What's gone on?' he said. The Gaelic accent was thick. 'In the name of Christ what's gone on?'

I shook my head. It seemed loose on my neck, almost as though I might shake it off. Maybe I pointed to the sheep-pen, maybe not. Whatever the reason he seemed to know what I was thinking, and began to climb the beach towards the crown of the island, dropping bucket and bundle as he went.

Half-blind with confusion, I followed, but before I could reach the boulders he was out of their shadow again, his face suddenly shining with panic.

'Who did that?'

'Jonathan,' I replied. I cast a hand towards the corpse, not daring to look back at him. The man cursed in Gaelic, and stumbled out of the shelter of the boulders.

'What have you done?' he yelled at me. 'My Christ, what have you done? Killing their gifts.'

'Just sheep,' I said. In my head the instant of Jonathan's decapitation was playing over and over again, a loop of slaughter.

'They demand it, don't you see, or they rise – '

'Who rise?' I said, knowing. Seeing the stones shift.

'All of them. Put away without grief or mourning. But they've got the sea in them, in their heads – '

I knew what he was talking about: it was quite plain to me, suddenly. The dead were here: as we knew. Under the stones. But they had the rhythm of the sea in them, and they wouldn't lie down. So to placate them, these sheep were tethered in a pen, to be offered up to their wills.

Did the dead eat mutton? No; it wasn't food they wanted. It was the gesture of recognition – as simple as that.

'Drowned,' he was saying, 'all drowned.'

Then, the familiar patter began again, the drumming of stones, which grew, without warning, into an ear-splitting thunder, as though the entire beach was shifting.

And under the cacophony three other sounds: splashing, screaming and wholesale destruction.

I turned to see a wave of stones rising into the air on the other side of the island –

Again the terrible screams, wrung from a body that was being buffeted and broken.

They were after the 'Emmanuelle'. After Ray. I started to run in the direction of the boat, the beach rippling beneath my feet. Behind me, I could hear the boots of the sheep-feeder on the stones. As we ran the noise of the assault became louder. Stones danced in the air like fat birds, blocking the sun, before plunging down to strike at some unseen target. Maybe the boat. Maybe flesh itself –

Angela's tormented screams had ceased.

I rounded the beach-head a few steps ahead of the sheep-feeder, and the 'Emmanuelle' came into sight. It, and its human contents, were beyond all hope of salvation. The vessel was being bombarded by endless ranks of stones, all sizes and shapes; its hull was smashed, its windows, mast and deck shattered. Angela lay sprawled on the remains of the sun deck, quite obviously dead. The fury of the hail hadn't stopped however. The stones beat a tattoo on the remaining structure of the hull, and thrashed at the lifeless bulk of Angela's body, making it bob up and down as though a current were being passed through it.

Ray was nowhere to be seen.

I screamed then: and for a moment it seemed there was a lull in the thunder, a brief respite in the attack. Then it began again: wave after wave of pebbles and rocks rising off the beach and flinging themselves at their senseless targets. They would not be content, it seemed, until the 'Emmanuelle' was reduced to flotsam and jetsam, and Angela's body was in small enough pieces to accommodate a shrimp's palate.

The sheep-feeder took hold of my arm in a grip so fierce it stopped the blood flowing to my hand.

'Come on,' he said. I heard his voice but did nothing. I was waiting for Ray's face to appear – or to hear his voice calling my name. But there was nothing: just the barrage of the stones. He was dead in the ruins of the boat somewhere – smashed to smithereens.

The sheep-feeder was dragging me now, and I was following him back over the beach.

'The boat' he was saying, 'we can get away in my boat – .'

The idea of escape seemed ludicrous. The island had us on its back, we were its objects utterly.

But I followed, slipping and sliding over the sweaty rocks, ploughing through the tangle of seaweed, back the way we'd come.

On the other side of the island was his poor hope of life. A rowing boat, dragged up on the shingle: an inconsequential walnut shell of a boat.

Would we go to sea in that, like the three men in a sieve?

He dragged me, unresisting, towards our deliverance. With every step I became more certain that the beach would suddenly rise up and stone us to death. Maybe make a wall of itself, a tower even, when we were within a single step of safety. It could play any game it liked, any game at all. But then, maybe the dead didn't like games. Games are about gambles, and the dead had already lost. Maybe the dead act only with the arid certainty of mathematicians.

He half threw me into the boat, and began to push it out into the thick tide. No walls of stones rose to prevent our escape. No towers appeared, no slaughtering hail. Even the attack on the 'Emmanualle' had ceased.

Had they sated themselves on three victims? er was it that the presence of the sheep-feeder, an innocent, a servant of these wilful dead, would protect me from their tantrums?

The rowing-boat was off the shingle. We bobbed a little on the backs of a few limp waves until we were deep enough for the oars, and then we were pulling away from the shore and my saviour was sitting opposite me, rowing for all he was worth, a dew of fresh sweat on his forehead, multiplying with every pull.

The beach receded; we were being set free. The sheep-feeder seemed to relax a little. He gazed down at the swill of dirty water in the bottom of the boat and drew in half a dozen deep breaths; then he looked up at me, his wasted face drained of expression.

'One day, it had to happen – ' he said, his voice low and heavy. 'Somebody would spoil the way we lived. Break the rhythm.'

It was almost soporific, the hauling of the oars, forward and back. I wanted to sleep, to wrap myself up in the tarpaulin I was sitting on, and forget. Behind us, the beach was a distant line. I couldn't see the 'Emmanuelle'.

'Where are we going?' I said.

'Back to Tiree,' he replied. 'We'll see what's to be done there. Find some way to make amends; to help them sleep soundly again.'

'Do they eat the sheep?'

'What good is food to the dead? No. No, they have no need of mutton. They take the beasts as a gesture of remembrance.'

Remembrance.

I nodded.

'It's our way of mourning them – '

He stopped rowing, too heartsick to finish his explanation, and too exhausted to do anything but let the tide carry us home. A blank moment passed.

Then the scratching.

A mouse-noise, no more, a scrabbling at the underside of the boat like a man's nails tickling the planks to be let in. Not one man: many. The sound of their entreaties multiplied, the soft dragging of rotted cuticles across the wood.

In the boat, we didn't move, we didn't speak, we didn't believe. Even as we heard the worst – we didn't believe the worst.

A splash off to starboard; I turned and he was coming towards me, rigid in the water, borne up by unseen puppeteers like a figure-head. It was Ray; his body covered in killing bruises and cuts: stoned to death then brought, like a gleeful mascot, like proof of power, to spook us. It was almost as though he were walking on water, his feet just hidden by the swell, his arms hanging loosely by his side as he was hauled towards the boat. I looked at his face: lacerated and broken. One eye almost closed, the other smashed from its orbit.

Two yards from the boat, the puppeteers let him sink back into the sea, where he disappeared in a swirl of pink water.

'Your companion?' said the sheep-feeder.

I nodded. He must have fallen into the sea from the stern of the 'Emmanuelle'. Now he was like them, a drowned man. They'd already claimed him as their play-thing. So they did like games after all, they hauled him from the beach like children come to fetch a playmate, eager that he should join the horse-play.

The scratching had stopped. Ray's body had disappeared altogether. Not a murmur off the pristine sea, just the slop of the waves against the boards of the boat.

I pulled at the oars –

'Row!' I screamed at the sheep-feeder. 'Row, or they'll kill us.'

He seemed resigned to whatever they had in mind to punish us with. He shook his head and spat onto the water. Beneath his floating phlegm something moved in the deep, pale forms rolled and somersaulted, too far down to be clearly seen. Even as I watched they came floating up towards us, their sea-corrupted faces better defined with every fathom they rose, their arms outstretched to embrace us.

A shoal of corpses. The dead in dozens, crab-cleaned and fish-picked, their remaining flesh scarcely sitting on their bones.

The boat rocked gently as their hands reached up to touch it.

The look of resignation on the sheep-feeder's face didn't falter for a moment as the boat was shaken backwards and forwards; at first gently, then so violently we were beaten about like dolls. They meant to capsize us, and there was no help for it. A moment later, the boat tipped over.

The water was icy; far colder than I'd anticipated, and it took the breath away. I'd always been a fairly strong swimmer. My strokes were confident as I began to swim from the boat, cleaving through the white water. The sheep-feeder was less lucky. Like many men who live with the sea, he apparently couldn't swim. Without issuing a cry or a prayer, he sank like a stone.

What did I hope? That four was enough: that I could be left to thumb a current to safety? Whatever hopes of escape I had, they were short-lived.

I felt a soft, oh so very soft, brushing of my ankles and my feet, almost a caress. Something broke surface briefly close to my head. I glimpsed a grey back, as of a large fish. The touch on my ankle had become a grasp. A pulpy hand, mushed by so long in the water, had hold of me, and inexorably began to claim me for the sea. I gulped what I knew to be my last breath of air, and as I did so Ray's head bobbed no more than a yard from me. I saw his wounds in clinical detail – the water cleansed cuts were ugly flaps of white tissue, with a gleam of bone at their core. The loose eye had been washed away by now, his hair, flattened to his skull, no longer disguised the bald patch at his crown.

The water closed over my head. My eyes were open, and I saw my hard-earned breath flashing past my face in a display of silver bubbles. Ray was beside me, consoling, attentive. His arms floated over his head as though he were surrendering. The pressure of the water distorted his face, puffing his cheeks out, and spilling threads of severed nerves from his empty eye-socket like the tentacles of a tiny squid.

I let it happen. I opened my mouth and felt it fill with cold water. Salt burned my sinuses, the cold stabbed behind my eyes. I felt the brine burning down my throat, a rush of eager water where water shouldn't go – flushing air from my tubes and cavities, 'til my system was overwhelmed.

Below me, two corpses, their hair swaying loosely in the current, hugged my legs. Their heads lolled and danced on rotted ropes of neck-muscle, and though I pawed at their hands,

138

and their flesh came off the bone in grey, lace-edged pieces, their loving grip didn't falter. They wanted me, oh how dearly they wanted me.

Ray was holding me too, wrapping me up, pressing his face to mine. There was no purpose in the gesture I suppose. He didn't know or feel, or love or care. And I, losing my life with every second, succumbing to the sea absolutely, couldn't take pleasure in the intimacy that I'd longed for.

Too late for love; the sunlight was already a memory. Was it that the world was going out – darkening towards the edges as I died – or that we were now so deep the sun couldn't penetrate so far? Panic and terror had left me – my heart seemed not to beat at all – my breath didn't come and go in anguished bursts as it had. A kind of peace was on me.

Now the grip of my companions relaxed, and the gentle tide had its way with me. A rape of the body: a ravaging of skin and muscle, gut, eye, sinus, tongue, brain.

Time had no place here. The days may have passed into weeks, I couldn't know. The keels of boats glided over and maybe we looked up from our rock-hovels on occasion and watched them pass. A ringed finger was trailed in the water, a splashless puddle clove the sky, a fishing line trailed a worm. Signs of life.

Maybe the same hour as I died, or maybe a year later, the current sniffs me out of my rock and has some mercy. I am twitched from amongst the sea-anemones and given to the tide. Ray is with me. His time too has come. The sea-change has occurred; there is no turning back for us.

Relentlessly the tide bears us – sometimes floating, bloated decks for gulls, sometimes half-sunk and nibbled by fish – bears us towards the island. We know the surge of the shingle, and hear, without ears, the rattle of the stones.

The sea has long since washed the plate clean of its leavings. Angela, the 'Emmanuelle', and Jonathan, are gone. Only we drowned belong here, face up, under the stones, soothed by the rhythm of tiny waves and the absurd incomprehension of sheep.

Human Remains

Some trades are best practised by daylight, some by night. Gavin was a professional in the latter category. In midwinter, in midsummer, leaning against a wall, or poised in a doorway, a fire-fly cigarette hovering at his lips, he sold what sweated in his jeans to all comers.

Sometimes to visiting widows with more money than love, who'd hire him for a weekend of illicit meetings, sour, insistent kisses and perhaps, if they could forget their dead partners, a dry hump on a lavender-scented bed. Sometimes to lost husbands, hungry for their own sex and desperate for an hour of coupling with a boy who wouldn't ask their name.

Gavin didn't much care which it was. Indifference was a trade-mark of his, even a part of his attraction. And it made leaving him, when the deed was done and the money exchanged, so much simpler. To say, 'Ciao', or 'Be seeing you', or nothing at all to a face that scarcely cared if you lived or died: that was an easy thing.

And for Gavin, the profession was not unpalatable, as professions went. One night out of four it even offered him a grain of physical pleasure. At worst it was a sexual abattoir, all steaming skins and lifeless eyes. But he'd got used to that over the years.

It was all profit. It kept him in good shoes.

By day he slept mostly, hollowing out a warm furrow in the bed, and mummifying himself in his sheets, head wrapped up in a tangle of arms to keep out the light. About three or so, he'd get up, shave and shower, then spend half an hour in front of the mirror, inspecting himself. He was meticulously self-critical, never allowing his weight to fluctuate more than a pound or two to either side of his self-elected ideal, careful to feed his skin if it was dry, or swab it if it was oily, hunting for any pimple that might flaw his cheek. Strict watch was kept for the smallest sign of venereal disease – the only type of lovesickness he ever suffered. The occasional dose of crabs was easily dispatched, but gonorrhoea, which he'd caught twice, would keep him out of service for three weeks, and that was bad for business; so he policed his body obsessively, hurrying to the clinic at the merest sign of a rash.

It seldom happened. Uninvited crabs aside there was little to do in that half-hour of self-appraisal but admire the collision of genes that had made him. He was wonderful. People told him that all the time. Wonderful. The face, oh the face, they would say, holding him tight as if they could steal a piece of his glamour.

Of course there were other beauties available, through the agencies, even on the streets if you knew where to search. But most of the hustlers Gavin knew had faces that seemed, beside his, unmade. Faces that looked like the first workings of a sculptor rather than the finished article: unrefined, experimental. Whereas he was made, entire. All that could be done had been; it was just a question of preserving the perfection.

Inspection over, Gavin would dress, maybe regard himself for another five minutes, then take the packaged wares out to sell.

He worked the street less and less these days. It was chancey; there was always the law to avoid, and the occasional psycho with an urge to clean up Sodom. If he was feeling really lazy he could pick up a client through the Escort Agency, but they always creamed off a fat portion of the fee.

He had regulars of course, clients who booked his favours month after month. A widow from Fort Lauderdale always hired him for a few days on her annual trip to Europe; another woman whose face he'd seen once in a glossy magazine called him now and then, wanting only to dine with him and confide her marital problems. There was a man Gavin called Rover, after his car, who would buy him once every few weeks for a night of kisses and confessions.

But on nights without a booked client he was out on his own finding a spec and hustling. It was a craft he had off perfectly. Nobody else working the street had caught the vocabulary of invitation better; the subtle blend of encouragement and detachment, of putto and wanton. The particular shift of weight from left foot to right that presented the groin at the best angle: so. Never too blatant: never whorish. Just casually promising.

He prided himself that there was seldom more than a few minutes between tricks, and never as much as an hour. If he made his play with his usual accuracy, eyeing the right disgruntled wife, the right regretful husband, he'd have them feed him (clothe him sometimes), bed him and bid him a satisfied goodnight all before the last tube had run on the Metropolitan Line to Hammersmith. The years of half-hour assignations, three blow- jobs and a fuck in one evening, were over. For one thing he simply didn't have the hunger for it any longer, for another he was preparing for his career to change course in the coming years: from street hustler to gigolo, from gigolo to kept boy, from kept boy to husband. One of these days, he knew it, he'd marry one of the widows; maybe the matron from Florida. She'd told him how she could picture him spread out beside her pool in Fort Lauderdale, and it was a fantasy he kept warm for her. Perhaps he hadn't got there yet, but he'd turn the trick of it sooner or later. The problem was that these rich blooms needed a lot of tending, and the pity of it was that so many of them perished before they came to fruit.

Still, this year. Oh yes, this year for certain, it had to be this year. Something good was coming with the autumn, he knew it for sure.

Meanwhile he watched the lines deepen around his wonderful mouth (it was, without doubt, wonderful) and calculated the odds against him in the race between time and opportunity.

It was nine-fifteen at night. September 29th, and it was chilly, even in the foyer of the Imperial Hotel. No Indian summer to bless the streets this year: autumn had London in its jaws and was shaking the city bare.

The chill had got to his tooth, his wretched, crumbling tooth. If he'd gone to the dentist's, instead of turning over in his bed and sleeping another hour, he wouldn't be feeling this discomfort. Well, too late now, he'd go tomorrow. Plenty of time tomorrow. No need for an appointment. He'd just smile at the receptionist, she'd melt and tell him she could find a slot for him somewhere, he'd smile again, she'd blush and he'd see the dentist then and there instead of waiting two weeks like the poor nerds who didn't have wonderful faces.

For tonight he'd just have to put up with it. All he needed was one lousy punter – a husband who'd pay through the nose for taking it in the mouth – then he could retire to an all-night club in Soho and content himself with reflections. As long as he didn't find himself with a confession-freak on his hands, he could spit his stuff and be done by half ten.

But tonight wasn't his night. There was a new face on the reception desk of the Imperial, a thin, shot-at face with a mismatched rug perched (glued) on his pate, and he'd been squinting at Gavin for almost half an hour.

The usual receptionist, Madox, was a closet-case Gavin had seen prowling the bars once or twice, an easy touch if you could handle that kind. Madox was putty in Gavin's hand; he'd even bought his company for an hour a couple of months back. He'd got a cheap rate too – that was good politics. But this new man was straight, and vicious, and he was on to Gavin's game.

Idly, Gavin sauntered across to the cigarette machine, his walk catching the beat of the muzack as he trod the maroon carpet. Lousy fucking night.

The receptionist was waiting for him as he turned from the machine, packet of Winston in hand.

'Excuse me . . . Sir.' It was a practised pronounciation that was clearly not natural. Gavin looked sweetly back at him.

'Yes?'

'Are you actually a resident at this hotel . . . Sir?'

'Actually – '

'If not, the management would be obliged if you'd vacate the premises immediately.'

'I'm waiting for somebody.'

'Oh?'

The receptionist didn't believe a word of it.

'Well just give me the name – '

'No need.'

'Give me the name – ', the man insisted, 'and I'll gladly check to see if your . . . contact . . . is in the hotel.'

The bastard was going to try and push it, which narrowed the options. Either Gavin could choose to play it cool, and leave the foyer, or play the outraged customer and stare the other man down. He chose, more to be bloodyminded than because it was good tactics, to do the latter.

'You don't have any right – ' he began to bluster, but the receptionist wasn't moved.

'Look, sonny – ' he said, 'I know what you're up to, so don't try and get snotty with me or I'll fetch the police.' He'd lost control of his elocution: it was getting further south of the river with every syllable. 'We've got a nice clientele here, and they don't want no truck with the likes of you, see?'

143

'Fucker,' said Gavin very quietly.

'Well that's one up from a cocksucker, isn't it?'

Touché.

'Now, sonny – you want to mince out of here under your own steam or be carried out in cuffs by the boys in blue?'

Gavin played his last card.

'Where's Mr Madox? I want to see Mr Madox: he knows me.'

'I'm sure he does,' the receptionist snorted, 'I'm bloody sure he does. He was dismissed for improper conduct – ' The artificial accent was re-establishing itself ' – so I wouldn't try dropping his name here if I were you. OK? On your way.'

Upper hand well and truly secured, the receptionist stood back like a matador and gestured for the bull to go by.

'The management thanks you for your patronage. Please don't call again.'

Game, set and match to the man with the rug. What the hell; there were other hotels, other foyers, other receptionists. He didn't have to take all this shit.

As Gavin pushed the door open he threw a smiling 'Be seeing you' over his shoulder. Perhaps that would make the tick sweat a little one of these nights when he was walking home and he heard a young man's step on the street behind him. It was a petty satisfaction, but it was something.

The door swung closed, sealing the warmth in and Gavin out. It was colder, substantially colder, than it had been when he'd stepped into the foyer. A thin drizzle had begun, which threatened to worsen as he hurried down Park Lane towards South Kensington. There were a couple of hotels on the High Street he could hole up in for a while; if nothing came of that he'd admit defeat.

The traffic surged around Hyde Park Corner, speeding to Knightsbridge or Victoria, purposeful, shining. He pictured himself standing on the concrete island between the two contrary streams of cars, his fingertips thrust into his jeans (they were too tight for him to get more than the first joint into the pockets), solitary, forlorn.

A wave of unhappiness came up from some buried place in him. He was twenty-four and five months. He had hustled, on and off and on again, since he was seventeen, promising himself that he'd find a marriageable widow (the gigolo's pension) or a legitimate occupation before he was twenty-five.

But time passed and nothing came of his ambitions. He just lost momentum and gained another line beneath the eye.

And the traffic still came in shining streams, lights signalling this imperative or that, cars full of people with ladders to climb and snakes to wrestle, their passage isolating him from the bank, from safety, with its hunger for destination.

He was not what he'd dreamed he'd be, or promised his secret self.

And youth was yesterday.

Where was he to go now? The flat would feel like a prison tonight, even if he smoked a little dope to take the edge off the room. He wanted, no, he *needed* to be with somebody tonight. Just to see his beauty through somebody else's eyes. Be told how perfect his proportions were, be wined and dined and flattered stupid, even if it was by Quasimodo's richer, uglier brother. Tonight he needed a fix of affection.

The pick-up was so damned easy it almost made him forget the episode in the foyer of the Imperial. A guy of fifty-five or so, well-heeled: Gucci shoes, a very classy overcoat. In a word: quality.

Gavin was standing in the doorway of a tiny art-house cinema, looking over the times of the Truffaut movie they were showing, when he became aware of the punter staring at him. He glanced at the guy to be certain there was a pick-up in the offing. The direct look seemed to unnerve the punter; he moved on; then he seemed to change his mind, muttered something to himself, and retraced his steps, showing patently false interest in the movie schedule. Obviously not too familiar with this game, Gavin thought; a novice.

Casually Gavin took out a Winston and lit it, the flare of the match in his cupped hands glossing his cheekbones golden. He'd done it a thousand times, as often as not in the mirror for his own pleasure. He had the glance up from the tiny fire off pat: it always did the trick. This time when he met the nervous eyes of the punter, the other didn't back away.

He drew on the cigarette, flicking out the match and letting it drop. He hadn't made a pick-up like this in several months, but he was well satisfied that he still had the knack. The faultless recognition of a potential client, the implicit offer in eyes and lips, that could be construed as innocent friendliness if he'd made an error.

This was no error, however, this was the genuine article. The man's eyes were glued to Gavin, so enamoured of him he seemed to be hurting with it. His mouth was open, as though the words of introduction had failed him. Not much of a face, but far from ugly. Tanned too often, and too quickly: maybe he'd lived abroad. He was assuming the man was English: his prevarication suggested it.

Against habit, Gavin made the opening move.

'You like French movies?'

The punter seemed to deflate with relief that the silence between them had been broken.

'Yes,' he said.

'You going in?'

The man pulled a face.

'I . . . I . . . don't think I will.'

'Bit cold . . .'

'Yes. It is.'

'Bit cold for standing around, I mean.'

'Oh – yes.'

The punter took the bait.

'Maybe . . . you'd like a drink?'

Gavin smiled.

'Sure, why not?'

'My flat's not far.'

'Sure.'

'I was getting a bit cheesed off, you know, at home.'

'I know the feeling.'

Now the other man smiled. 'You are . . .?'

'Gavin.'

The man offered his leather-gloved hand. Very formal, business-like. The grip as they shook was strong, no trace of his earlier hesitation remaining.

'I'm Kenneth,' he said, 'Ken Reynolds.'

'Ken.'

'Shall we get out of the cold?'

'Suits me.'

'I'm only a short walk from here.'

A wave of musty, centrally-heated air hit them as Reynolds opened the door of his apartment. Climbing the three flights of stairs had snatched Gavin's breath, but Reynolds wasn't slowed at all. Health freak maybe. Occupation? Something in the city. The handshake, the leather gloves. Maybe Civil Service.

'Come in, come in.'

There was money here. Underfoot the pile of the carpet was lush, hushing their steps as they entered. The hallway was almost bare: a calendar hung on the wall, a small table with telephone, a heap of directories, a coat-stand.

'It's warmer in here.'

Reynolds was shrugging off his coat and hanging it up. His gloves remained on as he led Gavin a few yards down the hallway and into a large room.

'Let's have your jacket,' he said.

'Oh . . . sure.'

Gavin took off his jacket, and Reynolds slipped out into the hall with it. When he came in again he was working off his gloves; a slick of sweat made it a difficult job. The guy was still nervous: even on his home ground. Usually they started to calm down once they were safe behind locked doors. Not this one: he was a catalogue of fidgets.

'Can I get you a drink?'

'Yeah; that would be good.'

'What's your poison?'

'Vodka.'

'Surely. Anything with it?'

'Just a drop of water.'

'Purist, eh?'

Gavin didn't quite understand the remark.

'Yeah,' he said.

'Man after my own heart. Will you give me a moment – I'll just fetch some ice.'

'No problem.'

Reynolds dropped the gloves on a chair by the door, and left Gavin to the room. It, like the hallway, was almost stiflingly warm, but there was nothing homely or welcoming about it. Whatever his profession, Reynolds was a collector. The room was dominated by displays of antiquities, mounted on the walls, and lined up on shelves. There was very little furniture, and what there was seemed odd: battered tubular frame chairs had no place in an apartment this expensive. Maybe the man was a university don, or a museum governor, something academic. This was no stockbroker's living room.

Gavin knew nothing about art, and even less about history, so the displays meant very little to him, but he went to have a closer look, just to show willing. The guy was bound to ask him what he thought of the stuff. The shelves were deadly dull. Bits and pieces of pottery and sculpture: nothing in its entirety, just fragments. On some of the shards there remained a glimpse of design, though age had almost washed the colours out. Some of the sculpture was recognisably human: part of a torso, or foot (all five toes in place), a face that was all but eaten away, no longer male or female. Gavin stifled a yawn. The heat, the exhibits and the thought of sex made him lethargic.

He turned his dulled attention to the wall-hung pieces. They were more impressive then the stuff on the shelves but they were still far from complete. He couldn't see why anyone would want to look at such broken things; what was the fascination? The stone reliefs mounted on the wall were pitted and eroded, so that the skins of the figures looked leprous, and the Latin inscriptions were almost wiped out. There was nothing beautiful about them: too spoiled for beauty. They made him feel dirty somehow, as though their condition was contagious.

Only one of the exhibits struck him as interesting: a tombstone, or what looked to him to be a tombstone, which was larger than the other reliefs and in slightly better condition. A man on a horse, carrying a sword, loomed over his headless enemy. Under the picture, a few words in Latin. The front legs of the horse had been broken off, and the pillars that bounded the design were badly defaced by age, otherwise the image made sense. There was even a trace of personality in the crudely made face: a long nose, a wide mouth; an individual.

Gavin reached to touch the inscription, but withdrew his fingers as he heard Reynolds enter.

'No, please touch it,' said his host. 'It's there to take pleasure in. Touch away.'

Now that he'd been invited to touch the thing, the desire had melted away. He felt embarrassed; caught in the act.

'Go on,' Reynolds insisted.

Gavin touched the carving. Cold stone, gritty under his finger-tips.

'It's Roman,' said Reynolds.

'Tombstone?'

'Yes. Found near Newcastle.'

'Who was he?'

'His name was Flavinus. He was a regimental standard-bearer.'

What Gavin had assumed to be a sword was, on closer inspection, a standard. It ended in an almost erased motif: maybe a bee, a flower, a wheel.

'You an archaeologist, then?'

'That's part of my business. I research sites, occasionally oversee digs; but most of the time I restore artifacts.'

'Like these?'

'Roman Britain's my personal obsession.'

He put down the glasses he was carrying and crossed to the pottery-laden shelves.

'This is stuff I've collected over the years. I've never quite got over the thrill of handling objects that haven't seen the light of day for centuries. It's like plugging into history. You know what I mean?'

'Yeah.'

Reynolds picked a fragment of pottery off the shelf.

'Of course all the best finds are claimed by the major collections. But if one's canny, one manages to keep a few pieces back. They were an incredible influence, the Romans. Civil engineers, road-layers, bridge builders.'

Reynolds gave a sudden laugh at his burst of enthusiasm.

'Oh hell,' he said, 'Reynolds is lecturing again. Sorry. I get carried away.'

Replacing the pottery-shard in its niche on the shelf, he returned to the glasses, and started pouring drinks. With his back to Gavin, he managed to say: 'Are you expensive?'

Gavin hesitated. The man's nervousness was catching and the sudden tilt of the conversation from the Romans to the price of a blow-job took some adjustment.

'It depends,' he flannelled.

'Ah . . .' said the other, still busying himself with the glasses, 'you mean what is the precise nature of my – er – requirement?'

'Yeah.'

'Of course.'

He turned and handed Gavin a healthy-sized glass of vodka. No ice.

'I won't be demanding of you,' he said.

'I don't come cheap.'

'I'm sure you don't,' Reynolds tried a smile, but it wouldn't stick to his face, 'and I'm prepared to pay you well. Will you be able to stay the night?'

'Do you want me to?'

Reynolds frowned into his glass.

'I suppose I do.'

'Then yes.'

The host's mood seemed to change, suddenly: indecision was replaced by a spurt of conviction.

'Cheers,' he said, clinking his whisky-filled glass against Gavin's. 'To love and life and anything else that's worth paying for.'

The double-edged remark didn't escape Gavin: the guy was obviously tied up in knots about what he was doing.

'I'll drink to that,' said Gavin and took a gulp of the vodka.

The drinks came fast after that, and just about his third vodka Gavin began to feel mellower than he'd felt in a hell of a long time, content to listen to Reynolds' talk of excavations and the glories of Rome with only one ear. His mind was drifting, an easy feeling. Obviously he was going to be here for the night, or at least until the early hours of the morning, so why not drink the punter's vodka and enjoy the experience for what it offered? Larer, probably much later to judge by the way the guy was rambling, there'd be some drink-slurred sex in a darkened room, and that would be that. He'd had customers like this before. They were lonely, perhaps between lovers, and usually simple to please. It wasn't sex this guy was buying, it was company, another body to share his space awhile; easy money.

And then, the noise.

At first Gavin thought the beating sound was in his head, until Reynolds stood up, a twitch at his mouth. The air of well-being had disappeared.

'What's that?' asked Gavin, also getting up, dizzy with drink.

'It's all right – ' Reynolds, palms were pressing him down into his chair. 'Stay here – '

The sound intensified. A drummer in an oven, beating as he burned.

'Please, please stay here a moment. It's just somebody up-stairs.'

Reynolds was lying, the racket wasn't coming from upstairs. It was from somewhere else in the flat, a rhythmical thumping, that speeded up and slowed and speeded again.

'Help yourself to a drink,' said Reynolds at the door, face flushed. 'Damn neighbours . . .'

The summons, for that was surely what it was, was already subsiding.

'A moment only,' Reynolds promised, and closed the door behind him.

Gavin had experienced bad scenes before: tricks whose lovers appeared at inappropriate moments; guys who wanted to beat him up for a price – one who got bitten by guilt in a hotel room and smashed the place to smithereens. These things happened. But Reynolds was different: nothing about him said weird. At the back of his mind, at the very back, Gavin was quietly reminding himself that the other guys hadn't seemed bad at the beginning. Ah hell; he put the doubts away. If he started to get the jitters every time he went with a new face he'd soon stop working altogether. Somewhere along the line he had to trust to luck and his instinct, and his instinct told him that this punter was not given to throwing fits.

Taking a quick swipe from his glass, he refilled it, and waited.

The noise had stopped altogether, and it became increasingly easier to rearrange the facts: maybe it had been an upstairs neighbour after all. Certainly there was no sound of Reynolds moving around in the flat.

His attention wandered around the room looking for something to occupy it awhile, and came back to the tombstone on the wall.

Flavinus the Standard-Bearer.

There was something satisfying about the idea of having your likeness, however crude, carved in stone and put up on the spot where your bones lay, even if some historian was going to separate bones and stone in the fullness of time. Gavin's father had insisted on burial rather than cremation: How else, he'd always said, was he going to be remembered? Who'd ever go to an urn, in a wall, and cry? The irony was that nobody ever went to his grave either: Gavin had been perhaps twice in the years since his father's death. A plain stone bearing a name, a date, and a platitude. He couldn't even remember the year his father died.

People remembered Flavinus though; people who'd never known him, or a life like his, knew him now. Gavin stood up and touched the standard-bearer's name, the crudely chased 'FLA-VINVS' that was the second word of the inscription.

Suddenly, the noise again, more frenzied than ever. Gavin turned away from the tombstone and looked at the door, half-expecting Reynolds to be standing there with a word of explanation. Nobody appeared.

'Damn it.'

The noise continued, a tattoo. Somebody, somewhere, was very angry. And this time there could be no self-deception: the drummer was here, on this floor, a few yards away. Curiosity nibbled Gavin, a coaxing lover. He drained his glass and went out into the hall. The noise stopped as he closed the door behind him.

'Ken?' he ventured. The word seemed to die at his lips.

The hallway was in darkness, except for a wash of light from the far end. Perhaps an open door. Gavin found a switch to his right, but it didn't work.

'Ken?' he said again.

This time the enquiry met with a response. A moan, and the sound of a body rolling, or being rolled, over. Had Reynolds had an accident? Jesus, he could be lying incapacitated within spitting distance from where Gavin stood: he must help. Why were his feet so reluctant to move? He had the tingling in his balls that always came with nervous anticipation; it reminded him of childhood hide-and-seek: the thrill of the chase. It was almost pleasurable.

And pleasure apart, could he really leave now, without knowing what had become of the punter? He had to go down the corridor.

The first door was ajar; he pushed it open and the room beyond was a book-lined bedroom/study. Street lights through the curtainless window fell on a jumbled desk. No Reynolds, no thrasher. More confident now he'd made the first move Gavin explored further down the hallway. The next door – the kitchen – was also open. There was no light from inside. Gavin's hands had begun to sweat: he thought of Reynolds trying to pull his gloves off, though they stuck to his palm. What had he been afraid of? It was more than the pick-up: there was somebody else in the apartment: somebody with a violent temper.

Gavin's stomach turned as his eyes found the smeared handprint on the door; it was blood.

He pushed the door, but it wouldn't open any further. There was something behind it. He slid through the available space, and into the kitchen. An unemptied waste bin, or a neglected vegetable rack, fouled the air. Gavin smoothed the wall with his palm to find the light switch, and the fluorescent tube spasmed into life.

Reynolds' Gucci shoes poked out from behind the door. Gavin pushed it to, and Reynolds rolled out of his hiding place. He'd obviously crawled behind the door to take refuge; there was something of the beaten animal in his tucked up body. When Gavin touched him he shuddered.

'It's all right . . . it's me.' Gavin prised a bloody hand from Reynolds' face. There was a deep gouge running from his temple to his chin, and another, parallel with it but not as deep, across the middle of his forehead and his nose, as though he'd been raked by a two pronged fork.

Reynolds opened his eyes. It took him a second only to focus on Gavin, before he said:

'Go away.'

'You're hurt.'

'Jesus' sake, go away. Quickly. I've changed my mind . . . You understand?'

'I'll fetch the police.'

The man practically spat: 'Get the fucking hell out of here, will you? Fucking bum-boy!'

Gavin stood up, trying to make sense out of all this. The guy was in pain, it made him aggressive. Ignore the insults and fetch something to cover the wound. That was it. Cover the wound, and then leave him to his own devices. If he didn't want the police that was his business. Probably he didn't want to explain the presence of a pretty-boy in his hot-house.

'Just let me get you a bandage – '

Gavin went back into the hallway.

Behind the kitchen door Reynolds said: 'Don't,' but the bum-boy didn't hear him. It wouldn't have made much difference if he had. Gavin liked disobedience. Don't was an invitation.

Reynolds put his back to the kitchen door, and tried to edge his way upright, using the door-handle as purchase. But his head was spinning: a carousel of horrors, round and round, each horse uglier than the last. His legs doubled up under him, and he fell down like the senile fool he was. Damn. Damn. Damn.

Gavin heard Reynolds fall, but he was too busy arming himself to hurry back into the kitchen. If the intruder who'd attacked

153

Reynolds was still in the flat, he wanted to be ready to defend himself. He rummaged through the reports on the desk in the study and alighted on a paper knife which was lying beside a pile of unopened correspondence. Thanking God for it, he snatched it up. It was light, and the blade was thin and brittle, but properly placed it could surely kill.

Happier now, he went back into the hall and took a moment to work out his tactics. The first thing was to locate the bathroom, hopefully there he'd find a bandage for Reynolds. Even a clean towel would help. Maybe then he could get some sense out of the guy, even coax him into an explanation.

Beyond the kitchen the hallway made a sharp left. Gavin turned the corner, and dead ahead the door was ajar. A light burned inside: water shone on tiles. The bathroom.

Clamping his left hand over the right hand that held the knife, Gavin approached the door. The muscles of his arms had become rigid with fear: would that improve his strike if it was required? he wondered. He felt inept, graceless, slightly stupid.

There was blood on the door-jamb, a palm-print that was clearly Reynolds'. This was where it had happened – Reynolds had thrown out a hand to support himself as he reeled back from his assailant. If the attacker was still in the flat, he must be here. There was nowhere else for him to hide.

Later, if there was a later, he'd probably analyse this situation and call himself a fool for kicking the door open, for encouraging this confrontation. But even as he contemplated the idiocy of the action he was performing it, and the door was swinging open across tiles strewn with water-blood puddles, and any moment there'd be a figure there, hook-handed, screaming defiance.

No. Not at all. The assailant wasn't here; and if he wasn't here, he wasn't in the flat.

Gavin exhaled, long and slow. The knife sagged in his hand, denied its pricking. Now, despite the sweat, the terror, he was disappointed. Life had let him down, again – snuck his destiny out of the back door and left him with a mop in his hand not a medal. All he could do was play nurse to the old man and go on his way.

The bathroom was decorated in shades of lime; the blood and tiles clashed. The translucent shower curtain, sporting stylised fish and seaweed, was partially drawn. It looked like the scene of a movie murder: not quite real. Blood too bright: light too flat.

Gavin dropped the knife in the sink, and opened the mirrored cabinet. It was well-stocked with mouth-washes, vitamin supplements, and abandoned toothpaste tubes, but the only medication was a tin of Elastoplast. As he closed the cabinet door he met his own features in the mirror, a drained face. He turned on the cold tap full, and lowered his head to the sink; a splash of water would clear away the vodka and put some colour in his cheeks.

As he cupped the water to his face, something made a noise behind him. He stood up, his heart knocking against his ribs, and turned off the tap. Water dripped off his chin and his eyelashes, and gurgled down the waste pipe.

The knife was still in the sink, a hand's-length away. The sound was coming from the bath, from *in* the bath, the inoffensive slosh of water.

Alarm had triggered flows of adrenalin, and his senses distilled the air with new precision. The sharp scent of lemon soap, the brilliance of the turquoise angel-fish flitting through lavender kelp on the shower curtain, the cold droplets on his face, the warmth behind his eyes: all sudden experiences, details his mind had passed over 'til now, too lazy to see and smell and feel to the limits of its reach.

You're living in the real world, his head said (it was a revelation), and if you're not very careful you're going to die there.

Why hadn't he looked in the bath? Asshole. Why not the bath?

'Who's there?' he asked, hoping against hope that Reynolds had an otter that was taking a quiet swim. Ridiculous hope. There was blood here, for Christ's sake.

He turned from the mirror as the lapping subsided – do it! do it! – and slid back the shower curtain on its plastic hooks. In his haste to unveil the mystery he'd left the knife in the sink. Too late now: the turquoise angels concertinaed, and he was looking down into the water.

It was deep, coming up to within an inch or two of the top of the bath, and murky. A brown scum spiralled on the surface, and the smell off it was faintly animal, like the wet fur of a dog. Nothing broke the surface of the water.

Gavin peered in, trying to work out the form at the bottom, his reflection floating amid the scum. He bent closer, unable to puzzle out the relation of shapes in the silt, until he recognised the crudely-formed fingers of a hand and he realised he was looking at a human form curled up into itself like a foetus, lying absolutely still in the filthy water.

155

He passed his hand over the surface to clear away the muck, his reflection shattered, and the occupant of the bath came clear. It was a statue, carved in the shape of a sleeping figure, only its head, instead of being tucked up tight, was cranked round to stare up out of the blur of sediment towards the surface. Its eyes were painted open, two crude blobs on a roughly carved face; its mouth was a slash, its ears ridiculous handles on its bald head. It was naked: its anatomy no better realised than its features: the work of an apprentice sculptor. In places the paint had been corrupted, perhaps by the soaking, and was lifting off the torso in grey, globular strands. Underneath, a core of dark wood was uncovered.

There was nothing to be frightened of here. An *objet d'art* in a bath, immersed in water to remove a crass paint-job. The lapping he'd heard behind him had been some bubbles rising from the thing, caused by a chemical reaction. There: the fright was explained. Nothing to panic over. Keep beating my heart, as the barman at the Ambassador used to say when a new beauty appeared on the scene.

Gavin smiled at the irony; this was no Adonis.

'Forget you ever saw it.'

Reynolds was at the door. The bleeding had stopped, staunched by an unsavoury rag of a handkerchief pressed to the side of his face. The light of the tiles made his skin bilious: his pallor would have shamed a corpse.

'Are you all right? You don't look it.'

'I'll be fine . . . just go, please.'

'What happened?'

'I slipped. Water on the floor. I slipped, that's all.'

'But the noise . . .'

Gavin was looking back into the bath. Something about the statue fascinated him. Maybe its nakedness, and that second strip it was slowly performing underwater: the ultimate strip: off with the skin.

'Neighbours, that's all.'

'What is this?' Gavin asked, still looking at the unfetching doll-face in the water.

'It's nothing to do with you.'

'Why's it all curled up like that? Is he dying?'

Gavin looked back to Reynolds to see the response to that question, the sourest of smiles, fading.

'You'll want money.'

'No.'

'Damn you! You're in business aren't you? There's notes beside the bed; take whatever you feel you deserve for your wasted time – ' He was appraising Gavin. ' – and your silence.'

Again the statue: Gavin couldn't keep his eyes off it, in all its crudity. His own face, puzzled, floated on the skin of the water, shaming the hand of the artist with its proportions.

'Don't wonder,' said Reynolds.

'Can't help it.'

'This is nothing to do with you.'

'You stole it . . . is that right? This is worth a mint and you stole it.'

Reynolds pondered the question and seemed, at last, too tired to start lying.

'Yes. I stole it.'

'And tonight somebody came back for it – '

Reynolds shrugged.

' – Is that it? Somebody came back for it?'

'That's right. I stole it . . .' Reynolds was saying the lines by rote, '. . . and somebody came back for it.'

'That's all I wanted to know.'

'Don't come back here, Gavin whoever-you-are. And don't try anything clever, because I won't be here.'

'You mean extortion?' said Gavin, 'I'm no thief.'

Reynolds' look of appraisal rotted into contempt.

'Thief or not, be thankful. If it's in you.' Reynolds stepped away from the door to let Gavin pass. Gavin didn't move.

'Thankful for what?' he demanded. There was an itch of anger in him; he felt, absurdly, rejected, as though he was being foisted off with a half-truth because he wasn't worthy enough to share this secret.

Reynolds had no more strength left for explanation. He was slumped against the door-frame, exhausted.

'Go,' he said.

Gavin nodded and left the guy at the door. As he passed from bathroom into hallway a glob of paint must have been loosened from the statue. He heard it break surface, heard the lapping at the edge of the bath, could see, in his head, the way the ripples made the body shimmer.

'Goodnight,' said Reynolds, calling after him.

Gavin didn't reply, nor did he pick up any money on his way out. Let him have his tombstones and his secrets.

On his way to the front door he stepped into the main room to pick up his jacket. The face of Flavinus the Standard-Bearer looked down at him from the wall. The man must have been a hero, Gavin thought. Only a hero would have been commemorated in such a fashion. He'd get no remembrance like that; no stone face to mark his passage.

He closed the front door behind him, aware once more that his tooth was aching, and as he did so the noise began again, the beating of a fist against a wall.

Or worse, the sudden fury of a woken heart.

The toothache was really biting the following day, and he went to the dentist mid-morning, expecting to coax the girl on the desk into giving him an instant appointment. But his charm was at a low ebb, his eyes weren't sparkling quite as luxuriantly as usual. She told him he'd have to wait until the following Friday, unless it was an emergency. He told her it was: she told him it wasn't. It was going to be a bad day: an aching tooth, a lesbian dentist receptionist, ice on the puddles, nattering women on every street corner, ugly children, ugly sky.

That was the day the pursuit began.

Gavin had been chased by admirers before, but never quite like this. Never so subtle, so surreptitious. He'd had people follow him round for days, from bar to bar, from street to street, so dog-like it almost drove him mad. Seeing the same longing face night after night, screwing up the courage to buy him a drink, perhaps offering him a watch, cocaine, a week in Tunisia, whatever. He'd rapidly come to loathe that sticky adoration that went bad as quickly as milk, and stank to high Heaven once it had. One of his most ardent admirers, a knighted actor he'd been told, never actually came near him, just followed him around, looking and looking. At first the attention had been flattering, but the pleasure soon became irritation, and eventually he'd cornered the guy in a bar and threatened him with a broken head. He'd been so wound up that night, so sick of being devoured by looks, he'd have done some serious harm if the pitiful bastard hadn't taken the hint. He never saw the guy again; half thought he'd probably gone home and hanged himself.

But this pursuit was nowhere near as obvious, it was scarcely more than a feeling. There was no hard evidence that he had somebody on his tail. Just a prickly sense, every time he glanced round, that someone was slotting themselves into the shadows, or that on a night street a walker was keeping pace with him, matching every click of his heel, every hesitation in his step. It was like paranoia, except that he wasn't paranoid. If he was paranoid, he reasoned, somebody would tell him.

Besides, there were incidents. One morning the cat woman who lived on the landing below him idly enquired who his visitor was: the funny one who came in late at night and waited on the stairs hour after hour, watching his room. He'd had no such visitor: and knew no-one who fitted the description.

Another day, on a busy street, he'd ducked out of the throng into the doorway of an empty shop and was in the act of lighting a cigarette when somebody's reflection, distorted through the grime on the window, caught his eye. The match burned his finger, he looked down as he dropped it, and when he looked up again the crowd had closed round the watcher like an eager sea.

It was a bad, bad feeling: and there was more where that came from.

Gavin had never spoken with Preetorius, though they'd exchanged an occasional nod on the street, and each asked after the other in the company of mutual acquaintances as though they were dear friends. Preetorius was a black, somewhere between forty-five and assassination, a glorified pimp who claimed to be descended from Napoleon. He'd been running a circle of women, and three or four boys, for the best part of a decade, and doing well from the business. When he first began work, Gavin had been strongly advised to ask for Preetorius' patronage, but he'd always been too much of a maverick to want that kind of help. As a result he'd never been looked upon kindly by Preetorius or his clan. Nevertheless, once he became a fixture on the scene, no-one challenged his right to be his own man. The word was that Preetorius even admitted a grudging admiration for Gavin's greed.

Admiration or no, it was a chilly day in Hell when Preetorius actually broke the silence and spoke to him.

'White boy.'

It was towards eleven, and Gavin was on his way from a bar off St Martin's Lane to a club in Covent Garden. The street still buzzed: there were potential punters amongst the theatre and movie-goers, but he hadn't got the appetite for it tonight. He had a hundred in his pocket, which he'd made the day before and hadn't bothered to bank. Plenty to keep him going.

His first thought when he saw Preetorius and his pie-bald goons blocking his path was: they want my money.

'White boy.'

Then he recognised the flat, shining face. Preetorius was no street thief; never had been, never would be.

'White boy, I'd like a word with you.'

Preetorius took a nut from his pocket, shelled it in his palm, and popped the kernel into his ample mouth.

'You don't mind do you?'

'What do you want?'

'Like I said, just a word. Not too much to ask, is it?'

'OK. What?'

'Not here.'

Gavin looked at Preetorius' cohorts. They weren't gorillas, that wasn't the black's style at all, but nor were they ninety-eight pound weaklings. This scene didn't look, on the whole, too healthy.

'Thanks, but no thanks.' Gavin said, and began to walk, with as even a pace as he could muster, away from the trio. They followed. He prayed they wouldn't, but they followed. Preetorius talked at his back.

'Listen. I hear bad things about you,' he said.

'Oh yes?'

'I'm afraid so. I'm told you attacked one of my boys.'

Gavin took six paces before he answered. 'Not me. You've got the wrong man.'

'He recognised you, trash. You did him some serious mischief.'

'I told you: not me.'

'You're a lunatic, you know that? You should be put behind fucking bars.'

Preetorius was raising his voice. People were crossing the street to avoid the escalating argument.

Without thinking, Gavin turned off St Martin's Lane into Long Acre, and rapidly realised he'd made a tactical error. The crowds thinned substantially here, and it was a long trek through the streets of Convent Garden before he reached another centre of activity. He should have turned right instead of left, and he'd have stepped onto Charing Cross Road. There would have been some safety there. Damn it, he couldn't turn round, not and walk straight into them. All he could do was walk (not run; never run with a mad dog on your heels) and hope he could keep the conversation on an even keel.

Preetorius: 'You've cost me a lot of money.'

'I don't see – '

'You put some of my prime boy-meat out of commission. It's going to be a long time 'til I get that kid back on the market. He's shit scared, see?'

'Look . . . I didn't do anything to anybody.'

'Why do you fucking lie to me, trash? What have I ever done to you, you treat me like this?'.

Preetorius picked up his pace a little and came up level with Gavin, leaving his associates a few steps behind.

'Look . . .' he whispered to Gavin, 'kids like that can be tempting, right? That's cool. I can get into that. You put a little boy-pussy on my plate I'm not going to turn my nose up at it. But you hurt him: and when you hurt one of my kids, I bleed too.'

'If I'd done this like you say, you think I'd be walking the street?'

'Maybe you're not a well man, you know? We're not talking about a couple of bruises here, man. I'm talking about you taking a shower in a kid's blood, that's what I'm saying. Hanging him up and cutting him everywhere, then leaving him on my fuckin' stairs wearing a pair of fucking' socks. You getting my message now, white boy? You read my message?'

Genuine rage had flared as Preetorius described the alleged crimes, and Gavin wasn't sure how to handle it. He kept his silence, and walked on.

'That kid idolised you, you know? Thought you were essential reading for an aspirant bum-boy. How'd you like that?'

'Not much.'

'You should be fuckin' flattered, man, 'cause that's about as much as you'll ever amount to.'

'Thanks.'

'You've had a good career. Pity it's over.'

Gavin felt iced lead in his belly: he'd hoped Preetorius was going to be content with a warning. Apparently not. They were here to damage him: Jesus, they were going to hurt him, and for something he hadn't done, didn't even know anything about.

'We're going to take you off the street, white boy. Permanently.'

'I did nothing.'

'The kid knew you, even with a stocking over your head he knew you. The voice was the same, the clothes were the same. Face it, you were recognised. Now take the consequences.'

'Fuck you.'

Gavin broke into a run. As an eighteen year old he'd sprinted for his county: he needed that speed again now. Behind him Preetorius laughed (such sport!) and two sets of feet pounded the pavement in pursuit. They were close, closer – and Gavin was badly out of condition. His thighs were aching after a few dozen yards, and his jeans were too tight to run in easily. The chase was lost before it began.

'The man didn't tell you to leave,' the white goon scolded, his bitten fingers digging into Gavin's biceps.

'Nice try.' Preetorius smiled, sauntering towards the dogs and the panting hare. He nodded, almost imperceptibly, to the other goon.

'Christian?' he asked.

At the invitation Christian delivered a fist to Gavin's kidneys. The blow doubled him up, spitting curses.

Christian said: 'Over there.' Preetorius said: 'Make it snappy,' and suddenly they were dragging him out of the light into an alley. His shirt and his jacket tore, his expensive shoes were dragged through dirt, before he was pulled upright, groaning. The alley was dark and Preetorius' eyes hung in the air in front of him, dislocated.

'Here we are again,' he said. 'Happy as can be.'

'I . . . didn't touch him,' Gavin gasped.

The unnamed cohort, Not-Christian, put a ham hand in the middle of Gavin's chest, and pushed him back against the end wall of the alley. His heel slid in muck, and though he tried to stay upright his legs had turned to water. His ego too: this was no time to be courageous. He'd beg, he fall down on his knees and lick their soles if need be, anything to stop them doing a job on him. Anything to stop them spoiling his face.

That was Preetorius' favourite pastime, or so the street talk went: the spoiling of beauty. He had a rare way with him, could

162

maim beyond hope of redemption in three strokes of his razor, and have the victim pocket his lips as a keepsake.

Gavin stumbled forward, palms slapping the wet ground. Something rotten-soft slid out of its skin beneath his hand.

Not-Christian exchanged a grin with Preetorius.

'Doesn't he look delightful?' he said.

Preetorius was crunching a nut. 'Seems to me – ' he said, ' – the man's finally found his place in life.'

'I didn't touch him,' Gavin begged. There was nothing to do but deny and deny: and even then it was a lost cause.

'You're guilty as hell,' said Not-Christian.

'*Please.*'

'I'd really like to get this over with as soon as possible,' said Preetorius, glancing at his watch, 'I've got appointments to keep, people to pleasure.'

Gavin looked up at his tormentors. The sodium-lit street was a twenty-five-yard dash away, if he could break through the cordon of their bodies.

'Allow me to rearrange your face for you. A little crime of fashion.'

Preetorius had a knife in his hand. Not-Christian had taken a rope from his pocket, with a ball on it. The ball goes in the mouth, the rope goes round the head – you couldn't scream if your life depended on it. This was it.

Go!

Gavin broke from his grovelling position like a sprinter from his block, but the slops greased his heels, and threw him off balance. Instead of making a clean dash for safety he stumbled sideways and fell against Christian, who in turn fell back.

There was a breathless scrambling before Preetorius stepped in, dirtying his hands on the white trash, and hauling him to his feet.

'No way out, fucker,' he said, pressing the point of the blade against Gavin's chin. The jut of the bone was clearest there, and he began the cut without further debate – tracing the jawline, too hot for the act to care if the trash was gagged or not. Gavin howled as blood washed down his neck, but his cries were cut short as somebody's fat fingers grappled with his tongue, and held it fast.

His pulse began to thud in his temples, and windows, one behind the other, opened and opened in front of him, and he was falling through them into unconsciousness.

163

Better to die. Better to die. They'd destroy his face: better to die.

Then he was screaming again, except that he wasn't aware of making the sound in his throat. Through the slush in his ears he tried to focus on the voice, and realised it was Preetorius' scream he was hearing, not his own.

His tongue was released; and he was spontaneously sick. He staggered back, puking, from a mess of struggling figures in front of him: A person, or persons, unknown had stepped in, and prevented the completion of his spoiling. There was a body sprawled on the floor, face up. Not-Christian, eyes open, life shut. God: someone had killed for him. *For him.*

Gingerly, he put his hand up to his face to feel the damage. The flesh was deeply lacerated along his jawbone, from the middle of his chin to within an inch of his ear. It was bad, but Preetorius, ever organised, had left the best delights to the last, and had been interrupted before he'd slit Gavin's nostrils or taken off his lips. A scar along his jawbone wouldn't be pretty, but it wasn't disastrous.

Somebody was staggering out of the mêlée towards him – Preetorius, tears on his face, eyes like golf-balls.

Beyond him Christian, his arms useless, was staggering towards the street.

Preetorius wasn't following: why?

His mouth opened; an elastic filament of saliva, strung with pearls, depended from his lower lip.

'Help me,' he appealed, as though his life was in Gavin's power. One large hand was raised to squeeze a drop of mercy out of the air, but instead came the swoop of another arm, reaching over his shoulder and thrusting a weapon, a crude blade, into the black's mouth. He gargled it a moment, his throat trying to accommodate its edge, its width, before his attacker dragged the blade up and back, holding Preetorius' neck to steady him against the force of the stroke. The startled face divided, and heat bloomed from Preetorius' interior, warming Gavin in a cloud.

The weapon hit the alley floor, a dull clank. Gavin glanced at it. A short, wide-bladed sword. He looked back at the dead man.

Preetorius stood upright in front of him, supported now only by his executioner's arm. His gushing head fell forward, and the executioner took the bow as a sign, neatly dropping Preetorius' body at Gavin's feet. No longer eclipsed by the corpse, Gavin met his saviour face to face.

164

It took him only a moment to place those crude features: the startled, lifeless eyes, the gash of a mouth, the jug-handle ears. It was Reynolds' statue. It grinned, its teeth too small for its head. Milk-teeth, still to be shed before the adult form. There was, however, some improvement in its appearance, he could see that even in the gloom. The brow seemed to have swelled; the face was altogether better proportioned. It remained a painted doll, but it was a doll with aspirations.

The statue gave a stiff bow, its joints unmistakably creaking, and the absurdity, the sheer absurdity of this situation welled up in Gavin. It bowed, damn it, it smiled, it murdered: and yet it couldn't possibly be alive, could it? Later, he would disbelieve, he promised himself. Later he'd find a thousand reasons not to accept the reality in front of him: blame his blood-starved brain, his confusion, his panic. One way or another he'd argue himself out of this fantastic vision, and it would be as though it had never happened.

If he could just live with it a few minutes longer.

The vision reached across and touched Gavin's jaw, lightly, running its crudely carved fingers along the lips of the wound Preetorius had made. A ring on its smallest finger caught the light: a ring identical to his own.

'We're going to have a scar,' it said.

Gavin knew its voice.

'Dear me: pity,' it said. It was speaking with *his* voice. 'Still, it could be worse.'

His voice. God, his, his, his.

Gavin shook his head.

'Yes,' it said, understanding that he'd understood.

'Not me.'

'Yes.'

'Why?'

It transferred its touch from Gavin's jawbone to its own, marking out the place where the wound should be, and even as it made the gesture its surface opened, and it grew a scar on the spot. No blood welled up: it had no blood.

Yet wasn't that his own, even brow it was emulating, and the piercing eyes, weren't they becoming his, and the wonderful mouth?

'The boy?' said Gavin, fitting the pieces together.

'Oh the boy . . .' It threw its unfinished glance to Heaven. 'What a treasure he was. And how he snarled.'

'You washed in his blood?'

'I need it.' It knelt to the body of Preetorius and put its fingers in the split head. 'This blood's old, but it'll do. The boy was better.'

It daubed Preetorius' blood on its cheek, like war-paint. Gavin couldn't hide his disgust.

'Is he such a loss?' the effigy demanded.

The answer was no, of course. It was no loss at all that Preetorius was dead, no loss that some drugged, cocksucking kid had given up some blood and sleep because this painted miracle needed to feed its growth. There were worse things than this every day, somewhere; huge horrors. And yet –

'You can't condone me,' it prompted, 'its not in your nature is it? Soon it won't be in mine either. I'll reject my life as a tormentor of children, because I'll see through *your* eyes, share *your* humanity . . .'

It stood up, its movements still lacking flexibility.

'Meanwhile, I must behave as I think fit.'

On its cheek, where Preetorius' blood had been smeared, the skin was already waxier, less like painted wood.

'I am a thing without a proper name,' it pronounced. 'I am a wound in the flank of the world. But I am also that perfect stranger you always prayed for as a child, to come and take you, call you beauty, lift you naked out of the street and through Heaven's window. Aren't I? Aren't I?'

How did it know the dreams of his childhood? How could it have guessed that particular emblem, of being hoisted out of a street full of plague into a house that was Heaven?

'Because I am yourself,' it said, in reply to the unspoken question, 'made perfectable.'

Gavin gestured towards the corpses.

'You can't be me. I'd never have done this.'

It seemed ungracious to condemn it for its intervention, but the point stood.

'Wouldn't you?' said the other. 'I think you would.'

Gavin heard Preetorius' voice in his ear. 'A crime of fashion.' Felt again the knife at his chin, the nausea, the helplessness. Of course he'd have done it, a dozen times over he'd have done it, and called it justice.

It didn't need to hear his accession, it was plain.

'I'll come and see you again,' said the painted face. 'Meanwhile – if I were you – ' it laughed, ' – I'd be going.'

166

Gavin locked eyes with it a beat, probing it for doubt, then started towards the road.

'Not that way. This!'

It was pointing towards a door in the wall, almost hidden behind festering bags of refuse. That was how it had come so quickly, so quietly.

'Avoid the main streets, and keep yourself out of sight. I'll find you again, when I'm ready.'

Gavin needed no further encouragement to leave. Whatever the explanations of the night's events, the deeds were done. Now wasn't the time for questions.

He slipped through the doorway without looking behind him: but he could hear enough to turn his stomach. The thud of fluid on the ground, the pleasurable moan of the miscreant: the sounds were enough for him to be able to picture its toilet.

Nothing of the night before made any more sense the morning after. There was no sudden insight into the nature of the waking dream he'd dreamt. There was just a series of stark facts.

In the mirror, the fact of the cut on his jaw, gummed up and aching more badly than his rotted tooth.

In the newspapers, the reports of two bodies found in the Covent Garden area, known criminals viciously murdered in what the police described as a 'gangland slaughter'.

In his head, the inescapable knowledge that he would be found out sooner or later. Somebody would surely have seen him with Preetorius, and spill the beans to the police. Maybe even Christian, if he was so inclined, and they'd be there, on his step, with cuffs and warrants. Then what could he tell them, in reply to their accusations? That the man who did it was not a man at all, but an effigy of some kind, that was by degrees becoming a replica of himself? The question was not whether he'd be incarcerated, but which hole they'd lock him in, prison or asylum?

Juggling despair with disbelief, he went to the casualty department to have his face seen to, where he waited patiently for three and a half hours with dozens of similar walking wounded.

The doctor was unsympathetic. There was no use in stitches now, he said, the damage was done: the wound could and would be cleaned and covered, but a bad scar was now unavoidable. Why didn't you come last night, when it happened? the nurse

167

asked. He shrugged: what the hell did they care? Artificial compassion didn't help him an iota.

As he turned the corner with his street, he saw the cars outside the house, the blue light, the cluster of neighbours grinning their gossip. Too late to claim anything of his previous life. By now they had possession of his clothes, his combs, his perfumes, his letters – and they'd be searching through them like apes after lice. He'd seen how thorough-going these bastards could be when it suited them, how completely they could seize and parcel up a man's identity. Eat it up, suck it up: they could erase you as surely as a shot, but leave you a living blank.

There was nothing to be done. His life was theirs now to sneer at and salivate over: even have a nervous moment, one or two of them, when they saw his photographs and wondered if perhaps they'd paid for this boy themselves, some horny night.

Let them have it all. They were welcome. From now on he would be lawless, because laws protect possessions and he had none. They'd wiped him clean, or as good as: he had no place to live, nor anything to call his own. He didn't even have fear: that was the strangest thing.

He turned his back on the street and the house he'd lived in for four years, and he felt something akin to relief, happy that his life had been stolen from him in its squalid entirety. He was the lighter for it.

Two hours later, and miles away, he took time to check his pockets. He was carrying a banker's card, almost a hundred pounds in cash, a small collection of photographs, some of his parents and sister, mostly of himself; a watch, a ring, and a gold chain round his neck. Using the card might be dangerous – they'd surely have warned his bank by now. The best thing might be to pawn the ring and the chain, then hitch North. He had friends in Aberdeen who'd hide him awhile.

But first – Reynolds.

It took Gavin an hour to find the house where Ken Reynolds lived. It was the best part of twenty-four hours since he'd eaten and his belly complained as he stood outside Livingstone Mansions. He told it to keep its peace, and slipped into the building. The interior looked less impressive by daylight. The tread of the stair carpet was worn, and the paint on the balustrade filthied with use.

168

Taking his time he climbed the three flights to Reynolds' apartment, and knocked.

Nobody answered, nor was there any sound of movement from inside. Reynolds had told him of course: don't come back – I won't be here. Had he somehow guessed the consequences of sicking that thing into the world?

Gavin rapped on the door again, and this time he was certain he heard somebody breathing on the other side of the door.

'Reynolds . . .' he said, pressing to the door, 'I can hear you.'

Nobody replied, but there was somebody in there, he was sure of it. Gavin slapped his palm on the door.

'Come on, open up. Open up, you bastard.'

A short silence, then a muffled voice. 'Go away.'

'I want to speak to you.'

'Go away, I told you, go away. I've nothing to say to you.'

'You owe me an explanation, for God's sake. If you don't open this fucking door I'll fetch someone who will.'

An empty threat, but Reynolds responded: 'No! Wait. Wait.'

There was the sound of a key in the lock, and the door was opened a few paltry inches. The flat was in darkness beyond the scabby face that peered out at Gavin. It was Reynolds sure enough, but unshaven and wretched. He smelt unwashed, even through the crack in the door, and he was wearing only a stained shirt and a pair of pants, hitched up with a knotted belt.

'I can't help you. Go away.'

'If you'll let me explain –.' Gavin pressed the door, and Reynolds was either too weak or too befuddled to stop him opening it. He stumbled back into the darkened hallway.

'What the fuck's going on in here?'

The place stank of rotten food. The air was evil with it. Reynolds let Gavin slam the door behind him before producing a knife from the pocket of his stained trousers.

'You don't fool me,' Reynolds gleamed, 'I know what you've done. Very fine. Very clever.'

'You mean the murders? It wasn't me.'

Reynolds poked the knife towards Gavin.

'How many blood-baths did it take?' he asked, tears in his eyes. 'Six? Ten?'

'I didn't kill anybody.'

'. . . monster.'

The knife in Reynolds' hand was the paper knife Gavin himself had wielded. He approached Gavin with it. There was no doubt: he had every intention of using it. Gavin flinched, and Reynolds seemed to take hope from his fear.

'Had you forgotten what it was like, being flesh and blood?'

The man had lost his marbles.

'Look . . . I just came here to talk.'

'You came here to kill me. I could reveal you . . .so you came to kill me.'

'Do you know who I am?' Gavin said.

Reynolds sneered: 'You're not the queer boy. You look like him, but you're not.'

'For pity's sake . . . I'm Gavin . . . Gavin – '

The words to explain, to prevent the knife pressing any closer, wouldn't come.

'Gavin, you remember?' was all he could say.

Reynolds faltered a moment, staring at Gavin's face.

'You're sweating,' he said. the dangerous stare fading in his eyes.

Gavin's mouth had gone so dry he could only nod.

'I can see,' said Reynolds, 'you're sweating.'

He dropped the point of the knife.

'It could never sweat,' he said, 'Never had, never would have, the knack of it. You're the boy . . . not it. The boy.'

His face slackened, its flesh a sack which was almost emptied.

'I need help,' said Gavin, his voice hoarse. 'You've got to tell me what's going on.'

'You want an explanation?' Reynolds replied, 'you can have whatever you can find.'

He led the way into the main room. The curtains were drawn, but even in the gloom Gavin could see that every antiquity it had contained had been smashed beyond repair. The pottery shards had been reduced to smaller shards, and those shards to dust. The stone reliefs were destroyed, the tombstone of Flavinus the Standard-Bearer was rubble.

'Who did this?'

'I did,' said Reynolds.

'Why?'

Reynolds sluggishly picked his way through the destruction to the window, and peered through a slit in the velvet curtains.

'It'll come back, you see,' he said, ignoring the question.

Gavin insisted: 'Why destroy it all?'

'It's a sickness,' Reynolds replied. 'Needing to live in the past.'
He turned from the window.

'I stole most of these pieces,' he said, 'over a period of many years. I was put in a position of trust, and I misused it.'

He kicked over a sizeable chunk of rubble: dust rose.

'Flavinus lived and died. That's all there is to tell. Knowing his name means nothing, or next to nothing. It doesn't make Flavinus real again: he's dead and happy.'

'The statue in the bath?'

Reynolds stopped breathing for a moment, his inner eye meeting the painted face.

'You I thought I was it, didn't you? When I came to the door.'

'Yes. I thought it had finished its business.'

'It imitates.'

Reynolds nodded. 'As far as I understand its nature,' he said, 'yes, it imitates.'

'Where did you find it?'

'Near Carlisle. I was in charge of the excavation there. We found it lying in the bathhouse, a statue curled up into a ball beside the remains of an adult male. It was a riddle. A dead man and a statue, lying together in a bathhouse. Don't ask me what drew me to the thing, I don't know. Perhaps it works its will through the mind as well as the physique. I stole it, brought it back here.'

'And you fed it?'

Reynolds stiffened.

'Don't ask.'

'I *am* asking. You fed it?'

'Yes.'

'You intended to bleed me, didn't you? That's why you brought me here: to kill me, and let it wash itself – '

Gavin remembered the noise of the creature's fists on the sides of the bath, that angry demand for food, like a child beating on its cot. He'd been so close to being taken by it, lamb-like.

'Why didn't it attack me the way it did you? Why didn't it just jump out of the bath and feed on me?'

Reynolds wiped his mouth with the palm of his hand.

'It saw your face, of course.'

Of course: it saw my face, and wanted it for itself, and it couldn't steal the face of a dead man, so it let me be. The rationale for its behaviour was fascinating, now it was revealed: Gavin felt a taste of Reynolds' passion, unveiling mysteries.

'The man in the bathhouse. The one you uncovered – '

'Yes . . .?'

'He stopped it doing the same thing to him, is that right?'

'That's probably why his body was never moved, just sealed up. No-one understood that he'd died fighting a creature that was stealing his life.'

The picture was near as damn it complete; just anger remaining to be answered.

This man had come close to murdering him to feed the effigy. Gavin's fury broke surface. He took hold of Reynolds by shirt and skin, and shook him. Was it his bones or teeth that rattled?

'It's almost got my face.' He stared into Reynolds' bloodshot eyes. 'What happens when it finally has the trick off pat?'

'I don't know.'

'You tell me the worst – Tell me!'

'It's all guesswork,' Reynolds replied.

'Guess then!'

'When it's perfected its physical imitation, I think it'll steal the one thing it can't imitate: your soul.'

Reynolds was past fearing Gavin. His voice had sweetened, as though he was talking to a condemned man. He even smiled.

'Fucker!'

Gavin hauled Reynolds' face yet closer to his. White spittle dotted the old man's cheek.

'You don't care! You don't give a shit, do you?'

He hit Reynolds across the face, once, twice, then again and again, until he was breathless.

The old man took the beating in absolute silence, turning his face up from one blow to receive another, brushing the blood out of his swelling eyes only to have them fill again.

Finally, the punches faltered.

Reynolds, on his knees, picked pieces of tooth off his tongue.

'I deserved that,' he murmured.

'How do I stop it?' said Gavin.

Reynolds shook his head.

'Impossible,' he whispered, plucking at Gavin's hand. 'Please,' he said, and taking the fist, opened it and kissed the lines.

Gavin left Reynolds in the ruins of Rome, and went into the street. The interview with Reynolds had told him little he hadn't guessed. The only thing he could do now was find this beast that had his beauty, and best it. If he failed, he failed attempting to secure his only certain attribute: a face that was wonderful. Talk of souls and humanity was for him so much wasted air. He wanted his face.

There was rare purpose in his step as he crossed Kensington. After years of being the victim of circumstance he saw circumstance embodied at last. He would shake sense from it, or die trying.

In his flat Reynolds drew aside the curtain to watch a picture of evening fall on a picture of a city.

No night he would live through, no city he'd walk in again. Out of sighs, he let the curtain drop, and picked up the short stabbing sword. The point he put to his chest.

'Come on,' he told himself and the sword, and pressed the hilt. But the pain as the blade entered his body a mere half inch was enough to make his head reel: he knew he'd faint before the job was half-done. So he crossed to the wall, steadied the hilt against it, and let his own body-weight impale him. That did the trick. He wasn't sure if the sword had skewered him through entirely, but by the amount of blood he'd surely killed himself. Though he tried to arrange to turn, and so drive the blade all the way home as he fell on it, he fluffed the gesture, and instead fell on his side. The impact made him aware of the sword in his body, a stiff, uncharitable presence transfixing him utterly.

It took him well over ten minutes to die, but in that time, pain apart, he was content. Whatever the flaws of his fifty-seven years, and they were many, he felt he was perishing in a way his beloved Flavinus would not have been ashamed of.

Towards the end it began to rain, and the noise on the roof made him believe God was burying the house, sealing him up forever. And as the moment came, so did a splendid delusion: a hand, carrying a light, and escorted by voices, seemed to break through the wall, ghosts of the future come to excavate his history. He smiled to greet them, and was about to ask what year this was when he realised he was dead.

The creature was far better at avoiding Gavin than he'd been at avoiding it. Three days passed without its pursuer snatching sight of hide or hair of it.

But the fact of its presence, close, but never too close, was indisputable. In a bar someone would say: 'Saw you last night on the Edgware Road' when he'd not been near the place, or 'How'd you make out with that Arab then?' or 'Don't you speak to your friends any longer?'

And God, he soon got to like the feeling. The distress gave way to a pleasure he'd not known since the age of two: ease.

So what if someone else was working his patch, dodging the law and the street-wise alike; so what if his friends (what friends? Leeches) were being cut by this supercilious copy; so what if his life had been taken from him and was being worn to its length and its breadth in lieu of him? He could sleep, and know that he, or something so like him it made no difference, was awake in the night and being adored. He began to see the creature not as a monster terrorising him, but as his tool, his public persona almost. It was substance: he shadow.

He woke, dreaming.

It was four-fifteen in the afternoon, and the whine of traffic was loud from the street below. A twilight room; the air breathed and rebreathed and breathed again so it smelt of his lungs. It was over a week since he'd left Reynolds to the ruins, and in that time he'd only ventured out from his new digs (one tiny bedroom, kitchen, bathroom) three times. Sleep was more important now than food or exercise. He had enough dope to keep him happy when sleep wouldn't come, which was seldom, and he'd grown to like the staleness of the air, the flux of light through the curtainless window, the sense of a world elsewhere which he had no part of or place in.

Today he'd told himself he ought to go out and get some fresh air, but he hadn't been able to raise the enthusiasm. Maybe later, much later, when the bars were emptying and he wouldn't be noticed, then he'd slip out of his cocoon and see what could be seen. For now, there were dreams –

Water.

He'd dreamt water; sitting beside a pool in Fort Lauderdale, a pool full of fish. And the splash of their leaps and dives was continuing, an overflow from sleep. Or was it the other way round? Yes; he had been hearing running water in his sleep and his dreaming mind had made an illustration to accompany the sound. Now awake, the sound continued.

It was coming from the adjacent bathroom, no longer running, but lapping. Somebody had obviously broken in while he was asleep, and was now taking a bath. He ran down the short list of possible intruders: the few who knew he was here. There was Paul: a nascent hustler who'd bedded down on the floor two nights before; there was Chink, the dope dealer; and a girl from downstairs he thought was called Michelle. Who was he kidding? None of these people would have broken the lock on the door to get in. He knew very well who it must be. He was just playing a game with himself, enjoying the process of elimination, before he narrowed the options to one.

Keen for reunion, he slid out from his skin of sheet and duvet. His body turned to a column of gooseflesh as the cold air encased him, his sleep-erection hid its head. As he crossed the room to where his dressing gown hung on the back of the door he caught sight of himself in the mirror, a freeze frame from an atrocity film, a wisp of a man, shrunk by cold, and lit by a rainwater light. His reflection almost flickered, he was so insubstantial.

Wrapping the dressing gown, his only freshly purchased garment, around him, he went to the bathroom door. There was no noise of water now. He pushed the door open.

The warped linoleum was icy beneath his feet; and all he wanted to do was to see his friend, then crawl back into bed. But he owed the tatters of his curiosity more than that: he had questions.

The light through the frosted glass had deteriorated rapidly in the three minutes since he'd woken: the onset of night and a rain-storm congealing the gloom. In front of him the bath was almost filled to overflowing, the water was oil-slick calm, and dark. As before, nothing broke surface. It was lying deep, hidden.

How long was it since he'd approached a lime-green bath in a lime-green bathroom, and peered into the water? It could have been yesterday: his life between then and now had become one long night. He looked down. It was there, tucked up, as before, and asleep, still wearing all its clothes as though it had had no time to undress before it hid itself. Where it had been bald it now sprouted a luxuriant head of hair, and its features were quite complete. No trace of a painted face remained: it had a plastic beauty that was his own absolutely, down to the last mole. Its perfectly finished hands were crossed on its chest.

The night deepened. There was nothing to do but watch it sleep, and he became bored with that. It had traced him here, it wasn't likely to run away again, he could go back to bed. Outside the rain had slowed the commuters' homeward journey to a crawl, there were accidents, some fatal; engines overheated, hearts too. He listened to the chase; sleep came and went. It was the middle of the evening when thirst woke him again: he was dreaming water, and there was the sound as it had been before. The creature was hauling itself out of the bath, was putting its hand to the door, opening it.

There it stood. The only light in the bedroom was coming from the street below; it barely began to illuminate the visitor.

'Gavin? Are you awake?'

'Yes,' he said.

'Will you help me?' it asked. There was no trace of threat in its voice, it asked as a man might ask his brother, for kinship's sake.

'What do you want?'

'Time to heal.'

'Heal?'

'Put on the light.'

Gavin switched on the lamp beside the bed and looked at the figure at the door. It no longer had its arms crossed on its chest, and Gavin saw that the position had been covering an appalling shotgun wound. The flesh of its chest had been blown open, exposing its colourless innards. There was, of course, no blood: that it would never have. Nor, from this distance, could Gavin see anything in its interior that faintly resembled human anatomy.

'God Almighty,' he said.

'Preetorius had friends,' said the other, and its fingers touched the edge of the wound. The gesture recalled a picture of the wall of his mother's house. Christ in Glory – the Sacred Heart floating inside the Saviour – while his fingers, pointing to the agony he'd suffered, said: 'This was for you.'

'Why aren't you dead?'

'Because I'm not yet alive,' it said.

Not yet: remember that, Gavin thought. It has intimations of mortality.

'Are you in pain?'

'No,' it said sadly, as though it craved the experience, 'I feel nothing. All the signs of life are cosmetic. But I'm learning.' It

176

smiled. 'I've got the knack of the yawn, and the fart.' The idea was both absurd and touching; that it would aspire to farting, that a farcical failure in the digestive system was for it a precious sign of humanity.

'And the wound?'

' – is healing. Will heal completely in time.'

Gavin said nothing.

'Do I disgust you?' it asked, without inflection.

'No.'

It was staring at Gavin with perfect eyes, his perfect eyes.

'What did Reynolds tell you?' it asked.

Gavin shrugged.

'Very little.'

'That I'm a monster? That I suck out the human spirit?'

'Not exactly.'

'More or less.'

'More or less,' Gavin conceded.

It nodded. 'He's right,' it said. 'In his way, he's right. I need blood: that makes me monstrous. In my youth, a month ago, I bathed in it. Its touch gave wood the appearance of flesh. But I don't need it now: the process is almost finished. All I need now –'

It faltered; not, Gavin thought, because it intended to lie, but because the words to describe its condition wouldn't come.

'What do you need?' Gavin pressed it.

It shook its head, looking down at the carpet. 'I've lived several times, you know. Sometimes I've stolen lives and got away with it. Lived a natural span, then shrugged off that face and found another. Sometimes, like the last time, I've been challenged, and lost – '

'Are you some kind of machine?'

'No.'

'What then?'

'I am what I am. I know of no others like me; though why should I be the only one? Perhaps there *are* others, many others: I simply don't know of them yet. So I live and die and live again, and learn nothing – ' the word was bitterly pronounced, ' – of myself. Understand? You know what you are because you see others like you. If you were alone on earth, what would you know? What the mirror told you, that's all. The rest would be myth and conjecture.'

177

The summary was made without sentiment.

'May I lie down?' it asked.

It began to walk towards him, and Gavin could see more clearly the fluttering in its chest-cavity, the restless, incoherent forms that were mushrooming there in place of the heart. Sighing, it sank face-down on the bed, its clothes sodden, and closed its eyes.

'We'll heal,' it said. 'Just give us time.'

Gavin went to the door of the flat and bolted it. Then he dragged a table over and wedged it under the handle. Nobody could get in and attack it in sleep: they would stay here together in safety, he and it, he and himself. The fortress secured, he brewed some coffee and sat in the chair across the room from the bed and watched the creature sleep.

The rain rushed against the window heavily one hour, lightly the next. Wind threw sodden leaves against the glass and they clung there like inquisitive moths; he watched them sometimes, when he tired of watching himself, but before long he'd want to look again, and he'd be back staring at the casual beauty of his outstretched arm, the light flicking the wrist-bone, the lashes. He fell asleep in the chair about midnight, with an ambulance complaining in the street outside, and the rain coming again.

It wasn't comfortable in the chair, and he'd surface from sleep every few minutes, his eyes opening a fraction. The creature was up: it was standing by the window, now in front of the mirror, now in the kitchen. Water ran: he dreamt water. The creature undressed: he dreamt sex. It stood over him, its chest whole, and he was reassured by its presence: he dreamt, it was for a moment only, himself lifted out of a street through a window into Heaven. It dressed in his clothes: he murmured his assent to the theft in his sleep. It was whistling: and there was a threat of day through the window, but he was too dozy to stir just yet, and quite content to have the whistling young man in his clothes live for him.

At last it leaned over the chair and kissed him on the lips, a brother's kiss, and left. He heard the door close behind it.

After that there were days, he wasn't sure how many, when he stayed in the room, and did nothing but drink water. This thirst had become unquenchable. Drinking and sleeping, drinking and sleeping, twin moons.

The bed he slept on was damp at the beginning from where the creature had laid, and he had no wish to change the sheets. On the contrary he enjoyed the wet linen, which his body dried out too soon. When it did he took a bath himself in the water the thing had lain in and returned to the bed dripping wet, his skin crawling with cold, and the scent of mildew all around. Later, too indifferent to move, he allowed his bladder free rein while he lay on the bed, and that water in time became cold, until he dried it with his dwindling body-heat.

But for some reason, despite the icy room, his nakedness, his hunger, he couldn't die.

He got up in the middle of the night of the sixth or seventh day, and sat on the edge of the bed to find the flaw in his resolve. When the solution didn't come he began to shamble around the room much as the creature had a week earlier, standing in front of the mirror to survey his pitifully changed body, watching the snow shimmer down and melt on the sill.

Eventually, by chance, he found a picture of his parents he remembered the creature staring at. Or had he dreamt that? He thought not: he had a distinct idea that it had picked up this picture and looked at it.

That was, of course, the bar to his suicide: that picture. There were respects to be paid. Until then how could he hope to die?

He walked to the Cemetery through the slush wearing only a pair of slacks and a tee-shirt. The remarks of middle-aged women and school-children went unheard. Whose business but his own was it if going barefoot was the death of him? The rain came and went, sometimes thickening towards snow, but never quite achieving its ambition.

There was a service going on at the church itself, a line of brittle coloured cars parked at the front. He slipped down the side into the churchyard. It boasted a good view, much spoiled today by the smoky veil of sleet, but he could see the trains and the high-rise flats; the endless rows of roofs. He ambled amongst the headstones, by no means certain of where to find his father's grave. It had been sixteen years: and the day hadn't been that memorable. Nobody had said anything illuminating about death in general, or his father's death specifically, there wasn't even a social gaff or two to mark the day: no aunt broke wind at the buffet table, no cousin took him aside to expose herself.

He wondered if the rest of the family ever came here: whether indeed they were still in the country. His sister had always threatened to move out: go to New Zealand, begin again. His mother was probably getting through her fourth husband by now, poor sod, though perhaps she was the pitiable one, with her endless chatter barely concealing the panic.

Here was the stone. And yes, there were fresh flowers in the marble urn that rested amongst the green marble chips. The old bugger had not lain here enjoying the view unnoticed. Obviously somebody, he guessed his sister, had come here seeking a little comfort from Father. Gavin ran his fingers over the name, the date, the platitude. Nothing exceptional: which was only right and proper, because there'd been nothing exceptional about him.

Staring at the stone, words came spilling out, as though Father was sitting on the edge of the grave, dangling his feet, raking his hair across his gleaming scalp, pretending, as he always pretended, to care.

'What do you think, eh?'

Father wasn't impressed.

'Not much, am I?' Gavin confessed.

You said it, son.

'Well I was always careful, like you told me. There aren't any bastards out there, going to come looking for me.'

Damn pleased.

'I wouldn't be much to find, would I?'

Father blew his nose, wiped it three times. Once from left to right, again left to right, finishing right to left. Never failed. Then he slipped away.

'Old shithouse.'

A toy train let out a long blast on its horn as it passed and Gavin looked up. There he was – himself – standing absolutely still a few yards away. He was wearing the same clothes he'd put on a week ago when he'd left the flat. They looked creased and shabby from constant wear. But the flesh! Oh, the flesh was more radiant than his own had ever been. It almost shone in the drizzling light; and the tears on the doppelganger's cheeks only made the features more exquisite.

'What's wrong?' said Gavin.

'It always makes me cry, coming here.' It stepped over the graves towards him, its feet crunching on gravel, soft on grass. So real.

'You've been here before?'

'Oh yes. Many times, over the years – '

Over the years? What did it mean, over the years? Had it mourned here for people it had killed?

As if in answer:

' – I come to visit Father. Twice, maybe three times a year.'

'This isn't your father,' said Gavin, almost amused by the delusion. 'It's mine.'

'I don't see any tears on your face,' said the other.

'I feel . . .'

'Nothing,' his face told him. 'You feel nothing at all, if you're honest.'

That was the truth.

'Whereas I . . .' the tears began to flow again, its nose ran, 'I will miss him until I die.'

It was surely playacting, but if so why was there such grief in its eyes: and why were its features crumpled into ugliness as it wept. Gavin had seldom given in to tears: they'd always made him feel weak and ridiculous. But this thing was proud of tears, it gloried in them. They were its triumph.

And even then, knowing it had overtaken him, Gavin could find nothing in him that approximated grief.

'Have it,' he said. 'Have the snots. You're welcome.'

The creature was hardly listening.

'Why is it all so painful?' it asked, after a pause. 'Why is it loss that makes me human?'

Gavin shrugged. What did he know or care about the fine art of being human? The creature wiped its nose with its sleeve, sniffed, and tried to smile through its unhappiness.

'I'm sorry,' it said, 'I'm making a damn fool of myself. Please forgive me.'

It inhaled deeply, trying to compose itself.

'That's all right,' said Gavin. The display embarrassed him, and he was glad to be leaving.

'Your flowers?' he asked as he turned from the grave.

It nodded.

'He hated flowers.'

The thing flinched.

'Ah.'

'Still, what does he know?'

He didn't even look at the effigy again; just turned and started

181

up the path that ran beside the church. A few yards on, the thing called after him:

'Can you recommend a dentist?'

Gavin grinned, and kept walking.

It was almost the commuter hour. The arterial road that ran by the church was already thick with speeding traffic: perhaps it was Friday, early escapees hurrying home. Lights blazed brilliantly, horns blared.

Gavin stepped into the middle of the flow without looking to right or left, ignoring the squeals of brakes, and the curses, and began to walk amongst the traffic as if he were idling in an open field.

The wing of a speeding car grazed his leg as it passed, another almost collided with him. Their eagerness to get somewhere, to arrive at a place they would presently be itching to depart from again, was comical. Let them rage at him, loathe him, let them glimpse his featureless face and go home haunted. If the circumstances were right, maybe one of them would panic, swerve, and run him down. Whatever. From now on he belonged to chance, whose Standard-Bearer he would surely be.

THE
DAMNATION GAME

Clive Barker

'It was an odd disease. Its symptoms were like infatuation –
palpitations, sleeplessness. Its only certain cure, death . . .'

Chance had ruled Marty Strauss' life for as long as he could
remember. Now at last luck was turning his way.

Parolled from prison, he becomes bodyguard to Joseph Whitehead,
one of the richest men in Europe.

But Whitehead has also played with chance – an ancient game
which gave him vast power and wealth, in exchange for his
immortal soul.

Now the forces he played against are back to claim what's theirs.
Terrifying forces, with the power to raise the dead; and Marty is
trapped between his human masters and Hell itself, with just one
last, desperate game left to play . . .

'I think Clive Barker is so good that I am almost literally
tongue-tied.' STEPHEN KING

'Clive Barker writes about horrors most of us would scarcely dare
imagine.' RAMSEY CAMPBELL

'The most impressive first novel I've read for a long, long time.
Touches of sheer brilliance throughout.' JAMES HERBERT

HORROR

Graham
Masterton
Ritual

The little town of Allen's Corners in rural Connecticut hid a
secret. A terrible, unimaginable secret. A secret that only the
children knew. It fed on their youth, ate away at their
innocence, and consumed their very souls with a twisted hunger
that could never be revealed – nor ever satisfied . . .

Le Reposoir was not on restaurant critic Charlie McLean's
itinerary. But since he had his son Martin with him, he was in
the mood to try something different. The restaurant owners,
as it turned out, were not interested in Charlie's patronage.
Or in getting a four-star rating. Martin, however, was
another matter. His tender youth would be just right for what
they had in mind . . .

HORROR

Graham
Masterton
Mirror

On the other side of the mirror lies a world beyond your darkest nightmares . . .

Screen writer Martin Williams is a man possessed. His obsession – 'Boofuls', the darling boy-angel of 30s Hollywood, whose horrific death was more spectacular than anything Hollywood ever dreamed up . . .

Now fifty years later all Martin wants is to make the movie that will bring Boofuls back to life. He can't believe his luck when he manages to buy a mirror from his idol's house. But that mirror was there when Boofuls died, and it has seen many things, more than the human eye can imagine . . .

Strange things happen in the mirror. Strange things happen to the people who try to probe its secrets. And Martin is about to enter the gateway through which all hell will break loose . . .

Also by Graham Masterton

REVENGE OF THE MANITOU   THE WELLS OF HELL
THE DEVILS OF D-DAY   THE HEIRLOOM
CHARNEL HOUSE   TENGU
NIGHT WARRIORS   DEATH TRANCE
DEATH DREAM   THE PARIAH

HORROR

<u>RELICS</u>

Shaun Hutson

When a hidden chamber filled with the skulls of children is discovered by an archaeological dig, the discovery triggers a series of murders in which the victims are horrifically mutilated. Inspector Stephen Wallace must discover the mad killer. Is it the sadistic thug responsible for organizing the barbaric dog-fighting? The mysterious recluse who holds Black Mass Orgies for heroin-addicted teenagers? Or is it, in fact, an evil so powerful, so obscene, that it threatens to engulf everyone? Something evil is waiting. Something monstrous is loose...

HORROR